BREATHING AUTUMN

FATED LOVE | BOOK ONE
MAELANA NIGHTINGALE

FATED LOVE PUBLISHING

AUTHOR'S NOTE & CONTENT WARNINGS

Dear Reader,

Thank you for choosing to read this story. Before you dive in, I want to provide a content warning for the themes and situations explored within these pages. This book contains mature and sensitive material, including references to alcohol, anxiety, assault, attempted sexual assault, light bondage, historical cheating, and historical child abuse. Other themes include historical death, depression, divorce, drug use, foster care, hospital settings, law enforcement involvement, nonconsensual drugging, and orphan experiences. Additionally, the story features profanity, rough sex, sexually explicit scenes, stalking, and toxic parental relationships.

These elements are integral to the characters' journeys and the emotional depth of the story, but I understand that some topics may be challenging or triggering for certain readers. Please prioritize your mental and emotional well-being as you read.

This story is about resilience, healing, and love, even in the face of hardship. If you choose to continue, I hope it will resonate with you and leave you feeling inspired.

Stay Naughty ♥ Mae

To everyone discovering love for the first time a little out of your prime—

this book is for you—the brave hearts who refused to settle, the dreamers who never gave up, and the souls who dared to believe that love doesn't have an expiration date. May this story remind you that love found later is no less magical—if anything, it's deeper, richer, and sweeter for the wait. Here's to second chances, bold beginnings, and the courage to open your heart.

♥ Unconditionally & Indefinitely ♥

CHAPTER ONE

THE FIRST DINNER

My daughter watches me with amusement dancing in her eyes as I struggle to drag my gigantic suitcase down the stairs.

"I thought you were only going to be gone for three days?" she teases, trying hard to contain her laughter.

"Yes, only three days and four nights, but I wanted options," I retort, a hint of defensiveness in my voice. "What if we go to the pool, or out to dinner, or for a night out somewhere else? I need to be prepared."

"You look like you're prepared for anything, that's for sure!" she replies, her grin widening.

Megan, my daughter, is living at home again. She's about to start her junior year at Marquette University. For the first two years, she lived on campus, but she quickly realized that it didn't make sense to bear the expense of housing when she could live at home.

Megan resembles me—not exactly like looking into a mirror, but close enough. We're both around five foot seven, with pale, freckle-covered Irish skin and long, straight strawberry-blonde hair. Our green eyes, however, are the real giveaway.

I never quite understood the frequent comments about my eyes until Megan provided a reference point. There are times when her eyes seem to change color—sometimes an unnatural shade of green, sometimes blue, and occasionally a striking teal. When she wears blue or stands in the sunlight, her eyes are mesmerizing. There's no question she's my daughter. Although I'm a bit heavier and more wrinkled than she is, the similarities are unmistakable.

I'm traveling to Dallas for my first national conference as a sales director. Until a few months ago, I was a sales assistant, but now, I've been promoted. It's a weekend conference, as most are, and I'm leaving on a Thursday—the conference runs from Friday through Sunday.

Having worked remotely up until now, I've never met any of my colleagues or clients in person. I know my team well from our frequent virtual meetings and phone calls, but the butterflies in my stomach are building as I anticipate meeting them face-to-face. I feel like I'm fourteen again, preparing for the first day of high school.

I work in the healthcare industry for Quisenbelt Technology, Inc., selling medical devices. Our sales team consists of five people, six including our leader. Despite knowing these people so well, I'm a bundle of nerves because I want to make a good first impression.

I glance at Megan. "Do you think they'll think I catfished them with my makeup and fancy lighting in all these virtual meetings?"

She bursts out laughing. "No, Mom, you're beautiful."

I smile at her, grateful for her presence. My ex-husband and I divorced when she was eight. We had two other children as well. Her brother, Kevin, is two years older than her, and her sister, Samantha—Sami—is two years younger.

We were married for eleven years before it all fell apart. People change a lot between twenty and thirty, and we married young. He was possessive, and there was some psychological abuse and infidelity. I came out of that divorce jaded and determined to be self-sufficient and alone.

I miss sex, sure, but the sex with my ex-husband wasn't great, and I definitely don't miss someone telling me what to do with my life all the time. It's been twelve years since the divorce, and I haven't had a single date. I've had offers—some I didn't even recognize until my kids pointed them out—but I wasn't looking, and none of those offers were enough to pull me back into the dating world.

Samantha just graduated from high school and went off to college in Michigan. So, apart from Megan living with me, I'm an empty nester and Megan is entirely grown up and self-sufficient. Lately, I've been thinking about putting myself out there again, trying to find "the one." I've heard of more miraculous things happening than finding love in your forties.

Heading off to Dallas for this conference, I'm thinking this might be my chance to put myself out there. I haven't been out with anyone but family and my best friend, Cara, in a very long time, and there will be a lot of smart, successful people there. I'm not going to tell Megan that, but that's part of why I packed so much—I want to dress to impress in any situation.

While I didn't share this with Megan, I did talk about it with Cara when we had dinner the night before.

"Autumn, you need to think about yourself," Cara said. "Being the hopeless romantic you are, I'm sure there will be someone there that lights a spark for you."

"We'll see," I replied. "I just haven't felt that 'thing' you feel when you know you want someone in so long. Maybe I'm just destined to be a spinster."

"Just find yourself a good fuck and worry about '*the one*' down the road."

I threw my napkin at her. "Cara, you know that's not me." I smiled, thinking for a minute. "But it *is* tempting."

We finished our dinner, talking about our kids and other parts of our lives. She hugged me, wished me good luck, and I went home to pack.

Cara has been divorced for about eight years, and like me, she hasn't really found anyone to settle down with. But unlike me, she hasn't remained chaste. Every few months, she finds some guy from a dating app or a bar and spends a couple of weeks just enjoying the sex. Even if the guys are interested in more, she never is. I applaud her, but I can't live like that. I'm thankful to whoever invented vibrators and leave it at that.

The drive from our home in Brookfield to the Milwaukee airport is short, and I'm grateful for the direct flight I found. Megan is kind enough to give me a ride. She helps me haul my gigantic suitcase out of the car, struggling a bit with its weight.

"I still can't believe you're bringing this much for three days," she says, tugging up the handle and pushing the suitcase toward me.

"I'll miss you, Megs," I say, ignoring her comment about the suitcase. "Don't burn the house down."

"I'll miss you too, Mom, and I won't," she replies, pulling me into a hug. As she drives away, I lug my suitcase into the airport.

When I land at Dallas Fort Worth, I navigate my way to baggage claim to retrieve my suitcase and then find my rideshare to the hotel near the Convention Center. It feels strange to be out traveling after being home for so long. The hotel is gorgeous, and I'm a bit in awe as I roll my suitcase into my room. Just as the door clicks shut behind me, my watch vibrates. I reach into my pocket and pull out my phone to check the group chat for my team.

I love my team.

They're more than just coworkers; they're friends. Cole Waters, my boss and the senior vice president of sales, is a couple of years older than me. He's also divorced with three kids, and we have bonded over our shared experiences in addition to the usual work banter. As the team's assistant for almost two years, Cole and I talked frequently, our conversations broken up into meetings and short chats throughout the day. When I got promoted, they didn't replace me, so I still handle a lot of the assistant duties, though some were passed on to an executive assistant at our corporate office in Columbus.

Tara Ellender is the only other woman on our team, and even though she's about twelve years younger than me, we get along really well. Tom Osler is the most senior of us, having been with the company for almost a decade before the merger that brought Cole on board. Sometimes Tom and Cole butt heads, which I assume is due to their differing tenures and approaches. Mark Tyson and Julio Cruz were both hired around the same time as me as part of the sales team expansion following the FDA approval of a new device.

Since this is the first conference I'm attending, Cole decided to bring the whole team along. Usually, only a few of us would go at a time, but for this one, it's everyone.

As I grab my phone, I see several more messages coming through from the group chat.

I glance at the clock on my phone—it's half past four. I wonder if that's enough time to shower. Probably not, since I like my hair to air dry.

Rummaging through my luggage, I find a cute, new blouse. It's mostly black with large blue flowers along the sides, giving the illusion that I'm a bit thinner. The blouse has a deep scooped back with one thin band across it—practically backless. I pair it with black slacks, ensuring they're wrinkle-free before laying them gently on the bed.

In the bathroom mirror, I assess my makeup and decide a full refresh is necessary. Washing my face, I set up my blank canvas. The anticipation of this in-person first impression has me fidgety and restless. But I manage to get my eyeliner symmetrical on the first try—a rare victory for me.

I run a brush through my strawberry blonde hair, deciding to leave it down and straight as usual. My hair is long enough to reach the small of my back, covering a lot while wearing the backless blouse. I packed all sensible shoes, having given up heels in my late twenties. Though I own cute shoes, even heels, I rarely wear them. Suddenly, I'm self-conscious about that.

What if Tara is wearing heels? What if they're expecting me to wear heels? Calm down, Autumn. They already know you.

With about twenty minutes before we're supposed to meet at the restaurant, I head toward the elevator. As I'm walking, I see a familiar face.

The white-haired man wears gray slacks and a white button-down shirt. His skin is paler than mine, or maybe he just lacks the full-body freckles my Irish father handed down to me. There's some extra weight around his middle, but overall, he looks good for his age. As I get closer, I definitely recognize his light blue eyes behind wire-rimmed glasses.

"Tom?" I ask.

"Autumn?" he replies, extending his right hand as I do likewise.

As he shakes my hand, he steps forward and hugs me. "It's so good to meet you in person," he says. "You're taller than I thought you'd be."

"Yeah?" I laugh, realizing I'm almost eye-to-eye with him. "Well, it's hard to tell height through a webcam."

We both laugh as he presses the button to call the elevator. The time is filled with small talk about our flights and the weather, soothing my nerves.

At the restaurant, the hostess checks our reservation and leads us to an eight-seat table encircling a hibachi grill. It's elevated with bar stools, and the far right part of the table is in the corner. Tom and I take seats to the left, continuing our small talk until Tara arrives.

I give her a big hug, thrilled to see her in person. Tara, my only female counterpart, sits in the back corner, commenting on how she doesn't like to sit with her back to the open restaurant. She's thin with a bit of a Barbie doll appearance, radiating sweetness with her Oklahoma accent. Her bleach blond, big hair and amazing figure undoubtedly make her the center of attention in many rooms.

Mark and Julio arrive together, led by the same hostess. Handshakes, half-hugs, and full hugs ensue around the table. They sit on the stools between Tara and Tom. It's like meeting long-lost friends, even though I've never seen them in person.

Finally, our fearless leader, Cole, walks in. I turn and look at him over my left shoulder as he says, "Look at all of you here in person."

Tom, Mark, and Julio all stand up to greet Cole. It's only later that I realize Tara and I were the only ones who didn't stand. I swivel my stool around, and by the time Cole is done shaking hands, he's standing right in front of me.

"Hey, Autumn," he says, placing his left hand on my shoulder, making brief but direct eye contact.

"Hey, Cole," I reply, feeling slightly caught off guard by how dazed the interaction leaves me.

He proceeds around the table to greet Tara. I slowly turn my stool back to face the table, trying to gather my thoughts. I've seen Cole Waters in hundreds, maybe thousands, of video calls. He was usually in a hoodie unless there were clients on, in which case he wore a long-sleeved button-down shirt.

Is there a term for the opposite of catfishing? Because if there is, Cole is it.

He exudes confidence—the kind that isn't arrogant or cocky but genuinely sexy. He's just over six feet tall and wearing a navy blue t-shirt that fits him perfectly. The sleeves accentuate his tan, muscular upper arms, and the shirt hugs his chest just enough to show off his definition. He has a hint of a dad bod stomach, but my eyes are drawn to his chest and arms. I feel something stir inside me that hasn't stirred in a very long time.

"Isn't that right, Autumn?" Tom asks.

"What?" I reply, snapping back to reality.

What in the actual hell? Did I just zone out, daydreaming about my boss's body? Snap out of it, Autumn. He is completely off-limits.

They all laugh.

"Sorry, I zoned out there for a minute." I smile.

"I was just saying how we both flew in from smaller airports, and DFW is so much bigger than our home airports," Tom says.

"Oh, yeah," I reply, my senses slowly returning.

As I glance back toward Tara and Cole, I realize that Cole has moved around and is pulling out the stool right next to me, leaving two vacant seats between him and Tara. A rush of electricity courses through my veins, and my heart quickens in my chest. I straighten my spine, try to flatten my stomach, and run my fingers through my hair, quickly recognizing I'm fidgeting.

Cole settles in next to me, his presence almost overwhelming. "So, how was your flight?" he asks, turning his attention to me.

"It was good, smooth," I manage to reply, trying to keep my voice steady. "And yours?"

"Pretty good too," he says with a smile that sends my heart into overdrive. "It's nice to finally meet everyone in person."

"Yeah, it is," I agree, feeling the warmth of his proximity.

I do my best to stay focused and engaged, but Cole's presence is a constant distraction. The small talk and camaraderie ease my nerves, but underneath it all, there's a spark I hadn't anticipated. And it's both thrilling and terrifying.

What the hell is wrong with me?

"Hey team, this is a special occasion, so feel free to have a glass of wine or two, or a cocktail—whatever your pleasure tonight," Cole says during a quiet moment. "We won't be able to do this every night we're here, but please, tonight is a celebration."

A minute later, a server arrives to take our drink orders. I spot a chocolate and Irish cream signature milkshake on the menu—it sounds delicious and makes my choice easy. The rest of the team orders wine and beer.

"Well, I guess that makes me the odd one out with my frou-frou drink," I joke after Tom orders last.

"Hey, the man said order whatever your pleasure," Mark says with a smile. "They all toast the same."

Mark gives off gentle giant vibes, even through a webcam. He's at least six foot four, a few inches taller than Cole, and large but fit. His skin is a beautiful shade of umber. His salt-and-pepper hair and well-groomed gray beard give him a distinguished look. He has such a good sense of humor and an ease about him—he makes everyone feel comfortable.

Everyone laughs at Mark's comment, and we engage in some small talk. I ask Tom how his wife is and how his son's new job is going. Mark joins in as we talk about our kids and how they're doing. Meanwhile, Julio, Tara, and Cole are engrossed in a conversation across the grill about college football. They all went to the University of Georgia, so they bond over Bulldogs sports. As the conversation naturally shifts away from me, Mark and Tom start talking more to each other.

"It really is good to meet you in person," Cole says quietly, and my breath catches in my chest.

He's leaning in, just inches from my ear, and when he speaks, his breath moves my hair and whispers across my ear. It sends a chill down my spine and heat to my groin. I bite my lower lip.

I turn my head toward him and meet his eyes. They are captivating—a dark, almost navy blue, like dark sapphires. I was never drawn into his eyes like this on the computer screen.

His complexion is sun-kissed, and his salt-and-pepper hair, more pepper than salt, is thick and well-groomed. He has a short beard and mustache, with lines around his eyes that make him look experienced and wise, not old.

He smells like heaven—earthy, spicy, and smooth, like velvet.

Smiling at me, his mouth so close to mine, I feel an intense desire just to kiss him. I swallow hard, my throat dry.

An expression crosses his face that I can't quite read. For a moment, I forget where I am.

I clear my throat. "Yeah, you too," I reply weakly, forcing myself to look away and focus on the rest of the team. "It's good to see the whole team in person and not just in little boxes on our computer screens."

But I can't help glancing back at him. He smiles at me, and I return a soft smile.

Damn, I'm like a moth to a flame, or maybe a moth to a bug zapper.

I swear he looks down at my lips before he swallows and leans back. As he moves away, I feel his hand on the back of my chair, his thumb lightly brushing across my back and hair as he removes his arm. More heat courses through me, and I almost feel lightheaded.

I take a deep breath, trying to steady myself. This is going to be an interesting trip.

Instantly, I become self-conscious about what the others might think of Cole's proximity to me. I barely hear Julio and Tara across the table talking about one of our competitors, and I use it as an escape.

"Oh, are they going to be here?" I ask, forcing myself to look away from Cole and focus on Tara.

"Yes, they are. While they're the competition, I'm looking forward to meeting some of them in person," Tara replies.

"Do you know who else will be here?" I ask, sparking a conversation within the whole group about clients and competitors.

The server brings our drinks, and sure enough, mine looks like a fancy dessert. I take one sip and realize it's strong—stronger than I expected. I probably have more liquor in this drink than all of my colleagues combined.

"That looks amazing," Tom says, leaning toward me for a closer look.

"It is. It tastes a lot like a whiskey-spiked milkshake," I say, smiling.

"Do you normally like whiskey?" Tom asks, providing a reason to focus in the opposite direction of Cole.

"I do. My brother is a bit of a whiskey—well, really, scotch—connoisseur," I say, nodding. "Although normally, I prefer it on the rocks or with soda, not this sweet."

Tom starts talking about the distilleries near where he grew up in Kentucky. The hibachi chef begins his show, and we all laugh—a lot. The server asks if we want another round of drinks. Everyone answers yes, except me. I order a glass of water.

"Not having another one?" Cole asks, leaning toward me. His voice is low, maybe even seductive.

His proximity quickens my heart again, sending an ache and heat to the juncture of my thighs. I clench my legs together, trying to contain the energy coursing through me.

"No, this one is strong. My cheeks are getting numb, and I haven't even finished it," I say, smiling and looking down at my drink, avoiding his gaze.

"Maybe you're just a lightweight," he jests, poking my arm with his elbow.

"Nah, I can handle my liquor. This is just seriously strong, and I haven't eaten in almost ten hours." I look up at him, our eyes locking for what feels like an eternity before Mark interrupts.

"I believe her," Mark interjects. "Sometimes those fancy drinks are ridiculously strong."

Cole raises his beer. "Well, maybe we should toast before Autumn finishes the rest of her drink then." He puts his arm on the back of my chair again.

Everyone looks at Cole, holding up their drinks. "To the best team I could ask for. I'm so glad to see us all together in person."

We cheer and toast.

"What are the plans for the next few days?" Tara asks. "I mean, outside of the conference."

Cole moves his arm off my chair to answer, and I exhale, realizing I had been at least partially holding my breath.

"Well, tomorrow night is the Meet and Greet for the whole conference. There will be drinks and a DJ. It's a chance for all the conference-goers to mingle. We'll be manning the booth all day, so outside of maybe breakfast, tomorrow is pretty well planned," Cole starts. "However, we can have dinner the next couple of nights, or if you all think of something fun, let me know. The big boss wants me to do some team-building exercises while we're here, and that might not be a bad idea." Julio and Mark groan, and Cole raises his hands in concession. "But tonight, I don't want to think about asking you fun facts about yourselves. I just want us to all relax and have fun."

"As long as you don't make us trust fall, I think we're good," Julio quips, making everyone laugh.

Julio has a physique almost the opposite of Mark's. He's about five foot four, maybe a hundred and thirty pounds, with bronze skin, brown eyes, and a thick head of black hair. His smile is contagious, and his sense of humor frequently borders on inappropriate but leaves us reeling often.

Once the laughter dies down, Cole continues. "We can take turns manning the booth in groups. Six of us could be overwhelming. We'll split into groups of three so the rest can look around the conference or attend some speaker sessions if they want."

Everyone nods in agreement. As we continue eating, the sounds of other tables' conversations and utensils fill the air.

"This is awesome," Tom says. "I've never been to one of these hibachi grills. I'm impressed."

"Yep, food and entertainment," Tara adds, and the team starts sharing their experiences at similar restaurants.

My watch vibrates. I glance at it and see a text message from Cara.

Cara

Found a new ex-husband yet?

I quickly swipe it away and pull out my phone, I quickly reply.

Me

At a work dinner, not a good time.

And then I make the mistake of leaving my phone to the right of my plate. She texts again, it appears on my phone screen.

Cara

> Well, if you haven't found an ex-husband, did you at least find a one-night stand?

I quickly turn off the screen, but it's too late. Cole catches sight of the message and laughs quietly. "That wasn't one of your kids, was it?"

I feel the heat rising in my cheeks. "No," I laugh uncomfortably. "That was my best friend, although maybe now my ex-best friend. She gets a little crazy sometimes."

"She divorced too?" he asks, his tone light but curious.

"Yeah," I reply, still trying to avoid looking directly at him.

"Maybe she's trying to live vicariously through you," Cole suggests with a chuckle.

"Maybe." I shrug. "But it's more like she's trying to get me to be more like her."

Cara

> Autumn, don't ignore me

Flashes across my screen and watch, so I put my phone on do not disturb and tuck it back in my purse. Cara will have to wait. We all finish eating while small talk continues.

Cole looks at his watch. "Hey team, this is a lot of fun, but booth setup is going to come up sooner than we think, and that jet lag will kick in. What do you say we call it a night?"

Standing up from the stool, I can feel the alcohol. I'm steady, but definitely aware of its effects.

As we step out of the restaurant, the heat and humidity hit us like a wall. We all groan and comment on it. I walk next to Tara, who was too far away to talk to during dinner. Mark and Tom are ahead of us, while Cole and Julio fall in behind.

"How's the wedding planning?" I ask her.

"It's good. You should get a save-the-date card in the next few weeks. We booked a venue for Valentine's Day next year."

"Aww, in Seattle, I assume?" I ask.

"Yeah, outside of Seattle, in Issaquah. It's beautiful. You can bring one of your daughters if you don't have a date." She hesitates. "I mean, I didn't mean it like that—"

"It's fine," I interrupt her, "I know what you mean. You're saying I can bring a plus one, regardless of who they are to me." I look at her and smile.

"Yeah, exactly." She smiles.

Julio comes up between us and puts his arms around both of us. "I'll be your plus one," he says, grinning.

Maybe he had more to drink than I thought he did.

"We'll see, Julio, we'll see," I say, laughing with Tara.

Julio is married with three young kids. He talks a big game, but we all know he loves his wife. He talks about her constantly, and their social media is filled with sickeningly sweet posts. Julio falls back again with Cole, staying about five yards behind Tara and me. It's only a five-minute walk back to the hotel. Tara, Julio, and Mark all have rooms on the twelfth floor, while Tom, Cole, and I are on the sixteenth floor.

"I don't know how that happened," Cole says. "We usually book our own rooms, but when the company does it, like this time, we're usually all together."

"No biggie," Tara replies with a smile. "We may have enough togetherness as it is." We all laugh a little.

The elevators are separated by floors one through fifteen and floors sixteen through thirty, so we have to take two separate elevators.

"See you all at breakfast around 6:30?" Cole asks. We all agree and go our separate ways. Tom, Cole, and I step into our elevator.

Cole and I reach for the button for our floor at the same time. Our hands touch, and a jolt of electricity courses through me. An intense burning sensation radiates from my hand, spreading through my veins and pooling at my center. For a second, I forget how to breathe.

"Sorry," he says, his expression unreadable yet almost alluring. I quickly look away.

"No, it's fine," I say weakly and push the button.

I am going to just ignore this, whatever "this" is. Maybe it's just the alcohol.

Cole clears his throat and turns to Tom. "So, how was the flight in from Little Rock?"

They continue their small talk until the elevator opens. Tom walks down the hall to the right; I knew he was that way from earlier. I turn left toward my room.

"Oh, you're down this way too?" Cole asks.

"Clearly," I state sarcastically.

Cole laughs, and I'm glad to have what feels like a more normal and typical interaction with him.

"I hope this conference lives up to whatever expectations you have," Cole says. The way he says it leaves me wondering if there's a meaning beyond the conference.

"Hopefully," I reply cheerfully. "Well, this is me." I stop in front of my door and reach into my purse for the key.

"Goodnight, Autumn. Sweet dreams," Cole says, and I look up to meet his eyes.

He winks at me before he turns and walks a couple more doors down and across the hall. That wink turns my legs into jelly, and I'm a little surprised I'm still standing.

"Goodnight," I reply as I hit the sensor with my key and open my door.

I slip inside, drop my purse on the floor, and lean my back against the door. I'm getting ready to give in to the jelly in my legs and slide down to sit on the floor when someone knocks. I freeze. I turn and look out the peephole—it's Cole.

Do I open it? Of course, open it, Autumn, fuck.

I open the door and lean against the edge, hoping it supports me. "Yes, Cole?"

"Hey, I just wanted you to know, since this is your first time traveling for the company, that you can open the minibar. The company will pay for it," he says, smiling and shrugging.

"Um, okay." I smile and glance at the minibar before looking back at Cole. "Good to know, thanks."

"Okay, goodnight for real," he says, starting to walk away.

"Goodnight," I reply, closing the door.

I lean back against it, my heart pounding. The encounter leaves me feeling a mixture of excitement and confusion.

CHAPTER TWO
THE MR. DARCY THEORY

I wait a minute, my heart pounding, then glance through the peephole again. He's gone this time. I kick off my shoes and decide a shower is essential. Between the lingering awkwardness, the alcohol, and the grime of travel, I need to wash it all away.

I slip into my usual routine. I place my watch on the charger and gather my sleep clothes, toiletries, and other necessities. Dropping my clothes on the hotel room floor, I head into the bathroom. I pause to examine myself in the mirror.

God, I wish I'd appreciated my body more when I was younger.

Three kids have left their marks—stretch marks and extra skin that defy any remedy. Breastfeeding means my breasts bear their own evidence of motherhood: slightly uneven, nipples not quite facing forward. I'm carrying about forty extra pounds, and though I carry it well, I'd be happier if they weren't there.

I turn on the shower, waiting for the water to heat before stepping in. The hot water cascades over me, soothing my nerves and relaxing every tense muscle.

When I'm done, I wrap my hair in a towel turban and another towel around my body, then head back to the bedroom. My pajamas feel exceptionally comfortable tonight. Suddenly, I remember my phone.

Oh crap, Cara.

I dig it out of my purse and see twenty-three messages from multiple people. With a sigh, I start answering them one by one.

Then, I open the thread with Cara.

Cara

Are you seriously ignoring me?

Does that mean it's good?

Or bad?

Come on, Autumn, tell me what's happening

That's it, I'm flying to Dallas to stalk you

You don't think I'm serious? I will do it

Booking my flight now

???!???!?!?!?!

Me

Oh. My. Gawd.

You're ridiculous

Can you talk?

My phone rings about two seconds later.

"Autumn, what's the skinny?" Cara asks.

"You're ridiculous, that's what's the skinny," I reply. Cara laughs. "We had a team dinner at a hibachi grill; my boss was sitting right next to me and saw your texts come through, so I put my phone on do not disturb. That's all."

"Yeah, yeah," Cara says, completely blowing me off, "How is it being with all those people in person? Any different than being with them on the internet?"

"It's the same," I hesitate a little, "for the most part."

"What's the other part?" Cara says in that tone of voice that tells me she thinks there is dirt coming.

"Cara," I say, clearly annoyed.

"Autumn, you know you'll tell me eventually, so just dish."

I sigh. "There is definitely chemistry with someone, but it's completely forbidden, so I just have to ignore it."

"Forbidden, why, because he's your boss?" The knowing tone in her voice catches me off guard and I don't answer.

Cara squeals, "I knew it, I fucking knew it. It's Cole Waters himself, isn't it?"

"How the fuck, Cara? *Are* you here in Dallas stalking me?" I ask as an accusation.

"Let me spell it out," she says in her true bitchy sarcastic tone, "the same Cole Waters you talk to on the phone for multiple hours a day about both work and personal stuff? You didn't realize y'all were bonding that way? I'm disappointed you didn't see it before, Autumn," she replies like she is lecturing me, "I thought you just didn't want to tell me, but I thought you *saw* it."

"I don't talk to him *that* much."

"Mmmhmmm," she says sarcastically, "Sure, that's why every time I call or stop by, it's always 'sorry I just got off the phone with Cole,' 'sorry, I have to finish this call up with Cole,' 'sorry, I'm waiting for Cole to call,' blah blah blah. And then half the time you talk to him, you aren't even talking about work." She sounds like she wants to say more, but she runs out of breath.

"Cara, he is my boss," I say firmly.

"Mmmhmmm," she says again. I sigh.

As she continues talking, continuing to go through my life with Cole as she knows it, I look through my other notifications. A message from my brother asking how my flight was, and then there's a message from Cole.

Cole

You felt that right? In the elevator?

My heart and breath stutter.

"Um, Cara?" I say a little weakly and hesitantly, completely interrupting her.

"What, Autumn?" She definitely caught the change in my tone.

"He wrote me, he texted me, I mean, he— oh, let me just start from the beginning. We were in the elevator together and we went to hit the button at the same time, our hands touched, it was insanely electric for me, but, maybe, it was for him too?" My voice rises in pitch substantially at the end of the question.

"Oh my, you had a Mr. Darcy moment?" she asks excitedly.

"What?" I'm confused. "I mean I know who Mr. Darcy is, but what is a 'Mr. Darcy moment' exactly?"

"You know? In the movie?"

"Which movie? Firth or Macfayden?"

"Macfayden, which doesn't matt— actually it does," she pauses, "So, you know when Matthew Macfayden is helping Keira Knightley into the carriage and then they zoom in on him flexing his hand? Because, well, chemistry, electricity, whatever you want to call it, that is the Mr. Darcy moment."

I stare at my phone, at the message from Cole.

"Cara," my voice is weak, "what am I supposed to say? He's my boss."

"Well, Autumn, I would go with honesty. Maybe you feeling *the thing* is more important than your job, I don't know, but you have to tell me what happens." Her voice is calm but I can tell she's almost giddy.

"Cara, I need to go. I need to think about this," I say, and I hang up, barely hearing her goodbye.

Cara

Let me know what happens - you're the best, bitch!

Me

okay lol, and no, you're the best

I stare at the phone, and I decide to go with a non-answer.

What can I say? That I fucking want you? That I want to kiss you? Come back to my door? Fuck.

I shift my focus to the other messages—Tara saying how nice it was to meet me, my brother asking about the conference, a few others. But I can't stop thinking about Cole. No response from him yet.

I head into the bathroom to pee one last time, then back in the bedroom, I turn on the TV and start scrolling through the channels. Ironically, *Pride and Prejudice* is on, the Matthew Macfadyen version, of course. I laugh to myself and settle in, hoping to drift off to dreamland.

I remember my phone is on Do Not Disturb. I reach over to turn it off, and there it is.

I drop the phone on the bed and lie back, thinking. Picking it up again, I type out a few responses, then delete them. He's probably watching those three dots appear and disappear.

Fuck.

I settle on a mix of honesty and reality.

His three dots linger for a long time, and I don't reply. He must be typing and deleting a dozen times.

I start to type "sweet dreams," but rethink the implications.

I sigh, thinking about raiding my mini-bar, but resist. I send a screenshot of the messages to Cara. I fall asleep sometime soon after Mr. Darcy proposes the first time, and I don't wake up until morning.

My alarm startles me awake. Whatever dream I was having slips away, but I remember feeling happy and reluctant to leave it. Groggily, I check my phone—no messages yet this morning. I stumble into the bathroom and start my morning routine.

I choose a bright royal blue blouse, knowing it will make my eyes gleam an almost unnatural shade of teal, and pair it with gray slacks. My makeup is light and natural, and I leave my hair down, straight and simple. As I finish getting ready, my phone buzzes with a new message.

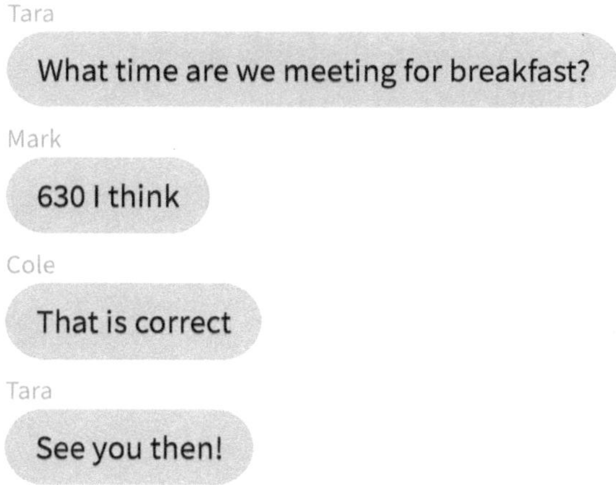

I glance at the clock; it's six now, and I'm pretty much ready to go. I give myself a final once-over in the full-length mirror and slip on my shoes. Opting for no purse today, I rely on my pockets. Grabbing my room key, debit card, and phone, I head out, hoping to beat both Cole and Tom downstairs.

Maybe I can avoid another awkward elevator moment.

I'm wrong.

As I open the door, I startle. Leaning against the wall directly across from my room is Cole, holding two cups of coffee and scrolling through his phone. He's ready for business in a dark gray button-down shirt and khaki slacks. He looks up, and our eyes meet.

I could get lost in those eyes, and, fuck, he looks sexy.

"Somehow I knew you'd be an early bird this morning," he says. "Here, I got you coffee, white mocha, no whip. I think I remembered that was your coffee of choice."

It takes me a minute to find my words. "Um, yeah, when I'm feeling indulgent anyway," I finally manage to say with a smile, taking the cup from his hand. "Too many calories for every day."

Our hands brush again, and there's that same electricity. We both look at each other, the eye contact lingering a bit too long. He clears his throat.

"Should we head down?" he asks, gesturing toward the elevators. I nod, and we start walking.

"Look, Autumn, I wanted to say I'm sorry," he sighs. "I am your boss. I put you in a position I shouldn't have with that text last night, and I truly am sorry."

"So, this is apology coffee?" I ask, holding up my cup, smiling to lighten the mood.

He laughs softly. "Something like that, yeah."

As we get in the elevator, the air between us feels thick, and neither of us knows what to say. I take a sip of my coffee, and he breaks the silence. "Is Samantha off at school already? I thought you said she was going in July for her scholarship program?"

"Yeah," I start, but I don't look at him. "It's kind of like a sorority, but it's not. They do a bunch of service projects before school starts—helping to get dorms ready, cleaning up the campus, and then they help other students move in. She's been there about a week and is loving it so far."

"Well, that's about the best we can ask for, that our kids are happy, right?" he says as the elevator doors open.

"Yep, for sure," I answer.

He gestures for me to get off the elevator first, and we walk into the hotel lobby.

"I have no clue where breakfast is," I laugh a little.

"I think it's this way," he says, pointing to the left. "I've heard it's a good spread."

We walk in silence for a minute. When we arrive at the buffet, it's an impressive spread, but I have butterflies in my stomach today, so I know I don't want much.

"I just want to grab a couple of things and then I'll hold down a table for us," I say.

"Not hungry?" Cole asks, a note of concern in his voice.

"Not much of a breakfast person, especially this early," I respond with a smile. He nods.

I wander through the buffet, picking up a blueberry muffin and a banana. Finding a table with a good view of the buffet, I sit down and watch the morning unfold.

Mark and Julio walk in and spot Cole at the omelet station. They join him, and soon the three of them head over to my table. Cole sits across from me instead of next to me, and I wonder if it's intentional.

Tara and Tom arrive shortly after. Tara, a kindred spirit, grabs a muffin and an apple, sparking some playful banter about genders and food choices. Before long, it's time to set up our booth.

Booth set-up starts an hour before the conference, so we have some time. The conference room is enormous, with over two hundred booths. As this is my first conference, I'm a little in awe.

Mark and Julio set up our demonstration devices while Tara and I arrange the rest of the table. We have pamphlets, cards, and, of course, swag. Little hand sanitizers with the Quisenbelt logo, pens, keychains, and under the table, fancy travel coffee mugs and other high-end items reserved for special clients or those who show significant interest.

Setting up is surprisingly fun. It's a bonding experience filled with laughter as things fall over or refuse to stay put. Cole and Tom, with their experience, offer helpful advice. Despite the chaos, we get the job done.

"Let's split up shifts," Cole suggests. "Did any of you want to see any of the speakers?"

"Honestly, I didn't get a chance to look yet," says Tara, visibly relieved when we all admit the same.

"Okay." Cole smiles. "Let's start with Autumn, Mark, and Julio in the booth. The rest of us can walk around and check out the other booths, and after lunch, we can switch. Sound good?"

We all nod. I'm left wondering if he's intentionally keeping some distance, but it's probably for the best, whether it was intentional or not.

The morning flies by in a whirlwind of activity. Our booth is near the entrance to the convention room, so people are still chatty and excited by the time they reach us. As I'm straightening out some pamphlets, I hear my name.

"Well, if it isn't Autumn Flynn in the flesh," he says. "Oh, and Mr. Tyson as well."

I turn around. "Dr. Gabari, it's so good to see you here," I say, reaching out to shake his hand. He grips mine a little too long.

"Tony, please, no need for titles," he replies, then turns to shake Mark's hand.

Dr. Anthony Gabari was one of my first sales at Quisenbelt. He's the epitome of tall, dark, and handsome, with olive skin and an Italian charm. From previous conversations, I know he's about five years older than me.

"How are things going at the practice?" I ask.

"Very well, actually. I just hired a new nurse practitioner; she's around here somewhere," he replies.

"Great, bring her by," Mark says. "We have lots of swag for our VIP clients!"

Tony laughs. "Will you be at the Meet and Greet tonight?"

"That's the plan," I say.

"Yessir," Mark says in almost unison with me, and we all smile.

"Well, maybe I can buy you a drink while we're there," Tony suggests.

"That would be great," I reply. "Are you here for the whole conference?"

"Yes, I'm speaking on Sunday. You both should come," he says, looking from me to Mark and back again. "And bring Cole too. I assume he's here."

"Absolutely, he is," I say while Mark hands him some of our swag. "Go explore; we'll be here all weekend!"

We exchange polite goodbyes, and Tony heads off to visit other booths.

I turn to Mark. "You know, this is fun, but being 'on' all the time is exhausting."

Mark chuckles. "It sure is, Autumn, it sure is."

Julio chimes in, "Well, if you need a break, please take one."

"Nah," I reply. "I just need to get used to not being able to turn off a camera and roll my eyes."

They both laugh, and we dive back into the busy, buzzing energy of the convention.

Lunch for those of us working the booths is catered separately from the conference attendees, but it's still a nice spread of sandwiches, fruit, vegetables, and other side dishes. Mark volunteers to watch the booth, allowing Julio and me to go eat. We run into everyone else almost as soon as we walk in. Tara sits next to me, and once again, Cole sits across from me.

We start talking about our mornings. Tara is excited about some of the booths she visited. Tom, a veteran of these conferences, talks about catching up with old friends and introducing us to people we should meet.

"What about you two?" Cole asks, "How was the morning in the booth?" He looks at both of us but then focuses on Julio, for which I'm grateful because every time our eyes meet, I get lost in them.

"We had a lot of people come by to get information, definitely some new clients in the pipeline," Julio says. "Oh, Dr. Gabari stopped by. I think he was particularly happy to see Autumn in person." He winks at me and smiles. "But he wanted to make sure to catch up with you too tonight, Cole."

Cole looks at me and smiles before quickly looking back at Julio. "Well, she is his favorite salesperson. He even asked if she could be his account exec now that he's moved beyond the sales stage. I assume you told him we'll be there tonight?"

"Yes, they, I mean Mark and Autumn, did," Julio replies.

"Speaking of tonight," Tara says with a heavy emphasis on 'speaking,' "Autumn, please tell me you brought a straightener?" She looks at me pleadingly.

"You're lucky, I did," I answer. "My daughter gave me grief about how much stuff I was bringing, but I did bring that."

"Thank goodness," Tara says with a smile. "I did not bring mine, and I think for my hair to go with my cocktail dress, I will need it."

"Absolutely, I can even help you. Maybe you can help me pin my hair up too?" I ask enthusiastically.

"Yes, definitely! I'm so glad you're here and prepared," Tara responds.

"Any of you boys feel like you're back in high school and the girls are talking about getting ready for homecoming?" Julio asks, making everyone laugh.

"Well, you know, us guys have it easy," Cole says. "We can just throw on a tie or a jacket over what we wore all day. The women, well, they have to change into cocktail attire, so count yourselves lucky."

Tara and I make arrangements to meet up before the Meet and Greet, then we head back to the convention room. After dropping off our plates, somehow Cole and I end up walking side by side.

"So Tony was happy to see you?" he asks.

"Yeah, it seemed that way," I answer. "But you know, I have to turn on that charm for the clients." I smile and make the mistake of looking up at him.

Those eyes are going to fucking kill me.

"Oh, I don't think you have to turn on anything for them to be excited to meet you," he replies.

I feel my cheeks burning with a blush that must be obvious to him. I pull my hair over my face, trying to hide.

We approach the door that separates the dining area from the conference hall, and he pushes it open with his right hand.

"Ladies first," he says, placing his left hand on the small of my back to guide me through the door.

I think it's an innocent touch, maybe something he would do for any woman he knows, but after he removes his hand, my back still feels warm from his touch. The absence of it is acutely felt.

CHAPTER THREE

THE MEET AND GREET

Around four o'clock, Tara and I head up to our rooms. She joins me in my room after fetching her dress and makeup from hers. As we begin the process of getting ready, I glance at Tara and say, "This really does feel like getting ready for homecoming."

She laughs. "It does!"

We chat about her wedding plans and my kids while I straighten her hair and she helps me style mine into an updo. Tara has chosen the classic little black dress—versatile enough to throw a cardigan over for a coffee shop visit on a Tuesday morning or, as she's done tonight, paired with heels and jewelry for a formal event.

I opt for a muted emerald green dress that brings out my eyes. It's a mid-length, mermaid dress with multi-thin strap shoulders and a low V-back. The best part? It has pockets. I realize I've unintentionally gone for a backless theme at this conference as I get ready with Tara.

"What kind of bra do you wear under that?" Tara asks, genuinely curious.

"So, I have two options," I say, taking them out of the suitcase. "I have this one that has the strap around the waist instead of higher up, but what I usually use is this," I pull out a black, sticky, push-up bra, "it has no straps at all, it sticks to your skin and holds the girls up. I never thought it would work for me, but my daughter insisted I try it, and sure enough, no issues."

"That is weird and amazing," Tara says with curiosity. "I'll have to try one of those."

We finish getting ready and slip on our shoes. I choose black strappy sandals, and Tara has heels that bring her up to my natural height.

"You ready?" Tara asks.

"Yep, let's go do this homecoming-esque thing!" I say, and we both laugh.

I text Cara on the way to the elevator.

Me

> Big Meet and Greet tonight, I'll update you after!

I decide not to wear my watch for this event. Putting my phone on silent, I tuck everything I need into my pockets. Tara assures me she can't even tell I have pockets. She's carrying a black wristlet just big enough to hold her phone.

"I haven't been to something like this in years," I say in the elevator, feeling a mix of excited anticipation and nervousness.

"I've been to a couple at conferences before," Tara replies. "They're usually fun. A lot depends on the venue and the music. I think this one will be good though because they have a real DJ."

As we walk toward the ballroom, we hear music blasting—Journey. We look at each other and laugh. The room has club vibes—dark with flashing lights, taking me back a decade or two. Most of the conference attendees are between thirty and fifty, so the music fits our demographic perfectly.

A dance floor dominates the center of the room, in front of a DJ booth. Two bars flank a long table covered in appetizers. I make sure to explore the appetizer table, knowing there will be alcohol involved. We finish snacking on some delicious little pastry bites when "Macarena" comes on.

Tara grabs my wrist, laughing. "Come on, I know you know this one."

Her laughter is infectious. We head to the dance floor, which is 95% female—this really is like high school.

Tara and I dance and have a great time. Just as the song is about to end, we notice the rest of our team—Mark, Julio, Tom, and Cole—standing by the appetizer table, watching us with amused expressions.

"Y'all should have joined us," Tara says in her amazing Southern accent as we walk up to them.

"It's more fun to watch," Cole says to her, glancing at me quickly before looking away.

"If they play the 'Cupid Shuffle,' I'll go out with you ladies," Julio says, "or 'The Electric Slide.'"

"I'll hold you to that." I smile at him.

"Oh, I know you will," he replies with a grin.

"You want a drink?" Tara asks me.

"Sure," I say as she pulls me away by the wrist again.

I glance back and catch Cole's eyes for a second before he looks away.

Was he watching us walk away?

Tara maneuvers me to the bar at the far end of the room. She's almost young enough to be my daughter, but she's fun, sweet, and kind of innocent. I'm glad to have this time with her.

Tara orders a vodka cranberry, and I decide to start strong with a Long Island Iced Tea. Between the sexual tension with Cole and my social anxiety, I realize I need something to help me relax. As soon as the bartender hands us our drinks, Dr. Gabari appears.

"Autumn, I'm glad to run into you so early tonight," Tony says, approaching from my right, with Tara on my left.

"Tony, good to see you. This is Tara Ellender; she's on my team at Quisenbelt as well," I reply.

"Nice to meet you, Tara," he says, extending his hand to shake hers. "Always happy to meet another member of the team."

"I've heard a lot about you, Dr. Gabari. I'm going to see if I can track down Mark and Cole for you," Tara replies. "I heard you'd want to see them as well?"

"That would be great." He smiles and nods.

Tara walks off. I'm not sure where our team is, but I know she'll find them. I feel a bit nervous about her leaving me, but Tony isn't exactly a stranger.

"I see you already have a drink." Tony smiles, gesturing at my Long Island. "I guess that means I need to hang around until you finish that one so I can buy you another."

I laugh. "I don't know that I'll want another one. This is pretty strong."

"I'll get you something, even if it's for a lightweight," he jokes. "In all seriousness, Autumn, it really is good to meet you in person. We've talked so much during the sales calls over the last year or so. I don't know if Cole told you, but I asked if you could be my account executive, even though I know that's not your normal position."

"He did mention that." I smile, taking a sip of my drink and putting it back down on the bar, still holding it with my right hand.

Tony reaches his right hand around and rests it gently on my left hand, the one not holding my drink.

What the actual fuck?

"You live in Milwaukee, right?" he asks, his finger trailing the back of my hand, sending a chill through me.

I try to move back a little without being rude. He's handsome, but he's also a client, and even if he wasn't, something about him feels very creepy.

"Yeah," I reply.

"You know I'm in Chicago?" he continues. "I'm not that far from you."

"I know," I say. "Mark and I were hoping to visit the practice sometime in the next couple of months. Speaking of which," I pull my hand away as I turn to look around, "I wonder if Tara found them yet."

As I turn back toward Tony, I realize he is looking me up and down, not even trying to hide it. A wave of discomfort hits me, and my stomach churns with nausea.

"You do look stunning tonight," he says, his left hand reaching up to touch the thin straps on my right shoulder, his eyes following his hand.

"Thank you," I say, backing away slightly.

He continues to run his fingers along my thin straps before grabbing my right hand and bringing it level with his face. "That's a beautiful bracelet, too."

"It was a gift from my brother," I reply, my voice tight.

He keeps holding my hand, and I seriously might be sick. Where is Tara? I don't want to be here.

I look past him and see Mark and Cole. As Tony's left hand moves to my right arm, grazing my inner arm with his thumb and making my skin crawl, my eyes meet Cole's. I can't quite read his expression—anger, jealousy, sadness, maybe. Cole slows and lets Mark walk ahead of him.

"Mark!" I say excitedly, pulling my right arm free from Tony's grip to give Mark a half hug, strategically placing him between Tony and me.

As Mark and Tony exchange pleasantries, I down the other half of my Long Island like a shot, setting the glass back on the bar a little too forcefully. I glance back at Cole, who is still walking toward us.

Suddenly, I feel both protective of and in need of protection from Cole. My emotions are a maelstrom inside me.

As he approaches, my fingers loop around his left wrist. His eyes widen slightly, and I gently guide him around behind Mark, stepping back to put more of a human buffer between Tony and me.

Cole looks at me, his narrowed eyes burning into mine, making me want to melt into a puddle at his feet. It's like he's trying to communicate telepathically.

Then he masks his expression with a smile and turns toward Mark and Tony. I exhale in relief.

"Tony!" Cole exclaims, extending his hand for a half-handshake, then placing his left arm around Tony's shoulder, almost forcing me back another few inches.

"Cole, it's good to see you and your team," Tony says, winking at me. "I was just going to buy Autumn here a drink. Do either of you want one? It's on me."

Cole looks back at me, then turns to Tony with a big smile. "Sure."

Tony signals the bartender over. I face the bar, feeling a wave of relief with both Mark and Cole now between Tony and me.

"Ladies first," Tony says, looking down the bar at me when the bartender approaches.

"Another Long Island?" she asks.

I start to object, but then, "You know what, yeah, I'll take another Long Island." I think I'm going to need to find a bathroom to text Cara. My brain is swimming, and I'm about to feed it more alcohol.

"Going for the hard stuff tonight, are we?" Cole asks quietly, his voice dripping with an emotion I can't name.

"Yeah, I guess so," I almost whisper, glancing at him and then quickly back down at my empty glass.

"I'll have what she's having," Cole says, smoothly wrapping his arm around my waist, pulling me into a small half-hug, then drawing his hand across my back.

It reminds me of the way my brother tries to comfort me. It's quick, just a few seconds, and it feels like a silent message—that he does feel protective of me. But it leaves me feeling more confused as my body fully registers every single millisecond his body is in contact with mine. As his fingers graze the bare skin on my back, I have to contain the shiver my body wants to release. I inhale sharply, and I'm sure he notices.

I need more alcohol. Either to kill my inhibitions or numb these sensations, because this man is going to be the death of me. I just need to survive two more days and then go back to seeing him on a computer monitor.

"You two are crazy," Mark says. "I'll have a light beer, whatever you have on tap."

Tony also orders a beer. Mark and Cole take a couple of steps back from the bar, forming a small semi-circle, with Tony and me as the bookends.

Small talk ensues—weather, flights, airports, business, anything mundane to fill the space. When the bartender returns with our drinks, Tony raises his glass for a toast.

"To meeting in person," Tony says, "and to a hopeful visit from Autumn and Mark in Chicago soon."

We all raise our glasses and drink.

"Yes, we've been talking about that since you're such a good client," Mark says. "Although it sounds like you already know that."

"Yeah, I told him we were talking about it just before you two came over," I add.

Tony then asks about a device we're not selling yet but is in the pipeline. Mark and I don't know much about it, but Cole does, so he starts explaining. He sets down his drink and pulls a pen and paper from his pocket to draw a diagram. As I watch him write and talk with his hands, I completely zone out. Watching his fingers move is electrifying, sending me into a fantasyland, imagining those fingers and hands on me. They all start laughing over something, snapping me back to reality. I take a big sip of my drink.

I really need to talk to Cara.

Mark reaches out to shake Tony's hand. "Hey man, we'll see you around, and we'll make it to Chicago. But I need to go meet up with some other people."

"No worries, I appreciate you taking some time for me tonight," Tony says.

Mark pats Cole's shoulder and walks away, leaving me in an awkward position with two men who clearly have intentions beyond business or friendship. One is completely creeping me out, and the other I'm pretty sure I would fuck in a public bathroom right now.

What the hell is wrong with me?

"Well, Cole, you need to make sure that you all don't let this one go," Tony says, gesturing toward me with his drink. "She's an asset for sure."

I smile, feeling the heat of a blush. Cole looks at me, and when our eyes meet, he says, "Oh, I have no intention of letting her go."

Even though I know I'm blushing, I now feel the blood drain from my face, butterflies swarm in my stomach, and both fire and ice flow to my core.

"I'm glad our good employees are appreciated," Cole says, looking back at Tony. "You know, if you feel that way about her, you should write a formal comment on our feedback website. It can help with her bonuses and raises, so you could make a real difference for her."

"Really?" Tony asks. "I'll be sure to do that," he says, winking at me.

"Well, I would certainly appreciate it if you would take the time," I respond, smiling at Tony.

"Oh, I can take the time for you." Tony grins.

Cole suddenly looks toward the other end of the room. "Tony, will you excuse us? I see some other people we need to chat with." Without giving Tony a chance to respond, he gestures for me to move.

"Thanks for the drinks, Tony," I say as we walk away.

Cole places his hand on the small of my back, guiding me to the other side of the room.

"Cole, who are we going to see?" I ask with a little giggle.

He leads me to a more private area near the wall, stops walking, and turns to face me.

"Nobody, Autumn, I just needed you out of that situation. I mean, it seemed like you needed out of that situ—fuck," he stammers, nervous in a way I've never seen before. Cole rarely uses profanity, at least not around me. "I mean, if I was wrong, I'm sorry, but—"

I interrupt him by placing my hand on his forearm, looking him in the eyes. A jolt of electricity courses through me. "No, you read the room right. Thank you."

"Autumn, I don't know how to ask this, but did he say anything inappropriate? Did he solicit you in any way? I'm asking as your leader; I just need to know," he says, running a hand through his thick hair.

"Cole, it wasn't that bad, but it could have gotten there if you and Mark hadn't walked up when you did," I admit, reluctantly removing my hand. "He was talking about how close we lived to one another and implying things, but he didn't outright say anything."

Cole closes his eyes and exhales deeply before looking at me again. "So, I did read that right. You weren't okay with that?"

"No, he made me very uncomfortable, so thank you," I say, intentionally wrapping my hand around his wrist and grazing my thumb across the back of his hand.

He flexes his hand, reminding me of Cara's 'Mr. Darcy moment' analogy. I laugh uncomfortably.

"What?" Cole asks softly, his eyes gentle, trying to understand.

"Nothing, just reminded me of something my friend Cara said," I sigh and let go of his arm.

"Is that the friend who's trying to live vicariously through you?" he asks with a soft smile.

"You could say that. Although if I followed her wishes, I'd probably be in a hotel room with Tony now," I laugh softly and roll my eyes.

A wave of emotions crosses Cole's face, but the expression he lands on tells me he doesn't find that funny at all. He replies seriously, "Well then, I'm very glad you're not."

I feel the heat in my face. I look at my feet, then "Cupid Shuffle" comes on and I look back up at Cole. He smiles.

I see Tara and Julio heading to the dance floor, laughing. Quickly finishing my drink, I hand the empty glass to Cole and join them. Mark and Tom appear out of nowhere and join Cole. Every time I glance at them, they are all smiling.

When the song ends, I excuse myself to the restroom. I do need to pee, but I also need a chance to bare my languishing soul to Cara. Leaving my laughing and happy team by the dance floor, I head off alone.

In the stall, I pull out my phone. I have messages from Cara, Samantha, and Cole.

What the? I never even saw Cole with his phone.

Cole

I can't watch this anymore, why is he touching you?

Sorry, probably too far

How long was he watching me with Tony? I didn't think he even knew anything was happening until he walked over. As I have the thread open, three little dots appear.

Cole

> You look beautiful tonight by the way

A light and happy feeling runs through me. It's been so long since a man I wanted to think I was beautiful actually called me beautiful.

Fuck, he has the thread open. He'll know I saw this. I decide to deal with it later.

Cara

> You better dish when it's over, bitch

Me

> It's not over, but oh my gawd, Cara, I don't know what to do.

> There's this other guy, a doctor, a client, that was trying to hit on me. He kept touching me and totally creeping me out.

> Cole was not okay with it and got me out of the situation, but Cole also kept touching me, and then I grabbed his wrist, and he did the Mr. Darcy flex

> Cara, I don't know, he's my boss - wtf am I supposed to do?

Then I flip over to another unread message.

Then my chats start blowing up so fast I can barely keep up.

Cara

I think you just ignore the fact that he's your boss and do whatever you would do if he wasn't - but I need the deets when you're able to talk

Me

Uggh …

Cara

I get it, but when was the last time that you felt like *this*

Me

You know it has been a long time

Cara

Exactly my point, you can always find another job, you may not ever find another Cole

You've waited a long time for this, you deserve to be happy

Those are the words I needed to hear. I feel like I come out of a fog and gain clarity. If this is real, and it sure as fuck feels real, nothing else should matter.

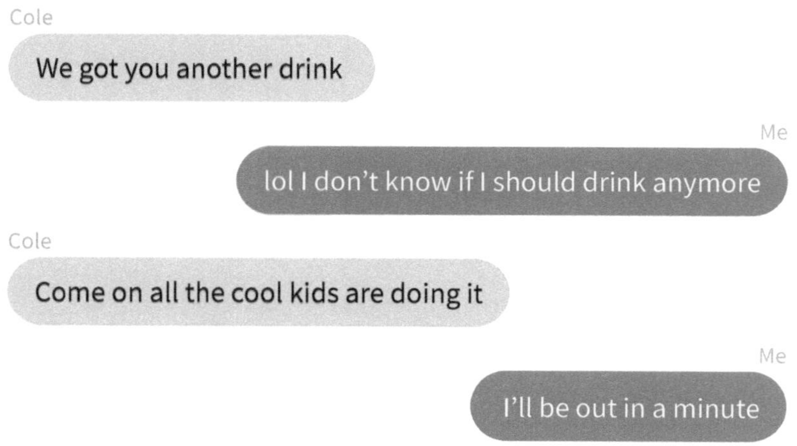

I put my phone in my pocket, finish up, wash my hands, fix some stray hairs in the mirror, and head back out to meet my team.

As I approach them, I see they're talking to another group from one of the pharmaceutical companies. Cole turns to me, hands me a drink, and as he does, he leans in, placing a hand on my waist and whispering in my ear, "I want to know where you keep a phone in that dress." His breath trails across my neck, sending electricity and warmth down my spine.

His scent envelops me, exhilarating and intoxicating. I turn my head toward him, fighting the urge to touch him, to kiss him. I take a breath before responding.

"That's for me to know and you to find out," I say softly, realizing too late how suggestive it sounds.

He arches an eyebrow, tilts his head, and a crooked, almost sinful smile materializes on his face. I look away, letting out a small, uncomfortable laugh, my eyes landing on the drink in my hand.

"What is this? Not another Long Island?" I ask.

"No," he responds, still with humor in his voice. "It's whiskey and ginger ale. Tom thought you might like it after your whiskey conversation yesterday."

I smile and take a sip. Cole turns back to the group and introduces me to the people I haven't met yet. There are eleven of us, and we enjoy making small talk, discussing business, and getting to know each other.

Cole frequently places his hand on the small of my back, often finding exposed skin whenever he can. I don't encourage him, but I certainly don't discourage it either. Every time his fingers find my bare skin, desire burns through me—heat in my veins, and vibrations in my nerves that settle at the junction of my thighs.

Tara slips over to me, saying she's exhausted and needs to get her heels off, so she's heading up to her room. She asks if I want to head up with her.

"No, I'm okay for now. That's what you get for wearing heels," I tease, bumping her shoulder lightly.

"I know, I know, you're older and wiser," she retorts.

"Ouch," I say, pretending to be offended.

"Like a big sister," she says, hugging me.

Tara says the rest of her goodbyes. Tom decides he probably needs to turn in too, as do a few people from the pharmaceutical company. The room starts to empty. It's nearing midnight, and we have to man a booth at eight in the morning. We decide it's time to head to our rooms. We split up by elevators again. Mark and Julio go to theirs, and four of the other group get in an elevator going to our floor.

As I go to step forward, Cole lightly puts his hand on my arm, smiles at them, and says, "We'll wait for the next one."

I glance at him, a mix of anxiety and excitement coursing through my body.

Why does he want me alone in an elevator?

I need to figure out my feelings quickly. My cheeks and nose are numb from the alcohol. I'm at that happy point of tipsy before I start feeling like crap, and honestly, I'm just happy. Although, I may not be in the best position to make decisions.

The elevator door opens, and we step in. I let him press the button, not wanting a repeat of last night. He stands slightly behind me and to my left. My heart races, butterflies swarm in my stomach, and the palms of my hands burn. I can't remember the last time I felt this way. I was probably a teenager. The anticipation and energy are overwhelming, not knowing his intentions or how I will react.

He moves in a little closer to me. The walls of the elevator are reflective but not mirrors, so I can sense what he's doing. I can tell he's looking at me. He raises his hand and moves toward me slightly but then puts it back down in his pocket. The air between us is thick with electricity, like a magnet drawing us together.

"So tomorrow," he finally speaks, his voice breaking the silence, "if you don't want a white mocha, what would you want?"

I turn and smile at him. There is hunger in his eyes—I'm not imagining it. I want to reach out and touch him. My left hand moves toward him slightly, but I drop it. The self-control required for me not to move into him should earn me an award of some kind.

"Um, honestly, most mornings I drink tea. From coffee shops, usually a nonfat chai latte."

"Tea, hmm, interesting," he says, looking at me.

I smile, wishing I could read his mind. The elevator doors open, and he gestures for me to step out first. My head starts to hurt from my updo, so I begin pulling the pins from my hair.

"Tara put these in so tight," I say, trying to fill the silence.

"I haven't seen you much with your hair up. It looked nice tonight," Cole says. "She did a good job."

I comb my fingers through my hair. "Today, I felt like she was the sister I never had," I say with a smile, wrapping my arms around myself to keep from reaching out to him.

"That's right, just a brother, right?"

"Yeah, Alex. He's three years older than me," I reply. "And you're one of seven or something crazy?"

He smiles. "Yeah, I'm the perfect middle of seven. The youngest is my only sister. I guess once they got the girl, they were done."

We reach my room, and I stop walking. He pauses too.

"Cole," I say softly, meeting his eyes. "Thank you for being my knight in shining armor tonight."

I take a chance and touch his arm, my thumb and index finger grazing his bare skin. He looks down at my hand.

"I'm just glad I could help," he says, looking back at me. I see the longing in his eyes. "Goodnight, Ms. Flynn."

"Goodnight," I say. He turns to leave. "Wait, Cole?"

He turns back. "Yeah?"

"Pockets," I say enthusiastically, smiling as I pull my room key and phone out.

He smiles. "Couldn't even tell."

"Goodnight," I say as I open my room door.

"Night," he responds and walks to his room. I watch him until he scans his key, then I walk into my room and immediately call Cara.

"Hey, Autumn," Cara answers the phone. I put her on speaker so I can change out of my dress and get ready for a shower.

I relay the entire evening to her—fixing Tara's hair, Cole's compliment, the dancing, Tony's creepy advances, Cole's rescue, the texts, and the elevator.

"Cara, I just don't know what to do," I whine.

"Here's the thing, Autumn," she says, surprisingly matter-of-factly, "you basically rejected him last night in those text messages. You kind of told him to stop without saying the words."

I sigh. "I can see that, and I accepted his apology coffee." I laugh a little.

"You did. So, Autumn, what is it that you want? That's the first thing you have to figure out."

"At first, I was worried about losing my job or him losing his, but after tonight, I think I just want him," I admit, realizing how true that is. "Cara, I haven't even dated or been attracted to anyone in forever. I don't even know what I'm doing."

"You need to do what comes naturally. It's like riding a bike. But if you want him, you need to let him know it's okay, that you're taking back that rejection. Even with the little I know about him from your conversations, one thing is clear—he's a gentleman. If he thinks you said 'no,' he's not going to push you. He may torture himself, but he won't pursue it."

"If you were me, what would you do?" I ask, knowing I might not follow her advice.

"I would text him tonight and tell him you enjoyed spending time with him. Nothing over the top like 'I want you now,' but enough to let him know you're thinking about him. Then tomorrow, turn on the charm, flirt with him, and find ways to touch him. You know he feels the same chemistry, so play on that."

"I think I can do that. It'd just be so different if we weren't here with the whole team," I say. "This all just caught me off guard. I know you say you saw it, but it all seemed like colleague friendship until I was here in person with him. How did it change overnight?"

"Pheromones," she laughs. "Y'all couldn't smell each other's pheromones through the computer."

We both laugh. "There might be some truth in that," I respond. "Thanks for being my sounding board, Cara. I could talk to the girls, but they would just make fun of me."

"I don't think they would," she says. "Now get some sleep soon. You'll need your beauty sleep for tomorrow."

"Thanks, I'll talk to you soon."

"You better," she says and hangs up.

I check my other messages. Both girls had written to me, making plans for the weekend Sami will be home. They reached out to Kevin too to see if we could make a weekend of it. It makes my heart happy that my kids want to spend time with each other and me. I have a couple of other messages from Cara, but I had already answered those when we talked.

I open my thread with Cole. There haven't been any messages since I was texting from the bathroom.

Me

Hey, I know I said it already, but thank you - you really were my knight in shining armor tonight

Well, maybe a shirt and tie lol

Cole

You should be sleeping, but you're welcome - again

Me

I still have to shower, but why aren't you sleeping?

Cole

I can't shut down tonight, too much going through my head

Me

I feel that - anything I can help with?

I know that was a loaded question, intentionally so. The three dots appear and linger. He's either writing a book or rewriting it again and again.

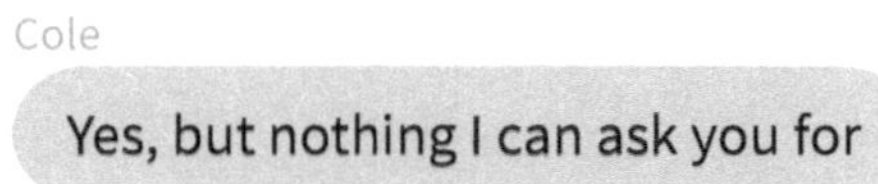

Now, I'm the one who can't decide what to say. I take an unreasonably long time to answer him.

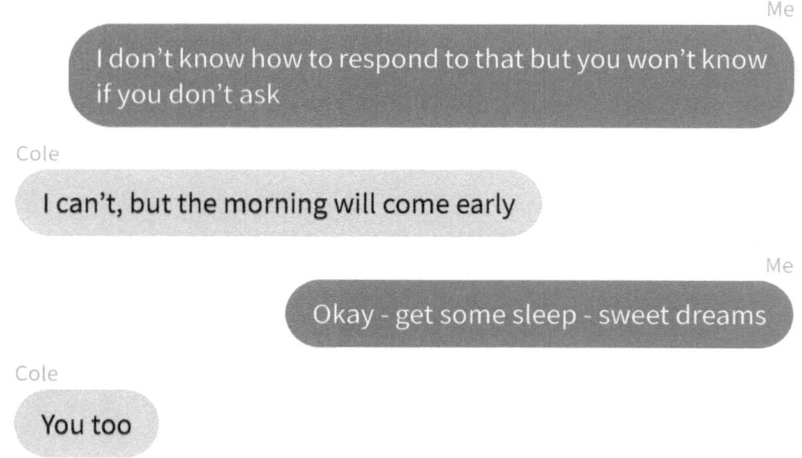

His responses feel cold, but I sense he's grappling with the same inner struggles I am. I shower, letting the hot water cascade over me. Even though I'm tired, I take the time to shave, exfoliate, and do all the things I sometimes skip. I just want to feel pretty and confident tomorrow. Sometimes I wear nice underwear even though nobody will see them because it makes me feel good, and this feels the same.

When I finally lay down in bed and drift off to sleep, I dream about Cole. It's been a very long time since my dreams about men featured anyone besides a faceless figure.

CHAPTER FOUR

THE YOU'RE WELCOME TEA

I wake up feeling surprisingly refreshed, despite the lingering effects of last night's indulgence and the few hours of sleep I managed. As I ease into the day, I take my time with my makeup, opting for a natural look—subdued and understated, a far cry from the more polished appearance I donned for the Meet and Greet. Today, I decide to go with the backless theme once more. This blouse, a deep forest green with a low V-back, features a delicate bow that ties at the base of my shoulder blades, and flowing angel sleeves that evoke a sense of whimsy and comfort. Paired with black slacks and the same strappy sandals from last night, I feel both grounded and just a little bit ethereal.

Cole's words about my updo still linger in my mind, so I decide to wear my hair half up. I pull back the strands just behind my ears and secure them with a gold and forest green comb clip. For the first time during this conference, I slip on a pair of earrings—long, gold dangles that complement the angelic sleeves and match the clip in my hair. I, again, ditch the purse for my pockets.

Before stepping out, I pause and glance through the peephole. Sure enough, there he is, scrolling through his phone, one cup cradled in the crook of his arm, the other in hand. My heart skips a beat, and a familiar warmth spreads through my chest. I take a deep breath, exhale slowly, and open the door.

Cole looks up, pocketing his phone with a casual ease that somehow feels intentional.

"Hey," I greet him, my voice soft and unsurprised to see him.

"Nonfat chai latte," he says with a smile, handing me the cup.

"You're too sweet, thank you," I reply, accepting it with a deliberate brush of our fingers. "So, if yesterday was apology coffee, what's this?"

He chuckles, a light sound that matches our easy stride towards the elevators. "I guess you could say it's 'you're welcome' tea."

"Cole, can I ask a favor?"

"You can always ask," he says, leaving the outcome open to interpretation.

"Would you stay in my group today? Just in case Dr. Gabari—Tony—comes around again?" I pause, the request hanging in the air. The truth is, I want him near for more than just that, but it's a convenient excuse.

"I was going to keep the groups the same, but yeah, I can do that," he agrees, before adding with a hint of mischief, "You know I separate you and Tara on purpose, right? It might seem a bit sexist, but we actually perform better when there's a female presence in the booth. It's not just us; you'll notice the trend at a lot of conferences."

"I had noticed and wondered about that," I admit.

"And I usually separate Tom and Mark, too. Their sales tactics are so similar that it's better to have one in each group," he continues. A small part of me wonders if he's just filling the silence, but for now, I'm content to let it be.

At breakfast, I grab a muffin and a banana again and settle at a table. It doesn't take long before Tara and the rest of the team filter in. The guys head straight for the hot food, while Tara comes over with her own muffin and an apple. We are, after all, creatures of habit.

"Autumn, my feet are killing me," she groans as she sits down. "I totally get why you gave up on heels when you were my age."

I chuckle, a knowing smile tugging at my lips. "I'll still wear them occasionally, but yeah, I gave up on heels around thirty. Being taller helps, but pregnancy changed my feet too. Now, even strappy shoes can be a challenge."

"Oh, the joys of getting older," she sighs just as the guys join us.

Cole surprises me by sitting to my left. After yesterday, I wasn't expecting it, but his proximity sends a flutter of excitement through me, a subtle thrill that prickles my skin and stirs something deep inside. Almost as soon as everyone is settled, Cole shifts into business mode.

"Alright, team, we're going to switch things up a bit today," he begins, his tone casual but focused. "Does anyone have any speakers they want to see, or anything specific planned for the day?"

"I don't today, but tomorrow, I'll want to see Tony speak. I think Autumn should too," Mark chimes in.

"Good to know. Anyone else?" Cole asks, glancing around the table. No one else pipes up, so he continues. "Alright then, here's the plan. Julio and I will swap today. The afternoon group could use his humor and charm, so I'll stick with Mark and Autumn in the morning, and Julio will go with Tom and Tara in the afternoon."

"Sounds good," Julio agrees with a nod.

Cole then shifts gears, his voice softening a bit. "Also, do you all want to have dinner as a team tonight, or would you rather take the evening to relax?"

"Well, we have to eat regardless," Mark says with a grin. "How about an early dinner? That way, we can still get to bed early. Last night was a bit late."

"Does that work for everyone?" Cole asks, his gaze sweeping the table. We all nod or voice our agreement. "There's an Italian restaurant about half a block from here. If no one objects, I'll make reservations there."

"No objections here," Tom chimes in. "I'm always down for Italian."

"Great, I'll book it for five. That gives us time to freshen up in our rooms if needed, but it's still early enough for a relaxed dinner."

Content with the plan, we all agree.

Not long after we settle into the booth, I'm grateful that Cole is by my side. Tony appears almost as soon as the doors open, but this time, he's brought along his new nurse practitioner.

"Good morning," Tony greets us with his usual charm. "This is Nicole Barnes, my new nurse practitioner. Nicole, meet Autumn, Mark, and Cole. Outside of Connor, our account exec, they're the ones we work with the most at Quisenbelt."

I extend my hand to Nicole, offering a warm smile. "I've heard so much about you, Autumn," Nicole says, casting a quick glance at Tony. "I think Dr. Gabari here is quite the fan."

"I think we've figured that out too," Cole interjects smoothly from my left, stepping forward to shake Nicole's hand. His movement subtly places me a bit further from Tony and Nicole, and Mark follows suit. I'm relieved not to have to respond directly—my knight in shining armor, indeed.

"So, Nicole, when did you start working with Dr. Gabari?" Cole asks, his tone light but purposeful.

Meanwhile, Tony's gaze lingers on me in a way that makes my skin prickle with discomfort.

"I started about six weeks ago, and I've already learned so much," Nicole replies, her eyes shifting between Cole and Tony.

"I'm sure you have," I say, aiming to deflect Tony's attention. "He knows his patients and his business."

Tony's smile is warm but pointed. "Well, you know yours too."

"Yes, she does," Cole adds, his voice carrying a quiet pride. "She's excellent at what she does, and so is the rest of my team." He turns to Mark. "Mark here is a wealth of knowledge as well."

"Nicole, let me grab some swag for you," I say, using it as an excuse to step away from Tony's gaze. I make a show of grabbing Cole's arm, as if I'm steadying myself, then let my hand glide across his back as I move behind him. It's a natural enough gesture, but in my head, I hear Cara's voice urging me to send all the subtle signals I can. I reach the box near Mark's feet, squat down, and gather a generous amount of swag for Nicole while the others continue their small talk.

Returning to Cole's side, I purposefully invade his personal space, positioning myself so that Tony would have to reach past Cole to touch me. As I hand the items to Nicole, my chest—cleavage and all—brushes against Cole's arm, sending a warm flush through my body. The sudden rush of heat makes my head spin slightly, and I feel my cheeks burn. I avoid looking at Cole, knowing that if our eyes meet, the intensity of my feelings will only amplify. But I hope—oh, I hope—he noticed.

"Welcome not only to Dr. Gabari's team but to ours as well," I say, my voice steady despite the storm of electricity coursing through me.

"Wow, that's a lot of swag," Nicole laughs, her eyes widening.

"Oh, do you need a bag?" Mark asks, already reaching down to hand her one. "We've got those too."

"How convenient," she chuckles. "I can use it for the rest of my swag around here too."

"Definitely," Cole says with a smile, his tone polite but dismissive. "I'm sure you have plenty of other booths to visit and speakers to hear. We'll see you at your talk tomorrow," he adds, directing the comment at Tony.

"Uh, yeah," Tony mumbles, a bit taken aback. "I suppose we should move on, see what else is out there."

"It was nice meeting you, Nicole," I say, leaning into Cole again as I extend my hand to her.

As they walk away and the distance between us grows, I glance at Cole. He's standing with his arms crossed, a quiet confidence about him. I squeeze his forearm, mouthing a silent "thank you."

He smiles, his eyes twinkling with understanding, and winks. "Anytime," he murmurs, just loud enough for me to hear.

Fuck, does he even realize what he's doing to me?

The morning unfolds smoothly, with a steady stream of people stopping by the booth, including some of our current clients. It's refreshing to meet them in person, and I'm relieved to realize that Tony is the only one who truly makes me uncomfortable. As the day goes on, it becomes clear how well Cole and I complement each other in the sales world. After two years of working together, we've developed an unspoken rhythm, a seamless partnership that feels almost effortless.

Whenever I can, I find subtle ways to touch Cole—whether it's resting my hand on his back while we talk or brushing against his arm as I walk by. The booth is small, which makes it easy to find excuses, and I take full advantage of that proximity.

By the time lunch rolls around, Cole seems to be in a better mood. He started the day a bit broody, but he's relaxed somewhat. He decides to leave the booth unmanned for a while, so we stash the swag behind the table and head to the dining hall. The rest of the team is already there when we arrive. After getting our food, I sit next to Tara, and, to my surprise, Cole takes the seat next to me once again.

"Okay, don't kill me," Cole begins, his tone almost apologetic as he raises his hands slightly in defense. "But we do need to do some team building at dinner." Mark and Julio groan in unison, their protests light-hearted but genuine. "I know, I know," Cole continues, "but we'll keep it casual—just a conversation. Throughout the afternoon, try to think of some things you all have in common or that you know you share with others in the group. Oh, and you can drink tonight, but it's on you—I can't expense it."

"Where's the fun in that?" Julio quips, making us all laugh.

After lunch, Mark, Cole, and I set out to visit more booths and maybe catch a speaker or two. The opportunities for flirtation are fewer in this setting, but Cole frequently rests his hand on the small of my back as we walk. Each time he pulls away, I feel a subtle ache, as if something is missing. His touch is more restrained than last night, but he still manages to find bare skin now and then, sending little jolts of electricity through me.

As we near four o'clock, we head back to the booth. Tara informs us that Tony had stopped by again, asking where I was.

"I don't know what we're going to do about that guy," Cole mutters, leaning against the table behind me, out of my direct view, while the rest of the team stands in front of me.

"Yeah, he's a little much with Autumn," Mark adds. "You both handled him well today, but with one more day here, I'll keep an eye out too."

"Thanks, Mark," I say, offering him a grateful smile.

Tara glances at me, her eyes curious. "Well, you *are* single, right? Is he not your type, or is it because he's a client?"

"Yes, and both," I reply, chuckling softly. "Honestly, he gives me the creeps a little—like a stereotypical used car salesman or something."

"I can see that," Tara nods. "He's not like that with me, but I haven't worked with him as much."

"And," I add, "you've got that rock on your finger."

"Maybe that's what you need," Mark suggests with a grin. "A ring, even if it's fake—guys like that might leave you alone."

"Maybe," I say with a shrug. "I'm not used to getting that kind of attention."

"Oh, I think you get that kind of attention more than you realize," Mark counters, raising an eyebrow. "Most men just aren't as forward as Tony. But, Autumn, you have to know you're a very attractive woman. Every guy that walks by this booth is happy to stop and talk to you—they're just not as obvious about it."

I feel the heat rise in my face as Julio chimes in, "Oh come on, you have to know that."

"You guys, stop," Tara intervenes, her tone protective. "You're making her uncomfortable. We all know Autumn is gorgeous, but you don't have to make her self-conscious about it."

From behind me, Cole clears his throat, his voice steady and serious. "Okay, well, whoever's around if Tony shows up again, just be mindful that he's bordering on harassment with Autumn." He steps forward, glancing at me briefly, his concern evident. "Let's just stay on guard."

"You still planning to watch him speak tomorrow?" Mark asks, looking at me.

"Yeah, I think I have to," I reply.

"Well, I'll go with you," Mark offers.

"Me too," Cole adds firmly.

"I haven't seen any of these interactions, but I can be there too if you need me," Tom chimes in.

"Best team ever," I say with a smile, feeling a deep sense of gratitude for the support surrounding me.

"Alright, if anyone needs to head upstairs before dinner, now's the time," Cole announces.

"I think I need to freshen up a bit," I say, already imagining the cool relief of getting my hair off my neck.

"Me too," Tara adds.

"Anyone else?" Cole asks, glancing around. The others shake their heads or shrug indifferently. "Okay, ladies, we'll see you over there in a few."

Tara and I head toward the elevators together.

"Are you going to change?" she asks.

"No, just going to touch up my makeup, reapply some perfume, and put my hair all the way up. It's sweltering outside," I reply.

"Good idea," she agrees. "I need to change my shoes. Even though these aren't heels, they're rubbing in the same spots as the heels did last night. I need to get them off."

"I totally get it. Meet you back here in ten?" I suggest as we split off to our respective elevators.

"Yep, that works for me," she says, heading to her room.

Upstairs, I touch up my makeup, opting for a lip stain to last through dinner. I take out my earrings, twist my hair up loosely but securely, and spritz on some body spray. Feeling a bit more refreshed, I head back toward the elevator, checking my phone as I go.

I smile at our exchange, then step out of the elevator and meet Tara in the lobby. Together, we walk over to the restaurant where the rest of the team is waiting.

"They wouldn't seat us until the whole party was here," Tom grumbles, a bit annoyed.

"So sorry," I apologize instinctively.

"Don't apologize," Cole says with a reassuring smile and a shrug. "You're actually a few minutes early. Our reservation isn't until five, and it's not quite five yet."

I glance at my watch—he's right. We still have almost ten minutes to spare. The hostess grabs the menus and leads us to our table. Cole, ever the gentleman or perhaps just a considerate boss, gestures for everyone to go ahead of him. Tara and I are at the back, so we're the last to follow. As we walk, Cole falls in behind me, and once again, I feel his hand on the small of my back for just a few seconds. But this time, as he drops his hand, it grazes over my ass—a touch that's new, and I can't quite tell if it's intentional. I inhale sharply, feeling a trail of heat in the wake of his hand.

When we reach the table, there's no choice left but for Cole and me to sit between Tara and Tom. I take the seat next to Tara, and as Cole settles in beside me, his leg brushes my arm. That simple, fleeting contact sends chills up my arm and lightning through my veins.

Seriously, Autumn, get your shit together.

CHAPTER FIVE

THE TEAM BONDING EVENT

After we've been seated for a few minutes, Cole leans in close, his breath warm against my neck and ear. "I'll buy you a drink if you want one," he murmurs, his voice laced with something that makes my pulse quicken.

I turn slightly to meet his gaze, allowing a slow smile to form. "I think I'm okay tonight. Maybe I should spend at least one evening here sober," I reply, deliberately holding his eyes for just a beat too long, letting the unspoken linger between us.

I order water, the only one at the table to do so. Once the food arrives and we've all started eating, Cole shifts into team bonding mode.

"I know, I know, this isn't exactly what you all want to be doing," he begins, his tone half-apologetic, half-serious. "But I think it's a good idea, and so do HR and my boss." He pauses, scanning the table before continuing. "We're each going to share something we know we have in common with at least one other person here. Then we can see if anyone else shares it, ask questions, or dig a little deeper—appropriately and within reason. Let's not let this go down the gutter, which I know it could very quickly with this team."

Laughter ripples around the table, breaking some of the tension.

"I'll start with Tom," Cole says, looking to his right, "and then we'll go around the table. I want you all to feel free to be open and honest, but let's keep it comfortable for everyone."

Tom clears his throat, visibly pondering his response. "Well, I think all of us, except Tara, have kids, so that's something we share."

"Very true," Cole agrees, nodding. "And I think we've all had plenty of conversations about our kids. Does anyone have anything to add?"

"I think all of y'all's kids are grown and out of the house, except for Julio, right?" Tara chimes in.

"I still have one at home," I say, glancing around the table. "But she's about to be a junior in college. They're all out of high school, though." I turn to Cole. "Cole, you still have one at home, too, don't you?"

"I do," he replies. "Well, at his mom's house most of the time, but same thing. He's my youngest, a sophomore in college."

"I still have one at home too—more like back at home," Mark laughs. "She's twenty-five and still figuring out life."

"So, Tom's the only true empty nester here?" Tara asks, looking around.

"Seems like it," Tom nods, a hint of pride in his voice.

"Alright, Julio, your turn," Cole says, shifting the attention.

"I'm taking the easy way out," Julio grins. "Tara, Cole, and I are all Georgia Bulldogs—we have that in common."

Laughter erupts again. "Maybe a little too easy," Cole teases. "Can you think of anything else?"

"Let's see." Julio taps his finger thoughtfully against his chin. "Well, sticking with the school theme, I think we all have master's degrees, right? So, we've all been down that road?"

Everyone nods in agreement. Then Cole chimes in, "Not to brag on her behalf, but Autumn has two of them."

A few curious looks circle the table, and I offer a modest smile. "I do. One in healthcare administration, but when I couldn't find the right job, I went back for my MBA. There was a lot of overlap in the credits, so it wasn't as much work as it sounds."

"Wow," Tom says, clearly impressed. "I had no idea."

"It's really not that big of a deal," I reply, shrugging it off.

"It is, but we'll let it slide," Cole says with a grin, his eyes lingering on mine for a moment. "Alright, Mark, you're up next. What've you got for us?"

Mark leans back in his chair, thoughtful. "I've been thinking about this. I'm pretty sure most of us don't live where we grew up."

"I do," I say, surprising a few of them. "I actually live about three blocks away from my childhood home. My kids even went to the same schools I did, for the most part."

"Nice," Mark nods. "I didn't know that."

"Neither did I," Cole adds, raising an eyebrow. "I knew you grew up in Wisconsin, but not that close."

"Yeah, my parents still live in my childhood home. It has its pros and cons," I say with a light shrug and a smile.

"Well, I moved from Oklahoma to Washington state, and I definitely miss being that close to my parents," Tara chimes in.

"I know most of your stories, but I'm curious—where did everyone else grow up and move to?" I ask, turning the conversation over to the group.

"I grew up in Kentucky and now live in Little Rock," Tom shares.

"My parents immigrated to Texas when I was a baby," Julio says. "Then we ended up in Atlanta, but after college, I made my way to Southern Colorado, and now I'm in Phoenix. We've bounced around a bit," he adds with a casual shrug.

"Nothing wrong with that," I say, nodding.

"Not at all," Mark agrees. "I've moved around too. For all you Bulldogs, I actually grew up in Athens, Georgia. Then I moved to Florida for a bit, and now I'm just outside Philadelphia."

"You know my story," Tara says.

"And mine," I add. "Although, when my ex-husband and I first got married, we lived in North Chicago for a while. I didn't move back to Milwaukee until after the divorce, mostly because I needed my parents' support."

"Nothing wrong with that either," Mark reassures me.

Cole takes his turn, his voice calm and steady. "Most of you know I grew up in Chicago, and now I'm in Fort Wayne. But after my ex-wife and I got married, we lived in Manhattan for a while. Once the kids were school-aged, we wanted to move to the suburbs, so we ended up outside Indianapolis before finally settling in Fort Wayne." He pauses, then gestures to Tara. "I guess that makes you next, Tara."

"My mind has been a bit one-track lately," Tara begins, a playful smile tugging at her lips. "But even though they didn't all work out, all of you have been married, and I will be in a couple of months."

"This is true," I say, returning her smile. "And hopefully it works out better for you than it did for me." I add the last part with a soft laugh, but there's a hint of wistfulness in my tone.

"Autumn, you can totally tell me if this is too much, but do you mind sharing what went wrong? Maybe it could help me down the road," Tara asks, her voice gentle but genuinely curious.

"No, it's fine, Tara," I say, aware that the entire table, especially Cole, is listening intently. I direct my words to her, but I speak slowly, choosing each one with care. "You have a big advantage over me—I was very young, only twenty-two, when I got married. I had Kevin, my oldest, when I was twenty-three. My twenties were a time of immense growth and change for both my ex-husband and me, and we eventually grew apart. But more than that, he became very controlling. He didn't want me talking on the phone with even my family, and he didn't like me going anywhere without him. The final straw was discovering his mistress." I pause, letting that sink in. "If we had met ten years later, I doubt we would've ever been married—or even dated—but I have three amazing children from that marriage, and for that, I wouldn't change a thing."

"Have you ever thought about getting married again?" Tara asks, her curiosity deepening.

I shrug slightly, feeling the weight of the question. "I have," I admit, careful with my next words, knowing Cole is likely listening closely. I swallow and take a breath. "When the divorce first happened, I was focused on my kids and getting through school as a single mom. I relied heavily on my parents for physical and financial support, so every moment not spent studying or working was dedicated to my kids. I fell into a pattern of being alone, I suppose." I pause, choosing my next words deliberately. "Up until now, I haven't had feelings like that for anyone since the divorce, which was a long time ago. It's not

that I wanted to be single all this time—it's just that the right person
hasn't come along. If I do take that leap again, it will have to be
with someone I trust completely, someone who makes me feel safe,
because my ex never did. They say the hardest part about dating a
woman who's been single for a while is that you're not competing
with other men—you're competing with how she treats herself."
Tara and Mark laugh, and I smile, feeling the truth in those words.
"But now, with all my kids out of high school, I have more time. So,
we'll see what happens."

Julio, likely trying to lighten the mood, chimes in with a grin.
"Man, don't you miss the sex?" He laughs, but the table falls silent.

"Julio," Cole snaps, his tone sharp, shaking his head in
disapproval.

Bless Tara, she doesn't miss a beat. "Oh, we girls do just fine
in that department without a man," she quips, making everyone
laugh. Then she turns to Cole. "What about you, Cole? Do you mind
sharing, or is that too personal?"

"No, it's fine," Cole says, glancing at me for just a second—a
look that feels charged with meaning. "My ex was very type A, very
career-driven, which was great at first. We also got married young—I
was twenty-two and didn't really know what I wanted to do with my
life. We went to college together, got married right out of school,
and had our first son almost immediately. She wasn't very interested
in being a mother, so I became the default parent. There was a lot
of resentment on both sides, and eventually, she cheated on me with
a partner at her firm," he says, looking at me again. "And that was
the end of that." Then he turns back to Tara. "And to preempt your
next question, after the divorce, I did a little bit of 'sowing my wild
oats,' you could say. But up until now," he adds, his tone and words
subtly mirroring mine, "I haven't felt the kind of chemistry with
anyone that made me want to risk getting my heart broken again."
He finishes with a shrug, but his words linger in the air.

"Who knew Cole Waters had a heart?" Julio jokes, then quickly
adds, "Just kidding, man, just kidding."

Cole laughs, breaking the tension, though I'm not sure if I
appreciate the shift in mood or not.

"Well, I think that was some solid bonding," Cole says, his tone lightening. "Good questions, Tara." Then he turns to me, his gaze lingering just a moment longer. "I guess it's your turn now, Autumn."

"Oh my," I start, feeling the weight of Tara's previous question hanging in the air. I decide to lighten the mood a bit. "I was going to say something different, but now I'm thinking we all have at least one sibling, right?"

Everyone nods in agreement. I glance at Cole with a teasing smile. "I think Cole here wins with his six siblings though."

Cole grins, a bit of pride in his eyes. "Yeah, I think I do have the most siblings."

Julio jumps in. "I've got four, so I'm next in line."

"Including step-siblings, I've got four as well," Mark adds.

"I just have one sister, Julie," Tara says, turning to me. "And you've just got Alex, right?"

"Yeah, one brother," I confirm, before looking at Tom. "What about you, Tom?"

"I have two—one brother and one sister," Tom replies.

Cole takes a deep breath, clearly about to steer the conversation into deeper waters. "Well, I guess that brings it back to me. Since we all have siblings, how about something we all definitely have—parents? I'm curious if any of you are comfortable talking about your relationships with them." He looks at Tom to start.

"My parents were married for over forty years before my dad passed away," Tom begins. "My mom is still with us, a spry ninety-three. We had an okay relationship—my dad was military, so our house ran like a tight ship. They were strict, but I always felt loved and supported, even if it wasn't always through words." He stops and turns to Julio.

Julio nods, picking up the thread. "Like I mentioned, my parents were first-generation immigrants. They came to the U.S. without speaking any English, so us kids had to help out a lot. They've been married over fifty years now, and we're a close-knit family. We all live in Phoenix, and on Sundays, everyone—kids, grandkids—gets together for dinner. It's a lot of people, but it's what keeps us connected."

"So, your whole family moved to Phoenix?" I ask, intrigued.

"Yep, the whole crew," Julio replies with a smile.

Mark takes his turn. "My dad was never really in the picture. I met him a few times, but I was mostly raised by my mom and an incredible stepdad. They've been together for about forty-five years, and they're still ridiculously in love—always gooey and sappy. My mom is pretty much always right, of course," he chuckles. "We're close. I've got a mix of step-siblings and half-siblings, and we make it a point to get together once a month."

Tara chimes in next. "I think most of you know this, but my parents are in Oklahoma. They were high school sweethearts and still live in the small town they grew up in. They've been married almost thirty-five years. Honestly, they're like magazine or TV show parents. Not perfect, but pretty close. They host parties, and my mom has a homemade dinner on the table every night by six. But trying to live up to them? Exhausting. I've learned that I'm not my mom, and we're not my parents. It's not going to be like that for us." She laughs softly before turning to me. "What about you, Autumn?"

"My story is pretty similar to yours, Tara," I say, gathering my thoughts. "My parents are wonderful—supportive, loving. My mom was the quintessential housewife, though now that they're older, they have some help around the house. I'll never be the kind of cook or housekeeper she was." I pause before sharing more. "My dad did cheat on my mom when I was in high school. We weren't privy to all the details, but they worked through it and have been married nearly fifty years now." I look at Julio, smiling. "We do Sunday dinners too, but with my kids spread out and my brother in the Pacific Northwest, they're not quite the same. Overall, my parents drive me crazy, but they're pretty great." I turn my gaze to Cole, ready for his response.

"Alright," Cole begins, taking a deep breath as if steeling himself. "I chose this topic because it gives me a chance to be a little vulnerable and bond with all of you." He pauses to take a sip of wine, the moment heavy with anticipation. "Most of you know I come from a big family, but when I was about twelve, protective services came and took the five youngest of us out of our home. My oldest brother had moved out and reported some of the things that happened to us to the police. After an investigation, they decided to remove us from the house."

He pauses again, letting the words sink in. I'm trying to process the weight of what he's sharing.

"Most of us have scars," he continues, his voice quieter. "Food was used as punishment, among other things." The atmosphere around the table grows thick with unspoken emotions as he takes another sip of wine, then clears his throat as if to steady himself.

"My brother wanted to take us in, but the courts turned him down, saying he wasn't old enough or stable enough to care for us. None of our other relatives wanted us, so we ended up scattered in the foster care system. In some ways, I'm grateful because it gave me the drive to be different, to not repeat the cycle. But it also probably led me into a bad marriage. My siblings and I are spread out across several states now. I'm close to my oldest brother, but the rest of us don't talk much. My parents ended up in prison. None of us, except maybe my sister, has contact with them. I don't even know if they're still in prison."

"Cole," I say softly, my voice barely above a whisper. He glances at me briefly before looking back at his drink, his expression guarded.

"Damn, man," Mark says, breaking the silence. "I thought my deadbeat dad was about as bad as it could get in this group."

Cole laughs softly, but it's a sound laced with discomfort. "It's not a happy story, but now you know a little more about me. Maybe too much, but it's out there. It shaped the kind of parent I am. I don't ever raise my voice at my kids, even when they probably need it. I also rarely yelled at my ex-wife, even when I probably should have. I was adamantly against any form of spanking or anything that resembled how my dad was. I guess I went too far in the opposite direction, but I'd rather be that way than repeat what I grew up with."

A heavy silence settles over the table, the weight of his words lingering in the air.

"Well, I definitely feel more bonded," Tara says, attempting to break the tension with a small laugh. We all chuckle, though the humor feels strained.

"Okay," Cole says, shifting the mood. "Let's finish eating, and then we can think about dessert."

As the others return to their meals, I glance at Cole, seeing him in a new light. This was the most vulnerable I've ever seen him. His left hand rests on his leg as he eats with his right. I can't resist—I reach over under the table and gently squeeze his hand, a surge of electricity jolting through me at the contact. I run my thumb over the back of his hand and lean in close, whispering, "I'm so sorry, Cole. That must have been hard to talk about."

He freezes for a moment, then squeezes my hand back, his voice low as he replies, "It's alright. It's something that needed to be shared at some point."

Reluctantly, I start to pull my hand away, but his fingers drag lightly against mine as if he's reluctant to let me go. I hope it was quick enough that no one else noticed.

Cole looks at me, his expression difficult to decipher, as if he's trying to read something in my face. His eyes trace the contours of my features, avoiding direct eye contact for a few seconds, and then they meet mine. The emotions I see in his gaze are a whirlwind—sadness, desire, hunger. His pupils dilate slightly, and I'm certain mine do the same.

"Anyone interested in dessert?" the waitress interrupts, breaking the charged silence between us.

"I'd love to look at a dessert menu," I say, turning to her with a smile.

"We can share the menu," Cole adds, shifting his gaze from me to the waitress.

She hands the menus around the table, and it seems like we're all in the mood for dessert tonight—maybe trying to soothe our emotions with something sweet after the heavy conversation.

"Oh, they have my favorite, tiramisu," I mention to Tara.

"One of my faves too," she agrees, "but I think I might go for the cheesecake instead. It's hard to resist."

I start to hand the menu to Cole, but as he takes it, our fingers brush. His touch lingers a moment too long, sending a tingle up my arm. He notices the goosebumps on my skin and narrows his eyes slightly, as if he's trying to read more into my reaction.

I drop my hands into my lap and focus on Tara while she orders her cheesecake. Tom decides to skip dessert, mentioning that he needs to call his wife and asking if he can head back early. Cole reassures him that it's no problem at all.

We finish our desserts, and as the bills are settled, I realize this is our last night together as a full team. As we start to get up, I feel a surge of boldness and decide to take another chance.

Turning toward Cole, I aim to squeeze his hand again, but he moves it just as I reach out. Instead, my hand lands on his thigh. I hesitate for only a second before I go with it, giving his thigh a gentle squeeze before trailing my hand up to his bicep. His eyes lock onto mine, narrowing just slightly as if he's trying to figure me out. I smile, leaving my hand on his arm as I stand up.

Cara would be so proud of me.

I almost think I hear him inhale sharply, but I'm already moving behind him, catching up to Tara before he can fully process what just happened. I loop my arm through Tara's, trying to ignore the heat and ache building in my core. She gives me a knowing smile.

"How are the feet?" I ask, trying to redirect my thoughts.

"I think they're better," she replies, "but I'm going to soak them tonight. We have some extra time!"

I glance at my watch—it's not even seven. "True," I agree. "They'll feel better tomorrow."

As we reach the front door of the restaurant, I turn back to see Cole trailing about ten yards behind us. "Come on, slowpoke," I tease, still holding onto Tara's arm.

"Looking at all of us, who would think you're the one who didn't drink tonight?" Cole jokes as he catches up.

I flash him a mischievous smile, biting my lower lip. I watch his eyes darken, his pupils expanding in response.

The hotel is just a short walk away, and Tara and I chat easily as we head toward the elevators. When we reach them, the group splits—Julio, Mark, and Tara head to one set, while Cole and I walk to the other.

I feel a strange, almost giddy sensation coursing through me—a mix of excitement and nerves, all fueled by my own hormones. I haven't felt this way in a long time.

"See you at breakfast," I say to the others as their elevator doors close.

I turn back to find Cole watching me, his expression almost puzzled.

I give him an innocent look. "What?" I ask as our elevator doors open. He doesn't answer, and we step inside, the tension between us thick and electrifying.

CHAPTER SIX

THE HALLWAY SPEECH

The elevator doors close, sealing us into a small, intimate space. Much like we were the night before, our positions mirror the previous encounter. This time, though, when I see his hand move in the reflection, reluctance doesn't win. Gently, he runs the back of his fingers from the nape of my neck to my waist, dragging slightly where my shirt is tied across my back. A silent question hangs in the air, testing how I will react.

A trail of electricity and warmth follows his touch. My breath stutters, but I don't pull away. His hand lingers on my waist for a few seconds—another test, perhaps—before he leans in close to my ear and whispers, "Oh, the things I want to do with you, Ms. Flynn."

The use of the word "with," not "to," catches my attention, making me want him more. His breath caresses the baby hairs on my neck, sending intoxicating waves through my body. Goosebumps are inevitable.

Turning toward him, I smile.

A sigh escapes him, as if he's been holding his breath, his body relaxing slightly. Surprised, he looks at me, perhaps expecting an argument, rejection, or hurt. Reaching up, he tucks a loose strand of hair behind my ear. My gaze is probably more than a little lascivious.

"Cole," I say softly, "you're still my boss."

Placing his hands in his pockets, he sighs and says, "I know."

The elevator doors open, and we step into the hall. Reality hits square in the face. Reasons to not pursue this flood my mind, despite my intense desire. Using Cara's logic, those five words I uttered in the elevator could be taken as a shutdown.

Utterly unnerved, my moral and ethical compass clashes with my heart and desires. Eyes closed, I take a deep breath.

I can find another job, but I may not ever find another Cole.

"Cole," I say softly, reaching for his forearm to stop him, turning him toward me as his hand slips from his pocket. I try to keep my voice steady, gentle. "I feel it too. But I don't want you to lose anything over this—over me. You've worked so hard to get where you are."

He lets out a quiet laugh, his eyes softening. "You're worried about me? That's so like you, Autumn. It's one of the things that makes you so endearing to everyone."

He looks at me for a brief moment before shaking his head and continuing to walk, my hand slipping from his arm.

"Cole," I call out as we approach my room, trying to catch up to the emotions swirling between us. "We're just really getting to know each other. I mean, yes, we've talked for years—"

He stops abruptly, cutting me off as we reach my door. His voice is low, almost a whisper, and he avoids my gaze. "Autumn, you can't be serious. We do know each other, but this"—he gestures between us, the intensity palpable—"this thing between us, it took me by surprise. Did I like talking to you? Did I find you attractive? Yeah, of course. But until that moment in the elevator two nights ago—maybe even a little before, at the restaurant—I didn't realize just how much I *want* you."

He pauses, taking a breath, as if weighing whether to continue. When he exhales, he finally meets my gaze, locking his eyes with mine for the first time since that moment in the elevator. His voice is raw with emotion as he continues, "I feel like I'd be willing to make big sacrifices for you. And you have no idea how much it infuriated me to see Tony touching you like that." His jaw tightens as he looks away, clearly fighting the images in his mind. "Honestly, Autumn, I think our normal working relationship is over, regardless of what happens here in Dallas. Even if I walk away right now, even if we never act on this, I'll always be thinking about it. And I'm not sure I can manage to keep you out of my physical vicinity during the normal course of business."

He looks me up and down, and the way he does it sends a wave of heat rushing through me. It's not creepy—it's intense, confident, and unmistakably masculine. My body responds instantly, every nerve alight, every part of me longing for him.

"Cole," I murmur, my voice pleading, his name hanging in the air between us, thick with unspoken desire.

In a heartbeat, he steps forward, his hands gently gripping my hips as he backs me up against the door. His lips hover inches from mine, and the scent of him—earthy, spicy, intoxicating—envelops me. The sensations coursing through my body are unlike anything I've ever felt before, an ache building deep inside me, wetness pooling at my core. Every inch of me is attuned to him, to the moment, to the inevitability of what's about to happen.

Holy fuck, did I break him? Did I push him to the edge where he's willing to risk everything for me?

I look into his eyes, repeating his name softly, "Cole—"

His voice drops to a near whisper, as if he's acutely aware that we're standing in a hotel hallway where anyone could walk by at any moment. "I'm not going to kiss you, Autumn, unless you ask me to. Look, I won't even touch you." He moves his hand from my waist to the door behind me, one hand resting above my right shoulder, the other beside my left hip. He leans in, his mouth so close to my ear that every breath, every word, sends waves of electricity through me. "I'm safe. I would be the safety you need and want. If we do this, I'm one hundred and ten percent in. I won't leave tomorrow, and I won't let them fire you."

He leans back slightly, his eyes locking with mine for the first time since the elevator. "If one of us has to lose a job over this, I'll be the one to fall on that sword. I tried, Autumn. For two fucking days, I tried. I tried to just get over it, and in those short two days, I realized I couldn't. I don't think I ever would. And then you touched me, again and again, and it gave me hope."

He pauses, then moves closer to my left ear, his voice dropping to a low growl that sends a shiver down my spine. "I have never wanted anyone this much in my life," he confesses, his words melting me from the inside out. "And it's far more than physical. You're smart, funny, and such a good person. You radiate beauty—you are beautiful—and you make everything around you shine. I didn't realize that until this weekend, and it surprised me. If we cross this line, I promise I'll do everything in my power to make your life better, to give you more, to make it worth it."

He pulls back slightly, his eyes boring into mine with an intensity that almost knocks the breath out of me. "I haven't felt this drawn to anyone in a very long time, maybe ever. I want you, Autumn. I want you to be mine, fully, unconditionally, and indefinitely mine." The end of his sentence is almost a growl, the word "indefinitely" lingering in the air between us.

Indefinitely? Did he just say indefinitely?

I'm speechless, my thoughts dizzying as I realize my hands have moved to his chest. My left hand is splayed out, while my right has balled up a part of his shirt. I'm biting my bottom lip, unable to move, unable to speak. The electric charges coursing through my body, combined with the weight of his words, have left me too overwhelmed to respond.

"Autumn, say something," he pleads, his voice filled with a quiet desperation as he pulls back slightly. His face falls, and he asks, "Do you want me to go?"

I shake my head no, but the words won't come. My lips part, but no sound escapes.

"Autumn, talk to me," he urges, his eyes searching mine, as if he's afraid I'm about to break his heart.

I tighten my grip on his shirt, dragging my gaze from his eyes to his lips, biting my bottom lip again.

I just want to kiss you.

"Autumn?" His voice is almost a whisper. "You've got to tell me what you're thinking."

I look back into his eyes, my voice barely audible as I finally speak. "If we cross this line, there's no uncrossing it."

He gently tucks loose strands of hair behind my ear with his right hand and murmurs, "I know, trust me, I know."

He leans his head against his hand, resting it beside my face, and I sense a shift in his posture as if he's bracing for rejection. I can't let him think that.

"Cole?" I say, my voice questioning as I pull him closer by his shirt.

His hand moves back above my shoulder, and he lifts his head, hope rekindling in his eyes as his face draws nearer to mine. "Autumn?" he whispers.

I draw him closer still, my lips brushing his ear as I whisper, "I think we should go inside the room now."

I drop my left hand and reach into my pocket for my room key. That's all the permission he needs. As soon as I pull it out, he swiftly takes it from me, his movements quick and decisive. With a single motion, he scans the lock, the green light flashing almost instantly, and before I can even process what's happening, he's backing me into the room.

The door closes behind us with a soft click, sealing us away from the outside world.

Once we're inside, Cole turns me against the wall, just to the side of the doorway, placing me in a position so similar to where we were moments ago, but now in the privacy of my room. The only light comes from the faint glow of the television on the hotel's welcome screen and the last remnants of daylight slipping through the edges of the drawn curtains.

"Autumn, are you sure?" His voice is hesitant, filled with doubt. "I really don't want you to feel like I'm pressuring you into anything."

"Cole," I say, clearing my throat to steady my voice. "Can you just shut up and kiss me now?"

His face transforms, lighting up with a brightness I hadn't seen before. It's as if the darkness that had been weighing on him lifts in an instant.

His next moves feel deliberate, as though he's thought about this moment a thousand times. He wraps his left arm around my waist, pulling me tightly against him, and I can feel the hard evidence of his desire pressing into the soft flesh between my hips. My hands flatten against his chest, then slide up to wrap around his neck. His right hand cradles my face, his thumb grazing along my jawline before tracing over my bottom lip. He lowers his mouth just inches from mine, searching my eyes one last time before closing the distance, capturing my lips with his.

The moment our mouths meet, it feels like an explosion ignites within me. The kiss is deep, filled with a hunger that leaves me breathless. His hand weaves into my hair, and the roughness of his facial hair against my skin is both exhilarating and tender. I lose track of time and place, lost in the sensation of his mouth moving against mine, tasting him, needing more. I reach up, my fingers threading through his hair, and pull him even closer, my body aching with desire.

His left hand moves slowly, deliberately, from my waist up to the side of my torso, his thumb slipping beneath the fabric of my shirt to brush against the bare skin of my ribs. The gentle caress sends a shiver through me, a soft moan escaping my lips as my body responds to his touch. My skin tingles under his fingertips, and when our mouths finally part, we're both breathing heavily, our foreheads nearly touching as we gaze into each other's eyes. His hand continues to move along my back and side, keeping the connection alive.

I realize he's still holding back, still worried about crossing a line, and I know I need to show him that I'm fully here, that I want this just as much as he does. With a sudden resolve, I begin unbuttoning his shirt. He glances down at my hands, then back up at my face, his expression softening as he gently tucks loose strands of hair behind my ear again. His other hand trails slowly down my ribs, sending another wave of electricity through my body.

It's clear now—there's no turning back. The desire between us is undeniable, and I'm ready to let it consume me.

"Cole?" I murmur as I continue working on the buttons of his shirt, my fingers trembling slightly with anticipation.

"Autumn?" His voice is thick with desire, his eyes following the path of his thumb as it traces along my cheekbone and jaw.

"It's been literally over a decade since I've done this," I confess, exhaling slowly to steady myself. "Please be patient with me."

His hand slips beneath my chin, gently tilting my face so our eyes meet. The intensity in his gaze is almost overwhelming. "First off, same," he says softly, "and I don't think I could ever be impatient with you."

"Same?" I echo, surprise lacing my voice.

"Same," he confirms, nodding slightly, his breath warm against my skin. "There was a time of sowing my wild oats, or whatever you want to call it, but I didn't like how it made me feel. I promised myself the next time would mean something." As I finish unbuttoning his shirt, he helps me slide it off his shoulders.

"I hope this means something then," I say with a smile, searching his eyes for reassurance.

"Honestly, Autumn, I think this means everything," he growls, his voice low and raspy, sending a shiver down my spine.

I reach behind his neck, pulling him into a hungry kiss, our mouths colliding with a newfound urgency.

As I pull back slightly, I find my voice again. "Also, because it's been so long, you don't have to worry about anything with me. My tubes were tied after Sami, so—"

Cutting me off with another kiss, his lips silence mine before I can finish. My hands slide down his torso, grabbing at the hem of the white t-shirt he's wearing beneath his button-down. He pulls back just long enough for me to tug the shirt over his head, revealing his chest—solid muscle covered in a light dusting of hair. I can't resist running my fingers through the soft curls, marveling at the warmth of his skin beneath my touch.

His hand glides up and down my bare back, each stroke sending shockwaves of pleasure straight to my core. I reach up, freeing my hair from its clip, letting it tumble around my shoulders. His hand tangles in it almost instantly, his fingers curling into the strands as if he's been waiting for this moment.

Finding the tie at the back of my shirt, he tugs on it slowly, untying the bow with deliberate care. His hands slide up my back, pushing the sleeves off my shoulders, then loop into the waistband of my slacks, easing them down just over my hips. As the cool air hits my exposed skin, he slides his hands over my cheeks, his touch firm yet tender. I'm suddenly grateful for the thong I chose and the time I took to prepare, realizing that maybe I'd hoped for this more than I admitted to myself.

My clothes fall in a soft heap on the floor, and he leans back, his eyes dropping to my bra with a soft chuckle.

"Interesting," he says, his voice full of amusement.

I blush, biting my lip as I smile. With a quick tug on the strings in the middle, my bra falls away, leaving me in just my thong and sandals. He pulls me close, pressing my bare chest against his, the heat of his skin searing into mine. He turns me away from the wall, guiding me backwards toward the bed. As we move, I kick off my sandals, not wanting anything to come between us.

As my knees hit the bed, I fall into a sitting position and immediately start unbuckling his belt. My fingers move quickly, unbuttoning and unzipping his slacks, and he groans softly as they slide down to the floor. He kicks off his shoes and socks, and I scoot further up onto the bed. Within seconds, he's beside me.

Cole lies on my right side, his hand gently tracing the contours of my face. "You are so beautiful," he whispers, kissing my forehead, then each cheek, before finally brushing his lips against mine.

In that moment, I feel completely cherished, safe, and this connection between us feels so much more than just physical. As his fingers move, I watch his eyes follow the path of his hand as it glides down my body. Every touch sends a jolt of electricity through me, my nerves alive with desire. He traces the curve of my breasts, the dip of my navel, and then softly brushes the inside of my thigh. His hand slowly makes its way back up, all the way to my mouth, where he kisses me deeply, as if he's trying to consume every part of me.

When our lips finally part, he begins a slow descent down my body, his mouth leaving a trail of heat in its wake. He kisses along my jawline, nibbles at my earlobe, and then moves down my neck until he reaches my breasts. He takes his time, teasing me, kissing around my left breast and nipple, deliberately avoiding the sensitive peak. He moves to my right breast, repeating the same torturous process, leaving me trembling with anticipation, my nipples aching for his touch. Just when I think I can't take any more, he finally takes my nipple into his mouth, his tongue swirling around it. The sensation makes me gasp, my back arching instinctively. He shifts to my other breast while his hand begins to explore my inner thighs, teasing, taunting, driving me wild. My fingers rake through his hair, scratching down his back as I'm consumed by the pleasure he's giving me.

He continues his journey down my body, and I cling to his hair until he's out of reach. When he reaches my waist, he slowly slides my thong down my legs, groaning as he feels how wet I am. His hunger for me is palpable, and he gently bites and sucks on my inner thigh.

I know I'll have a mark there tomorrow, a hidden reminder of this night, proof that it wasn't just a dream. My hips naturally tilt toward him, silently begging him to come closer. After what feels like an eternity of teasing my inner thighs with his mouth, leaving me even more soaked and desperate for him, he finally slips two fingers inside me. He hooks his fingers up, finding that perfect spot almost immediately. My body responds, trying to draw him even closer, and he groans, parting my folds and letting his mouth find exactly where I need him to be.

And fuck, my body craves him. His tongue circles and his fingers maintain a perfect rhythm, and I feel the orgasm building quickly, the days of tension between us coming to a head. I grind into his mouth and hand, pushing his fingers deeper, and when he groans, the vibration is the final push I need. My muscles clench around his fingers as the orgasm rips through me, and he groans again, his voice full of satisfaction.

"Fuck, Autumn," he sighs, moving back up my body.

He wraps my hair in his hand, pulling my mouth to his. His facial hair is wet, and I can taste myself on his lips—it's so fucking hot. I wrap my arms around him, my hands sliding gently up and down his back. When I pull back slightly, he looks at me with a hint of curiosity. I reach up, tracing his cheekbone with my fingers, and he turns his face to kiss the inside of my palm.

The hunger within me flares, and I draw his attention back to my face, running my thumb across his lips and down his chin. I whisper, "I just really need you to fuck me now."

Cole arches an eyebrow, a sly smile playing on his lips. "You want me to ask again?" I tease, but he shakes his head.

"Your wish is my command," he replies, his tone dripping with a mix of humor and need.

He hooks his thumb into his boxer briefs, smoothly ridding himself of them. For someone out of practice, he moves with the ease of a man who knows exactly what he wants. He settles between my legs, hovering just outside of me, almost as if he's savoring this moment, teasing both of us.

He looks up at me one last time, asking silently if I'm sure. I nod, and that's all he needs. He thrusts into me hard, filling me completely, and all I can think is that this is exactly what I've been waiting for.

"Fuck," I whisper, my head falling back as he thrusts into me. He's thick, filling me completely, making me feel whole in a way I hadn't realized I was missing. I wrap my legs around him, pulling him deeper, and he groans, the sound vibrating through my body as he moves in and out of me. He slows down, trying to make it last, his mouth finding mine in a heated kiss.

"God, you feel so good," he whispers, his face nuzzling against the side of mine.

I adjust my legs, angling him just right so he hits that perfect spot with every thrust. The pleasure builds quickly, each stroke pushing me closer to the edge. The time he's inside me feels both infinite and far too fleeting.

His ear is right next to my mouth, and I whisper, almost pleading, "Come with me?"

I can't control the moans escaping my lips—it all feels so incredibly good. As the orgasm builds, I grab his arm, my nails digging into his skin, probably leaving marks.

"Fuck, Autumn," he groans, thrusting into me one last time. My body convulses as I feel him pulsing inside me, our climaxes merging into one overwhelming sensation. His face lifts to mine, and he kisses my forehead tenderly. We stay like that, entwined, savoring the moment for what feels like an eternity.

"I think you deserved for that to last longer," Cole says with a soft laugh as he shifts to lie beside me, his lips brushing mine gently. "Don't get me wrong, it was amazing."

"That was pretty amazing for me too." I smile, still catching my breath. "I'm pretty sure I asked you to finish it."

"And didn't I say I'm all in?" he replies with a satisfied chuckle, pulling me close, my head resting on his chest.

"So we can do it again," I tease, laughing softly.

He tightens his hold on me, chuckling. "You know how we were comparing you and Tara getting ready to homecoming night? Well, this kind of feels like a high school dance night now too."

I laugh, the comparison amusing me. "No, this was so much better than that. I'm not disappointed at all."

"At all?" he asks, playing with a strand of my hair. "Not even worried about the consequences?"

"At all," I assure him, smiling. "You said you'd fall on that sword, so I have nothing to worry about."

He rolls into me, capturing my mouth in a long, slow kiss that leaves me breathless. So fucking intoxicating.

Resting his forehead against mine, his voice is tender. "I haven't been this happy in a long time, Autumn."

"Me either," I admit, lacing my fingers with his. "Now the hard part is pretending this didn't happen tomorrow."

He chuckles, "I think that will be easier tomorrow than it was today, at least for me. Getting a piece of you might just satiate me a little." He glances over my body again, his smile playful. "Or maybe not, but it was a good thought," he laughs, running his hand across my breasts. I inhale sharply, my body already craving more.

We lie there for what feels like hours, tracing the contours of each other's bodies, fingers laced together, talking softly.

Eventually, Cole voices what we've both been avoiding. "I want to stay with you all night, but I don't know how smart that would be with so many people we know around."

"No, I understand," I say, nodding. "And we have an early morning."

"Seriously, Autumn, I don't want you to read into me leaving. If you want me to stay, I'll stay," he says, looking into my eyes with sincerity.

"It's really okay," I reply with a playful smile. "And how am I going to call Cara and tell her about you if you're still in my bed?"

He laughs, kissing me deeply one last time before gathering his clothes. He dresses just enough to cross the hall, then leans down to kiss my forehead. I watch him through the peephole as he walks back to his room, my heart still racing, my body still tingling from the afterglow.

CHAPTER SEVEN
THE TRIP EXTENSION

I lean against the door, still wrapped in a sheet, my heart pounding in disbelief.

Fuck, did that just happen?

I grab my phone and sit on the bed, trying to collect myself. It's one o'clock in the morning in Milwaukee, but I need to talk to someone who understands.

The phone rings twice before Cara answers, her voice groggy. "Hey, Autumn, what's the update?"

"Cara," I say, my voice carrying a tone I barely recognize.

"Oh shit, did he kiss you?" she asks, suddenly more awake.

"Cara," I repeat, the word heavy with everything that's happened.

"What?" she practically screams, "He fucked you? Are you fucking serious?"

"Dead serious," I reply, and she squeals in delight. "And I'm deliriously happy."

"Oh, Autumn, I'm so happy for you! This is the start of something, right? Not just a one-night stand?"

"God, I hope not," I say, feeling the warmth of his words all over again. "He said he's all in, 110% in. And Cara?"

"Yeah?"

"He said that if it becomes an issue at work, he'd fall on that sword for me. He gave me this whole speech... I was fucking speechless. You know I'm never speechless."

"Are you kidding me? He gave you a whole speech?"

"He did," I say, my voice softening as I recall his words. "And it was probably the most romantic thing that's ever happened to me in my life."

"I'm so happy for you! But what happens now?"

"I don't know," I admit. "We've got one more day of the conference, and we'll have to play it cool with the team tomorrow. But after that... I guess we'll take it day by day. But, Cara, I believe him. I believe he's all in."

"I don't even know him, but I believe him too," she says with certainty.

I laugh. "I guess I should go shower now. I'm still just wrapped in a sheet."

"Well, you had to call me the second he left, right?" she teases.

"Of course," I reply. "I'll keep you posted. I'm going to shower and try to get some sleep."

"Sweet dreams, Autumn," Cara says, and we hang up.

I glance down at my phone, seeing a few messages. One stands out, and I respond immediately, my heart skipping a beat.

Me

I'll probably do it

Cole

Stay with me in Dallas for an extra night or two?

I want to do this right, you were supposed to fly home early Monday, right?

Me

I was, 8am, and I can't think of a single reason not to say

Cole

Stay til Wednesday?

Me

I'll look at flights

Cole

I'll find us another hotel, I just need more time with you before we go home

Me

I have absolutely no objections to more time together

Cole

I feel like this went zero to sixty and we need to spend some time in between lol

Me

lol I agree, but I did like sixty

Cole

Trust me - me too, I'll probably be dreaming about it

Me

Hey Cole?

Cole

Autumn?

Me

Can you approve my time off for the next few days?

Cole

Oh my ... yes.

Me

Thanks, I have something kind of important to do

Cole

I actually lol'd

Me

Good, I should probably shower now

Cole

Okay, have a nice shower, I'll be envisioning you in the shower

Me

I'll be envisioning you while I'm in the shower too

Cole

You're going to make it hard for me to act normal around you tomorrow talking like that

Me

We just have to hold it together for like eight hours, I believe in us

Cole

I think you have more faith than I do

I finally turn on the shower, letting the warm water cascade over my skin. The heat soothes my over-stimulated nerves, washing away the lingering tension. I close my eyes and simply savor the sensation, the warmth calming me, grounding me in the reality of what just happened. After a few moments, I wrap myself in a towel and climb into bed, not even bothering with pajamas. The cool sheets feel luxurious against my bare skin as I sink into the mattress.

Sleep comes quickly, my mind and body wrapped in a cocoon of bliss and happiness, the events of the night playing softly in my dreams.

My alarm sounds bright and early. I look at my phone.

Cole

Me too, best night of sleep in a long time, I think you might be good for me

Me

I would probably have slept even better if you stayed, I think you're good for me too

Cole

I'll stay tonight, we can test that theory

Me

Can't wait, but I need to get ready now

Cole

Alright, you get ready, I'll see you in a few

Before I get dressed, I realize I need to let Megan know I won't be home on Monday. It's about eight in the morning her time, so I hope I'm not waking her as I dial her number.

"Hey, Mom," Megan answers, sounding wide awake.

"Hey, Megs," I reply, trying to keep my tone casual. "How are you?"

"I'm good. How's the conference?" she asks.

"It's going well. I was actually calling to let you know I'll be extending my trip for a couple of days. I'll probably be home on Wednesday," I say, hoping I sound normal.

"Mom?" she says, her voice laced with suspicion. "What aren't you telling me?"

"Nothing, just staying a couple of days to get some work done," I say, trying to sound convincing.

"I don't believe you. You're not telling me something," she presses.

"Megs," I say, feeling a bit exasperated.

"You met someone," Megan declares, her tone triumphant. "Mom, I want to hear all about it."

"Why do you have to know me so well?" I sigh, giving in. "Yes, I did meet someone, but I'll tell you everything when I get home."

Megan squeals in delight. "Kevin is going to freak the f out—he swore you'd never date again."

"Megan, don't tell him yet," I plead. "Let me figure out exactly what's happening first. Just because you can hear it in my voice doesn't mean you need to tell everyone."

"You're ruining the fun part, Mom."

"Just wait until I get home, okay?"

"Okay," she sighs, then adds softly, "and Mom?"

"Yeah, Megs?"

"I love you, and I'm happy for you."

"Thank you, sweetie. I'll see you in a few days," I say, feeling a warmth in my chest.

"Okay, bye, Mom."

"Bye," I reply, pressing end on the call, a smile lingering on my lips.

As I pick out my clothes, I decide to go intentionally conservative, wanting to make things as easy on Cole as possible. I choose gray slacks and a black long-sleeve blouse—full coverage in the back, and no cleavage showing, at least not if I button it all the way. My makeup is minimal, just enough to look polished but natural. I realize this look might also help with the Tony situation since we're going to watch him speak later. Clearly, I'm not dressing to lure anyone in.

Before stepping out, I glance through the peephole. There he is. I open the door with a smile.

"Careful, Mr. Waters, you'll have me expecting this kind of treatment every morning," I tease as he hands me my cup and kisses the top of my forehead.

"I wouldn't mind getting you coffee or tea every morning if it means you're in my bed every night," he says, his voice soft but full of intent.

"Zero to sixty, huh?" I say, grinning at him.

He chuckles, his eyes sweeping over me. "Looks like you toned down your wardrobe today," he observes, gesturing with his coffee cup.

"I did," I admit. "Two reasons—the main one is Tony's speech, but I also thought it might make things a little less... tempting for you," I add with a playful smile.

"Maybe," he says, his gaze warm and inviting. "But I think you could wear a potato sack and still be tempting to me," he laughs. "So, what did Cara say? I know you must've called her."

I laugh. "She actually wasn't too over the top, just said she was happy for me. You know what's crazy?"

"What's that?" he asks as we step into the elevator.

"She said she knew," I say, leaning against the elevator wall. He looks at me, puzzled. "The second I told her it was someone I work with, she knew it was you. She said whenever she came over or called, I was always talking to you, about to talk to you, or talking about you. It's crazy because I didn't even feel this between us until the restaurant on Thursday night. It's just... weird."

"Me either," he admits. "Don't get me wrong, Autumn, you're gorgeous—I've thought that since your first interview," he laughs, "and I definitely saw you as more than just a coworker." He reaches up, brushing his thumb over my bottom lip. "But this intense chemistry? I didn't see it coming."

The elevator doors open to the lobby as he continues, "At the restaurant on Thursday, when you turned and looked at me after I sat down next to you, it was like it sparked a fire. And the more I tried to put it out, the bigger it grew. I think it's wild that she saw it too, but sometimes it's easier to see things from the outside."

"Ready for today?" I ask as we walk into the breakfast area.

"I think so, but I can't wait until tonight," he says, grinning. "Muffin and a banana?"

I laugh. "I am predictable, aren't I?"

With my muffin and banana in hand, I take my regular spot. Cole joins me after meeting the guys at the buffet. Tara takes her usual seat on the other side of me. It all feels so routine, yet there's this undercurrent of electricity between us. It's easier to manage today, though.

"So, here's the plan," Cole begins, addressing the team. "Dr. Gabari is speaking at two o'clock. Mark, Autumn, Tom, and I will all attend. We'll keep the same booth schedule as yesterday—Mark, Autumn, and I in the morning, with Julio, Tom, and Tara in the afternoon. Tom, you can join us when it's time for the speech." He pauses. "Also, I know people have flights out tonight and tomorrow morning, so we'll skip any kind of team dinner tonight. But don't worry—we'll be seeing each other a lot more often."

The morning in the booth is much like the day before. I don't change much, finding small opportunities to touch Cole, while he gets a little bolder in his flirting. Mark notices the change but only comments on how happy Cole seems.

"I am, Mark," Cole says, a contented smile on his face. "It's just a good day."

"Happy to see you so happy," Mark responds. "Hope it stays that way."

"That's the plan," Cole says, stealing a quick glance at me.

Tony and Nicole don't stop by the booth in the morning, which is a relief. I'm not in the mood to deal with them today. Lunchtime arrives, and we fall into our routine. I hadn't fully registered that the tables in the dining hall are covered with tablecloths until Cole's hand slides up my thigh under the table. The touch startles me, but it also feels completely natural. I place my hand across my lap, occasionally lacing my fingers with his. The rest of the team seems oblivious, but the thought of getting caught only adds to the thrill.

After lunch, we have a bit of time before Tony's talk, so the six of us use it to start breaking down the booth, making it easier to wrap up at the end of the day. About twenty minutes before two, we head over to the exhibit hall where the speakers are set up. We find seats midway back, making sure to say hi to Nicole so she knows we're there. I take a seat on the end of our row, with Cole to my left, then Mark and Tom beside him.

Once we're settled, Cole crosses his arms, but not before sneaking a few soft touches along my arm. Occasionally, I reach across as if adjusting my left arm and subtly lace our fingertips together. Tony's talk is informative, shedding light on his professional world, and he even mentions our device and how it's helped his patients. Despite how uncomfortable he makes me, I realize we'll have to find a way to continue working with him.

Tony's speech lasts about an hour. Afterward, we approach the stage to congratulate him. We all shake hands, offering our praise, and then Tony turns directly to me.

"Autumn, when are you flying back?" he asks.

"Early tomorrow morning," I reply.

"How about you have dinner with me tonight?" he suggests.

I hesitate, searching for a way out. "I'm not sure—"

Cole steps in smoothly, cutting me off. "We're having a team dinner tonight, at least for those of us not flying out."

"Oh, that's too bad," Tony says, sounding disappointed.

"We'll be headed to Chicago sometime soon. We can all have dinner then," Mark adds, trying to steer the conversation away.

"Well, Autumn isn't that far from me—just an hour or so north. I'm sure we can find time for dinner back home," Tony persists.

"I don't know, she's a busy woman," Tom interjects, his tone light but firm.

At this moment, I'm filled with gratitude for my team.

"We can always try," Tony says, a hint of persistence in his voice.

"You can sure try," Cole replies, and I catch the underlying challenge in his tone, even if Tony doesn't.

We exchange pleasantries and say our goodbyes to Tony and Nicole before heading back to the booth to finish packing up.

As we walk, I feel compelled to express my gratitude. "I just want to say I love this team. Thank you all for having my back in there. That would've been hard to navigate alone without coming off as rude." I pause, glancing at each of them. "And we know how important his account is, so we can't afford to lose it."

"Happy to help," Mark says with a smile.

"Me too," Tom adds, nodding.

Cole looks at me, his voice serious. "You know I won't let him make you uncomfortable if I can help it."

"I know," I reply, genuinely touched. "And I appreciate all of you. Thank you. Also, I'm really glad he only has my work contact information."

They all laugh in response.

As we dismantle the booth, it hits me how much I'm going to miss this time with Tara. I tell her she has to text and call more, and I promise to do the same. She agrees, saying she'll miss spending time with me too.

Finally, it's time for everyone to part ways. Tom and Julio are flying out tonight, and Mark is staying with family for the next two nights before his flight on Tuesday evening. That leaves just Tara, Cole, and me at the hotel tonight. Tara has a red-eye flight in the morning, so she politely declines Cole's offer to have breakfast with us, which I suspect was more out of courtesy anyway.

Cole mentions to the group that he'll be staying in Dallas for a couple more days "on business," and that I'll be taking a couple of days off, returning to work on Thursday. No one seems to read anything into it—Mark is also taking Monday off, and we've all been working hard all weekend.

We exchange goodbyes and hugs, the familiar bittersweet feeling of the end of a conference settling in. I ask Tara if she'd like to join Cole and me for dinner, but she declines, saying she needs to pack, unwind, and get to bed early. I give her one last hug before she heads to the elevator.

As the doors close behind her, Cole and I turn to head to our own elevator, a quiet anticipation building between us.

CHAPTER EIGHT

THE MOVIE NIGHT

As soon as the elevator doors slide shut, Cole wastes no time. His hand finds the base of my neck, and before I can catch my breath, his mouth is on mine. The kiss is deep, unhurried, leaving me lightheaded and craving more by the time the elevator jerks to a halt.

"I've been wanting to do that all day," he murmurs against my lips, his voice thick with a mix of satisfaction and something more.

"Me too," I admit softly, my words barely more than a breath.

We step out of the elevator, and Cole's tone shifts, taking on a practical edge. "Here's what I'm thinking for tonight," he begins, glancing at me to gauge my reaction. "Tell me if you're not on board. Let's both ditch these stiff work clothes, get comfortable, and then either your room or mine, we can order takeout, maybe watch a movie. Just unwind."

I can't help the playful smile that tugs at my lips. "So, Netflix and chill?"

His laughter is easy, unguarded. "I hadn't thought of it that way, but yeah, I guess that's exactly what I'm saying. Does that work for you?"

"I'm one hundred percent on board with that plan," I reply, my smile widening.

"Your room or mine?" he asks, his gaze warm, full of a kind of anticipation that mirrors my own.

I shrug, thinking it over. "Honestly, I don't care. But I probably have a lot more stuff than you, so it might be easier if we stick to my place. But really, Cole," I pause, meeting his eyes, "I just want to be with you. The where doesn't matter."

He smiles, that genuine, slightly lopsided smile that makes my body tingle. "Alright, let me go change and grab a few things. I'll be over in a bit," he says, stopping in front of my door.

Before I can respond, he places his hands on my shoulders, leaning in to press a tender kiss to the top of my head. I melt, as I have so many times already. It's a gesture that's quickly become his signature—unassuming, not driven by desire, but by something deeper, something that makes me feel safe and cherished. No one has ever kissed me like that, with such unspoken care. It's a rare kind of intimacy, one that speaks volumes without a word.

Once inside my hotel room, I slip out of my work clothes and into my favorite pair of soft, black leggings and an oversized green, off-the-shoulder t-shirt. The bra is the first thing to go, but I pull on a black tank underneath, just for a bit of modesty. I gather my hair into a messy bun, remembering how Cole once mentioned he liked it up, though he seems to like it just as much tangled in his hands.

As I settle into the comforting rhythm of my space, I realize I haven't updated Cara since last night. Grabbing my phone, I fire off a quick text, knowing she'll want to hear every detail.

Me

Cole is getting some stuff to spend the night in my room, he asked me to stay until Wednesday, with him

Cara

Shut the front door, you're staying right?

Me

I am, he's finding us another hotel, Cara, am I crazy, is this too fast?

Cara

Does it feel too fast?

Me

No, it feels like we've been together for years in some ways

Cara

then no, you follow your heart or your …. lol

Me

Oh my … Cara

Cara

You cannot tell me that's not part of it

Me

Oh, it is, lol

Hey, off subject, I think all my kids are going to be home this weekend, Sami wants to do pizza in Chicago, you want to come?

Cara

Absolutely, then I can be there while you explain this all to your kids

Me

Facepalm, okay, leave me alone for tonight, please?

Cara

I will but I want deets in the morning

I grab my fuzzy socks from my luggage, slipping them on and feeling a little more cozy. I glance in the mirror, and for a moment, I appraise myself—a forty-something woman in comfortable clothes, doing her best to look cute. Cole didn't seem to mind the stretch marks and extra skin last night, so tonight, I'm determined not to let those thoughts creep in. I flick on one of the nightstand lamps, letting the soft light set a relaxed, inviting atmosphere.

A knock at the door pulls me from my thoughts. I check the peephole, just to be sure, and then swing it open. Cole stands there with a small bundle of things, dressed in gray sweatpants and a blue t-shirt that makes his eyes even more striking.

"Hey, gorgeous," he says with that easy smile. "You look comfortable."

"So do you," I laugh, closing the door behind him.

He wastes no time pulling me into a long, lingering kiss. God, I could get lost in this man.

"We're going to end up with chapped lips if we keep this up," I tease.

"I think we'll survive," he replies playfully, brushing his thumb over my bottom lip. "First question of the night—what do you want for dinner?"

"Why is that always the hardest question?" I groan.

"Let's see what's nearby that we can have delivered. Are you hungry now?"

"Yeah, pretty hungry," I say, sinking onto the couch. The room is small, but there is a coffee table in front of the couch, which faces the television. Cole joins me, and we start scrolling through options on his phone.

"Cole?" I ask, breaking the comfortable silence.

"Autumn?" he answers, his tone mock-serious.

"Does it feel to you like we've been doing this for years already?" I ask, meeting his eyes. "Like, these conversations, looking for food—it just feels so natural. It doesn't feel new."

He kisses my temple, his lips warm and reassuring. "Yeah, it does. I've been trying to figure out how to describe it, but that's exactly it. And it's crazy, especially since we've both been alone for so long."

"Right?" I laugh. "Like it should be more awkward?"

"Exactly," he agrees as we go back to scrolling through his phone. I lean my head on his shoulder, feeling that inexplicable ease between us.

"I'm pretty easy when it comes to food. I'm not a huge fan of seafood, but I can eat it if I have to. Otherwise, I can find something almost anywhere. Maybe we should consider what it'll do to our breath," I add with a laugh.

"I brought my toothbrush," he says, chuckling.

"Let's just go with a standard American chain—something simple and no fuss."

He nods, and we quickly settle on a place. He orders a burger; I opt for a turkey avocado sandwich. Now, all that's left is to wait.

"You haven't touched the mini-bar?" he asks, glancing at the untouched bottles.

"No, despite appearances this weekend, I don't actually drink that much."

"I wiped mine out between Thursday and Friday nights, trying to figure out how to handle you," he admits with a laugh. "After I texted you Thursday night, I was sure you wouldn't go for this. And then Friday..." He trails off, his expression shifting. "The way you looked in that dress, the way Tony was eyeing you like a predator... and then, the way you touched me, how you didn't flinch when I touched you back," he sighs, "it left me genuinely confused."

"I was confused too," I say, meeting his gaze. "The logical part of me kept saying you were off-limits, that I shouldn't even entertain the thought." I clear my throat, my voice rising into a playful, sing-song tone. "But then, while I was texting in the bathroom on Friday, Cara said, 'You can always find another job, but you may not find another Cole.' And that was it. Those words cleared everything up for me."

"So, you're saying I should be thanking Cara for all of this?" He gestures around the room, a teasing grin on his face.

"I think I would've gotten there eventually, but she definitely sped things up. Without her, I probably would've tortured us both for weeks or even months, clinging to my ethics like it was some unshakable moral high ground."

"Speaking of which." Cole shifts forward, turning to face me with a seriousness that tugs at the easy rhythm of our evening. "At some point, I'm going to have to tell Pete and Lauryn." Pete is his boss, our chief operations officer, and Lauryn is their HR partner. I start to object, but he gently places a finger on my lips, stopping me.

"I looked up the policy on the intranet," he continues, his voice steady. "The responsibility is mine alone. The policy says leaders can't engage in 'inappropriate' relationships with subordinates. Otherwise, it's discouraged but not outright prohibited. The language makes it clear—I'm the one who'd face the consequences, not you."

He takes a deep breath, and I can see the weight of this on him. "Pete likes me. He brought me over in the merger, and we've worked together for almost two decades. I think we can work something out, but I need to go to them before they hear it from someone else."

"Cole," I say, my voice tight with concern, "I think we should wait. Not because I'm unsure about us, because I am sure, but I just think it's better to wait a bit."

He nods, his gaze softening. "I agree. But I also know it'll be better coming from me. If someone else reports it, Pete might not be able to help."

I reach up, my thumb brushing across his cheekbone, and then I lean in, kissing him softly. "Okay," I whisper against his lips, "I trust you."

I rest my head on his shoulder, and he wraps his arm around me, his hand rubbing my shoulder in slow, comforting circles. The moment feels fragile yet strong, like something precious we're both carefully holding, knowing that honesty and timing are just as important as the feelings we share.

A knock at the door interrupts our cozy evening, and Cole glances at his phone. The food isn't supposed to arrive yet. He gets up, checks the peephole, and then turns back to me with a raised eyebrow. "Someone sent you flowers."

Curiosity piqued, I move to the door as he steps aside. A delivery person stands there holding an enormous bouquet of roses. I thank them, take the bouquet, and bring it inside, glancing at Cole with a questioning look.

"Don't look at me," he says, hands up in mock surrender. "I wish I'd thought of it, but it wasn't me."

I reach for the card nestled among the flowers, already suspecting who it's from. As I read the familiar name, I can't help but roll my eyes. Of course, I should have guessed.

Autumn,

It was wonderful meeting you in person. You are more stunning in person than I imagined in all those virtual meetings. I hope you will find some time to have dinner with me soon.

Yours, Tony Gabari

I hand the card to Cole, who takes one look and chuckles. "Wow," he says, shaking his head. "This guy is seriously hung up on you."

I snatch the card back, rolling my eyes. "They are beautiful, but he thinks I'm flying out tomorrow. What does he expect me to do with them? And why do I have to live so effing close to him?"

Cole leans against the wall, arms crossed, a thoughtful expression on his face. "From a guy's perspective, he's probably hoping that when you see the flowers, you'll reach out to thank him, and maybe he'll get to see you tonight."

"Seriously?" I ask, incredulous.

"Seriously," he confirms, his face mirroring the gravity of his words.

"I'm not even going to acknowledge it."

Cole tilts his head, considering. "Maybe you should. But wait a couple of days. Then, let him know you're seeing someone. Tell him you appreciate the gesture, and you're glad to work with him, but you're spoken for."

I sigh, knowing he's right. "You're right, that would be the best way to handle it. It's just that he gives me the creeps."

Cole laughs, a deep, easy sound. "For a solid twenty-four hours, I thought I was creeping you out too."

"No, no, no," I quickly reassure him, smiling. "You're not creepy. I'm sorry I even made you think that."

"Food's almost here," Cole says, glancing at his phone. "Hopefully, the next knock on the door will be our dinner."

"Good, because I'm starving," I say, patting my stomach.

Right on cue, the food arrives. We settle in to eat, the conversation flowing easily as we start to learn more about each other.

"Favorite genre of music?" he asks between bites.

"All of them," I reply, but his skeptical look makes me laugh. "I'm serious! The only music I don't like is the kind where I can't understand the words—like heavy metal and mumble rap. But as long as I can understand the lyrics, or if there aren't any, like with classical or EDM, I'm good with anything."

"Alright, fair enough," he concedes. "But what do you listen to the most?"

"It's shifted over the years. I grew up on my parents' music from the sixties and seventies, then got into country during my preteen years, and punk rock in my teens. I bounce around, but if I had to choose, country and punk rock or alternative are probably my favorites. What about you?"

"I'm a country fan," he says, nodding. "But I like a lot of other genres too. I didn't listen to much music as a kid, but at my first job in Fort Wayne, they played country all the time, and it just stuck with me."

He pauses, then asks, "What's your favorite song?"

"Oh, that's tough," I say, thinking. "It really depends on my mood, but some of my top picks would be 'Chasing Cars' by Snow Patrol, 'Wonderful Tonight' by Eric Clapton, and 'Crash Into Me' by Dave Matthews." I laugh softly. "I could go on."

"You are such a girl," he teases.

"Oh, I know," I reply with a grin. "What about you?"

"I probably shouldn't have made fun of you," he admits, looking a little sheepish. "My all-time favorite song is 'The Dance' by Garth Brooks."

"That's a good one," I say, squeezing his hand. "I'm sure it has a lot of meaning for you, in multiple ways."

"Yeah," he says, his voice softening. "It's tied to my childhood, my marriage, life in general." He laughs, but there's a touch of nostalgia in his eyes.

"Sometime, we'll have to talk more about that childhood of yours," I say, threading my fingers through his. "But only when you're ready."

He chuckles, a sound tinged with something deeper. "Well, at some point soon, you'll see the scars. They kind of speak for themselves." He looks down at his lap, and I can feel the shift in his mood, his whole body seeming to draw inward.

"Hey," I murmur, gently lifting his chin until his eyes meet mine. "I don't think I'm capable of intentionally hurting you. I can't promise I'll never do something that might hurt you, but it would never be on purpose."

His hand cups my face, his thumb grazing softly across my cheekbone. The tenderness in his touch contrasts with the weight of the moment.

"I see your pain," I continue, my voice steady. "I think I've seen it all along. I know you've been hurt, and the last thing I want to do is add to that."

His hand moves to the nape of my neck, and he pulls me closer. The kiss that follows is more desperate, more passionate than any before. We're sitting side by side on the couch, but he pulls me onto his lap, holding me close. When the kiss ends, he rests his forehead against my chest, not in a way that's suggestive, but in a way that's searching for comfort. I run my fingers through his hair, tracing along the back of his neck, my other hand soothingly caressing his back. We stay like this for what feels like an eternity, wrapped in a quiet understanding.

Eventually, he reaches up, takes my hand, and lifts it to his lips, pressing a kiss into my palm. His eyes find mine, and there's an intensity there that almost feels like it's burning through me.

"I'm going to say something, Autumn," he begins, kissing my palm again. "And you're probably going to think I'm crazy. Maybe I am. But I don't want it to scare you, okay?"

"Okay," I whisper, my heart suddenly pounding with a mix of anticipation and fear.

"I know the first time we kissed was yesterday. I know we haven't had much time together like this. But..." He sighs, as if searching for the right words. "I think your friend Cara was right. This has been building for a lot longer than either of us realized." He pauses, and I run my fingers through his hair again, offering silent encouragement. His eyes lock onto mine, filled with something raw and unfiltered. "I need to tell you that I am absolutely head over heels for you. And... I think I may have already fallen in love with you."

He finishes by placing my hand against his face, kissing my palm one last time.

His words leave me speechless, just like the night before. I study his face, searching for any hint of doubt, but all I see is sincerity. "Autumn?" he says softly, almost pleading. "Talk to me. Please don't let that scare you off."

I lean in, kissing him just above his right eyebrow, my hands cradling his face as I savor the closeness. Being perched on his lap, I'm slightly elevated, giving me the perfect angle to trail a series of gentle kisses across his forehead, moving slowly to his left temple. I continue down the line of his cheekbone, each kiss deliberate, until I reach his mouth. When our lips meet, it's not the desperate, passionate kiss from earlier—it's soft, tender, a slow dance of tongues as if we both want to savor every moment, making it last.

He pulls back slightly, his eyes searching mine. "Autumn?" he starts, but I place a finger over his lips, silencing him with another kiss.

His hands find my hips, and I instinctively move against him, feeling the heat between us intensify. In one swift motion, he pulls off both of my shirts, and I start tugging at his, needing to feel his skin against mine. He tips me back onto the couch, positioning himself over me, his mouth trailing down to my breast. He takes my nipple into his mouth, his hand moving to caress the other, sending a shiver through me. I grab his shirt again, and he pauses just long enough to pull it off, then leans back down, our bodies flush.

I run my nails up his back, and he groans in response, bringing his face close to mine again. He studies me for a moment, his gaze intense, before capturing my lips in a deep kiss. His mouth begins a slow descent down my body, each kiss igniting a fire beneath my skin. When he reaches the waistband of my leggings, he peels them off, standing up to fully remove them, and as he does, he discards the rest of his clothes too.

For a moment, I just look at him, taking in every inch of his body, the way his muscles move, how utterly gorgeous he is. And then the thought hits me—he is mine.

As he moves to climb back on top of me, I place a hand on his chest, pushing him back into a sitting position on the couch. I straddle him, and the look in his eyes tells me he understands exactly what I'm about to do. I keep my gaze locked on his as I reach down, guiding him inside me. I lower myself slowly, savoring the sensation of him filling me completely. Just like the night before, it feels as though he's the missing piece of me I've been searching for.

"Fuck, Autumn," he whispers, the words barely audible.

I press my finger to his lips again as his hands explore my body, moving from my breasts to my hips, then down to my ass as I begin to move. I spread my knees wider, taking him deeper, feeling the fullness of him within me. He groans, pulling me closer, burying his head in my cleavage as I continue to move, a slow, rhythmic dance that sends waves of pleasure through both of us.

I feel his muscles tighten beneath me, a telltale sign that he's close. With one final, deliberate movement, I plunge down, taking him fully inside me. His body tenses, and I feel him throbbing deep within as he clings to me, his hands gripping my back, pulling me as close as possible to him.

As his body relaxes, he trails his hands lightly up and down my back, the touch so gentle it almost tickles. I run my fingers through his hair, down his neck, holding his head tenderly in both hands.

After a few moments, he looks up at me, and I lean down, kissing him softly.

"I think I might be falling in love with you too," I whisper against his lips before kissing him again, sealing the promise of something deeper between us.

CHAPTER NINE

THE ZERO TO ONE HUNDRED

Cole had pulled the comforter off the bed, and now we're curled up under it on the couch, still naked, just enjoying the warmth of each other. I'm sitting beside him with my legs draped across his lap, my head resting on his chest, his arm wrapped securely around me. We've been silent for a while, our hands and fingers lazily tracing each other's skin, simply listening to the rhythm of our breathing.

"Autumn," Cole says softly, breaking the silence. I look up at him, and he smiles. "You've got to stop doing that silence thing to me."

"The 'silence thing' is a good thing," I reply, intertwining my fingers with his. "There have been very few times in my life where I've been rendered speechless."

"Speechless, huh?" he says, turning slightly so he can see my face better.

"Yes, speechless. Both last night and tonight. I'm sure it won't be a regular occurrence, but so far, you're two for two."

He grins, playfully suggesting, "Maybe we should put some clothes on. I actually want to watch a movie with you—pretend this is something close to a normal relationship."

I drag out my response, "I guess," with an exaggerated sigh, making him laugh.

We reluctantly separate and gather our scattered clothes. I head to the bathroom and almost laugh out loud when I catch a glimpse of myself in the mirror—my hair is a wild mess. I work the hair tie out and step out to find my hairbrush.

As I'm brushing through the tangled mess, I ask Cole, "Why didn't you tell me my hair was a disaster?"

"If I told you I didn't notice, would you believe me?" he asks with a smile, pulling me into his arms. He's still shirtless but has his sweatpants back on.

"No, no, I wouldn't," I laugh, looking up at him.

"It might sound cheesy, but even with the crazy hair, you're beautiful," he says, his smile warm and genuine.

"Okay, that *is* a little cheesy," I tease, smiling back as he kisses my forehead.

"So, you really want to watch a movie, huh?" I ask, raising an eyebrow. "Anything in particular?"

"Yeah, but no—nothing specific. Let's just see what's on," he replies.

We settle on a movie that strikes a good balance—some rom-com elements with a bit of action. We turn the television toward the bed and snuggle up before hitting play. I nestle into the crook of his arm, absently playing with his chest hair while he rubs my back. Amazingly, we actually watch the whole movie, though my mind is spinning the entire time.

As the credits roll, I prop myself up on my elbow, looking at him. "Hey," I start, feeling a flutter of nerves. "Now you're going to think *I'm* the crazy one—like certifiably crazy—and you can absolutely say no."

"Okay," he says, a bit skeptically, waiting for me to continue.

"So my kids are planning a thing this weekend. Kevin and Sami are coming home, Cara's going to join us, and we're heading to Chicago for pizza and whatever other trouble we find." I pause, running my hand through the hair on his chest, feeling a little vulnerable. "I think you should come," I add, biting my bottom lip.

He laughs, "Oh, so now we're talking zero to one hundred, instead of zero to sixty. You want me to meet the family?"

"Yeah, I guess that is exactly what I'm saying. Cara already knows, and Megs figured out there was 'someone' the second I extended my trip. Even though I asked her not to, I'm sure she's told Kevin and Sami." I look at him, searching for his reaction. "It'll be like ripping off a bandaid, and it'll give us a chance to spend more time together—maybe outside of a bedroom," I add, wrinkling my nose playfully.

He smiles, but there's a thoughtful look in his eyes as he sighs. "This whole thing is just so different. I was so young the last time I was in any kind of relationship, at least at the beginning."

"Me too," I admit. "But I think being older, wiser, and waiting until it felt right really does make a difference."

"Okay," he finally says. "Let me figure out the logistics, but I'm on board if you think it won't be too much for your kids."

"One hundred and ten percent in, right?" I ask, needing to hear his commitment.

"That's what I said," he replies, kissing my forehead.

"There's just one thing," he adds. "No social media until I've talked to Pete and Lauryn. We can take all the pictures you want, but we just can't post them yet."

"I'm okay with that," I say, nodding. "I'll make sure my kids know too—they'll respect it."

Not long after, we drift off to sleep, his warmth beside me a comfort I hadn't realized I craved. I wake with the first light of dawn, and Cole is still deeply asleep, his back turned to me. In the soft morning light, I notice the scars he mentioned. They crisscross his back like a brutal map, all carefully placed to remain hidden beneath a shirt.

My heart aches as I reach out, gently tracing the lines of his scars. Some are so deeply etched, raised like the ridges of old wounds that never truly healed. My chest tightens with sorrow and anger. How could anyone do this to a child? He said he was twelve when they took him out, meaning this all happened before then. The trauma he carries must be woven into the very fabric of who he is.

I move closer, pressing gentle kisses along the highest scar, from his left shoulder to his right. As I reach the last one, he stirs, rolling onto his back to face me. His expression is unreadable, as if he's trying to gauge my reaction, trying to understand what I'm thinking. Without a word, he pulls me into the space beneath his arm, and I rest my head on his chest. His fingers trail lightly over my back, and I place my hand on his chest, feeling the steady beat of his heart beneath my palm. He covers my hand with his, holding it there, grounding us both in the silence.

After a few moments, he finally speaks. "I have an 8 a.m. meeting with Pete to debrief on the conference. I'll head back to my room for that, then I'll come back. We both need to pack up a little—we're moving to a very nice hotel downtown. I made sure they have room service."

"Okay," I reply softly, lifting my head to look at him. "I'll shower and get ready while you're in your meeting."

He nods, kissing me on the forehead before slipping out from under me. "I'll shower too, get my stuff together. Maybe afterward, we can go find a place for brunch?"

"I love brunch," I say, smiling up at him, the thought of more time together filling me with warmth.

He grins back, and with one last kiss, he heads out the door, leaving me with the lingering comfort of his presence.

Standing in the shower, I realize something that almost catches me off guard—I feel genuinely happy. It's a kind of happiness I haven't felt in a long time, one that's different from the joy I get when my kids are together and content. This is deeper, almost like a sense of inner peace that I wasn't sure I'd find again.

But how is that even possible? It's only been two days.

I step out of the shower, grateful for the foresight to pack my oversized suitcase with plenty of options. I dig out my favorite jeans from the bottom and pair them with a black tank top and a thin green cardigan. The tank top shows just enough cleavage to be flattering without being too much. I opt for a bit more makeup today, still keeping it natural but with a touch more emphasis, and quickly run a brush through my hair before packing up the rest of my things.

Once everything is in order, I sit down, my thoughts already drifting to Cole, and start typing out a text to him.

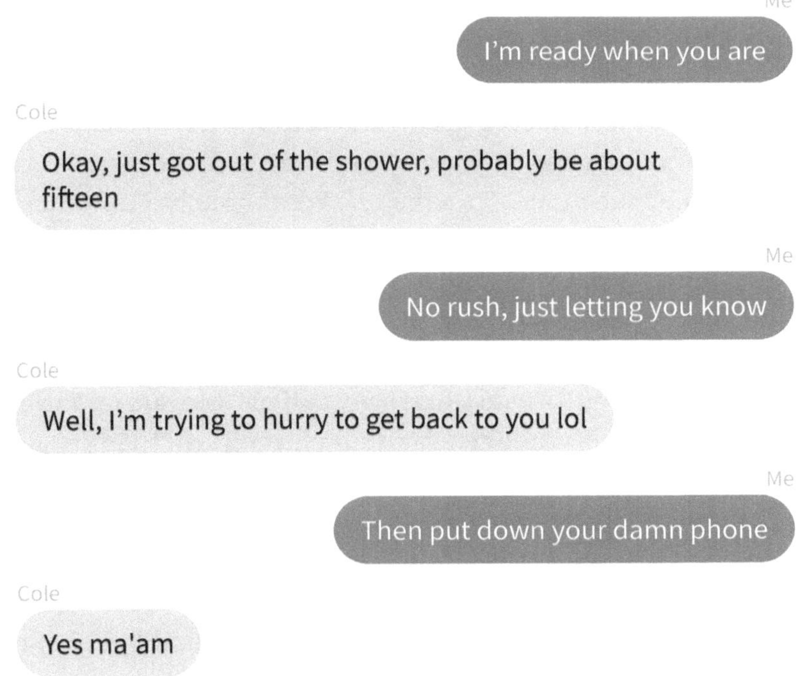

He arrives at my door almost exactly fifteen minutes later, rolling a small suitcase with a compact backpack slung over his shoulder.

"So, my suitcase is definitely bigger than yours," I say, laughing as I glance at the difference.

"Well, you have to bring more stuff than me," he replies with a smile. "You ready? I haven't called the rideshare yet, but I can. They'll be here quickly."

"Yeah, let's go."

Without a second thought, he takes charge of my luggage, loading everything into the car before we start the drive into downtown Dallas. It's not until we pull up to the entrance that I realize where we are—the Ritz-Carlton.

"Are you kidding me?" I ask, turning to Cole with wide eyes.

"Nope, not kidding." He grins. "But don't get too excited or used to it. I had a lot of points saved up, and I figured this was a good way to use them."

We're too early to check in, but they hold our bags, and we set off to find brunch. We discover a charming little French restaurant nearby and enjoy a leisurely meal filled with delicious food.

"So, before this weekend," Cole begins, chuckling, "what should I know about all these people you're about to introduce me to?"

I smile, thinking about my kids. "Let's see... Kevin is super smart and very protective of me. He's the one who thought I'd never date again, but Megan thinks he's going to be thrilled."

"He's twenty-two, twenty-three?" Cole asks.

"Twenty-two, turning twenty-three in December. He's been out on his own for over a year now. He works as a loan officer for a mortgage company in Madison." I pause to sip my coffee. "Megan, on the other hand, is fiercely independent, even though she's still living at home. She's my mini-me, most like me in both personality and looks."

"Oh, so there's another one of you?" he teases.

"Yep, a twenty-year-old version," I laugh. "She'll be twenty-one in October. And then there's Samantha, or Sami. She's the typical baby of the family—maybe a little spoiled but also incredibly grateful for what she has. She's the most introverted of the three. Kevin has a good relationship with both girls, but the girls can be hot and cold with each other. Still, they're all great kids... or adults now, I suppose."

Cole looks at me warmly. "Well, you raised them, and even though I haven't seen it firsthand, I'm pretty sure you're an amazing mom."

I feel a flush of warmth in my cheeks and smile at him. "Finally, there's Cara," I say, switching gears. "She's a spitfire and kind of my opposite—the yang to my yin, you could say. She's the most likely to say something incredibly inappropriate, but she'll probably tone it down around my kids."

Cole laughs, "How did you two meet?"

"Me and Cara?" I ask, and he nods, waiting for the story. "Kevin was best friends with her son back in elementary school. We bonded over their sports and school activities. Even though the boys drifted apart in high school, Cara and I stayed close. She's really my only true friend. I have plenty of acquaintances, but when it comes to someone I can truly rely on, it's her."

Cole nods thoughtfully. "I get that. While Pete and his wife, Laura, feel like family, the only person I'd call a trusted friend is my oldest brother. It's strange, isn't it? You know all these people from work or school, but they're not really friends."

"Exactly," I say, feeling a deep connection to what he's saying. "I've bonded with so many people over the years in similar situations, but they're just acquaintances. I have hundreds of people on social media, but only a few real friends." I pause, considering.

"Speaking of brothers, I'd definitely consider my brother Alex—Alexander Liam Flynn," I laugh, "he uses his full name for business, so we tease him about it—a close friend. But he has his own life. He moved to northern Oregon about eight years ago, and we usually only see each other once a year. And if we do see each other more than that, it's usually for something serious—a funeral or a hospital visit. Occasionally, we get together for happy events, like graduations or weddings. He came out for both Sami's high school and Kevin's college graduations, which were just a few days apart in May."

"My oldest brother, Carson—they named us all with C names," he laughs softly, "moved to Indianapolis when I moved to Fort Wayne to be closer to me and another one of our brothers, Cameron, who lives outside Cincinnati. We try to have dinner a couple of times a month to catch up. Some of our siblings, especially our sister, didn't agree with Carson's decision to report our parents. We were all separated, and the foster system wasn't kind to us all. I was lucky in that way, but they would've preferred to stay where they were, rather than go through what happened."

I reach across the table, touching his hand gently. "Cole, you can't make them see it the way you and Carson do. But that doesn't mean it wasn't the right thing to do."

He sighs, nodding. "I know, but some days it's harder than others. Sometimes, hearing about your family, it just makes me miss something I never had. Not that I don't want you to talk about them—I do. It's just... it makes me realize what I lost, or never really had. Even the family I made after that was so dysfunctional. Trusting anyone has been really hard for me."

"No family is perfect," I say softly. "But I know I'm lucky. I still don't understand how my mom forgave my dad for cheating, but she did. Sometimes, I think my parents hold it against me that I couldn't forgive Steve for doing the same."

I let go of his hand and take a moment to eat, gathering my thoughts. Then I continue, "Cole, there's something else you should know. It's not exactly a big secret, but it's important for you to understand where I'm coming from, my life before you, before this weekend."

He looks at me with curiosity, his eyebrows lifting slightly. "Are you about to tell me about the skeletons in your closet?"

"Not exactly," I laugh, "but kind of. A lot of people, especially the kids' friends, make assumptions when they visit." I pause, trying to find the right words. "I live in a beautiful, large house in a nice neighborhood. When Steve and I separated, I was a stay-at-home mom with a degree but no recent or relevant work experience. I was in a terrible place, both emotionally and financially, and the kids were struggling too. My parents and Alex bought the house for me, and they made the payments until almost two years ago."

Cole looks stunned. "They bought you a house?"

I nod. "Not just a house—a very nice, very large, forever home. My grandparents had recently passed away, and Alex used his inheritance to help buy the house, with no expectation that I'd ever be able to pay him back. When my mom was going through cancer treatment, he paid the mortgage." I pause, letting that sink in. "About two months after Steve and I separated, they sat me down in my parents' living room. My kids were in another room with Alex's wife, Claire. My dad looked at me and said, 'You have so much to worry about right now, and the last thing we all want is for you to worry about where you'll live.' Then Alex handed me the keys and the paperwork."

I glance at Cole, who's clearly trying to process what I've just told him. "The look on my face back then was probably very similar to yours right now. That's also why I live so close to my parents."

"That's insane," he says, shaking his head. "In the world I come from, I can't even comprehend a family doing that for their child or sibling."

"Up until that moment, I couldn't either. But people who come to my house make certain assumptions. There were times when I couldn't even pay the utility bills," I admit. "My brother and my parents are amazing—they're not perfect, but I'm incredibly grateful for them. I just think you should know if you ever make it to my house. It's a conversation I've never had before because I haven't dated anyone since then."

"Not if—it'll be when," he says with a smile. "And wow, they expect nothing in return?"

"The house is still in my parents' name. They've adjusted their will so that Alex gets the house they're living in, plus an investment account my dad has. I get my house, and we'll split everything else. Alex will be reimbursed for all the help he gave me when my parents pass, if that makes sense." I shrug. "And I was expected to start paying the mortgage, utilities, and everything else as soon as I could. I'm doing that now, but they paid off so much of it over the years that, after a refinance, my payment is pretty low."

"Well, maybe I should prepare you for how not big and beautiful my house in Fort Wayne is," he says with a laugh.

I laugh, teasing him. "I'll just picture the worst bachelor pad I can imagine, and then I should be pleasantly surprised, right?"

"Yeah, probably." He grins. "Michelle—my ex—has had a high-earning career for a while, so the kids love spending time with me, but they prefer her house. More space, more things to do—she could always buy them the latest toys and gadgets. My place was filled with cheaper entertainment, like board games, and while they loved it, it wasn't their first choice."

"Tell me about your kids," I prompt, just as the waitress refills our drinks. We've been lingering long after finishing our meal, comfortable in each other's company.

"You know a lot already, but my boys are twenty, twenty-three, and twenty-six," he begins. "Matthew, my youngest, is still in college. He lives at his mom's place but spends a lot of weekends with me. He's quiet until he's not," he adds with a chuckle. "He's also an amazing artist. Tyler, my middle son, graduated from college a year ago and is now a history teacher at a middle school in Indianapolis. We catch up over dinner about once a month. He's the most like me, but he's also the one with the most issues with his mom. Then there's William—he insists on being called William now. It used to be Will or even Willie when he was younger, but now it's just William." He laughs, but there's a touch of sadness in his voice.

"He's my oldest and works in sales for a company that makes restaurant equipment. He'd like to think he's very different from me, but we're more alike than he realizes. Our relationship is the most strained. He was the oldest when we divorced, and he still holds some resentment about it. He'll be the tough one if you ever meet my kids because, even now, he's holding out hope that his mom and I might get back together." He pauses and then asks, "Did any of your kids go through that?"

"No, actually," I say. "All three of them have pretty strained relationships with their father, especially Kevin. I tried really hard not to speak negatively about him when they were younger, but they formed their own opinions. Now that they're adults, I'm more open about things, but I still try not to villainize him."

I pause, debating whether to share more, but then decide to be honest. "Right after I moved out, Steve moved his mistress in. The kids didn't handle that well. He married and divorced her within two years, and then there was a series of live-in girlfriends—none lasting more than a year or two. The kids would get attached, and when the relationships ended, it broke their hearts. I think that's part of why I didn't even entertain the idea of dating. He'd break their hearts, and I'd be the one picking up the pieces. When Kevin was in high school, he caught Steve cheating twice on whoever the woman of the moment was. He lost a lot of respect for him after that."

"That sounds similar to what my kids went through," Cole says, nodding. "Michelle had several men move in over time, and when those relationships ended, the boys felt like it was their fault sometimes." He shrugs, looking thoughtful. "I never really put it together before, but that's probably part of why I never entertained dating either. If I brought someone into their lives, I'd want to be sure it wasn't temporary. I wanted to give them more stability, not less."

"Well, that got deep fast," I say, trying to lighten the mood a bit. "But it sounds like we have some similar experiences when it comes to our divorces and our kids."

"Yeah, it did get deep, didn't it?" He laughs, a warm sound that eases some of the tension. "You know, that's an interesting thing about us." He gestures between us. "We've had so much small talk over the last two years of working together that now, most of our conversations are deep. Things we might not talk about with someone we just started dating for weeks or months—or even longer—are already on the table for us. I think that foundation of friendship is also why we, well, accelerated, I guess, the physical side of things faster than I normally would." He laughs again and reaches over to touch my hand, sending a pleasant shiver up my arm.

"Yeah, I mean, I haven't dated since I was a teenager," I laugh, "but I never imagined I'd just jump into bed with someone at this point in my life. I guess you're the exception." I smile at him, and he laces his fingers with mine, the gesture feeling so natural.

"Speaking of which," he glances at his phone, "I think we can check into our room now."

"Oh, 'speaking of which,' huh?" I tease.

"Yeah." He grins, looking around the restaurant. "I think it's time for us to get out of such a public space." His half-smile is filled with promise, and I can't help but laugh, feeling a rush of excitement.

CHAPTER TEN

THE DISTRACTION

As we walk back to the hotel, I realize I never asked, "How did your meeting with Pete go?"

"It went well," Cole replies, his tone easy. "He was pleased with how the conference turned out for us, and he liked that we had some solid team bonding. I did mention Dr. Gabari, and while Pete isn't thrilled about it, he thinks we handled it well as a team. He suggested you just tell Gabari you're seeing someone and see if that puts an end to it."

"That's a relief," I say, feeling a weight lift. "I'm glad Pete knows, at least."

When we arrive at the hotel, Cole checks us in, and sure enough, we're staying here practically for free, just paying the tax. The place is stunning, and our suite is like a small apartment. I'm a bit in awe as I take it all in.

"As I said, don't get used to this," Cole says with a chuckle as he wraps his arms around me from behind, pulling me back against him. "This is way beyond my usual budget, but I figured if I was going to do this, I'd do it right." He kisses the top of my head, his lips warm and tender. "And the best part is, with room service, we don't have to leave this room until Wednesday afternoon unless we want to."

"That sounds divine," I murmur, leaning back into him, feeling completely content.

He brushes my hair aside, pressing his lips to the sensitive spot just under my ear, sending a shiver straight through me. A soft moan escapes as his lips travel to my earlobe, which he takes into his mouth before descending back down to my neck. With measured movements, the shoulder of my cardigan is gently pushed aside, leaving a trail of kisses across my skin.

Turning me to face him, his mouth finds mine, and my arms instinctively wrap around his waist. The kiss is slow, tender, and electrifying, a wave of heat coursing through my body. The cardigan slips from my other shoulder, and I let it land in a soft heap on the floor. A hand rests on the small of my back while the other cradles the nape of my neck, pulling me closer with gentle yet undeniable pressure.

After a moment, he leans back, brushing loose hair from my face, his eyes full of desire. A kiss lands on the top of my forehead before he reaches behind me to lift my tank top. I raise my arms as the fabric is pulled over my head. His fingers tracing the lace of my bra across the top of my breasts sends a thrill through me. As his fingers reach the end of the lace, his eyes meet mine, and then another kiss finds my lips. His hands move to unclip my bra, the straps sliding off my shoulders before it joins the pile of clothes on the floor.

Guiding me backward toward the bedroom, his hands rest on my ribs just below my breasts. The bed catches me as I back into it, and with quick, practiced motions, my jeans and underwear are unbuttoned and slid down. I kick them off along with my shoes, feeling the cool air on my skin.

A playful smile curves my lips as I grab the sides of his shirt. "I think you're a little overdressed."

The grin that spreads across his face is followed by the swift removal of his pants and shoes. My hands lift his shirt over his head before he gently pushes me further up the bed, guiding me with an arm around my back.

Tracing the line of my jaw with his thumb, he grazes my lower lip before kissing me deeply once again. Lips trail down my neck and chest, and as he nears my nipple, my hand finds its way up his back, fingers tangling in his hair. His mischievous eyes meet mine just before he captures my hand, running his other hand down my arm. Before I realize it, both my wrists are pinned above my head with one hand.

Another kiss claims my mouth before his attention shifts to my breasts. His fingers trace the edges of each breast, spiraling inward with excruciating slowness. My back arches in response, prompting him to tighten his grip on my wrists. Gentle fingertips graze my nipples, and a deep ache pools within me. My back arches again, drawing a quiet chuckle from him as warm breath caresses my skin. His hand cups my left breast, thumb teasing the nipple, while his mouth closes over my right, the combined sensation making everything else fade away.

Instinct drives my body to tilt my pelvis toward him, an involuntary response to the intense pleasure. The attempt to move my hands is met with a firm but gentle hold, keeping them pinned. The orgasm builds, overwhelming and unstoppable, until my body convulses with a powerful release.

"Cole," I gasp, his name a plea as his hand moves from my breast to the sensitive area between my thighs. Fingers slide inside, prompting a push toward him, craving more. His mouth follows his hand down my body, bringing my wrists down over my head and holding them against my chest as his mouth continues its journey lower.

The withdrawal of his fingers leaves a deep ache for more, and his hand spreads my legs apart. Lips find my right thigh, kissing a slow path upward before repeating the journey on the left, deliberately avoiding the area I need him to touch most. My hands twist in his grip, earning a tighter hold. As his mouth returns to my left thigh, his thumb grazes my center, drawing a sharp inhale from me.

The control slips for both of us as he spreads me open, his tongue exploring with a deliberate pace. Every pass over that perfect spot makes my toes curl, my hips pushing toward his mouth. When his tongue plunges inside, his thumb circles in just the right way, and my back arches, a moan escaping. Fingers replace his tongue, curling inside and finding that sweet spot, while his mouth continues its relentless teasing. The pressure on my wrists intensifies, keeping them pinned as the orgasm builds once more.

"Fuck, Cole," I breathe as he drives me over the edge. The release is powerful, leaving my body trembling in its wake.

The climb up my body is followed by a kiss that's deep and filled with passion, the taste of me still lingering on his lips. The gentle withdrawal of his fingers leads to a slow, teasing graze across my mouth. My lips part, and I suck on his fingers, savoring the taste before he pulls them away, leaning in for another kiss and releasing my wrists. His hand cups my breast as my nails trace down his upper arms, earning a moan against my mouth.

With a push on his shoulder, the unspoken signal is given, and he allows me to roll us over so I'm on top. Straddling him, I lean down for a kiss before sitting up, taking him in my hand. His hands press into my thighs as his eyes close, anticipation written across his features. With a deliberate movement, I position him beneath me, sinking down until he fills me completely.

Our gasps mingle as I adjust, the sensation perfect and overwhelming. The rhythm I set is a quick, hungry chase for release. "Fuck, Autumn," he groans as I tilt my head back, driving him deeper with each movement.

His thumb finds that sweet spot between us, circling with expert precision, pushing me toward another climax. The build is quick, and soon I'm convulsing around him, the pleasure spilling over.

Once I've stilled, he sits up part way, wrapping his arms around me, flipping us over without leaving me empty. Grabbing the headboard, he thrusts into me with a force that sends ripples of pleasure through my entire body. My legs wrap around him, one hand gripping his upper arm, the other tangled in the hair on his chest. The intense rhythm drives me to another level of ecstasy, and when he finally releases, I feel him pulsing inside me. His hand slips from the headboard as I trace down his chest, guiding him to my mouth in the aftermath.

Breathless and spent, he collapses beside me, leaving a warmth in his wake. The room fills with the sound of our breathing, a shared silence that speaks volumes.

He lies on his back, and I roll over to rest my head on his chest. His fingers gently weave through my hair while my hand settles on his chest, finding comfort in the steady rhythm of his heartbeat. We stay like that for what feels like hours, wrapped in peaceful silence.

After some time, Cole rubs his hand over mine and quietly asks, "You still awake?"

"Yeah," I reply softly, "just listening to your heart."

He kisses the top of my head and gives my hand a gentle squeeze. "I need to run to the bathroom," he says reluctantly. "I don't want to move, but I have to."

I slide off him with a smile. "Nature calls," I say, looking up at him.

Leaning down, he kisses me gently before getting up. The moment his warmth leaves, a chill sets in, so I decide to either put on some clothes or get under the blankets. The blankets win. I pull down the sheets and comforter on the bed—still mostly untouched despite all we've done—and tuck myself in.

When he returns, he slips on his boxer briefs but quickly joins me under the blankets. I settle back onto his chest, his fingers resuming their gentle play through my hair and down my back. He grabs his phone from the nightstand, checking his work emails and texts.

"See? Don't you wish you'd asked for a few days off too?" I tease, glancing up at him.

"Actually, yes, I do," he admits. "But I told Pete I'd be intermittently available since I was at the conference all weekend, and he was fine with that. I've got an auto-responder on my email, so I'm covered." He lifts the sheets slightly and peers down, a playful smile on his lips. "You're still naked under there?"

"Uh, yeah," I say, looking up at him. "I didn't even leave the bed, just climbed under the blankets. I was cold after you left."

"I'm glad I can keep you warm," he says, his voice softening. "Autumn?"

"Cole?"

"How the hell did we live without this for so many years?"

"I have no idea," I reply, smiling. "I mean, I've got a small arsenal of toys, but it's not the same."

"A small arsenal?" He laughs, his eyes lighting up.

"Uh, yeah. I think a lot of single women do," I say with a laugh. "But they can't kiss you, rub your back, or tell you they're falling in love with you."

"Interesting," he says, grinning. "When I make it to your place, you'll have to show me this arsenal."

I laugh. "Most of them were gifts from Cara. It's a running joke—every birthday, Christmas, sometimes Valentine's Day, she tells me she's bought me a new boyfriend, and lo and behold, he's battery-operated."

Cole laughs. "I think most guys just stick with their hands. I know there are things out there, like pocket pussies and whatnot, but I'm pretty sure most single guys don't have an arsenal of toys. Though, as Tara said about women doing fine on their own, we do too. But it's so much better with someone else."

"Here's my question," I say, a mischievous smile tugging at my lips. "How are you so good at it when you've been out of practice?"

He laughs, a deep, warm sound. "I'll take that as a compliment, but I could ask you the same thing. Maybe it's just because we're such a good fit for each other."

"That's a little cheesy," I tease, "but it feels that way."

Cole's phone rings, and he glances at the screen. "I need to take this," he says, keeping one arm wrapped around me as he answers. His voice remains steady and professional, but as the minutes tick by, I start to feel restless.

A mischievous idea forms, and I let my hand trail down his chest, my fingers brushing along the waistband of his boxers. I feel his muscles tense under my touch, a subtle sign of the effort he's making to stay composed. When my hand slips inside his boxers, finding him already hard, I start stroking him, cupping him gently as I reach lower. His grip tightens on a fistful of my hair, pulling me up to meet his eyes. He shakes his head at me, but there's a smile playing on his lips.

With a playful shrug, I shift on top of him, my movements slow and intentional. He continues his conversation, trying to maintain normalcy, but I can tell he's struggling. I start at his chest, trailing kisses down between his nipples, over his navel, and down to the waistband of his boxers. Another glance up at him earns me another head shake, but he's still smiling. I slide his boxers off and toss them aside, then move back on top of him.

Starting at his navel again, I work my way down, taking him in my hand and stroking him. My lips follow, and soon I have him in my mouth, using both my hand and mouth to stroke him in tandem. The taste of myself on him from earlier only intensifies my desire. I can hear him struggling to keep up his conversation, but eventually, he gives in.

"Hey, something just came up. Can I call you back in a few?" he says, his voice a little strained. After a brief pause, he adds, "Okay, talk to you soon." His phone drops onto the bed, and his hand grips my hair as he moans, "Autumn, fuck, you're insane."

I don't stop, and it doesn't take long before I feel him start to come, the salty taste filling my mouth. His grip on my hair tightens as I finish, then let him slip from my mouth, trailing kisses back up to his lips.

"Sorry, was that distracting?" I ask with a teasing smile.

"Very," he says, his breath still ragged. "I thought we were trying not to get each other fired."

I laugh and shrug. "Guess I got a little carried away."

"Honestly, you can distract me like that anytime," he murmurs, pulling me in for another kiss. Then, leaning back, he adds with a grin, "You know, now that I think about it, I don't think I've had a woman go down on me since I was a teenager."

"Seriously?" I laugh, raising an eyebrow.

"Seriously," he chuckles. "I almost thought it was a myth at this point."

"Wanna know a secret?" I ask, my tone turning playful.

"What's that?" he asks, intrigued.

"I don't know if this is fair or how other women feel, but it's true for me," I say, meeting his gaze. "I know some women don't do it at all, but the more loved and satisfied I feel, the more I want to do it. If I don't feel loved or fulfilled, I have little interest."

"Well, okay then," he says, laughing softly. "I'll do my best to keep you loved and sated." He kisses my forehead gently. "But I really do need to return that call. Can you behave?"

"How about I take a shower?" I suggest. "That should buy you some time."

"Sounds like a plan," he agrees, already reaching for his phone.

As he dives back into his call, I rummage through my luggage, gathering what I need for a long, warm shower. The water feels heavenly, and by the time I step out, I'm dressed in cozy pajama pants and a tank top with a built-in bra. Once again, I'm grateful for the endless options in my gigantic suitcase.

CHAPTER ELEVEN
THE RELATABLE CHEESE

When I step into the living room area of the suite, I find Cole on the couch, dressed in sweatpants and a T-shirt, his laptop open on his lap. The casualness of it makes me smile. Grabbing my phone, I sit down beside him, resting my head—wet hair and all—on his shoulder as I start scrolling through my notifications.

The moment feels so natural, as if this is how it has always been and how it always will be. There's a weight to that thought, a sense of gravity that's almost suffocating if I let myself dwell on it. But when I stop thinking and just let it be, it feels easy, perfect.

It feels like forever.

With that comforting thought, I decide it's time to make plans for the weekend. I start by texting Megan, feeling a quiet excitement about what's to come.

Me

Hey Megs, you busy?

Megan

No, just reading, what's up?

Me

I wanted to ask you something and then talk about this weekend

Megan

Okay

Me

First - did you tell Kevin and Sami why I stayed in Dallas? I know I asked you not to, but I need to know

Megan

I plead the fifth

Me

lol okay - so don't freak out okay?

Megan

No promises

Me

I'm bringing him home with me this weekend

Megan

No fucking way

Mom, this must be serious, you sure you just met this guy?

Me

No, I didn't just meet him, but the romantic side of this just started

Megan

It's Cole isn't it? It's got to be Cole

A sudden laugh escapes me, and Cole glances over, curious. I hold up my phone, showing him the last couple of messages.

"How did everyone realize this was happening except us?" I ask, still smiling at the absurdity of it all.

He chuckles, leaning in to kiss the top of my head. "Maybe we were too close to see it," he says softly, a warmth in his voice that makes the moment feel even more special.

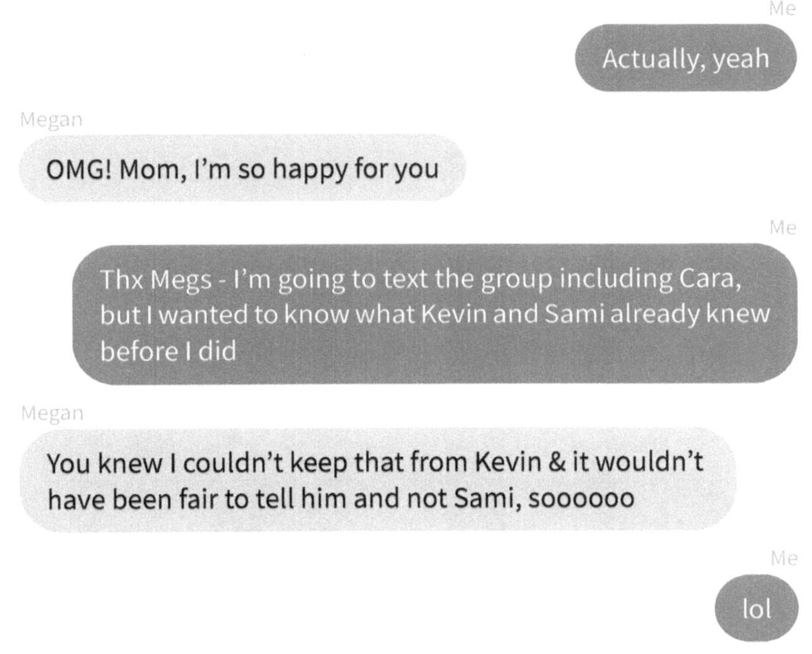

I open the group chat for the kids, Cara, and me.

Kevin

Yes, and I have questions for you

Sami

So excited, it was my idea remember

Cara

Oh, I'm not missing this one

Me

So I know Megan already spilled the beans to Kevin and Sami and I have filled Cara in on part of this

Megan

Hey I tried to plead the fifth

Kevin

That's what my questions are about, but I think she called me about half a second after she found out

Me

Not surprised

So here's bigger news, I'm bringing him home with me this weekend

Cara

Shut the front door

Kevin

?!?!?!?!

Me

Y'all need to be nice, please

> And Cara and Megan already know, but it's Cole, you know, my boss, and while we figure out some things this needs to be on the DL as y'all would say

Sami

> Mom, stop trying to be cool, but are you fucking serious? Cole?

Kevin

> Well at least we know he's financially stable lol

> And you didn't just meet him which was our biggest worry - we were prepared for an intervention and a talk about sex in the modern age

Me

> Oh my … Kevin!

Kevin

> Seriously, Megan thought it was some guy you just met, we were concerned, so this is a relief and I think I might actually be able to be happy for you

Cole laughs softly, and I realize he's reading over my shoulder.

"Hey now," I tease, turning to him with a playful smile. "No eavesdropping on my text messages."

"It's hard not to when they're right in front of me," he replies, grinning. "But I have to admit, it's pretty entertaining."

Sami

> You're going to make him meet all of us at once, I mean Megs and me sure, but you're going to expose him to Kevin and Cara right away?

> I hope he's brave

"You still reading over my shoulder?" I ask, keeping my eyes on the screen.

"No, you scolded me," he laughs, the sound warm and easy.

"I was just kidding," I say with a grin. "I don't think I have anything I'd want to hide from you. Megan is asking if you're staying at the house and if you'll come up with me when I go home on Wednesday."

"I figure yes to the first, unless there's a reason you'd prefer otherwise," he replies. "As for the second, I probably need to go home, do some laundry, and re-pack my suitcase, but I could be there by Thursday if that works for you."

"I'm good with both of those answers," I say, smiling. "You'd drive, right?"

"Yeah, probably," he says thoughtfully. "I'll check flights, but I doubt there's anything direct, and it's only a five-hour drive. Actually, I might make it there late Wednesday." He nudges me playfully with his shoulder.

I laugh, feeling a warmth spread through me. "I wouldn't mind that," I say, glancing back at my phone with a smile.

Kevin

Oh, great, you're going to let the unstable child meet him first

Megan

Hey!

Sami

Megs, I expect a full report

Megan

Of course

Me

Y'all are ridiculous - but he will stay at the house and he'll drive up from Fort Wayne either Wednesday night or Thursday during the day

Megan

Yesss! I do get to meet him first!

Kevin

You going to bring him to Sunday dinner with the grandparents?

Me

Shit, I didn't even think about that

Kevin

Well you should, or you should send him home on Sunday morning lol

We should tell Uncle Alex his appearance is requested for Sunday dinner this weekend, he's going to shit bricks and then he'll be elated

"That was amazing and exhausting," I say, putting down my phone with a satisfied sigh.

"Yeah?" Cole asks, his eyes full of warmth.

"Yeah," I reply, smiling. "My kids are super excited to meet you."

A couple of hours pass as I get bored and eventually turn on the TV, settling on a home improvement show. Cole closes his laptop and turns to me. "You hungry?" he asks.

"I am, though it feels early. But I'm ravenous," I admit.

"Well, you've been burning some extra energy these last couple of days," he says with a playful elbow to my side. "Let's check out the room service menu."

We order food—enough to keep us from having to leave the room for a while, with extra snacks and drinks. As we sit at the fancy dining room table, eating, I decide to take a chance and ask Cole about his childhood.

"Do you want to tell me more about your childhood?" I ask gently.

"I can try," he says after a moment, his voice tinged with hesitation. "Sometimes I don't articulate well. The therapist I saw as a teenager said I regress when I talk about it, that I don't communicate like an adult. But it's been a while."

"I've seen the scars," I say softly, "otherwise, I might wonder if it was really that bad. But, Cole, I can't even imagine someone doing that to a child."

"I was one of the 'good kids,'" he says, using air quotes. "So my scars aren't as bad as some of my brothers'." He pauses, and I look at him, offering silent support. "Basically, we were expected to be seen and not heard, to do our chores and not cause trouble. At four, I was washing and folding laundry, running the dishwasher, and even making meals."

"Seriously?" I ask, shocked.

"Seriously," he nods. "If something was wrong—like if my mom didn't like how the towels were folded, or if dinner was overcooked or undercooked—we'd be punished. The severity of the punishment depended on how much my dad had to drink that day."

He takes a few bites of food before continuing. "If he'd had too much to drink, there was almost no punishment because he wasn't capable. If he was sober, the punishments were light. But in between... it could be anything from being whipped to cigarette burns. It never happened to me, but a couple of my brothers had their heads held underwater in the bathtub. They'd withhold food from us, too. My sister was sometimes chained to the bed."

A horrible thought crosses my mind, and I hesitantly ask, "Do you think your dad ever—"

"I don't know," he cuts in, his voice tight. "She's the most defensive of our parents, so it's hard to believe that. But at the same time, she wasn't even five, and I wouldn't be surprised.

"When Carson went to the police, he had the scars to back up what he was reporting. They pulled us out of the house within twenty-four hours, and we never went back," he continues.

"Did you end up bouncing around in foster care?" I ask, my heart aching for the little boy he once was.

"I was lucky, luckier than most of my siblings," he says with a small shrug. "But the home I was placed in regularly had six to ten kids coming and going. My foster mom was great, but she had too many of us to really make a significant impact. I kept to myself, focused on being a good kid and a good student. I stayed with her for six years. She made sure I had regular therapy and medical care, which probably made a huge difference. She passed away a couple of years ago, but she was the closest thing to a mom I had."

"Cole," I reach out and touch his hand, "I'm so sorry."

"It's not your fault, but thank you," he says, squeezing my hand. "I think when I met Michelle, I didn't recognize it at the time, but I was drawn to how she mothered me. And I don't mean just a little maternal—you're a *little* maternal," he smiles at me, "but she full-on mothered me. She picked out my clothes, bought my favorite snacks, reminded me of everything from brushing my teeth to going to bed. She even checked in on my grades through college and chastised me if they weren't an A or B. It wasn't until we had kids that I realized what was happening, and it hit me like a brick to the face."

"I can see that," I say softly.

"I started to resent it," he continues, his voice thoughtful. "I wanted to be respected as an adult, but she emasculated me, talked down to me in front of the kids. Things went downhill quickly after that. Even sex was on her terms—when she wanted it, how she wanted it. My desires didn't seem to matter." He shrugs, a hint of sadness in his eyes. "That's probably why I went a little wild after we separated, but I quickly realized that wasn't what I wanted either."

He looks at me, his gaze serious. "I think all this time, I've just been waiting for you. How's that for cheesy?" he says, a smile breaking through the seriousness.

"That is cheesy," I laugh, "but I relate to that cheese. I feel the same way, as silly as it sounds." I reach over and place my hand on his forearm. "Maybe starting as colleagues worked out in our favor. I don't know how our relationship would have grown if we'd been in person more. I've been thinking about how everyone around us seemed to know before we did. We had something blossom over those two years, and maybe it wouldn't have been the same if we'd been together more."

He nods, his expression thoughtful as he considers my words, and for a moment, we simply share the quiet understanding between us.

"Or," Cole begins, "maybe this all would have started a long time ago."

"That's possible," I reply, smiling at the thought. "It's just strange—I have all the excitement of a new relationship, but it also feels like it's been there forever, like there's always been an *us*, and like there always will be."

He looks at me intently, then reaches out, pulling me from my chair and into his lap. His eyes lock onto mine as his hand brushes my cheekbone, his thumb tracing the line softly before he cups the back of my neck, drawing me in for a long, deep kiss. He tastes like chocolate cake, and I wish the kiss could last forever.

When he pulls back, his expression is serious. "Autumn, I don't know how I got this lucky, but I swear, if you break my heart... " He rests his head against my chest, his vulnerability palpable.

"I'm more worried about you breaking mine," I whisper, wrapping my arms around him and kissing the top of his head. "This is so intense, it's terrifying. If you're feeling that, I'm feeling it too."

"Yeah," he says, looking up at me, his voice tinged with apprehension. "It just feels too good to be true, like I'm waiting for the other shoe to drop. You literally scare me because it's been two days, and I already feel like I'd follow you off a cliff. I honestly don't think I've ever felt this way about anyone."

"I'm not leading you off a cliff," I assure him with a soft smile, "as long as you don't lead me off one. And I feel the same way." I kiss his forehead gently. "Maybe we should watch a funny movie or something, tone down all this intensity."

"That's probably a good idea," he agrees, laughing softly.

I stand up, grab his hand, and lead him to the couch. Handing him the remote, I say, "You pick—whatever you want. I just want to snuggle with you."

He puts his feet up on the coffee table, and I tuck mine under me, leaning into him. He picks one of those silly, funny movies that's exactly what we need. We laugh, roll our eyes, steal kisses, and exchange playful touches. When the movie ends, we head to bed, and for the first time in our whirlwind romance, we just snuggle and sleep. There's no need for anything more—just the warmth of his body next to mine. I drift off into one of the best nights of sleep I've had in a long time, comforted by the simple closeness we share.

CHAPTER TWELVE
THE FLIGHTS HOME

Tuesday unfolds in much the same way as the day before. Cole works while I snuggle up next to him, either scrolling through my phone or watching TV. I try not to be too much of a distraction—our playful moment was fun, but I know he needs to focus.

As we eat dinner that evening, the reality that this is our last night of our little hiatus begins to sink in. Tomorrow, we'll have to figure out how to make this work in the context of our regular lives.

"But I don't want to," I whine, feeling a pang of reluctance.

"Me either," he admits. "But in a couple of nights, I'll be in your bed, so there's that."

"There is that," I say with a smile. "You know, I've never had sex in my house, so that will be new and different."

"I get to be your first—how special," he teases.

"That's not the only thing that's special," I laugh, appreciating the lightness he brings.

"I land in Indianapolis at two, should be home by five. If I move quickly, I can be in your bed by midnight at the latest," he says, a playful twinkle in his eye.

"You don't have to rush," I say, though part of me hopes he does.

"Funny you should say that, because it's not a have to. I definitely want to," he replies. "I don't know how I'm going to concentrate on anything without you. The only reason I managed today was because you were right here, within reach. It's like, if I can't touch you, you might disappear." He laughs, but there's a sincerity beneath his words.

"Maybe that anxiety—or whatever it is—will fade over time," I suggest.

"Are you sure?" he asks, a touch of skepticism in his voice.

"I feel like it has to," I say with a laugh. "I don't think we can sustain this level of intensity forever."

A few hours later, we crawl into bed for the last time in this luxurious hotel room. Laying my head on Cole's chest, I run my hand through his chest hair. It feels like home—like home is a person, not a place.

Propping myself up on my elbow, I lean in and kiss him softly. His hand moves up from my hip to my breast, and then he gently guides me onto my back. This time, making love with Cole feels different—deeper, more intimate. Everything is slow, gentle, and full of emotion.

His kisses are tender, trailing down my body with an intentional gentleness that makes me feel cherished. His fingers lightly tease my inner thighs before slipping inside me, moving with a softness that matches the tenderness in his eyes. He massages me slowly, his thumb creating a rhythm that mirrors the deep connection between us. He kisses me again, our mouths and bodies moving together in perfect harmony. As I come around his fingers, our moans mix softly in the quiet room.

Cole rolls us over, sitting back against the headboard, pulling me into his lap. My legs wrap around him as he guides himself inside me, our movements slow and synchronized, our bodies fitting together perfectly. I wrap my arms around his neck, and he holds me close, his arms around my waist. I've never felt this physically close to anyone before.

When we're done, I feel completely loved, cherished, and fulfilled. We stay wrapped in each other's arms, never leaving the bed, falling asleep naked and content, knowing that whatever comes next, we'll face it together.

In the morning, I wake up before Cole. My body is wrapped around his, my arms draped over him, his back turned to me, exposing the scars etched into his skin. I can't help but start tracing them gently, kissing each one as if I could make them disappear, the way my kids used to believe a kiss could magically heal their scrapes and bruises. When my fingers graze a scar near his side, he stirs, grabbing my hand and rolling onto his back. His eyes meet mine as he reaches up to lightly trace my jawline.

"Apparently you're awake," I say softly. "Sorry if I woke you."

"You can wake me anytime," he replies, his voice gentle. "I can't imagine being upset at you for that." He studies me for a moment. "You did that the other morning too—traced my scars."

"I did," I admit, suddenly self-conscious. "I'm sorry. Is that not okay?"

"No, it's okay," he reassures me. "It's just... no one's ever done that before. Other women—Michelle, even my high school girlfriends—either avoided them or pretended they didn't exist. People like to say that scars are cool on men, but they don't always feel that way."

"I want to fix them," I say, my voice barely above a whisper. "I know I can't, but I wish I could make them softer, less painful, maybe turn the memories into something that doesn't hurt so much. I want to kiss them away like I did when my kids bumped their heads."

"I wish it were that easy," he says, a hint of sadness in his voice. "But I appreciate the gesture, and I appreciate you. And honestly, I don't think I would've been able to appreciate you like this twenty years ago. I've been through a lot to get to this point, but damn, I wish I'd had more years with you."

"You have me now," I remind him gently. "And I think we should be grateful for what we have instead of what we missed." I lean in and kiss him softly.

"You're right," he agrees, though there's a touch of wistfulness in his tone. "It's just that hearing about your family makes me think about what I didn't have. Your world has been so different from mine."

"Well, welcome to my world," I say with a smile. "You're part of it now. My kids are already excited to meet you, and I'm sure my parents and brother will be too once I tell them you exist," I laugh. "They're not perfect, but they're a lot better than most."

"It doesn't take much to be better than mine," he says with a half-smile.

"That's not your fault," I say, kissing him again.

"I know," he nods, "and thank you for letting me into your world."

We spend the rest of the morning ordering breakfast, eating together, and packing up. When it's time to leave, we head to the airport. Cole's flight takes off earlier than mine, so I walk him to his gate. Just before he boards, we share a lingering kiss.

"See you tonight," he says with a big smile.

"Hopefully," I respond, my heart feeling both full and heavy.

"Even if it's three in the morning, I'll be there," he promises.

I watch him board the plane and then make my way to my own gate. As I sit down to wait for my flight, I pull out my phone.

Cole

I miss you already

Me

Oh, so we're one of *those* couples

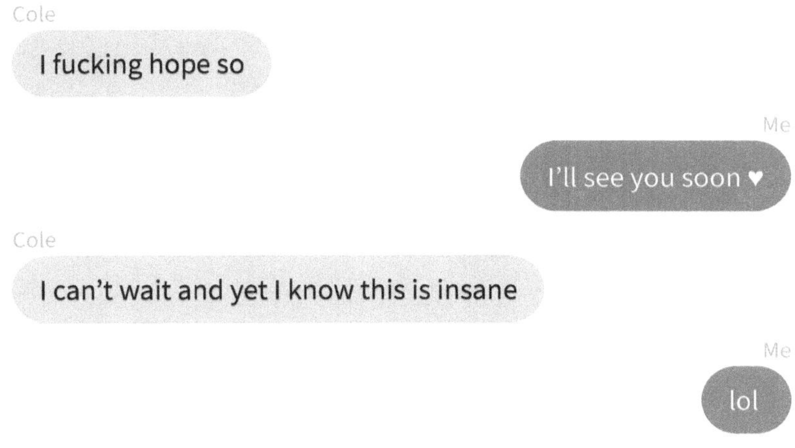

As I hit send, a notification comes in from Megan.

I don't even have time to put my phone away before a text from Kevin lights up my screen.

Me

Oh, you don't want Megan to have that much of a headstart on you, huh?

And I can do lasagna since my baby boy is requesting it lol

Kevin

Heck no, I want to get to know this guy, neither sister is going to ask the same questions I will

Me

As long as you're nice

Kevin

Mom, believe it or not, I do not want to scare him off, if he makes you happy I want him to stay

Me

Kev, that might be one of the nicest things you've ever said to me lol

Kevin

I have my moments

Me

Love you, see you Friday if I don't talk to you beforehand

Kevin

Don't forget the lasagna

Me

Can you pick up a tiramisu for dessert with said lasagna?

Kevin

I sure can - it's on my way

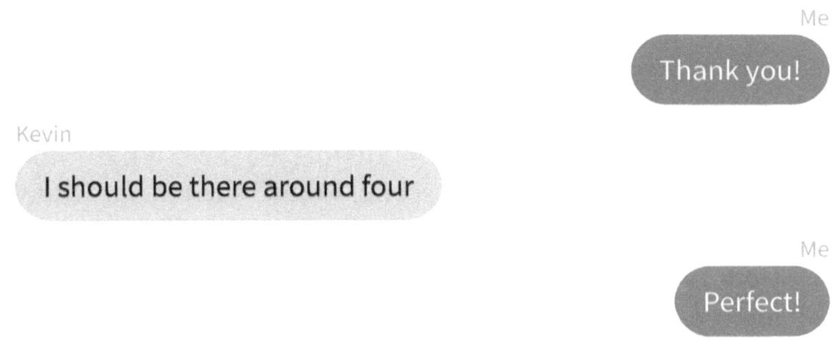

Cole is right—my family is amazing. My plane boards, and I manage to catch some sleep on the flight. We touch down in Milwaukee just after three, and timing works out perfectly. As I step outside, Megan pulls up to the curb right on cue.

"Well, hey there, my no-longer-single mother," Megan teases, loading my suitcase into the back of the car. She studies me with a playful grin. "You look different—happy, maybe even glowing," she laughs.

"Oh, Megan," I sigh, rolling my eyes. "I hope you're joking."

"No, I'm serious," she insists. "Your eyes are smiling. You look genuinely happy. So, when's he getting to the house?"

"Sometime late tonight," I say. "He'll probably leave Fort Wayne around five or six, depending on any delays."

"I'm waiting up with you," she declares. "I'm not missing this, even if he doesn't get here until after midnight."

"Whatever you need to do, Megs," I laugh. "By the way, Kevin is coming in Friday afternoon. He requested lasagna for dinner."

"That's a great idea, Mom! Kevin can be smart sometimes."

I furrow my eyebrows, confused by her enthusiasm.

"Oh, come on," she says, rolling her eyes right back at me. "You make it all from scratch. It's a chance to show off your cooking skills, and we all come in to help as a family. It's like a postcard-perfect scene when you make lasagna. You know, 'look at how perfect our little family is.'"

"I totally bought into it," I admit with a smile. "I even asked Kevin to pick up tiramisu."

"See? Sometimes he's a smart guy," she laughs. "Plus, it puts us all in the kitchen, gives us a chance to talk to Cole without it feeling like some formal interrogation."

"I can't believe I didn't think of all that," I say, shaking my head.

"Well, you're new to the dating scene, Mom," she teases. "But what have Kevin and I always asked for when we bring someone new home—even just a friend?"

I roll my eyes again, but she's right.

We pull into the garage, and I head straight to the laundry room, dumping all my dirty clothes into the washer. I lug the rest of my things up to my bedroom. Then I strip the bed and plan to wash the sheets and blankets once the washer is free. I vacuum the bedroom and tidy up the master bathroom, making sure there are extra towels. Meanwhile, Megan takes charge of the main areas—the kitchen, the powder room, and the guest bathroom. Nothing's terrible, but everything needs a little fine-tuning.

Megan looks at me, her expression softening. "Mom, don't worry too much. I took good care of the house while you were gone, and I prepped because I knew you'd freak out if the house was a mess once you knew he was coming."

"It's just weird," I admit. "I've never even had a guy pick me up at the house. You kids have had more dating experience here than I have."

"I know," she says gently. "But we all want this to be amazing for you. I know you think Cara and Kevin are going to be ridiculous, but they won't be. They want to show him why he should want to be with you and be a part of this family." She smiles. "Sami and I do too, but I think that's what you expect from us."

"This is true," I say, feeling a warmth spread through me.

My phone rings, and I glance at my watch—it's Cole. I scramble to find my phone, finally answering it a little out of breath.

"Hey," I say, trying to catch my breath.

"You okay?" he asks, a laugh in his voice.

"Yeah, just couldn't find my phone." I laugh along with him.

"Oh, is that all?"

"Yes, that's all. How are you doing?"

"I'm good. I should be able to head out of Fort Wayne in about twenty minutes," he says, and I glance at the clock—it's just about five. "So, I should be there around ten your time, unless there's crazy traffic."

"Sounds good," I reply. "Megan refuses to go to bed until you get here, so we'll both be waiting for you."

He chuckles. "I can't wait."

"See you soon. Call me if anything changes."

"I will," he promises.

It's about a quarter to ten when Cole calls again.

"Hey, Cole," I answer.

"Hey there, beautiful. I'm just on your side of downtown Milwaukee. I should be there in about fifteen minutes."

"Okay, I'm sure you'll have no issues, but Megan says to tell you her black Jeep is in the driveway in case that helps," I laugh.

I can hear the smile in his voice. "Got it. Does it matter where I park?"

"Anywhere in the driveway is fine. None of us are going anywhere until Saturday, I don't think," I say. "We can rearrange cars before Sami and Kevin get here if we need to."

"Sounds good."

About fifteen minutes later, Megan spots headlights in the driveway and gets very excited. "There are headlights, Mom!" she squeals.

"How are you more excited than I am?" I tease.

"Mom, I've been waiting for this for like a decade," she says, her tone making it clear this should be obvious.

Megan opens the front door just as Cole walks up. Our grand foyer with its huge staircase and double front doors greets him. To the right is a large living room, and to the left, a spacious kitchen with a massive island and kitchen table. Behind the stairs, the family room leads out to the patio and pool. Beyond the kitchen is the formal dining room, bathroom, and my office. The house is always a little impressive to first-time visitors, and I can see the surprise on Cole's face as he takes it all in.

I hug him, but he only half-hugs me back, still absorbing everything around him. Leaning in close, I whisper in his ear, "Now you know why I had that conversation with you."

"Uh, yeah," he murmurs, still in awe. "Holy shit."

"Cole, this is Megan. Megan, this is Cole," I say, introducing them.

Cole extends his hand, but Megan walks right past it and hugs him instead.

"She's a mini-you," he laughs, and Megan grins at me.

"Let me take you on the grand tour," Megan offers, "Mom gets embarrassed, so I'll show off for her."

Megan proceeds to give Cole the full tour of the main level, pointing out everything she finds particularly cool. When they reach the patio and pool, Cole turns to me, surprised.

"You have a pool?" he asks.

I shrug, but Megan jumps in. "And a hot tub and a sauna," she adds, pointing toward the sauna area.

Cole steps out onto the patio with Megan, taking in the outdoor kitchen, extensive patio furniture, and everything else.

"There's a point to this besides me trying to show off," Megan says, slipping into her best infomercial voice. "For the low, low price of loving my mother, this can all be yours." She gestures dramatically around the space.

I burst out laughing, caught off guard. "Megan!" Then I turn to Cole. "I swear I had no idea she was going to do that."

"That was pretty funny, though," Megan says, her grin wide.

Cole laughs too, though I can tell he's a bit overwhelmed.

"Megan, thank you for the grand tour," I say, "and for thoroughly overwhelming him. But you can continue your antics tomorrow."

Megan isn't done yet, though. She switches back to her infomercial voice. "Well then, let's go get your suitcase and show you to the bedroom," she says, making a grand gesture.

I look at Cole and mouth, "I'm sorry." He just smiles at me.

When we finally get to the bedroom and Megan has left us alone, I close the door behind us.

"Holy fuck, Autumn," he says quietly, looking around. "I think you undersold this. I mean, I knew you said a big fancy house, but this... this is not what I expected. I think you could fit half my house in your bedroom."

The bedroom is indeed impressive. There are double doors leading in, with an ornamental oak headboard on the king-size bed to the left. A sitting area with a loveseat, chaise lounge, and coffee table is set up to view the large-screen television, which is also viewable from the bed. The far wall is mostly windows, letting in plenty of natural light during the day. The entrance to the large, five-piece bathroom is to the right, past the foot of the bed, with a spacious walk-in closet beyond. Skylights in the bedroom and bathroom add to the open, airy feel during the day. The entire master suite is about eight hundred square feet, and I can tell it's overwhelming him too.

"I know," I say softly. "I know when I told you about how I got the house, it sounded crazy, but now you understand."

"Your brother and your parents bought you this?" he asks, still processing. "They could have found you a little townhome somewhere, but they bought you *this*?"

"Uh, yeah," I reply in a sarcastic, matter-of-fact tone before adding more seriously, "I know, it's insane. And I really had no idea Megan was going to do that." I laugh. "She completely caught me off guard."

"She's funny," he says with a smile. "And she is a mini-you."

"The kids all say their goal this weekend is to make you want me more than you already do," I tell him. "Kevin said they want to sell you on the package deal that comes with me so that you'll stick around because they already believe you make me happy."

"Autumn, I don't think I can want you more than I already do," he says, his voice full of warmth. "But if they want to add some cherries on top, I have no objections."

I move closer, grabbing the belt loops of his jeans and pulling him toward me. "Welcome to my big, fancy home," I say, kissing him deeply.

He wraps his arms around me, melting into the kiss.

"How was the drive?" I ask once we pull apart.

"It was good, except for a small stretch near Chicago," he says, "but nothing awful."

"Good," I say, kissing him again. "Make yourself at home. If you need anything or if I need to make space for you, just let me know. I put extra towels in the bathroom, but that probably won't matter until tomorrow. Just tell me if you need anything."

He pulls me close, his voice a low whisper in my ear. "Right now, I just need you." His words send a wave of warmth and desire through me, settling deep inside.

"Then take me," I whisper back.

He lets out a sound that's somewhere between a growl and a groan, quickly pulling my shirt over my head and unbuttoning my jeans. I unhook my bra and start working on his shirt. We kick off our shoes and strip down in seconds, both of us eager and hungry for each other.

There's no foreplay this time—he pushes me onto the bed, pulls my hips to the edge, and lifts my knees over his arms. He takes me with an intensity that's animalistic and raw. It's hot and urgent, making me feel wanted, needed, and loved in a completely different way than the tender lovemaking of the night before. When we're done, he collapses beside me, both of us breathless.

He looks at me, a little sheepish. "Sorry, not sure what came over me."

I laugh, brushing his apology aside. "Don't be sorry—that was pretty hot. You wanted something, and you took it."

"I guess I did," he laughs, the tension easing.

"Now come cuddle with me," I say, pulling him closer.

"Yes, ma'am," he replies with a grin.

We snuggle up together, and within moments, we're both fast asleep, wrapped up in each other's warmth.

CHAPTER THIRTEEN

THE ASSHOLE BOSS

Thursday morning starts with my alarm blaring, and Cole groans beside me, mumbling something about it being too early.

"Well, you see," I tease as I sit up, "I have this asshole boss who expects me on camera at eight in the morning, so I have to get ready."

He pulls me back down onto the bed, chuckling. "Yeah, he sounds like an asshole," he says with a grin. "Speaking of which, I'm not sure how we're going to do that camera thing today."

"I've already figured it out, unless you have any objections," I say. "I'll work from my office, and you can use either the desk in Kevin's room or the dining room. Just turn on a background blur or use a fake background—even if you don't, no one would recognize where you are anyway."

We both get ready, though it takes me a bit longer than it does Cole. He opts for the dining room, and soon we're logging in for our morning meeting. We discuss updates from prospective clients, and then Cole shares that he'll be working on the conference schedule over the next few days, letting us know when and where we'll all be going.

"We've registered for seven more conferences in the next six months," Cole says, "so I'll be figuring out who goes where and sending it to Pete for approval by the end of the weekend. Also, I'm canceling the morning meeting tomorrow."

I struggle to keep a straight face but manage it. Cole wraps up the meeting, and I head into the dining room.

"Want some breakfast?" I ask.

"Yes, and coffee," he laughs. "I hope you have coffee."

"We do," I assure him with a smile. "Megan probably already brewed some—she has summer classes at nine on Tuesdays and Thursdays."

Cole shuts his laptop and follows me into the kitchen. There's a plate of freshly baked muffins on the island with a note from Megan.

"She baked these this morning," I say, smiling at Cole. "I also have eggs, cereal, bagels—whatever you want."

"These smell amazing," he replies, gesturing to the muffins. "I don't need anything fancy. I'll stick with these."

I turn on the electric kettle and pull two mugs from the cabinet. "So, this is almost embarrassing," I admit, "but you pretty much knew my coffee preferences before we even got to Dallas. How do you take your coffee?"

He smiles. "Almost black, just a splash of milk or cream and a little sugar." I pull the milk out of the fridge, put it on the island along with the sugar dish, and pour him a cup of coffee. The tea kettle signals it is ready and I start steeping my tea.

"This feels pretty natural, despite your kitchen being ridiculously big and fancy," he laughs.

"It does," I agree. "But tell me, how did you know I like white mochas? I don't even remember having that conversation."

"I don't remember exactly when, probably some pre-meeting small talk," he says. "I vaguely recall you and Tara chatting about it during pumpkin spice latte season—neither of you got the hype. Somehow, it stuck with me."

"Maybe those are the kinds of things other people saw that we didn't," I muse. "Do you think the team is completely in the dark?"

"Not completely. Tara's sharp—she can read a room, and Mark made a comment about our moods," he says. "I don't think they'll be surprised when it comes out, except maybe Tom, but I doubt anyone realizes that line has already been crossed."

"I was thinking the same," I say. "What's on your agenda for the rest of the day?"

"I need to draft the conference schedule and then meet with Pete later to go over it," he says. "He usually doesn't object. I wish I could always schedule myself to go with you, but that's not realistic."

"I know," I say with a smile. "I've just got to follow up on leads from the conference—emails today, phone calls tomorrow or Monday."

"Not too bad for either of us," he says, "and outside of my meeting with Pete, we don't need to be in separate rooms."

"We can work here," I suggest, gesturing to the island, "or in the family room where the couch is much more comfortable than these bar stools."

"I vote for comfort," he says. We finish our coffee and muffins, then grab our laptops and settle into the family room, ready to work side by side.

He settles into the couch, casually kicking his feet up on the coffee table. I curl up sideways, my back pressed against the armrest, and nudge my fuzzy socked feet into the warmth of his thigh. We don't need to fill the space with words. The soft click of our laptop keys and the quiet of our shared presence are enough. Every so often, he reaches over, his fingers brushing against my legs or massaging my feet, a tender reminder that this—right here—is exactly where we're supposed to be.

After a while, he glances up, breaking the silence. "I've got a question for you," he says, his voice curious but laced with something deeper. "If you had a choice, would you want me to go with you to Denver or San Francisco?"

I laugh lightly, tilting my head to look at him. "Who would go with me to the other city?"

"San Francisco? Probably Tara and Mark," he muses. "And Denver, Julio and Tom."

A smile tugs at the corners of my mouth as I consider. "Then come with me to Denver. I'll have Tara in San Francisco. But watch that preferential treatment," I tease, nudging him playfully with my foot.

He chuckles, squeezing my foot in response. "Oh, believe me, I'm trying. But it's tough imagining you going off somewhere without me." There's a softness in his eyes as he finishes typing, then passes me his laptop. "Okay, take a look at this. Tell me what you think."

I take the laptop, scanning the screen. Over the next six months, we have seven conferences lined up. We're each attending four, with three overlapping. And for the one he's not coming with me, he's paired me with Tara.

"I think it looks good," I say, meeting his gaze. "But do you think anyone will question you being at three of my four?"

He grins, shaking his head. "Nah, I spaced them out. Plus, I'm pretty sure Dr. Gabari will be at two of them, and I can use that as an excuse—big client, needs special attention, and all that. Especially after that inappropriate behavior he showed you last time."

I hand him back his laptop, the memory of Gabari's uncomfortable advances flickering briefly before Cole asks, "Did you reach out to him yet?"

I sigh, shaking my head slightly. "Honestly, it slipped my mind the last few days. I'll send him an email now."

"Copy me on it," Cole says, then reconsiders. "Actually, blind copy me and Pete too. Then forward us any response."

"Okay," I say, turning back to my laptop to type, my fingers moving quickly across the keyboard. The small act of crafting the email feels strangely intimate, like a shared secret between us.

Dr. Gabari,
It was truly delightful to have the opportunity to meet you face-to-face during our time in Dallas. Mark and I are eager to visit and look forward to coming to your practice soon.
I wanted to express my sincere gratitude for the lovely roses; they added a special touch to our day. I truly appreciate the thoughtful gesture, and while I am flattered, I want to ensure

*there's clarity regarding my availability. I am already involved
in a committed personal relationship and my focus is solely on
maintaining a professional working relationship.*
*Thank you once again for your kindness. We plan to be in
touch shortly to coordinate our upcoming in-person visit.*
Thank You Again, Autumn

I hand my laptop to Cole, seeking his approval on the email draft. He nods, satisfied, so I hit send. Just as I do, my watch vibrates—Megan's texting, asking if we want her to bring lunch. Cole is all for that suggestion, and I quickly call Megan to place our orders.

Forty-five minutes later, Megan sweeps through the door, and we gather at the kitchen island. The scent of takeout fills the room as she distributes the food.

"So, Megan," Cole begins, curiosity evident in his tone, "what are you studying these days?"

"My major is environmental science, for now," she replies, a hint of uncertainty in her voice. "But I'm not sure I'll stick with it."

"What do you want to do after school?" he asks, genuinely interested.

"I want to move to Oregon and work with my Uncle Alex," she says, her eyes brightening. "I love it there—it's beautiful, and he needs people."

I start to elaborate, "Alex is—"

But Megan cuts me off with a dramatic clearing of her throat, adopting her best exaggerated British accent. "I think you mean *Alexander Liam Flynn*," she announces, then bursts into laughter.

I can't help but smile at her theatrics. "Yes, Alexander Liam Flynn," I play along, "*esquire*, you forgot that part, Megs. Anyway, he's an environmental attorney specializing in forestry and the logging industry."

Megan tosses napkins onto the counter in front of us, grinning. "Yeah, I want to be a professional tree-hugger," she says with a laugh.

"My dad thinks it's dumb—probably a lot of people do—but that's what I want to do."

Cole's expression softens as he responds, "I don't think that's dumb at all," drawing a smile from Megan.

"He works with logging companies to help them stay within legal boundaries and comply with regulations," I add, looking at Megan. "And you're right, Megs—the Pacific Northwest is stunning."

"I've never been," Cole admits, a note of excitement in his voice. "I'm really looking forward to Tara's wedding because of that. I've always wanted to visit that part of the country."

"Tara works with you guys, right?" Megan asks, curiosity piqued.

"Yeah," I confirm. "She's originally from Oklahoma but lives in Seattle now. The wedding is on Valentine's Day."

"I've never understood why people do that," Megan muses.

"Do what?" I ask.

"Take away a romantic holiday by making it their wedding anniversary too," she explains. "When I get married, I want to space it out from Christmas, my birthday, Valentine's Day, and even the 4th of July."

"The 4th of July?" Cole raises an eyebrow.

"Yes, because fireworks are *so* romantic," she says, pressing a hand to her heart and gazing dramatically at the ceiling.

"My daughter, the actress," I tease.

"I'm just a romantic, Mom, that's all," she replies, laughing.

Cole chuckles, shaking his head. "I'm not sure if this makes me glad or sad that I only have boys."

Megan's ears perk up. "You have boys? How old are they? Are they single?"

Cole laughs, and I roll my eyes. "He has three boys, and they line up a lot like you three, just a little older," I answer.

"Interesting," Megan says with a mischievous grin.

"My youngest is your age," Cole adds, "and as far as I know, they're all single."

"Don't encourage her," I laugh, shaking my head.

We finish our lunch, and Megan heads to her room, no doubt to dive into her homework.

"Is she always like this?" Cole asks, a smile playing at the corners of his mouth.

"Not always," I reply, grinning. "She's just a little amped up with you here." I pause, studying his face. "Kevin's going to be too, I think. Sami, well, she's the wild card."

"When will they be here?" he asks, leaning back. "I might need a nap first." We both laugh.

"They'll both be here tomorrow," I say. "Sami midday, and Kevin around four. He made a special request for lasagna, so I guess I'm making that tomorrow. Sami will probably monopolize the laundry room, but she's usually the quiet one."

"Zero to one hundred," he says with a knowing smile.

"Yep." I wrinkle my nose, apologetically. "Sorry."

"It's fine, Autumn," he says, reaching over to rest his hand on my thigh. "It's really nice to see you in an environment that's not work-related," he pauses, his voice softening, "or, you know, bedroom-related. You really light up around Megan, and I have a feeling that when all your kids are together, you'll really shine."

"I don't know about shine," I say, my heart swelling, "but it fills me with joy when they're all together, especially when it's by their own choice, like this weekend."

"Well, I guess we'll see if you shine," he teases. "I've got to jump on this meeting with Pete. It shouldn't take too long."

"Okay, I'll be here," I say, starting to clean up the counter.

He walks over, gently turning me toward him, and kisses me. Then, with a tender kiss on my temple, he heads to the dining room for his meeting.

A little later, Cole and I settle back into our spots on the couch, comfortably absorbed in our work. Just before four, Megan strolls into the family room, her backpack slung over one shoulder and a duffle bag in her hand. She stands in front of us, miming a phone to her ear, silently asking if either of us is on a call.

"No, you're good, Megs," I say, glancing up from my laptop. "What's up?"

"Sooo," she begins, drawing out the word with a playful grin, "just wanted to let you know I'm heading to Stacey's for the night."

Megan has maintained a second home with Stacey, her best friend for nearly a decade, for almost as long as I can remember.

"Yeah?" I ask, curious. "What time will you be back?"

"Planning on barely beating Sami here," she replies. Then, in an exaggerated whisper, she cups her hand around her mouth, pretending to keep her voice low as she shoots a conspiratorial glance at me, "I figured you might want the house to yourself before the whole fricking family descends for the next two nights."

I laugh, appreciating her humor and thoughtfulness. "That's very considerate of you."

"I know," she says with a dramatic shrug, flipping her hair over her shoulder like a diva. "You know how to reach me if you need me. I'm alarming the house on my way out, so you'll know if anyone shows up."

"Okay," I laugh again, then glance over at Cole.

He smiles, a hint of mischief in his eyes, and winks at me. "I think I'm okay with that plan too," he says, his tone warm and teasing.

CHAPTER FOURTEEN

THE TEENAGE DREAMS

I prepare a simple baked chicken and rice dinner, pairing it with a bottle of wine. With just the two of us here, it feels cozy and intimate, so we decide to eat at the kitchen island, enjoying the easy flow of conversation.

"This really is a beautiful kitchen," Cole remarks, glancing around appreciatively. "And unlike some houses, I can tell you actually use it the way it's meant to be used."

I smile, setting down my fork. "Just wait until tomorrow," I say, a hint of anticipation in my voice. "Lasagna nights are a whole different level of chaos."

"Oh yeah?" he asks, intrigued.

"Yeah," I nod. "Megan thinks Kevin requested it not because he's craving lasagna, but because he loves the atmosphere of it. I make everything from scratch—the noodles, the sauce, all of it."

"Seriously?" He looks at me, clearly impressed.

"Yep," I confirm. "It's a recipe handed down from my grandmother on my mom's side. Now that the kids are older, everyone pitches in, so it becomes this big family event. We've got mixers and food processors going, Kevin usually handles the garlic bread, but sometimes I'll make rosemary garlic bread from scratch. The kitchen feels like Thanksgiving with all the laughter and conversation. The few times Kevin has brought a girl home, he's always requested lasagna. Which is why Megan suspects it's more about the tradition than the dish."

Cole leans back, a look of nostalgia crossing his face. "I can't even remember the last time I had a real, home-cooked meal, let alone one made entirely from scratch. Maybe I've never even had that."

"When money was tight," I explain, "I had to get creative. Cooking from scratch was often cheaper, especially when buying ingredients in bulk. It also meant there were usually plenty of leftovers, which helped stretch the budget. But more than that, it was about making sure my kids had good, nourishing meals."

"Well, I'm already impressed," he says with a warm smile. "I can't wait to see what this lasagna night is all about."

"I'm honestly a little excited for it," I reply, feeling the flutter of excitement at the thought of sharing this tradition with him.

He takes a sip of his wine, then looks at me with a playful glint in his eyes. "You know what I want a tour of now?"

"What's that?" I ask, curious.

"I want a tour of this small arsenal you've got," he says, his grin turning devilish.

I laugh, shaking my head at his teasing as the warmth between us deepens. The evening feels intimate, like a shared secret unfolding in the soft light of our kitchen. I walk over to him, and he swivels his stool toward me. Stepping between his spread legs, I lean into him, pressing my lips to his. "Well, the arsenal isn't in the kitchen," I murmur against his mouth.

Laughing, he steals another kiss. "Lead the way."

Taking his hand, I guide him up the staircase to the master bedroom. As we step inside, I glance back at him. "It was nice of Megan to leave us alone for the night."

"I'm not complaining," he replies, his voice low and warm.

I gently push him onto the bed, his eyes never leaving mine. "Wait here."

He grins, clearly intrigued. I disappear into the walk-in closet and return with a black, locked case that resembles an oversized makeup box. Setting it beside him, I notice his raised eyebrows.

"Before we dive into this world of surprises," I say, laughing, "just remember that I only bought one thing in this box. The rest were gifts from Cara—whether as gag gifts or not."

He nods, the memory of our earlier conversations evident in his eyes. "I remember."

"Almost nothing in here is charged or has batteries, so if you're looking to play tonight, you might be out of luck." He chuckles, and I continue, "Most of what I have are different kinds of rabbits. I've never quite had the courage to ask if the ones Cara buys me are ones she's also bought or tried herself." I laugh, pulling the key from my nightstand. "This is a little embarrassing for me, so be nice."

"I just want to know what a rabbit is," Cole says, laughing.

I feign surprise. "Have you been living under a rock?" I open the box and pull one out, holding it up. "See? Rabbit," I say, pointing to the little ears.

"Wow, Ms. Flynn," he says, peering into the box, "that really is a small arsenal."

He starts pulling items out, examining them with a mix of curiosity and amusement. He picks up a butterfly-shaped toy that looks almost flat, aside from a few nubs, and raises his eyebrows at me.

"That one just sits in your underwear, controlled by a remote app on your phone," I explain. He laughs, and I add, "So it could be used in public, by myself, or whatever. I haven't used it much."

"Or when we're at a conference, out to dinner with the team?" he suggests, one eyebrow arched.

"I suppose that could be an option," I laugh, imagining the possibilities.

He pulls out a few more rabbits, then holds up a long wand with a disc-shaped end, giving me a questioning look.

"That," I say, clearing my throat, "is a G-spot stimulator."

"Interesting," he muses, turning it over in his hands. "And what about this one? It looks like a rabbit, but what's this third part for?"

I raise my eyebrows, challenging him to figure it out. I watch as understanding dawns on his face, his eyes widening.

"Oh," he says, his gaze snapping back to me. "Wait, Autumn... Have you? Would you?" He stumbles over the question, but I know exactly what he's asking.

"Um, yes, and yes," I admit, feeling a blush spread across my cheeks.

"That is so hot," he murmurs, his voice rich with desire as he guides my hips toward him. "You're so full of surprises."

Judging by his reaction, I can tell this will be part of his plans for tonight—or at least the near future. If he hasn't had a woman go down on him since high school, I figure that will be a first for him.

"Eventually, the surprises will run out," I say with a smile.

"Maybe," he concedes, his eyes darkening with intent. "But I actually think they won't. I think you'll keep amazing me."

He digs through the box, picking up a flower-shaped toy, raising his eyebrows again. "And this one?"

I laugh. "That's supposed to simulate oral sex."

He tosses it back into the box, shaking his head in disbelief. "I didn't even know half of these things existed."

"If it weren't for my crazy friend, I wouldn't either," I say, still laughing.

"Well, I guess we should be grateful for your crazy friend," he says, pulling me closer, his voice a low rumble that sends a shiver down my spine.

He's still seated on the bed, and I'm standing between his legs, our breathing syncing in the quiet intimacy of the moment. Without warning, he wraps his arms around my thighs and, in one fluid motion, stands and flips me onto my back on the bed. I shriek softly, laughter bubbling up as the sudden movement surprises me.

He swiftly pulls off his shirt, then reaches for mine, tugging it over my head with an ease that sends a shiver through me. His hands find the waistband of my leggings, and in one nearly seamless movement, he removes them along with my thong and socks. Suddenly, I'm bare before him, and he quickly sheds the rest of his own clothes.

For a moment, he just looks at me, his eyes sweeping over my body like I'm a masterpiece hanging in a gallery. "You're so fucking beautiful," he murmurs, his voice thick with admiration.

He pulls my hips to the edge of the bed, hooking my legs over his arms again. I'm expecting a repeat of last night, but then he drops to his knees, his lips trailing along the inside of my thigh. The touch is electric, sending heat pulsing through me as I gasp. He teases me with his lips, tongue, and fingers, skimming the sensitive skin of both thighs but deliberately avoiding the place where I ache for him most.

I'm desperate for him now, my body straining toward his touch, but he leaves me wanting. With a powerful movement, he stands and pushes me further back onto the bed, climbing on top of me and kissing me deeply. His hands are everywhere, exploring, teasing, without ever breaking eye contact.

When his fingers finally slip between my thighs, he enters me with two, drawing a sharp inhale from my lips. "Fuck, Autumn," he groans, his voice ragged. "You're so wet. I love how wet you get."

I bite my lip, a soft moan escaping as his words ignite something deep within me. He continues to explore, his lips trailing down my neck, kissing slowly across my collarbones. My hands find their way to his back, my nails raking down his skin, into his hair, massaging the back of his neck as he moves lower, his mouth finding my breasts.

He expertly works his mouth over my nipples, each flick of his tongue sending waves of pleasure through me. I feel his hand shift, his thumb entering me as his fingers move toward the mattress, his outer fingers spreading me open. His middle finger grazes a forbidden target, a place that sends a jolt of sinful pleasure through my body, scratching an itch I didn't even know I had.

He pulls his hand away and kisses me deeply, his lips capturing mine as I feel him pressing against my entrance. When he enters me, I can't control the moan that escapes. He sits back on his knees, pushing lightly on the inside of my thighs as he begins to move, each thrust sending me spiraling closer to the edge. His left thumb circles my most sensitive spot, driving me wild as I push my pelvis toward him, my body coiling tighter with every movement.

My climax builds, tension wrapping around every nerve, until, finally, it breaks. I grip his forearm, my hand tightening as the waves of orgasm crash over me. Slowly, I release, my body melting back into the bed as my muscles start to relax.

He pulls out, his eyes dark with intent as he pushes himself downward with his right hand, searching for the other entrance he wants to explore. I lift my hips, pushing toward him in encouragement.

"Fuck, Autumn," he breathes, his eyes locking with mine, blazing with desire. "Are you sure?"

The low, rumbling timbre of his voice and the fire in his gaze send a fresh wave of arousal through me. I bite my bottom lip, nodding as I exhale a breathy, "Yeah. I'll tell you if you need to stop."

Pushing toward him again to encourage him, he enters. A brief sting of pain is quickly replaced by a euphoric pleasure. I grab his left hand, guiding it back to my center. His fingers slide inside me, and I arch my back, the sensation overwhelming in the best possible way. He starts slow, building intensity, his movements growing faster and harder. I wrap my legs around him, losing myself in the rhythm, the sensation, the heat.

His fingers leave me, but his thumb continues its relentless circling of my swollen nerves. I feel my body on the verge of another explosion, and I look at him, breathless. "Come with me," I plead, my voice trembling with urgency.

As the muscles in my pelvic floor tighten in a pleasure-filled rhythm, my orgasm crashes over me, pulling him with me into the same euphoric wave. He groans, deep and primal, and I feel the pulsing of his release, the final, perfect harmony to our shared crescendo.

I barely get a minute to savor the bliss of lying next to him, my body still humming with pleasure. But then I sit up, pressing a kiss to his cheek. "I have to go clean up. I'll be right back."

Laughing with twinkling eyes, he responds, "Okay, but hurry back."

When I return, I lean down and kiss him, slow and lingering. His gaze shifts to the bed, the scattered toys, and the open box. "What a shame we didn't even use any of them," he says with a playful smirk.

"We have time," I reply, smiling. "And like I said, we'll need batteries."

"You should remedy that," he teases, and I laugh.

"Want to take a shower with me?" I ask, my voice soft but inviting.

"Oh, I would love to," he responds, his tone full of anticipation.

I lead him to my shower, a spacious haven with dual shower heads. "I've had this shower for years," I admit with a laugh, "but I've never had the opportunity to really enjoy it with someone."

"Well, we'll fix that now," he says, his grin widening.

The next twenty minutes are spent beneath the warm cascade of water, our bodies pressed together, finding every excuse to touch and explore each other. We take turns soaping up, kissing, and lingering over every curve and plane. Just before we finish, I wash and condition my hair, relishing the simple intimacy of the moment.

Wrapped in towels, we head back to the bedroom. He slips into a pair of boxer briefs, while I choose bikini-cut underwear and a mid-thigh-length t-shirt. After I pack up the toys and tuck the box back into the closet, I feel his arms wrap around my waist from behind.

"If you had told me two weeks ago that you were the kind of woman who had all these toys and was willing to fulfill all my teenage boy fantasies, I'd never have believed you," he says, his voice warm and a little awed. "Now, the cooking lasagna from scratch and baking? That I would have believed."

I turn in his arms, wrapping mine around his neck. "Never judge a book by its cover," I say with a knowing smile. "And for the record, those teenage boy fantasies? They have everything to do with how you treat me and how well you know my body. They aren't things I'd do with just anyone," I pause, my gaze steady on his, "or even with you, if the circumstances weren't right."

"Noted," he says softly, his smile deepening as he presses a kiss to my forehead.

"I'm hungry," I say, glancing at him with a playful grin. "Want to rummage around the kitchen with me?"

He smiles, nodding. "Yeah, I'm hungry too."

We make our way to the kitchen and settle on the simplicity of cereal. I grab the bowls and milk while he sits on a barstool at the island, watching me with that easy, comfortable gaze I've come to adore.

"You know what I'm grateful for?" I ask, pouring the cereal.

"What's that?" he asks, his tone curious.

"I'm grateful that when I'm with you, I don't even think about my insecurities."

He looks surprised, almost disbelieving. "You have insecurities?"

"Well, yeah," I say with a soft laugh. "I'm not a spring chicken anymore." He chuckles, but I continue. "Seriously, I've got stretch marks, extra skin, saggy boobs from having and breastfeeding kids, and just from aging. I'm definitely carrying around some extra weight," I tap my belly just above my pubic bone, "and there are times when I'm totally self-conscious about it. But when I'm with you, all of that just fades away."

He leans forward, his eyes full of sincerity. "Autumn, you're fucking gorgeous. Yeah, neither of us looks like we did in our twenties, but I don't see a single thing wrong with you. It feels like your body was made for me."

I feel a warmth spread through me at his words. "It feels that way to me too," I admit, smiling as I shrug. "Like you're the missing puzzle piece, both physically and emotionally."

He smiles, his eyes softening. "And sometimes, like just now, with that little shrug, you're absolutely fucking adorable, and I just want to hold you."

"Well," I say with a teasing smile, "let's finish our cereal, and then we can go snuggle, and you can do just that."

And that's exactly what we do. After we finish our cereal, we head back to my bedroom. I turn on an old movie, something comforting and familiar. We brush our teeth and go through our night routines, a peaceful rhythm we've already settled into. And for the fifth night in a row, I fall asleep in his arms, feeling absolutely, blissfully happy.

I'm awakened from a deep sleep by the soft, gentle touch of Cole's hands gliding up and down my back. I'm lying on my stomach, arms tucked under my pillow, and I can't help but moan, a sound that's part waking, part pleasure, as his hand moves tenderly across my skin. He leans over me, his breath warm on my earlobe before he kisses down my neck, trailing across my shoulder blades and then back up, all while his hand continues its soothing caress.

After a few moments, his hand moves to the side of my breast, tracing the curve before sliding down to my thighs, his fingers dancing along the creases where my legs meet my ass cheeks. He carefully avoids where the hunger is building, teasing me as he shifts from one thigh to the other.

"Autumn?" he murmurs.

"Mmmhmm," I reply, still lost in the sensation.

"I just wanted to make sure you were awake," he says softly.

I roll toward him, meeting his gaze. "I was just enjoying the way you were touching me," I say, smiling.

His eyes are intense, dark with desire, but he doesn't smile. Instead, as soon as I turn to face him, he places his hand on my neck and kisses me, softly at first, then deeper, with a tenderness that makes my heart flutter. I reach up, my hand cupping his face, and he groans into the kiss, a sound that sends shivers down my spine.

My hand trails down to his chest, but he catches it, bringing it to his lips to press a kiss into my palm. His fingers then find their way under my shirt, caressing my breasts with gentle reverence before he tugs at the waistband of my underwear. I help him slip them off, then assist as he removes his, guiding them down his legs and off his feet.

Kissing me again, with a gentle nudge of his knee, he parts my legs, his gaze locking with mine. I gasp as he slowly pushes into me, his movements tender and unhurried, each stroke filled with a deep, quiet intensity that makes me feel cherished.

He leaves a trail of kisses along my neck, his lips eventually finding mine again as his pace begins to quicken. Shifting angles, he finds the perfect spot, and as he moves, his kisses grow more urgent, more fervent. My body responds to the rhythm, and I feel the tension building, the edge approaching. I moan, the sound caught in my throat as I reach the brink, my body convulsing around him as I fall over into release. His groan follows, and he doesn't stop until he finds his own climax a few moments later.

Rolling onto his side, he faces me, fingers brushing tenderly across my face as he tucks a strand of hair behind my ear.

"I think you've made me the luckiest girl in the world," I whisper softly, the words a gentle confession.

"Oh no, Ms. Flynn," he whispers back, his voice full of warmth and sincerity. "I am definitely the lucky one."

I smile, feeling the honesty of his words wrap around me like a warm blanket. As he gently kisses the top of my head, I drift back to sleep in his arms, utterly content and blissfully happy.

A few hours later, the morning sun filters through the skylight, filling the bedroom with a soft, golden light. I glance up at Cole and find his eyes already open. Smiling, I run a finger lazily down his chest.

"Good morning, beautiful," he says, his voice still husky with sleep, as he trails his hand down my back.

"Hey," I reply softly. "Did you sleep?"

"Not really," he admits.

I prop myself up on my elbow, searching his face with concern. "What's wrong?"

He laughs softly, shaking his head. "Nothing's wrong—actually, I think the problem *is* that nothing's wrong. I just don't know how I'll ever go back to a life where I don't wake up next to you."

"So don't," I say with a smile, lacing my fingers with his as he runs his other hand through my hair.

"If only it were that simple," he sighs.

"Someday it will be that simple, if we both want it to be," I assure him. "But first, you have to survive Sami, Kevin, and lasagna night."

He grins. "You know what I'm most worried about?"

"What's that?"

"That it's going to make me want to stay even more," he laughs.

"It might," I say, smiling back at him, "but that's better than the opposite. Now, come on, grumpy pants, let's go find some breakfast."

He lifts the blanket and glances down. "I think you mean grumpy *no*-pants," he jokes.

I laugh and kiss him before getting up to find my underwear and leggings. While I'm dressing, Cole calls Pete, telling him he has some personal things to take care of and is taking the day off.

"I think I'm a bad influence on you," I say, teasingly.

"Maybe," he replies with a smile, "but on Monday, it's back to reality. Today, I want to be fully present, and I want to give you all my attention."

His words bring a smile to my face as I settle at the kitchen island to start making a shopping list. "Do you want to go shopping with me, or should I send Sami and Megan to the store?" I ask.

"That's up to you," he says. "I'm good with either."

"Maybe I'll send them," I decide. "Especially if they want me to make bread—it's time-consuming." He chuckles.

Smiling at him, I suggest, "If we're staying in, I'll have you park in the garage so none of the kids have to block each other in. Are you good with that?"

"You want me to park in your garage, huh?" he says, his tone laced with playful innuendo.

I laugh, playfully hitting his chest. "That too, but I also mean it literally."

He grins. "I'll go do that now."

"I'll kill the alarm and open the garage door," I say, walking over to the security box and disarming the system.

Cole pulls his black SUV into the garage, parking it next to my Audi coupe. As he steps out, he looks at my car with a smirk. "I don't think we pay you that well," he teases.

I laugh. "Oh, you don't. That's another gift courtesy of my brother."

"Does he keep anything for himself?" Cole chuckles.

"Yeah, he has two houses, a condo, a few cars, and a daughter in grad school with no student loans. His wife's a corporate attorney too, so between the two of them..." I shrug. "The car was a gift when you promoted me. He said I needed something impressive if I was going to be impressing doctors."

"He's not wrong," Cole laughs.

"He also drove it for almost two years before handing it over to me," I say, grinning. "Used giving it to me as an excuse to buy a new one. But that SUV over there?" I point to the other side of the garage. "It's about fifteen years old and still reliable. I drive it when I'm not feeling fancy or when I need to fit more than one other adult in the car."

"You keep surprising me," he says, shaking his head. "Or maybe it's your family that does."

"Cole," I step closer, wrapping my arms around him, "I know I'm lucky, and I'm deeply grateful for everything my family has done for me. Sometimes, I even feel guilty about it. If it weren't for my brother and his success, I might be living out of that old SUV." I gesture toward it.

He kisses me, and I reach down to take his hand, leading him back inside, closing the garage door behind us as we go.

"I know you took the day off," I say as we walk back into the house, "but I need to at least check my email."

I log on and have a few sales lead responses. I schedule time with them to talk next week. Then there is a response from Dr. Gabari.

Autumn,

I am glad you liked the roses and, while I respect your desire to maintain a solely working relationship, I am disappointed.

I do look forward to seeing you in person again soon.

Yours,

Tony

I show the email to Cole, and he immediately rolls his eyes. "Forward that to Pete and me," he says, his tone laced with mild irritation. "My gut tells me not to respond and let Mark handle the meetings with him later on, but we'll see if Pete has a different take."

"Okay," I agree, quickly forwarding the email as requested.

After reviewing my calendar for the upcoming week, I close my laptop with a sense of satisfaction. "I wonder if my boss will notice I signed off early today," I tease, glancing at Cole with a playful smirk.

He chuckles, the sound deep and warm. "Oh, he definitely notices, but I don't think he cares. He probably encouraged it, honestly. Though, to be fair, I doubt he knows what anyone on the team is doing today, so you're not exactly an exception."

"It's kind of cute when you talk about yourself in the third person," I say, my smile widening.

Just then, my phone rings. I glance at my watch. "It's Pete," I say, giving Cole a pointed look. "So, you might want to stay quiet."

He playfully mimes zipping his lips, earning a quick grin from me before I answer the call.

"Quisenbelt, this is Autumn Flynn," I say, slipping into my professional tone.

"Hey, Autumn, it's Pete."

"Hey, Pete! How are you?" I ask, keeping my voice light and friendly.

"Good, good. I heard the conference went well. Cole mentioned you brought in a lot of leads," Pete says, sounding pleased.

"Yes, quite a few," I confirm. "I reached out to all of them yesterday and have a few initial meetings lined up for next week."

"That's great, Autumn," he says, then jokes, "Maybe you can secure that end-of-year bonus early."

I laugh softly. "That would be fantastic."

Cole raises an eyebrow, clearly curious, but I wave him off with a smile.

"So, I was calling because I know Cole took today off, or I'd run this by him directly, but I want to address the situation with Dr. Gabari," Pete continues, his tone shifting to something more serious.

"I'm assuming you saw my email?" I ask, already anticipating where this is going.

"Yes," he replies, pausing briefly. "First, Autumn, I want to apologize. You shouldn't have to deal with this kind of behavior. If he were one of our employees, he'd likely have been written up or even fired by now. This isn't something you should have to manage."

"Thank you," I say, genuinely appreciating his concern. "I do want you to know that the team—Cole and Mark in particular—were incredibly supportive when it came to him."

"I'm glad to hear that," Pete responds. "Here's what I'm thinking, Autumn: I know Dr. Gabari is expecting an in-person visit, and that's fine. But rather than just you and Mark going, I'd like Cole and me to join as well. It'll give Dr. Gabari an ego boost, showing him he's important enough to warrant executive attention, but more importantly, it'll provide you with added protection and a buffer."

"I think that's a great idea," I say, feeling a sense of relief. "He's a big account, but the whole situation makes me uncomfortable."

"Exactly," Pete agrees. "Cole sent me your conference schedule. I don't know if you've had a chance to see it yet, but I'll go over it and find a time in the next few weeks when we can visit his practice."

"Sounds good," I reply. "I really appreciate your help with this."

"Anytime," Pete says warmly. "Have a good weekend, Autumn."

"Thanks, you too," I say, hanging up the phone.

Cole looks at me expectantly. "That was about Dr. Gabari, I assume?"

"Yeah," I nod. "Pete wants to come along when we visit him in person. He wants you there too."

"I'm okay with that," Cole says, his expression thoughtful. "Pete has a way of being firm without coming off like a jerk. Maybe he can put an end to this nonsense once and for all."

"I hope so," I say, feeling a bit more at ease.

CHAPTER FIFTEEN
THE LASAGNA NIGHT

Megan bursts through the door, her eyes wide with a hint of panic. "Mom? Is everything okay?" She hurries into the kitchen, then relaxes when she spots Cole. "Oh, thank goodness. I didn't see your car, and it freaked me out."

I can't help but smile. "Megan, you're such a drama queen. I had him move his car into the garage so you all wouldn't have to block each other in."

Her expression brightens. "That makes sense. Sami's only about ten minutes out."

"Perfect," I say, handing her the shopping list. "I'm sending you girls to the store."

She looks at the list, then at me with a raised eyebrow. "Geez, Mom, you're not even going to let her set foot in the house?"

"Of course you don't have to rush out the second she arrives," I laugh.

"Can we get stuff for breakfast pizza on Saturday too?" she asks, already thinking ahead.

"Why not?" I reply with a grin.

She grabs a pen and scribbles more items on the list. I hand her my debit card, and she takes it with a nod.

A few minutes later, Sami walks in. She and Kevin resemble their father more than they resemble me. Sami is taller than both Megan and me, with dark, wavy hair that falls just past her shoulders and striking blue eyes. Sami and Kevin also don't have the freckles that sprinkle across our noses.

"Well, hello, my baby girl," I say, wrapping her in a warm hug.

"Hey, Mom," she replies in her soft, natural tone. "I have so much laundry to bring in from the car."

I laugh, shaking my head. "We can help you with that—or make Kevin do it when he gets here." I take her wrist and gently guide her into the kitchen. "Sami, this is Cole," I say, introducing them with a smile. "And Cole, this is Samantha."

Cole extends his hand to her. "Nice to meet you, Samantha," he says warmly.

She shakes his hand, returning his smile. "Nice to meet you too."

"Do you prefer Sami?" Cole asks, his tone considerate.

"Usually, yes," she replies, "but family can call me Samantha."

"Mom is making us go to the store," Megan chimes in, twisting a face at her sister.

"For lasagna stuff?" Sami asks knowingly.

"Of course," Megan replies in a sing-song voice.

"Do you want to start the laundry first?" I ask Sami.

"Nah, I'll wait until later. Let's get shopping over with," she says.

"Let's go. I'll drive," Megan offers, already heading for the door.

"Bye, girls," I call out as they leave, feeling the warmth of home settle around me.

Cole looks at me thoughtfully. "I gather they're pretty different," he says, picking up on the contrasts between my daughters even from that brief interaction.

"Very," I reply. "They're like night and day. Sami can be hard to read. Sometimes I think she's sad, but she's not. Other times she seems fine or even happy, and then she's upset a few minutes later. It's gotten better as she's grown older, but as the baby of the family, she was the most affected by the revolving door of women her dad brought into her life. I'm not sure how she'll handle this situation, to be honest."

"That's understandable," Cole says. "They've never seen you in this kind of relationship."

"Exactly," I agree, pulling out ingredients to start making the bread. I mix yeast, sugar, and warm milk in a bowl, beginning the process.

"Starting dinner already?" Cole asks, watching me.

"Just the bread," I say with a smile. "It takes a while to give it time to let it rise and do it right."

"Doesn't everything worth it take time?" he says with a wink, making me smile.

We spend the next little while chatting, waiting for the girls to return. Cole asks more about my kids—their personalities, how they grew up, and how our custody arrangements worked.

"We started with a three-day/four-day split," I explain, "but it was too much for the kids. With his work schedule, they hardly saw him. Eventually, we settled on me having them about seventy percent of the time. He would take them every other weekend and during some of their school breaks. The rest of the time, they were with me. What about you?"

"We ended up where you did, with me not having them as much," he says, his voice tinged with a hint of regret. "I couldn't afford a good lawyer, but she could. As they got older, they sometimes chose to stay with me more, but other times they wanted to be at her place because she wasn't around much. They could get away with things, have parties, get into trouble—typical teenage stuff."

"That sounds like a teenager's dream but a parent's nightmare," I respond, understanding the worry behind his words.

"Exactly," he says. "Especially with William. He had a really tough time with the divorce and turned to substances and other things for a while. He's doing much better now, but those were rough years."

"I'm surprised none of my kids went down that path," I admit. "I think they all grew up too fast, especially Kevin. He felt like he needed to be the man of the house."

"With two younger sisters and a mom, I think a lot of guys would feel that way," Cole says gently.

"Probably," I say, sighing. "I just wish he hadn't taken so much on himself. When are you going to tell your kids about us?"

"I've been thinking about that," he says, pausing to gather his thoughts. "I think when we can find a time for you to meet them, I'll talk to them."

"I think that's fair," I say, appreciating his thoughtfulness. "I probably wouldn't have told my kids yet if the circumstances were different."

Just then, the girls return, arms full of groceries. Sami starts putting things away, and as she grabs some cheese off the counter, she glances at me. "Want me to start prepping the tomatoes?" she asks.

"Sure," I say with a smile. "You know exactly what you're doing."

Sami makes a point of setting the cutting board and food processor on the island, instead of on the counter where she usually works. It's a subtle gesture, one that Cole might not notice, but Megan and I do. It's her way of trying to create a connection, of making herself part of the moment. She begins coring and seeding tomatoes, tossing them into the food processor with practiced ease.

"I'll start the rest of the sauce," Megan says, grabbing another cutting board and expertly chopping an onion.

Cole, observing the easy rhythm between them, asks if they even need a recipe anymore.

Sami laughs, her mood light. "We've done this so many times, I think I could make lasagna in my sleep."

I smile, sensing her contentment in being here, involved in the process. It's a rare moment when she's so at ease, and I'm grateful for it.

"Oh, Kevin called while we were at the store," Megan says, her voice pulling me out of my thoughts. "He got out of work early, so he'll be here closer to two."

I glance at the clock—it's already half past one.

"Okay," I nod, "as long as he remembers to pick up dessert."

"He'll remember," Sami says with quiet confidence.

Sami finishes pureeing the tomatoes in the food processor just as Megan starts sautéing garlic and onion in a stockpot. The kitchen hums with the comforting sounds and smells of a family meal coming together.

Right then, Kevin walks in, juggling several bags in his arms. "There's my beautiful mother," he says with a grin, giving me the best hug he can manage without dropping anything. Before I can introduce him to Cole, he's already one step ahead. "And you must be Cole," he says, glancing at his full hands. "I'll shake your hand in a minute." He smiles, and Cole laughs, the easy camaraderie between them evident.

Kevin makes his way around the kitchen, giving Megan a half hug as she continues sautéing, and then does the same to Sami before finally setting the bags down.

"So," he begins, pulling out two tiramisus from one of the bags, "here's dessert." I raise an eyebrow, and he grins. "Oh, come on, Mom, you know we usually devour one, and we've got an extra person this time." I laugh as he digs further into the bags, revealing two bottles of Cabernet.

Then, with a slightly guilty expression, he produces a bottle of Dewar's 25 Year Scotch, setting it on the counter in front of Cole. "And this," he says, "is courtesy of my mom's brother. I think I'm supposed to interrogate you under the influence of alcohol."

Cole picks up the bottle, inspecting the label with a chuckle before looking at me with amusement.

"Kevin," I say with annoyance, "he did not need to know that yet, and for the record, that scotch is older than you."

Kevin grins. "I agree, Mom. If I'd known more, I wouldn't have spilled the beans, but remember, we were planning an intervention."

"Oh, I heard about that a little, but why an intervention?" Cole asks and looks at me.

Surprisingly, Sami speaks up first. "Well, you see," she starts, "when Megan told us that Mom was staying in Dallas and it involved a guy—"

Megan cuts in, "Because I can read Mom like a book."

"Yes, because she can read Mom like a book," Sami continues, rolling her eyes, "we all jumped to the conclusion that she'd met some random guy. We thought she'd lost her mind—she's been single forever and hasn't really seen anyone outside of us, our grandparents, and Cara in ages."

"I'd show you the group text," Kevin adds, looking at Cole with a grin, "but let's just say we were a little too worried."

Sami picks up the story again. "So, we were planning an intervention, you know, 'the talk,' the whole nine yards."

"At that point, I called Uncle Alex because I was concerned," Kevin says. "He's more of a father figure to us than an uncle."

Megan, turning from the stove with the wooden spoon still in hand, looks directly at Cole. "Then we found out it was you," she says, pointing the spoon at him for emphasis, "and we were all like, 'well, never mind, that's cool.' But Kev had already talked to Uncle Alex, so then he had to update him, and well..." She trails off, pointing the spoon toward the bottle of Scotch in Cole's hand.

Cole laughs, shaking his head as he looks at the bottle. "I see," he says, the warmth and ease of the moment settling in around us.

"Here's my only question," Cole says, his tone serious yet curious, as all four of us turn our attention to him. "You hadn't met me before, so why did it make a difference once you found out it was me?"

Megan throws her arms in the air dramatically, her reaction so sudden that it startles both Cole and me in a humorous way. "Oh, *come on!*"

"Like, you do know we've been listening to at least one side of your way-too-long boss-employee conversations," Sami begins, picking up where Megan left off. She emphasizes her point by holding up two fingers. "*For two years.* Sometimes we only hear Mom's side, but sometimes you're on speaker, or through Bluetooth in the car, or even over the computer. We've been spectators to this happening."

Cole and I exchange a look. He smiles, and I shrug. "What's hilarious," I say, "is that we didn't see this coming."

"Are you serious?" Kevin says, turning his gaze to me. "I didn't even *live* here during those two years, and I saw it. I was actually hoping for it," he adds, glancing at Cole. "Because I could tell he made you happy." He looks back at me. "Every time you talked to him or just finished talking, you had this huge smile plastered on your face."

I feel my cheeks flush with warmth.

"So," I ask Kevin, "why didn't you assume it was him when I extended my trip?"

"Because," Megan interjects, drawing everyone's attention, "I figured if it was Cole, you would've told us. You were so secretive and weird about it. I thought maybe it didn't matter what we saw because, well, he's your boss, so I figured you wouldn't go there—even though maybe you should."

I laugh and turn to Cole. "Are they overwhelming you yet?"

"Actually, no," he responds, chuckling. "It's kind of entertaining. But I didn't see it either." He sets the bottle of Scotch down and leans back in his barstool. "Don't get me wrong, I knew I was attracted to her, but she was my employee. I didn't think those feelings would ever overpower the fact that I'm her boss."

"But then *they did*," Megan swoons, drawing laughter from everyone.

Kevin walks over to Cole and extends his hand. Cole stands to meet him, their heights nearly equal. Kevin, with his thick, dark hair and blue eyes that match Sami's, looks every bit the confident young man I'm so proud of.

Kevin places his left hand on Cole's shoulder. "We'll talk later, but it's good to meet you," he says, his tone even and sincere.

"You too," Cole replies, shaking his hand.

I find myself watching the interaction in awe. When did my little boy grow into a man who can go toe-to-toe with someone twenty years older, matching their confidence and presence? It's a bittersweet realization, and I feel a swell of pride mixed with a twinge of nostalgia.

"Cole has sons," Megan says matter-of-factly, drawing everyone's attention back to her. "So, *maybe* we'll have more brothers someday."

I glance at Cole, a little apologetic, but he's laughing.

"I suppose that's within the realm of possibilities," he says with a grin, directing his warmth toward Megan.

Megan and Sami continue working on the sauce, with Sami browning the meat, while I focus on the bread. Meanwhile, Kevin takes it upon himself to teach Cole how to make pasta dough. Once the bread is in the oven, I join them, guiding Cole through the process of making lasagna noodles and showing him how I blend the perfect mix of four cheeses for the filling. The kitchen buzzes with laughter and easy conversation as the girls take charge of layering the lasagna into the pan.

At one point, while Cole and I are rolling out noodles, I catch Kevin's eye and mouth, "*Thank you.*" He smiles and winks, his support filling me with warmth.

After four hours filled with laughter and conversation, dinner is finally ready. As the girls set the dining room table, Kevin opens the Cabernet, pouring everyone a glass and pausing to ask Cole if he'd like one. Kevin, who usually takes the head of the table, leaves it open this time, so Cole and I sit together on one side while the kids take the other. It feels just right—like a perfect fit.

Before we start serving, Kevin stands and raises his glass. "To new beginnings," he announces.

We all raise our glasses in a toast, and I can't help but laugh. "Y'all are putting a lot of faith into a relationship that's only a few days old," I tease.

"Psssh," Megan dismisses with a wave, "this is like two years old. Y'all just didn't start touching each other until a few days ago."

Cole chuckles, turning to me with a knowing smile. "It does feel that way," he says softly, and I lean in to kiss him.

"Moooom," Sami groans, and all three of them make exaggerated gagging sounds, their laughter filling the room.

Dinner is amazing—full of rich flavors and lively conversation. After we've eaten our fill, the girls and I begin clearing the table. Meanwhile, Kevin grabs a couple of rocks glasses, fills them with ice, and picks up the bottle of Scotch from the kitchen. He turns to Cole and says, "Come with me out to the patio by the pool."

The sun is setting, casting a warm glow over everything, and even though it's still warm outside, the atmosphere is peaceful. I know Kevin wants to have a conversation with Cole, likely fulfilling whatever promises he's made to my brother. As they head outside, the girls gather around me, ready to talk.

"Mom, I really like him," Sami says, her voice warm with approval. "He handled everything we threw at him, including just dealing with us being ourselves," she adds with a laugh.

"Seriously, Mom," Megan chimes in, grinning. "If we could all be so lucky. And Cara is going to love him."

"Are you bringing him to Sunday dinner with Grandma and Grandpa?" Sami asks, curiosity in her tone.

"I haven't talked to him about it yet," I admit. "I figured we'd get through tonight first, and then I'll bring it up."

"I think both Grandpa and Uncle Alex will like him too," Megan says with confidence.

"You think so?" I ask, a little surprised.

"I know so," Kevin's voice cuts in from behind me.

Startled, I turn around with a small laugh. "How long have you two been standing there?"

"Just long enough to hear that last part," Kevin replies.

"So, I take it your interrogation went well?" I ask, laughing as I glance at Cole, who chuckles along with me.

Kevin nods, a grin spreading across his face. "Yeah, well, he's definitely nothing like Dad."

Cole, leaning casually against the doorframe, raises an eyebrow, clearly caught off guard by the bluntness. He observes, "That's a lot of confidence for just a few hours of conversation."

Kevin glances back at him. "If you knew the comparison, you might not think so. It doesn't take much to beat those expectations."

Megan chimes in, her voice hesitant, "Yeah, our dad is…" She trails off, searching for the right words.

"Our dad is a total and complete dick," Kevin says bluntly. "Like, the king of assholes."

The room falls quiet for a moment, all of us absorbing the weight of his words.

"I know that's not the most polite way to put it," Kevin continues with a shrug, "but it's true."

"He's not wrong," Sami adds, her voice steady. "Dad's a womanizing piece of shit."

Megan looks around the room, trying to lighten the mood. "Well, this is fun," she says dryly. "But seriously, Cole, I think the point is even we all like you a lot more than our father. Our uncle is going to be thrilled."

Cole remains leaning against the doorframe, his eyes soft as he meets my gaze. He smiles, and I feel a wave of warmth.

"Anyone want tiramisu?" Sami asks, breaking the tension, and we all laugh.

We decide to have dessert in the kitchen, gathered around the island. Throughout the evening, Cole finds little opportunities to touch me—a gentle brush of his fingers through my hair, a hand resting on my arm. Each touch sends a spark through me, making me feel both electric and content.

"Hey guys," Megan says, looking up from her tiramisu. "We got the stuff to make breakfast pizza. Should we prep it tonight or make it in the morning?"

"In the morning," Kevin says, stifling a yawn. "I'm actually pretty beat."

Megan teases him, "You're turning into an old man. It's only nine."

Kevin laughs. "When you have to get up for work at six every day, nine starts to feel late."

"Truer words have never been spoken," I say, smiling as I run my hand down Cole's back. "We should probably turn in soon too."

"What time are we heading south tomorrow?" Megan asks.

"I was thinking around four," I reply. "We can have an early dinner and still have time for something else if we want."

"Did you talk to Cara about it?" Megan asks.

"Not yet. I haven't spoken to her in a couple of days," I admit.

"That's crazy," Sami says, shaking her head. "I don't think you've ever gone twenty-four hours without talking to her."

"I think she's giving us space," I say, feeling my cheeks flush slightly. "Time to figure things out."

"I'll let her know the plan," Megan offers. "She'll let us know if she has any other ideas."

"Sounds good," I say, grateful for her help.

Sami opens the dishwasher, then turns to us and then Kevin with a playful grin. "Okay, you old folks go to bed. Megs and I can finish up here."

"You sure?" I ask, knowing how much there is to clean.

"Yes, Mom, we're sure," Megan replies firmly.

I hug each of the kids, and Cole exchanges pleasantries before we head off to bed. As we walk down the hallway, I feel a sense of peace settling over me, knowing that for the first time in a long while, everything feels just right.

CHAPTER SIXTEEN

THE AMAZINGNESS

As soon as the bedroom door closes behind us, Cole wraps me in his arms and kisses me. It's a long, tender kiss, followed by a few quick ones that send a wave of warmth and energy through me.

"I know that was probably a lot—maybe zero to two hundred?" I ask with a laugh, searching his eyes for any sign of overwhelm.

"That was wonderful, Autumn," he replies, his voice soft. "They're amazing, and it's clear how much they love you."

"They do," I say, my heart swelling with pride and affection.

"Kevin was right about lasagna night," he continues, brushing a stray lock of hair behind my shoulder, the touch sending a delightful shiver down my spine. "That was some pretty impressive family time."

"It didn't start out that way," I admit, smiling at the memory. "It was just a special meal at first, but as the kids got older and started helping more, it became the amazingness you saw tonight."

"Amazingness is the perfect word for it," he says, his eyes warm. "Remember how I told you that you radiate beauty? That definitely radiates to your kids."

I reach up and pull him into another kiss, our lips meeting with a mix of tenderness and desire. His hands move down my back, leaving a trail of goosebumps in their wake. As he guides me toward the bed, we strip off our clothes, leaving only my bra and his boxer briefs by the time my legs touch the edge. He quickly removes the last barriers between us, and I'm lost in the heat of his touch.

Our kiss deepens, becoming more urgent, and his hands slide down my sides, his thumbs grazing my nipples, sending sparks of pleasure through me. He gently pushes me onto the bed, his arm under my back, pushing me further onto the mattress with him. His mouth and hands move with a kind of desperation, kissing down my neck to my breasts, his touch both demanding and reverent. I rake my nails up and down his arms, tangling them in his hair as he moves back up to kiss me.

His fingers find their way between my legs, and he groans when he feels how ready I am for him. "Fuck, Autumn," he whispers, his voice thick with need.

"Cole," I whisper back, my voice trembling, "I need you."

He looks into my eyes, his hand moving to the nape of my neck as he kisses me deeply and pushes inside me. I wrap my legs around him, trying to pull him even closer.

His mouth moves to my neck, then to my shoulder, his weight grounding me, comforting me. As we move together, I'm overwhelmed by a sense of being needed, safe, and profoundly loved. The emotions swell inside me, and tears prick at the corners of my eyes as Cole reaches his climax. He props himself up on his arms, trailing kisses up my neck and across my jaw until our lips meet again. I pull him closer, kissing him deeply, needing him to feel how much this moment means to me.

When he pulls back, he notices the tears on my cheeks and gently wipes them away. "Autumn, what's wrong?" he asks softly, concern etched on his face.

"Absolutely nothing," I sniffle, managing a smile. "I'm just happy."

"Happy tears?" he asks, a hint of a smirk playing at his lips.

I nod, confirming, "Happy tears."

He laughs softly. "That's a first for me."

"Me too," I admit with a gentle smile.

He shifts to lie beside me, his fingers tracing tender patterns over my face and down my body, then back up again. His touch is reverent, as though he's cherishing every inch of me, and I find myself captivated by the concentration on his face as he watches his fingers move over my skin. I rub my hand gently from the back of his head down to his shoulder blades and back, and we stay like this in comfortable silence, simply savoring the moment.

Eventually, he looks back into my eyes and kisses me softly. "I was going to apologize for the quickie, but you seem okay," he jokes lightly.

"Yeah, I'm more than okay." I smile up at him, feeling a deep contentment. "Pretty happy."

"Good," he says, brushing a kiss on my forehead before standing up. "I'm going to find some clothes. I know they won't come in here, but it feels a little weird with your kids out there."

I laugh softly. "I get it."

He heads off to clean up and find some clothes, and I do the same—washing my face, brushing my teeth, and slipping into some sleep shorts and a tank top. When I return to bed, I curl up next to him, snuggling into his chest. He wraps his arms around me, kissing the top of my head, and in that moment, everything feels just right.

"I'm almost afraid to ask," I start, a playful smile tugging at my lips, "but what did Kevin ask you?"

Cole chuckles. "Actually, he didn't ask me anything. He told me things. I mean, I responded, of course—it was a two-way conversation—but he wasn't really fishing for information."

I prop myself up on my arm, curious. "Really?"

"Really," he confirms, pulling me back down to rest on his chest.

"Well, what did he tell you then?" I ask with a soft laugh, intrigued.

"Nothing too surprising," Cole begins, his voice gentle. "He mentioned the house—that when their dad left and moved his mistress in, you were almost catatonic, like you weren't even functional." He pauses, perhaps to gauge my reaction, but I just keep running my fingers through his chest hair, staying calm. "He said it took you a long time to recover emotionally, and that's why your brother is so protective of you and generous with you now. But mostly, he told me how much they all want you to be happy. They were worried you'd stay single forever."

"I might have," I admit with a small laugh, the reality of that possibility not lost on me.

Cole laughs softly, his hand moving up and down my back in soothing strokes. "I told him a bit about my background too, even though he didn't ask. I think he was surprised to hear that I'd been single for a long time as well."

"That's so different from their father," I say, shaking my head slightly. "He always started his next relationship before ending the one he was in. I'm sure that struck a chord with Kevin."

"It seemed that way," Cole agrees. "He also told me he's scared to be in a relationship himself. He's worried he might have inherited some of his dad's traits and doesn't want to end up treating anyone the way his dad treated women."

"He told you that?" I ask, surprised by Kevin's openness.

"He did," Cole replies. "I told him that from what I've seen so far, I don't think it's possible. He's too aware of it to let himself treat someone that way. But he just said, 'Maybe.'"

"I always wondered if he felt that way, but he's never said anything to me."

"I think he only shared it with me to emphasize just how bad things were with his dad."

"Was that the whole conversation?" I ask, still processing what I've heard.

"Yeah," Cole says with a laugh. "Outside of talking about the weather and the pool. Honestly, it just made me want to time travel back to when all that was happening and hug you, to tell you everything would be okay."

He kisses the top of my head, and we fall into a comfortable silence, his hand still tracing patterns on my back.

"Cole?" I ask softly, wondering if he's still awake.

"Yeah?" he responds, his voice steady.

"Does this all feel too fast to you?" I ask, needing to know if he shares my uncertainty.

"Yes and no," he sighs. "Logically, when I think about it, this is ridiculously fast. But as far as how I feel? No, it feels like this is exactly where we're supposed to be."

"That's how I feel too," I say, relieved to be on the same page.

"I do have to figure out how to handle this with work," Cole says thoughtfully. "Part of me thinks I should address it right away, but another part of me thinks maybe I should wait."

"That's up to you," I say, trusting his judgment. "You know Pete better than I do."

"I just feel like I want to keep this to ourselves for a while, like it's something sacred," he says with a laugh. "I sound so cheesy—I would never have said something like that three weeks ago."

"I know what you mean," I laugh with him. "It feels too private, too special to share with everyone just yet."

"Exactly," he agrees.

"Speaking of moving too fast," I say, "Sunday evening is always dinner with my parents, so it's up to you whether you want to stay or head out before that."

"I'll stay," he says, without hesitation.

"Well, that was easy," I say, a little surprised by his decisiveness.

"I have to go back to Fort Wayne on Monday, but I want to spend every second with you until then," he says, pulling me closer.

"It's going to be weird sleeping without you," I admit, snuggling deeper into his embrace.

"I'm not even sure I'll be able to sleep without you," he responds, his voice low. "But I guess we'll find out."

"Maybe I'll just chain you to my bed," I joke, a mischievous grin on my face.

He lets out a devilish laugh. "I'd probably enjoy that."

"I would too," I say, feeling the heat rise between us again.

"Another one for my teenage boy sex dreams catalog," Cole jokes, his tone playful.

"You know," I say, looking up at him with a flirtatious smile, "I wouldn't mind if you tied me up either."

"Be careful what you wish for," he teases, his hand running down my back, sending shivers through me.

"I don't want to be careful with you," I whisper, sliding my hand down his chest and into his shorts, feeling his immediate response to my touch. As I wrap my hand around him, he inhales sharply.

"Autumn," he murmurs, his voice filled with longing.

I lean in to kiss him, then whisper against his lips, "Shhh."

I kiss my way down his neck, feeling his hand tighten in my hair, the other gripping my arm. My lips trail down his chest, past his navel, and I pull down his shorts, continuing my path until I reach my destination.

I take him into my mouth, feeling his body react instantly, his back arching as he moans. His hand guides my movements, tangled in my hair, and I synchronize my hand with my mouth, moving in rhythm as he moans with each motion. The taste of him, mixed with the memory of our earlier encounter, ignites my own desire.

"Holy fuck, Autumn," he whispers, his voice barely audible as he nears the edge.

Soon, I feel him start to pulse, and I taste him as he releases. He gently pulls me back up to him, kissing my forehead and wrapping me in his arms.

"Yeah," he laughs softly, holding me close, "I'm never letting you go."

CHAPTER SEVENTEEN

THE BEST FRIEND

The next morning, I wake up to the smell of sausage cooking. As I stir, Cole wakes up too, stretching beside me.

"Are the kids making breakfast?" he asks, his voice still heavy with sleep.

"Certainly smells like it," I reply, smiling as the familiar scents waft through the room.

"What exactly is breakfast pizza?" he asks, curious but already smiling.

"Oh, it's amazing," I say, my enthusiasm clear. "It's biscuit dough for the crust, white pepper gravy for the sauce, then scrambled eggs, sausage or bacon, all topped with cheese."

"Okay, sold," he says, sitting up a little.

"It's another one of those things I made that was pretty cheap back when things were tough," I explain. "The kids love it."

"Well, let's go try it," he says, grinning. "After we get dressed, of course."

"Of course," I laugh.

We both get dressed, opting for comfortable clothes. I quickly brush my hair and twist it into a messy bun before we head downstairs. The kitchen is bathed in sunlight, filled with the sound of laughter and chatter. The country radio station plays softly from Megan's speaker.

"Well, hey, sleepyheads," Megan calls out when we walk in. Then she slips into her exaggerated British accent to ask, "Did the wonderful smells of our kitchen rouse you from your sleep?"

"Actually, yeah," I admit with a laugh.

The girls are in leggings and t-shirts, while Kevin, as usual, is in basketball shorts and shirtless.

"Pizza's already in the oven," Kevin says. "Shouldn't be too long now."

"Looks like we're having a lot of pizza today," Sami adds with a chuckle.

"Very different kinds of pizza, though," I say, smiling.

"Truth," Sami agrees.

"So, Cole," Kevin says, turning to him, "Megan mentioned you have three boys?"

"Yeah, they're twenty-six, twenty-three, and twenty," Cole says. "They're close to your ages."

"Still at home?" Kevin asks.

"No, well, my youngest is, but he's usually at his mom's because it's closer to his school. The other two are on their own now. They live in Indianapolis, so not too far from me."

"You're in Fort Wayne, right?" Sami asks.

"Yeah," Cole confirms.

"For *no-ow*," Megan chimes in, her tone full of playful implication as she grins.

Cole glances at me and smiles. "Yeah, probably for now."

I look at Megan, trying to keep the conversation light. "He has kids and ties too, so we'll cross that bridge when it's time."

But Cole surprises me, saying, "I don't have ties to Fort Wayne like you do here. I'm pretty sure when that time comes, it'll be here."

Megan grins triumphantly. "See, Mom? Just listen to us—we know what's up." She adds a chin lift at the end for emphasis.

Cole continues, "I don't have kids still living with me, or parents with Sunday dinners a couple of blocks away. My home isn't a forever home that my kids will want to return to with their kids. You all are lucky to have this, and I wouldn't take it away from any of you."

"Mom," Sami says, her voice thick with emotion, "you need to keep him."

I laugh, touched by her sincerity.

"No, seriously," Kevin adds, "we were worried during our intervention phase that you'd find someone who would move you away or just want to stay with you because of what you have here," he says, gesturing around the house.

Cole wraps his arm around my waist, pulling me closer as he laughs. "I was already gone before I even knew this place existed."

"I can attest to that," Megan says, grinning. "I saw the saucer eyes when I was showing him around the house."

"Megan!" I exclaim, playfully tossing a kitchen towel at her. Everyone laughs.

Kevin nods, more serious now. "I'm sure Mom told you, but despite how Megan jokes about it, we're all a little self-conscious about this place. People see it and make assumptions."

Cole nods, understanding. "She mentioned she's self-conscious about it, but not that you all felt the same."

"Yeah, it's all of us," Sami says. "Not that we don't love and appreciate the house, because we do."

The timer dings, and Kevin pulls the breakfast pizzas out of the oven, the aroma filling the kitchen. He slices and serves them while Sami grabs hot sauce from the fridge, and Megan takes drink orders. Soon, we're all gathered around the island, digging in.

"Oh," Megan says between bites, "I talked to Cara. She's going to be here around two. She'll hang out for a bit, and then we can all drive down together."

"Thanks, Megs, sounds good," I reply. "She's not upset that I haven't called, is she?"

"No," Megan assures me, grinning. "She said she figured you were too busy being 'twitterpated.'"

I groan, feeling the heat rise in my cheeks. "Oh geez."

"Is she wrong?" Kevin teases, laughter in his voice.

I roll my eyes, unable to hide my smile. "I guess not."

Cole wraps his arm around my shoulders, pulling me closer as he kisses my temple. The kids exchange a quick, knowing look, their silent conversation almost palpable.

Sami clears her throat, bringing us back to logistics. "So, what cars are we taking down? Because we won't all fit in any one of them."

Kevin jumps in. "I was thinking I'd drive you two and Cara in Mom's SUV. Then Cole and Mom can take either his car or the Audi—if that's cool with everyone."

"Oooh," Megan chimes in with a grin, "you should let Cole *drive* the Audi."

I laugh. "That's fine with me. What do you think, Cole?"

"I don't know many guys who would turn down that offer," Cole says with a chuckle.

"Well, that's settled then," Kevin declares, satisfied.

"This breakfast pizza is amazing," Cole says, clearly impressed.

"Isn't it, though?" Sami agrees, her pride evident.

After breakfast, we all go about our routines—taking turns in the shower, getting ready for the drive into Chicago. Kevin helps Sami haul in her laundry, and she starts her marathon loads. Before long, it's nearly two, and Cara will be arriving soon.

As I'm finishing up, Cole looks at me with curiosity. "Anything I need to know about Cara that you haven't already told me?"

"Not really," I say, thinking it over. "I've pretty much covered it. She and I went through similar things, but we reacted differently. I avoided men completely; she, well, she tends to use them. I don't always agree with how she handles things, especially when someone gets hurt, but most of the time, she's upfront about her intentions."

Cole laughs, shaking his head. "So, she makes other men pay for what was done to her?"

"In a way," I reply. "But she usually finds men who are looking for the same thing—a casual hookup. It's rare that someone gets attached, because she's clear from the start. The only time it becomes an issue is if they don't have that talk before things get physical, which doesn't happen often."

"Good to know," he says, nodding thoughtfully.

"I think she's just going to be curious about the guy who got me to jump back in the pool," I say with a laugh. "But I hope she'll be on her best behavior in front of the kids."

Cara shows up at the house without knocking, which is normal for her, but I can see it throws Cole off a bit. I probably should have warned him about that.

Cara stands tall at five foot ten, with bleach-blonde hair and cinnamon-brown eyes. She's curvier than I am, with a little more weight in all the right places. Today, she's wearing black jeans and a royal blue button-down tank top that flatters her figure.

"Autumn, bitch, what is happening?" Cara greets me with her usual flair.

"Can you please tone it down?" I say, hugging her.

She tilts her head, sizing up Cole as she approaches him. "Oh, this must be the man himself," she says, then glances back at me, mouthing, "*He's hot*," before reaching out to shake his hand. "Congratulations," she says to him, adding with a smirk, "on taking her second V card."

"Cara!" I snap, but Cole just laughs, clearly amused.

"Okay, I'm done," she says, throwing her hands up in mock surrender. "Best behavior from here on out."

Just then, Megan rounds the corner. "Cara!"

"Hey, Megs," Cara says, turning her attention to her. "Thanks for keeping me in the loop."

"That's what surrogate daughters are for," Megan quips.

"Where are Sami and Kevin?" Cara asks, scanning the room.

"They're around here somewhere. I'll find them," Megan says, leaving to track them down.

Cara turns back to me, pulling me into another hug. "Seriously, forgive my crassness," she says, glancing between Cole and me. "I'm really happy for both of you," she adds, pointing at me, "but especially you."

Kevin and Sami enter the room, exchanging hugs and pleasantries with Cara. I catch Cole's eye, giving him an apologetic look, but he just smiles, clearly entertained.

We all move to the kitchen and settle around the island. Megan efficiently hands out drinks before Cara starts in with her usual antics.

"Okay, pop quiz," Cara announces, her eyes locking onto Cole.

She launches into a rapid-fire series of questions, and Cole handles each one with ease.

"Marriages?" she asks.

"One," he replies.

"Kids?"

"Three, all boys."

"Favorite music?"

"Country."

"Favorite movie genre?"

"Action."

"College?"

"University of Georgia for undergrad, Indiana for grad school."

"Major?"

"History and an MBA."

The kids and I watch the exchange like a tennis match, amazed at how smoothly Cole keeps up with her.

"How long have you been at Quisenbelt?"

"Nine years."

"And before that?"

"Ten years at the company that merged with them."

"Do you own a passport?"

"Yes."

"Have you used it?"

"Not recently."

"Parents?"

He hesitates. "I'll pass on that one." Cara glances at me, and Cole follows her gaze, but I shake my head slightly, signaling her to move on.

"Siblings?"

"Six. I'm one of seven, and the only girl is the youngest."

"Wow, where do you fall in the lineup?"

"Dead center—number four."

"Awww, a middle child," she says with a playful smile, exchanging a look with Megan. "If you could travel anywhere, where would it be?"

"Ireland."

"Cool, awesome honeymoon destination," she says with a wink, making me roll my eyes. "Do you read?"

"Yes."

"What kinds of books?"

"Mostly nonfiction—business and history, but sometimes mysteries and suspense."

"Chocolate or vanilla?"

"Vanilla."

Cara pauses, as if searching for more questions, then shrugs. "That's all I got. But just so you know, if you break her heart, I'll make sure they never find the body," she says, making everyone laugh, including Cole and me.

Kevin chimes in, joking with Cole about surviving the grilling. Meanwhile, Cara nudges me and whispers, "What's the deal with the parents?"

"Not now," I murmur, nudging her back with my elbow.

"So, which restaurant are we going to?" Cara asks, shifting gears.

"Lincolnwood," I reply.

"And the car situation?" she asks.

"Kevin had a plan, we all agreed to it, so you're stuck with it," I tease.

"As long as I don't have to drive so I can drink, I'm good," she jokes.

Kevin assures her that with Sami and Megan underage and him volunteering to drive, she's in the clear.

"I'm going to steal your mom for a few," Cara announces, grabbing my arm and pulling me into my office before shutting the door behind us.

"Autumn, first off, he is *fucking hot,*" Cara says, shaking her head in disbelief. "But more importantly, are you happy?"

"Extremely," I reply, my smile genuine.

She hugs me tightly. "I'm so happy for you," she says, then pulls back, her expression more serious. "But what's the deal with his parents?"

I sigh, knowing this conversation was inevitable. "Cara, this isn't something to joke about or tease him about. It's really sensitive."

"Do you think I'm a monster?" she asks, her tone a mix of concern and defensiveness.

"No, but I know you sometimes use humor as a defense mechanism," I say gently.

She nods, understanding. "Okay, I promise I won't say anything, especially not a joke."

"The kids don't know either, so please," I add, needing her to understand how important this is. She makes a gesture, crossing her heart.

"When he was twelve, he and his siblings were pulled out of their home by protective services. He ended up in foster care," I explain.

"Fuck, that's rough," she says, her usual bravado dimming.

"He has scars, Cara," I continue, my voice somber. "Bad ones. It looks like he was flogged. Whatever happened, it was awful."

Cara's face turns serious in a way I've rarely seen. "Oh, fuck, Autumn. I'm sorry I even asked."

"You didn't know," I say, offering her a small smile. "Just leave it alone with him, okay?"

"Okay," she agrees, her tone sincere.

We head back out to the others, the atmosphere lightening as we rejoin them.

"You done with your grilling?" Kevin asks Cara with a grin.

"Oh, I'm sure I'll come up with more questions," she replies, winking at him.

I walk over to Cole, wrapping my arms around his waist. He pulls me close, kissing the top of my head. In that moment, I feel warm and safe, the rest of the room fading away.

"They're pretty cute, huh?" Cara's voice cuts through my little bubble, snapping me back to reality. I turn and give her a playful scowl.

"Yeah, we figured that out already," Megan adds with a smirk.

As we wrap up some small talk and catch up on everyone's lives, it's time to head to the pizza place in Chicago. I make sure Kevin knows the route, then watch as he backs my SUV out of the garage. I hand Cole the keys to the Audi.

"You sure about this?" he asks, his tone a mix of excitement and caution.

I shrug, smiling. "If anything happens to it, I've still got the other car. It's just a car, after all."

"I don't plan on hurting it," he says with a grin, clearly eager.

We get in, and I input the address. We're on the road just a minute behind Kevin and the others. My eclectic playlist fills the car, and Cole seems to know most of the songs. He enjoys the Audi's power, especially when accelerating onto the freeway, but for the most part, it's a regular car ride, just as I expected—comfortable and easy.

Even though it's a Saturday, we arrive early enough that there's no wait for a table. Once seated, I can tell Cara is making a conscious effort to be on her best behavior. She asks Sami about school and Megan about her summer classes. The dinner is full of laughter, conversation, and the easy banter that comes with being surrounded by loved ones.

Cole's hand slips under my hair, his thumb tracing slow circles at the base of my neck. The sensation sends chills down my spine, and when I glance at him, he's smiling that knowing smile. His hand moves down, grazing my arm before resting on my upper thigh. I feel a rush of heat as his fingers play with the inseam of my jeans, so close to where I'm already aching for him. I inhale sharply and grab his hand, squeezing it as a warning. He squeezes back but then gives me a devilish grin and returns to his teasing.

He leans in, his lips brushing my ear as he whispers, "I can't wait to have you all to myself later." His voice is low, just for me, and it sends a thrill through my body.

As he pulls back, he locks eyes with me, his gaze intense, full of promises. He slides his hand down my leg, resting it closer to my knee, his thumb still gently stroking my thigh.

"I have an idea," he says, his tone quiet but not quite a whisper.

"What's that?" I ask, curiosity piqued.

"You should set Cara up with Dr. Gabari," he suggests, laughing softly.

I nearly spit out my drink, laughing at the absurdity of it.

"What's so funny over there?" Cara asks, looking at us.

"Cole's over here trying to play matchmaker for you," I reply, still chuckling.

"Oh?" Cara raises an eyebrow, intrigued. "Do tell."

"Remember that doctor I told you about from the conference?" I say, wrinkling my nose.

She rolls her eyes. "The one who sent you roses?"

"Yep, that one."

"Well, normally I'm not the type to take another girl's leftovers, but I'm always down to meet a man," she says with a playful smirk.

"Cara," I laugh, "we were joking."

"Well, if you need me to take one for the team, there have been worse things," she says, sipping her wine.

Kevin facepalms while Megan speaks up. "Seriously, Cara, do you have no self-control?"

"I'm just trying to make your mom's life easier, jeez," Cara says, shrugging as she lifts her glass.

Sami turns to me, curiosity evident. "A doctor sent you roses?"

"Yeah," I nod, "but he was a little too forward."

"So you *could* have hooked up with a stranger?" Megan asks, her tone teasing.

I laugh. "Could have, yes. Would have? Absolutely not."

"But our intervention *was* a real possibility?" Megan presses.

"I guess you could say that," I say, glancing at Cole. "Cole was my knight in shining armor, saving me from the doctor's advances."

"It wasn't hard," Cole adds. "The guy's lucky I just ran interference and didn't do more. But that was the moment I knew," he says, brushing my hair behind my ear. "I knew we'd either end up here, together, or she'd break my heart."

"Well, if that isn't so sweet it makes my teeth ache," Cara teases, turning to me. "Was that before or after the Mr. Darcy moments?"

Cole gives me a questioning look.

I take a sip of wine, trying to hide my blush. "After the first one, barely before the second," I admit, staring at my glass.

Megan looks between the three of us, while Kevin pretends not to hear any of this, and Sami gives Cara a *"what the hell"* look.

Cole turns to me, still smiling. "What exactly is a 'Mr. Darcy moment'?"

Before I can answer, Megan jumps in, "It's the hand thing, isn't it? It has to be the hand thing."

"Yes, Megan," I start, "it's the hand thing."

I finish the rest of my wine in two quick gulps. Cole is still looking at me, curious, but Megan commands his attention.

"Do you know who Mr. Darcy is?" she asks him.

"From *Pride and Prejudice*, right?" Cole replies.

"Yeah, have you seen the movie?" Megan asks, getting more animated.

"No, I read the book in college," he says.

Megan leans in, clearly excited. "So, there's this moment in the movie—the first time Mr. Darcy touches Lizzie. He just helps her into the carriage. But when he walks away, after letting her hand go, they zoom in while he flexes his hand because, well, chemistry. He felt everything he needed to feel in those two seconds."

Cole turns back to me. "The elevator?" he asks, his voice soft.

I smile, half-nodding. "Yeah."

"And the second?"

I clear my throat. "Right after you led me away from Tony, just before the Cupid Shuffle, and then I went to the bathroom to spill my soul to Cara."

I glance at Cara, who grins back at me.

"I remember that," Cole says. "You grabbed my hand when you told me I did the right thing. I'm pretty sure I should thank Cara for the bathroom pep talk." He smiles at me, his eyes full of gratitude.

Cara shrugs, flipping her hair. "It's what I do."

"And what exactly did you do?" Sami asks, her curiosity piqued. "What did you say to her?"

"I basically told her to leave her work ethic and morals at the door and follow her hormones instead," Cara says, shrugging again.

"Cara!" Kevin exclaims, throwing his napkin on the table.

"What, Kev? I think we're looking at the best possible outcome here," she says, gesturing toward me and Cole with her wine glass.

Cole turns to me, his eyes filled with warmth. "Wait, you talked to her about us after the elevator? That first night?"

"Yeah," I admit. "Even before I saw your text."

He places his hand back on my thigh, giving it a gentle squeeze.

"Mom," Megan says softly, "I feel like we need to hear this entire story."

"You will, Megs, but not tonight," I reply, knowing this isn't the time.

"Okay, one question," Megan says, determined. "If the first chemistry moment was on night one, how long did it take you to figure out this was a thing?"

I glance at Cole as he starts to answer. "I'm pretty sure we both knew on night one," he says, smiling at me. "But work ethic and all that being what it is, night three was the pivot point, I guess."

I shrug, smiling back at him.

"I was done fighting it at the end of night two," he continues, "but your mom was harder to read until the next day."

"Then I was probably a little too obvious," I laugh.

"At the end of dinner on night three, maybe," he agrees. "But I still wasn't sure until you asked me to kiss you."

"You asked him to kiss you?" Megan asks, her voice softening. "That's so sweet."

"More like demanded," I joke.

"Yeah," Cole chuckles, "you *were* a little demanding."

"I didn't hear you complaining," I tease back.

"My understanding is he gave you a big romantic speech first, though," Cara says, grinning.

Cole laughs, looking at me. "Is there anything you didn't tell her?"

"I didn't tell her the content of the speech," I reply, smiling. "And yes, there's plenty I haven't told her."

"Not yet." Cara winks. "But she will."

Kevin laughs, shaking his head. "Cole, maybe someday when this isn't so weird—because, you know, she's my mom—you can teach me your ways of making women ask you to kiss them."

"Oh, this was a first," Cole says, laughing. "The speech wasn't planned, and even when I finished, I wasn't sure if she wanted to kiss me or tell me to fuck off."

"That's because I didn't say anything at all," I laugh.

"Because he left you speechless," Cara teases, winking at me.

I squeeze Cole's hand, feeling incredibly lucky.

"I think you're both just really lucky you found each other," Sami says softly, her voice full of sincerity.

"Me too," Cole agrees, looking at me with a tender smile.

We finish dinner, and Cara picks up the bill, insisting it's a special occasion and not to argue.

CHAPTER EIGHTEEN
THE OVERWHELM

As we're leaving the restaurant, Cole asks if I mind taking a detour on the way home. I tell him I don't mind at all.

He's unusually quiet as we drive further into Chicago. We exit on Belmont, heading into Avondale. After a few minutes and several blocks, he pulls up to a brick apartment building. He sits there, staring out the window, not saying a word.

"Cole," I say softly, my voice filled with gentle curiosity.

"This is where I grew up," he finally says, pointing to a second-floor corner apartment. "That one, right there on the corner."

I hesitate for a moment, then ask quietly, "Before or after?"

"Before," he replies, his voice tinged with a mix of nostalgia and something deeper.

"Have you been back here?" I ask, sensing the weight of the moment.

"A couple of times," he says after a pause, "but not in the last ten years or so."

I reach over and gently caress the back of his neck, offering silent support.

He turns to me, his eyes meeting mine. "Someday, I'll tell you everything, but not tonight."

"Cole," I say, keeping my voice soft and reassuring, "you don't have to tell me anything unless you're ready."

He takes my hand from the back of his neck, kisses it softly, and holds it in his lap as we drive away. The silence between us is comfortable, filled with unspoken understanding. The radio plays quietly, my playlist miraculously leaning toward country on the nearly two-hour drive back to my house. I let him be, knowing that, sometimes, just being present is enough.

Cole parks the car in the garage and turns off the engine. He just sits there for a moment, lost in thought.

"You okay?" I ask, squeezing his hand.

"Yeah," he replies, squeezing back, then sighs. "Let's go inside."

As we walk into the house, I hit the garage door button. My SUV is parked inside, but the house is unusually quiet.

"I think the kids might have already gone to bed," I say, then notice a note on the kitchen island. "Oh, they went to a movie and took Cara's car. They'll be back around midnight," I say, glancing at Cole.

Without warning, he moves quickly toward me, pulling me into a deep, passionate kiss. My hands instinctively rise to his face, holding him close. When he pulls back, his eyes are filled with intensity as he rests his forehead against mine.

"Thank you," he whispers.

"For what?" I laugh softly, surprised by his sudden shift.

"For just being you," he says, his voice thick with emotion. But then his mood darkens slightly. "Fuck, Autumn, the contrast between dinner with your family and how I grew up—how my kids grew up."

He lets go of me, turning away as he leans on a bar stool, his posture tense.

"The way you've mothered your kids," he continues, "it's like nothing I've ever experienced—not as a child, not as a father."

"They were my whole life, for a long time," I say gently. "Some people tell me that's a bad thing. And I could only do that because I had financial support from others."

"It's not a bad thing," he says, his voice rising slightly as he turns to face me, crossing his arms over his chest. "I think most kids could live in cardboard boxes and be happy if their mothers loved them half as much as you love yours. I didn't even have to see you mother them to know that. The way they interact with you, with each other—that's all you. And I don't know whether it makes me sad and angry for my own experiences, or for my boys, or just grateful to have you in my life now."

I stay quiet, wrapping my arms around myself as I let him speak. He was silent during the entire car ride—this has clearly been building inside him. He leans against the island, staring down at his feet, still lost in thought.

"I think," he begins, his voice softer now, "the hardest part isn't about how I was raised—I couldn't control that. It's about how my boys were raised. They're not close to their mother or me, and they're not super close to each other. It makes me wonder if I could have given them a better life if I'd made different choices earlier on."

I walk over to him, closing the distance between us. "Cole, I've played the 'what if' game more times than I can count. My kids deserved a better father, no doubt about that. But if I hadn't been with Steve, I wouldn't have them, and they wouldn't be who they are."

I reach up and gently cup his cheek. "We can't change the past, and we can't fix everything for them. All we can do is love them as best we can. The fact that you care this much speaks volumes. They must feel that, even if it's not shown the way we do in our family."

He remains silent, still looking down at his feet, lost in his thoughts.

"I'm not perfect," I continue. "The kids could tell you plenty of stories about times I messed up, missed events, or wasn't there when they needed me. You're just seeing a snippet, and believe me, they're all on their best behavior."

He opens his arms, wrapping me in a tight embrace. "I think you need to meet my boys sooner rather than later," he says, his voice lighter now. "Maybe we can have them up for a lasagna night." He smiles softly, a hint of hope returning to his eyes.

"I'm sure the kids would love that," I reply, smiling back. "Now, can you stop being all broody?" I tease, standing on my toes to kiss him. "We have the house to ourselves, and you had me all hot and bothered back at the restaurant."

He laughs, his mood lifting as he pulls me closer, the tension of the evening melting away as we focus on the here and now.

"All hot and bothered, huh?" he says, the tension in his face easing as his eyes brighten.

He runs his hands down my back, the warmth of his touch sending a shiver through me.

"Yeah," I whisper, leaning in to kiss him. I take his hands and lead him upstairs to the bedroom.

As I close the door behind me, Cole steps closer, backing me against the door, his arms bracing above my shoulders. He kisses my forehead and sighs, his voice soft as he asks, "Where have you been my whole life?"

His words, his breath, the nearness of him—it all sends a jolt of electricity down my spine. I grab his shirt and yank him closer, kissing him with a hunger that's been building all night. I pull his shirt over his head, and he quickly responds by tugging me closer by the belt loops of my jeans, working them down over my hips. I kick off my jeans and shoes as he peels my shirt off.

I start unbuckling his belt, pushing him toward the bed. His hands glide up and down my arms, leaving trails of heat in their wake, the warmth pooling in my core as my desire for him intensifies. I drop his pants to the floor, and he kicks them off along with his shoes. I'm about to push him onto the bed, but he has other plans.

In a swift motion, he pulls me around, and before I can react, I'm on my back beneath him. He pins my arms above my head with one hand, a move that's becoming a frequent routine. His other hand finds my breast, and his mouth captures mine in a deep, passionate kiss. My back arches into him as the need for him builds.

He trails kisses along my jawline to my neck, each touch igniting sparks inside me. The ache for him is almost unbearable as he moves his lips across my collarbone. I try to pull my hands down to touch him, but he tightens his grip on my wrists, holding me captive in the most delicious way.

He takes my nipple into his mouth, his hand continuing to tease the other, rolling and pinching with just the right pressure. Slowly, he moves his mouth down my body, releasing my wrists as his hand slides down my arm, then along my ribs. His fingers trace up my inner thigh, from my knee to the wetness that's been waiting for him. He slips his fingers inside me, and I moan, arching into him, my hands tangling in his hair.

He groans, and his tongue slides down the slit of my center, his mouth working in tandem with his fingers. The rhythm he sets is perfect, a harmony of sensation that sends me spiraling toward the edge.

"Don't stop," I beg, my voice barely a whisper. He doesn't, maintaining the pace until I'm convulsing around his fingers. With a low groan, he moves back up, covering my body with his, his mouth claiming mine once more.

I wrap my arms and legs around him, pulling him closer, and he doesn't hesitate. He enters me, and it's more than just physical—it's a feeling of completeness, of being whole. He pulls me to the edge of the bed, standing as he lifts my knees over his arms, thrusting into me with an urgency that mirrors my own. I grip the sheets, biting my bottom lip to stifle the sounds of pleasure. His groan fills the room as he reaches his climax, the throbbing intensity pushing me over the edge once more.

Lowering my legs, he leans over me, trailing kisses from my navel to my breasts, up my neck, and finally, his lips find mine again. This kiss is slow and tender, a contrast to the passion we just unleashed.

He gently kisses my temple before lying down next to me. I roll into him, resting my head on his chest, and he wraps his arm around me, holding me close as we both catch our breath, content and complete in the aftermath of our connection.

After a few minutes of comfortable silence, Cole runs his hand through my hair and asks, "Did you really talk to Cara about the elevator before you even saw my text that night?"

I laugh softly, my fingers tracing patterns in his chest hair. "Yeah, I was on the phone with her when I checked my messages and saw your text. It wasn't just the elevator, though—it was the restaurant too. But when our hands touched in the elevator, that was pretty definitive."

"Honestly, if Tom hadn't been in there with us, I don't know what I would have said or done," Cole admits. "Especially if I had known you felt it too."

"We still ended up here," I say, smiling. "Just with a couple more days of sexual tension. But I knew you wanted to touch me that second night in the elevator—I saw your hand moving in the reflection on the metal wall."

"Would you have stopped me?" he asks, his voice low.

"No," I reply, meeting his gaze. "I wanted to touch you too. I had my logical concerns—hell, I still do—but I wouldn't have stopped you."

"One of the reasons I didn't is because we had both been drinking, a lot," he says thoughtfully. "I didn't want that to be the reason either one of us didn't stop."

"That's actually pretty sweet," I say, touched by his consideration. "And the next night, I was completely sober."

"I know," he says with a chuckle. "I knew everything you did before we got on the elevator was all you—not influenced by alcohol. Monday's going to be hard, though. I'm afraid."

"Yeah," I agree, a hint of melancholy in my voice. "It'll be our new normal. Back to the old normal, but with a twist."

Just then, we hear the kids come in. "I guess I should get some clothes on and go check on them," I say reluctantly.

Cole sighs, "Me too. Just give me a minute."

I slip into sleep shorts and a tank top with a built-in bra, while Cole throws on sweats and a T-shirt. We head downstairs to see the kids. They look surprised to find us still awake, but each of them gives me a goodnight hug, telling me they enjoyed dinner and the movie.

As the girls head upstairs, Kevin lingers behind for a moment.

"Hey," he starts, his tone a bit more serious, "I wanted to let you know I talked to Uncle Alex. I didn't want to keep that from you. He's good, really happy for you. He said he might come out for Thanksgiving, but more likely in the spring. He wants you to call him sometime soon."

"I will," I assure him. "When Cole goes back to Fort Wayne."

"That's what he figured," Kevin says with a nod. "Megan mentioned Cole's coming to dinner tomorrow?"

"Uh, yeah," I say, glancing at Cole, who just smiles.

Kevin chuckles, "Have you told them yet?"

"No, not yet," I laugh, feeling a little sheepish. "I guess I should make that call tomorrow when they get home from church."

"Yeah, I kind of figured that hadn't happened," Kevin says, pausing for a moment. "It's been a little... fast."

Cole and I both laugh at that. Kevin says goodnight and heads upstairs, leaving Cole and me alone in the quiet kitchen.

"So, what do I need to know about your parents?" Cole asks, curiosity evident in his voice.

I take his hand and lead him to my office, where I show him a large family photo. "My parents had these done a couple of years ago and gave Alex and me these huge prints as gifts."

Cole studies the picture as I continue. "My dad, Liam, worked in finance until he retired a couple of years ago. My mom, Emily, has a degree in English but was a stay-at-home mom and later an incredible housewife. She had cancer about ten years ago, and it was rough—really rough—on both of them, but she's been in remission for a while now. My dad's more the type to hire someone to fix things than do it himself. I've never really seen him work with his hands."

Cole points at the photo. "So, this is your dad and mom, and I assume this is your brother?"

"Yeah," I confirm, pointing to the picture. "And that's Kiersten, my niece, next to Megan. My parents wanted this picture to be just our genetic family, but..." I move over to another picture. "This is Alex, his wife, Claire, and Kiersten."

Cole starts looking around the room, taking in the various photos. "Are these the kids' senior pictures?" he asks, noticing the large portraits of my children.

"Yeah," I say, moving closer to the photos. "And these are all of them as babies."

"Wow," Cole says, pausing at Alex's wedding picture where I'm standing next to Claire as her maid of honor. "Megan really is a mini-you."

"She is. I was her age in that photo," I say with a smile.

"These are your parents too, right?" he asks, looking at a picture from Kevin's college graduation.

"Yeah, that's the most recent picture I have of them in here—it was just a couple of months ago."

He turns toward the bookshelves behind my desk, running his fingers over the spines of the books in my extensive fiction collection. "Have you read all of these?" he asks, sounding impressed.

"I have," I say with a laugh. "That's where all my free time went up until, y'know, like a week ago."

"Is that why Cara asked if I read?" he chuckles.

"Probably."

"And this is where so many of those meetings and phone calls with me happened?" he asks, a smile playing on his lips.

"Yes, especially if we had to be on camera," I say, smiling back. "If no cameras were involved, I sometimes did my morning meetings in bed. Don't tell my boss," I joke.

"My lips are sealed," he says, his smile widening. "Well, your workspace is much nicer than mine."

"Until I took the job with Quisenbelt, this was a reading and craft room. But it has made a nice office," I say, glancing around the room. "Also, the couch folds out into a bed, so it doubles as another guest room if I ever need it."

"I know you and Megan didn't show me the whole house, but how many bedrooms are there?" he asks.

"Officially, five, plus the office and two bedrooms in the basement that aren't to code, so we can't count them. But they're set up like guest rooms, so really, eight."

"So," he says a bit cautiously, "if I did bring my boys here to meet you, there would be places for all of them?"

"Yeah," I answer, smiling reassuringly. "There would be. And if you really do want to do that soon, we should do it while it's still warm so they can use the pool. When you combine a lasagna night with a poolside barbecue the next day, things get even better around here," I tease, pulling him closer by his waist.

"Do you grill, too?" he asks, a hint of a smile playing on his lips.

"I'm sure I'm capable," I say, grinning. "But Kevin likes to man the grill—has since he was about fifteen. I'm sure he'd share with you and the boys, though. He's a little old-fashioned and sexist that way."

"I can't imagine Kevin being really sexist about anything," Cole says thoughtfully. "More like chivalrous."

"Kind of like you," I say, kissing him softly. "Let's go to bed."

CHAPTER NINETEEN
THE PARENTS & THE POOL

We all sleep in that morning, and by the time Cole and I stir, it's already past ten. The kids haven't been up for much longer. When we finally make our way to the kitchen, the comforting aroma of French toast greets us. Sami is at the stove, flipping slices with the effortless grace of someone who's done this a million times. Kevin is perched at the kitchen island, his fingers flying over his laptop keyboard, while Megan is absorbed in her phone, scrolling with intense focus.

Breakfast is a relaxed, quiet affair. Afterward, the kids scatter, each off to do their own thing. By noon, I realize I need to call my parents and let them know Cole will be joining us for dinner. The thought of that call sends a flutter of nerves through me, though I can't quite pinpoint why.

"Hi, Mom," I say as she picks up on the second ring.

"Hey, Autumn! How are you, sweetheart?" Her voice is warm, as always.

"I'm good—actually, I'm really good," I respond, my words tumbling out a bit too fast. "That's why I'm calling."

"Oh, you have good news?" she asks, her voice lighting up with curiosity. "Let me get your dad." I hear her calling for him, and the familiar rustling as she puts me on speakerphone. "Okay, Autumn, we're both here."

"Hi, Dad," I begin, a bit more tentatively now. "First, I wanted to let you know that all the kids are here this weekend, so the whole crew will be at dinner tonight."

"That's great! We're looking forward to it," my mom says, her enthusiasm genuine.

"And... well, here's the news: I've met someone. It's already pretty serious, so I'm bringing him to dinner too." The words hang in the air, and the silence that follows is a beat too long.

"Mom?" I prompt, unable to keep the anxiety out of my voice.

"We're here, Autumn," she finally says. "I think we're just a little surprised. How long have you known him?"

"Well, I've worked with him for about two years, but we only just met in person last weekend," I explain. "The kids have met him, and they really like him."

"Autumn," my dad interjects, his voice careful, "are you dating your boss?"

I pause, feeling the weight of the question. "Dad... yes, technically I am, but we're figuring that part out."

"Liam, that's really none of our business," my mom chimes in, a note of firmness in her tone. "Are you happy, Autumn?"

"I am. I'm very happy," I say, the truth of it settling in as I speak.

"Well, then we're happy for you and we look forward to meeting him," she says with finality.

"Thanks, Mom," I reply, relief washing over me. "We'll see you guys soon."

"See you soon. Love you, Autumn. Bye," she says, and the call ends with a click.

I lower the phone, feeling Cole's presence beside me, his eyes searching mine. He could only hear my side of the conversation, but he seems to know there's more beneath the surface.

"How did that go?" he asks gently.

"With my mom, it went fine," I say, hesitating for a moment. "My dad... well, I think he's a bit wary about the situation. He's a businessman, after all, and he guessed it was you. So, there's that."

I look down at the phone, still warm in my hand, and Cole pulls me close, pressing a tender kiss to my temple. "I guess that's one advantage I have—no parents to please," he says with a soft laugh.

"Cole," I murmur, a small smile playing on my lips, "that's terrible."

"I know," he replies, his grin widening. "But hey, silver linings." I nudge him playfully with my shoulder, and he wraps his arm around me, his warmth seeping into me. "It'll be okay," he reassures me.

"I know," I say, my voice softening. "I think my dad will like you. You're both businessmen, and I'm sure you'll connect on that level." I pause, the next words more difficult. "But... there's one thing that might be on his mind. He won't say it, but when he cheated on my mom, it was with one of his employees. So, he might be projecting a little."

Cole nods, understanding flickering in his eyes. "Yeah, I don't think he'd say that out loud, even if he's thinking it," he says, pulling me closer and kissing my temple again. "Zero to two hundred."

Megan saunters in a few minutes later, her tone playful as she announces, "I'm staying at Stacey's again tonight, so you'll have the house all to yourselves—again." Her sing-song voice is loaded with implication, and I can't help but chuckle.

Soon after, Kevin and Cole help Sami load up her car with laundry and other essentials she's taking back to school. We all begin getting ready to head over to my parents' house. Sami drives her car so she can leave directly from there, and the rest of us pile into my SUV. Though it's only three blocks away, the high nineties and oppressive humidity make walking out of the question. As we drive, I can't help but feel a mix of anticipation and nerves. This dinner will be the start of something new—a new chapter, a new beginning. And despite the lingering doubts, I find myself excited for what lies ahead.

As we pull into my parents' driveway, I can feel Cole's unspoken thoughts hanging in the air between us—their house is modest, about half the size of mine, lacking the grandiosity and polished facade that defines my home. But it's comfortable, lived-in—a place where memories are etched into the walls. I catch a glimpse of my mother opening the front door, her face lighting up as she steps outside to greet us, with my father following close behind.

My mother fusses over Kevin first, her hands reaching to straighten his collar before moving on to embrace the girls. Finally, she turns her attention to Cole and me. She pulls me into a tight hug, and I can feel the warmth and love in her embrace. When she releases me, she faces Cole with an expectant smile.

"Cole Waters. It's nice to meet you, Mrs. Flynn," he says with a touch of formality, his voice steady.

"Please, call me Emily," she insists, her smile widening. "It's so nice to finally meet you. And this," she gestures to my father, "is my husband, Liam."

My dad offers Cole a firm handshake, his expression inscrutable. He doesn't say much, just nods before turning to hug me, the silent protector as always.

"So, Autumn," my mom begins, a hint of excitement in her voice, "I decided to order out for today rather than cook. The food will be here in about forty-five minutes."

"Oh, Mom," I say, touched by the gesture, "you didn't have to go to all that trouble."

"It's no trouble at all," she replies, her smile softening. "Much easier than cooking."

As the minutes tick by, I watch Kevin make a deliberate effort to draw my dad out of his shell. It's a dance I've seen before, Kevin's natural charm working its magic as he nudges my dad into conversation. Soon enough, my dad and Cole are talking business, delving into the intricacies of healthcare investments and retirement plans. My dad, ever the finance man, quizzes Cole on his future strategies, and I can't help but be impressed by Cole's confident, well-thought-out responses. His plans are far more comprehensive than mine—no surprise there, given how long it took me to establish a full-time career.

By the time the food arrives, the atmosphere has shifted. Kevin, Cole, and my father, Liam, are laughing easily together, the initial tension having dissolved into mutual respect. My mom pulls me aside, her voice low as she asks, "How happy are you, really? Did you expect this when you went to Dallas?"

I smile, giving her the details I'm comfortable sharing. Her eyes light up with genuine happiness for me, and she squeezes my hand.

"He's so different from Steve," she observes, her tone thoughtful. "Even in the way he carries himself and interacts with the kids."

"I know, Mom," I say, my heart swelling. "I'm pretty head over heels right now."

"Samantha and Megan seem to like him too," she notes. "Samantha could've been a challenge, but she genuinely seems to like him."

"Yeah," I agree, a small sigh of relief escaping me. "She was the one I was most worried about. But Cole's been wonderful with them, all three of them. And Alex even sent Kevin on a bit of a fact-finding mission, though I'm not sure whether it was to get information or give it. Either way, it went well."

"This is really fast, Autumn," my mom cautions, her concern peeking through. "I just feel like you need to be a little cautious."

"I know, Mom," I say, my voice softening as the truth settles in my heart. "But I think I'm already in love with him."

"Oh, Autumn," she says, her eyes misting with emotion. "I'm so happy for you. Just promise me you'll be careful."

"I will," I assure her, knowing it's a promise I intend to keep.

Dinner is pleasant, the conversation flowing easily as we let the kids take the lead, their laughter filling the room. When it's time to leave, we all give Sami a big hug and send her off back to school. The drive back to my house is quiet, the evening settling in as Kevin and Megan pack up to head out—Kevin to his apartment, Megan to Stacey's. Finally, it's just Cole and me, the house suddenly feeling both large and intimate at the same time.

"I think that went well, Autumn," Cole says, leaning casually against the arm of the couch in the family room. "Your dad had to warm up a bit, but once he did, I think it went okay."

"I do too," I reply, feeling the lingering tension finally dissipate. "Sometimes the anticipation is the worst part."

"Sometimes anticipation is nice," Cole says with a slow smile, his eyes locking onto mine. "Or maybe it just makes what comes after even better."

The look in his eyes as he finishes speaking is downright devilish, charged with a lust that sends shivers racing down my spine, leaving trails of heat in their wake. I clear my throat, caught off guard by the intensity of my reaction to his words, to the deep, sultry tone of his voice, to the way his eyes seem to undress me right where I stand. He's so damn sexy, and the best part? He's all mine.

"Sometimes," I manage to whisper, my voice barely audible, betraying just how breathless he's left me.

He steps closer, and when he reaches me, he brushes the back of his hand along my cheek. That simple touch ignites a fire deep inside me, and my eyes flutter shut without my permission. When I open them again, his thumb tracing along my jawline, I'm met with a gaze that's even more intense, burning right through me. My legs feel weak, and my palms tingle with a fiery sensation. In this moment, there's no trace of the vulnerability he's shown before. Everything about him now feels raw, animalistic, like a predator honing in on his prey—and I'm more than willing.

His hand slips into my hair, and he leans down, capturing my lips with his. Heat floods my body, desire igniting every nerve. As he pulls back, he drags my bottom lip between his teeth, the sensation sending a shockwave straight to my core. He kisses his way along my jawline to my ear, whispering in a voice that sends electric currents through me, "You're wearing far too many clothes for this adventure."

His breath on my neck makes my toes curl. He tugs at my waistband, dropping to his knees as he pulls down my jeans and underwear in one swift motion. I step out of them, and he runs his hands up my legs, his fingers leaving trails of fire as he kisses up the inside of my thigh. Just before reaching the apex of my thighs, he stands, slipping his hands under my shirt and tearing it off over my head with a controlled urgency. He kisses me again, this time with a hunger that borders on desperation, his tongue exploring mine with fervor. He reaches behind me, unhooking my bra with practiced ease, sliding it off my arms. I grab at his shirt, and he obliges, whipping it off over his head.

I press my hands to his chest, but he grabs my wrists, his grip firm yet gentle.

He steps back, guiding me toward the patio door with a wicked smile. "Come swim with me," he says, his voice a low, seductive purr.

"Cole," I laugh softly, "you're insane."

"I know," he replies, opening the patio door and leading me out into the moonlight.

"I think now you're overdressed," I tease, glancing down at his waist.

His response is swift—he drops his pants and boxers, leaving him gloriously naked as he continues to lead me toward the pool. We reach the stairs, and he backs down them, still pulling me with him, stealing soft kisses with nearly every step. The water is warm, inviting, and we wade deeper until it's up to my waist.

He places my hands back on his chest, brushing the back of his hand over my cheek once more. His other hand travels down my side, his thumb grazing over my nipple, causing me to inhale sharply. He smiles at my reaction, running his thumb over my bottom lip before pulling my body into his, kissing me with that same insatiable hunger. Without breaking the kiss, he turns me, backing me against the side of the pool. His mouth moves in smooth kisses down my neck, his hands caressing my breasts before finding them with his mouth.

His fingers slide down to my center, pushing inside me, and I gasp as he explores, his mouth returning to mine in a passionate kiss. His fingers continue their rhythm, teasing me until I'm nearly coming undone. Then, with a swift motion, he lifts me by my thighs, seating me on the edge of the pool. He guides my legs to open wider, his lips and tongue trailing slowly from my knee up the inside of my thigh. I lean back on one hand, the other tangling in his hair. As he reaches my center, he slows down, teasing me with his breath, sending jolts of anticipation through me.

When his mouth finally meets the source of my desire, I gasp, my hips trying to rise, but his hands hold me in place. He moves with expert precision, bringing me closer and closer to the edge until I can't hold back. My climax crashes over me, sending waves of pleasure rippling through my body, and I feel the gush of fluid my body releases at its height. I squeal, biting my lip to keep from crying out too loudly, the sensations amplified by the water.

I'm still trembling, lightheaded from the intensity, but I manage to reach down, running my fingers through his hair as he looks up at me, his face glistening. He pulls me back into the pool, his hands hungry, touching me everywhere, his mouth seeking mine with renewed urgency.

Without warning, he maneuvers us out of the pool and onto the daybed beside it. He trails kisses from my hip up to my neck, finally capturing my mouth again. He spreads my thighs with his legs and thrusts inside me, drawing moans from both of us. Everything about him feels perfect, the way he fills me, the way he moves, hitting every spot with precision. He leans back, signaling with his hands for me to roll over, and I comply easily.

He positions himself with one knee on the daybed, the other foot on the ground, pulling my hips into him as he thrusts harder. Each movement sends shockwaves of pleasure through me, and I can't hold back my moans, though I try to keep them quiet. With one final thrust, I feel the pulse of his release inside me, and he collapses next to me on the daybed.

I'm lying on my stomach, facing Cole, my body still wet from the pool. His hand traces over my back, leaving trails of goosebumps as his fingers gently move over my skin. In this moment, I am utterly satisfied, completely content. I never want it to end.

Cole breaks the silence, moving his hand up to brush my hair out of my face. "I'm going to miss you in a way I don't think I've ever missed anyone," he says, his voice soft and sincere.

"Maybe you can dream of me," I say with a sleepy smile.

"I don't think that's a maybe, Ms. Flynn," he replies, his smile matching mine. "And I don't think I'll need to be sleeping to be dreaming of you."

"When do you have us scheduled to work together again?" I ask, my eyes growing heavy.

"Three weeks," he says. "But you're only a five-hour drive away. I don't see myself staying away for three weeks." He laughs, the sound warm and comforting.

"Maybe it would be good for us," I tease, "to take a break, let my body recover."

Cole chuckles. "Oh, you need recovery time?"

"Not now, but at this rate, I will," I reply, leaning over to kiss him.

"Maybe I need to try harder," he says, a playful challenge in his tone.

"Oh," I kiss him again, "you definitely don't need to try harder."

"Is that your way of telling me you're satisfied?" he asks, a bit too much inflection in his voice.

He kisses my forehead, and I sigh, "Very," before adding, "That doesn't mean I don't want more of you though."

He smiles, laughing softly. "But," I start, "even though I'm very content right now, maybe we should go inside."

"Maybe," Cole agrees.

He stands and reaches out a hand to help me up. As he pulls me to my feet, he draws me into his arms, holding me like he can't get close enough, and kisses me deeply. It's just the two of us, standing naked under the moonlight with the pool reflecting its soft glow, and I know this is a moment I'll never forget.

CHAPTER TWENTY

THE SEPARATION

The next morning, we both log on to our morning meeting, sharing brief glances that speak volumes more than any words could. Cole wraps up his other meetings, and then it's time for him to pack up and head home. The reality of his departure starts to settle in as we find ourselves standing in my garage, next to his SUV. He leans me back against the cool metal, his hands firm on my waist as he kisses me deeply, as if he's trying to imprint this moment onto both of us.

"Drive safe," I say softly, my voice tinged with the ache of goodbye.

"Fuck, I don't want to go," he murmurs, pressing his forehead against mine. The raw honesty in his voice tugs at something deep inside me.

"I know," I whisper, my hands cradling his face. I kiss him gently, trying to pour all my reassurance into that one touch. "But we'll figure this out. I know we will."

He sighs, a mix of frustration and resignation in his breath. "Isn't there some bullshit about leaving you wanting more and distance making the heart fonder and all that?"

"There are bullshit sayings about both," I laugh softly, the sound more melancholy than amused. "I guess we'll find out if they're true, though I wish we didn't have to." I pause, my thumb tracing the curve of his cheekbone. "As much as I hate to admit it, this did all happen so fast. Maybe a little space will help us both ground ourselves again."

"I hate it, but I agree," he says, his voice laced with reluctance.

I pull him into a long hug, holding him close, savoring the feel of his body against mine. It's like I'm trying to memorize every detail before he leaves.

"Be safe," I murmur as we finally pull apart, my heart tightening in my chest. "I'll miss you."

"I could stand here and kiss you goodbye all day," he says with a small, bittersweet smile, "but I guess at some point, I have to leave." He leans down, kisses the top of my head, and then strokes my hair with such tenderness that it makes my chest ache. "I'll miss you too," he adds, his voice thick with emotion.

He gives me one last kiss on the top of my head before reluctantly opening his car door. As he backs out of the garage, I stand there, my arms wrapped around myself, feeling the weight of his absence already settling in. I watch until he reaches the end of the driveway, and then I turn, closing the garage door behind me.

I step back into the house, into the life I had just ten days ago. But it isn't the same—it can't be. I'm different now, changed in ways that I'm only beginning to understand. No matter what happens from here on, I know I'm not the same woman who stood in this foyer just over a week ago. On every level imaginable, I am changed.

I find myself sitting on the steps in the foyer, my thoughts swirling around everything that's happened. I pull out my phone and call Cara. I need to decompress, to talk it through, even if there are parts of this that I want to keep to myself, parts that feel too sacred to share with anyone. Cara agrees to come over for dinner, and it's a small comfort to know that, Megan or no Megan, I won't be alone tonight.

After I hang up, I stay there on the stairs, lost in thought. I think about what dating was like when I was younger, how everything felt so intense, yet somehow less complex. The hormones were powerful, sure, but the emotions were different. Even when I dated Steve and thought I'd found the love of my life, it didn't feel like this. There's an intensity with Cole that's unlike anything I've ever experienced. I don't know if it's the sudden, overwhelming physical connection or if I'm just completely in love with him. But whatever it is, this is different—different from anything I've ever felt in my life.

I pick up my phone and text Alex, asking if he's busy. Less than twenty seconds later, my phone rings, his name flashing on the screen.

"Hey, Alex," I answer, a smile already forming.

"Hey, baby sister," he replies, his voice warm and familiar. "So, I take it your whirlwind, crazy weekend is over?" He chuckles softly, and I can't help but smile wider.

"Yeah," I say, unable to keep the happiness out of my voice.

"Autumn," he begins, his tone shifting to something more serious, "I only have one question. That's it. You don't have to tell me anything else." He pauses, and I can almost hear him considering his words. "Are you happy?"

"I am, Alex," I reply, my voice steady. "So happy. I'm still processing, but I'm really, really happy."

"When Kev first called me, he was freaking out," Alex says, his voice lightening. "He thought it was someone you'd just met, and they were worried about you. But after hearing enough conversations between you and Cole over the last couple of years, that killed all their concerns. And Autumn?"

"Yeah?" I prompt, curious about where he's going with this.

"Kevin probably doesn't want me to tell you this, but he said seeing you two in person was—what was the word he used? 'Impressive.'" Alex continues, a hint of admiration in his voice, "He said he's never seen two people drawn together like magnets the way you two are. Even said he could see it just in how you looked at each other. He talked about his friends' relationships, Steve's escapades, even Claire and me, and said he's never seen anything like it."

I pause, trying to find the right words to respond. "Alex, it's intense. It's so intense. There was no fighting it for either of us, which is scary, in some ways. I'm a little grateful he went home so I can process and ground myself a little."

"I can understand feeling scared," Alex says, his voice gentle. "Just be careful, but enjoy it. Autumn, if this is everything everyone seems to think it is, you deserve this. You deserve happiness, you deserve love. You're such an amazing person, and after Steve... " He pauses, and I can hear him take a deep breath. "Well, I thought I'd never see you happy in that part of your life again. I'm really, really happy for you."

Tears well up in my eyes, the warmth of his words overwhelming me. "Alex, you really are the best brother. Thank you for always being my rock." My voice catches, and I sniffle, trying to hold back the tears.

"Autumn, are you crying?" Alex asks, a hint of humor in his voice.

"Just a little," I admit, laughing softly through the sniffles.

"Maybe those feelings are a little intense," he teases, his laughter light and comforting.

"Maybe," I agree, wiping away the tears that have escaped.

"I'm going to try to bring the family home for Thanksgiving," Alex says, his tone more serious again. "But we had other plans this year, so I'm not sure it's going to work. It may not be until spring or summer that we get out there, but we'll see."

"I'll actually be out your way in February," I mention. "Well, the Seattle area, for a wedding."

"I think I could find a way to drive a few hours to see you then," he says, and I can hear the smile in his voice. "I have to run—I've got a meeting to get to. But I love you, Autumn. I'm happy for you."

"Love you too, Alex. Talk to you soon," I say before we hang up.

Deciding I need to shake off the lingering heaviness, I head upstairs for a long, hot shower. The water cascades over me, grounding me, bringing me back to my own space. Once I'm dressed—just leggings and a comfortable shirt, since it's a casual dinner at home with Cara—I text Megan to see if she'll be home for dinner. She replies that she won't be back until late, which is just as well. I kind of want to talk to Cara without the kids around.

I busy myself picking up around the house, throwing some laundry in the wash. It all feels like a strange return to normalcy, as if I'm coming down from the adrenaline rush of a roller coaster ride. My body is decompressing from the constant sexual tension and, well, the sex. The day is starting to feel more ordinary, more familiar, though there's an undercurrent of exhaustion running through me. Even though everything with Cole felt so natural, it was on an elevated level that I'm not used to sustaining. Now, I just feel drained.

I glance at the clock—Cole should be almost home by now, but he'll still be driving, so I call him.

"Hey there," he answers, his voice warm and soothing.

"Hi," I say softly, not realizing until now that hearing his voice is exactly what I needed.

"You okay?" he asks, concern lacing his words.

"Yeah, just wanted to hear your voice," I admit, the simplicity of the truth catching me off guard.

"I miss you too," he says, and I can hear the sincerity in his tone.

"You almost home?" I ask.

"Yeah, about twenty minutes out," he replies. I can hear the faint sounds of traffic in the background.

"Drive okay?" I ask, needing the comfort of small talk.

"Yeah, not bad," he says, and then adds, "I used the time in the car to call my boys."

"Yeah? How did that go?"

"I didn't tell them anything specific, but I'm taking all three of them to dinner on Friday. I told them I had something to tell them, so I'll talk to them all together then."

"That sounds like a good plan," I say, feeling a little lighter. "I talked to my brother earlier. I don't know everything Kevin told him, but he's happy for me. Genuinely happy."

"I'm just glad that *you're* happy, Autumn," Cole says, and I can feel the warmth of his smile through the phone.

I laugh softly. "Me too, but it helps if there isn't any drama."

Cole chuckles. "Yeah, there's that. Other than talking to the boys, I've just been listening to music, trying to decompress a bit."

"Yeah," I laugh, "I've been doing some of that too. Cara's coming over for dinner."

"Say nice things about me," he teases.

"I don't think that'll be a problem," I say with a smile. "You gonna make me be on camera at eight in the morning?"

"Absolutely," he laughs. "I want to see your face."

"So you'll torture everyone else just for me? I see how you are."

"I think it's only you and Tara that stress about it," he says, still chuckling.

"Blame society for that one, not us," I laugh along. "You do know that's six in the morning for Tara, right?"

"Oh, I know. She has reminded me. But it's only three times a week, and nobody from work bothers her after about two her time."

"Ah, the joys of working on a national level."

"Yeah, it has its pros and cons for sure," he says, his tone softening. "I think these are the kinds of conversations everyone else heard and could read, but we couldn't."

"You're probably right. Just normal conversations, but they come so easily for us."

"It's nice that it comes easy," he says. "I'm about to get off the freeway—"

I interrupt him, grinning. "How does the freeway feel about that?"

He bursts out laughing. "Okay, I'm about to exit off the freeway," he corrects himself, still laughing. "I can call you back when I get unloaded."

"No, that's okay. Cara will be here shortly, but I'll let you know when I'm alone again."

"I like it better when you're alone with me," he says, his voice dropping to a more intimate tone.

"Me too," I admit, "Tonight will be weird."

"It will," he agrees. "I'll talk to you later, Autumn. Miss you."

"Miss you too," I say, and as I hang up, I quietly whisper, "*I love you,*" to the empty room.

Taking a deep breath, I tuck my phone in my pocket and head to the kitchen to start on some mundane tasks, like unloading the dishwasher. About twenty minutes later, Cara walks in, and the first thing she does is give me a big, tight hug.

She plops down on one of the bar stools, her eyes bright with curiosity. "Okay, Autumn, dish. No kids, no Cole, just dish."

"I don't even know where to start, Cara," I say, feeling the blush rise to my cheeks. "It's all just so much, so intense, so fast, and so amazing."

"So, the sex, I take it, is not an issue?" she asks, grinning like a cat who caught the canary.

I laugh, shaking my head. "No, absolutely not. And I know it's been a while, but, fuck... it's so good. Like, best of my life good."

Cara shrieks with delight. "I knew it! I fucking knew it! You two orbit around each other."

"I guess Kevin said something like that to Alex," I laugh, still blushing.

"Oh, we had a conversation, the kids and I, on the way home from the restaurant. Sami said it's like watching a romance novel or movie in real life."

"Sami said that?" I'm surprised, caught off guard by her insight.

"Yeah," Cara says, her smile softening. "She's a little floored by the whole thing, but she's so happy for you."

My eyes start to tear up again, and I laugh, feeling a little ridiculous. "What the fuck is wrong with me, Cara? I keep crying for no reason."

"I'm pretty sure you're insanely in love," she says, her tone both teasing and serious.

"I think so too," I admit, my voice quieting. "You know, on the second night, he said he thought he was already falling in love with me. We haven't said anything since then, but that's what it feels like. Fuck, I feel like I just got off a roller coaster, and I want to get back on."

"Are you scared?" she asks, her voice gentle.

"A little," I admit. "I don't think there's anything in him that could intentionally hurt me, but it's just so intense. If something goes wrong... if it turns... it would be rough."

"I know," she says softly. "That's exactly the kind of shit I try to stay away from."

"I know you do," I laugh, feeling a bit lighter. "What do you want for dinner?"

"Here's my thought," she says, leaning in conspiratorially. "Let's order pizza, sit on the couch, and watch chick flicks for a few hours. Let you come down off that roller coaster a little easier."

"That sounds amazing," I say, relief washing over me.

And that's exactly what we do. I order pizza, we open a bottle of wine, and we settle into the family room. Cara insists on watching *Pride and Prejudice*, so we do, and then we follow it up with a romantic comedy before she heads home.

She gives me a big hug at the door. "I'm happy for you, Autumn. I just have a feeling that this will all work out."

"Me too," I say, closing the door behind her, the quiet of the house settling in around me like a warm blanket.

I clean up the wine glasses and pizza boxes, putting the leftovers away, and then head to the family room to fold the blankets we used. I'm just smoothing out the last one when Megan comes in, her presence bringing a comforting sense of normalcy.

"Hey, Mom!" she greets me with a brightness in her voice.

"Hey, Megs. How are you?" I ask, sensing something more in her tone.

"I'm good. How are you?" she asks, her voice layered with something deeper, maybe curiosity or concern.

"I'm good," I reply, giving her a reassuring smile. "Cara just left. I think I'm just decompressing a bit."

To my surprise, she rushes at me and wraps her arms around me in a tight hug.

"Mom, we're all so happy for you," she says, her words full of sincerity. "He's amazing, and he's going to set some high bars for Sami and me."

Her words warm my heart, and I hug her back, feeling a wave of gratitude wash over me. "I'm glad you like him," I say softly. "I'm hoping his kids feel the same way."

"They'll love you. They have to," Megan insists with the unwavering confidence only a daughter could have.

"We'll see," I say, my voice tinged with a hint of caution. "They've lived a very different life from you three, so they might react differently." I pause, thinking about the potential challenges. "I'm worried they'll react more like you do with your dad's new people."

"I sure hope not," she says with a knowing smile. "But he hasn't dated much either. We're jaded in that area; his kids probably won't be."

"I guess we'll find out," I say, laughing softly. "Apparently, Kevin's lasagna night plan sold though, because Cole thinks we should do that when you all meet his kids."

"Mom!" Megan exclaims, her excitement bubbling over. "We should do a pool barbecue!"

I laugh, nodding. "I said the same thing to Cole. I told him we should do it while it's still warm enough to use the pool."

"Great minds," she says with a laugh. "You have an early morning, right?"

"I do," I reply, glancing at the clock.

"Well, you get off to bed. I have some homework to finish before class tomorrow."

"Okay, Megs. Love you!"

"Love you too, Mom!"

I head upstairs, and as I do, I hear Megan plop down on the couch with her bag. The thought of going to bed alone tonight feels strange and a little hard to reconcile. I go through my nighttime routine—the brushing of teeth, the application of night creams, the familiar rituals that usually bring comfort. But tonight, they feel a bit emptier.

Dressed in soft pajamas, I slide into bed and rest my head on the pillow Cole has been using. The faint scent of him still lingers, and I inhale deeply, wanting to hold onto that part of him just a little longer.

As I lie there, I hear the soft buzz of my watch on the nightstand. I reach for my phone, and sure enough, it's him.

"Hey you, I was just thinking about you," I answer, a smile tugging at my lips. "My bed smells like you."

"Oh, does it now?" he replies, a hint of mischief in his voice.

"Yeah, and it made me miss you," I admit, feeling the distance between us in the quiet of my room.

"I miss you too," he sighs, the weight of it clear even through the phone.

"You in bed yet?" I ask, picturing him there, wishing I was next to him.

"Not yet, but clearly you are," he laughs.

"I just got here. Megan just got home a few minutes ago."

"Yeah? How was your time with Cara?" he asks, his voice softening, genuinely interested.

"It was good. We ate pizza, drank wine, and watched some movies. Just chilled on the couch."

"No third degree?" he teases.

"No, not really. She asked a couple of questions, but nothing too intense. She did say the kids and she talked on the way home on Saturday, and they all like you and us."

"I like them and us too. What movies did you watch?"

I tell him, and he laughs when I mention *Pride and Prejudice*.

"I think Cara just needed to watch it with me," I explain.

"That whole part at dinner was embarrassing and enlightening," he says, the memory still fresh.

"Yeah, I'm just not used to talking about this kind of thing with anyone," I admit, feeling a bit vulnerable.

"Me either. Hey, Autumn?"

"Yes, Cole?"

"I don't know how I'm going to sleep tonight without you," he says, his voice tinged with longing.

"Drugs?" I joke. "Just kidding, it will be hard for me too. But I have this pillow that smells like you I can snuggle with; that might help."

"Maybe next time I need to steal something of yours," he laughs.

"Or I can come sleep in your bed, and then your bed can smell like me."

"That would work too," he says, the idea clearly appealing to him.

"In your bachelor pad?" I tease.

"Yeah, I guess you could call it that. It's not nearly as comfortable as your house."

"Cole, I could be with you in a cardboard box and be happy."

"I see what you did there, turning my words back around on me."

"Yeah, but it doesn't make it any less true," I say softly, meaning every word.

"What am I going to do with you, Autumn?"

"What do you want to do with me, Cole?" I ask, letting the question hang between us, heavy with possibilities.

"Now, if that isn't a loaded question."

"Just a little," I say, the tension between us crackling through the phone.

"I'd answer it, but then it would be even harder for me to sleep."

I laugh, knowing exactly what he means. "Probably me too. Maybe we save that for a night when we don't have to be functional so early in the morning."

"Yeah, maybe you can tell me about how you use your arsenal when you're alone, but not tonight," he says, his voice dropping to a playful whisper.

"Cole Waters, now what am I going to do with you?" I tease, half-serious, half-flirting.

"Whatever you want, because I would let you."

"Oh, the thoughts running through my head," I joke, trying to keep the conversation light. "Maybe I'll just ask you for a raise."

"Wow," he says, feigning hurt. "Is that all you want from me?"

"You know better than that."

"I do." He pauses, the mood shifting back to something tender. "We probably should get some sleep, and it will take me a little bit to come down off the high of even talking to you."

"Me too," I say, feeling that same mix of exhilaration and exhaustion. "Dream of me."

"Oh, I will. I miss you. I'll see your pretty face in the morning."

"Miss you too. Goodnight."

As I hang up, it strikes me that our "miss yous" could easily be "love yous." I know we'll get there eventually. I turn on some old, boring movie to fall asleep to and curl up with the pillow that smells like him, holding it close. The scent of Cole, the lingering warmth of our conversation, and the comfort of the familiar help me drift off faster than I expected.

CHAPTER TWENTY-ONE

THE SON CONVERSATIONS

T he next morning, when my alarm wakes me up, I'm pleasantly surprised by how well I slept. Maybe I really did need that decompression. I stretch, feeling more rested than I expected, and get out of bed to start my day. After washing my face and putting on some light makeup, I throw a cozy sweater over the tank top I slept in and make my way down to the office. It's a familiar routine, but there's a lingering sense of contentment from the night before that makes everything feel a little lighter.

I settle into my chair and, for the first time this morning, pick up my phone. As the screen lights up, I notice several notifications in the team chat. Curious, I unlock my phone to see what's been going on while I was still waking up.

Cole

Just a heads up, Pete is also jumping in the meeting today

Julio

Are we in trouble?

Cole

I sure hope not

Tara

Uggh, okay let me do my hair

Cole

I don't know that he cares that much about what you look like

Tara

Well I don't want to look like I just rolled out of bed

Cole

Fair

Mark

Sometimes I'm grateful I was born a man

Julio

Says all men

Tara

Then be nicer to us

Me

So many messages so early in the morning

Tara

?!?!?!

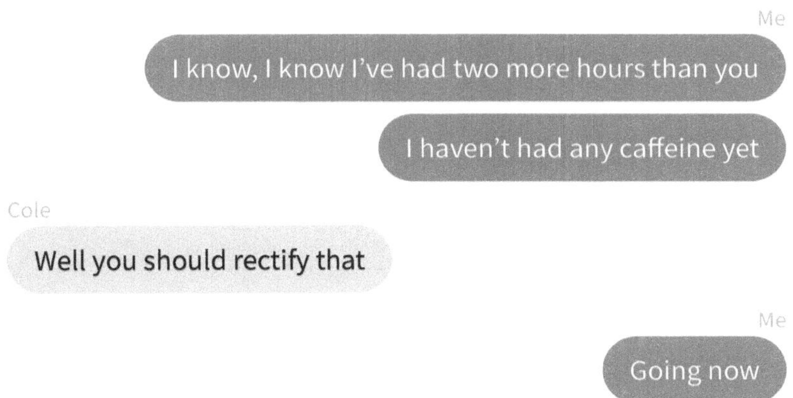

The house is quiet as I start the tea kettle, the familiar sound of boiling water adding a sense of calm to my morning. I lean against the counter and check my phone when I feel another notification come in.

I finish steeping my tea and head back to my office, where I test my camera, adjust the lighting, and go through all the usual rituals to get myself ready to go online. Once everything looks right, I log into the meeting a few minutes early. It's just Julio, Cole, and me at first.

"Hey there, Autumn," Julio greets me.

"Good morning, guys," I reply, smiling at them both.

"Good morning," Cole says, and I catch the warmth in his smile that makes my heart do a little flip.

Within about thirty seconds, the rest of the team joins the meeting, including Pete, who takes charge right away.

"Hey, guys. Cole, do you mind if I commandeer the beginning of this meeting?" Pete asks.

"Nope, go right ahead, sir," Cole says, taking a sip of his coffee.

Pete, who's older than the rest of us by a good fifteen or twenty years, exudes confidence. His weathered face and piercing blue eyes give him a wise, no-nonsense look, and though he's never come off as cocky to me, I can see how some might think so. With his blonde-gray hair and commanding presence, he's not someone you easily ignore.

"Okay," Pete begins, "I just wanted to drop in and say what a great conference you all just had and go over some plans going forward, including the proposal Cole has given me for a conference schedule."

We all nod in agreement as Pete continues.

"So, I only made one change to one of the conferences he proposed. Here's the list, and I'll send it out after the meeting with dates. First up, the third weekend of August, we'll have the Nashville conference. Cole, Mark, and Autumn will attend. Then, the second weekend in September in Miami, we'll send Tara, Julio, and Tom. Sorry, Tara, I know that's about as far as we can fly you, but I think you'll do well there."

"No worries," Tara says with a smile. "I'll be fine."

Pete continues, "Then, the fourth weekend in September, we'll send Cole, Autumn, and Julio to Chicago. Autumn, you might even get to sleep in your own bed." He laughs. "That was half the reason for the swap I made, just for the travel cost savings, even if it's just flights. But both Cole and Autumn should be able to drive."

I smile, appreciating the thoughtfulness. "I might appreciate my own bed over a hotel," I say.

Pete goes on with the list. "The third week in October, we'll send Tom, Tara, and Julio to Las Vegas. Sorry to the rest of you—I know that's a coveted destination," he says with a chuckle, and we all laugh. I know he swapped Cole and me out of Vegas to send us to Chicago instead, but nobody else would. "Then, the first weekend in November, Cole, Tara, and Mark can head to St. Louis. There's a break around the holidays when there aren't many conferences, and we don't want you all to travel anyway. So, the third weekend in January, Cole, Autumn, and Tom will head to Denver. Good luck with the snow and cold that time of year. And finally, the last conference until we start looking at spring, the second weekend of February, we'll send Autumn, Tara, and Mark to San Francisco. Tara, I wanted to check if that was okay since your wedding is just around the corner then."

Tara, with her charming Oklahoma accent, chimes in, "Nope, that'll be fine. It'll be a good distraction." We all laugh, easing the mood.

"Any objections to any of that?" Pete asks, looking around. We're all silent, nodding in agreement. "Cole, you okay with that one swap?"

"Yeah, no objections," Cole replies, sounding perfectly content, likely because the swap still has us working together.

"Now, onto less pleasant matters," Pete says, and I hold my breath a little. "About this business with Dr. Gabari..." I exhale as he continues, "I talked to Autumn last week, but I think Mark, Cole, Autumn, and I should all go meet up with him, and soon. I think if Cole and I show up too, it'll stroke his ego some and maybe ease some of the inappropriate pressure he's been putting on Autumn. I'm thinking next week, so I have my assistant reaching out to him to set up a dinner and a meeting. Any objections from those of you who need to travel for that?"

"No," I say, relieved. "I appreciate your help with this. I know it's a delicate situation."

"It is," Pete agrees. "If he were our employee, it would be different, but since he isn't, we have to handle it with kid gloves."

"I'm good with that," Mark says.

"Me too," Cole adds.

"Alright, that's settled. I'll let you know the details when I have them," Pete says. "Cole, I'm going to drop off now—the meeting is yours. Thanks for letting me intrude."

"Thanks, Pete," Cole says, and the rest of us exchange pleasantries as Pete leaves the call.

"Okay," Cole begins, once Pete has dropped off the call, "just making sure—nobody has any issues with the schedule? Tara, I know a couple of those trips might be rough for you."

"I'll be okay," Tara replies with her usual optimism. "For Miami, y'all already make me get up at the butt crack of dawn, and the one before the wedding will be a great distraction."

"Alright," Cole says with a laugh, "how are all the leads from last weekend going?"

We go around the virtual room, each of us giving updates on our leads and touching on a few personal notes—wedding plans, kids, spouses, and whatever else comes up in casual conversation. It's a relaxed, friendly atmosphere, and soon enough, we all sign off to tackle the rest of our day with clients and prospective clients.

Almost as soon as the meeting ends, my phone rings.

"Hey," I answer, smiling.

"Hey you," Cole says, his voice warm and familiar. "You good with that swap from Las Vegas to Chicago?"

I laugh. "Would it matter if I wasn't? But no, I'm good with it. It gives me an excuse to not need a hotel room and stay in yours."

"Autumn Flynn," he says in a mock accusatory tone, "do you think that's appropriate?"

"I honestly don't care if it's appropriate," I reply, laughing. "So, Nashville, Chicago, Denver, right?"

"Yeah, and I'll go to St. Louis without you, and you'll go to San Francisco without me."

"But I'll have Tara," I tease.

"Yes," he laughs, "you'll have Tara, although I'm hoping that's a little different."

"Oh, it's definitely different," I chuckle. "Are you upset he pulled us from Vegas?"

"No," Cole replies, his tone thoughtful. "Honestly, I'd rather do Vegas with you when we can really enjoy it, not just squeeze in a few experiences between conference events."

"I've never been to Vegas," I admit.

"Are you kidding me?" He sounds genuinely surprised.

"Nope, never."

"Well, then even more reason I want to take you there when we can really experience it and not just shove some experiences in between conference events."

"Are you a Vegas expert?" I ask, laughing at the thought.

"No, I've been a couple of times, but never the way I wanted to," he says. "I feel like with you, I might actually feel the magic."

"Isn't all the time you spend with me magical?" I tease.

"You have no idea how magical I think time with you is," he replies, his voice softening in that way that always makes my heart skip.

"I think I have an inkling," I say, smiling to myself, knowing how much we both treasure these moments.

The next few days settle into a comfortable routine. Good morning texts, goodnight phone calls, and little messages exchanged throughout the day. I snuggle with a pillow that still smells faintly like Cole, and it all starts to feel like a new normal, something I could really get used to.

Friday morning, however, brings a slight shift. Pete calls to let me know he's set up a meeting with Dr. Gabari for the following Tuesday and Wednesday. Tuesday night, we'll have dinner at a restaurant with Dr. Gabari and some of his staff, and on Wednesday, we'll spend time at the clinic. Almost as soon as I hang up with Pete, Cole calls.

"Hey, are you okay with Pete's plan?" he asks, concern in his voice.

"Yeah, I think so," I reply, feeling more resolved after hearing the details.

"I have another big meeting that day, so I might be a little late to the dinner. Just wanted you to know. I'll be there, but not at the start."

"I'll be okay," I say, laughing softly. "I'll have Mark and Pete."

"Yeah, you should be fine. Also, tonight's my dinner with the boys."

"Oh, right, it is Friday, isn't it?"

"It is," he confirms.

"How are you feeling? You nervous?" I ask, sensing a bit of anxiety from him.

"Kind of, yeah. Mostly about William. I think Tyler and Matthew will be fine; they'll probably wonder why I'm making such a big deal about it."

I chuckle. "Yeah, it's funny—when the kids start dating someone, they don't sit us down to tell us. I was thinking about that the other day."

"Yeah, I think we're more worried about them than they are about us," Cole says, the smile evident in his voice.

"I think that's good, though. It means we've taught them that we love them unconditionally, so they aren't as worried about our approval."

"True, I can see that," he agrees.

"When and where is this dinner?" I ask.

"We're going to this little Mexican restaurant down the street. It's a hole in the wall, but we've gone there for years for celebrations. We're meeting around six."

"Okay, make sure you get any major life updates from them first," I tease.

"I probably should, but they know I want to tell them something, so they may not give me the opportunity."

"I guess you'll find out," I say, smiling.

We hang up, and I go about my normal afternoon. Around fifteen minutes before six, I text Cole, telling him I'm thinking of him and wishing him good luck. He thanks me, and I don't hear from him again until after nine.

My phone rings, and I answer it immediately, feeling a bit anxious.

"Hey," I say.

"Hey, Autumn," Cole replies, but I can tell something's off.

"What's wrong?" I ask, my heart sinking.

He sighs heavily. "It went a lot like I thought it might. Matthew and Tyler are good—Tyler's actually elated—but William, William is not okay."

"Cole, I'm so sorry."

"It's not your fault, don't be sorry. He held it together in front of his brothers, but once they left, he really let me have it. Asked how I could do this to his mom, all the things I feared he might say. It's just... it's so hard, Autumn. Michelle and I have been separated for over a decade. How can he still have this much magical thinking left?"

"I don't know," I say gently, "and I don't think you can change it overnight. All you can do is love him through it."

Cole sighs again, sounding weary. "I probably said things I shouldn't have said tonight. About Michelle, about myself."

"You might have," I acknowledge, "but you can apologize or reframe it. I'd do it soon, though."

"I told him I'd call him in the morning."

"Maybe you should do something with him tomorrow," I suggest. "What do you do with your boys? Play golf? Go fishing?" I laugh softly. "How do I not know this?"

Cole chuckles a little. "Not much of that, especially not with William. But there's a car show tomorrow in Indianapolis. Maybe we can wander around and talk."

"I think that's a stellar idea."

"But I was thinking about driving up to see you," he says, and I can hear the longing in his voice.

"I'll be here," I say gently. "And I'll see you on Tuesday if not before. It won't go over well if you rush away from whatever you're doing with him to drive to me."

"You're right, as always," he says, resigned.

"Cole, I'm not always right."

"So far, you are," he insists. "Let me text him."

The phone goes silent for a minute, and then Cole says, "Okay, he's good with the car show. It's not really my thing, but it is his, so maybe we can bond a bit and reset."

"That's a good idea. Also, are you telling me that maybe I can win him over with the Audi?"

I catch Cole off guard, and he snickers. "Yeah, Autumn, that might actually help, as ridiculous as it sounds."

"See? I knew my brother gave me that car for a reason."

"I want to kiss you right now," he sighs.

"I would like that too. You're so far away, and your smell is fading from this pillow."

"Soon," he promises. "Are you staying in a hotel for the Dr. Gabari meeting?"

"I don't think so, unless I stay in yours."

"Well, maybe plan on that, or I can come and make your bed smell like me again."

"I could bring the pillow with me," I laugh. "On another note, we have that next week, then like ten days later, Nashville. I was thinking, if you want to arrange a weekend here with your kids, maybe we do it the weekend after Nashville or the one after that?"

"Isn't that Labor Day?" he asks.

"Oh, you're right, it is. That might make it even better. What do you think?"

"I think that sounds like a good tentative plan. Let me talk to the boys."

"Yeah, whatever you need to do. But it would be a good weekend to do a pool barbecue and all that. If they have girlfriends or friends, that's fine too—whatever makes it easier on them."

"You're amazing, Autumn. I'll talk to them and let you know."

"I'll have Megan and Sami invite some friends, give them some female incentive."

"You do not talk like the mother of girls," he laughs.

"I've had a few years of practice being the mother of both girls and a boy."

"This is true."

"But seriously, a pool party with college-age girls? Come on."

"You're playing dirty, Ms. Flynn."

"I'm just using the assets I have at my disposal. I think that's just good business sense. I'm trying to sell your boys on something, am I not?"

"You are, and I can't believe I've never thought of it that way."

"Maybe thinking like the amazing salesman you are will help you tomorrow. Pull some emotion out of it, but not too much. He's your son, your oldest son, and you love him."

"You continue to amaze me," he sighs.

"I just care about you and want to make your life easier."

"Autumn, I adore you. You may see me tomorrow night yet."

"We'll see. I wouldn't complain, but William is more important tomorrow."

"He is, but we'll see. I can sacrifice some sleep."

I laugh, "I'm sure you can—I've seen it."

We talk for a few more minutes, saying our goodnights. Once again, I fall asleep hugging my Cole-scented pillow, feeling the mix of hope and longing that seems to have become my constant companions.

When I wake up the next morning I already have a text from Cole. I slept in and he did not.

Cole

> Good morning beautiful

> Meeting William in about thirty, I'll have my phone but I might be slow

The texts came in over an hour ago, but I respond anyway.

Me

> Sorry, I slept in - Have fun! I'll be around when you're done

I get up and start my usual Saturday routine—brewing a cup of tea, tossing some laundry in the wash, and just moving through the morning at an easy pace. It's comforting to sink into the familiar tasks, letting my mind wander as I fold clothes and tidy up the house.

Megan comes down after a while, and we chat for a bit before she heads out to meet up with friends. It's nice to have those little moments with her, just touching base before she goes off to do her own thing.

Almost two hours pass before my phone buzzes with a new message from Cole. My heart does a little flip as I reach for it, eager to hear how things are going with him and William.

Cole

> Hey there, it's going well I think, but still not where I'd like to be

Me

> It'll take time, you just want him open and talking to you

Cole

> Yeah, we're there

Me

> Just enjoy time with him

This Saturday would have felt perfectly normal just a few weeks ago, but now it feels oddly quiet. The kids aren't around, Cara is off spending time with her own family, and Cole is busy with his boys. The stillness of the day makes me feel restless, anxious even, in a way I haven't felt in a while. I try to shake off the unease by picking up a book and curling up in the family room to read. The words help a little, offering a brief escape, but it's not the same as having Cole or the kids around.

A little after five, my phone rings. It's Cole.

"Hey you," I answer, feeling my mood lift just hearing his voice.

"Hey, Autumn. I just wanted you to know that I'm taking William to dinner. It has been a good day. As much as I want to, I don't think I'm going to make it up there tonight."

"It's fine," I say, pausing to let him hear the smile in my voice. "I may be more patient than you think I am."

"You may be, but I am not patient," he replies with a chuckle.

"Tuesday," I remind him, laughing softly. "You just have to wait until Tuesday. Where are you going to eat?"

"His favorite steakhouse," Cole says, "hoping to score some points that way."

"Well, you enjoy. You can call or text later—I'll be here."

"I miss you, Autumn."

"Miss you too," I reply, adding a quiet "I love you" after I disconnect the call.

I spend the next few hours reading, making myself a simple dinner, and taking a long shower to unwind. Megan texts to let me know she won't be home until after midnight, so I settle into bed with a home improvement show playing softly in the background. Around nine, my phone rings again. It's Cole.

"Hey," I answer, feeling the familiar warmth that comes with hearing his voice.

"Hey, how are you?" he asks.

"I'm good," I say, laughing a little. "It was a really quiet day, which would have been normal a couple of weeks ago, but it's weird now."

"I can understand that," he says, laughing with me.

"How did dinner go?" I ask, shifting the conversation.

"It went well. I think we're in a good place, or at least, I got him to a good place. He's willing to come and meet you and your kids, give it a chance. He still has this fantasy that his mom and I will end up together. I don't know if anything will change that. Her parade of men certainly hasn't. Maybe this will."

"I'm glad it went well," I say, relieved for him.

"Me too," he says, then pauses. "Autumn?"

"Cole?"

"Do you think you could come down this way and have dinner with just William and me next weekend?"

"Yeah, I probably could. You don't want to include the others?"

"I think the other two will thrive in the chaos of your kitchen. I'm not sure William will. I think it might be better if he meets you more privately."

"I don't think there will be any issue with that, Cole," I say, smiling. "And then I can see your bachelor pad," I tease.

"I'm looking forward to you making my bed smell like you," he replies, his voice heavy with suggestive undertones.

A rush of warmth spreads through me, and I laugh. "Don't get me all hot and bothered if you're not here to do anything about it."

"You have your arsenal," he teases, his laughter a little wicked.

"I do, but I'd rather have you."

"I'd rather you have me too," he admits, "and this conversation is turning me on a little too much."

"Oh yeah?"

"Yeah, the things I want to do with you."

"Cole, I want you to do all the things with me," I say, my voice dipping into a more sultry tone.

"You're killing me, Autumn."

"I don't think that's death you're feeling," I tease.

Cole laughs. "No, but it's something I'm going to have to take care of before I sleep."

"Me too, I'm afraid. Just think of me—I'll think of you."

"There's no one else I would picture at this point. It's all you, all Autumn, all the time."

"I fucking miss you," I say, laughing at how much I mean it.

"I miss fucking you," he replies, his voice rich with desire.

"Cole Waters, why I never," I say in mock offense.

"Don't act like you don't remember asking me to fuck you that first night," he laughs.

"Oh, I do, and I'm sure I'll do it again," I say, matter-of-factly.

"I won't mind if you do."

"I'm sure you won't. You didn't complain then either."

"Tuesday can't come fast enough," he says with a sigh.

"I agree. I do miss you."

"I know. I miss you too. I'm going to go take a cold shower," he says, and we both laugh. "I'll talk to you in the morning?"

"Yeah, I'll talk to you in the morning."

We hang up, and I'm left feeling incredibly turned on. Without hesitation, I reach for my favorite rabbit from the nightstand and take care of myself—twice—all while imagining Cole's hands on me, his voice in my ear. Afterward, I drift off to sleep, still clutching the pillow that carries his scent, the longing for him fading into my dreams.

I want to hear about your fantasies

Cole

I will tell you, but not until I can see you

Me

Would it help if I told you I used my favorite rabbit to take care of myself last night after we got off the phone?

Cole

Fuck, Autumn, what are you doing to me?

Me

I don't know what I'm doing to you, but I know what you're doing to me

And what I want you to do to me

Cole

Oh, please share

Me

What was it you just said? Not until I can see you

Cole

That is what I said

Me

So ditto

Cole

I feel like you are quickly becoming my whole world

Me

Also ditto

The three dots linger on my screen, and just as I start wondering what's taking him so long, my phone rings instead—I smile.

"Yes?" I answer in a flirtatious tone.

"Autumn," Cole almost rasps, his voice more serious than the playful one I used. He pauses, and I can almost hear the weight of what he's about to say. "I really wanted to do this in person—"

I quickly interrupt him, thinking I know exactly where this is heading. As much as I want to hear those words, I want them face-to-face. "So wait. I think I even know what you're going to say, but wait."

"You think you know, huh?" he teases, though there's a hint of curiosity in his voice.

"Yeah, I mean, I could be wrong, but I'll see you in three days."

"Seriously, woman, what am I going to do with you?"

"Hopefully keep me," I reply with a smile he can probably hear.

"That is my plan."

"Mine too," I say, letting the conversation settle back into something lighter. "What are you doing today?"

"Just normal weekend stuff—laundry, packing for the trip to Chicago."

"Are you going to stay at a hotel or with me?" I ask, the question coming out more suggestively than I intended.

"Either way, I'm staying with you," he laughs. "But where do you want me?"

"Well, that's a loaded question," I laugh, "Maybe back in my pool."

"Back in your pool, huh?"

"Maybe," I admit, blushing even though he can't see me. "That was... let's just go with intensely satisfying."

"Oh, I know," he says, a hint of pride in his voice. "Even if I hadn't known, your body told me so."

"I know it did," I reply, trying to keep it light. "In that rare occurrence of extreme client satisfaction."

"I think you using business language to describe sex might be hotter than you mean it to be," he laughs.

"Probably," I laugh. "But anyway, my house or a hotel?"

"I think you just sold me on your house."

"There's no guarantee Megan won't be here."

"I know, but there's a chance."

"There is a chance."

Eventually, we get off the phone, and I go about the rest of my Sunday. I spend some time reading, trying to distract myself from the growing anticipation. Megan and I have a quiet dinner together, where she asks about my week. I fill her in on the plans for Tuesday and Wednesday, mentioning that we might stay in Chicago or come back home. She's fine with either, but her focus quickly shifts to what I'm going to wear to the dinner.

"Um, maybe that green dress I took to Dallas," I say.

"Mom, isn't that the one you were wearing when Cole totally fell head over heels for you?" she asks with a knowing grin.

"I don't know if that's exactly how it went, but yeah."

"You should wear something else, save that for another sentimental occasion. What about that blue dress? It's sexy and more formal."

I know the one she's talking about. It's strapless, with a corset top that turns my eyes a striking shade of teal.

"I'm trying not to make this doctor think he has a chance, Megs," I say, considering her suggestion.

"Well, the blue dress and the green dress send the same message, so I say go with the blue. Are you sure it's that formal?"

"I think so. It's in the MVP dining room of a really nice restaurant."

"Well, take that cute black cardigan. It can keep you warm and make it look more casual if you need to."

"That's a good idea, Megan. I guess I will wear the blue one."

"Are there going to be other women there?" she asks.

"Pete is bringing his wife, and Nicole, the nurse practitioner, will be there, at least, if not more."

"Okay, cool, so you won't be the lone female."

"No, I shouldn't be."

"You should find out what Pete's wife is wearing if you can."

"I might do that tomorrow," I say, thinking that's actually a solid plan.

Later, as has become the norm in my new routine, Cole calls just as I'm settling down to sleep.

"Hey you," I answer, feeling instantly calmer.

"Hi, beautiful. How are you?"

"I'm good, tired but good. You?"

"Glad we're this much closer to Tuesday," he laughs.

"Yeah, me too."

We chat about our days, updating each other on the usual—kids, work, life in general. It's comforting, these nightly talks, and even when we're apart, they help me feel connected to him in a way that nothing else does.

"Goodnight, Autumn. I miss you," he says softly.

"Miss you too. Goodnight," I reply, the unspoken "I love you" sitting on the tip of my tongue as I hang up.

I fall asleep easily, still holding onto the pillow that smells like him, knowing that in just a few days, I won't need it as a substitute.

CHAPTER TWENTY-TWO
THE BLUE DRESS

The next morning unfolds with our usual team meeting, marking the start of a typical Monday. During the meeting, Cole informs the team that he'll be driving up to Chicago on Tuesday afternoon for our dinner with Dr. Gabari. He mentions that he has a meeting that will run right up to the start of dinner, so Mark and I are expected to join Pete without him initially. Although he had already told me all this, the realization hits me that I won't see him before the dinner on Tuesday, and it leaves me feeling a little unsettled.

Almost immediately after the meeting ends, my phone rings. It's Cole.

"I was just going to call you," I say as I pick up.

"Oh, were you?" he teases.

"Yeah, it hit me during the meeting that I won't see you until we're already at dinner."

"Yeah, I know. That might be interesting," he replies, his voice playful but with a hint of something more.

"Interesting, huh?" I ask, adding a little extra inflection to my voice.

"Yeah, but we'll figure it out. You know it's formal, right?"

"Uh, yeah," I say, relieved that I had the foresight to ask Pete's wife what she's wearing. "I was going to ask Pete to talk to his wife to see what she was wearing, but I have a cocktail dress I'm planning to wear."

"Okay, yeah. Pete and I are going full suit. I told Mark too, so it's not just pants and a blazer or sport coat, but a full suit."

"Yeah, like a step below a tuxedo," I laugh.

"Exactly, so I just wanted to make sure you got the memo too."

"You'll probably be sexy in a suit," I say flirtatiously.

"Autumn Flynn, will you stop making this even harder?" he groans, but there's a smile in his voice.

"This or you?" I laugh.

"Woman, what am I going to do with you? Seriously. And I don't know what you'll be wearing tomorrow, but my guess is you'll be the sexiest person in the room."

"I was in a bit of debate about that," I admit, "I didn't want to give Dr. Gabari more eye candy than necessary, but then I decided I didn't care."

"Oh yeah?"

"Yeah, Megan helped me decide which dress to wear. I think it's a good choice. I may see if Mark and I can meet up first, though, so I'm not walking in alone."

"I think Pete has a plan for that too. I'll just be the one lagging behind you. I'm assuming you're not taking your SUV?"

"No, I have to let the valets have some fun too," I laugh.

"Yeah, you're going to pull up and turn heads for sure," he laughs.

"My brother would be proud," I chuckle, "That was his whole intent when he gave me the car—for exactly this kind of occasion."

"He would be proud. You should tell him," Cole laughs.

"I will, after the fact."

Cole laughs too. "I can't wait to see you."

"But, unfortunately, you have to."

"Yes, unfortunately."

"Are you getting a hotel room at all?" I ask.

"I am. I'll go and do my meeting there before dinner."

"I was thinking about it—I think we should just go to the hotel."

"Yeah? Why is that? What happened to the pool?" He sounds a bit disappointed.

"I'm more thinking of logistics and time," I say.

"Yeah?"

"Why waste time driving when I could spend it with you?"

"I get that, but," he hesitates.

"But?"

"I'm staying at the same hotel as Mark and Pete, so that may raise red flags, and I have a funny feeling you will not be unnoticeable tomorrow night," he says, and I blush even though he can't see me.

I sigh. "Okay, what time are we getting to the practice on Wednesday?"

"Well, luckily, Pete has a board meeting in the morning, so we won't go to the practice until around eleven."

"Okay, so what about your clothes?" I laugh. "You can't wear the same suit the next day."

"This is true. Let me think about that—you may have to take me back to the hotel."

"I mean, that's where I'm supposed to be taking you anyway, right? We'll figure it out."

"That is where you would be taking me anyway," he laughs. "Also, just so you know, I'm going to reserve us adjoining rooms in Nashville—to avoid all this."

"Oh yeah? How are you going to professionally make that request?" I laugh.

"I'm going to ask that we have three rooms all together and preferably two of them adjoining. Then we just have to make sure we get the adjoining ones."

"We'll see how that works, but I like the way you're thinking."

"I'm trying," he sighs.

"Any more thoughts about telling Pete?" I ask gently.

"No, I still think we should wait. I know it's a risk, but I'm just not ready to let those two worlds collide all the way yet," he says, sounding torn.

"I understand. I trust you."

"I'm glad you trust me." He pauses. "I could talk to you all day, but I have to get to this other meeting in a couple of minutes."

"Okay, I'll talk to you later."

"Yes, you will."

We hang up, and I dive into my workday, responding to emails and making phone calls that I've been putting off over the last few weeks. It's a busy day, and I manage to distract myself fully with work. By the time the workday ends, I'm ready for dinner with Cara and Megan. When Cole calls me later in the evening, I'm thoroughly exhausted but happy to hear from him.

"So, here's my thought," Cole says with a playful tone, "you bring stuff just in case, I'll have a bag ready to grab too, and whatever happens, happens."

I laugh, shaking my head. "I'm glad you said you have a thought because that isn't a plan."

"No, no it's not," he admits, chuckling. "But we'll have to see what happens. I think we're going to have to go with the flow."

"Okay, I guess we'll see what happens," I reply, feeling the excitement bubbling up for what's to come.

"No matter what happens, I'm getting a piece of you tomorrow," he says, his voice laced with confidence and a hint of something more seductive.

"Well, aren't you just sure of yourself?" I tease.

"Pretty confident at this point," he laughs.

"We'll see if you're on good behavior," I warn playfully.

"I'm planning on not being on good behavior," he responds, the grin evident in his voice.

"Cole Waters, you are going to corrupt my innocence," I say, trying to keep a straight face.

He laughs deeply, the sound filling me with warmth. "I'm excited to see you," I add, my tone softening.

"Me too. I miss you."

"Yeah, I miss you too. One more night. Then I'll see you this weekend too, to meet William."

"Yeah, I'm excited for that too."

"Good," I say, smiling to myself. "Maybe this will stop feeling like a whirlwind at some point."

Cole laughs again. "Maybe."

We eventually get off the phone, and I settle in for the night.

The next day is a whirlwind in itself, filled with preparations leading up to dinner. Mark texts me with a plan—we will meet in the lobby of the restaurant, and he will arrive early to ensure I shouldn't have any awkward moments alone with Dr. Gabari.

I slip into my blue cocktail dress, feeling a thrill of confidence as I look in the mirror. The dress is elegant, with a maxi-length asymmetrical skirt and a slit that teases at my mid-thigh. The strapless top, with its hidden boning and built-in corset, gives me all the support I need, so I ditch the bra and opt for black strappy heels that give me just enough height to keep the dress from dragging.

I curl my hair into soft waves, and with Megan's help, we style it into a waterfall braid that leaves the length flowing down my back. I go a bit heavier on the makeup, just enough to last through the evening without looking overdone. A silver and sapphire tennis bracelet graces one wrist, while a delicate silver necklace with a heart pendant and matching earrings complete the look. I slip on my watch and grab a small clutch for my phone, ready to head out.

Before I leave, I ask Megan what she thinks. She grins and tells me I look stunning, snapping a few pictures to send to her siblings and her uncle.

"Mom, I don't know how Cole is going to not touch you," she laughs. "He's like a magnet to you when you're in leggings and a t-shirt."

"I don't know, Megs, guess we'll see," I laugh back.

I back the Audi out of the garage, and Megan closes the door behind me as I leave. I've packed an overnight bag with clothes for the clinic tomorrow, just in case. As Cole said, we'll see what happens. He calls me as I'm getting on the freeway.

"You on your way?" he asks.

"I am. I'm on track to be there right when Mark is expecting me."

"Okay, I'm about to go into this meeting. I'll see you soon."

"I can't wait," I say, the excitement clear in my voice.

"Me either. The anticipation may kill me."

"Well, Megan thinks seeing me may kill you," I laugh.

"I think you're just going to kill me, period, Autumn," he sighs with a playful exasperation. "But dead or alive, I'll see you soon."

As I hang up, I can't help but smile, the anticipation of seeing him again making the drive feel both too long and too short. The night ahead is full of possibilities, and I can't wait to see how it all unfolds.

I arrive at the restaurant exactly when Mark is expecting me. As I pull up, the valet swiftly opens my door and offers his hand to help me out. When he calls me "miss" instead of "ma'am," it brings a small, unexpected smile to my face.

As I walk into the restaurant, I spot Mark, who immediately shakes his head with a grin.

"Autumn, you're supposed to be making this guy *not* want to say inappropriate things to you," he laughs.

"But I'm also supposed to be formal." I shrug with a playful smile.

"Cole is going to have a heart attack when he sees you," Mark says, and for a moment, I'm at a loss for how to respond. Thankfully, Pete and his wife, Laura, arrive just then, sparing me from having to think of a reply.

"Autumn," Pete greets me, giving me a quick, appraising look—not in a way that makes me uncomfortable, but enough to notice. "It's so good to meet you in person. This is my wife, Laura."

"Very nice to meet you, Laura," I say, shaking her hand warmly.

Pete speaks briefly with the hostess, and we're led to a private dining room where it's just the four of us for the time being.

"My understanding is Dr. Gabari is bringing several of his staff," Pete says as we settle in. "I wanted us to get here first, so we were somewhat established before he arrived. Autumn, the plan is for Cole and me to sit next to you at the table so we can provide the best protection, if you will, that way. I talked to Cole about it but didn't get the chance to mention it to you. Sorry about that. I'm hoping he'll be here earlier than he thought."

Laura takes a moment to compliment me, her tone genuine. "You look lovely. I can see why you're having to beat them away with sticks."

"Oh, you're so sweet. You look gorgeous too," I reply, feeling a little self-conscious under the attention.

"I might, honey," she says with a smile, "but I'm about fifteen years older than you, and it shows. I'm sure you're a huge asset on the sales team. Even though it shouldn't be about looks, it never hurts."

I can feel the warmth rising in my cheeks. I've never thought of myself as unattractive, but I've never really considered myself beautiful either. When people focus on my appearance, it makes me a bit uncomfortable.

"How did you ever do that to your hair?" Laura asks, admiring my hairstyle. "Did you go to a salon?"

"No, I have a twenty-year-old daughter who lives with me. She comes in handy for things like this," I laugh.

"Oh, I can imagine," she chuckles.

Just then, Dr. Gabari and his team walk in. Pete subtly positions himself slightly in front of me but off-center, taking the lead in making introductions around the room. Dr. Gabari is a bit more restrained than he was in Dallas, but I can still feel his gaze as he looks me up and down before shaking my hand.

He leans in just close enough to whisper, "You look stunning, Autumn," before moving on to greet Mark. Thankfully, he doesn't linger in front of me as I had feared.

As the introductions continue, my watch vibrates, alerting me to a new message. I glance down discreetly to read it.

Well, Mark thinks you look so good he had to warn me about it, I think you should find a reason to head to the ladies room

"Excuse me," I say, "work message," taking my phone out of my clutch.

"No problem, Autumn, do what you need to do," Pete says.

Why would he feel like he needs to warn you? Lol He said something weird to me too, and okay, but only because it's you asking me to

"Hey, Pete, I need to take this real quick. I'll be right back," I say, trying to keep my voice steady.

"Okay, Autumn. We'll save your seat along with Cole's," Pete replies with an understanding nod. "Take your time."

I walk slowly toward the lobby, phone in hand, and just as I near the restrooms, I feel a hand wrap around my wrist. Startled, I turn and find Cole gently pulling me into a small, secluded room. It's likely an old payphone area, now unused and out of sight. His left hand slides around my waist, and his right still holds my wrist as he draws me closer.

"Well, hello," I say, a little breathlessly, caught off guard but thrilled to see him.

He pushes me away just enough to take a long, slow look at me, his eyes raking from my feet all the way up to my face. The hunger in his gaze is undeniable, but coming from him, it's a look I don't mind one bit.

"Hi," he finally says, his voice low and warm. "You're tall tonight."

"Heels." I shrug with a small smile.

He runs his thumb along my jawline and pulls me into a kiss. It's not long, but it's enough to quench a bit of the longing that's been building between us. When he leans back, I instinctively reach up to wipe his mouth.

"You've got a little lip gloss on you," I say, smiling as I wipe it away. His eyes meet mine, and though he's not smiling, there's an intensity in his gaze that sends a shiver through me.

"You okay?" I ask softly, noticing the seriousness in his expression.

"Yeah," he says, his voice steady. "I just don't know what I'm going to do with you. You are absolutely stunning tonight. There's probably not a man in this restaurant who isn't looking at you."

"Well, you're the only one going home with me," I reply, giving him a reassuring smile.

"Thank God for that," he murmurs, his relief evident.

"What does Mark know?" I ask as I reach up to fix the collar on his jacket and straighten his tie, trying to keep the moment light.

"I'll tell you about that later, but not everything," he says, brushing a stray curl back into place.

"Are we walking back in there together?" I ask with a grin.

"Yeah, well, not *together*, together, you know what I mean." He laughs.

He pulls me in for a careful hug, his hand trailing down my back, leaving a trail of warmth in its wake. I quickly check to make sure there's no makeup smudged on him, and then, with a final glance, we head back to the private dining room. He places his hand on the small of my back as he opens the door, and together—but not too together—we walk in, ready to face the evening ahead.

CHAPTER TWENTY-THREE
THE NIGHT OF TOO MUCH WINE

"Look what the cat dragged in," I say with a playful smirk as we walk into the room, gesturing toward Cole.

"Cole!" Pete exclaims, his voice full of warmth. "I'm so glad you could make it."

As Cole shakes hands with everyone, I take a moment to admire him from a distance. He looks incredibly sexy in a dark gray suit with subtle pinstripes, a stark white shirt, and a royal blue tie that matches my dress almost perfectly. The sight of him sends a rush of warmth through me, a mix of pride and desire that's hard to ignore.

We all take our seats at the dinner table. Laura ends up on my right instead of Pete, with Cole on my left. This seating arrangement makes me feel a bit more comfortable, especially with Dr. Gabari seated almost directly across from me. As the servers circulate, offering us a choice of red or white wine, Cole and I both opt for the white. I take a sip as soon as my glass is poured, hoping it will help settle my nerves.

"That is a beautiful tennis bracelet," Laura comments as I set my glass down.

"Thank you," I reply, smiling. "It was a gift from my brother for my fortieth birthday. Sapphires are my favorite stone."

"Did he give you the necklace and earrings too?" she asks, clearly interested.

"The earrings, yes. The necklace, no. It was my grandmother's."

"They're all beautiful," she says with genuine admiration. "And by the way, you don't look over forty."

"Thank you, that's sweet," I say, feeling a little flattered.

While Laura and I chat, Cole leans in toward me, prompting me to lean in as well. His hand gently lands on my upper arm as he turns slightly away from the table and whispers in my ear, "Tony did talk about you while you were gone. Just stick close to me tonight."

His breath on my ear sends the usual electricity through me, but his protective tone leaves me feeling warm, but also a little anxious. When he looks back at me, his eyes lock onto mine with an intensity that's both comforting and serious.

"Understand?" he asks, but it's clear this is more of a command than a question. Whatever was said while I was out of the room has left him visibly tense, maybe even angry.

I nod and quietly say, "Yeah," before taking another sip of my wine, trying to mask the sudden spike in tension with the warmth of the alcohol.

The servers move efficiently, refilling my glass as needed and bringing out baskets of bread. I pull my chair a little closer to the table, wanting to maintain some semblance of grace despite the increasing anxiety. As I adjust, I suddenly become aware that the slit in my dress is facing Cole. His hand discreetly finds its way onto my bare thigh under the tablecloth, and I can feel the heat of his touch. Without drawing attention, I switch my wine glass to my left hand and drop my right hand into my lap, placing it over his, keeping the connection between us while maintaining the facade of casual conversation.

Laura and I continue to talk about children, jewelry, and fashion, while Cole discusses business with Mark. I'm grateful that I'm not being pulled into conversation with Tony, at least for now. When our food arrives, Cole reluctantly withdraws his hand to eat, which is both a relief and a disappointment. I miss the physical connection, but I also don't want him to get into any trouble with Pete.

"Autumn," Nicole says from across the table, drawing attention back to me. "I have to know if you did your hair yourself."

Before I can respond, Laura jumps in, "I asked her that already—her daughter did it for her." I smile at both women, appreciating Laura's camaraderie.

"You have kids?" Nicole asks, sounding genuinely surprised.

"I do," I reply, smiling warmly. "I have three—twenty-two, twenty, and eighteen."

Just as I finish speaking, Tony stuns the entire table into silence asking, "Their dad out of the picture?"

The silence is thick, and it's clear no one knows how to respond. After a moment, I muster a calm reply. "Not out of their picture, no."

Sensing the awkwardness, Laura quickly shifts the conversation, turning to Cole. "You have three kids too, right?"

Cole's hand finds my thigh again under the table, grounding me as he answers. "Yes, I have three as well. They're close in age to Autumn's." He glances at me, and our eyes meet for a moment that feels just a bit too long, filled with unspoken words.

As the conversation resumes around the table, Laura leans in closer to me, her voice low and apologetic. "That was awful. I am so sorry."

I shrug, trying to brush it off. "That's part of why you and Pete are here tonight. He's been saying things like that."

As we wrap up our meal, Pete stands up and walks over to where Cole and Mark are sitting. He leans down between them, and they both turn toward him for a conversation that, judging by their body language, is serious. I know I'll hear about it later, but for now, I focus on the mini-dessert buffet the restaurant has set up, along with coffee, tea, and more wine. We all get up from the table to mingle, and I can't help but notice Pete heading straight for Tony, with Cole and Mark close behind.

Laura and I gravitate toward the desserts, but our attention is clearly divided as we watch the unfolding conversation. From a distance, it looks tame, but the tension in the air is palpable.

"I think he crossed the line too many times for Pete with that last question," Laura says, her voice low but firm.

"I hope so," I reply, feeling a surge of relief that someone else sees how inappropriate Tony has been. "And I hope Dr. Gabari listens."

We pretend to focus on the desserts, taking turns glancing over at the conversation. Laura and I quietly narrate to each other what we observe, turning the situation into a sort of covert operation. It's oddly comforting to have this kind of interaction with another woman, especially in a situation that's been so tense.

I see Cole's body language tense up a couple of times, his shoulders stiffening as he listens to Tony. Pete seems to notice too because he places a calming hand on Cole's arm and says something that makes Cole back away slightly, though he doesn't go far. Cole turns and looks at me, and I offer him a soft, reassuring smile before turning my attention back to Laura.

"I've known Cole a long time," Laura says thoughtfully, her eyes on the men. "He would never behave the way Dr. Gabari did, but I can tell he's a little smitten with you."

My heart skips a beat. This is Pete's wife—how do I even begin to respond to that?

I clear my throat, trying to keep my voice steady. "Cole is a gentleman, for sure. He and I have bonded a lot over the last couple of years. I know this is upsetting to him. He was my knight in shining armor in Dallas when this all started."

"I'm sure he was," Laura replies with a knowing smile. "Cole deserves some happiness. He's been broody and alone since I first met him, but you're right—he is a gentleman, such a sweetheart. There's just something about the way he looks at you. I think he adores you."

I can feel the heat rising in my cheeks, and I'm at a loss for words. "Laura," I begin cautiously, "you know he's my boss, right?"

"Yes, I know that," she says with a laugh, her eyes twinkling. "But where there's a will... " She trails off with a singsong tone and a shrug.

I can't believe this conversation is happening. To cover my flustered state, I ask for more wine and down it a bit too quickly. As I'm trying to collect myself, Nicole approaches us with a cautious look.

"I'm so sorry about that," Nicole says, her voice tinged with concern.

"It's not your fault," I assure her, shaking my head. "I'm just hoping tomorrow at the clinic is a little better."

Nicole offers a small, hopeful smile. "I think it will be."

Eventually, Pete and Mark finish their conversation with Tony and update Cole, before they approach us. Pete wraps an arm around Laura, and they exchange pleasantries with Nicole. Then Pete looks at Nicole with a more serious expression.

"Can you excuse us for just a minute, Nicole? We need to talk to Autumn."

"Certainly," Nicole replies, stepping away gracefully.

I take another sip of my wine as Nicole walks away, trying to brace myself for whatever Pete has to say next. He turns to me, his expression serious but with a hint of frustration. "I think we have him where he should be, but he is a persistent prick."

I glance down at my wine glass, feeling a mix of relief and unease.

"I read your email to him about the roses, and so did Cole," Pete continues. "We both thought it was pretty clear, but Tony, well, he thought it left the door open. I had to have Cole back off because he was getting a little heated." Pete laughs, but there's no humor in it. "Mark and I set him straight, though. We made it clear that you're not interested, and even if you were, it would be an unethical boundary to cross."

"So, tomorrow?" I ask, already dreading the next day's encounter.

"Tomorrow," Pete says, pausing as he searches for the right words. "Tone down the wardrobe." He immediately winces as Laura smacks him in the chest. "Okay, that was the wrong choice of words. I'm not victim-blaming, I promise. But maybe wear something more conservative and uninviting. Not because you should have to make yourself less appealing," Pete pauses as Cole snickers without humor and rolls his eyes, "but it can't hurt. Cole, Mark, and I will all be there. We can't stop him from saying some things, but we can stop him from touching you or from saying everything he's thinking."

"This is just wrong," Laura interjects, her voice filled with frustration. "Have you talked to Lauryn about this?"

"I haven't, but I will," Pete responds, sounding a bit defensive.

Laura looks directly at Cole, her tone softening but with a clear edge of protectiveness. "You need to protect her at all costs."

Cole's expression hardens as he looks at me and then back at Laura. He crosses his arms over his chest, a clear sign of resolve. "I will, even if it means losing a client."

Pete sighs, a hint of resignation in his voice. "I wasn't sure how much of what I was hearing was exaggerated," he says, "but after what he said when you left the room, and what he said across the table, it's just wildly inappropriate."

"What did he say when I left the room?" I ask, feeling a chill run down my spine.

There's an uncomfortable silence as Mark, Pete, and Laura exchange glances. Finally, Cole breaks the tension. "I'll tell you later," he says, and I feel a collective sigh of relief from everyone.

"Mark told you?" Pete asks, directing the question at Cole.

"Yeah," Cole replies, his tone grim. "Almost as soon as I walked in the room."

Pete nods, then forces a smile onto his face as he suggests, "Okay, let's go mingle. We still have a job to do."

Mark heads off toward Dr. Gabari's staff, while Pete turns to Cole with one last directive. "Seriously, if we lose him as a client, we lose him. Don't let him treat her that way."

"I have no intention of letting him get close to her," Cole assures him.

Pete gives a final nod and moves off to mingle, Laura following closely behind. Cole starts to walk away too, but I grab his arm, turning him toward me.

"What did he say? Why are they all acting like this?" I ask, the anxiety in my voice hard to hide.

Cole looks at me, his expression softening, but he shakes his head. "I will tell you later, I promise, but not now."

I sigh, feeling the tension in my shoulders. Without thinking, I ask for and quickly down another glass of wine.

"How many glasses have you had?" Cole asks, chuckling softly.

"Too many," I admit, feeling a bit unsteady.

"You're not driving," he says, more of a statement than a question.

I reach into my clutch and hand him my valet ticket. "No, you are."

He raises his eyebrows at me, a mix of surprise and amusement crossing his face.

"Nobody's going to question it tonight," I say, smiling up at him. "Between what both Mark and Laura have said and the fact that I've been drinking a lot, it's fine. Wasn't the plan, 'We'll just see what happens'?"

He smiles, shaking his head as he pockets the valet ticket. "You're right. We'll just see what happens."

"Come on," Cole says softly, holding out his elbow to me.

I slide my hand under his arm, grateful for his steady presence as we head over to speak with some of Dr. Gabari's staff I haven't had much interaction with yet—his office manager, Keith, and his accountant, Jeremy. The conversation starts with the usual pleasantries, the kind that feel almost obligatory at these events.

Keith mentions that patients have had great success with our device, which has led to growth in their practice.

"That's great," Cole responds, his tone genuinely pleased. "It's always good to know we're helping people. Sometimes we get stuck behind the numbers."

"Totally understandable," Jeremy chimes in with a grin. "I do that too. But at the end of the day, we're saving and changing lives."

The small talk stretches on longer than I'd like, and before I know it, I'm face to face with Tony. Nicole stands beside him, while Cole stays close to me, his presence reassuring.

"Autumn, I am so sorry if I have offended you in any way," Tony says, his tone overly sincere. "You are a very attractive woman and hard to resist."

I feel Cole stiffen beside me, the tension radiating from him. I hold my composure, keeping my voice steady. "Tony, I'm flattered, but this all needs to remain strictly business."

"I think your colleagues have made that clear," he replies, casting a glance at Cole before returning his gaze to me.

I maintain my smile, trying to steer the conversation back to neutral ground. "We just had a pleasant conversation with Keith and Jeremy about how our device is helping people, and that's wonderful."

"It is," Tony agrees, though his tone is less enthusiastic now.

I turn to Nicole, offering her a warm smile. "Nicole, it's been so nice getting to know you better tonight."

"It has been," she replies, her own smile genuine.

After a few more goodbyes and pleasantries, we move past them. With Dr. Gabari's team now gone, a collective sigh of relief seems to pass through our group.

"I have the board meeting in the morning, so the plan is to meet in the lobby of his building at eleven," Pete says, settling the check for dinner.

"Autumn," Laura says, her voice light and teasing, "I know you had a lot of wine, which is understandable," she laughs, "but you're not driving, are you?"

"No, Cole took a ride share here, so I gave him my valet ticket. He'll drive," I assure her.

"Okay, just making sure," Laura says, then turns to Cole. "You only had one, right?"

"Yeah, I figured a little while ago that I'd be driving," he says, giving me a knowing look.

"Well, let's get out of here," Pete announces.

Cole furrows his brow slightly as Pete insists we get my car first from the valet. I just shrug in response.

When they pull up my car, Pete's reaction mirrors Cole's from earlier. "I don't think we pay you that much," he jokes.

"You don't," I laugh, leaving it at that.

The valet opens my door, but Cole helps me in, his hand lingering just a moment longer than necessary.

"Have fun driving that," Pete says, exchanging a laugh with Mark.

"I'll try," Cole responds with a grin as he slides into the driver's seat.

We drive to his hotel, where he parks in front of the luggage loading area. "Give me five minutes, wait here," he says, his voice gentle.

"Okay," I reply, pulling my phone out of my clutch and leaning my head against the cool glass of the window. The night feels strangely off, like a puzzle piece that doesn't quite fit, so I lock the doors as I watch Cole walk into the hotel. With a sigh, I reach down, push the heel straps off my shoes, and kick them off, relishing the relief.

I check my messages, noticing a few I'd missed after turning off my notifications once Cole arrived at the restaurant. As I scroll through them, I try to shake the lingering unease from the evening, hoping that whatever comes next will help settle the disquiet in my mind.

Cara

Holy fuck girl, Megan sent me that picture, you trying to seduce every man in town?

I laugh and respond.

Me

No, just one

I have a few messages waiting for me—Tara wishing me luck with Dr. Gabari, and Sami and Megan both checking in on my night. I quickly respond to all of them, letting them know everything's fine, just a bit overwhelming. Just as I finish typing, there's a tapping on the glass. I nearly jump out of my skin but quickly realize it's just Cole. I unlock the doors, feeling a little silly for being so jumpy.

Cole tosses a bag and his suit jacket into the backseat before sliding into the driver's seat. He loosens his tie with a relieved sigh before starting the car. As he puts it in drive, he glances over at me. "You alright, Autumn?"

"Yeah, I think so. There was a lot that happened tonight," I reply with a small laugh, trying to shake off the lingering unease.

He drives for a couple of blocks before turning into an empty parking lot. I look around, confused. "Where are you taking me?" The way I say it, I can tell I've had too much to drink. My words aren't slurred, but they don't sound quite right.

Without a word, Cole turns to me, pulls me close, and kisses me deeply and passionately. It's the kind of kiss that erases the tension of the evening, even if just for a moment.

"I just needed to do that," he says with a laugh as he buckles his seatbelt. "Now I'll take you home."

"Cole?" I ask as he merges onto the freeway.

"Autumn?" he responds, his tone playful yet attentive.

"I think I had too much wine," I admit, laughing at myself.

"I think you did too," he says with a smile, his hand resting reassuringly on my thigh.

"What does Mark know? What did Tony say? And why is Pete's wife telling me you're smitten with me?" I lean my head back against the cool glass, feeling the effects of the wine.

Cole sighs, his thumb absentmindedly brushing against my thigh. "Mark knows that I have feelings. He asked in Dallas," he pauses, "before we did anything. He knows I'm attracted to you, but he doesn't know that it's been acted on or that it's reciprocated."

"Okay, and Tony?" I ask, trying to piece together the puzzle of the evening.

Cole's driving becomes a bit more aggressive as he accelerates around another car.

"Hey," I say, half-serious, half-teasing, "be nithe to my car." I slur slightly, and Cole laughs.

"How can you be this adorable even when you're inebriated?" he teases.

"You're avoiding the question," I point out.

He sighs heavily, clearly reluctant to tell me. "I wasn't there, but he said something along the lines of, 'She is just asking for me to do dirty things to her all night. She's the most fuckable thing I've seen in a long time.'" He accelerates again, passing another car with more force than necessary.

"What?" I sit up straight, the shock sobering me up instantly. "What the fuck is wrong with him?"

Cole glances at me briefly, his jaw tight. "Yeah, hence Pete with the tone down the wardrobe comment; he didn't mean it how it sounded. Tony said it in front of Nicole and Laura, it wasn't even locker room banter or whatever you might call guys talking to guys."

"Holy fuck," I say. "What the hell is wrong with him?"

Cole steals a glance at me. "Yeah, that was pretty much the consensus."

"None of his own people said anything?"

"I don't know for sure, but not loudly in the moment, that much I do know. They also are all his employees."

"Okay, and Laura?" I ask, curiosity piqued.

Cole smiles, glancing at me. "I think you're going to have to explain that one to me."

"When you all were talking to Tony and Laura was talking to me, she mentioned she's known you for a long time and that she could tell you're smitten with me," I say, laughing. "I mean, she's not wrong."

"No, no she's not," Cole agrees, smiling. "But how did you respond to that?"

I speak slowly, the wine still influencing my words, though not slurring. "Um, I told her that you and I had bonded over the last couple of years, that you were a gentleman and my knight in shining armor. She said, 'where there's a will, there's a way,' encouraging me to do something about us." I laugh, finding the whole situation amusing in my tipsy state.

"Autumn, I'm not sure that's funny," he says, though he's smiling too.

"Oh, it's funny," I insist, laughing even more. "Under the circumstances, it's funny. You do realize nobody questioned that you were driving my car and that I was going home while you were supposedly going to a hotel a couple of blocks away?"

"I do realize that," Cole says, a knowing look on his face. "But I'm almost positive there will be questions to answer tomorrow."

"Maybe." I shrug, looking out the window, feeling the cool glass against my skin.

"Autumn?" Cole's voice is soft, pulling me back from my thoughts.

"Cole?"

"You look beautiful tonight. You are stunning," he says, his voice sincere.

"Thank you," I murmur, shifting to lean toward him. I place my hand on his thigh, leaning over the console to rest my head on his shoulder.

"Now hopefully you're not too inebriated when we get to your house." He laughs, the warmth of his voice vibrating through his chest.

"I'll be fine," I assure him, "but if not, you have my permission to still do whatever you want to me."

Cole laughs, the sound rich and warm. "You're insane."

"I know."

I call Megan from the console. "Hey, Mom," she answers almost immediately.

"Hey, Megs, Cole is driving my car back. I had a little too much wine. Can you just make sure the door between the garage and the house is unlocked? I don't think I brought the house keys."

"Uh, yeah. Are you on the Bluetooth in the car?" Megan's tone shifts, clearly catching on.

"Um, yeah," I reply.

"Hi, Cole," Megan says, her tone playful.

Cole laughs. "Hey, Megan."

"She looked good tonight, didn't she?" Megan teases.

"She's stunning, Megan, and you did a great job with her hair."

"How drunk is she?" Megan asks, a mix of humor and concern in her voice.

"I'm right here," I interject, a little offended but also amused.

"Like nine glasses of wine drunk," Cole says, trying to keep the tone light.

"Isn't that like two bottles of wine?" Megan sounds surprised.

"About," Cole confirms.

"I feel like there's a story," Megan says, clearly intrigued.

"There is, but I'll let her tell you when she's sober," Cole laughs.

"Okay, the door is unlocked. See you soon, you crazy lovebirds."

"Bye, Megs," I say, disconnecting the call. "She's the best," I sigh, feeling a wave of gratitude for my daughter.

"You won the daughter lottery," Cole says with a chuckle. "So, sapphires, huh?"

"What?" I ask, not quite following.

"At dinner, you told Laura that sapphires are your favorite," Cole reminds me.

"Oh, yeah," I say, looking down at the bracelet on my wrist. "They are."

"Even more than diamonds?" he asks, genuinely curious.

"Yeah, they remind me of the ocean and the sky. Your eyes are the color of sapphires," I add, glancing up at him.

Cole laughs softly. "I haven't heard that one before."

"Well, it's true," I say with a sigh. "Your eyes are a unique shade of blue; they're so dark, but just like sapphires."

"Autumn, sweetheart?" His voice softens, and I can hear the concern.

"Yeah?"

"I'm sorry about tonight."

I lift my head from his shoulder and look at him, puzzled. "What do you have to be sorry about? Nothing is your fault."

"I know that, but it doesn't feel that way. I feel like I should have protected you better," he says, his voice tinged with frustration.

"You did everything in your power. I'm not upset with you at all. You don't need to apologize," I assure him, meaning every word.

I lean my head back on his shoulder as faint music plays through the speakers. I recognize the song—"The Dance"—and turn up the volume slightly. Cole sighs and kisses the top of my head, a gesture that feels both comforting and intimate. More music follows, but we leave the volume alone, letting the quiet moments stretch between us as we drive. It isn't until we're turning into my driveway that he speaks again.

"You awake?" Cole asks gently.

"Yeah," I sigh, feeling a mix of exhaustion and contentment.

"It's barely ten. Let's get you some water and some sleep," he suggests.

"It doesn't feel that early," I laugh softly.

"I'm sure it doesn't to you," he says with a grin.

Cole pulls into the garage, parks, and then walks around to the passenger side to help me out. The door to the house swings open, and Megan appears, looking both concerned and amused.

"You need any help?" Megan asks, eyeing me with a knowing smile.

"Actually, yeah, can you grab my bag from behind the driver's seat?" Cole asks, his tone grateful.

"Yeah, on it," Megan replies, moving quickly to retrieve the bag.

"Also, your mom is going to need a lot of water," Cole says with a laugh.

"Okay," Megan laughs, clearly entertained by the situation.

"I'm right here," I grumble, feeling a bit like a child being fussed over.

"We know you are," Cole says, his voice warm as he kisses my temple and leads me into the house.

"You going straight upstairs?" Megan asks as she follows behind us.

"Yeah, I think so," I reply, trying to sound more composed than I feel.

Megan heads up the stairs ahead of us and leaves Cole's bag in the room. Cole is helping me up the stairs, and I'm grateful for his support because I'm definitely unsteady, the room spinning slightly with each step.

"Hey, Megan," Cole starts as we reach the top, "I hate to ask, but two more favors?"

"What do you need?" Megan asks, ever the helpful daughter.

"Can you find some pajamas for your mom and also take her hair down and brush it out? I don't think I could do that without hurting her," he says with a chuckle.

"I can do both," Megan agrees. "Can you grab a couple of bottles of water out of the fridge?"

"Yeah, thank you, Megan," Cole says, his tone full of appreciation.

At this point, I don't care that they're talking about me like I'm not there. Megan sits behind me on the bed, and the room spins worse when I close my eyes, so I keep them open as she gently undoes the plaits in my hair. Cole returns while she's brushing it out.

"Hey," I say softly, "thank you."

He looks at Megan, then back at me. "You don't need to thank either of us."

"Okay, that should keep it from tangling worse overnight," Megan says, setting the brush aside. "Let me grab her something to sleep in."

She disappears into the closet and comes back with a pair of soft sleep shorts and a tank top, setting them on the bed.

"You got her from here?" Megan asks, looking at Cole.

"Yeah, thank you, Megan," Cole replies.

"Night, Mom," Megan says, her voice gentle as she stands up.

"Goodnight, Megs, love you," I murmur.

"Love you too, Mom," she says, closing the door behind her as she leaves the room.

I stand up, feeling a bit wobbly but determined to stay steady.

"Where are you going?" Cole asks, half-amused, half-concerned.

"I need to pee," I laugh, "Is that allowed?"

Cole laughs, loosening his tie. "Yes, that's allowed."

I manage to make it to the bathroom, where I take care of business, then wash my face and brush my teeth. When I finish, I look up in the mirror and see Cole leaning against the doorframe between the bedroom and bathroom, watching me with a soft smile. His tie hangs loosely around his neck, his shirt untucked and partially unbuttoned.

I turn around and walk to him, wrapping my arms around his waist and leaning into his chest. He kisses the top of my head, and we stand there quietly for a few minutes, the moment feeling intimate and comforting.

I pull back slightly and look up at him. "You did look sexy in that suit," I say with a smile. "You look pretty sexy like this too."

He runs his fingers through my hair, the gesture tender. "You were all the pretty things, including sexy, and you still are."

"Cole?" I say, my voice small.

"Autumn?" he replies, his tone matching mine.

"I'm going to need your help getting this dress off."

He laughs, the sound warm and familiar. "I figured that, but you're going to have to tell me how."

I laugh along with him. "I mostly just need help because of all the boning."

"Boning?" he echoes, still chuckling.

"That's what these steel devices of torture are called, silly."

"Really?" he asks, intrigued.

"Really. They were originally made out of whale bones, so the name stuck."

"How are you this smart when you can barely stand up and walk?" he teases, his voice full of affection.

"That's not smart, that's just random knowledge," I reply, shrugging.

He laughs again. "Okay, come back into the bedroom, and let's get you out of that dress."

I lift my arm to show him where the zipper is, and he carefully finds it, slowly unzipping the dress. I immediately feel a sense of relief as the tightness loosens around me. I peel the corset off my body, and it falls to the floor in a heap. He picks it up, feeling the steel boning in the corset.

"Yeah, that doesn't seem like it'd be very comfortable," he says, shaking his head.

"The price of beauty." I shrug. "That's also why I like the green dress more—no heels, no corset."

He grabs the shirt Megan picked out for me and slips it over my head, helping me push my arms through the straps.

"Wait, why are you putting clothes on me? Isn't that the opposite of what we do?" I tease.

He laughs. "Usually, yes."

He places the shorts by my feet and helps me step into them, steadying me as I pull them up.

"Now, let's get you into bed," he says, turning down the blankets. I crawl in, feeling the comfort of the cool sheets against my skin.

I drink an entire bottle of water as I watch him strip down to his underwear and throw on some sweats. Then he climbs into bed next to me, and I instinctively roll into him, snuggling close.

"Cole?"

"Autumn?" he replies softly.

"I'm sleepy," I say, my voice heavy with exhaustion.

Laughing quietly, he says, "I'm sure you are. You can just go ahead and sleep, it's fine."

He strokes my hair, planting soft kisses on my head and rubbing my back until I drift off to sleep, feeling safe and cared for in his arms.

CHAPTER TWENTY-FOUR
THE COMPRESSION BRA

I wake up in the middle of the night, the darkness pressing in around me. My head is pounding, and I instinctively reach for my phone. It's almost three in the morning. I sit up slowly, the room spinning slightly as I do. My hand fumbles for the water on my nightstand, and I'm relieved to find that either Cole or Megan left ibuprofen and acetaminophen for me. Grateful, I take both, washing them down with a few more sips of water.

As I turn to look at Cole, I see he's still facing away from me, sound asleep. I quietly slip out of bed and head to the bathroom. When I return, I slide back into bed, this time lying on my left side so I'm facing him. Last night he was incredible—such a gentleman, making me feel safe, cared for, and, most importantly, loved.

I scoot closer to him, gently pressing a kiss between his shoulder blades before wrapping my arm halfway around him and resting my head against his back. I'm not expecting any response, but he surprises me by grabbing my hand and rolling over to face me. He kisses my forehead and pulls me closer, guiding my head onto his chest.

"You okay?" he asks, his voice low and soft, filled with concern.

"Yeah, just a headache," I whisper with a soft laugh, feeling the comfort of his presence. He runs his hand down my arm, a soothing gesture that calms the last remnants of unease.

"Cole?" I whisper, barely audible.

"Autumn?" he responds, his voice gentle.

I prop myself up on one elbow so I can see his eyes. My hand finds its way to his cheekbone, and I trace the familiar lines of his face before leaning in to kiss him. It's a tender kiss, slow and meaningful, and when I pull back, I look into his eyes, searching for the right moment.

It comes quickly, naturally. "I love you," I say, my voice steady despite the surge of emotion.

His response is immediate. He reaches up, his hand cradling the nape of my neck, and pulls me in for another kiss, soft but deep. As he kisses me, he gently rolls us over so I'm lying on my back, but he doesn't press his weight onto me. He breaks the kiss and runs his thumb over my cheekbone, his eyes intense as they search mine.

"I love you too," he says, his voice thick with emotion.

Tears well up in my eyes and begin to fall as I pull him closer for another kiss, this one gentle and full of unspoken words.

"Autumn," he begins, his voice trembling slightly, "I'm not even sure that love is a strong enough word for how I feel about you."

Tears slip down my face and onto the pillow, and I nod, understanding exactly what he means. "Me either," I whisper, my voice breaking. "I'm just so grateful for you."

He gently wipes away my tears and presses a kiss to my forehead. "Me too," he murmurs, his voice filled with sincerity.

He lies down next to me, wrapping me in his arms in a comforting spooning position. As he kisses the top of my head and strokes my hair, I feel a deep sense of peace wash over me. His presence, his love, it's all so overwhelming, but in the best possible way. With him holding me, I drift back to sleep, feeling more loved and secure than I ever have.

Cole's alarm goes off, and I wake up still nestled against him. "What time is it?" I ask.

"Seven. I figure we need to leave by nine, that would give us both time to get ready," he answers.

"Yeah, I know I need to shower," I say, turning toward him, "Wanna shower with me?"

He smiles. "I don't think I'd ever turn that down."

I make sure we have everything we need and start the shower. I get in first and the warmth and steam feel amazing this morning. I still have a little bit of a headache, but it's not awful. Cole joins me a minute later. He pulls me into him and kisses me.

"You do remember us talking in the middle of the night, right?" he laughs.

"Yes, and I still mean it," I say.

"Just making sure that wasn't the wine talking."

"No, not the wine, and thank you. Thank you for last night, for being a gentleman, for everything."

"I knew when I got back to the car after grabbing my bag that was what you needed. I like taking care of you," he pauses and lifts my chin to meet my eyes, "loving you."

"I'm sorry I had so much wine, it was just all a lot."

"It was a lot, for me too. I think everyone understood why you were drinking," he laughs.

I kiss him again and then we actually shower, taking moments to flirt, touch, and soap each other up, but we do need to get ready to leave.

"I hope you're coming back here tonight," I say.

"That's the plan, and Autumn?"

"Yeah?"

"I was thinking I'll just stay until Friday or you can come with me back to Fort Wayne on Thursday since you're coming down this weekend anyway. We can figure out logistics later."

"That sounds perfect," I say.

After Cole gets out, I stay behind to wash and condition my hair. When I finally step out, wrapped in a towel, I realize I haven't decided what to wear. I stare at my clothes, feeling a bit lost.

Cole notices my hesitation and laughs. "You okay?"

"Yeah, I just don't know what to wear that will keep Tony from being a creep," I admit, holding up an old brown pantsuit with weird puffy hips.

"It shouldn't matter what you wear; he should have self-control," Cole says, though his expression shows he understands my dilemma.

"I agree," I say, pulling out a cream blouse to wear under the suit. I joke about wearing a compression sports bra to flatten my chest, and Cole half-seriously agrees that it might not be a bad idea.

"I'm a bad judge," Cole adds, "I think you look sexy and inviting in anything, especially just a towel." I look at him and smile.

Once I'm dressed, I feel frumpy and unattractive, but that's kind of the point. My makeup is subdued, and I pull my hair up in a severe twist. Cole, however, still thinks I look hot, though he acknowledges I tried to downplay it.

"Yeah," Cole says, "you're still hot, but you tried."

"I did try, and you might be the only one who thinks so," I say, "I smell food. I think Megan is cooking."

Cole puts on his t-shirt and then his button-down. I fix his collar while he tucks in his shirt. When he is ready, he wraps his arms around me and kisses me softly. Then we head downstairs. Megan has made eggs, hash browns, and sausage.

"Hey," she says as we walk into the kitchen, "I thought you might need some grease in your stomach."

"It smells amazing, Megs, thank you," I say, "How do you know about alcohol and grease?" I laugh.

"Mom, I might live at home, but I still have friends and I *am* a college student." She rolls her eyes.

Cole laughs. "I take it you haven't had to do that for your mom before, then?"

"No, she occasionally gets a little tipsy with Cara, but no, never like that," she answers.

"Last night was an exception," I say, "and wine makes my head spin more than other things, in general."

"You want to tell me what happened?" Megan asks, "Because clearly you weren't upset with Cole."

"No, Cole was amazing." I smile at him. "That doctor that was hitting on me in Dallas, he said some very inappropriate things to me, and even more inappropriate things to others. Then there were a couple of things our team said about me and Cole. I don't know, it was just a lot, and by the time I realized how much I had, it was too late."

"Like how inappropriate?" Megan asks, looking between me and Cole.

Cole clears his throat. "When she left the room he said something to everyone else in the room describing what he wanted to do to her; that's the nice way of putting it."

"And he's supposed to be a professional?" Megan asks while handing me a plate of food.

"One of the top in his field," Cole says.

"I assume that's why you're dressed like that," she says, laughing.

"Yep," I laugh.

"Victim blaming at its finest," Megan says.

"That too, but I do *not* want a repeat of last night," I say.

"Me either," Cole says.

"So you said some of your team said things?" she asks, "Are you still on the down-low?"

I laugh. "Yeah, but I think they still see it. Cole wants to wait to talk to them about it, and I'm okay with that, but we're not invisible."

"It will impact one or both of our jobs in some way," Cole says, "She can't report to me, so something will change. I'm just not ready for that yet."

"You haven't said that to me before," I say.

He shrugs. "It's part of why I don't want to say anything yet."

"You won't lose your job, will you?" Megan asks, looking between us.

"Probably not either of us, just some kind of lateral move, but if one of us does, it would be me, not your mom," Cole says.

"That's rough," Megan says.

"Yeah," I say, "but people have said things to both of us now, letting us know they see the spark, so I don't know how much longer we'll be able to wait."

"To be fair," Cole says, "they both only said they see it from me, so you're doing a better job than me."

"Yeah, but then I gave you my valet ticket and had you drive me home last night," I pause to emphasize, "*in front of them.*" I shrug.

"If Pete asks me, I won't lie," Cole says, "but I'm not volunteering yet. I'm thinking we wait until this conference schedule is over."

"February?" I ask.

"Yeah, I know it seems like a long time, but it establishes us a little bit and gives me some time to figure out a plan to propose about how we make this work."

"Awe, just before Valentine's Day," Megan interjects. Cole and I both smile at her.

We finish eating, I hug Megan goodbye, and we head for the practice. Cole decides I should drive my own car, just to make the optics better. His car is at the hotel, so his plan is just to tell them I picked him up. Cole has to take some business calls while we're driving down to Chicago so that also makes it better that he isn't driving.

We arrive at Dr. Gabari's office building, and the lobby wait is brief. Mark shows up within minutes, and Pete isn't far behind. Neither of them acknowledges my appearance, which feels both unsettling and oddly appropriate. A part of me is relieved they don't mention anything about Cole driving me home, though their silence leaves me uneasy.

As we navigate the practice, the cramped hallways of a medical office remind me that there's little room to breathe, let alone escape. Pete and Cole subtly position themselves between me and Dr. Gabari, ensuring there's no opportunity for Tony to catch me alone. We spend an hour and a half touring the office, meeting his staff. Nicole, ever gracious, tries to make me feel at ease, but Cole keeps close, allowing her only brief moments to connect with me.

Pete arranges for a catered lunch for the staff, but instead of joining them, we head out to a local steakhouse. As soon as I settle into the car, I pull my hair down, letting it fall naturally, and undo the top buttons of my blouse. Cole chuckles softly, his eyes warm. "That's more like you," he says, the tension between us easing just a bit.

Lunch is a surprisingly pleasant affair. Laura joins us, and I find myself sitting between her and Cole. As we settle in, Pete remarks, "Well, that went much better than last night."

Cole nods in agreement. "Definitely."

Laura, with her perceptive gaze, turns to me. "So, I take it he behaved himself today?"

I laugh lightly, a bit of the tension lifting. "Pete and Cole didn't give him a chance to misstep. But no, he wasn't inappropriate."

She nods approvingly, giving Cole a glance. "Good job, that's exactly how it should be."

Cole's smile in response is small but genuine.

The conversation flows easily as we catch up on life outside of work. I'm pleasantly surprised by how much I enjoy getting to know Laura. We exchange contact information, a silent agreement to stay in touch. As we part ways, I hug Pete, Mark, and Laura, feeling a warmth I hadn't expected.

The official story is that I'm dropping Cole off at the hotel, where he'll grab his things and head home. But in truth, he's planning to drive up to Milwaukee to spend the night with me, and I can hardly contain my anticipation.

At the hotel, there's a quiet urgency between us. With only twenty minutes before he has to vacate the room, there's no time for anything more than a squeeze of the hand, his eyes saying what we don't dare risk with a kiss—especially with Pete and Mark nearby. I squeeze his hand back, a silent promise, before heading home, a smile playing on my lips. Tonight can't come soon enough.

On the drive home, I blast my favorite music, letting the loud, pulsing beats wash away the tension of the day. By the time I pull into the driveway, I'm in a good mood, lighter somehow. I quickly shed my work clothes for something more comfortable—leggings and a tank top. The compression bra and those ridiculous pants are finally a thing of the past. When I open the door for Cole, I can't help myself—I practically leap into his arms.

Laughing, he catches me with ease and kisses me before wrapping me up in a tight hug. My toes barely touch the floor as I breathe in the familiar scent of my perfume mingling with his cologne. "I think someone's happy to see me," he teases, setting me down gently.

"Just a little." I smile up at him, my heart full.

Strong arms pull me back into his embrace, and we stand there in the doorway, the door still wide open, as if time itself has paused just for us. The way he holds me—tight, grounding, necessary—makes me feel like I'm exactly where I belong. We're both still, not a single movement beyond the rise and fall of our chests as we breathe together. The simple proximity of his body to mine stirs something deep inside me, an ache I can't ignore.

Eventually, he pulls back slightly, his hand finding the back of my neck as he leans in for a kiss. It's one of those slow, tender ones, filled with love more than hunger. His lips are soft, lingering, and I melt into it.

"I should probably grab my stuff from the car," he murmurs with a small smile.

"I guess," I reply, though I'm reluctant to let him go. "You can pull into the garage. I'll open the door."

"Okay," he says, giving me a quick kiss on the forehead before heading outside.

I wait for him at the door between the house and the garage, anticipation bubbling inside me. When he comes back in, bags in hand, he looks around. "Megan's Jeep isn't here. Is she home?"

"Nope," I say, unable to keep the grin off my face. "She went to Chicago with friends about an hour ago. She won't be back until after midnight."

The door barely clicks shut before he drops his bags and pulls me into a fierce kiss, this one full of urgency. The heat between us is immediate, electric, and I feel it all the way to my core. As he walks me backward toward the family room, he discards his shoes.

My hands find their way to the buttons of his shirt, working them loose as he tugs at the hem of my tank top. I raise my arms, letting him pull it off in one swift motion, and then I'm back to unbuttoning his shirt. It falls to the floor along with his undershirt, and my fingers eagerly find his belt. His pants and boxers follow suit, a crumpled pile at his feet. He turns us so that his back is to the couch and he sits, peeling off my leggings and underwear with a mix of tenderness and urgency.

I straddle him as he leans against the back of the couch, his hands trailing down from my armpits to my hips, leaving a trail of fire and electricity in their wake. His touch is both familiar and thrilling, and I shiver as his hand moves to caress my breast, his mouth finding the other. My back arches naturally, my body responding to him as if it has been waiting for this moment all day.

Lips travel up my neck, finding mine again, and our kiss deepens, his hands exploring every inch of my skin. I break the kiss to rise slightly above him, and he takes the cue, positioning himself beneath me. Our eyes lock as I lower myself onto him, and the sensation is overwhelming. I bite my lip, a sharp inhale escaping me as he fills me completely.

Our mouths find each other again as he gently rocks my hips with his hands, each movement deliberate and powerful. We savor the feeling, the connection between us deepening with each passing second. The build-up is slow, steady, and as I feel the orgasm cresting, I break the kiss. My back arches, my head tilting back, as he buries his face in my chest and my body shudders with release.

He pushes us over so that he's on top, and the rhythm changes. It's primal now, fierce and unrestrained, and I brace my hand against the arm of the couch to keep us steady. The sound of our bodies meeting, the wetness between us, heightens everything, making my head spin. When he reaches his peak, I feel him pulse inside me, and his body collapses toward mine. I wrap my arms around his neck, pulling him into another kiss, softer this time.

When our lips part, he brushes a stray lock of hair from my face, a quiet smile playing on his lips. "Hi," he whispers, his breath warm against my skin.

"Hi," I reply, laughing softly. "I feel better. What about you?"

"Yeah—better." He grins. "We'll go with that."

He sits up, and I push myself up on my elbows, snuggling against him. For some reason, today, I feel small, but in the best way—safe and secure in his arms, exactly where I want to be.

CHAPTER TWENTY-FIVE
THE REAL DATE

We sit there, entwined in each other's warmth, letting the world outside fade away. After a while, Cole breaks the silence with a rumble in his stomach. He grins. "I'm getting hungry. How about we get dressed and find something to eat?"

Laughing, the sound vibrating pleasantly through me, he suggests, "You know, I've never actually taken you out on a real date. Want to go out for dinner?"

I raise an eyebrow, a smirk tugging at my lips. "You mean, like, an actual date?"

"Yeah, like a real date," he says, taking my hands and then guiding them around his waist, pulling me closer.

"I think I'd like that," I reply, leaning in to kiss him softly.

"Alright then," he says, smiling against my lips. "You go get dressed, and we'll figure out where to go."

I head upstairs, feeling a flutter of excitement. I pull on a pair of jeans that hug in all the right places and a black top that's just revealing enough with its peek-a-boo sleeves. A swipe of mascara, a touch of lip gloss, and I slip into my sandals. When I come back downstairs, Cole's eyes light up.

"You look cute," he says, his voice warm with approval.

"Thanks," I reply, feeling a little glow inside.

"You know this area better than I do. Where do you want to go?"

I think for a moment, then suggest, "We've had steak two nights in a row. How about Italian or Mexican?"

"Let's go Italian," he decides.

"Perfect. There's a little Italian place just a couple of blocks from here. It's cozy, not too crowded."

"That sounds great," he says, his hand finding mine as we head to the garage.

As we reach the door, an impulsive thought strikes me, and I can't help but laugh at myself. "Okay, Cole, don't overthink this," I say with a teasing grin.

He looks at me, puzzled, but intrigued. I open a cabinet and pull out a garage door opener and a key. Holding them out to him, I watch his expression shift from curiosity to something deeper.

"Autumn?" he says, taking the items from my hand, his eyes searching mine.

"I trust you," I say simply. "That's the garage door opener—it used to be in Kevin's car—and the key to the garage door."

Staring at me, he seems momentarily stunned, and I can't help but laugh again. "Seriously, don't read too much into this," I say. "The kids all come in through the front door now, and there's a code if they need to get into the garage. I haven't given you the house alarm codes," I pause, my smile softening, "yet."

Pulling me close, he kisses me, a blend of amusement and affection in his eyes. "This feels all backward sometimes," he murmurs, his laughter mixing with mine. "You just gave me the key to your house, and we're only now heading out for our first real date."

I cover my mouth, realizing the irony, and laugh out loud. "I didn't even think of it that way, but yes, that is exactly what just happened."

He wraps his arms around me. "Let's take my car this time," he suggests.

"Fine by me," I reply, feeling a rush of anticipation.

Dinner is different. For the first time, we're out in public without having to hide, without the weight of secrecy. In my neighborhood, there's a chance I'll run into someone I know, but none of them would know Cole or have any context beyond us being on a date. It feels natural, easy—like we're just a couple, enjoying an evening out.

As we settle into the booth, the conversation flows effortlessly. We share stories from our younger years, laughing over high school antics, before the conversation turns more serious.

"I feel like we probably should have talked about this sooner," Cole says, his tone turning thoughtful. "We both know it's been a while, but what's your dating history like?"

I raise an eyebrow at him, pretending to be offended. "Are you asking about my body count, Mr. Waters?"

He laughs, a deep, warm sound. "I guess I am. That's what they call it these days, right?"

I smile, leaning back in my chair. "It's not very exciting. Between eighteen and twenty, I slept with four men and married the last one. You're number five." I pause, watching his reaction before continuing. "My first was my high school sweetheart. Then there was a guy I dated for a few months, followed by a one-night stand with a high school friend—who I'm still friends with, by the way—and then Steve."

"A one-night stand, huh?" he says, his voice laced with curiosity.

"Yep," I reply, shrugging. "And you're the first person I've ever told about it. It was completely consensual; we were both in a rough spot emotionally, between relationships. It was what we both needed that night. He's married now, with a daughter. Middle school-aged. I don't think he ever told anyone either." I take a sip of my wine, feeling the warmth spread through me. "That's probably my biggest skeleton. What about you?"

"You didn't tell Steve?" he asks, his eyes narrowing slightly.

"Nope," I admit. "He was even more conservative than me when it came to that kind of thing. I thought it would make him mad. Maybe that should have been a red flag. I was number two for him, but then he turned into a womanizing jerk, so there's that."

I look at Cole, curiosity bubbling up. "What about you?"

"Yeah, mine's a bit more extensive, but not by much," Cole chuckles, the sound carrying a touch of self-reflection. "I was fourteen when it all started—my childhood was way different from yours. By the time I graduated high school, I'd been with five girls, all of whom I dated for at least a couple of months, though nothing lasted longer than a year. There was one more in college before Michelle, so she was number seven. After the divorce, there were three more—flings I regret. They mostly involved too much alcohol, and honestly, I didn't enjoy them. I just felt worse afterward."

"So, that makes me number eleven?" I ask, stretching out the last word and wrinkling my nose in playful disbelief.

"Yeah," he says, meeting my gaze.

I laugh lightly. "Well, still double me."

"True," he admits, a grin tugging at the corners of his mouth. "But I had a four-year head start on you."

"Were you honest with Michelle when you had this talk with her?"

"Actually, no." He shrugs, the motion almost dismissive. "I didn't tell her anything before college."

"So she thought she was number two?" I ask, a little surprised.

"Yeah, she did."

I shake my head, chuckling. "We were both young and kinda stupid."

"Maybe," he concedes with a shrug. "What about boyfriends before eighteen?"

"A few," I say, reminiscing. "My first love was when I was thirteen, and he was seventeen, which seems insane to me now, but back then, no one could've convinced me otherwise. It lasted about three months, and it was my first real heartbreak. After that, I dated someone two years older for almost two years—and before you ask, no, I didn't give it up to him. When he graduated, that was the end of us." I shrug, smiling at the memory. "Then there were two real relationships, both about six months. The second one was the one I finally did give it up for. And after that, I think I did a short stint of sowing my wild oats with little flings before Steve.

"What about you?" I ask, curiosity getting the better of me.

"Nothing serious before Michelle," he admits. "The closest was when I was fourteen—she was fifteen, and it lasted about nine months. But nothing longer. I think that's part of why I ended up proposing to Michelle. She stuck around. I don't think I actually thought about whether either of us was truly happy. She was there, and she was willing to be there."

I smile at him, understanding. "You know, when Steve and I got engaged, my mom told me she thought I was more in love with the idea of having a family than I was with Steve. I argued with her at the time, but in hindsight, she was right. I wanted the white picket fence, someone to marry and have kids with, preferably someone with a career that would let me stay home with them. I didn't think much about *my* happiness either—I just wanted the dream."

"How many times have you been proposed to?" Cole asks, a teasing smile playing on his lips.

"Uh, three times, but two were Steve, so I'm not sure they all count," I laugh, shaking my head at the memories. "Once when I was eighteen—he was serious, though maybe that one shouldn't count either. Then Steve proposed in the middle of a fight—another red flag I missed—and then the real proposal, with the flowers, the romance, the whole shebang." I look at Cole. "I'm assuming Michelle was it for you?"

"Yeah, she was the only one," he says, his tone more reflective now. "And it wasn't even a big romantic gesture. More like a discussion. I mean, I asked, but it was more, 'Hey, do you think we should get married?' than anything grand."

He looks at me, his eyes holding a question. "I saw your brother's wedding pictures. I'm guessing you had a big wedding?"

"Yep, a big, big church wedding. Three hundred guests, the full ceremony—it lasted over an hour. The reception was massive too." I sigh, thinking back. "I'm not sure I'd do it that way again. It wasn't bad, but it was so much money for such a short amount of time."

"The actual wedding or the time married?" He grins, the teasing back in his voice.

"Both," I laugh, nudging him playfully. "What about you?"

"We did the courthouse thing," he says. "Honestly, if I ever did it again, I'd want a real wedding, but not as big as yours."

"There's a happy medium," I say, thinking about it. "I think Tara's is going to be something in between. She's having fewer than a hundred people, a quick exchange of vows, and then a party."

Cole nods, smiling at the idea.

"So, was Michelle your first real bad breakup?" I ask, curiosity laced with empathy.

"Yeah," he says, a wry smile tugging at his lips. "I guess she was."

"That explains the sowing-your-oats phase a bit," I muse. "Steve was probably my third real heartbreak, but it was the first one without teenage hormones. And even though I was glad to be rid of him," I pause, choosing my words carefully, "the things he did at the end were pretty awful. I think I just didn't want to put myself in a position to let that kind of thing happen again. The night Kevin talked to you—the one with my brother's bottle of scotch," I laugh softly, shaking my head, "that was more about how much my life had changed than it was about Steve. I had this comfortable life—big house, several cars, staying home with the kids, throwing them these great birthday parties—and then suddenly, I was destitute. The courts imputed income on me because of my degree, so I didn't get alimony, and the child support was laughable. That's what really got to me, and I spent a lot of time beating myself up for ending up in that position. I've even told my girls to always have a way out, to never be financially dependent on anyone."

"I get that," Cole nods, his voice gentle. "My situation wasn't quite like yours. I had a decent-paying job, but she made three times as much, so my life changed a lot too. Yours was more dramatic, and I don't want to take away from that, but I understand."

"It's not a competition," I say, reaching across the table to touch his hand, feeling the warmth of his skin beneath mine. "We were both put in tough spots. You had to work your way through it, while my family stepped up and basically rescued me. Our stories are similar, but neither is better or worse, just different."

Cole takes a sip of his wine, a sigh escaping him. "After Michelle... God, she was such a bitch," he says, shaking his head in disbelief. "Any woman who was even nice to me in those first few months I thought might be the answer to my problems. But they weren't—they were just more problems." He laughs, the sound tinged with irony. "So I gave up on the whole idea. If you hadn't come along, I don't know if or when that would have ever changed."

"I honestly didn't pay attention to anyone," I admit, swirling the wine in my glass. "A couple of years ago, Kevin told me that some of his teachers, and even a few of his friends' divorced dads, tried hitting on me, but I shut them all down without even noticing. I didn't pick up on any of it." I shrug. "So I don't know how many there were, but until you walked into that hibachi grill two weeks ago, nothing had stirred in me since Steve. And honestly, nothing stirred in me like that with Steve either."

I reach out and touch his hand again, my voice softening. "I was drawn to you in a way I've never felt before," I confess, looking down as I swirl my wine. "You mentioned something about the way I looked at you that night in the restaurant?"

"Yeah," he says, his voice taking on a thoughtful tone. "When you turned and looked at me, when we made eye contact for the first time after I sat down, there was an intensity there. I don't know how to describe it, but it felt like I saw my whole world in your eyes." He laughs, rolling his eyes at himself. "It sounds so cheesy, but it's true."

I laugh, feeling the warmth of his words. "For what it's worth, the first time I felt something was when I watched you walk over to Tara. But after that, when you leaned over to me and were inches from me, saying how happy you were to see me in person—your breath on my neck, my ear—it sent chills and heat through me at the same time. And then I turned, and you were right there, just inches away, and that was it. I was done, gone. So yeah, you probably saw me seeing my whole world in your eyes too." I smile at him, taking another sip of wine.

"So, definitely before the elevator?" he teases, laughing. "And what about me walking over to Tara?"

"I was just enjoying the view." I smile back, a hint of mischief in my voice. "I don't know, you were a pleasant surprise in person—taller, sexier, all those good things. I just wanted to touch you. But then, when our eyes met, it caught me off guard—the intensity."

He blushes slightly, laughing. "Well, I guess I'm flattered. I was pleasantly surprised by you too. I mean, all I'd ever seen was your face and your hair, so seeing the whole you was pretty enticing. Especially walking back to the hotel that night behind you, because before that, you were sitting, so I couldn't take all of you in." He winks at me. "And seriously, all these years, that was the first time you felt that?"

"Uh, yeah," I admit, swirling my wine again. "I mean, have I noticed attractive men? Sure. But have I ever wanted to do anything about it? No." I smile, thinking of Cara. "Cara points out men all the time, but I never wanted to act on it—until then."

We eat in comfortable silence for a few minutes before curiosity gets the better of me. "When did Mark ask you about it?"

"Uh, at the Meet and Greet, while you were in the bathroom." Cole chuckles, glancing at me with a knowing smile. "He said, 'I see the way you're looking at her, and I know she's off-limits, but you two would be good together.' I told him that if you weren't off-limits, I would've already acted on it. He just laughed. That was the entire conversation."

"Well, that explains what he said to me on Tuesday night," I say, the pieces falling into place.

Cole looks at me, curiosity piqued. "What did he say? You mentioned something weird?"

I laugh, recalling the moment. "When I walked into the lobby of the restaurant, he shook his head at me and said something about how I was supposed to stop Dr. Gabari from making inappropriate comments. Then he added, 'Cole is going to have a heart attack when he sees you.' It was weird at the time—I couldn't figure out why he'd say that. But now it makes sense."

Cole laughs too, a hint of mischief in his eyes. "You know, when I pulled you into that little side room, I had plans for... more, I guess. But I quickly realized that if I disheveled you at all, it would be obvious. And with how perfect you looked, I couldn't risk walking back into that room with you looking any different than when you walked out."

"Disheveled, huh?" I tease, raising an eyebrow.

"Yeah," he admits, laughing with me. "If you'd been wearing something like that green dress from the Meet and Greet, I might have gotten away with more. But you were pretty buttoned-up—hair and makeup flawless. I couldn't risk it."

I chuckle, shaking my head. "But if I hadn't walked out of that room, Tony wouldn't have had his chance to be an ass."

"This is true," Cole nods thoughtfully, "but if Tony hadn't had that opportunity to show his true colors, Pete might not have realized just how bad he really is. That incident sealed it for him."

"You're right," I concede. "I guess I'm glad Tony had the chance to prove what an asshole he is. Did Pete or Mark ask you anything about going home last night?"

"Nope," he says, shaking his head. "Maybe they didn't want to know, but they're aware you went home, and they know you didn't drive yourself."

"Maybe they didn't ask so they could have plausible deniability." I laugh, imagining the unspoken conversations.

"Maybe, but I'm sure they've made some assumptions. Like I said, if Pete asks me outright, I won't deny it. The main thing is, until February—or whenever I decide to tell him—there can't be any special treatment. You can't get anything the others don't, and I'm not worried about that. But that's where the legal lines get crossed versus just company policy."

"No, that makes sense," I agree. "And it's what they're trying to avoid by having policies like that in place."

"Exactly. That, and avoiding the disruption a breakup could cause."

"Let's not even think about that," I say quickly.

"No, let's not," Cole agrees, smiling at me warmly.

After dinner, I order a tiramisu to go. Cole comments on my love for it, and I just shrug, smiling. On our way out of the restaurant, he takes my hand, and it feels like the most natural thing in the world, yet entirely new at the same time. We haven't had much time for these simple, normal interactions, and it feels refreshing.

When we get back to the house, for the first time, Cole uses his own garage door opener and pulls into the garage. It feels like a quiet step forward, a symbolic move in this connection we've been carefully nurturing.

CHAPTER TWENTY-SIX
THE BACHELOR PAD

Thursday morning starts like any other with our regular team meeting, and we manage to get some solid work done. After a productive morning, Cole brings up logistics for the weekend, his tone casual but tinged with anticipation.

"I've got a plan if it works for you," he begins. "I say we head down to my place today. That way, you can settle in before dinner with William tomorrow. Then, I'll bring you back up here Saturday or Sunday."

"That works for me," I reply, nodding. "Are you sure you want to drive me back? I could just drive down myself."

"I'm sure," he laughs, his eyes twinkling. "It gives me an excuse to spend more time with you."

Smiling, I feel a warm flutter in my chest. "Okay, let me gather some things."

Up in the bedroom, I pack a bag for the weekend, carefully choosing what to bring. As I zip it up, Cole steps into the room, his presence filling the space.

"How's it going?" he asks, leaning against the doorframe.

"All set," I reply, patting the bag.

"Great. I was thinking we'd head out in about twenty minutes if that works for you. We should hit my place around seven and avoid most of Chicago rush hour."

"Sounds good to me," I say, smiling up at him.

He brushes a strand of hair out of my face, pulling me closer until our bodies are flush. "I think it's going to be weirder for me having you at my place than being here, but we'll see." He laughs, the sound vibrating pleasantly between us.

"Why do you think that?" I ask, intrigued.

"I'm just not used to having anyone in my space," he admits. "Matthew comes over occasionally, but other than that, I'm usually alone."

"Maybe it'll be a good kind of weird," I suggest, grinning up at him.

"Oh, I don't doubt that," he murmurs before kissing me, his lips soft against mine.

"And I can make your bed smell like me," I tease, wrapping my arms around his waist.

"That's exactly what I'm counting on," he laughs. "Even the memories of you in my bed will help when you're not there."

"Memories help me too," I say softly, understanding the comfort of familiar scents and thoughts.

"Alright, let's get this downstairs and get going," he says, lifting my bag off the bed with ease.

Once we're in the car and on the road, I call Megan to let her know our plans and that I'll be back by the end of the weekend. With that taken care of, I settle into the ride, enjoying the easy conversation and music that fills the car. We make a few pit stops, because my bladder is notorious on long drives, and we finally pull into his driveway a little before eight.

As the house comes into view, I glance at Cole and laugh. "You definitely undersold this place."

"It's not your house," he says, shrugging as if it's nothing special.

"Yeah, but this is a really nice house," I reply, taking in the two-story structure, the three-car garage, and the well-manicured yard. It's impressive in a quiet, understated way.

He opens the garage, revealing a space filled with weights and workout equipment. "So, this is where the muscles come from," I tease, giving his bicep a playful squeeze.

Laughing, he leads me inside. The garage opens into a bright, spacious kitchen that flows into an equally large great room with a dining area and living room. It's open, airy, and modern, with high-end appliances that make mine look outdated. Despite its bachelor pad potential, the house feels lived-in, with plants adding warmth, though there's a noticeable lack of personal photos or art.

"Cole, this is really nice," I say, genuinely impressed. "Between some of the things you've said and my jokes about picturing the worst bachelor pad imaginable," I laugh, shaking my head.

He leans back against the kitchen island, smiling. "I did alright for myself and the boys," he says, pride evident in his voice. "Let me put your bag in the bedroom. The master is on the main floor, and the boys' rooms are upstairs."

I follow him into his bedroom, taking in the simple yet cozy decor. The furniture is understated but comfortable, and there's even a small couch near the window. I catch a glimpse of the master bath—a luxurious five-piece setup with a tub that practically invites long, relaxing soaks.

"Yeah, I could be very comfortable here," I say, tugging him close by his belt loops.

"Yeah? You think so?" he asks, his voice low and inviting.

"Definitely. It's a lot newer than my house too," I add, running my fingers along the fabric of his shirt.

"It is," he agrees. "It was a new build when I bought it about seven years ago."

"You're the only one who's ever lived here?" I ask, curious.

"Yep, just me and the boys."

"Still weird to have me here?" I ask, searching his eyes.

He laughs softly. "Yeah, actually, it is. I don't know how to describe it—it just makes me feel vulnerable. It's something I've never shared with anyone. Just like you said you'd never had a guy in your house, I've never had a woman here. I've had very few people here at all, just the kids and, rarely, their friends."

"Cole, that makes sense," I say, understanding the significance of what he's sharing. "My house has been like Grand Central Station for the last ten years. I'm used to kids bringing people in and out, Cara dropping by, my parents, their friends—everyone coming by the house. I'm used to having people around. You're not." I smile at him, squeezing his hand. "I get it."

He smiles at me, his eyes warm. "You hungry?"

"Yeah, dinner sounds good."

"Want me to wow you with my cooking skills? Or we could order in," he chuckles, a playful glint in his eye.

I grin. "I'll leave it up to you. You've been full of surprises today."

"How about we just order pizza tonight, and I'll make you breakfast in the morning?"

"That sounds perfect," I say, wrapping my arms around his neck and kissing him.

He takes my hand and leads me back to the living room, guiding me to the couch. After ordering the pizza, we settle in, scrolling through the options on the television. We find a movie we've both been talking about watching but decide to wait until the pizza arrives to start it.

Everything feels so natural—eating pizza, snuggling up to him, and watching a movie. It's the kind of normalcy we haven't had much of, and I savor it. I know he's not completely comfortable with me being here, that he has his reasons, so I don't push him. I just let things flow.

When the movie ends, I tell him I need to monopolize the bathroom for a few minutes. I brush my teeth, wash my face, and go through my bedtime routine. When I come out, he's already changed into sweats and a t-shirt, and he looks so effortlessly sexy that I have to restrain myself from jumping on him.

He trades places with me in the bathroom, and while he's in there, I change into sleep shorts and a tank top. I'm brushing my hair when he comes back out, and I catch him just watching me.

"What?" I smile, feeling his gaze on me.

"I'm just taking you in," he says, a softness in his voice. "You, in my bedroom, just being your normal, adorable self."

"Adorable, huh?" I tease.

"Yeah," he says, moving toward me. "The cute faces you make, the way you move." He pulls me into a close embrace.

"Well, when I saw you come out of the bathroom, I wanted to attack you," I admit, smiling up at him. "So maybe you're adorable too. Although I'd probably say more like sexy."

"Attack me?" he laughs.

"Something like that," I laugh along with him.

He kisses me softly, lingering just enough to make my heart race. "Let me go turn off the lights. I'll be right back."

"I'm not going anywhere," I say, my voice soft with anticipation.

He moves through the house, turning off the lights in the kitchen and living room, and switching off the television. I lean against the frame of his bedroom door, watching him, waiting. When he looks at me as he walks back, I see the hunger in his eyes, and he quickens his pace.

He reaches me in a heartbeat, one arm sliding around my waist, the other hand gripping the back of my neck, his fingers tangling in my hair. He pins me against the wall just inside his bedroom door, his kiss deep and hungry. My hands grip his shirt, pulling him closer, and I lose myself in him, floating in a sea of sensation.

He turns us, backing me toward the bed. With a swift motion, he pulls my tank top over my head and drops to his knees, tugging off my shorts and underwear. His touch is primal, savage, as his hands travel up my legs and over my chest. He grips my upper arms, pushing me back onto the bed with a controlled force that sends a thrill through me.

As he strips off his shirt and pants, I can't tear my eyes away from him. His hands glide up my inner thighs, leaving a trail of fire in their wake. As he gets closer to my center, my skin buzzes with anticipation, every nerve ending on high alert. He teases me, trailing his fingers back down to my knees and repeating the motion, driving me to the edge of madness. I clutch the sheets, my back arching with every near-touch, desperate for more.

Finally, he gives in, sliding his fingers inside me while his other hand continues its relentless teasing. He curls his fingers just right, and I feel the sharp rise of a powerful orgasm building, my body on the brink, aching for release.

"Fuck, Cole," I whisper, gripping the comforter as pleasure overtakes me. He responds by roughly fondling my breast, his fingers working inside me with perfect precision. Just as I'm about to tip over the edge, his hand slides back down my body, grazing my inner thigh. It's enough to send me spiraling into ecstasy, my body convulsing as waves of pleasure crash over me and waves of fluid are released from me.

I'm aware of the wetness on me, under me, and as his hand moves up my body, I feel it dripping from him too. He uses his soaked hand to caress my breast, then lowers his mouth to my nipple, tasting me with a groan of pleasure.

"God, Autumn," he murmurs, his voice thick with desire as he kisses me, his hunger matching mine. I'm barely able to catch my breath, my body still shuddering beneath him. He pulls back slightly, his eyes dark and intense as he traces my lips with his fingers. Understanding his silent command, I open my mouth and gently suck on his fingers, earning a deep groan from him before he claims my mouth again.

His hand finds its way to the back of my neck, gripping my hair as his lips trail down my neck. He takes his time with my nipples before dropping to his knees at the edge of the bed, pulling my legs toward him. His mouth finds the sensitive bundle of nerves at my core, and I gasp as his tongue enters me. He replaces his tongue with his fingers, expertly working me from the outside with a rhythm that sends me spiraling again.

My body tightens, my toes curling as I grip the comforter, unable to control the primal moans escaping me. He's relentless, his mouth and fingers driving me to another shattering release, my body convulsing around him as he tastes every bit of me.

He stands, using the momentum to push me further onto the bed, climbing over me with a sense of urgency. He turns me to my side, lifting my leg and positioning himself between mine. Gripping my leg for leverage, he enters me, and just like before, he fucks me hard and deep. I brace myself against the headboard, each thrust sending pleasure radiating through me.

I reach the peak once more, coming hard just as he does, my muscles clenching around him, drawing out every last bit of pleasure. When he's spent, he lays behind me, spooning me, and we take a long time to catch our breath, the room filled with the sound of our slowing heartbeats.

When I finally regain the ability to speak, I whisper, "Cole?"

"Autumn?" His voice is breathless, laced with the remnants of our shared intensity.

I turn toward him, needing to see his face. "I'm pretty sure that was the best sex of my life," I say, a soft laugh escaping me.

He smiles, his hand lazily tracing patterns over my skin. "I'm glad you're satisfied."

"Satisfied isn't a strong enough word." I laugh again, still riding the afterglow.

I reach up, gently brushing my thumb across his cheekbone before leaning in to kiss him. He's still catching his breath, so it's just a brief, tender kiss. A few moments later, when his breathing steadies, he gestures toward the end of the bed and says, "I'm pretty sure you created a small lake down there."

I laugh, feeling a flush of warmth spread through me. "I think you had a little something to do with that. I didn't do it all on my own."

"Yeah, that might be true," he agrees, kissing my temple. "That was pretty amazing for me too."

"I know you were pretty selfless tonight," I say, my voice soft with gratitude. "Thank you."

"Maybe not as selfless as you think," he murmurs, a playful grin tugging at his lips. "I love it when your body reacts to me like that."

"I swear you were made for me," I say, my hand trailing down his arm, savoring the connection between us.

"It does seem that way." He smiles, his eyes full of warmth.

"Hopefully, that's a good enough memory for your bed," I tease, laughing softly.

"Come here," he says, his laugh quiet but full of affection. He pulls me closer, lifting my mouth to his, kissing me deeply but tenderly. "I love you, Autumn."

"I love you too."

CHAPTER TWENTY-SEVEN

THE AMAZING DINNER, THE FLOWERS, & THE EX

S ometime during the night, we manage to slip under the covers, though neither of us bothers getting dressed. We stay wrapped around each other, barely moving, and it feels like heaven. When I wake, sunlight is filtering through the window, and I feel the soft glide of his fingers tracing down my side.

"Good morning, beautiful," he murmurs, pressing a gentle kiss to my temple.

"Hey you," I reply, turning to smile at him.

"Did you sleep okay?" His voice is soft, still carrying the warmth of sleep.

"Wonderfully, actually," I say, feeling more rested than I have in a long time.

"Good," he says, his smile widening. "I promised you breakfast, so I'll get on that in a minute."

A sudden thought strikes me, and I laugh. "Cole, did we sleep through the meeting?"

"Check your phone," he suggests, kissing me once more before climbing out of bed.

I realize I have no idea where my phone is; everything happened so quickly last night. I throw on a sheet from the bed and wander into the living room, eventually finding my phone nearly dead in my bag. Wrapping the sheet tighter around me, I sit on the couch and open my phone to find our team chat buzzing with messages.

I glance up at Cole, surprised. "I didn't even feel you move."

He smiles, a warm glint in his eyes. "You were sleeping pretty soundly."

I chuckle, shaking my head. "I'm a bad influence on you—taking another day off because of me. That's two Fridays in a row."

"Or maybe it's because you're good for me," he says with a laugh. "I'm starting to see the benefits of taking a break."

"Maybe." I smile, feeling a little flutter in my chest. "I guess I should plug in my phone and put on some clothes."

I walk into the kitchen, wrapped in a sheet, and kiss him before heading back to the bedroom to get dressed. As I brush out my tangled hair—a reminder of last night's adventures—I can't help but smile. When I return to the kitchen, Cole is nearly finished with breakfast, whipping up breakfast burritos with peppers, onions, and all the fixings. The aroma fills the kitchen, making my stomach rumble.

We eat together, laughing and talking. It's nice to see him more relaxed, the tension from last night seemingly gone. As I check my phone, I notice messages from several people, including Megan and Cara, who are both upset that I didn't text them last night.

I really need to be better about that. But, damn, Cole is distracting.

"So, what's the plan with William?" I ask between bites.

"We'll need to drive down to Indianapolis," Cole says, pausing to take a sip of coffee. "I told him we'd meet for dinner around six. It'll put us right in the middle of rush hour, but he works until five."

"Okay, so we should leave here between three and four?" I suggest.

"Yeah," he agrees with a smile. "And I'm definitely going to need a shower."

"Me too," I laugh. "Is there anything I need to know about William that you haven't already told me?"

Cole thinks for a moment, then shrugs. "Not much. Just be yourself. If you're you, I think he'll like you, whether it's right away or over time. We can't force it."

"That's fair," I nod. "I get that."

We both take showers and get dressed for dinner. As we make the bed, which we thoroughly destroyed last night, I can't help but feel a mix of anticipation and nerves about meeting William.

As we start the drive to Indianapolis, I turn to Cole, curious. "If I remember right, you said your other two boys would probably do better in a group setting, but William might not handle it as well, right?"

"Yeah," Cole says, glancing at me. "He gets overstimulated and is a bit more emotional than the other two. I just think he'd appreciate getting to know you one-on-one before dealing with your kids and his brothers all at once."

"That makes sense," I agree. "Do you think he'll be okay with us touching and all that?"

Cole hesitates, then says, "Honestly, I'm not sure. It might bother him, but then again, maybe that 'magnetic' thing your kids noticed could help. If he sees what they saw, maybe he'll understand that this is the real deal."

I smile, touched by his words. "Awwww, you think this is the real deal?"

"Autumn," he sighs, shaking his head with a grin, "you're adorable."

"You keep using that word to describe me," I laugh.

"It's the best word for you," he says, his smile widening.

"Okay, so be myself, but watch his reactions. Got it."

"Yeah," Cole says, his tone a little more serious. "And, Autumn?"

"Yes, Cole?"

"If he gets mean or says something abrasive, try to brush it off. He doesn't mean it—he's just struggling to cope with all of this."

"Don't worry," I say, reaching over to place my hand on his thigh as we drive down the highway. "I'll be fine."

We pull up to the restaurant around a quarter to six. Cole gets out and comes around to open my door, offering his hand to help me out of the car. I chose to wear jeans and a simple green shirt—not overly sexy, but it feels right for tonight. Cole is dressed in jeans and a button-down shirt he's left untucked, looking effortlessly handsome.

We wait in the lobby for William, anticipation buzzing between us. "Here he is," Cole murmurs as he spots his son. He greets William with a half hug, his voice warm. "Hey, buddy. How was your day?"

William doesn't look exactly like Cole, but the resemblance is there. They're about the same height, with dark hair—William's without the salt that peppers Cole's—and the same eye color. Their facial features share similarities, though William's nose is a bit flatter and his eyes are set slightly differently. He's dressed in gray dress pants and a blue polo shirt, a classic casual Friday look in the corporate world.

"Hey, Dad. It was good, productive," William replies.

"Good, that's the way workdays should be," Cole says, then turns to me, his hand resting on the small of my back. "William, this is Autumn."

I reach out to shake William's hand, noticing his slight hesitation before he finally takes mine. "It's really nice to meet you. Your dad has told me a lot about you," I say, offering a warm smile.

"You too," William says with a laugh, glancing at Cole.

Cole steps up to the hostess to get our table, and William surprises me by making small talk. "Was the drive down from Fort Wayne okay?" he asks.

"Yeah, we hit a bit of rush hour traffic once we got to Indianapolis, but it wasn't too bad," I reply.

"That's good. I think it's worse going the other way, with people leaving Indianapolis to head toward Dad's house."

"That's what it looked like, but you and your dad would know better than me," I say, appreciating his attempt at conversation.

As Cole returns, William asks, "Dad says you're from Milwaukee?"

"Yeah, a suburb, actually—Brookfield, on the west side of the city," I answer.

"I went to Marquette, so I'm familiar," William says, nodding.

I glance at Cole in surprise. "Your dad didn't tell me that. My daughter's a junior at Marquette."

Cole shrugs, looking a bit sheepish. "I guess it just never came up."

William and I both laugh, shaking our heads. "Seriously?" I ask, still chuckling.

"What?" Cole asks, genuinely confused, which makes William and me laugh even harder. In that moment, I know everything is going to be okay.

Dinner is pleasant and relaxed. Cole and I aren't overly affectionate, but there are plenty of flirtatious looks and gentle touches. He puts his arm around me a couple of times and even kisses me on the temple once. William doesn't visibly react, which I take as a good sign.

William talks about his job and jokes about following in his dad's footsteps in sales. He asks a bit about my kids, and I answer honestly, enjoying the ease of the conversation. We linger at the table long after we're done eating, chatting for about an hour. Cole assures the waitress he'll tip her well for the extended stay.

As we're leaving the restaurant, I turn to William and say, "It was really nice to meet you." On a whim, I ask, "Would it be okay if I gave you a hug?" He doesn't even hesitate, wrapping me in a warm, if brief, hug.

"We'll have to have you and your brothers over to our house sometime soon, so you can meet my kids," I suggest.

"That would be nice," William says, sounding sincere.

Cole hugs his son goodbye, and I step back, giving them a moment for a private conversation. When Cole returns to me, the smile on his face is genuine, his happiness radiating through the night.

As Cole reaches me, he wraps his arm around my waist, pulling me close and kissing my temple. Once we're settled in the car with the doors closed, he can't contain his excitement. "That was amazing, Autumn."

I smile, feeling the warmth of his happiness. "Yeah, I think it went really well."

He pauses before backing out of the parking space, turning to look at me with a mix of awe and gratitude. "That went better than I could have hoped for. Seriously, you amaze me."

The drive back to his house feels easy and light. We talk about the dinner, and Cole shares his thoughts on how he thinks his other boys will handle things. We even start making plans for Labor Day weekend, with Cole planning to talk to all the boys in the next couple of days to finalize everything. His happiness is so genuine, it's infectious.

We're just a couple of blocks from Cole's house when my phone buzzes with a text from Megan.

Megan

> Mom, someone sent you flowers, do you want me to open the card?

Me

> Yeah, please do, because I'm 99.9% sure it wasn't Cole

Megan

> Okay one sec

"Fuck," I say, catching Cole off guard.

"What?" he says, looking at me concerned.

"Tony Gabari sent me flowers," I pause for emphasis, "*to my house.* He has my address, Cole. My house isn't even in my name, how does he have my address?"

Cole is silent, but I can tell his mood has shifted. We pull into his garage as the message from Megan with the picture of the card comes through. I read it out loud to Cole, and then he hits the dashboard of his car.

Autumn,

I know we are supposed to be keeping things strictly business, but I just can't help but think about how good we would be together. Please let me know when you are free for dinner.

Yours,

Tony Gabari

Cole picks up his phone and dials a number, his expression shifting into something more serious. He glances at me and gestures for silence.

"Hey, Pete, sorry to bother you this late on a Friday," Cole says, his tone calm and businesslike.

There's a brief pause, then Cole continues, "Yeah, it is important. Anthony Gabari sent Autumn flowers to her house." He listens for a moment, his jaw tightening slightly. "No, Pete, her house isn't even in her name—it's in her parents' name. He would've had to dig to get her address." Another pause. "I'll send you a picture of the card." He listens again. "Okay, I'll let her know. Keep me posted after you talk to Andy and Lauryn." Another pause. "Thanks, Pete. Talk soon."

Cole ends the call and leans back in his seat, staring up at the roof of the car with a frustrated sigh. "Fuck," he mutters, clearly agitated. "Tell Megan to make sure the alarm is on all the time. I don't think he'd go that far, but I don't like the idea of her being alone there right now."

I nod, concern gnawing at me. "What did Pete say?"

"He's going to talk to Andy now," Cole explains, referring to our chief compliance officer. "They'll figure out what needs to be done. Can you send me the picture of the card so I can forward it to Pete?"

"Yeah," I say, already reaching for my phone.

"Let's go inside," Cole says, squeezing my hand for reassurance.

Once we're inside the house, I settle onto a barstool at the kitchen island and call Megan while Cole paces the kitchen, clearly on edge.

"Megan wants me to call Kevin," I say after hanging up, and Cole nods in agreement.

"Hey, Kev," I say when he answers.

"Hey, Mom, what's up?"

"So, you know that doctor who's been way too forward with me?"

"Yeah, the one in Chicago, who was also in Dallas?"

"Yeah, him. He sent flowers to the house, so he knows our address. I'm in Fort Wayne with Cole, and Megan wants to know if you can stay at the house tonight and tomorrow."

"Are you fucking kidding me, Mom?"

"I wish I were, Kevin, but I'm not."

"Yeah, I'll call Megan. I'll be there in less than two hours and stay until you and Cole get back."

"Thanks, Kev. Love you."

"Love you too."

As I hang up, Cole's phone buzzes with a new message. He glances at it and lets out a frustrated laugh. "This night went to shit so fast," he says, tossing his phone onto the counter.

"What is it?" I ask, nodding toward his phone.

He gestures for me to take a look, and I see the message on his lock screen.

Michelle

I hear William got to meet your new flame, good luck with that, I'm sure you'll fuck it up somehow

CHAPTER TWENTY-EIGHT

THE NIGHT THAT WENT TO SHIT

"Cole," I say softly, watching him pace the kitchen, his hands running through his hair in frustration. I step closer, reaching up to place my hands gently on his chest.

"Just don't, Autumn," he snaps, his voice sharp. "Just give me a minute."

I don't move. I refuse to let him spiral like this.

"Cole, look at me," I say, my voice still soft but firm enough to cut through his agitation.

He stops and meets my gaze. I take hold of his wrists, gently pulling them down from his head, and wrap his arms around me.

"Cole, I'm here. I'm not going anywhere—not because of Tony, Michelle, or anyone else," I say, my thumb grazing his bottom lip as I cup his cheek. "Tony is an issue we'll deal with. Michelle is just trying to get under your skin. Don't let her."

He leans his forehead against mine, his breath warm on my skin. "It's just so much at once," he admits, his voice strained.

"I know, Cole. It's a lot for me too."

Lifting his head, he starts to speak again, worry creasing his brow. "And Michelle—she's a bitch, but that means William must have talked to her, so maybe it didn't go as well as we thought—"

I cut him off gently but firmly. "Cole, you can't stop him from talking to his mother. Nothing in that message suggests William said anything negative about you, me, or us. She's trying to get under your skin, to manipulate you, to make you react and strain your relationship with William. Don't take the bait."

He looks at me, processing my words. "Cole, seriously, she's trying to terrorize you. She's a fucking emotional terrorist. Don't let her win."

His gaze intensifies, and then he kisses me, his hand moving to the back of my neck, pulling me closer as his lips press urgently against mine.

When he breaks the kiss, he rests his forehead against mine, his breath steadier. "You're right. You're a hundred percent right. My instinct is to call or text William, but that would undo everything we achieved at dinner."

"Exactly," I agree. "You know how she is. Remember how I told you I did everything in my power not to villainize Steve? I guarantee she's doing the opposite, villainizing you at every opportunity."

He takes a deep breath, nodding as the tension begins to ease from his shoulders. "I know you're right. Thank you," he whispers, holding me close.

Cole's phone rings, and I see Pete's name flash on the screen. He answers quickly.

"Hey, Pete," Cole says, his tone calm but focused.

I catch a few words here and there, but nothing that gives me any real context. When Cole hangs up, he looks at me, a mix of relief and resolve in his eyes.

"Andy's going to have Tony served with a cease and desist letter tomorrow," Cole explains. "If he continues to harass you, we can take him to civil court, maybe even criminal court. Pete's pulling you completely off his account. You won't have to deal with him anymore, except maybe at conferences."

"Okay," I nod, absorbing the information. "I think I'm okay with that. I'll call Kevin and let him know so he can update Megan."

"Good," Cole says, then adds, "I'm going to call William."

I start to object, worried he might get drawn into something negative, but he stops me gently. "Autumn, I'm just going to thank him again for his time and tell him how much we enjoyed dinner. I want to reinforce all the positivity and the beautiful energy you brought tonight."

I can't help but smile at him. I lean in, kiss him softly, and then dial Kevin. As I explain everything, Kevin listens carefully, his protective instincts kicking in. He assures me he'll keep Megan informed and that he'll stay on alert until Tony is served on Saturday. He's worried, but he understands the plan.

Cole and I finish our calls around the same time.

"How'd it go?" I ask, watching his expression.

"Well," he says, a smile tugging at his lips, "William said he enjoyed dinner too. He mentioned that he can see we're a good match and that he's looking forward to spending more time with us and getting to know you better."

"See?" I say, my smile widening as I lean in for another kiss. "It's all going to be okay."

But just as our lips are about to meet, my phone rings.

It's Alex. I answer immediately. "Hey, Alex."

"Autumn, Kevin just called me. What the fuck is going on?"

"Well, hi to you too," I reply, my voice laced with sarcasm.

"Autumn!" he snaps, his tone sharp and concerned.

I take a deep breath and explain everything to him. He agrees with the plan to serve Tony with a cease and desist letter, but then drops a surprise on me. "I told Kevin to take Megan back to his place instead. If there's any real concern this guy might do something, they just shouldn't be there at all. They're going to arm the house and leave."

"Um, okay," I say, trying to process this new twist. "I guess that's a plan too."

"Autumn, I know it might seem like I'm overreacting, but when Claire was in criminal law, these were the scariest cases. Things can escalate so quickly."

"Alex," I begin, but my voice falters as a tightness grips my chest. My eyes start to burn.

"It'll be okay, Autumn," he says, his tone softening. "I'm not trying to scare you. I just want to be extra cautious—an abundance of caution, that's all."

I sniffle, fighting back the tears. Cole's eyes meet mine, filled with concern. He walks over, gently stroking my hair, grounding me.

Alex continues, more gently now, "You remember my friend Jamie from law school?"

"Yeah," I manage, "he was in your wedding."

"Right. He runs a private investigation and security company in Milwaukee now. I'm going to reach out to him tomorrow, see if we can figure out whether this guy is just being a creep or if we have something to worry about."

"Okay," I say, my voice barely above a whisper. "I'm okay with that."

"I'm sorry, Autumn. I didn't mean to upset you. I just... if something happened to you... just, please, be careful."

I swallow hard, my throat tight. "Yeah, I'm with Cole," I say, my voice cracking. "We're in Fort Wayne."

"Good. Just stay there until I hear back from Jamie." I glance up at Cole, who watches me with a mix of concern and curiosity.

"Okay," I say, trying to keep my composure. "Just keep me posted, please."

"I will. I love you, Autumn. I'm really sorry this is happening," he says, his voice filled with genuine concern.

"Love you too. Talk soon." I end the call and look up at Cole, but I can't find the words. Instead, I lean into his chest, letting the tears come. Softly, quietly, he just holds me, offering the comfort I desperately need without asking for explanations.

When I finally manage to gather myself, I explain everything Alex said. "He's going to have his friend Jamie look into Tony, just to see if there's something more serious going on."

Cole nods, his hand gently resting on my neck, guiding me back into his embrace. "I think that's a good plan. I'm pretty sure Tony isn't dangerous, just persistent. But it's smart to find out if there's more to be concerned about."

I don't respond, just let myself melt into the comfort of his arms. He whispers in my ear, "And I don't mind you staying here either."

We stay like that for a moment longer until, unexpectedly, I start laughing. The sound catches both of us off guard.

"What a fucking night," I say with a rueful smile.

Cole smiles back, his own tension easing. "Yeah, just a bit of an emotional rollercoaster for both of us."

I laugh again, the absurdity of it all hitting me. "I need to wash my face."

Cole brushes a strand of hair out of my face and kisses my forehead before stepping back to let me go. I head to the bathroom, and when I catch sight of myself in the mirror, I almost laugh again. I'm a mess—red as a tomato, with swollen eyes and smeared makeup.

I take my time, splashing cold water on my face, trying to calm the heat in my cheeks and reduce the swelling in my eyes. Finally, when I look a little more like myself, I leave the bathroom, feeling slightly more put together.

I find Cole back in the kitchen, scrolling through his phone. He looks up when I walk in. "You okay?" he asks, concern softening his voice.

"Yeah, I think so," I reply, though my voice sounds smaller than I'd like.

"Want to watch a movie or something? Just try to forget all this?" he suggests with a gentle smile.

"Yeah, that sounds good. I just need you to hold me," I admit, feeling vulnerable.

"That," he says, pausing as he walks toward me, "is definitely doable."

When he reaches me, he places his hand on my cheek, his thumb softly tracing my cheekbone before he presses a tender kiss to my forehead. Grabbing a blanket from the back of the couch, he gently tugs me down beside him. I curl up with my head in his lap, and he stretches his legs out, propping them on the coffee table. Draping the blanket over us, he turns on the TV and picks a light, silly comedy. As we watch, his fingers thread through my hair, and he rubs my back, the simple touch soothing me.

After the movie ends, Cole suggests we go to bed, and I agree. I realize I'm still wearing the clothes from dinner, and Cole, too, is still mostly dressed, though he's ditched his button-down. I grab a tank top from my bag and slip into bed wearing just that and my underwear. Cole joins me in his boxers, and he wraps his arms around me, holding me close all night. I feel safe, loved, and warm, and I'm overwhelmed with gratitude for him.

We sleep late into Saturday morning, both of us needing the rest after the emotional and physical exhaustion of the night before. When I finally stir, I feel him still spooning me, his hand gently tracing down my arm.

"Good morning," I say softly, my voice still heavy with sleep.

"Good morning," he replies, kissing my hair. "You know, I was lying here thinking."

"Yeah? About what?" I ask, turning to face him.

"That today marks three weeks," he says with a quiet laugh. "And it's been the most intense, longest three weeks of my life."

I meet his gaze, and he brushes a strand of hair out of my face. I place my hand on his cheek, my thumb tracing the short beard along his jaw, but I stay silent, just absorbing his words.

"Seriously," he continues, holding my eyes with his, "I don't think I'm the same man I was a few weeks ago. And it doesn't feel like just three weeks—it feels like I've known you forever."

I run my thumb back over his jaw, and he says, "Autumn, I love you. I love you more every day."

He leans in to kiss me, his lips tender and gentle, and warmth spreads through my entire body.

"I love you too," I whisper as I pull back slightly, "and more every day."

As his mouth meets mine again, his hand begins to explore my body, and I wrap my arms around him, holding him close. There's so much emotion in every touch, every kiss, that it all feels more intense, more profound. His lips trail soft kisses and playful nips down my body as his hands slowly remove the few pieces of clothing I have on. My hands never leave his skin, needing to feel him—his hair, his shoulders, his strong arms, his capable hands.

His mouth and fingers find all the places my body craves, but today, it's more than just physical. It's as though he becomes a part of me, and as my body reaches the peak of pleasure, I'm overwhelmed with a flood of happiness and love. He's like a drug—a drug I desperately crave, a drug I can't imagine living without. He is my everything.

He moves back on top of me, kissing me deeply as he enters me, and in that moment, I feel whole again, like he's the missing piece of me, the one that completes me. When he breaks the kiss and our eyes meet, I see everything I'm feeling reflected back at me. As he reaches his climax, he kisses me once more, and we roll to our sides, still connected in every way. We lay in silence as he slowly withdraws, but he keeps me close, wrapping his arm around me and pulling me into him. I bury my face in his neck, feeling the steady rise and fall of his breath, and he just holds me, as if he never wants to let go.

When we finally stir from our embrace, I check my phone. There's a missed call and voicemail from Pete, along with several text messages from the kids, Cara, and Alex. I play the voicemail from Pete on speaker so Cole can hear it too.

"Hey, Autumn, I wanted to reach out to you directly instead of just going through Cole. I'm really sorry about everything that's happened. I wanted to let you know that Dr. Gabari was successfully served with the cease and desist letter this morning. He immediately contacted Andy and assured him that he's done and won't reach out to you anymore. I hope this resolves it once and for all. Again, I'm so sorry."

Cole shrugs slightly. "I guess we'll see, but I really hope it's over."

"Yeah," I agree, feeling a mix of relief and uncertainty. "I'm going to call my brother and fill him in."

Cole nods and kisses my forehead, offering silent support. I call Alex, and he's relieved that we've taken this step. He hopes it's the end of the drama too. He also tells me that Jamie, his friend, has someone keeping an eye on Tony over the weekend, just to make sure he stays in Chicago. If anything changes, Jamie will let us know. Jamie also shared that Tony's criminal record is clean—no charges for stalking, assault, or domestic violence. He's been married three times, each lasting less than five years, but there's no history of violence.

"All of that sounds like good news," Cole says. "You're lucky to have your brother."

"I am," I reply, reflecting on Alex's protectiveness. "He was pretty shaken last night, and that's not like him. He doesn't get scared easily."

"He clearly loves you. I'm sure the thought of someone hurting you is terrifying for him," Cole says, his tone gentle.

I send a quick thank-you text to Pete and respond to the other messages. As Cole makes us lunch, the day begins to feel more normal, a welcome shift from the intensity of the night before.

While we're eating, I look at Cole, feeling the need to check in. "I know everything spiraled quickly after my brother called last night. How are you holding up? Especially with William?"

He smiles at me, his eyes warm. "I'm okay. I think I was good even before Alex called. You were right—William is fine. And Michelle... what did you call her?"

"A fucking emotional terrorist," I say with a laugh.

"Well, you nailed it. She's been that way the entire time I've known her, and I never really saw it exactly that way."

"I was married to someone like that too," I say, recalling my own past. "My therapist actually used the comparison to a terrorist during our sessions. I wouldn't be surprised if I get a similar message from Steve at some point. He always took pride in thinking I couldn't move on after him, like he's so irreplaceable."

Cole grins. "I think Michelle and Steve would get along great then. I'm pretty sure she feels the exact same way."

After lunch, Cole and I both agree it's time to shower and clean up. Since Cole's shower isn't as spacious as mine, we take turns. While he's in the shower, I take my time—shaving, exfoliating, and doing all the little things that help me feel refreshed and pretty. I dab on some perfume and, feeling playful, spray a bit on the pillow I've been sleeping on, smiling to myself as I do.

When I step out of the bedroom, I find Cole in the kitchen. He greets me with a kiss on the forehead and then says, "I think we should go out tonight, like a real date."

I smile up at him, warmth spreading through me. "I'd like that."

We end up going out for dinner and a movie. It's exactly what we need—a distraction from everything and a chance to just be normal. Walking hand in hand to and from the car, laughing over dinner, and snuggling up to him in the movie theater feels so wonderfully ordinary, and yet, it's everything.

On Sunday morning, after talking it over with Cole, I decide to call Alex. I'm supposed to have our regular Sunday dinner with my parents, but I'm unsure about what to do given everything that's happened. Alex reassures me that Tony hasn't done anything concerning—nothing that raised any red flags with Jamie, who thinks it's safe for us to head back to my house if we want. Still, Alex asks if Cole is willing to stay with us, and I can tell my brother isn't thrilled about the idea of me going home, but he also doesn't want to alarm our parents.

I talk to Cole, and he agrees to stay for a couple of days, but reminds me that we both have flights to Nashville on Thursday. He's also reluctant to leave me alone at the house, but he'll have to drive home before flying to Nashville.

"Are you sure you're okay with this? I know it would have been easier to stay at your place," I ask as we're driving.

"Autumn, Megan needs to be home, and I don't care where we are as long as I'm with you," he says, then chuckles softly. "More cheesiness I didn't think I was capable of."

"I'm a bad influence on you," I laugh, feeling a little lighter.

"No, you're the best influence on me," he replies, reaching across the console to squeeze my thigh.

We arrive at the house almost simultaneously with Kevin and Megan. After freshening up, we head to dinner with my parents. The atmosphere is more relaxed this time since they've already met Cole, and Kevin does a great job of keeping my dad engaged in the conversation again.

After dinner, Kevin comes back to the house with us. He checks all the ground floor windows and the egress windows in the basement, making sure everything is locked and the sensors on the alarms are working properly—at Alex's request, of course. He asks if we're sure we're okay, and we reassure him that we are. He gives Megan and me big hugs, shakes Cole's hand, and then heads back to his place.

The whole day and night feel almost normal, but there's this strange shadow hanging over everything. Megan has the flowers from Tony sitting in the kitchen. I take them to the garage and throw them away, vase and all, trying to rid the house of that lingering unease.

CHAPTER TWENTY-NINE

THE FIRST TWO NIGHTS IN NASHVILLE

The next few days pass without much incident. I'm a little disappointed when my period arrives—it was bound to happen eventually. It doesn't stop us from being close, but it does slow us down a bit. Cole and I fall into our usual rhythm, working side by side. We separate for meetings when necessary, but otherwise, we're on the family room couch, always finding small ways to stay connected—his hand on my leg, my head resting on his shoulder.

On Wednesday, Cole heads back to his house to pack and prepare for his flight out of Indianapolis to our conference in Nashville. It'll be just over twenty-four hours until we see each other again, but when we say goodbye, it feels like we're parting for much longer.

That night, as I lay down in bed, I find myself missing him more than I expected. I reach for my phone and send him a text.

Me

I miss you

Cole

So we are one of *those* couples

Me

lol, yes, you willed it into existence

Cole

I miss you too, and now I get the pillow thing, this pillow does smell like you

Me

I have one that smells like you too, so I'll hug it and bury my face in it all night

Cole

You ready for this weekend?

Me

I think so, we'll be with Mark, so for whatever reason, that makes me more comfortable than if it were anyone else on the team

Cole

Yeah, me too, maybe Tara

We talk a little longer, savoring the connection even from a distance, before saying goodnight. I fall asleep quickly, already looking forward to the next day.

In the morning, Megan has a class, so I drive myself to the airport in my SUV. After going through security and finding my gate, I check my phone and see texts from both Cole and Alex.

Shortly after I put my phone away I get another notification.

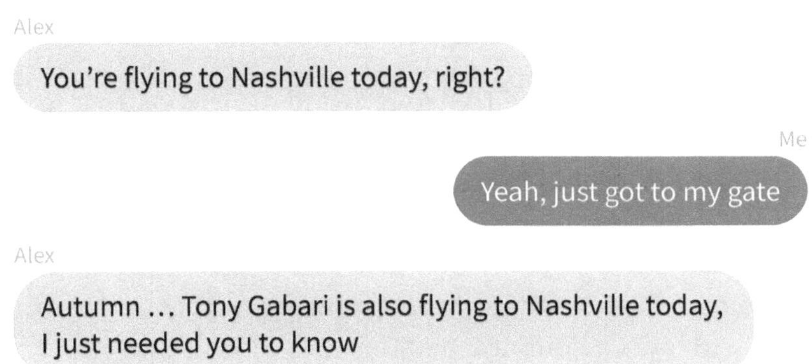

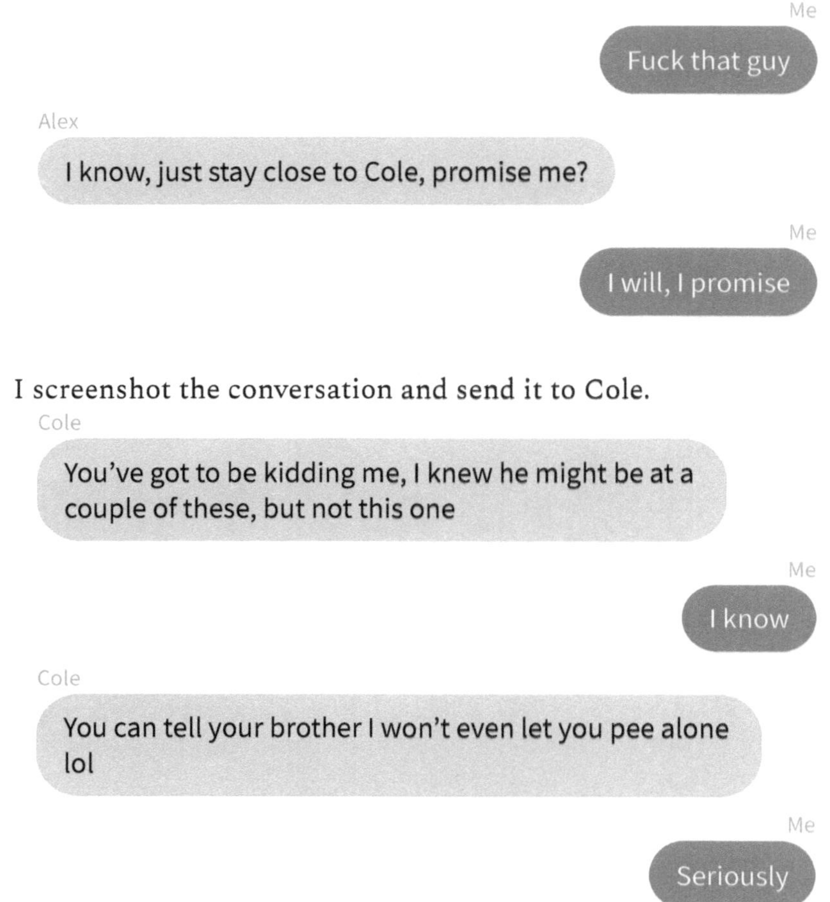

I screenshot the conversation and send it to Cole.

The flight is smooth, and true to his word, Cole is waiting for me at the gate. He pulls me into a quick hug and kiss before we head off to baggage claim. In public, we're cautious, keeping our displays of affection to a minimum, but once we're away from prying eyes, we start to relax.

At the hotel, Cole checks us in and manages to get our three rooms in a row, with ours adjoining.

"We should probably sleep in the one furthest from Mark's room," he jokes with a knowing smile as we ride the elevator.

"Probably," I agree, smiling back. "At least this way we have two bathrooms," I add with a laugh.

Once we're settled in our rooms, the doors between them are immediately propped open. Cole texts Mark to check how far out he is, and we learn he'll be there in time for dinner. They finalize the plans, and we both get dressed and ready to meet him.

Dinner with Mark is pleasant, filled with catching up and casual conversation. But beneath the table, Cole's fingers play a different game. He lightly touches my inner thighs, tracing the inseam of my jeans, occasionally grazing just close enough to my center to send jolts of electricity through me. The teasing is maddening—intensely arousing and slightly frustrating as the need for him builds inside me. Cole, however, keeps his expression completely composed, chatting with Mark as if nothing is happening.

Several times, I swat his hand away, but each time, he only returns with more persistence. The wetness between my thighs grows, and the ache for him intensifies, leaving me torn between desire and annoyance. Cole, of course, finds this incredibly amusing.

At some point, the conversation turns to the recent events with Dr. Gabari. Cole fills Mark in on the flowers, the cease and desist letter, and everything else that's transpired over the past week. Mark suggests that maybe we should skip the cocktail hour tomorrow night, or at least that I should. We agree it's probably a good idea, but decide to play it by ear, depending on how the day unfolds.

As the three of us ride the elevator back to our rooms, Cole positions himself slightly behind me, his hand sneaking along the inside of my thighs, teasing its way up to the juncture of my legs—all while maintaining a perfectly normal conversation with Mark. I'm the one struggling to keep it together. When Mark gestures for me to step off the elevator ahead of him, it takes me a beat too long to realize what's happening.

"Sorry, zoned out for a minute," I stammer, while Cole stifles a laugh that's a little too amused.

I head into the room between Cole's and Mark's, offering a quick goodnight. As soon as the door shuts behind me, I'm already moving toward Cole's room, the door barely closing behind me before I'm stripping off both our clothes with a speed I didn't know I possessed. My hands fumble with his belt and pants while his grip tightens around my neck, pulling me into a hungry kiss. As soon as his pants hit the floor, I peel off my own jeans and underwear. I push him onto the bed, straddling him, finding him more than ready for me.

He tugs at my shirt, so I pull it off over my head, leaving us both half-dressed—his shirt still on, my bra still in place. I lower myself onto him, the sensation overwhelming in its intensity.

"Autumn," he breathes out with a laugh, a mix of surprise and arousal in his voice.

"Shhhh," I murmur, leaning down to kiss him, silencing any further protest.

Our hips find a fast, desperate rhythm as I sit up, using one hand on the bed for balance. His hands move over my still-covered breasts before he sits up, flipping us over without breaking our connection. He pushes my bra down beneath my breasts, his mouth and hands devouring me. Then, standing, he drags me to the edge of the bed, lifting my legs over his arms. I brace myself against the bed, each thrust sending shivers of pleasure through me until, in a frenzy of chaos, we reach our climax together—my body contracting around him as his releases inside me in deep, palpable throbs.

Dropping my legs, he climbs up my body to find my mouth again, flipping us so I'm back on top. I sit up, straddling him once more, breathless and spent. We're both still half-dressed—his shirt still on, my bra askew—but I can't help but collapse beside him, laughing.

"You better now?" he asks, grinning as he catches his breath.

"Yeah," I reply, still panting. "I was at the point where I either needed to fuck you or kill you, so yeah."

He laughs, rolling over to face me. "I think you made the preferable choice."

"For both of us," I agree, smiling.

"You know this reaction doesn't exactly discourage my behavior," he teases, still amused.

I narrow my eyes at him playfully. "Maybe next time I'll opt for the other option."

"You're cute when you're trying to be menacing," he says, pulling me into another kiss.

Eventually, we manage to move, putting on clothes to sleep in. I snuggle up to Cole, my head resting on his chest with an arm and a leg draped over him. His hand gently strokes my hair and runs down my back, soothing me. As I drift off to sleep, I feel safe, loved, and completely satisfied.

The next morning, as we get ready to head down to breakfast with Mark, I decide to wear my backless green shirt with angel sleeves.

"I remember taking that shirt off of you the first night we were together," Cole says with a smile before leaning in to kiss me.

"I remember that too," I reply, smiling as I wipe the lip gloss off his mouth with my thumb.

We head down to breakfast and meet Mark before setting up the booth for the day. It's a relatively uneventful day—Cole behaves himself, mostly keeping his hands to himself. True to his word, he sticks close by, even waiting outside the restroom when I go in and making sure Mark is with me whenever he needs to step away. We don't see Dr. Gabari at any point, so we decide it's safe to attend the cocktail hour that evening.

Before we get ready, Cole finds a professional way to suggest I dress a bit more conservatively. "Hey, Autumn, I don't know what dress you brought for tonight, but the last two Tony saw you in probably aren't the best idea," he says with a smile, earning a laugh from Mark.

"I have something a little more subdued, and you're not going to leave my side, right?" I ask.

"No, I won't leave your side," Cole promises, exchanging a knowing look with Mark that I'm not supposed to notice.

I choose a black lace dress, reminiscent of the one Tara wore in Dallas, but with a second layer for modesty. The main dress is a simple knee-length A-line, while the outer layer is ankle-length lace. It has a halter top, so there's no cleavage, and my back is still almost completely covered. I keep my hair natural and my makeup understated.

Cole helps me button the halter top, then steps back to look at me, letting out a sigh. "You still look stunning. Maybe we really do need to consider that burlap sack next time," he teases, kissing my cheek with a smile.

Mark meets us in the hall, and together we head down to the cocktail hour. This event is much more subdued than the last one—classical music plays softly in the background, and the lighting, though dim, is brighter than at the last one. It's purely a social hour, with appetizers and mingling. As we move from table to table, Cole keeps a hand on the small of my back or my upper arm, a subtle gesture that I know he'll pass off as protective if Mark asks.

Just as we're talking about heading back to our rooms, we hear a familiar voice. Dr. Gabari is approaching, but instead of addressing Cole or me, he calls out to Mark.

"Mark Tyson, good to see you," he says as he walks toward us.

In an instant, Cole shifts, positioning himself in front of me while keeping his hand on my arm. Mark raises a hand, signaling Tony to stop. But before any of us can react further, another man—big, imposing, and quietly standing in the corner with a drink—steps in front of Tony. He's about the same size as Mark, but with a much more intimidating presence.

The stranger extends his hand toward Tony. "Tony Gabari, right?"

Tony, clearly thrown off, hesitates. "Yes, that's right."

"Why don't we have a chat?" the man suggests, guiding Tony away from us.

I glance at Cole, confusion written all over my face. "That was weird, right? What just happened?"

Cole and Mark look just as bewildered as I feel. We sip our drinks in silence, all of us suddenly hyperaware of our surroundings.

A few minutes later, I notice Cole stiffen, his gaze focused behind me. I turn to see the same man who had intervened with Tony walking toward us.

"Autumn Flynn?" he asks, and Cole instinctively pulls me closer, my back pressed against his chest.

"Yeah?" I respond, my tone skeptical.

The man extends his hand to me. "My name is Danny. I'm a friend of Jamie's—who, I believe, is a friend of your brother's?" He glances around, his eyes darting back and forth. "I think I got that right," he adds with a smile. He reaches into his pocket and hands me a business card for a private security firm, identifying him as a personal security guard.

I feel Cole's muscles relax behind me, and I let out a breath I didn't realize I was holding. But a part of me bristles, even though I know I shouldn't. "Wait, did my brother hire you?"

Danny senses my unease and raises his hands slightly in a placating gesture. "Not exactly," he explains, looking from Cole to Mark before continuing. "Jamie asked me to look into the situation. I worked with him a while ago, and he knew I was here in Nashville. He explained what was happening and asked if I could keep an eye out for you if I had the time. No one hired me or told me what to do—just a favor, really. I wasn't planning to approach you or Dr. Gabari unless something happened, but when he approached you, I felt the need to step in. I don't think he'll bother you again here in Nashville. We had a chat, and he understands that you'll enforce that cease and desist if he tries anything. I also gave him my business card, so as far as he's concerned, you do have personal security. Hopefully, that keeps him away permanently."

I stand there, processing everything, unsure of what to say. Danny turns to Cole and extends his hand. "You must be Cole. Sorry to intrude or make things awkward, but after what I was told, I wasn't going to let him approach her."

Cole shakes his hand. "No, we appreciate it. It was just surprising."

Finally finding my voice, I add, "Yes, surprising, but thank you. I do appreciate it."

Danny shakes Mark's hand as well before telling us he'll be around and to call or text him if we need anything. He heads back to the corner of the room, blending in with the crowd.

"Remind me never to cross you, Autumn Flynn," Mark says with a laugh, taking a sip of his drink.

I realize I'm still pressed against Cole and step forward, turning to face him. "Uh, yeah, I don't know whether I want to hug my brother or kill him."

"I'd go with hugging," Cole says with a half-smile.

"That was pretty impactful, Autumn," Mark adds. "If I were Tony, I wouldn't even think about approaching you again."

"Hopefully," I reply, still processing everything.

As the night winds down, the crowd thins out, and we decide it's probably time to call it a night. We're all fairly quiet as we ride the elevator up to our rooms, the weight of the evening still lingering in the air. Mark and Cole agree on a time to meet for breakfast, and I just nod, my thoughts elsewhere.

Once we're back in our rooms, Cole is the one who quickly crosses through the adjoining door. Without a word, he wraps me in his arms, pulling me close and holding me tight.

"You okay?" he asks softly.

"Yeah," I reply, resting my head against his chest. "I'm grateful, honestly. I just wish Alex had told me, but maybe Jamie didn't mention it to him either. It would've been nice to know someone was running interference."

"I think that interference was necessary, and I'm grateful for it," Cole says, his voice firm but gentle. "I just want you to be safe."

"Men," I say with a sigh, but I can't help smiling up at him. "Also, I'm wondering if Mark thought anything of you pulling me back into you like that and me just staying there."

"Let me show you something," Cole says, handing me his phone.

Mark

I don't know how you do it, man, I know you're head over heels for her and yet you maintain that professional image, I still think you two would be great together

Cole

Autumn?

Mark

Seriously? Who else would I be talking about?

Cole

lol just making sure and you're right we would be good together, she's a challenge for me every day

Mark

someday you're going to slip, and I just hope I'm here to see it

Cole

lol are you hoping for my downfall?

Mark

nah, man, I'm hoping for your happiness

I finish reading the exchange on Cole's phone and look up at him, trying to process it all.

"I don't think Mark was surprised," Cole says, noticing my reaction. "That's why I wanted to show you. Under the circumstances, I think he expected it."

"Is that what that look was between you two when you said you wouldn't leave my side?" I ask, piecing it together.

"Exactly." He smiles. "That was Mark's way of silently telling me I was torturing myself."

I hand his phone back and straighten the collar of his shirt. "Do I torture you, Mr. Waters?"

"Undeniably," he says, pulling me in for a kiss. "You absolutely torture me."

"Can you help me out of this dress?" I ask, turning around and lifting my hair.

"Autumn Flynn, are you asking me to undress you?" he teases.

I smile at him over my shoulder as his fingers deftly undo the buttons at the back of my neck. The anticipation builds as he unzips my dress, his lips trailing kisses down my spine, sending shockwaves through me. He turns me to face him, guiding the dress off my shoulders until it falls to my feet, leaving me in just a thong.

"Okay, well, thanks," I say playfully, pretending to walk away.

Cole grabs my hips and pulls me back toward him. "You're not going anywhere," he murmurs before his mouth claims mine.

I wrap my arms around his neck as he leads me through the door into his room. "I think you're a little overdressed," I whisper, my fingers already working on the buttons of his shirt.

"More than a little," he agrees, smiling as he begins to shed his clothes. He drops to his knees, sliding my thong down, and kisses the inside of my thigh on his way back up. The anticipation is electric as he pushes me onto the bed and moves on top of me, his fingers exploring until he finds just the right spot inside me. I gasp as he hits it, my body arching into him.

I feel his lips curve into a smile against my skin as he trails kisses down my body, finally reaching my center. His tongue works in perfect harmony with his fingers, sending waves of pleasure crashing over me. My hand grips his hair as the orgasm overtakes me, leaving me trembling and weak beneath him. He moves back up, gently entering me, and sits up on his knees, pulling me into his lap. This time, he moves slowly, savoring every moment, taking his time inside me. As he reaches his climax, he pulls me closer, sitting me up so we're face to face, and kisses me deeply, our connection solidified in that moment.

We lie together for a while, letting the calm settle over us before finally getting up to take showers. Once I'm done, I check my phone and see a few messages waiting for me.

I call Cara and fill her in on everything that happened. She laughs and tells me my life is starting to sound like a soap opera, which makes me laugh too. Then I call Alex to tell him about Danny. He hadn't known, but he's relieved Jamie took action. After answering texts from all three of my kids, I feel like life is normal again. I drift off to sleep next to Cole, feeling content and at peace.

CHAPTER THIRTY

THE RAINSTORM & THE CHALLENGE

Saturday passes without much excitement beyond the conference itself. Cole and I both notice Danny nearby, always close to our booth, yet never obvious about it. The day goes smoothly, with plenty of sales leads and high spirits all around. Toward the end of the day, Cole brings up dinner plans, and Mark not-so-subtly excuses himself.

"I'm really exhausted and want to turn in early," Mark says, then adds with a nudge to Cole, "but you two should go enjoy dinner without me."

"You sure?" Cole asks, though it's clear he already knows the answer.

"Yeah, I'm sure," Mark replies.

Cole turns to me, his eyes warm. "You want to have dinner?"

"Sure," I say, smiling at him. "Sounds fun." Once again, Mark gives Cole a look I'm not supposed to notice.

After closing down the booth, Cole checks his phone and finds a small restaurant a few blocks from the hotel. It's a little out of the way, so we figure we're less likely to run into anyone we know.

The restaurant turns out to be a cozy, hole-in-the-wall place, and it really isn't crowded. We have a lovely dinner, our fingers and hands frequently finding each other across the table. I have a few glasses of wine, and by the time we're ready to leave, I'm feeling warm and content.

As we step outside, we discover the weather has changed. A light rain is falling, not enough to cool the air entirely but enough to take the edge off the heat.

I smile at Cole. "You mind getting a little wet?"

"I think I can handle it," he replies with a grin.

It's about four blocks to the hotel, and we're halfway there when the light rain turns into a downpour. We're soaked within moments, water dripping from our hair and faces. Laughing, I pull Cole into a small alcove next to a brick building, offering some shelter from the storm.

I turn from the street to look at Cole, still laughing, but his expression is serious, his eyes dark with hunger and desire. He takes my breath away as he pins me against the brick wall, his mouth crashing onto mine, his hands gripping my hips. The sound of the rain, the water streaming down us, amplifies the heat between us.

He pulls back slightly, breathing heavily. "God, Autumn, the things you do to me."

I don't say anything, just smile softly, my breath mingling with his. He laughs, then tenderly places his hand on my cheek, his thumb grazing my cheekbone as he studies my face. Then he leans in again, his body pressing against mine, his mouth desperate for me.

I wrap my arms around his neck, rising on my toes to be closer to him. Even under the building's cover, some raindrops still find us, landing on our hands, hair, and cheeks. Water runs off both of us as we lose ourselves in each other, completely absorbed by the moment.

Eventually, the rain begins to subside, and Cole pulls back, his eyes slowly traveling up from my feet until they meet mine. His voice is low and rough when he finally speaks. "I think I need you in my bed now."

We step out onto the sidewalk, where the rain is still falling softly. I can't help but look up, stretch out my arms, and spin slowly, feeling unbelievably happy. This moment feels magical. Cole laughs, and when I stop spinning to look at him, he grabs my hand, and we start walking quickly toward the hotel.

As we approach the entrance, the valets stop us, directing us to use a different door to avoid tracking water through the lobby. I laugh again, the sound bubbling up as we head toward the side door of the hotel.

The side door leads us into a stairwell. The door closes with a resounding echo, followed by my laughter, which reverberates off the walls. Cole turns to me, his eyes darkening more with desire. In an instant, he pushes me up against the wall, pinning my wrists above my head with one hand. His lips crash into mine with a hunger that takes my breath away, while his free hand trails down to my breasts and then slips inside the front of my pants.

"Cole," I laugh, the sound bouncing off the walls.

"Shhh," he murmurs against my lips, his voice low and urgent.

With a swift motion, he undoes my pants, allowing his hand full access. My hands are still pinned above my head as his fingers slide inside me, and I gasp, not caring that we're in a public stairwell. His movements are both deliberate and perfect, and it doesn't take long before I feel the heat building, my body nearing its peak.

"Cole," I whisper, almost pleading.

He doesn't stop, and as I reach the edge, a moan escapes me, echoing through the stairwell. Cole releases my wrists, and I collapse into him, wrapping my arms around his neck. We hear voices from the stairs above, and with a mischievous smile, he quickly buttons my pants and leads me through the door to the elevator.

Once we're alone again, and the elevator doors close, he pulls me back into him, my back pressed against his chest. I can feel how turned on he is, his arousal pushing into my lower back. His hands roam over my chest and down to my crotch, and then back up again. As the elevator stops, he grabs my hand and pulls me toward our rooms. The hallway is blissfully empty, and I'm relieved. He scans his key card, and as the door opens, he pushes me backward into his room.

We start tearing off each other's wet clothes, leaving puddles of water on the floor. My hair drips as we peel away the layers. Once we're finally undressed, he pushes me onto the bed and is almost instantly on top of me, inside me. The urgency between us is palpable, but after a moment, I push at him, signaling for him to flip over. He pulls me on top of him, and I straddle him, but instead of staying there, I lean down to kiss him, my mouth trailing a line from his jaw to his navel.

When I take him into my mouth, his breath hitches, and his hands tangle in my wet hair, which brushes against his hips and thighs. He groans, the sound raw and deep, as I move with a ravenous hunger for him.

Just as I feel him tense, on the brink, he stops me, pulling away only to guide me back to his mouth with a fistful of my hair. He kisses me hard, then flips us over again, driving into me with a force that leaves us both gasping. He thrusts with intensity until finally, he releases, filling me completely. We collapse together, breathless and sated.

I lace my fingers with his, and he brings my hand to his lips, kissing it tenderly.

"That was," he pauses, still catching his breath, "hot."

I laugh, feeling a lightness I haven't felt in a long time.

"God, I love the sound of your laughter," Cole says, his voice warm.

I laugh again, unable to help myself. "We might have to sleep in my room tonight," I suggest, still grinning.

"And why's that?" he asks, raising an eyebrow.

"Because of all the rain," I say, giggling. "I'm pretty sure this bed is a little wet now."

"Wet isn't always a bad thing," he replies with a smirk, "but you might be right."

Eventually, we gather up our soaked clothes, laughing the whole time. Cole can't stop laughing at me, and I can't stop laughing at the situation. As we hang our wet clothes in the bathroom to drip dry, he pulls me into his arms and kisses me.

"I love you so much, Autumn," he murmurs.

I smile, my heart swelling. "I love you too. You're good for me."

"Ditto," he says, pressing a kiss to my forehead.

We end up falling asleep in my room that night, and the next day at the booth, we're both in high spirits. Mark can't help but notice.

"There's something different about you two," he comments, eyeing us with curiosity.

Cole shrugs casually. "Maybe it's the weather," he says, trying to keep a straight face while I have to stifle a laugh.

Mark, oblivious to the underlying joke, continues, "Did you two get caught out in that rain last night?"

I quickly look away, struggling to contain my amusement, while Cole smoothly responds, "Just for a minute or two."

The day goes by quickly as we wrap up the conference and pack up our booth. The three of us have dinner together, and Cole and I sit next to each other, exchanging subtle touches. Mark notices our moods again.

"I don't know what's different about you two, but I like it," he says with a smile. "You're both just so happy."

Cole shrugs again, glancing at me with a knowing look before turning back to Mark. Mark laughs softly but doesn't push further.

After dinner, we walk back to our rooms. Cole and I maintain appearances by entering our separate rooms, but as soon as I'm in mine, I slip through the adjoining door to find him waiting.

"He knows, doesn't he?" I say, still smiling. "He has to know."

Cole chuckles. "He might. Apparently, you're glowing today, and that's something you can't hide."

I smile, playfully swatting him on the chest. "I don't think it was just me who was glowing."

"Last night was pretty amazing," he says, pulling my hips against his.

"It was alright," I tease, shrugging nonchalantly.

Cole laughs. "What am I going to do with you?"

I lean in close, whispering against his lips, "Anything you want."

He lets out a low, primal growl, taking up the challenge as his mouth crashes into mine, his hands already tugging at my clothes.

The euphoria from the night before still courses through me, and I'm instantly aching for his touch. After he strips me of my clothes, he gently pushes me back onto the bed and begins his delicious assault of sensual torture.

He pins my wrists above my head with one hand, then releases them, whispering, "Don't move."

His fingertips trail from my wrists down to my armpits, then along my ribs. When he reaches my waist, he traces back up, circling my breasts without ever touching the peaks. The teasing makes my back arch, my pelvis tilting toward him, seeking more. He laughs softly, running his fingers down the center of my chest to my navel and back up, continuing to tease my breasts. The ache intensifies, my nipples painfully tight, and the desire between my legs becomes almost unbearable.

My back arches again, and finally, he ends some of my torment by taking one of my nipples into his mouth, his hand moving to the other. I bring my hand down to the back of his head, but he quickly puts it back above my head with a chuckle.

"Stay," he commands in a raspy voice.

I moan as his mouth and hand work my sensitive nipples, the warm wetness of his mouth and expert tongue on one while his fingers roll, flick, and pinch the other. The sensations build to a crescendo, and I feel the throbbing between my legs as my body climaxes just from the attention to my nipples. He must feel me shaking beneath him because he laughs softly, clearly enjoying his effect on me.

He leaves one hand on my chest, expertly working my nipples, even managing to stretch his hand between the two, his smallest finger on one, and his thumb on the other. His mouth and other hand move to my thighs, and while he kisses and licks up and down my right inner thigh, his fingertips gently brush the inside of my left thigh. The wetness builds, the ache for him growing with every passing second.

When I raise my hips, seeking relief, he pushes them back down into the mattress with his other hand. I grip the pillows above my head, moaning in frustration and anticipation. He runs his hands up and down my inner thighs, barely grazing my lips, teasing me mercilessly. The ache becomes torturously overwhelming.

"Cole," I whisper, pleading softly. "Please."

His hands return to my inner thighs, and his fingers finally enter me. I sharply inhale, followed by a loud moan of relief. He moves back up, his mouth finding my breasts again while his fingers work inside me, hitting all the right spots. He trails kisses down my body, meeting his hand with his mouth, his tongue circling and fluttering over the most sensitive area of my body. When he pulls back and blows gently on me, my hips buck involuntarily. He alternates between licking and blowing, teasing me until I'm trembling with need. Finally, he puts his mouth back on me, sucking and licking until I reach one of the strongest climaxes of my life, the pleasure pooling beneath me.

Entering me with his tongue, he moans against me, then moves his wet hand to explore more forbidden areas. He circles the rim and slowly enters with a finger, my hips rising to meet him. He shifts up my body, his mouth finding mine again, the taste of me still on his lips, and I'm even more turned on than I thought possible.

Quickly, he is thrusting inside me as he sits up on his knees, using his thumb to massage my sensitive nerves while he hits the perfect spot inside me. My body reaches another apex, convulsing around him. He pulls out, moves lower, and explores the forbidden area he craved. Slowly, he pushes in, and I moan, biting my lip as ecstasy overtakes me. He uses his fingers inside me, too, working both entrances until I'm a trembling, moaning mess.

Unable to contain my pleasure, I grab a pillow, covering my face as I bite down to muffle my sounds. He continues, pushing me over the edge again, this orgasm leaving me faint and weak. As I drop the pillow, I watch his face as he finally reaches his climax, collapsing beside me, both of us spent.

I roll into him, barely able to breathe, my head swimming with the intensity of it all. We lie there for a few minutes before Cole kisses the top of my head. He pulls me up with him as he stands, saying, "Come shower with me."

"Okay," I reply, laughing softly. "But you might have to hold me up."

We shower together, the smaller hotel shower feeling more intimate than the one at home. My body is still ravaged and weak, and I appreciate him soaping me up and kissing me frequently.

As we climb into bed that night, knowing we'll be going home to our separate places tomorrow, I realize it will be a long time before I stop thinking about Nashville.

CHAPTER THIRTY-ONE

THE GIRLS' NIGHT & THE ART EXHIBIT

When I get home, I text Cara, asking if she wants to come over for dinner. She replies almost instantly, eager as always. We decide on Chinese takeout, and soon we're sitting at my kitchen table, sipping wine, and digging into the feast laid out before us. As the wine loosens our tongues, Cara dives right in with the questions—those deliciously embarrassing ones only a close friend would dare to ask. And honestly, I'm dying to spill.

"So, how was the whole adjoining rooms situation in Nashville?" she asks, her eyes gleaming with mischief.

I let out a long, dramatic sigh. "Cara, I don't think I'll ever forget Nashville. It was... hands down the best sex of my life."

Her laughter bubbles up, contagious and warm. "Alright, spill the tea, woman! I need details."

I indulge her, recounting the storm, the stairwell, the sheer intensity of it all.

"Autumn Flynn, you wild thing," she exclaims, shaking her head in mock disbelief. "I can't believe *you* let that happen. But damn, it sounds hot."

I smile, a little lost in the memory. "It just felt right, you know? I can't imagine letting anyone else do that in public. But with him... I wanted it. I wanted him. So much."

We chat a little more about the weekend, the conversation flowing easily between us. Then I turn the tables, curious about her romantic escapades. Cara's been seeing someone steadily for about four weeks now, which, for her, is practically a committed relationship.

"Same weekend me and Cole started up, huh?" I tease, nudging her. "I knew I was a trendsetter."

She laughs, rolling her eyes, and we dive into the juicy details of her fling. It feels good, this exchange, this unfiltered honesty. I'm reminded, as I sit there with her, how lucky I am to have a friend like Cara—someone who gets me, who's been there through it all, and who can always make me laugh, no matter what.

Cole and I talk late into the night, our conversation stretching nearly two hours before we finally hang up and try to sleep. The silence that follows is unsettling; it feels strange to fall asleep alone after so much connection. But as the days pass, we settle back into our usual rhythm—work, quick calls between meetings, and longer conversations at night. There's something comforting about waking up to his sweet texts, and I'm beginning to believe that this distance, as challenging as it is, might actually be making my heart grow fonder.

We start planning for Labor Day weekend, when his boys will come up. Our first order of business is the menu—pizza on Friday night, lasagna on Saturday, and a poolside barbecue on Sunday. We let the kids know they can invite friends to the barbecue, which thrills William—he's excited to reconnect with some old friends from his Marquette days. Cara is joining us too, with her two kids and possibly her new beau in tow.

Despite our excitement, Cole and I don't have any plans to see each other before Labor Day. It's shaping up to be our longest stretch apart since we crossed that invisible line a few weeks ago. It's not for lack of wanting—we both have kids, appointments, and the relentless demands of adult life, all three hundred miles apart.

Our nightly phone calls are becoming a lifeline, filled with laughter, innuendos, and that sweet cheesiness that only deepens our connection. We miss each other terribly, and it's obvious to anyone who knows us. Even Megan asks daily why I don't just drive down to Fort Wayne. Some days, I'm tempted.

And then, on a Friday morning, Cole surprises me by suggesting just that.

"Hey, what if you come see me this weekend?" Cole suggests when he calls after our morning meeting. His voice carries that familiar warmth that always makes me smile. "I've got that thing for Matthew on Saturday afternoon, but if you can be here, come with me."

I hesitate, trying to gauge the implications. "Let me talk to Megan. I'm sure she'll be fine with it. Are you sure you want me there, though?"

Matthew, Cole's youngest, has a piece in an art exhibition at his university—a big moment for him.

"Absolutely," Cole replies, his tone sincere. "I'd love for you to be there. Honestly, I think Matthew would be excited to meet you too. William's already said some nice things about you, and both William and Tyler will be there, so you'll meet them ahead of next weekend. And, if you come, bring something nice to wear for the gallery—not too formal, but no jeans."

"Okay, I'll talk to Megan and call you back."

What I don't tell Cole is that I'm a little nervous—okay, more than a little. I know Matthew's mom, Michelle, will be there. The idea of coming face to face with her makes my stomach knot. I'm sure Cole's thought about it too, maybe that's why he wants me there, though he hasn't said as much. When I talk to Megan, she's not just fine with it—she's encouraging, which helps ease my mind.

I call Cole back. "Alright, I'll be there. I'm leaving shortly. I can't wait to see you—I miss you."

"I miss you too, Autumn. I'm so glad you're coming."

"Cole, I have a question," I begin, hesitating. "I'm assuming Michelle will be at this thing, right?"

"Uh, yeah, she'll be there, but it's a pretty big exhibit. We might not even run into her."

"Okay," I say, though my nerves are still there. "It just makes me a little anxious."

"Now, who's letting her get in their head?" he teases, and I can hear the smile in his voice.

"It's not about me," I explain. "I'm more worried about how it could affect you."

"Autumn," he says, his voice softening, "everything's easier with you by my side. I can't imagine your presence making anything worse. If anything, you'll keep me calm if she decides to be difficult."

"Okay," I sigh, relieved. "Just wanted to make sure. If my boss lets me out early, I can probably be there around five."

"I think that can be arranged," he laughs.

"Alright, I'll call you when I'm on the road."

"You bringing the Audi?"

"Was planning on it, unless you object."

"No objections here. I actually thought that's exactly what you should do."

I raise an eyebrow, even though he can't see it. "Are you planning on showing off my car along with me?"

"Maybe," he laughs, not even trying to hide it. "Couldn't hurt."

"Cole Waters, what am I going to do with you?"

"Didn't you already answer that question? Anything you want? I'll stick with that."

"You might regret that," I tease.

"I really don't think I will," he chuckles. "Alright, I'll let you go so you can get on the road."

"Okay, love you. See you soon."

"Love you too."

I pull up to Cole's house just before five, and he's already outside, practically vibrating with anticipation. The moment I park, he's at my car door, opening it for me. He pulls me into his arms and kisses me deeply, like he's been starving for it. That night is perfect—he cooks me dinner, we create more memories in his bed, and I sleep better than I have in weeks, wrapped up in him.

We sleep in the next morning, savoring the rare luxury, and then share a leisurely breakfast before starting to get ready for Matthew's exhibition. I shower first, letting the warm water ease the remnants of sleep from my body. While Cole takes his turn in the bathroom, I focus on my makeup. I keep it simple yet elegant—just a touch of eyeliner and eyeshadow to make my eyes pop, but otherwise, I keep it subdued. I know Cole loves my green top with angel sleeves, so I slip into that, feeling the soft fabric drape perfectly over my curves. Paired with black slacks that hug my hips just right, I feel confident, attractive, and ready.

When Cole emerges from the shower, his eyes rake over me, taking in every detail. "I approve," he says, a smile playing on his lips.

"Oh yeah? Was I seeking your approval?" I tease, raising an eyebrow.

"Maybe, maybe not." He grins, stepping closer to pull me into his arms.

"Cole, you're all wet," I laugh, gently pushing him away.

"I have good memories of you all wet," he murmurs, a playful glint in his eyes.

"Oh, I know, but we have to leave soon," I remind him, though my voice is tinged with a hint of reluctance.

"Fine, later," he concedes, kissing me on the forehead.

I pin my hair half-up, letting the rest cascade down my back, and add a pair of gold dangle earrings. The look is nearly identical to what I wore that first night we spent together in Dallas, and I wonder briefly if I'm doing this for Cole, for myself, or perhaps even for Michelle. In the end, it doesn't really matter.

Cole dresses in dark gray slacks and a lighter gray button-down shirt. He debates the tie, ultimately choosing one that nearly matches the green of my top. After a moment of hesitation, he decides to wear a blazer, and the result is striking. He looks incredibly handsome, the kind of man who turns heads without even trying.

"I approve too," I say, smiling as I take him in.

"Good," he replies with a satisfied nod. "You ready?"

"Yeah," I say, tossing him the keys to the Audi.

He laughs, catching them easily. "Okay, let's go."

I don't bother with a purse; my driver's license and debit card are tucked into my phone case.

We arrive at the art gallery about thirty minutes later, and Cole wisely opts for valet parking. The valet opens my door, offering a hand as I step out, and I wait for Cole to join me. Most of the men walking in are dressed in blazers or sport coats, so I'm glad Cole decided to go that route too.

As we enter, ushers hand us a program, which helps us navigate the exhibit and find Matthew's work. We stroll through the gallery, taking in the art, and I'm pleasantly surprised by how passionate Cole is about certain pieces. It's a side of him I hadn't fully seen before, and it makes me smile.

We turn a corner into the third open room, and Cole spots William and Tyler. William greets me with a hug, and Cole introduces me to Tyler, who is the spitting image of his father—tall, handsome, with that same easy charm. It's like seeing a younger version of Cole, much like Megan is a younger version of me. Both boys are enthusiastic about the upcoming weekend, and hearing their excitement fills me with warmth. I know it must make Cole just as happy.

"Matthew's just around the corner," William says as the small talk winds down.

"Let's go," Cole says, his tone eager.

We step into the next room, and I spot Matthew right away. He resembles William—though Matthew has his own distinct presence. His brothers have already greeted him, so their exchange is casual, but when Cole hugs him and introduces me, there's a warmth that makes me feel instantly welcomed.

"Thank you so much for coming," Matthew says, his gaze shifting between Cole and me. "I'm really happy to meet you. William and Dad have told me a lot about you."

I smile at him, feeling the sincerity in his words. "I've heard a lot about you too."

We spend time admiring Matthew's piece, a stunning sculpture of a man and woman, naked and intertwined, holding each other with a tenderness that feels almost sacred. I ask him about it, and he explains how he first drew it from live models, then brought it to life in the sculpture. It's beautiful, an arresting piece that commands attention. I tell him as much, and the pride that lights up his face is unmistakable. It's clear he's poured his heart into this work, and seeing it appreciated brings him a quiet joy that I'm grateful to witness.

From behind us, a voice with a distinct New York accent cuts through the air. "There are all my boys."

While Cole and William stay relatively composed, I notice Matthew and Tyler tense up immediately. It's an all-too-familiar reaction, reminiscent of how my own children respond to their father. My maternal instincts kick in, and I turn around, only to pause as Cole steps slightly in front of me.

Michelle, Cole's ex, sweeps in, hugging William and Tyler before turning her attention to Matthew, showering him with overly enthusiastic praise for his art, all while completely ignoring the actual sculpture.

She's shorter than I imagined, maybe five foot three, with dark hair, brown eyes, and olive skin. She's a bit heavier than I expected—not overweight, but certainly not the towering, slender figure my insecurities had conjured up.

After her dramatic display with Matthew, she finally turns to Cole and me. "Cole," she says, her tone icy, devoid of any warmth. No greeting, no pleasantries—just his name.

"Michelle," Cole replies calmly.

She immediately shifts her attention back to the boys.

"Mom," William interjects, trying to smooth over the awkwardness, "this is Autumn."

Michelle turns her gaze to me, scanning me up and down before responding flatly, "Yeah, I figured that."

Tyler looks mortified, and Matthew tries to busy himself with another artist nearby. Cole chuckles softly, glancing at me with a slight shrug. "Okay, then."

"Mom," William says again, his tone a mix of frustration and disbelief.

"She won't last. Don't get attached," Michelle snaps.

Cole starts to say something, but William beats him to it, his voice sharp. "What the hell is wrong with you? Is civility above you?"

"Will, you know how these things go," she retorts, dismissively.

"It's William," he corrects, his voice firm. "And I know how they go *with you*. You're right. But I'm pretty sure this is different, and unless you want these things to be awkward for all of us forever, you could try acting like an adult."

The air stills as everyone processes his words. Michelle, clearly stunned, rolls her eyes and turns away with a huff. "Fine, it's nice to meet you, Autumn. I guess we might be seeing you around."

"Mom," Tyler and William say in unison, their exasperation palpable.

Matthew catches my eye and, with a wry smile, quietly remarks, "Well, this is fun."

I can't help but laugh, the tension breaking for a brief moment.

Michelle's head whips around. "Is something funny?"

I meet her gaze, taking a moment to steady myself. "No, actually, nothing about this is funny—except for what Matthew just said." I glance at him with a smile before continuing. "William is right. We're probably going to run into each other at more of these events, celebrating these amazing young men you've raised. And at bigger moments, like graduations, weddings, grandchildren's birthdays, it would be nice if we could be on good enough terms that their faces don't look like this every time we're in the same room." I gesture to each of the boys, who all look pointedly at her.

Cole's hand finds the small of my back, his thumb brushing gently against the bare skin there. He takes a deep breath before speaking. "Michelle," he says, his voice steady, "none of us want this to be difficult. We all just want to coexist in a situation that's beyond the boys' control. So, let's try this again. Michelle, this is Autumn. Autumn, Michelle."

Taking Cole's cue, I extend my hand. Michelle hesitates but eventually offers a soft, reluctant shake. "Nice to meet you, Autumn," she mutters before turning to Matthew. "I'll see you at home," she says, then walks away.

She barely glances at his sculpture—doesn't even really see it. Tyler looks completely floored by her behavior, stunned into silence. Meanwhile, William and Matthew seem less affected, almost as if they find the absurdity of it amusing.

Matthew catches my eye, his lips curving into a playful smile. "Weddings and grandchildren, huh?"

I shrug, and he chuckles. His sense of humor is infectious, and I can already tell he and Megan will get along just fine.

Cole, clearly trying to mend the awkwardness, looks at his sons with a mix of pride and a need to smooth things over. "How about dinner with us? My treat," he offers.

Matthew is the first to respond. "As long as it's after six—I have to stay until then."

"That works," Cole agrees.

Tyler and William exchange a look before William turns back to Cole. "Yeah, actually, I'd really like that."

"Me too," Tyler adds.

As Cole makes plans with them, I take the opportunity to wander through the rest of the room, letting the art distract me. I startle slightly when I feel Cole's hands on my hips, his breath warm against my ear as he whispers, "Have I told you lately that I love you? Because that was amazing."

I turn to him, smiling. "That was a lot, and we'll talk later when we're alone."

He studies me, his brows furrowing in curiosity. "Nothing bad," I assure him, "just something I noticed."

He raises an eyebrow, still skeptical, but I lean in and speak softly. "Tyler and Matthew reacted to her before she even said a word, the same way my kids do when they see their dad. All my maternal instincts kicked in. They're relaxed around you, so whatever doubts you have about them preferring her—you're wrong."

He takes a moment to process my words, then smiles, pressing a kiss to my forehead. We head back over to say goodbye to Matthew, who surprises Cole by asking, "Hey Dad, I know Autumn's staying with you, but do you mind if I crash at your place tonight?"

"I'll never mind you staying with me," Cole says, his voice warm. "It's your home too."

"Awesome, thanks. I just don't want to deal with the fallout tonight," Matthew admits.

"You shouldn't have to deal with it at all," Cole says, his tone protective.

Matthew just shrugs, resigned. "She'll be too pissed at William to call him, so if I'm there, I'll have to hear about it."

Cole looks like he's about to say something, but I gently squeeze his arm, signaling him to hold back. "So, Matthew, how long will your art be in the gallery?" I ask, smoothly changing the subject.

We chat about the exhibit for a bit longer before saying our goodbyes. Cole gives Matthew a hug, and we catch up with Tyler and William, who are still exploring the gallery. Eventually, we part ways, heading back to Cole's house to relax before dinner.

Once we're in the car, Cole glances at me. "So, what was that about? What did you observe?"

"As soon as Matthew and Tyler heard her voice, their body language changed. They went on the defensive—it made them uncomfortable, just like my kids when Steve shows up at an event."

"They never talk about her negatively, not like your kids do about Steve," Cole muses. "Today was the first time I've seen them really upset with her, aside from the usual fallout when she ends relationships and disrupts their lives."

I chuckle softly. "Men don't always express these things the same way. Kevin has his sisters to vent to, but your boys might not feel comfortable complaining to you about her. And even if they do, you can't vilify her or agree with them unless they directly ask. That's why I stopped you from speaking earlier. In all the times you've heard my kids complain about Steve, I've never added my two cents. It's about taking the high road. They're entitled to their feelings, and you can comfort them, but you can't commiserate because, deep down, they still want a relationship with their other parent. You don't want to be the one who tarnishes that bond, especially with Michelle. If you say something negative about her, and they don't agree—or even if they do but later change their minds—they'll turn on you fast."

Cole is quiet, absorbing my words. I add gently, "If you stick to the high road, your relationship with them will be stronger. If they ask for your opinion, give it, but don't volunteer it."

He glances at me, a mix of admiration and curiosity in his eyes. "How did you get so smart?"

I laugh. "Years of therapy. Also, I think they're closer to each other than you realize."

He nods thoughtfully. "It's possible."

A few hours later, we head out to dinner with the boys. The conversation flows easily, and I learn a lot about them. They ask about my kids, and I answer honestly. Cole isn't shy about showing affection, frequently rubbing my back or running his fingers through my hair, even kissing my temple a few times. They don't flinch or seem uncomfortable, which I'm grateful for—he keeps it family-friendly.

After dinner, the boys spend some time admiring my car, discussing engines and transmissions—a topic they all bond over. Matthew follows us back to Cole's house, where we spend a bit more time talking in the kitchen before he heads upstairs.

Cole wraps his arms around me, holding me close. "Thank you," he whispers, his voice full of emotion.

I look up at him and kiss him softly. "You're very welcome."

"I know I've asked this before, but where have you been my whole life?" Cole says, his voice filled with genuine curiosity.

I smile, meeting his gaze. "Pretty sure I was waiting for you to show up in mine too."

Later, after we retreat to the bedroom and close the door behind us, Cole brings up the afternoon with a thoughtful expression. "William really surprised me today. I didn't expect him to react like that. I'm not sure he would have if we hadn't had dinner with him a couple of weeks ago."

"Maybe," I say with a shrug, "It surprised me too. But it seemed like Tyler was the most affected by the whole thing. Matthew, on the other hand, almost expected it. I think William was hoping she wouldn't behave that way but wasn't shocked when she did."

"Yeah, Tyler probably talks to his mom the least. William calls her pretty often, probably like you and Megan, and Matthew lives with her, so he's in the thick of it all. Tyler's more independent—he doesn't spend much time talking to either of us."

"He's a mini-you, though," I say with a smile. "He looks so much like you."

Cole chuckles. "He does. Maybe that's why he's not as close to Michelle."

"That's a possibility," I laugh, the sound lightening the mood.

Cole's expression softens as he pulls me into his arms. "I love it when you laugh," he murmurs, kissing me gently.

"We have to be quiet," he whispers, drawing me closer still.

Maybe it's the need to be quiet, or perhaps it's the emotions of the day, but tonight, Cole makes love to me with a tenderness that's different from our usual intensity. His movements are slow, deliberate, and full of love, each touch deepening the connection between us. When we finally drift off to sleep, I'm nestled in his arms, blissfully content and completely sated.

CHAPTER THIRTY-TWO

THE PIZZA & THE HOT TUB

Sunday morning, Cole makes breakfast for the three of us. I'm grateful for the extra time with Matthew, getting to know him better and seeing the bond he shares with his father—being able to see Cole be a father. As we linger over coffee, I call my parents to let them know I won't make it to Sunday dinner. Kevin and Megan are going in my place. My mom jokes about how serious things must be with Cole if I'm skipping our traditional family meal—she's not wrong.

I will need to head back home mid-week to prepare for the upcoming weekend, but I decide to stay a bit longer, savoring more time with Cole—and, as it turns out, with Matthew too. He seems in no hurry to return to his mom's, sticking around despite work and school obligations.

Being at Cole's house for an extended stay allows me to see him in his element. He sticks to his routine, working out at the end of every workday. While I don't watch him the entire time, I certainly enjoy the sweat-glistened skin moments I do.

Wednesday arrives, and it's time for me to head back to Wisconsin. Even though we'll see each other on Friday, our goodbye feels like we're parting for weeks. Matthew finds our melodramatic farewell amusing, giving me a big hug before I leave. I promise them both I'll see them in a couple of days, then head home.

Back in Wisconsin, Megan is thrilled to see me. Since I hadn't been traveling for work until July, she's gotten used to me being around all the time. On Thursday, Megan, Cara, and I dive into preparations for the influx of house guests.

Megan takes charge of the guest rooms, meticulously cleaning and setting up the upstairs and both basement bedrooms with fresh bedding, towels, snacks, and beverages. She even creates a thoughtful welcome note with the Wi-Fi password and a reminder that guests are welcome to use the kitchen and common areas anytime.

Cara and Megan team up for a grocery run, stocking up on everything we'll need for the weekend—dinner ingredients, a wide array of snacks, fruit, and drinks, both alcoholic and non-alcoholic. Megan spends hours ensuring both the indoor and outdoor kitchens are fully stocked and accessible. She even gathers every spare towel in the house, placing them in the storage cabinet by the pool.

By Thursday night, as we collapse into bed, the house feels perfectly prepared for our guests. Sami and Kevin are expected to arrive by noon on Friday, with Cole and his kids following around four. Just as I'm settling into bed, my phone rings—of course, it's Cole with our nightly call.

"Hey, you," I answer, my voice warm with anticipation.

"Hey," Cole replies, the familiar comfort of his voice instantly soothing. "How was your day?"

"Productive, very productive," I laugh softly, thinking about how much we managed to get done.

"Good, are you ready for this? Feeling anxious?"

"I think I'm less anxious than Megan," I chuckle, "but yes, we're ready. What about you? Are you anxious?"

"I am," he admits, "but I've got a feeling everything's going to go well, so it's more excitement than anxiety."

I smile at the thought. "I could go with excited too. And I'm definitely excited to see you."

"Yeah? You missing me?" I can hear the smile in his voice.

"Always."

"I miss you too."

"How many cars are you all bringing up here?" I ask, curious about the logistics.

"I think two, maybe three. William's driving, and so am I, but Tyler might drive separately. He and William are still figuring it out. Matthew's riding up with me, but he might go back with William if I stay longer."

"Are you thinking about staying longer?" I ask, letting a playful undertone slip into my voice.

"How could I not? You're irresistible," he teases.

"Am I now?"

"Very. I'm surprised I ever let you leave my side," he laughs.

"'Let me,' huh?"

"Yeah, maybe we should revisit that idea of chaining you to the bed."

I laugh. "I don't think I'd mind."

"I don't think you would either," he chuckles, the sound rich and warm.

"Maybe someday we'll find out."

"Maybe," he says, his voice dropping a notch, "also, maybe you should make sure you have batteries for your...arsenal," he adds with a mischievous laugh.

"Cole Waters, you're going to corrupt my innocence."

"Oh, I'm pretty sure it's you corrupting me, Ms. Flynn."

"I get the feeling you want to do dirty things to me."

"That might be true," he says, his voice softening, "but I really just want to do nice things to you—whether they're dirty or not."

"I like nice things. We can probably arrange that."

"You're making the wait until tomorrow much harder," he murmurs.

"Maybe that's the plan," I laugh. "Harder, more anticipation. And you'll still have to wait a few hours."

"I know," he sighs. "It'll be late tomorrow night before I get you to myself."

"And we'll have to be quiet, but I think we'll survive."

"Oh, you mean you don't want all six of our children to hear us? How unadventurous of you," he laughs.

"Yes, I'm completely lacking in adventure," I tease.

"In all seriousness, Autumn, I'm really excited about this. Thank you for making it happen."

"I'm excited too. I think it's going to be good for all of us."

"Me too."

We say our goodnights, and I fall asleep quickly, even though I miss his scent on the pillow—it faded after I washed the sheets. I can't wait to have it back.

In the morning, I have my usual meeting with the team before Megan and I sit down for breakfast. We both opt for nice shirts and jeans, our hair styled similarly, making us look more alike than ever. Sami and Kevin arrive around noon, they park their cars on the gravel at the far side of the garage, ensuring no one will get blocked in later. Once their luggage is stowed in their rooms, we gather in the kitchen for a light lunch.

Kevin, dressed in a flattering polo that shows off his upper arms, looks every bit the part of the confident professional. Sami, in jeans and a shirt from one of her favorite bands, has even put on makeup—a rare occurrence that Cole has never seen before, so it'll be a new look for him.

As we eat, Kevin and Sami pepper me with questions about Cole's kids, while Megan, who's already exhausted this topic, listens quietly. Kevin, William, and Cole all work in white-collar fields, so I expect they'll have plenty in common. Matthew, still in college, aligns well with Megan and Sami, while Tyler, though a bit of the odd man out, is a history teacher—he'll have common ground with Kevin, who minored in history. There's potential for connection all around, but I can't shake the nervousness building inside me as the time of their arrival draws near. My stomach flutters, and my hands tingle with anticipation.

Megan catches me fidgeting and laughs. "Mom, you've already met them, and they like you. You're weird."

"I know," I admit with a sheepish grin.

When Cole and his kids arrive, William is right behind him. They don't pull into the garage, probably thinking it might be too much, but instead park along the side of our circular driveway, leaving space for easy access to the street. Kevin and I head outside to greet them and offer help with their bags. Introductions flow smoothly—Cole's three sons, all in shorts and polo shirts, look like they might have coordinated, though I suspect it's just coincidence.

As everyone steps inside, Megan and Sami introduce themselves. Matthew immediately jokes about how much Megan resembles me, prompting Cole to comment that it's even more noticeable today. Megan and Sami then show Cole's kids to the guest rooms, playfully suggesting they can duke it out over who gets which room. Matthew claims the upstairs bedroom without much fuss, leaving William and Tyler to take the basement rooms, putting Matthew on the same floor as Megan, Sami, and us.

Megan gives a quick tour of the house, pointing out the essentials like the bathrooms, snacks, and anything else they might need, careful not to overwhelm them with too much information. Cole, who has never had a full tour himself, seems to take everything in with quiet appreciation.

In the basement, we have another family room, a wet bar, and a cozy theater area with recliners and a large screen. The kids explain that it was more popular when they were in high school, but it's rarely used now—though everyone is welcome to make themselves at home there if they like. Megan also breezes through the upstairs bedrooms, making it clear who sleeps where without dwelling on it too long. Matthew's room, nestled between Sami and Megan's, has always been the guest room, thanks to its fewer windows and more central location.

With bags dropped off and everyone settling in, we regroup in the kitchen. Between the island and the large kitchen table, there's plenty of room for all eight of us to gather comfortably. Cole suggests we stick to the kitchen for now, saving the formal dining room for lasagna night. It's a smart call—it keeps the atmosphere casual, and everyone seems at ease as we settle in for the evening.

Megan serves beverages while we wait for the pizza to arrive. When Sami grabs a wine cooler, Matthew turns to Cole and asks if it's okay for him to have one too. It's another glimpse into Cole's parenting style and the respect his kids have for him. Cole nods, telling Matthew to take it easy. Both Megan and Sami are underage, though Megan is just shy of turning twenty-one, and I've always allowed them a drink or two on special occasions.

Kevin and William hit it off almost instantly. As the oldest siblings, they share a natural bond. Kevin, with his athletic build, might seem intimidating at first glance, but he's doing a great job of keeping things relaxed and approachable. William, though less of an athlete, connects with Kevin over their shared experiences and interests.

When the pizza arrives, Cole and Matthew retrieve it from the door, and soon everyone is eating and chatting, the room buzzing with laughter. Conversations flow easily, with each of the kids occasionally surprising their siblings with unexpected answers. Kevin even surprises Sami and me when he casually mentions that he's been dating someone for a couple of months. Megan doesn't seem surprised at all—when I look at her, she just shrugs, clearly in the loop.

Cole and I continue to be openly affectionate, something that has become second nature around my kids and Matthew. The only unknowns were how Tyler and William would react, but they seem unfazed. After we finish eating, Tyler and William ask if they can use the hot tub.

"Of course," I say, smiling.

Megan quickly asks if they'd mind if she joins them, and they're happy to have her along. Soon, Matthew and Sami decide to join in as well. Kevin opts out, and Cole and I volunteer to clean up the kitchen while the kids head to the hot tub.

As the evening settles in, Cole and I remain in the kitchen, listening to the sounds of laughter and chatter from outside. I'm tidying up when I pass by Cole, who's sitting on a bar stool. He reaches out, pulling me between his legs, his hands cupping my hips.

"Hey, you," he says, his voice low and warm.

"Hi," I reply, leaning in to kiss him.

"I'm pretty happy with how everything's going so far. You?"

"Listening to them all laughing out there? Yeah, it makes me pretty happy," I say, smiling before kissing him again.

Just then, Kevin walks into the kitchen and hesitates. "Sorry," he says, a bit sheepishly.

"You're fine, Kev. What's up?" I ask, while Cole drops his hands like we've been caught doing something we shouldn't in a moment of teenage awkwardness.

"I think I'm going to join them outside. It's too hot for the hot tub, but I figured I'd sit out there with them. Just grabbing a drink first."

"I agree, it's way too hot for that," I laugh.

Kevin grabs a beer from the fridge and gives me a quick side hug before heading out to the patio.

"And then there were six," I say with a smile, turning back to Cole.

"And then there were six," he echoes softly, pulling me in for another kiss.

We decide to linger in the kitchen for a while, eavesdropping on the laughter spilling in from outside. While we're there, I start prepping breakfast for the next day. Cole joins me, helping to cook the eggs and sausage for the breakfast pizzas. With so many of us, I'm making five pizzas, and I'm grateful for my double ovens. Once everything is prepped, we wrap the pizzas in foil and tuck them into the fridge, ready for whoever wakes up first to pop them in the oven.

As we finish up, there's not much reason to stay in the kitchen, other than to listen in on the kids. But honestly, I'm eager to have some time alone with Cole. We head out to the patio to check on them and say goodnight.

When we step outside, it's clear they're in their own world. They barely notice us as they laugh together, even Kevin, who's perched on a high stool next to the hot tub, level with the others.

"Well, you guys look like you're getting along," I say, leaning against the doorframe with a smile.

Matthew and Megan are too caught up in their laughter to respond, but Kevin grins at me. "I think we're doing okay," he says, before joining in their laughter.

I can't remember the last time I saw my kids laugh this hard. It fills my heart with joy.

"Just remember we have neighbors," I remind them with a smile. "And, by the way, breakfast is prepped in the fridge. Whoever's up first can throw it in the oven."

"Breakfast pizza?" Sami asks, her eyes lighting up.

"Yep, breakfast pizza," I confirm.

"How many did you make?" she asks.

"Five, so we should be good. But we can only bake four at a time."

"No problem. It'll probably be me, maybe Kevin, but we've got it covered," she says with a grin.

"You heading to bed?" Kevin asks.

"I think so. Keep them in line," I tease, smiling at Kevin.

"If you think I can control them, you're mistaken," Kevin replies, and all six of them burst into laughter.

I roll my eyes playfully. "Goodnight, kids," I say and am met with a chorus of "Goodnights" in return.

Before we head inside, Cole approaches and leans in close to William, whispering something. They exchange a few words, both smiling, before William rolls his eyes and laughs. "Goodnight, Dad," he says.

Cole walks back to me, tilting his head with a quick gesture for me to follow him. As I close the patio door, I glance back at the kids one last time, smiling at the sight of them all so happy. Cole grabs my hand, walking backward toward the stairs, his face lit up with genuine happiness.

"Well, aren't you happy?" I ask, matching his smile.

"Deliriously," he replies, his eyes sparkling.

When we reach the stairs, Cole turns around but keeps hold of my hand. As soon as the bedroom door closes behind us, he pulls me into a kiss, but then suddenly he pulls back, pacing the room with restless energy.

"Autumn, this is so fucking amazing," he says, words tumbling out in a rush. "This is beyond anything I hoped for. Our kids are all together, laughing and happy. I haven't seen William laugh like that in ages. Matthew, sure, but William? No way. It's like I'm waiting for the other shoe to drop, but this... this is just so fucking amazing."

I can't help but smile and laugh a little at his excitement. "Would it change if you thought they were laughing at us?" I tease.

He stops and looks at me, grinning. "No, it wouldn't. But I don't think they are."

"I don't either," I say, "but look at you—I don't think I've ever seen you this happy."

He glances up at the ceiling, still pacing, his excitement palpable. "I'm so happy, I can't even list all the things that went right tonight."

"It's good, Cole. Really good, but," I say, watching him with fondness. But then I pause, and his smile falters, like he's bracing for something bad. "All this energy you're burning pacing the floor? I can think of better ways to use it."

His smile returns, and he steps forward, wrapping me in a tight embrace, lifting me off my feet. "I love you, Autumn. I love you so much."

I laugh as he sets me back down, and when his mouth meets mine again, the kiss is deep and lingering. When he pulls back, he says, "You and that laugh are going to be the death of me."

I place my hand on the back of his neck, pulling him closer. "Cole, seeing you this happy makes me happy. The kids are just the cherry on top."

He leans his forehead against mine, holding the moment, then lets out a soft laugh. "I do have a lot of fucking energy right now."

"Fucking energy, huh?"

"What am I going to do with you? You and your dirty mind?"

"I don't know, what do you *want* to do with me?" I ask, my voice teasing.

"Everything. You might want to lock the door," he says with a laugh.

I grin, turning to lock the door, and before I know it, he's grabbed me from behind, pulling me back against his chest. His hands roam immediately—one up to my breasts, the other slipping into my pants.

"Cole!" I half-shriek, half-laugh, surprised by his sudden move.

He leans in close to my ear, his voice a low whisper. "What did I tell you about that laugh?" He laughs softly, then adds, "Remember, you said we'd have to be quiet."

He uses his chin to nudge my hair aside, taking my earlobe into his mouth before trailing his lips and tongue down my neck. The ache for him builds instantly. One hand finds a sensitive nipple while the other explores deeper in my leggings, his fingers moving with perfect precision. As he continues to kiss and lick the tender spots along my neck and ear, my body responds with a quick, intense buildup toward climax.

As I moan, my thighs clenching, he whispers in my ear, "Come for me, Autumn." The warmth of his breath on my skin and the relentless movement of his fingers push me over the edge. I come undone, and he turns me around, kissing me deeply, pulling me as close as he can.

In one fluid motion, he lifts my shirt over my head, unhooks my bra, and slides my pants off. When I reach for his shirt, he grabs my wrists, leaning in close to my ear. "No, this is about you tonight," he rasps, his voice thick with desire.

The heat of his words sends a rush through me, leaving me weak in the knees. He backs me toward the bed, pushing me down onto it before tearing off my thong. I expect him to tease, but he doesn't. His fingers find their mark, and his mouth follows, his tongue moving between my thighs as his other hand caresses my breast. I gasp, my body trembling with each touch.

"Fuck, Cole," I whisper, my voice breathless.

He responds with a low groan, his fingers delving deeper, his tongue working with maddening skill. The coil in my core tightens, the pressure building almost to the point of pain, desperate for release. My hips move instinctively toward him, urging him deeper, harder. My hand finds his hair, gripping it as my body reaches the brink.

And when I finally break, he doesn't stop. He pushes me through one orgasm after another until I'm left trembling, the sheets beneath me damp with sweat and release. I'm wrecked, utterly and completely, my body teetering on the edge of collapse.

He doesn't relent. His mouth trails up my body, pausing at my breasts, his face glistening with the evidence of his efforts. When his mouth meets mine, the kiss is fervent, almost desperate. His fingers continue their relentless rhythm until he coaxes yet another orgasm from me. I break the kiss, tilting my head back, only for his lips to find the sensitive spots on my neck.

When he finally brings his fingers to my mouth, I do exactly what he wants. He groans, a sound of pure satisfaction. "Fuck, Autumn, I think you're shaking," he whispers, laughing softly.

"Mmmhmm," is all I can manage, my voice weak with pleasure.

"I'm not done with you yet," he says, and I hear the sound of his zipper. I'm not sure if I'm relieved or disappointed, but when he strips off his shirt and rolls me onto my side, I know I want more. He positions himself behind me, his left leg between mine, and after a brief exploration with his fingers, he pushes inside me. He's so hard, and the sensation is almost too much for my already oversensitive body. I gasp loudly as he enters me.

"Shhh," he whispers, playfully smacking my ass, and I stifle a moan.

He begins to move, thrusting with just the right amount of force, using my elevated leg as leverage to keep us steady. When he finally reaches his climax, he fills me completely, then drags my leg back across his chest, leaning down to kiss me before collapsing beside me on the bed.

I lie there, shaking, every muscle in my body weak from exhaustion and pleasure. I manage to reach out, resting my hand on his chest. He places his hand over mine, looking at me with a satisfied grin.

"I hope you're satisfied," he teases with a small laugh.

I try to swat at him, but my arm barely moves. "I think you took all my energy and added it to yours," I whisper.

He laughs. "But are you satisfied?"

"Considering I'm shaking and can't move? Yes, I'd say so."

"Better than that night at my house?" he asks, a hint of challenge in his voice.

"Oh, are you trying to top that?" I reply weakly, smiling.

"Maybe." He shrugs.

"Yeah, better," I admit, "but you still might have to beat Nashville."

He laughs, leaning in to kiss me. "I love you, Autumn."

"I love you too," I whisper back, my body finally starting to relax in his embrace.

THE OVERWHELM PART TWO

Saturday morning unfolds slowly, with everyone sleeping in. Cole and I eventually make our way downstairs just before noon, finding Sami the only one awake, lounging in the kitchen and scrolling through her phone. She tells us she didn't put the breakfast pizzas in the oven because no one else was up yet, but the ovens are preheated and ready.

"What time did you all finally come in?" I ask, curious about their late-night antics.

She laughs, "Around two."

"Oh, to be young again," Cole says with a smirk.

Sami grins, looking between the two of us. "We didn't even realize it was that late. After you went to bed, we mostly stayed out of the hot tub—that's too long to be in there. Kev started the firepit, and we just sat around talking."

"Well, I'm glad you all seem to be getting along," I say, genuinely pleased.

"Yeah, we talked a lot. They asked about Dad, and we ended up comparing all the crappy things their mom has done with the crappy things our dad has done. I think it was a relief for them to know we have a shitty parent too," she says with a shrug. "But then we moved on to school, friends, jobs, music—you know, the usual. We even found out that William is friends with Stacey's older brother. Megan probably met him at Stacey's graduation party, if not before."

"Small world," I say, smiling at the connection.

"It really is," Sami agrees.

Soon, Kevin, Megan, and Matthew make their way downstairs together. Kevin gives me a hug and ruffles Sami's hair, while Matthew walks up to Cole and playfully shoulder-checks him.

"I guess we should get the pizza in the oven," I say with a smile.

The kitchen quickly fills with the chaotic energy of young adults. William and Tyler join us, drawn by the noise. Megan turns on some music, and the room buzzes with conversation and laughter. I lean against the island, watching it all unfold, a content smile on my face. Cole comes up behind me, rubbing my back for a moment before wrapping his arm around me and pulling me closer. I look up at him, and he just smiles, pressing a soft kiss to my temple.

The banter flows easily between the two sets of siblings, with teasing and playful jabs flying back and forth. Kevin volunteers to pick up tiramisu for dessert, and William asks if he can join him. I decide to skip making bread today and tell them to grab some garlic bread from the store as well.

As breakfast winds down, the kids begin to trickle away—some to shower, others to get dressed or just relax. Megan lingers to help clean up, but soon she heads upstairs too, leaving Cole and me to savor the quiet moments before the day's activities pick up again.

I turn to Cole with a soft laugh. "I think this is going to be okay."

"Yeah," he agrees, wrapping me in his arms, "I'm a little floored."

"We should probably get dressed too," I suggest. "It's funny—same people, but somehow eating dinner in the dining room in our pajamas feels weird."

He laughs, a mischievous glint in his eye. "You know what the first step to changing clothes is, right?"

I smile, and we head upstairs together.

By the time Kevin and William return from the store, the kitchen is buzzing with activity as lasagna night kicks off. Cole and I don't have to lift a finger—the kids have it all under control. They pair off naturally—Kevin and William take on the pasta dough and garlic bread, Megan and Matthew tackle the sauce with some help from Sami and Tyler, and Sami and Tyler handle the cheese mixture and a salad. When everything is prepped, Megan and Sami begin assembling the lasagnas.

Just as they start, William suddenly says he needs some air and steps outside to the driveway. After a minute, Cole glances at me and then follows him out. A few minutes later, my watch buzzes—it's a message from Cole asking if I can join them outside. I quietly tell Megan and head out front.

William is visibly upset, pacing and running his hands through his hair, a frustrated energy radiating from him. Cole gives me a soft smile as I approach. "Hey," he says gently.

"What's going on?" I ask, looking between the two of them.

Cole lets out a small laugh. "Remember all those feelings I had after we went to Chicago with Cara and the kids?"

"Yeah," I smile, "a little overwhelmed?"

William gives me a brief, tight-lipped smile, but it quickly fades as he resumes pacing, his frustration clear. I notice how much he mirrors Cole's mannerisms when upset. "You know," I say softly, "your dad does that exact same thing when he's upset—pacing like that."

William pauses, glancing between us, then runs his hand through his hair again, a mirror image of his father.

"Hey," I say, taking a few steps closer to him. "I know this is overwhelming. All of you, even my kids, have been handling this better than I could have hoped, but it's still a lot. Everything's happening so fast, and it's okay to feel overwhelmed."

"It's not just that," William says, turning to face me. "Yeah, this all happened fast, but the first time I saw how happy Dad was with you, it didn't bother me. But now, seeing this," he gestures toward the house, "I realize I didn't grow up like your kids. My mom... she's just so fucking selfish, and I keep thinking how different my life could've been if she were a different person."

I give him a moment to collect his thoughts, glancing at Cole, who looks at me, uncertain how to respond.

"William," I say softly, "I'm going to tell you the same thing I told your dad when he expressed very similar feelings to me." He nods, listening. "For many years, my kids were my entire world. Some people might say that wasn't healthy, but I could only do that because my parents and brother supported me financially. If I had to work full-time, it would've been different for them too. And trust me, I'm not perfect. My kids can tell you plenty of stories about my mistakes. They also have another parent who doesn't deserve any credit for how great they are. I know you shared some stories last night—they can relate to you on that."

He remains silent, so I take a chance, stepping forward to hug him. He clings to me, almost desperately, and begins to cry. It feels both natural and strange, comforting this young man who, despite his size, seems so much like a child in this moment. His sobs are heart wrenching and I have to fight back my own tears.

I hear the front door open and close, and William quickly lets go of me, turning away. I turn to see Tyler standing there, concern etched on his face.

"Everything okay?" Tyler asks.

Cole nods. "Yeah, just give us a few minutes."

Tyler nods, starts to walk back to the house, but then he stops, turning back to William. Walking past me, he grabs William's shoulders, turning him to face him. Then, in a move that's both masculine and deeply empathetic, he puts his hands on the back of William's neck and looks him in the eyes. I take a step back, wrapping my arms around myself, giving them space.

"Hey, man, whatever you're feeling, we're all feeling it. You just might be feeling it more intensely," Tyler says, his voice steady. "I know you've always held out hope that maybe she'd be the mom we needed, but... people don't change, William. They just don't. I know dredging up all those shitty memories last night and then seeing this today—it's such a fucking contrast. I get it. But you have Dad, and you have me and Matthew. You have family that cares about you." He glances over William's shoulder at me and Cole, who's now standing next to me with his arm around me. "And I'm pretty sure this family we just met will be the same. Now we just have to hope Dad doesn't fuck it up," Tyler adds with a smile, and I see William's shoulders shake with quiet laughter. Cole pulls me closer, kissing my hair.

William hugs Tyler and quietly says, "Thank you."

Tyler leans back, giving William a light punch on the shoulder before heading back inside. As he passes Cole and me, he smiles but doesn't say anything. William takes a deep breath, then turns back to face Cole.

"I think," William starts, then pauses, sniffling and gathering his thoughts. "I think when you first told me about Autumn, I reacted the way I did because I always thought you were the one who could change Mom. *You* were the one who could fix her because no one else could." He pauses again, taking another deep breath. "I know that's insane. But then I met Autumn," he glances at me with a soft smile, "and she is not Mom." He laughs, and Cole chuckles softly beside me. "Seeing how happy you are with her, how natural you two are together... that didn't bother me. But now, seeing this, seeing the mother she is and hearing stories from her kids, it's just a lot."

"Your dad felt the exact same way the first time he came here and met my kids," I say gently. "I know it's overwhelming."

"But it's overwhelming in a good way," William says, his voice thick with emotion. "I feel like I'm grieving for the life I could've had, for what I'll never have, but not because this is bad—because it's so good."

I give William another quick hug, which he returns. "I'm going to go inside and give you two some time," I say, stepping back.

Cole smiles at me as I head back into the house. They don't return for about twenty minutes, but when they do, William looks calmer, his face no longer flushed, his eyes clearer. No one makes a big deal about their absence or how long they were gone, and the evening continues with the same warmth and ease as before.

Cole meets my eyes and gestures for me to follow him. He leads me to my office, the only room on the main level with a door besides the bathroom, and closes it behind us. The moment we're alone, he pulls me into a tight hug.

"I just need to decompress for a minute," he says, his voice heavy with emotion. "How did I miss all of this?"

"Miss what?" I ask, a small laugh escaping me.

"How did I miss how much they hate their mom? All these years, I thought they preferred her—every single one of them. I knew their relationships with her weren't perfect, but I always thought they chose her over me."

He starts pacing the room, his agitation clear. I can't help but smile.

"What?" he asks, noticing my expression.

"You're pacing, just like William," I say softly. "And, Cole, I don't think you missed anything. I think it was her—Michelle. She probably said or did things that made you believe they preferred her. That's the only explanation I can think of." I pause, considering my words. "When I saw how Matthew and Tyler reacted to her, I knew something was off. But maybe it's because I'm a mom, and I could sense it. My instincts kicked in to protect them, just from their body language."

Cole stops pacing for a moment, his expression troubled. "I always thought William was such a mama's boy, but now I see he just wanted her to be the mom he needed. She never gave him that. And I can relate to that—I never had a mother who cared. Hell, I never had a parent who cared, but I accepted that a long time ago."

"Cole," I say gently, "I'm pretty sure Michelle made you feel inferior. I saw how you reacted when she texted you that night. She knows how to push your buttons, to make you feel like a failure as a father and probably as a husband too. Steve did the same to me—made me feel like I was an inadequate wife and partner. I think she told you things like the kids preferred her or didn't want to be with you, and you believed her. It's not about being smart; it's about being manipulated."

Cole looks almost stunned, his jaw dropping slightly as if he's about to say something, but then he snaps it shut and resumes pacing. I stay quiet, giving him space to process. Eventually, he stops and turns back to me.

"This is insane," he says, shaking his head. "Thinking of all the things she's told me over the years, I can't believe I didn't see through it."

"It's not about intelligence," I say with a small laugh. "It's about your heart. She messed with your emotions, not your brain. And your history with your parents probably didn't help."

"She's been messing with my emotions since the day I met her," he mutters.

"Honestly, Cole, I think she's worse than Steve ever was. Steve was an asshole and a cheating womanizer, but he never tried to manipulate the kids like that. He always respected that I was their mother and didn't try to drive a wedge between us. Michelle, on the other hand, is something else entirely. The way she acted at the art exhibit... I've never seen anything like it, and I have plenty of divorced friends. It was brazen."

Cole shrugs, the resignation clear in his voice. "I'm so used to it, nothing she does surprises me anymore. It's exactly what I expected of her."

"You're desensitized, which is probably a good thing in some ways. But the silver lining is that your kids are adults now. You only have to deal with her at random important events."

"That's true. It's been easier since Matthew turned eighteen."

I walk over to him and pull him into a hug. He cups the back of my head, threading his fingers through my hair, and kisses me deeply.

When he pulls back, he looks at me with a soft smile. "I feel like even if I *do* fuck this up like Tyler joked about," he laughs, "you've already made my life better. If you hadn't come into it, I don't know how long I would've kept going with things as they were."

"I hope you don't mess it up," I say, laughing lightly.

"Me too. But I'm 99% sure that if one of us does, it'll be me."

I kiss him softly, letting the moment linger before we rejoin the kids in the kitchen. They're back to their usual antics, the room filled with laughter and playful chaos. Dinner is ready not long after, and we all gather in the dining room, where the conversation flows as easily as the wine. The table is alive with energy as we dig into salad, lasagna, garlic bread, and more wine. The laughter is constant, and the room never quiets.

As the meal winds down, Megan suggests we play Cards Against Humanity, and the idea is met with unanimous excitement. We grab the decks and move to the family room, where everyone finds a comfortable spot—whether it's on the couches, chairs, or even the floor. Playing a game so full of off-color humor with six barely-adults is absurdly fun, and the addition of a little alcohol makes it even more hilarious. We play until about eleven, finally deciding we're exhausted from laughing so hard.

Kevin heads outside to start the firepit, while Sami and Tyler decide to call it a night. Cole and I also decide it's time to turn in, leaving the other four kids to hang out by the fire until the early hours of the morning.

CHAPTER THIRTY-FOUR
THE REVELATIONS

In the morning, Sami and I dive into making breakfast—French toast from three entire loaves of bread, sausage, bacon, scrambled eggs, and hash browns. The aroma fills the house, slowly waking everyone up, and they start trickling into the kitchen. When Megan doesn't appear, I send Sami to wake her up.

It's around ten, and with the pool party starting at noon, the house buzzes with activity. Everyone pitches in to set up snacks and drinks. Kevin, William, and Tyler take charge of the outdoor kitchen, forming burger patties and prepping other meats for the grill. Kevin makes a quick run to the store for two extra propane tanks, just in case. Preseason football is on, so Cole sets up the game in both the family room and on the small outdoor screen. Afterward, everyone heads off to get ready.

I slip into a sundress over what my kids jokingly call my "old lady swimsuit." It's got compression in the abdomen and a short skirt that helps me feel more comfortable about the areas where I carry extra weight. I'm not sure I'll get in the pool today, but I want the option.

Cole is the same—board shorts and a t-shirt, but he's doubtful he'll get in the water.

Sami and Megan are both in shorts over their bikini bottoms, with crocheted swim cover-ups over their tops. The boys follow Cole's lead, all wearing board shorts and t-shirts, except Kevin, who's already shirtless.

About thirty minutes before the party, Cara arrives with her two sons and her new beau, Blake. He seems like a good fit for her, and I can't resist teasing her about how I've inspired her to settle down. I also repay the favor by playfully warning Blake that if he hurts her, he'll have to answer to me.

Stacey and her brother are the next to arrive, which makes William happy. It's funny how Megan and William had this small-world connection before there was ever a Cole and me. My parents show up shortly after, clearly in awe of how well all six kids are getting along. As the afternoon progresses, more guests arrive—mostly the kids' friends, along with a few more of mine and Cara's.

The weather is perfect, and the day unfolds beautifully. Kevin mans the grill for most of the time, handing off duties to others when he needs a break. With nearly sixty people coming and going throughout the day, it's a lot to manage, but everything flows smoothly.

As the party winds down, the last guests are Stacey, her brother, and Cara with her group. They help with the cleanup, wrapping up leftover food. I send Cara home with some potato salad and other extras. Stacey and her brother are the final ones to leave, and by then, everyone is exhausted but happy.

"That was fun, Mom," Megan says, sinking into the couch. "We should do that more often."

"I agree," I say, smiling at her.

The kids all collapse in the family room, catching the end of the football game. Meanwhile, Cole and I head to the kitchen to finish putting away the food. As we work, I can tell he's just as pleased with how the day went as I am.

"Are you leaving with the boys tomorrow?" I ask, glancing at Cole.

"Not a chance," he replies with a smile. "Though I think Matthew might head back to my place. He mentioned that William's going to take him by his mom's to pick up some things."

"Isn't that a bit further from his school?" I ask, recalling the logistics.

"Yeah, about fifteen minutes further. But honestly, I'm just happy he wants to stay at my place. I'm not going to argue with him."

"Definitely not," I laugh, sharing his relief.

We finish tidying up the kitchen, say goodnight to the kids, and head upstairs, leaving them sprawled out in the family room. As we walk away, we both notice Megan's legs draped across Matthew's lap on the couch. It doesn't necessarily mean anything—Megan is a lot like me, always affectionate. I've seen her cuddle up with girlfriends and even Kevin like that more times than I can count. Still, we notice.

The next morning, everyone is moving at a slow pace. Cole takes charge and sets up a breakfast burrito bar, which quickly becomes a hit. As the morning goes on, his boys, Sami, and Kevin start packing up, preparing to head out. Around noon, the house fills with the sound of goodbyes and hugs. I'm embraced warmly by all three of Cole's boys, and Sami gives Cole a big hug. The girls exchange hugs with the boys, and I can't help but notice Cole's raised eyebrow when Matthew kisses Megan on the cheek during his goodbye. Finally, the three cars pull out of the driveway together.

As we walk back into the kitchen, I casually glance at Megan. "Looks like you and Matthew bonded pretty well."

"Yeah, he's awesome," she replies with a smile at Cole, then looks between the two of us. "Wait, do you mean *bonded*?" she asks with a teasing tone before laughing. "First off, I already see all three of them as more like cousins or something, so eww. Second, if I didn't, it would be Tyler. And third, you know he's gay, right?"

She looks at me, then back and forth between Cole and me, her expression shifting to surprise when she realizes Cole's reaction.

"Wait," Megan says, turning to Cole, "you didn't know? Seriously?" She covers her mouth, trying to stifle a laugh.

"Megan, is that something you're assuming?" I ask, my voice calm.

"No, he told us," she says, sounding a bit defensive. "I would never assume—you raised me better than that. He mentioned it casually, like we should've known. He said his mom didn't know, but William and Tyler weren't surprised and seemed to have known for a while. He didn't say anything about you two, though. We just figured everyone knew."

I glance at Cole. "You didn't know?"

"No," he says, shaking his head slightly. "And I don't care. It makes a lot of sense honestly, but no, I didn't know."

"Well, hopefully, he doesn't want to kill me now," Megan says with a nervous laugh.

"Megan," I say gently, "if he told all three of you, he probably expected it to get back to us. It might have been intentional. And if not, he clearly doesn't care if most people know."

"No, he doesn't care—just his mom. That's the weird thing. He made such a big deal about how disappointing it would be to her. I just assumed it was like one of those things where we tell you things we don't tell Dad. He really didn't say anything about you," she adds, looking at Cole with a hint of regret. "He made it sound like he just didn't want to tell his mom."

A few seconds of silence pass. "Well, I think I'm just going to pretend this conversation didn't happen," Cole says with a laugh. "Honestly, I don't care. Now that I've had a moment to process, it really does make a lot of sense, but yeah... He hasn't told me yet, so for now, I'll just let it be."

"That's probably for the best," I say, nodding.

"Maybe then he won't want to kill me for telling you," Megan adds with a relieved laugh.

I decide to shift the conversation. "So, tell me about this girl Kevin is dating," I ask, genuinely curious.

"She's cool. I met her when Uncle Alex sent me to stay at Kevin's apartment for the weekend. Otherwise, I might not have known." Megan pauses, then adds, "Mom, he's super worried he's going to mess it all up. He's in his head about it. I think he needs Uncle Alex—or maybe Cole," she says, turning to look at him, "to talk to him. He's so anxious about screwing it up that he probably will, just because of that."

"I don't know that I'm the best resource in that area," Cole says with a chuckle. "Your uncle might be better."

"Maybe," Megan replies thoughtfully, "but Uncle Alex started dating Aunt Claire when he was nineteen. He doesn't have anything recent to go on."

"My experience isn't much even if it's more recent," Cole laughs.

"Yes, but it is more recent," Megan teases, joining in the laughter.

I can't help but smile at their exchange. "Anything new I need to know about you and Sami?" I ask with a laugh.

"Nope, we both still like boys—at least I do. I can't speak for her, but our standards are high, so I'll let you know if someone comes along who meets them."

"That's my girl," I say, laughing. "I had to wait for someone who met my standards too."

"Aww," Megan says, playfully making a gagging gesture.

Cole and I burst out laughing, the warmth of the moment wrapping around us like a comforting embrace.

Later that night, after dinner, Cole and I are curled up on the couch in the family room. Megan is sitting in the chair next to me, and we're all watching a movie when Cole's phone buzzes. He checks it, then looks at me with a troubled expression.

"What is it?" I ask.

Wordlessly, he hands me his phone.

Michelle

> What the fuck? Matthew is moving in with you? This wasn't even worth a conversation?

"How am I supposed to respond to that?" Cole asks, clearly frustrated.

"You don't," I say flatly, handing his phone back. "You can't block her in case there's an emergency with the kids, but you should definitely ignore her."

Before Cole can respond, his phone rings. It's Matthew. Cole answers, and Megan pauses the movie.

"Hey, what's up?" Cole says. We can only hear his side of the conversation, and it's clear from his tone that something's up. "I figured—she texted me," he adds, rolling his eyes and leaning back against the couch. "Okay, yeah... No, that's fine." He pauses for a long moment, then his expression shifts to concern. "Seriously?" Another long pause, and then he looks over at Megan. "Yeah, she's actually right here," he says before holding the phone out to her. "He wants to talk to you."

Megan takes the phone, and her face immediately hardens. "Hey," she says, then listens for a moment. "Are you fucking kidding me? What a fucking bitch." She listens for a while, her eyes darting between Cole and me. "No, I don't think so. My mom told him to ignore it." She pauses again, then asks, "You want to talk to him again?" After another pause, she hands the phone back to Cole. "Okay, here he is. Good luck."

Cole takes the phone and continues, "Hey... No, that's fine too. Send me a list, and I'll have them deliver stuff in the morning... Okay, Matthew. Love you. Bye." He ends the call and looks at Megan.

"What?" she asks, catching his gaze.

I nudge Cole. "She can commiserate. We can't," I remind him gently.

He considers it for a moment, then leans back on the couch, staring at the ceiling.

"You okay?" I ask, concerned.

"Yeah, I'm fine," he replies, sitting up with a sigh. "But I'm going to have to go home tomorrow," he says, looking over at Megan.

"Yeah, I think so," Megan agrees. "If it were me, I'd want Mom home."

She hesitates, glancing at Cole before turning to me. "Matthew's mom threw all his shit out the window when he was trying to load it into William's car. Breakable things—like his computer, his art, everything."

I sit up, shocked, and look at Cole. His face reinforces the truth in her statement.

"Yeah," he confirms, his voice heavy. "That's the story I got too. All three of them were there. Tyler tagged along to help, so they're all probably not okay right now."

"If our dad did that, Kevin would probably punch him," Megan says, "but that's probably not a solution in this situation."

"Megan," I sigh, "that wouldn't be a solution in your situation either."

"True," she concedes with a smirk. "But we'd all feel better afterward. Can I get Matthew's number?"

"Yeah," Cole says, unlocking his phone and handing it to her. She quickly enters Matthew's contact information.

"What are you having delivered in the morning?" I ask.

"Just groceries," Cole replies. "We left the house pretty bare when we came up here."

"Well, that's easy enough," I say. "Do you think you should drive back tonight?"

"Maybe," he says, his voice tired. "But I'm exhausted and emotional, and it's probably not the smart decision. Tyler said he'd stay at my place with Matthew. That's where they left his car, but he'll have to leave early to get to work.

"Do you want to come with me?" Cole asks, his voice tentative.

I glance between Cole and Megan, and I can see that Megan is thinking the same thing I am. "I want to," I admit, "but I think I shouldn't. I think you and your boys need some time to heal and bond, just the four of you—especially you and Matthew."

"You're probably right," he says, leaning back and looking up at the ceiling again. "Fucking Michelle."

"Cole," Megan says softly, her voice curious yet hesitant, "how were you ever married to a woman like that? I mean, Mom and my dad... if he hadn't cheated on her, she might not have been super happy, but he's not like your ex. He's a bit narcissistic and controlling, and yeah, he can't be alone, so he's always got a flavor of the month, but he would never do something like that to us."

"Honestly, Megan," Cole replies, his tone reflective, "I don't really know. I had a rough childhood, and I think she took advantage of that. She emotionally manipulated me—used my vulnerabilities against me."

"How long were you married to her? I know you had three kids like Mom and my dad, but how long?" Megan asks, her curiosity piqued.

"Just over ten years," he says, a hint of regret in his voice. "And she was unfaithful too, so it's a pretty similar story to your mom's."

Megan shakes her head. "I think you should both be grateful they cheated—it got you away from them. They're both awful, but seriously, Cole, I don't know how your boys do it."

"Well," Cole sighs, "I guess we're about to find out how they handle her at her worst." He runs his fingers through his hair, his gaze distant. "This is an escalation for her, though, and I hate to say it, but it's probably a reaction to our relationship," he adds, glancing at me.

Megan lets out a small laugh. "I'm pretty sure none of them are going to speak to her for a while. Matthew is seriously pissed, and Tyler might be even more so. I think because he's a teacher, he relates to the kid in all of them, and he just fucking hates how she's treated them."

Cole looks at her with a mix of disbelief and sadness. "You know what's weird, Megan? Up until this weekend, I thought they preferred her and her house over me."

Megan hesitates, her eyes shifting between Cole and me. "Okay, don't get mad, but I don't think you've ever heard this." She pauses, biting her lip. "Fuck, they'll kill me."

She glances between us, hesitating, then focuses on Cole. "So, that night in the hot tub, Kevin told your boys about Mom—how she was when Dad cheated, how broken she was," she says, giving me a sympathetic look. "Anyway, they said you were the same way. They treated you like a bomb that could go off at any moment because you were so broken. They were just waiting for the anger to come, but it never did—or at least they never saw it."

She pauses, gathering her thoughts. "They all love you, Cole. They worried you were broken beyond repair, and they didn't want to put more stress on you. Like even giving them rides to school or trying to keep track of all their activities. They went to their mom's house not because they wanted to, but because they thought being with you was too stressful for you. They prefer you, your house, everything about you as a parent, but they were just trying to protect you." She hesitates again, tears on her cheeks. "They'll kill me if they know I told you this."

"Megan," I say gently.

"I know," she says, "but I thought he should know."

I look at Cole, who's turned away, his expression unreadable. I reach out to touch him, and though he flinches slightly, I continue, letting my hand rest on his shoulder. He leans into me, his head finding its place on my shoulder, his face buried in my neck and hair. I feel and hear him sigh deeply. I glance at Megan and mouth, *"Thank you."* I run my fingers down the back of his head and neck, offering silent comfort.

After a few moments, Cole finally looks up. "Do you want to finish the movie?" he asks, and we all share a soft laugh.

Megan restarts the movie, and Cole holds me close. Throughout the film, I notice Megan texting, and I assume she's talking to Matthew, which brings a different kind of warmth to my heart.

That night, when we go to bed, Cole needs me in a way that feels different from any other time we've been together. It's as if the roles have reversed; the way I once craved his presence like a drug is how he's clinging to me now. I love him fiercely, giving him everything I can. For the first time in our relationship, he falls asleep with his head on my belly instead of me on his chest. I stroke his hair and rub his neck until he drifts off, and every time I wake up during the night, he's still there, holding on to me like a lifeline.

CHAPTER THIRTY-FIVE
THE INFORMAL PROPOSAL

The next morning, I help Cole pack up. He decides to take the day off for personal reasons, and I send him off in his SUV, feeling a mix of worry and relief. He calls me frequently from the road, and I can finally breathe easier when he reaches home and finds Matthew safe and sound. I give him space, waiting for him to call me that night.

When my phone rings and I answer with a simple "Hey, you," his response is immediate and heartfelt.

"I love you," he says, his voice filled with emotion.

"I love you too. How's Matthew?"

"I think he's going to be okay," Cole replies, a note of relief in his tone. "Some of his art was broken, and it might not be repairable, but he has this perspective about artists and how their work reflects their personal pain. I don't fully understand it, but he seems at peace with it."

"I'm glad he's okay, Cole. I'm glad he has you."

He laughs softly, though there's a trace of bittersweetness. "Well, there are two sides to that. If he didn't have me, he'd still be there and maybe his stuff wouldn't be broken."

"But he wouldn't be in a good place emotionally," I point out gently.

"True. How are you? Was your day okay?" he asks, his concern evident.

"Yeah, it was fine. I miss you, but I'm okay otherwise."

"I miss you too, so much," he says, a smile in his voice. "But your pillow here still smells like you."

"Yours too," I reply, my own smile spreading.

"I have plans with all three boys for dinner on Friday. I think it'll be good for us."

"That's great, Cole. I think it will be really good for all of you. You have some time to make up with them."

"I agree," he says, then adds with a laugh, "But I'm not sure when I'll see you again, and that hurts a little."

"We'll be okay," I reassure him. "We went two years being awesome friends and co-workers before this. We'll be fine."

"I know, but I still miss you and will keep missing you."

"I miss you too," I say softly. "But I'll see you in my dreams tonight."

"Oh, you know I'll dream of you, Autumn."

"You should tell me about your dreams," I tease, laughing. "I'll do the same. Then we can be all hot and bothered by the time we see each other again."

"I'll count the minutes," he jokes, his voice warm and playful. "Even without sharing dreams."

"Me too," I say, feeling the warmth of his words linger long after the call ends.

We spend nearly three weeks apart, relying on phone calls and texts to bridge the distance as we gear up for our upcoming conference in Chicago. This time, we'll be joined by Julio instead of Mark, and as the days pass, our excitement to see each other again grows.

"You getting a hotel room?" I ask, casually probing.

"I don't think so," he replies. "But that might mean some early mornings."

"Yeah, but it also means you'll be in my bed, exactly where I want you."

"Oh, Ms. Flynn, you want me to hold you?"

"I want you to do a lot more than hold me," I tease, and we both laugh.

During this time, Megan has stayed in constant contact with Matthew. She keeps me updated, telling me that none of the boys have spoken to their mother since that night, despite her many attempts. Cole confirms this, mentioning the flood of texts and missed calls he's been receiving and ignoring—desperate messages from Michelle, pleading to know if her "babies" are alive.

I keep Cara in the loop, and she finds the whole situation both hilarious and devastating, calling my life a soap opera. She can't imagine either she or her ex ever treating their kids the way Michelle did.

With a little more time to myself, I've been able to catch up with some of my other friends. Laura and I have chatted a few times, and I've spent a lot of time talking to Tara between meetings, getting updates on her wedding plans and her life. I'm excited to see her again, maybe in February, although there's also the company holiday party in December.

The week of the Chicago conference arrives, and Cole plans to drive up on Thursday. But by Tuesday, his anxiety gets the best of him, and he decides to make the drive on Wednesday instead. I'm thrilled he'll be here sooner than expected—this has been the longest we've been apart since our whirlwind romance began. But then he calls me while driving up with some unwelcome news.

"Hey, you," I answer, smiling at the sound of his voice.

"Hey. Have you had a chance to look through the full program schedule for the conference?" he asks.

"No, why?" I ask, feeling a hint of unease.

"Julio just called and let me know that Dr. Gabari is speaking. He thought we should know if we didn't," Cole says, pausing. I feel my stomach tighten—I haven't thought about Dr. Gabari since Nashville. "Autumn?" he prompts.

"Yeah, I heard you. I'm going to call my brother."

"Okay, that's a good plan. I'm sorry... I'll see you soon."

"Can't wait. Love you."

"Love you too."

I call Alex, and he tells me he'll reach out to Jamie. An hour later, Alex calls me back.

"Hey, Alex," I answer.

"Hey. Jamie's going to send someone or be there himself on Saturday and Sunday, but he doesn't have anyone for Friday. Just be careful, stick close to Cole," he says with a laugh. "I'm sure you will, but you know what I mean."

"I do, Alex. Thank you."

"Hypervigilance, you promise?"

"I promise. Love you."

"Love you too," he says, and we hang up.

I call Cole and fill him in. He jokes about not letting me pee alone again, but it gets me thinking.

"Cole?"

"Autumn?"

"I think we either need to get a hotel room for Friday or skip the cocktail hour."

"Yeah?"

"Yeah. I'll need somewhere to get dressed, and it's too much to drive back and forth to Milwaukee."

"Maybe we'll just skip it," he suggests. "Especially since Jamie doesn't have anyone there. It'll make things easier all around."

"I'm okay with that. What are you going to tell Julio about not having a hotel room?" I laugh.

"I'll just tell him I'm staying with a friend and I'm on your way, so we're carpooling."

"Technically, that's the truth," I say with a grin.

"Exactly. Also, I'm about forty-five minutes out."

"Yay! I can't wait to see you. Oh, and I know we need time alone, but Cara texted and asked if we wanted to go to dinner with her and Blake."

"Sure, we can do that if you want. We have to eat sometime, right?"

"True," I laugh, already anticipating the moment I'll see him again.

When Cole finally arrives, I practically attack him the moment he steps into the garage. I barely let him get out of the car before I'm on him, my excitement palpable. But he manages to slow me down just enough to get us inside the house.

"I take it Megan isn't here?" he laughs, as I finally let him catch his breath, still trying to undress him in the living room, just inside the garage door.

"Nope," I reply, my tone teasing.

"Autumn, you're insane," he says, brushing a stray lock of hair from my face while I work on the buttons of his shirt.

"Maybe, but only for you," I say with a playful grin. I pause, feigning hesitation. "I mean, I can stop if you want me to."

"That's the last thing I want," he says, swiftly shrugging off his shirt and pulling me closer.

His hands slip under my shirt, exploring the skin of my back before unhooking my bra and moving around to my front. I focus on his belt, unfastening it as he works on my pants. My body hums with anticipation as he slides my pants down to my knees, and I kick them off eagerly.

He pushes me toward the family room, clearly intending to guide me to the couch. But I have other ideas. I turn him around and push him down onto the couch, straddling him before he can react. Our eyes lock as I pull him into a deep, hungry kiss, feeling the tension of weeks apart melt away. His hands find their place on my hips, guiding me as I lower myself onto him, feeling whole again, like the world isn't right unless we're this close.

It's a quick, intense connection, the kind that leaves us both breathless and satisfied within minutes. When it's over, I stay straddling him, our bodies still intertwined. My arms rest around his neck as I continue to kiss him, savoring every moment. His hands roam my back, my ribs, my arms, my thighs, as if he's trying to memorize the feel of me.

"I missed you," he says, his smile warm and genuine.

"I might have missed you too," I reply, teasingly downplaying just how much I've longed for him.

We stay like that for a while, kissing and snuggling, before we eventually pull ourselves together to get ready for dinner. But even as we dress, we can't keep our hands off each other, both of us craving any form of physical connection after being apart for so long. Every touch, every kiss, every brush of our fingers feels electric, a reminder of just how deeply we've missed each other.

We meet Cara and Blake at the same cozy Italian restaurant where Cole and I had our first real dinner date. It's one of those charming little places where the staff doesn't mind if you linger at the table, which suits us perfectly. The atmosphere is warm and familiar, and although Cole and I are still a bit handsy, Cara and Blake seem just as affectionate. I enjoy getting to know Blake better—he works in the pharmaceutical business as a reimbursement specialist, so our professional worlds overlap a bit, making conversation easy. We talk about his kids, and he asks about ours. It's a relaxed, pleasant evening.

After we order dessert, Cara gives me a look. "Um, Autumn?" she says, her voice laced with hesitation.

I glance at her, raising an eyebrow in question.

"Not to make things awkward, but Steve and Vanessa just walked in behind you," she says.

I turn, and sure enough, there's my ex with his current girlfriend. This one isn't a fiancée or wife—at least not yet. I turn back to Cara and shrug. "Thanks for the heads-up."

Cole, curious, glances over his shoulder. Steve is about the same height as Cole—it's clear where Kevin gets his height. He's almost completely gray now, clean-shaven, with deep-set blue eyes, and tonight he's dressed in a shirt and tie. Vanessa, who's about twelve years younger than me, has always weirded out our kids a bit—she hadn't even finished puberty when Kevin was born. She's pretty, with pale skin, long dark wavy hair, and chocolate-brown eyes. Tonight, she's wearing a little black dress, and I have to admit, she looks good.

I give Cole a playful backhand to get his attention back on me, and we both laugh.

"Are you going to say hi?" he asks.

"If I have to," I reply with a smile. "It's unlikely he'll miss seeing both Cara and me, so I'll probably have to. But I promise, even if it's unpleasant, it won't be as bad as meeting your ex," I add with a grin, and Cole laughs.

Cara chimes in, "Yeah, that sounds like it was a one-of-a-kind experience. Steve might be cold or a little rude, but he won't be abrasive. He'll probably turn on all his gaslighting charms. Have your kids told him about Cole?"

"I don't know, honestly. They haven't mentioned it to me, and I haven't asked," I say. "Kevin went golfing with him last weekend, so it's possible."

Cole's arm is draped over the back of my chair, and I feel his thumb gently brushing my shoulder, his fingers occasionally running through my hair. His touch is comforting, but I can tell having Steve behind us makes him a little uneasy and his moves are possessive. I keep my hand on his thigh, offering silent reassurance, until dessert arrives and I need both hands.

The evening continues pleasantly, and I almost forget that Steve is even there—until I see Cara's eyes flicker up, signaling someone's approach. Sure enough, Steve walks over, leaving Vanessa at their table. None of us stand as he nears.

"Hey, Cara," Steve greets, then turns to me with a smile. "Autumn, lovely, as always."

"Hey, Steve, fancy meeting you here," I reply, clearing my throat. "This is—"

He cuts me off. "Cole, I assume. The kids told me." He extends his hand, and Cole shakes it, though he doesn't say anything.

"Yeah," I continue, "And this is Blake." Blake extends his hand, and they shake as well.

"I figured it would be rude not to say hi once I saw you here," Steve says smoothly. "I'll leave you to it, but it's good to see both you ladies, as always." He glances between Cole and Blake. "You're both very lucky men to be with these two. Autumn, give me a call sometime this weekend about Megan's birthday, if you get a chance."

"I'll be at a conference, but I'll try," I say with a polite smile.

"Nice meeting you both," Steve adds with a half-wave before heading back to his table. Cara quietly lets us know that Vanessa looks visibly annoyed.

Once he's out of earshot, Cara can't hold back a laugh. "What a fucking douche."

I almost spit out my wine, laughing at her bluntness.

Blake looks puzzled. "I don't get it. He seemed pleasant enough."

Cara exchanges a look with me before explaining, "That was him being over-the-top, 'I'm such a great guy.' Those were his gaslighting charms. That's not how he'd have talked to either of us if you guys weren't here."

"Truth," I add. "That was his absolute best behavior—the way he'd act in front of the kids' teachers so they wouldn't think he's an asshole."

"Well, I'll take that over what happened at Matthew's exhibit," Cole says with a smile.

"Me too," I agree as Cole pulls me closer and kisses my temple. "And I guess that answers the question of whether or not my kids had mentioned anything to him."

We finish our dessert and another glass of wine, enjoying the rest of the evening's conversation. As we leave, we have to walk past Steve and Vanessa's table, so I figure it would be rude not to acknowledge them.

I stop by their table, just close enough to be polite but not to engage in a conversation. "Nice to see you, Vanessa," I say with a smile. "Hope you both have a great night."

As we walk away, Cole grabs my hand and pulls me closer before opening the car door for me. "You know he got one thing right?" he says, holding me close.

"Yeah? What's that?" I ask, curious.

"I am a lucky guy," he says, kissing me softly. Then, as he opens the car door, he adds with a grin, "And he was right about something else—you do look lovely."

When we arrive home, Megan is there, and I'm a bit surprised by how genuinely happy she seems to see Cole. We chat in the kitchen, and all the while, Cole's fingers move gently through my hair and down my back, sending shivers through me that I'm not sure he even realizes he's causing. It's as if every touch ignites something deep inside me, and I can feel the warmth spreading throughout my body.

Megan says goodnight and heads upstairs, leaving us alone. I turn to Cole, running my fingernails lightly down his arms and then up his back. He pulls me close, our bodies flush, and instead of what I expect, he surprises me by simply holding me in a long, tender embrace. I can feel his breath, steady and warm, and the rhythmic beat of his heart against mine.

When he finally loosens his grip, he kisses my forehead and murmurs, "I really missed holding you."

"I missed you too," I reply softly. "Want to hold me in the bedroom?"

He smiles. "How could I say no to that?"

We head upstairs, and as soon as the bedroom door closes, he pulls me into another embrace, his hand gently resting on the back of my neck as he kisses me. His kiss is soft, full of emotion, and his hands stay steady—one around my waist and the other on my neck. It's a kiss that says everything without needing to say a word.

When we pull apart, he looks into my eyes and kisses the top of my forehead. "I love you so much, Autumn. 'Love' really doesn't feel like a strong enough word."

I run my hands and nails up and down his arms. "I love you so much too," I whisper, kissing him softly, my hand resting on his cheek, my thumb tracing his bottom lip.

He laughs, recalling, "Remember those first days we were together in Dallas when I said something like, 'I swear to God if you break my heart'?"

"Yeah, I remember." I smile back.

"Well, I'm pretty sure at this point, you could do more than break it—you could shatter me," he says, a hint of vulnerability in his voice.

"Cole, I still can't imagine ever hurting you," I say, my hand trailing down from his cheek to his chest. "Is something on your mind? Are you okay?"

"Yeah," he replies, though his voice is tinged with introspection. "It's just... even this short time apart made me realize how much I need you. It's crazy to feel this much, this soon. I've never felt this much before, maybe only for my kids, but never for anyone else."

"Cole," I say gently, "I can't promise we'll never fight or that it'll always be perfect. But I'm terrified too, because everything I feel with you is *so* intense. I'm pretty sure you could shatter me too." I smile softly, pressing my finger into his chest. "But I love you so much, and I need you so much. It's like a part of me is missing when I can't touch you," I admit with a small smile. "I survived while you were gone, but I didn't like it."

"I didn't like it either." He smiles, brushing his thumb along my cheek.

"You know what I think?" I say, leaning in closer.

"What, Autumn?" His voice drops, husky and laced with anticipation, turning me on even more.

"I think you should make love to me now," I whisper, my fingernails grazing down his chest.

"Is that all you ever think about?" he teases, laughing softly.

I let my hands wander lower, feeling his body's response to me, and he inhales sharply. "I'm pretty sure I'm not alone," I whisper with a knowing smile.

"What am I going to do with you?" he murmurs, smiling as he kisses me gently.

"Love me forever," I reply, surprising him with the seriousness in my voice. He expected something playful and erotic, but my words catch him off guard. He kisses me again, deeper this time. "Grow old with me," I add, followed by another kiss. "Never leave me," I whisper, feeling the intensity between us. "Change my last name."

His mouth and hands become hungrier, more desperate. "Make love to me," I finish.

He pulls me toward the bed and sits. His hands move from my thighs up to my ribs and back down, following the curves of my body with his eyes. My hands find his hair, raking through it and down his neck, as he lifts my shirt over my head and draws me closer. His hands quickly find my breasts, his mouth following, sending shivers through me as my head tilts back naturally. His grip on my back tightens.

I gather his shirt at the base of his neck, and he pulls it off, tossing it aside. His hands work their way down to my pants, removing them swiftly. Even though he's still wearing his, he draws me close, his fingers finding their way to the most sensitive part of me. A soft moan escapes my lips, bringing a smile to his.

Still standing, he rests his forehead on my belly, one hand holding me close while the other works me into a frenzy, his fingers moving expertly. As my climax builds, I grip his hair, my body tightening, and when I finally come undone, I feel my body throbbing around his fingers.

He looks up, pulling me down for a kiss, his mouth moving hungrily from my lips to my neck and down to my breasts. I work on removing his pants, and when they're finally off, he flips me onto the bed, kissing his way up my body, from my inner thigh to my belly, past my navel, and up to my lips.

He enters me slowly, and I gasp, overwhelmed by the feeling of being so completely filled by him. He guides my legs around him as he moves, slowly and gently, making love to me with an intensity that leaves us both breathless. He shifts us so that he's leaning back against the pillows, pulling me on top of him. We move together in perfect harmony, our bodies synchronized as if we've been doing this for years. As I reach another climax, my nails digging into his back, I feel him reach his too, filling me as my body trembles around him.

We stay like that for a while, our breathing slowing as we kiss softly, savoring the closeness. Eventually, he looks at me, a smile playing on his lips. "Did you seriously ask me to change your last name?"

"Uh, yeah," I reply flippantly and then laugh. "Did that just register?"

"It registered the first time." He grins. "I just wanted confirmation."

"That wasn't a formal proposal, Mr. Waters," I say, still laughing softly. "But it was an answer to the question you asked me."

He laughs too. "Well, yeah, I mean, a formal proposal should have flowers and some kind of grand gesture. You'll have to do better next time."

"Under the stars, where dreams come true," I muse, "with flowers, music, and a ring."

"God, I love you," he whispers, "and that laugh." He pulls me in for another kiss, and in this moment, everything feels perfect.

CHAPTER THIRTY-SIX

THE CHICAGO CONFERENCE

Thursday morning, we wake up for our usual morning meeting and then get ready to head down to Chicago for dinner with Julio. I joke with Cole about how ridiculous it is to drive four hours just for dinner, but he insists it's worth it to stay at my house and avoid the risks of being in a public hotel together. I smile and tell him he's driving.

"I'm good with that." He grins.

Since it's a long drive, we agree on an early dinner, planning to meet Julio at five. We choose a nice steakhouse just a block from his hotel. When we arrive, I greet Julio with a big hug, while Cole shakes his hand. It's great to see him again.

Dinner is pleasant, filled with easy conversation. Julio catches us up on his wife and kids, and Cole and I share updates on ours. Cole talks about the drama with Michelle and Matthew, carefully leaving out anything involving me. Julio is just as shocked as we were that any parent could treat their kids like that.

Then Julio asks about Dr. Gabari, and I explain that I'll have security on Saturday and Sunday, but not Friday. Cole chimes in, telling Julio he promised my brother he wouldn't let me out of his sight—not even to use the restroom. That's part of why we're carpooling to the conference. We all agree that while we don't think Gabari is dangerous, he makes everyone on the team uncomfortable.

As the conversation continues, I can't shake the anxiety building inside me. It's strange because I hadn't thought about Gabari since Nashville, but now, an ominous feeling lingers. I don't share this with Cole or Julio, but it sits heavy in my chest.

We finish dinner by seven, and the drive back to my house puts us home just after nine. Despite the early return, we'll still be sleep-deprived in the morning, needing to leave around five to get to the convention hotel in time to help Julio set up the booth.

We just sleep. I snuggle up to Cole, feeling safe and warm in his arms, and drift off quickly. When the alarm blares at four in the morning, it's jarring, but we manage to get up and out of the house on time.

As we load into the car, I can't help but notice how good Cole looks. His button-down shirt fits perfectly, and the way he's rolled up his sleeves highlights the definition in his forearms, making me bite my lip.

"What?" he asks, catching the look on my face.

"Nothing." I smile. "I just have a little crush on you."

Laughing, he leans over to kiss me. Even though fall is creeping in, it's warm today. I'm wearing a sleeveless lavender button-down shirt and black pants that, judging by Cole's lingering glances, accentuate my curves nicely. I have a black cardigan with me, but for now, I leave it off. My makeup is simple, letting my freckles show, and my hair is down, straight and long. I didn't have the energy for anything more today.

Setting up the booth is a blast. Julio is in a great mood, cracking jokes, and Cole and I can't stop laughing. The morning is busy with a steady flow of sales leads. True to his word, Cole waits outside when I head to the bathroom, and between him and Julio, I'm never left alone. We split our lunch break, with Cole and I grabbing a quick bite before returning to the booth so Julio can eat.

The afternoon slows down, and we talk about the evening's Meet and Greet, which promises live music and an open bar. Most people seem to have left early to get ready for the event, and by five, the convention hall is starting to empty out.

Just as we're closing up the booth, a group of people stops by, showing a lot of interest in our products. We stay and talk to them, and by the time we're wrapping up, the convention hall is eerily quiet and nearly empty.

"I have to pee," I say, laughing as I look at Cole.

"Okay." He smiles, then glances at Julio. "You good with the booth for a couple of minutes? We'll be back to help lock everything up."

Julio nods, and Cole and I head out the side door to the hallway. I leave him leaning against the wall between the men's and women's restrooms, scrolling through his phone, while I head into the ladies' room. After I finish, I wash my hands and take a moment to smooth my hair and brush away a few stray mascara flakes. As I do, that unsettling feeling returns, creeping up my spine.

As I walk out of the bathroom, turning the corner of the L-shaped hallway, I come face to face with Dr. Gabari. The sight of him sends a jolt through me.

"Autumn Flynn," he practically sings my name, his voice dripping with unsettling familiarity. "How nice to see you here, back in my hometown."

I try to sidestep him, but he moves to block my path. "Please, just don't," I say, trying to keep my voice steady.

He steps closer, forcing me to retreat. "Don't what?" he asks with a twisted smile. "Don't tell you how beautiful you look?"

His eyes rake over my body, making my skin crawl. I instinctively put my hands out in front of me, trying to create some distance. He takes another step forward, and I step back, feeling a sickening wave of nausea rise within me.

"We would be so good together," he murmurs, closing the gap between us. "I could make you feel things you've never felt before," he continues, his tone dark and suggestive. Another step forward, another step back. "Every time I see you, I think about what your lips taste like," he says, his eyes lingering on me in a way that leaves no doubt he's not talking about my mouth. "I imagine it's sweet."

I try to move to the side, but he blocks me again, backing me further into the bathroom. My back hits the wall, and I can still see the main hallway, but I feel trapped. Panic starts to set in, my breath quickening as I desperately scan for Cole.

Should I yell? Scream? The building feels so empty, I can hardly breathe.

"I've never been with a redhead," he says, his voice low and predatory. "Do the drapes match the curtains?"

"Tony, please just stop," I manage to say, but my voice is weak, the fear tightening its grip on me.

He steps even closer, cornering me in the narrow space. My heart pounds as I realize just how trapped I am.

Where is Cole? Did he go into the men's room?

"This color looks pretty on you," Gabari says, his gaze trailing down my body again. "Autumn, I could give you the world—trips to Paris, Rome, wherever you want to go. Cars, houses, anything you desire."

I turn my head away as his face inches closer to mine. Is he going to try to kiss me?

Summoning all the strength I can muster, I say, "What I want, Dr. Gabari, is for you to leave me the fuck alone."

He smirks, his eyes darkening with twisted pleasure. "Who would have thought you'd have such a dirty mouth? I can think of better things for you to do with that dirty mouth."

Panic surges through me. "Tony, stop," I say, pushing against his chest, but he's unyielding, a solid wall of muscle.

"I think it's time you stop playing hard to get," he says, his hand gripping my arm. I flinch as his fingers dig into my skin.

I can't believe this is happening. "I'm not fucking playing. Back the fuck off!" I try to yell, but my voice comes out weaker than I intend, the fear choking my words.

He runs his hand down my arm again, pinching my skin, and I feel my strength waning. My limbs grow heavy, the panic suffocating me. I try to push him away, but it's as if all the fight has drained from my body. I close my eyes, turning my face away, trying to shut him out.

Why do I feel so weak? Why am I shutting down?

I feel his breath, warm and invasive, on my face and neck. His presence overwhelms me, suffocating and terrifying. Just as I brace myself for the worst, I suddenly sense him pull away. I hear voices, other people, but they're distant, like echoes in a fog. I open my eyes, struggling to process what's happening.

Cole is there, and so is Julio, along with two other men I don't recognize. Cole, usually so calm and composed—my forever pacifist—has Gabari pinned against the wall across from the bathroom, his forearm pressed firmly against Gabari's neck. The tension in Cole's jaw is something I've never seen before—pure, unfiltered rage.

Cole's voice, shouting "What the fuck is wrong with you?" is the first thing that breaks through the haze in my mind.

Julio is suddenly in front of me, his face blurry as he asks, "Are you okay, Autumn?"

I blink, trying to focus, but I see more than one of him. Two men I don't know are also asking if I'm okay, and that's when I realize I'm crying—my face is soaked, my nose congested. I think I held it together until Cole pulled Gabari off me, but I'm not sure. It's like I've lost chunks of time.

Tears are flowing so fast I can't see clearly, and my throat is tight, words tangled up in the overwhelming emotions. I wrap my arms around myself and manage a nod to Julio. One of the other men reaches out, meaning to comfort me, but I flinch, and all three of them immediately step back, giving me space. I appreciate the gesture, even if I can't express it right now. My legs give way, and I slide down the wall, sinking to the floor, burying my face in my hands.

Suddenly, I feel hands gently trying to pull mine away from my face. Instinctively, I flinch and jerk my hands away, my body reacting before my mind can catch up.

"Hey, hey." Cole's voice is soft, calming. "It's just me."

I look up at him, and everything inside me crumbles. I lean into him, collapsing into his arms, sobbing uncontrollably. He holds me, his arms secure and steady, then slowly pulls me out of the bathroom and into the main hallway. One of the men I don't know is standing guard, arguing with Tony, blocking him from leaving. Cole sits down beside me against the wall, keeping me close, his presence grounding me in the chaos.

"Go get security," Cole says, his voice steady but filled with tension. I assume he's speaking to Julio, but everything is still so muddled.

My sobs begin to slow, but I still can't fully process what's happening around me. The world feels distant, muffled, like I'm hearing it all through water.

Two male security guards arrive, along with a man in a suit who I assume is the hotel manager. I hear Dr. Gabari trying to explain that he was attacked for no reason, his voice slippery and defensive. The noise around me is overwhelming—confusion, anger, too many voices. I catch snippets of conversation between Julio and Cole about Andy and a cease and desist letter. But it's all so fragmented, my ears ringing; everything is softened and dreamy.

Soon, Chicago Police Officers arrive, not just security. A female detective, dressed in plain clothes, approaches me, her demeanor calm and professional. She gently guides me out of the hall and into another room with a table and chairs, where I sit down, feeling numb. She tells me she'll need to ask me some questions, but I can take my time. I nod, but the words feel far away, like they're meant for someone else.

A few minutes later, Cole appears in the doorway, his expression a mix of concern and resolve. Squatting down in front of me, he strokes my hair. "They need information from Alex," he says gently.

I nod again, still not finding the words. He asks if I want to make the call or if he should. My hands are trembling as I unlock my phone, find my brother's contact, and hand it to him. Cole stays close, his voice low and steady as he talks to Alex, keeping me tethered to reality with his presence.

"Hey, Alex, it's Cole," he begins, his voice steady despite the tension in the air. "I know we've never spoken, but there was an incident with Dr. Gabari." He pauses, listening to my brother's response. "No, no, she's okay—physically, at least—and I think she will be otherwise, but the police are here, and they need some background on the situation." Another pause. "Okay, thank you. That would be great."

Cole turns toward the detective, holding out the phone. "Can you talk to her brother? He needs a fax or email to send some information, including a copy of the cease and desist letter this asshole was served to stay away from her."

"Yeah," the detective replies, taking the phone from him.

Cole sighs, running his fingers gently through my hair as he stands beside me. His touch is comforting. I can hear the detective talking to Alex, giving him her contact details, but it all feels distant, still like I'm listening from underwater.

There's some conversation, but the only part that really sticks is when she says, "Yes, sir, but it was only an attempt. She'll be okay. Do you want to talk to her?"

The detective looks at me, her expression soft. "I think your brother just really wants to hear your voice."

I reach out, taking the phone. My voice is small, almost unrecognizable to me as I say, "Alex." I feel Cole exhale beside me, a release of tension that had been coiled tight in him.

"Autumn, do you need me to come home?" Alex's voice is calm, but I can hear the worry beneath it.

I take a deep breath. "No, I'll be okay. Just in shock, I think."

"Okay," he says, his tone shifting into something more focused. "I'm going to tell you some things; it's a lot of information. You can hand the phone to Cole when I'm done so he can hear it too, just in case you're not processing or remembering everything, okay?"

"Okay," I manage.

"Jamie is sending over everything to the police, including a contract he just created and I signed for personal security going back to before Nashville. It explicitly states you're afraid of this guy. Danny wrote something up after Nashville, so they'll have that too. Jamie is going to file for a No Contact Order based on Sexual Misconduct as soon as the courts open in Cook County on Monday morning, which is better than the cease and desist letter. If he contacts you at all, in any form, even from jail, it will be a misdemeanor, and if he does it again, it will be a felony."

He pauses, letting that sink in before continuing. "If he is convicted of a felony, he can lose his license to practice medicine, so I'm hoping that's enough to keep him away," he says, his voice a mix of hope and frustration. "I already told the detective that, and she agreed it was a good plan. Do you understand?"

"Okay," I whisper, feeling the weight of it all. It's a lot to take in, but I grasp the essentials.

"Autumn," Alex's voice softens, "did he touch you?"

I'm silent for a moment, the question hanging heavy in the air.

"Autumn?" he repeats, his tone gentle but insistent.

"No," I say, then pause. "Well, yeah, but just my arms. It was mostly just stuff he said, and he had me backed into a corner."

"Okay, thank God," he breathes out. "I love you. I'll call you later after you've had some time." There's a pause, and I remain quiet. "Can you give the phone back to Cole?"

"Yeah," I say, my voice shaky but steadying. "Love you, thank you." I hand the phone to Cole.

"Hey," Cole says into the phone, pausing as he listens, while the detective turns her attention to me, asking more questions.

"When you were talking to your brother, was that the answer to whether he touched you?" she asks, her voice careful, kind.

I swallow hard, trying to keep my composure. "Uh, yeah."

Deep breaths, Autumn. Don't start crying again. Why am I so tired?

"He ran the back of his hand down my arm and squeezed them both hard enough to pinch, but otherwise, he didn't touch me. I'm sure if he hadn't been stopped, he would have done more," I admit, my voice shaking but clear.

The detective nods, giving me a piece of paper. "Fill this out in the next twenty-four hours and email it to me, but you don't have to do it tonight."

I barely register Cole saying goodbye to Alex, but he turns back to us, asking if he can take me home now. The officer tells him I'm free to go, but that he needs to check with the other officers to make sure he is as well.

Cole squats down next to me, handing me back my phone. He brushes my hair out of my face, his touch tender, and I take my phone, but otherwise, I don't react. I'm too drained, too overwhelmed.

"Hopefully, I'll be just a minute, and then I'll take you home," he says, his voice barely above a whisper.

I nod, sniffling, trying to pull myself together as I wait for him to come back and take me somewhere safe, somewhere away from all this.

A uniformed officer enters the room, leaning in to whisper something to the detective. She nods, her gaze shifting toward me, concern etched in her expression.

After the officer exits, the detective steps closer, her voice gentle. "Autumn, you mentioned that he squeezed your arms so hard it felt like he pinched you?"

I nod, the memory still fresh and unnerving.

"Okay," she continues softly, "We're going to have paramedics take a look at you. They found some things on Dr. Gabari, and we need to make sure you're okay."

Her tone is reassuring, but I can tell she's not telling me everything. I simply nod again, my voice absent.

It feels like an eternity before Cole reappears, but finally, he does, and this time he's accompanied by the uniformed officer and paramedics. Relief and fear churn together as he approaches.

"Sorry I took so long," Cole says softly, his voice filled with unspoken concern. "I had to talk to Pete and Andy too. Pete's on his way—he'll finish the conference with Julio. So when we can leave, both of us can just go home."

He takes a deep breath, his body language making me feel like something heavy is coming. He hesitates, clearly not wanting to say what he has to, but finally, he meets my eyes. "They thought it would be best if I tell you this next part." His voice is strained. "When they put him in handcuffs and searched him, they found an empty syringe and needle on him, along with vials of medication, another syringe, and some kind of powder in a bag."

I feel my stomach drop. Cole's words hit me like a physical blow, and I barely manage to nod as tears begin to spill from my eyes again.

"They're going to check you out," he continues, his voice steady but tender. "Then they'll need to take you to the hospital to run some tests. I can ride with you in the ambulance if you want."

My voice fails me, so I just nod, the tears running freely down my face.

The detective steps forward, clearing her throat. "Autumn, can you show the paramedics where you felt the pinch?"

The paramedic, a woman with a calming presence, steps up. "Ms. Flynn, I'm Hannah. I'll be with you in the ambulance. Can you show me or tell me about this pinch?"

I manage to point to my right shoulder, the words barely escaping my lips, "My deltoid."

Hannah examines the area, nodding to the detective before taking out her equipment. "Okay, I'm going to take your vital signs," she says, meeting my eyes with a steady, reassuring gaze. "Autumn, I don't want you to be scared. We think we know what he gave you, and it shouldn't be dangerous—just something to make you sleepy and easier to control. But we need to take you to the hospital to make sure that's all it was."

I nod, a soft smile pulling at my lips as I offer her my arm.

As she wraps the blood pressure cuff around my arm, the detective speaks up again. "We also need the bloodwork for evidence, to prove he drugged you."

I nod again, glancing at Cole. He continues threading his fingers through my hair in a comforting rhythm.

I stay silent, not moving, not speaking, just trying to process everything.

Hannah finishes taking my vitals, jotting down notes before looking back at me. "I think you can probably walk, but just in case, my colleagues are bringing the stretcher. We'll leave as soon as they're ready."

Cole squats down in front of me, trying to meet my eyes. "Autumn?" His voice is tender, concerned.

I finally meet his gaze, and it's all too much. The tears come again, my sobs breaking the silence.

"Autumn," he sighs, his own voice thick with emotion. "Sweetheart, I am so sorry." He stands and pulls a chair close, sitting in front of me. Leaning into him, I bury my face in his neck, his familiar scent and the feel of his familiar facial hair against my skin offering a small comfort.

Someone else comes in, asks a question, but I don't catch any of it. Cole answers, his voice low and calm.

"Autumn, do you think you can come with us now?" he asks softly.

I nod, feeling drained but ready to leave this place behind.

He stands, gently pulling me to my feet, wrapping his arms around me. His hand strokes my hair, and he kisses the top of my head before whispering, "Okay, let's go."

CHAPTER THIRTY-SEVEN

THE DOCTOR AND THE DRUG TEST

When we arrive at the hospital, they swiftly move me to a secluded room. Cole and the detective stay by my side. A nurse in light blue scrubs enters almost immediately, her demeanor calm and reassuring.

"Hi there, I'm Carrie," she introduces herself, her smile warm. "Do you mind if I call you Autumn?"

"That's fine," I reply as she begins attaching various monitoring equipment to me, her movements efficient yet gentle.

"And this is your partner?" she asks, her eyes flicking to Cole.

I can't help but chuckle softly at the title. "Yeah, Cole," I confirm, glancing over at him. He meets my gaze and takes my hand, his hold reassuring.

"Okay, Autumn, I'm going to draw some blood now," Carrie explains, her voice steady. "We need to check a few things before deciding on an IV or any further treatment. We'll also keep an eye on how you're feeling—let us know if anything changes, okay?" She pauses, waiting for my nod before continuing. "The most senior attending doctor here tonight, the one that should probably see you, is male. Are you comfortable with that?"

"Yeah, that's fine," I say, my voice steady though my mind feels like it's racing.

She begins the process, her hands moving quickly as she switches out the tubes on the needle, each one filling with my blood. It feels like everything is happening at lightning speed. "We'll also need a urine sample when you can. There's a cup in the bathroom; it doesn't need to be a clean catch, just enough to check for anything that might not show up in your blood."

"Okay," I agree, feeling slightly overwhelmed but grateful for her straightforwardness.

Carrie continues, her tone reassuring. "Hannah said she already told you, but we think we know what's in your system, and you should be fine. Depending on the lab results, you might be out of here pretty quickly." She smiles at me, and it's like a small beacon of hope in the sterile room.

"Thank you," I murmur, trying to absorb everything.

"If you start feeling anything other than tired," she turns to Cole, "or if she gets really lethargic and can't respond to you, push this button." She points to the call light.

She looks back at me. "Also please push it after you pee." Looking back at Cole, she adds, "Don't let her get up by herself, so if you're not comfortable taking her, you can hit the call light for that too."

Cole nods, his hand squeezing mine gently, a silent promise that he's got me.

"Dr. Gomez will be in shortly," Carrie says before turning to the detective. "Did the paramedics hand off the vials and other samples to the lab?"

"Yes, ma'am," the detective responds, her voice as calm and steady as ever.

The room falls quiet for a moment as Carrie leaves, but Cole's hand in mine keeps me grounded. Despite the whirlwind of medical procedures and questions, I feel a strange sense of peace with him beside me.

About five minutes later, a young doctor steps into the room. "Hey there, I'm Dr. Gomez," he greets us with a warm smile. "First, let me say how sorry I am that this happened to you."

Shaking Cole's hand, he deliberately avoids touching me, a thoughtful gesture that I immediately recognize. He pulls up a chair, motions for the detective to join us, and then begins speaking, his tone calm but serious.

"Alright, let's go over what we know so far and discuss the possible steps from here. I believe in making sure my patients are fully informed, so unless you'd prefer not to hear everything..." He trails off, waiting for my response.

"No, I want to know," I reply, pausing for a moment before turning to Cole. "But, hold on. Can you get Alex on the phone?" I hand Cole my phone, and he nods, understanding without question.

I look back at Dr. Gomez. "Sorry, my brother is very protective. If he hears it from you, it'll save us from having to explain it all over again."

Dr. Gomez nods, a small smile of understanding on his lips. "That's a good idea. You might not be able to process everything right now, so it's helpful to have extra ears."

Cole quickly dials Alex, explains the situation, and sets the phone on my lap with the speakerphone on. Alex's voice crackles through, confirming he can hear us.

"Alright," Dr. Gomez begins, his expression turning serious again. "I just ask that you let me get through everything before asking questions. I've done this more times than I'd like to admit, and I've learned to address most questions as I go along—including those that may be important for legal reasons, not just for your immediate care."

I nod, bracing myself.

Dr. Gomez continues, "What we're primarily concerned with are the empty vials they found on him." He glances at the detective before focusing on me. "We believe he administered something we refer to in the medical field as a 'B52.' It's a combination of drugs used to sedate psychiatric patients who are agitated or violent. Paramedics and emergency personnel sometimes use it for similar reasons. The 'B' stands for Benadryl, which, when injected, makes you much sleepier than a typical pill would. The '5' is for five milligrams of haloperidol, or Haldol, an antipsychotic that, in your case, would make you weaker and even more drowsy than the Benadryl alone. Lastly, the '2' represents two milligrams of lorazepam, commonly known as Ativan. This is where our main concern lies. Lorazepam is a benzodiazepine that can suppress the entire central nervous system, making it harder for you to breathe."

He pauses, his eyes flicking to the detective, who nods in acknowledgment, before looking back at me. Cole's grip on my hand tightens, grounding me as the weight of Dr. Gomez's words sinks in.

"The reason we're particularly worried about the lorazepam is that the usual dose for an adult is one or two milligrams. The vial found on him contained twenty milligrams, and it was empty." Cole drops his head, running his fingers through his hair. "We don't know how much he gave you, but the fact that you're doing as well as you are right now is a really good sign. This happened about two hours ago?" He glances at the detective again, who nods. "Injected lorazepam peaks at around three hours, so once we pass that mark, you should be in the clear."

He clears his throat before continuing, "We're going to start you on antibiotics and antivirals as a precaution, just in case there was anything harmful on the needle or in the solution that could cause an infection."

Cole's head drops again, his hand squeezing mine even tighter.

"I'm sure law enforcement or EMS already mentioned this, but there was another vial he had with him," Dr. Gomez begins, his voice steady, yet I can sense the gravity behind his words. "The cap was still on, so we're not concerned about it, and your symptoms would have been very different if any of that had been in the syringe he used. The drug in that vial was rocuronium."

Glancing at the detective first, he turns back to me. "Rocuronium is a drug we use in the operating room and occasionally in the emergency room. It's a paralytic."

The word hits me like a punch, and I inhale sharply, my eyes widening in disbelief. The detective pauses her note-taking, and I hear a muffled gasp—both from Cole beside me and Alex through the phone. The room seems to contract around me, the air thick with tension.

For the first time, Dr. Gomez reaches out, lightly resting his hand on my arm. The warmth of his touch is grounding. "If he had used it, the effects would have been immediate. But I wanted you to hear this from a doctor, to understand it before it's potentially brought up in court. Rocuronium is typically used when we need to perform a procedure very quickly—it acts like an anesthesia, mainly to put a breathing tube in someone in an emergency situation."

He pulls his hand back, his expression softening as he continues. "There was also a small plastic bag with some kind of powder. While we're waiting for lab confirmation, we strongly suspect it's Rohypnol, commonly known as 'roofies' or 'the date rape drug.' It's another benzodiazepine, and the combination of the two could have been extremely dangerous. However, we're relatively confident it didn't enter your system. Rohypnol typically needs to be ingested with food or drink, and again, your symptoms don't align with that."

His gaze shifts to Cole, then returns to me, his voice carrying a gentle yet firm authority. "Over the next few days, I want you to drink plenty of water. This will help your kidneys and liver process everything out of your system. Be hyper-aware of any unusual sensations in your body. We'll give you a phone number to call if you have any medical questions or concerns.

"Based on what we know—and it was fortunate that he still had the remaining vials on him, allowing us to identify them—we're confident that everything will clear your system within thirty-six hours. The Benadryl will be out by morning, the lorazepam by tomorrow night, and the Haldol, which takes the longest, should be gone in thirty to thirty-six hours. Watch for extreme lethargy and any trouble breathing. You might experience mild hallucinations or very vivid dreams. If those continue beyond tomorrow night or become extreme, please call immediately."

Dr. Gomez looks around the room, taking in our varied expressions, and then sighs softly. "Alright, that's everything. What questions do you have?"

I shake my head, still processing. Cole glances at me, then back at the doctor. "I can't think of any right now. It's overwhelming, but thank you for everything. Alex?"

"Yeah, I've got a few questions, mostly legal," Alex replies, his voice steady but tinged with a hint of detachment. "Sorry, I'm a lawyer—I'm in business mode right now. I'll process the rest later tonight, I'm sure."

"No worries, it's good you were listening," Dr. Gomez says, nodding in understanding.

Alex exhales audibly, gathering his thoughts. "Okay, so both Haldol and Ativan are controlled substances, right?"

"Haldol isn't, but Ativan is. It's a Schedule IV controlled substance," Dr. Gomez clarifies.

"Would most doctors have these drugs in their clinics?" Alex presses.

Dr. Gomez pauses, considering. "No, not typically. Unless it's a psychiatric or maybe neurology clinic. Ativan might be found in some specialties, but it's not common."

"What about that paralytic—rocuronium? Is that something most doctors would have access to?" Alex's tone is sharp, and I notice the detective jotting down notes as Cole gently squeezes my hand, his thumb tracing soothing circles on my skin.

"If they work in an emergency room or an operating room, yes. It's also carried on some ambulances for intubation, but it's definitely not something a doctor would just have in a regular clinic," Dr. Gomez explains.

"Alright, that's it for me," Alex says. Then, addressing me, he adds, "Autumn?"

"Yeah?" My voice feels small, the weight of everything starting to settle in.

"Have Cole or Megan call me when you get home, okay?"

"Yeah," I reply, glancing at Cole for reassurance.

"Thanks, Dr. Gomez, that was very helpful. I appreciate it," Alex concludes.

"Of course," Dr. Gomez says. "I'm all for providing as much information and transparency as possible in situations like this."

"Good," Alex responds, his voice turning steely. "And, Autumn, if the prosecutor doesn't take care of it, we will. By the time Jamie and I are done with him, that fucker will never practice medicine again."

Dr. Gomez looks momentarily taken aback while the detective and I exchange uneasy laughs. Cole just shakes his head, a wry smile playing on his lips.

"Thanks, Alex. We'll talk soon," I say, and he hangs up. Turning to Dr. Gomez, I shrug. "Protective brother."

Dr. Gomez smiles, a hint of sympathy in his eyes. "They don't usually share non-medical information with me, but... it was a doctor who did this?"

Cole lifts my hand to his lips, brushing a tender kiss across my fingers. "Yeah," I answer softly. "Unfortunately."

Dr. Gomez shakes his head, about to say something when Carrie, the nurse, walks back in, handing him a set of papers without a word.

"Alright, a couple of the blood tests will take longer, and we still need a urine sample, but the preliminary results are exactly what we expected—nothing more than the three drugs we discussed," Dr. Gomez says, his tone reassuring. "Do you think you can give us that sample now? If everything checks out, we can have you out of here in about an hour."

"Yeah, I think I can manage," I reply, nodding.

Cole helps me to the bathroom, his hand steadying me as we walk. The nurse checks the sample quickly, confirming nothing unexpected, but they'll send it off to the lab, too.

Dr. Gomez and Carrie return about an hour later, handing me prescriptions and discharge instructions. "You're free to go," Dr. Gomez says with a reassuring smile.

As we wait, Cole is busy texting, his phone buzzing every few minutes. I don't ask who he's messaging—I'm too drained to care right now and I'm relatively sure he's talking to my family and work people.

"How are we getting back to the hotel?" I ask, realizing I haven't thought that far ahead.

"I had Julio bring your car here. He's pulling it up out front," Cole replies.

I blink, surprised by the thoroughness. "Um, okay... How is he getting back?"

"I can take him," the detective offers. "I need to head back there anyway—we just got the search warrant for Gabari's hotel room."

I glance between them, then shrug, feeling a strange mix of relief and exhaustion. "Okay then."

As we step out of the emergency room, I wrap my arms around myself, trying to hold together the fragments of my shattered composure. But Cole is there, his arm firmly around my waist, anchoring me to reality. The night air is cool, a stark contrast to the sterile chill of the hospital. Julio is waiting at the entrance, standing beside my car, trying—and failing—not to look too pleased with himself for having driven it here. He hands the keys to Cole with a quick, almost sheepish smile.

"You sure you're good? Need anything else?" Julio asks, concern lining his voice.

"Yeah, we're good," Cole replies, his tone reassuring. "Her daughter knows we're on our way to her house. The house has a security system, and her brother is arranging additional security if we need it."

I glance up at him, my brow furrowing with unspoken questions. He catches my look and offers a small, reassuring smile. "I'll explain in the car," he says softly.

Cole opens the passenger door and helps me in with a gentleness that makes my heart ache. He closes the door and exchanges a few more words with Julio, giving him a brief, brotherly hug before finally sliding into the driver's seat. As we drive off, I feel a sense of déjà vu wash over me—much like the night he drove me home after too much wine, when Tony Gabari was also somehow involved. I curl up against the cool window, trying to make sense of everything that's happened.

As we merge onto the highway, Cole reaches over and rests his hand on my thigh. Instead of flinching away, I find myself craving the connection. Without hesitation, I scoot closer, resting my head on his shoulder and wrapping my left arm around his. The silence between us is heavy but comforting, a shared space where words aren't necessary.

"Autumn?" he murmurs after a while.

"Cole?" My voice is still small, almost fragile.

"Megan called Cara. They'll both be at the house when we get there. I thought you might need someone... I don't know, not male," he adds with a soft laugh. "At least for a while."

His thoughtfulness touches me, though I don't respond right away. It's sweet, and I do appreciate it, even if I can't find the words.

He continues, "And what I said earlier is true. Jamie's arranging for someone to stay at the house if we need it. The person assigned to you for the weekend will be at the house instead, and he's working on overnight coverage for Saturday and Sunday. Your brother's also having exterior cameras installed tomorrow. I'm not sure it's all necessary—they took Tony away in handcuffs—but your brother pointed out he has money, so bail won't be an issue."

A small laugh escapes me, surprising even myself.

"What?" Cole glances at me, clearly caught off guard by my reaction.

"That's what he was telling me," I say, shaking my head in disbelief. "How he could give me the world, take me to Europe, blah, blah, blah." Another laugh bubbles up, this one a little more genuine.

Cole chuckles softly. "I think you're a little slap-happy or delirious."

I shrug, not entirely disagreeing. "Cole?"

"Yeah, Autumn?"

"Where were you?" The question slips out, and I feel the tension in him immediately, a subtle shift that speaks of guilt and regret.

Sighing deeply, he squeezes my thigh and presses a kiss to the top of my head before answering. "I was waiting for you when Julio came over and said some doctors were asking for me by name. I swear I looked around before I left, and I was only gone for a very short time. But it was long enough."

"Is that who else was with you? Those doctors?"

"Yeah," he admits, his voice heavy with regret. "I knew one of them. I told them to walk and talk so I could get back to you quickly. I'm so sorry, Autumn."

His voice cracks at the end, and it breaks my heart to hear the pain in it. "Cole, it's not your fault," I say, my own voice steadying as I try to soothe him. "I didn't mean to make you feel guilty by asking. I just wanted to know."

I shift closer, still leaning on his shoulder, and start to run my hand up and down his upper arm, a small gesture meant to comfort him.

"It's not your fault any more than it is mine. And I'm really glad you came back when you did."

He kisses my head again, a tender response that says more than words ever could. And with that, we fall back into the quiet, the highway stretching out before us like a promise of eventual peace.

As we pull into my neighborhood, the quiet hum of the car is broken by Cole's voice, tinged with hesitation. "Autumn, there's something else I need to tell you."

I turn to him, my curiosity piqued. "Okay."

He hesitates for a moment, then says, "Pete knows... about us."

The words land heavily, and I sit up straighter, my eyes searching his face.

"The police were asking a lot of questions, and I wasn't going to lie to them," Cole continues, glancing at me briefly before returning his focus to the road. "So when I called Pete, I told him."

"And?" I prompt, my voice steady despite the sudden flutter in my chest.

"He wasn't surprised. Said he saw it coming, pretty much assumed it already happened." Cole sighs, the weight of the situation evident in his tone. "He told me that making sure you're okay is the priority, so he'll keep it to himself for now. But he's lost plausible deniability, which was the only reason he didn't flat-out ask me after we were with him in Chicago. If Andy asks him, he'll have to tell him."

Cole pauses again as we pull into the garage, the conversation lingering in the air like unfinished business. "Pete said he'd talk to me about it later next week, when we're not in the middle of all this. It's just not his priority right now."

Taking a deep breath, I let his words settle. "What about Julio?" I ask, needing to understand the full scope.

"We didn't have a direct conversation about it, but everyone there knew I was the only person you'd let near you. I'm not sure how he interpreted that, and I don't know how much he overheard of my conversations with either the police or Pete."

Nodding in understanding, I acknowledge the unspoken complexities. "I'm pretty sure you and Kevin are the only men I'll let near me for a while," I say softly, the vulnerability in my voice surprising even me.

"Well, I guess that's good," he says as he looks up at the door to the house that just opened in front of us and Kevin is there with Megan.

CHAPTER THIRTY-EIGHT

THE STATEMENT & THE TRUTH

The moment I step through the door, the kids and Cara rush toward me, their faces full of concern, their touches gentle but overwhelming. Their good intentions are palpable, but it's just too much for me right now.

I squeeze Kevin's arm, forcing a small smile. "I just need to take a shower and decompress, okay?"

Cole hasn't touched me since we got out of the car. I can't decide if I'm grateful or if it just makes me feel sad. I turn to him, reaching out to place my hand on his cheek. "Give me a little bit, okay?"

"Whatever you need, Autumn. You do what you need to do," he replies softly. "But if you're going to shower, can Megan sit in the bedroom with you? Just in case, since they said you're a fall risk."

I nod, appreciating his concern, and Megan, uncharacteristically quiet, follows me upstairs. The murmur of voices drifts up from below as I make my way to the bathroom.

In the shower, I let the hot water run until it's tepid, hoping it will wash away the remnants of this day. I pull on my most comfortable clothes—fleece-lined leggings, a super-soft tank top, and a cozy sweatshirt. Even though it's not cold outside, I add fuzzy socks for maximum comfort. I brush out my hair and twist it into a loose, messy bun, not caring that it will dry into a wild tangle.

Megan sits on the chaise in my room, still quiet but present. "Kevin ordered your favorite comfort food and ice cream," she says softly. "It'll be here soon."

As we quietly descend the stairs, I hear Kevin's voice, but it's only his voice, so he must be on the phone.

When I turn the corner into the family room, everyone looks at me. Kevin glances up and smiles. "She just came downstairs. Do you want to talk to her?" He pauses, listening, then nods. "Okay, here's Mom."

He hands me the phone, and I see Alex's name on the screen. A wave of relief washes over me; I don't know who I thought he was talking to, but clearly, something was giving me anxiety.

"Alex?" I say, bringing the phone to my ear. Cole moves closer, his presence a steadying force.

"Hey, baby sister, you hanging in there?"

"Yeah," I say, a small smile tugging at my lips. "I showered. That helped." I feel Cole's body relax slightly beside me, mirroring my own sense of relief.

"Well, I've got some good news for you," Alex says, his tone lightening. "On a couple of fronts."

"Yeah? What's that?"

"They denied a bail hearing until Monday morning at eleven. By then, the protective order will be filed, so he won't be able to get near you." Tears stream down my face, a mix of relief and release. Cole's fingers trace a gentle line down my back, and I feel the tension in him ease. "There'll be a hearing for the order, hopefully by Wednesday afternoon, but you don't need to go. Jamie will handle it. Dr. Gabari will have to appear, either virtually or in person, but I really don't think you should be there."

"Okay," I manage to say, my voice thick with emotion as I sniffle.

Alex half sighs, half laughs. "This was supposed to be good news, so why are you crying?"

I laugh through my tears, wiping my face with the back of my hand. "Because I'm a girl," I joke weakly. "I think I'm just relieved." Cole relaxes further beside me, and I marvel at how in tune we are with each other, even in moments like this.

"You should be," Alex says, his tone gentle. "I'm still going to have cameras installed tomorrow, but you don't need security—not now that we know he can't go anywhere until at least Monday. I've asked Kevin to make sure Cole has my contact information in case we need to coordinate. But I think it might be a good idea if Megan stays with a friend and you go to Fort Wayne with Cole for the next week or so, just until we know the outcome of everything."

Tears well up again, and I can't bring myself to respond.

"Autumn?"

"Yeah, I understand, that's probably a good idea," I say, my voice trembling slightly. I look up at Cole, wiping at my eyes. "I'm sure Megan can stay at her dad's, Cara's, or Kevin's if she can't stay with a friend."

Megan gives me a questioning look, and I manage a soft smile in return.

"I love you, baby sister." Alex's voice is tender on the other end of the line.

"I know you do, that's never in doubt." My voice wavers. "I don't think I can repeat all that without crying. Can you tell Cole?"

"Of course. I already filled in Kevin, but I'll talk to Cole. You can hand him the phone."

"Okay, here he is. Talk to you soon," I say, handing the phone to Cole.

As Cole walks away to speak privately with Alex, I turn to Megan. "He thinks we shouldn't be at the house if the bail is granted on Monday. We're good until then, but there might be a couple of days between when he could post bail and when the protective order is fully in place." I sniffle and grab a tissue, wiping my nose and eyes. "He wants me to go to Fort Wayne. I'm sure he thinks it'll be safer there."

Cara wraps me in a comforting hug and then looks at Megan. "Of course, Megan. If you don't have anywhere else to go, you're more than welcome to stay at my house."

"Your place is closer to school for her than my apartment," Kevin adds.

"Alex thinks it'll just be until Wednesday, but he mentioned a week, probably to cover all possibilities," I say with a shrug.

The doorbell rings suddenly, and I jump. Instantly, all three of them rush to comfort me.

"It's just the food, Mom," Kevin says gently. "I should have warned you they were almost here. I'm sorry."

"It's okay, Kev," I say, trying to smile through the lingering anxiety. "I think I'm just going to be jumpy for a while." I squeeze his hand and walk off to find Cole in my office.

When I enter, I see him on the phone, leaning against the table at the far end of the room, his gaze fixed on the floor. I catch the tail end of his conversation, and my heart tightens as I realize he's explaining why he wasn't there when everything happened. I appreciate that Alex likely asked, but the last thing I want is for Cole to feel guilty. It's not his fault that this guy is a monster—blaming him would be like blaming me for wearing a pretty dress.

"I didn't even think of that, but I suppose it's possible," Cole says into the phone. "They gave statements to the detectives, but I was too focused on Autumn to hear what they said."

Looking up, he notices me standing there. Our eyes meet, and his expression softens. "Yeah, it would be good to know that, at least," he continues. "It would also add to the proof of intent."

As he speaks, Cole walks over to me, wrapping an arm around my waist and pulling me close. He kisses my forehead tenderly, and when he starts to let go, I cling to him, not ready to lose the comfort of his embrace. He smiles gently, appreciating my need for closeness.

"Please, keep us posted," Cole says into the phone, his voice soft as he kisses my forehead again. "She can stay with me in Fort Wayne as long as necessary, that's not an issue at all." He listens for a moment, then adds, "She's right here. Do you want to talk to her?" Another pause. "Okay, thanks. Here she is."

I take the phone from Cole, my eyes never leaving his. "Hey, Alex."

"Hey, I just wanted to say goodbye and tell you I love you again," Alex says, his voice filled with warmth.

I chuckle softly, feeling a bit lighter. "I know, Alex. I love you too."

"Okay, I'll talk to you soon. Be safe," he says.

"I will. Bye," I say, ending the call but keeping my focus on Cole.

I look at Cole, worry lacing my words. "I hope Alex wasn't too hard on you."

He shakes his head gently. "No, much like you, he wasn't. My own guilt might be another story, but Alex didn't add to it." Reaching out, he brushes a stray hair that's fallen from my bun out of my face, his touch as soft as his voice.

"I heard you explaining everything to him," I say, my voice tinged with concern. "I don't want you to feel guilty about any of this."

"Alex thinks it's possible that Tony arranged for me to be called away," Cole explains with a slight shrug. "If that's true, it would add to the proof of intent and make it even harder for him to get bail. We think that might come out in the statements, but we won't be able to pull those until Monday morning. Jamie's planning to attend the bail hearing, and he might be able to make a statement on your behalf."

"What exactly did they arrest him for?" I ask, the question surfacing before I can stop it. "I don't even know what the charges are."

Cole pauses, as if weighing his words. "I thought Alex would've told you. Sorry. They arrested him for aggravated stalking, which is a felony. The second violation of the cease and desist letter, combined with the fact that he physically restrained you, elevated the charge from stalking to aggravated stalking. Alex says Claire thinks he might be able to plea down because his record is clean. But if he violates the protective order after that, the consequences will be severe, both personally and professionally. There's also the possibility that additional charges could be brought against him, depending on the prosecutor."

I'm stunned, the reality of it hitting me like a wave. "Cole, I haven't even given them my statement yet."

He steps closer, pressing a kiss to my hair. "I know, but between what the four of us witnessed, the documented history from Andy, Alex, and Jamie, and the drugs they found on him... well, it was enough for the officers on the scene. Plus, there were cameras in the hallway, including one positioned to monitor the bathroom entrances, so they didn't need your statement to understand what happened."

I swallow hard, trying to process it all. "At some point," I murmur, "I'll tell you everything, but I need to hear your side too. Cole, I was so scared." My voice cracks, and tears start to well up again. I take a deep breath, trying to steady myself. He moves to hold me, but I put up a hand. "Just a minute—if you hug me now, I won't be able to stop crying." I manage a small, shaky laugh, and he looks at me with such understanding that it makes my heart ache.

"I didn't even realize you all were there until you had him pinned against the wall. It's like I completely checked out, left my own body."

He waits a beat, then asks with a soft smile, "Can I hug you now?"

I nod, and as he pulls me into his arms, he says, "Autumn, I totally get it. That's what I used to do when my dad would punish me." His voice is steady, but I can feel the depth of his empathy as I wrap my arms around him. "I'd go somewhere else in my mind. The good part is, I don't fully remember those moments—just the aftermath. Maybe it'll be the same for you. Plus, he drugged you, so there are probably gaps in your memory related to that."

He takes a deep breath, holding me close. Then, after another moment of contemplation, he continues, "I know you told Alex that Tony didn't touch you, and I want you to write your statement before I tell you what we saw because I don't want to influence your memory. But I'm sure you lost some time, Autumn. When we got there, his hands were definitely on you."

I look up at him, confusion clouding my expression.

"I know you checked out, and that's okay," he says gently. "But we all saw it, and the cameras picked it up. It wasn't just me."

"Cole..." I say his name slowly, like it's longer than just four letters. He hugs me tighter, as if he can hold all the pieces of me together.

"Let's go eat," he suggests softly. "Then you can write your statement, and after that, I'll tell you whatever you want to know."

I take a deep breath, wiping the tears from my eyes, and nod. He kisses my temple, a tender gesture that steadies me, and together, we go to join Cara and the kids for dinner. As we sit down, Cole hands Kevin his phone back.

We sit down to dinner without mentioning what happened, just focusing on each other's company. I ask Kevin about his girlfriend—someone I've heard about but haven't met—and while he doesn't share much, given the circumstances, it's enough to make me laugh a few times. The food is comforting, and the ice cream afterward is a small indulgence I didn't realize I needed.

After dinner, I convince Cara that she should go home. I know she has things to take care of in the morning with Blake, and though she doesn't say it, I suspect he's waiting for her to return. I thank her, hug her, and assure her that I'll be fine. She teases me again about living such a soap opera life before promising to call me in the morning.

Kevin tells me that Alex asked him to stay the night until after the cameras are installed, so he plans to stick around. Everyone seems to relax a little now that they've seen me acting more like myself, even though I still don't feel quite like me. I'm just glad they feel better.

Once Kevin and Megan head to bed, I find the statement form the detective gave me. Cole and I sit down at the kitchen table to fill it out. The form says someone else can write it as long as I sign it, so I ask Cole if he will. He hesitates but then agrees.

"I just know if I start crying, I won't be able to see well enough to keep writing, and it'll take forever. I just want it over with," I explain.

"It's fine, Autumn," he says, though I can see the strain in his eyes. "It'll be hard for me too, but I need to hear it anyway."

I nod, then begin to recount everything as I remember it. I make sure to mention that from the moment I yelled at Tony to stop until Cole had him pinned against the wall, I completely checked out. I don't remember anything in between.

As Cole writes, I notice him taking deep breaths, especially when he's writing down the quotes. He clarifies a few things to make sure he gets it right, but at some point, I can see him slip into business mode, distancing himself emotionally to get through it. I do cry, but not as much as I thought I would. Once he finishes, I read through it, sign it, and use the scanning app on my phone to send it to the detective. When it's done, I look at Cole, and he knows what I'm going to ask.

"Okay, your turn," I say gently. "Might as well rip off the band-aid."

Cole takes a deep breath, and I can see how much he doesn't want to do this. I know he doesn't want to hurt me, and he's already feeling the weight of his own guilt after hearing what I went through.

"Autumn," he begins, then sighs.

"Cole, it's okay," I reassure him. "I need to know, and I'd rather hear it from you than read it in a police report."

He nods, taking another deep breath. "Alright. You know that when we turned the corner, we were only about thirty feet away from you?"

"Yeah, that sounds right," I reply, trying to brace myself.

"But we couldn't see you until we were much closer, so we didn't see everything," Cole says, his voice heavy.

"Cole," I say, a touch of impatience in my tone, needing him to just say it.

He swallows hard before continuing. "From what I could see, you had your fists against his chest, trying to push him away. But he had one hand trying to undo your pants and the other under your shirt, on your chest." He pauses, watching my reaction as I flinch. "Julio and I both pulled him off of you. It wasn't just me."

I'm confused. "I definitely don't remember that. When I saw you, it was just you with him, and Julio was right in front of me."

Cole laughs uncomfortably. "That's the part you're concerned about?" I shrug, and he shakes his head. "That was probably about thirty seconds after we pulled him off you. I honestly think you didn't check back in until Julio spoke to you. And then I think you checked out again when you sat down against the wall. The other two with us made sure Tony didn't go anywhere. I was trying to talk to you before I touched you, but you didn't even know I was there until I did. I was trying not to startle you." He pauses, running his hand through his hair in frustration. "The only reason I touched your wrists was to try to get you to look at me, to make sure you knew it was me."

"You talked to me before you touched me?" I feel a little sick, realizing I don't remember his voice, though I'm grateful I responded to his touch.

"Yeah," he says softly. "I said your name a few times, told you it was me. But until I touched you, you were oblivious." He reaches for my hand, and I lace my fingers with his. The relief is palpable—as I don't flinch from him. "I think you missed most of the conversation with the security guards who got there first. Julio had to have Andy send him the cease and desist letter so he could show it to them, and that's when they called the police. I think more time passed than you were aware of. But I was with you against that wall the whole time, at least until the detective, who specializes in this kind of situation, came and pulled you into that private room."

"Cole." I shake my head in disbelief. "That all felt like thirty seconds, maybe a couple of minutes."

"From the time I got you to look at me and then managed to get you into the hallway, it was probably almost twenty minutes before the detective came and took you to the other room," he explains, his thumb gently stroking the back of my hand. "Security and police tried to ask you questions, but you didn't speak to anyone—not them, not me, not anyone—until they told you that Alex needed to hear your voice."

"I don't remember anyone asking me questions except when Julio asked if I was okay," I say, still trying to process how I blocked all of that out. "Then she came and said she'd take me somewhere away from the chaos. But I don't remember her asking questions, and then you asked me about calling Alex."

"I know, Autumn," Cole says softly. "I had a feeling that's about all you remembered." He grazes his thumb over my hand again. "I was relieved when you talked to your brother. I was kind of surprised when you took the phone from her."

I smile, almost laughing. "Well, that was still a pretty one-sided conversation. I didn't respond to most of what he said. I do remember you talking to him when I gave you my phone, though. I don't think I missed anything there."

"I think once they got you out of that hallway, you were more aware," he says. "Not yourself, but aware."

"Did you tell Alex?" I ask, meeting his gaze. "Did you tell him what you saw?"

"Yeah, I did," he says, holding my gaze. "I think this is going to haunt both you and me for a while." He takes a deep, shaky breath. "Autumn, I'm so sorry I wasn't there. I don't know if it'll make me feel better or worse if we find out that Tony had them call me away on purpose, but I need you to know that I am *so* sorry, I—"

"Don't," I snap, surprising myself with how stern my voice sounds. Cole looks taken aback, so I soften my tone. "Cole, don't. I know you feel guilty, and if I were in your shoes, I would too. But this is not your fault."

"Autumn, I—"

"Cole, don't." I interrupt him again, and before I realize what I'm doing, I quickly move from my chair to his lap, my lips meeting his in a kiss that's needy, desperate. My body finally starts to relax as he hesitates, then kisses me back, his hands finding me—one on my cheek, the other around my waist.

I pull back slightly, searching his face, my thumb brushing over the familiar feel of his short facial hair. "This isn't about us. *We* are okay. I may not be okay, but *we* are. I love you, and if you need to hear me say I forgive you, I do."

"Autumn, you're way too selfless," he says, his voice full of frustration. "You shouldn't be worrying about me right now. That should be the last thing on your mind."

"This isn't selflessness," I say, shaking my head. "It's selfishness." He looks at me, confused. "I *need* you to be my rock. I need you to be strong for me because you're right—I am going to feel this for a while. I don't need you riddled with guilt or feeling so much of *my* pain. I need you to be my strength." I can almost see the gears turning in his head as he processes what I've just said. "I need you not to be broken too. This is entirely selfish."

He studies my face, running his thumb across my cheekbone, clearly trying to piece it all together.

"I need you to treat me like you did yesterday," I say softly. "Because every time I sense your hesitation to touch me, it's a reminder."

He sighs, the weight of my words settling in. "I just don't want to force any kind of proximity or touch that you don't want. I don't want to make things worse or trigger you in any way."

I run my hand through his hair, down the back of his neck. "Cole, we are okay. This is still fresh, but I already know that your touch is okay. It helps." I take his hand and place it on my chest, over my heart. "I am still yours. I still need to laugh with you, kiss you, just be with you." I rest my hand on his face, running my fingers through his short beard again. "I just need you to love me the way you always do."

He looks at me, still questioning, but then his hand moves to the back of my neck, guiding me into another kiss, this one long and tender. And in that moment, I feel the reassurance I've been seeking all along.

CHAPTER THIRTY-NINE

THE LAKE & THE CARDBOARD BOX

I wake up from the nightmare with a gasp the terror still clinging to me like a dark shadow. In the dream Tony Gabari had managed to trap me in a closed locked room instead of a bathroom doorway and the fear felt so real it's hard to shake even now.

The room is pitch black and for a moment I'm disoriented my heart racing. But then I feel Cole beside me his warmth his steady presence.

When I finally wake, the room is bathed in sunlight, a stark contrast to the darkness of my dreams. I must have slept for hours. I turn to see Cole lying beside me, his back facing me. Gently, I start tracing the familiar scars on his back with my fingers, feeling the roughness, the history in each one. He stirs, rolling over to face me.

"Good morning, beautiful," he murmurs, a sleepy smile spreading across his face before he kisses the top of my head.

"Morning," I reply softly. "Did you sleep okay?"

"Eventually," he says, brushing a stray lock of hair from my face. I close the distance between us, nestling my face into his chest, feeling the steady beat of his heart beneath my cheek.

We lie there in comfortable silence, his hand occasionally stroking my hair, his lips brushing the top of my head. It's a simple, quiet moment, but it feels like everything I need right now.

Eventually, we rouse ourselves and head downstairs. It's late—almost lunchtime—and Megan and Kevin have prepared a spread of brunch for us. As we enter the kitchen, the company installing the security cameras arrives. Kevin has been coordinating with Alex and knows exactly what needs to be done. Sixteen cameras are going up around the property, a fortress being built to protect me.

As the installation nears completion, Kevin steps away to give Alex an update over the phone. Cole leans in close, his breath warm against my ear. "We might have to turn off the cameras by the pool on occasion," he whispers, a mischievous smile playing on his lips.

I give him a playful nudge in the chest, but I can't help laughing, my cheeks flushing with warmth. The way he kisses me in that moment, with all the ease and familiarity of before, makes life feel like it's slipping back into place.

He narrows his eyes at me, a teasing glint in them. "I think I want to take you out tonight. Dinner somewhere nice, if you're up for it."

A genuine smile spreads across my face. "I'd like that."

The rest of the afternoon passes in a comfortable rhythm. Kevin and Cole watch some college football, their banter filling the room, while Megan and I talk in the kitchen. I can tell this whole ordeal has shaken her, but she's glad to spend some normal time with me.

Eventually, Kevin heads back to his apartment, and Megan, after some gentle encouragement, decides to go ahead with her plans to hang out with friends. For a moment, it feels like everyone is trying to cling to the semblance of normalcy, but there's an unspoken understanding that everything could change if Dr. Gabari gets out on bail.

As the evening approaches, Cole squeezes my hand, a small, reassuring gesture. "I'm taking you someplace nice," he says with a smile. "You might want to dress up a little."

I nod, feeling a flutter of excitement that I haven't felt in a while. I choose a forest green top that brings out the color of my eyes, pairing it with black pants and a touch more makeup than usual. I grab a black sweater on the way out to Cole's car, feeling a bit like I'm stepping into another world—one where danger doesn't lurk in the shadows.

We pull up to a valet at a restaurant I've never been to before, nestled along the Milwaukee Bay. The ambiance is warm and inviting, with dim lighting and an intimate atmosphere. They seat us in a small, circular booth in the corner, making the space feel even more secluded, like it's just the two of us in the world. We can't keep our hands off each other, the connection between us seem like it's growing stronger with each passing moment.

As the night unfolds, I'm increasingly grateful that Cole brought me here. Something has shifted in him. Maybe it's the aftermath of what happened, or perhaps it's the fact that Pete now knows about us, freeing Cole from the need to hide. His public displays of affection are more confident, more unrestrained. The dinner turns into a beautiful blend of shared laughter, stolen glances, and soft, lingering touches.

Even the server notices, smiling as she approaches with our check. "You two lovebirds are so cute," she says, and I can't help but blush, feeling a warmth that reaches all the way to my soul.

After dinner, instead of handing the valet our ticket, Cole takes my hand, his eyes sparking with excitement. "Come walk with me," he says, a boyish grin tugging at his lips.

I slip on my sweater, then take his hand again as he leads me down to the lakefront. The night is clear, with an almost full moon casting a silvery glow across the water. The city lights drown out most of the stars, but a few manage to pierce the darkness. I stop to take in the serene view, and Cole releases my hand to move behind me, his hands gently settling on my hips. He leans in and presses a soft kiss to my hair, the warmth of his breath on my neck sending a shiver down my spine.

"It's beautiful," I murmur, my voice barely above a whisper.

"It is," he agrees, his lips brushing my ear. "But not as beautiful as you."

His words make me smile, but instead of replying, I wrap his arms around me, pulling him closer. We stand there in silence, the sound of the water lapping at the shore mingling with the distant hum of the city. After a few minutes, Cole gently turns me to face him. His eyes lock onto mine, and I'm captivated by the depth of emotion I see there. The soft breeze off the lake heightens every sensation, making the moment feel even more intense.

He leans in slowly, kissing me with a tenderness that makes my heart flutter. In some ways, it feels like our first kiss all over again—fresh, new, filled with unspoken promises. As the kiss deepens, the world around us fades away. I forget where we are, lost in the warmth of his embrace. When we finally pull apart, the look in his eyes—a mixture of affection, desire, and something deeper—makes my breath catch. There was a time when I didn't understand these expressions, but that feels like a lifetime ago.

In this moment, I know with absolute certainty that this man loves me more than I've ever been loved before. He would go to the ends of the earth for me, with me—I can see it in his eyes, written across his face. His hand rises, gently brushing a few strands of hair away from my face. The words that come next, spoken in this moonlit and starry embrace, will stay with me forever.

"Autumn?" he asks softly.

"Cole?" My voice betrays the depth of my emotions, completely entranced by him.

"Do you remember, before that dinner where you had too much wine, I told you I had something I wanted to tell you? And you told me to wait until we were in person?"

"I do." I smile, the memory surfacing easily. "Because I thought I knew what you were going to say."

"I think you might have," he chuckles softly, "but then you kind of stole my thunder in the middle of the night." He laughs again, a sound that makes my heart light. "So I kind of want to rectify that."

"Okay," I say, still lost in his eyes, the moon reflecting in them like a promise.

"You and me, this," he gestures between us, "this connection we have—it feels like forever." He laughs, a bit self-conscious. "I know, it sounds cheesy, but it's like a flame that doesn't even flicker in the wind. It's just... constant. I love laughing with you, playing with you, making love to you. But it's the quiet moments, the unspoken things that pass between us, that speak to my soul." He pauses, his thumb tracing along my jaw, sending warmth radiating through my body. "This recent drama also taught me something—it's how I wait with bated breath when I'm worried you're not okay and the immense relief I feel when I know you are." His voice lowers, the words heavy with meaning. "I don't know what label to put on it, Autumn, but this—what we have—it's beyond the normal realms of emotions and labels, at least anything I've ever felt. Whatever it is, it's us, it's uniquely ours, and it's stronger, deeper, more profound than love or anything else I've ever known."

I can't help but smile, my voice coming out weakly. "I think you just outdid your hotel hallway speech." I laugh a little, and he smiles, his thumb tracing my jaw again. "But I agree," I continue, my voice still soft, "it is hard to explain." I pause, searching for the right words. "You're my anchor, Cole—a comfortable place that feels like home. Like home isn't a place, it's a person. With you, I feel like I can be completely me, without masks, without changing who I am." His eyes are so intense, watching me, and I swallow, trying to hold back tears. "You are my sanctuary," I say, laying my hand on his chest, feeling the steady beat of his heart beneath my palm. "My solace. I feel how much you love me and accept me, every part of me." My voice trembles as I meet his gaze again, tears stinging my eyes. "It's not just love—you're right. 'Profound' is the perfect word. It's a profound sense of belonging whenever we're together, and it started the very first night in Dallas. You make me feel grounded, loved, cherished, sexy." I smile through the tears that start to fall, and he smiles back softly. "But most importantly, you make me feel safe. You are my home, and being with you feels like, for the first time in my life, I've found where I truly belong. I do love you, Cole, but it's so much more than that."

He wipes my tears with his thumbs, his eyes never leaving mine. "Happy tears?" he asks, a gentle smile on his lips.

"Yeah," I whisper, "happy tears."

Cole's hand slides to the back of my neck, his fingers threading through my hair. His other hand cups my face, his thumb brushing along my bottom lip, then tracing my jaw. He pulls me closer, his kiss intense and emotional, filled with all the spoken and unspoken words, the need, the love, and the desire we both feel.

We stay by the water for a while longer, soaking in the night air, before finally retrieving the car and heading home. The drive is filled with the quiet intimacy of his fingers trailing along my inner thigh and my nails lightly running up and down his arm. By the time we pull into the garage, all I can think about is getting him into my bed.

We walk inside, and I immediately reset the alarm from "away" to "home." Even though Tony is in jail, the need to stay vigilant lingers. Meanwhile, Cole's hands are all over me, his lips pressing against my neck, his touch both comforting and electrifying. He guides me upstairs, his intent clear, and as soon as we enter the bedroom, he pulls me close, one hand tangling in my hair, the other wrapping around my waist. His kiss is intense, full of unspoken desire.

He spins me around, guiding me back toward the bed, his hands roaming up and down my ribs, grazing the sides of my breasts. I'm already so turned on that it hardly matters what he does next—every touch feels like fire. As my legs brush against the bed, he starts to undress us both, and I let him, my body responding to his every move.

Our kisses are intoxicating, and I don't want them to stop. My hands wander across his body, memorizing every curve and muscle. I step out of my pants when he needs me to and momentarily separate so he can pull my shirt over my head. The moment my back hits the bed, he's with me, his mouth still on mine, one arm bracing himself while the other explores every inch of me he can reach.

I feel him between my legs, and then he's inside me, filling me completely. I wrap my legs around him, savoring the connection, the feeling of being whole with him. When our lips aren't entwined, our eyes lock, and the intensity of his gaze captivates me.

Tonight's intimacy is everything I need—slow, tender, deeply connected. This isn't the night for wild passion or endless waves of pleasure; it's a night of deep, emotional connection. The fact that Cole seems to know this, or maybe needs it too, is just another testament to how in tune we are with each other, and I love him even more for it. After his orgasm crests, he pulls back to look at me, his eyes full of love before he lies down beside me. I look at him, feeling the depth of my love and need for him all over again.

I roll toward him, my fingers threading through the hair on his chest. "I love you. Thank you."

He looks at me with a soft smile. "I love you too." He pauses, then adds with a playful laugh, "You're welcome? I guess."

"Seriously," I say, smiling back at him. "I needed that. I needed this whole night. Thank you."

He laces his fingers through mine, bringing my hand to his lips for a gentle kiss. "I needed it too, so thank you as well," he says, his smile warm and sincere.

I let out a contented sigh. "Now I think I just need to cuddle," I say, my voice a little whiny, but filled with contentment.

He chuckles softly. "That I also need. Let me clean up, and then we can go to bed."

I wash my face and brush out my hair, then slip into my sleep shorts and a tank top. When I climb into bed beside Cole, he suggests we turn on a movie. Ironically, *Pride and Prejudice* is on. He glances at me, and I shrug with a smile, so he starts the movie. I fall asleep quickly, feeling safe and content in his arms. In the morning, Cole tells me he watched the whole thing.

"You slept well," Cole says, his voice gentle. "I didn't, but I'm glad you did."

"I'm sorry you didn't," I reply, my fingers threading through the hair on his chest, trying to soothe him.

Sighing, he kisses the top of my head. "I think I'm just worried about you. I know you're doing okay, but I can't shake this feeling that I failed you. And I know you don't want me to feel that way, but I do." He laughs softly, but it's tinged with sadness. "I think I'm worried about failing you again."

"I hope we never find ourselves in a situation like that again," I say, trying to reassure him.

"Me too," he sighs, his voice heavy with concern. "You're always going to draw people to you, but you went a lot of years without anything like this happening."

"I did." I pause, then add with a light laugh. "I also didn't know people were drawn to me."

Cole chuckles, then checks his phone. "Let's head downstairs. There's a surprise waiting for you." He kisses my temple, a playful smile spreading across his face.

"A surprise, huh?"

"Yeah, courtesy of Megan."

When we get downstairs, I see Megan, Sami, and Cara waiting for me. I hug Sami tightly, my eyes welling up with tears.

"I'm glad you're okay, Mom," she whispers.

"I'm so happy to see you," I reply, my voice thick with emotion.

"Your girls thought you might want a little girls' day, or at least a morning," Cole says as Sami looks past me to him.

"Yeah," Megan chimes in. "I thought maybe brunch and getting our nails done might be nice."

I smile, feeling touched by their thoughtfulness. "That sounds amazing. I just need to get dressed."

"No rush," Megan says with a smile. "We have time."

As I head upstairs, I overhear Cara and Cole talking in low voices. Their tone makes me uneasy, so when I reach the top, I ask Cole to join me.

"What's going on?" I ask, trying to keep my voice steady. "Why all the whispering?"

He meets my gaze and sighs, his expression betraying his reluctance. "It's nothing, really. Nothing we don't already know."

"Then why don't you want to tell me?" I ask, frustration creeping into my tone.

Cole inhales deeply, then lets out a sigh. "Alex says Claire thinks there's a good chance they'll give Tony bail. His lawyers might argue that both violations of the cease and desist were in public places during the course of business—"

"So attacking and drugging me is just business as usual?" I interrupt, my anger rising.

"No, of course not," Cole says, trying to calm me. "But his presence in the building was. And he has a spotless record."

I walk over to the bedroom window, staring out at the driveway. Cole follows, placing his hands gently on my upper arms.

"Jamie is going to request to make a statement on your behalf," Cole continues. "They don't always allow that at bond hearings, but if he can, they think it could make a big difference." He pauses, then adds, "Your brother wants us to go to Fort Wayne tonight because if they grant bail, Tony could be out by noon tomorrow."

I remain silent, processing the news.

"He wants you and Megan out of the house before the hearing," Cole says, but I sense there's more he isn't telling me.

"I know that, but what else?" I ask, turning to face him.

He looks down at his feet, then exhales loudly. "The way things are right now, the actual criminal trial might not happen until January, maybe December," he explains. "So if he gets bail—"

"I could have to stay in Fort Wayne for months?" I finish for him.

"Potentially," he sighs, crossing his arms over his chest, looking up at the ceiling. "I know it's not ideal—"

"Cardboard box, Cole," I interrupt.

He looks at me, confused.

"Do you remember when I told you I could live in a cardboard box as long as I'm with you?" I remind him, stepping closer. "Or when I said that wherever you are is home? *You* are my home, my sanctuary."

"But Megan," he says, still worried. "She's your home too."

"She is," I agree. "But she's an adult. Sami lives here too, when she's not at school. They both have options—they can stay with their grandparents or their dad. Megan can probably get back on campus if needed, or Alex might even get her an apartment."

"Autumn," Cole begins, still uncertain.

"Cole," I respond more sharply than I intend. "First, we're putting the cart before the horse here. We won't know anything until Monday, and even then, it's not certain what will happen. Second, if the worst-case scenario is that Megan lives on campus and Sami stays with family during her school breaks, that still puts us in a much better situation than many others."

Cole looks at me, processing my words. His voice softens. "Cara and Megan both thought this would be devastating for you. Even Alex thought so."

"Will it be different? Yes. An adjustment? Absolutely," I admit. "But devastating? No. They've never seen me in a healthy relationship, so they don't understand. Devastated would be if I had to go somewhere *without* you, not *with* you."

Cole sighs and pulls me into his arms, holding me tightly and kissing the top of my head.

I pull back slightly to look at him. "Is this why you couldn't sleep last night?"

He smiles up at the ceiling and nods. "Yeah, actually."

"Well, let this be a lesson," I say, kissing him softly, my tone gentle. "Talk to me, don't hide things from me. And no more putting the cart before the horse."

"Yes, ma'am," he replies with a small laugh.

I laugh too. "Okay, I have questions."

"Shoot."

"When do we need to leave for your place?"

"I'd like to leave by four or five. I have to work tomorrow, but you don't. Lauryn and Pete are giving you the week off, paid, without using your PTO. I was going to tell you that later."

"Is that a choice or a mandate?" I ask, raising an eyebrow.

"Honestly, I'm not sure. I thought they were just being considerate of the situation." He shrugs. "When they told me, I thought it was a good idea, so I didn't question it."

"Can you find out? I'll take Monday off regardless, but I'd like to know."

"Yeah, I'll check," he says.

"Do you know where Megan is going?"

"She's staying at Stacey's tonight and tomorrow. If Tony gets out on bail, she's supposed to call Alex and figure out the next step."

I nod. "So, Alex will probably get her an apartment."

"He didn't say that," Cole responds, shaking his head.

"He doesn't have to." I smile knowingly. "That's how he operates. He'll likely get her something big enough for Sami too." I pause, considering. "Okay, I guess I need to get ready for this girls' day and then come back to pack?"

"That's the plan," he confirms.

"Okay, well, since you're not joining us," I smile at him, "if I throw a bunch of stuff together, can you pack it in the suitcases?"

He laughs. "Yeah, Autumn, I can handle that." He shakes his head slightly, looking at me with admiration.

"What?" I ask, curious.

"You're just amazing," he says, his voice filled with warmth. "Every time I think I've got you figured out, you surprise me."

"Maybe you should just expect to be surprised," I tease, shrugging playfully.

"I think I'm learning that quickly," he says, tracing his thumb along my jaw, then over my bottom lip before pulling me into a tender kiss.

"Okay, go tell them I'm fine. But don't mention the apartment idea—Megan might get her hopes up," I say with a laugh. "I'll be down and ready to go in about thirty minutes."

"Got it. And, Autumn?"

"Cole?"

"I love you," he says, his smile full of affection.

"I love you too," I reply, feeling a deep sense of peace as he heads downstairs to update the others.

CHAPTER FORTY

THE STAY IN FORT WAYNE

I throw a pile of clothes onto the bed and pull my suitcases out of the closet. After some quick organizing, I decide to pack just a few nicer work outfits, knowing that most of my work will be remote and that we can come back here on weekends if needed. Once I'm ready to go out with the girls, I head downstairs.

"You ready?" I ask as I reach the bottom of the stairs. The girls all turn to look at me with the same confused expression that Cole had earlier.

"What?" I laugh, a bit self-conscious.

"Are you sure you're good with this?" Cara asks, concern evident in her voice.

"Yeah, I am. We don't know what's going to happen yet. I'll miss you all, but Fort Wayne isn't that far. Look at how much time Cole and I have spent together living at that same distance." I turn to Sami. "And Fort Wayne is closer to Ann Arbor than either is to Milwaukee. It'll be an adjustment, but it's not the end of the world."

"You'll be further from me and Kevin," Megan says, her disappointment clear.

"I know, but it's still driveable, and I'm sure Alex has a plan for you if we need it," I reassure her. "It won't be much different from when you lived on campus. We don't have to avoid the house entirely; we just need to be more cautious if we're here. It'll be easier if we're just not around, but that's still putting the cart before the horse. By Monday afternoon, this might all be moot."

Cara glances at Cole and laughs. "Okay, you weren't lying—she's really fine."

Megan hugs me tightly. "I'll miss you, though."

"I'll miss you too, but we'll see each other, and we can talk all the time. Maybe we can find a cute hotel in Gary and we can all meet there," I joke.

"That's not a bad idea," Cole muses with a grin.

I smile at him. "Hey, I threw a bunch of stuff on the bed and pulled out the suitcases. If you're not comfortable—"

"It's fine, Autumn," he interrupts, smiling warmly. "I'll take care of it."

I turn back to the girls. "Seriously, are you all ready?"

"Yeah," Megan says, nodding. "Let's go."

The day with the girls is exactly what I need. Brunch is delicious, and getting manicures and pedicures is both practical and fun—something I've been needing to do anyway.

While our feet are soaking, Megan looks over at me. "Hey, Mom, you know my birthday is in like two weeks?"

I smile, teasing her. "I'm pretty sure I was there when you were born, so yeah, I know."

Sami and Cara laugh, and Megan rolls her eyes, but she smiles too.

"Dad wants to do something big, which I think is weird because he didn't for Kevin. But he wants to have a big party, and he wanted to coordinate with you," Megan says.

"Are you okay with that, Megs?" I ask, wanting to make sure she's comfortable.

"Yeah, I just think it's weird. But he wants you to call or text him or whatever," she says.

"He mentioned it, but without many details. I'll reach out to him this week," I assure her. "And Megs?"

"Yeah?"

"I will be here for your birthday, no matter what. We'll figure it out."

"Thanks, Mom," she says, her smile widening. "That does make me feel better."

"I won't miss your twenty-first birthday. I promise."

When we return to the house, I find that Cole has already packed my suitcase. I add my toiletries, and then we all prepare to leave around the same time. We take Cole's car, leaving both of mine in the garage. If we need to figure out logistics for getting one of my cars later, we can handle it then.

I hug Cara, Sami, and Megan, and then our four cars pull out of the driveway in a small caravan. We follow Sami for most of the drive until she heads toward Michigan, and we continue toward southern Indiana.

As we part ways on the freeway, Cole says, "You know, I didn't even think about how much closer you'll be to Sami. That's a silver lining."

"It is," I reply with a smile, feeling a bit lighter. "She's close enough that we could just meet for dinner, really."

We arrive at Cole's house around ten. As we walk in, Matthew greets us with a warm hug and helps carry in my things. It hits me then—Cole hasn't told his boys anything about what's been happening. Matthew knew I was coming, but he's completely unaware of the drama that unfolded over the last few days. As we're unpacking, Matthew casually asks Cole how the conference went. Cole hesitates, glancing at me before answering.

"There's a lot to catch you up on," Cole says, his tone gentle, "but not tonight."

"You didn't tell them?" I ask, a little surprised.

"I was focused on you," he replies with a small smile. "I'll fill them in, just not tonight." Matthew nods.

I shrug, replying, "It's fine. Just caught me off guard."

That first night, all we do is sleep. Cole holds me close, and for the first time in days, I feel genuinely safe. His presence is a comfort, and I drift off easily in his arms.

In the morning, his alarm pulls us both from sleep. As he gets ready for his morning meeting, I listen in, finding it hard to concentrate on anything else. They have questions—questions Cole seems unsure how to answer—but he still sounds as confident as ever. Julio must have told them something, but clearly not everything. As soon as the meeting ends, my phone buzzes. Tara is calling, but I let it go to voicemail, texting her instead that I'll call later.

"That wasn't fun," Cole says, leaning down to kiss my forehead.

"You handled it well, given the circumstances," I reassure him.

Later, Cole calls Pete to clarify if my time off is mandatory. It's not, but they're strongly encouraging me to take the week. They talk for about twenty-five minutes, with Pete avoiding any mention of our relationship.

"Okay," I say after Cole hangs up. "I'll take the week off, but I'm going to need a bookstore."

Cole smiles, relieved. "That can definitely be arranged."

The rest of the morning is filled with a lingering anxiety. Chicago is an hour behind Fort Wayne, so we don't hear anything until almost one. Finally, Alex's name pops up on my phone.

Alex

> You and Cole have a few minutes? I have Jamie on the phone too

As soon as my phone rings, I answer and immediately put it on speaker so Cole can hear too. We're both leaning against the kitchen island, eyes fixed on the phone as we wait.

"Hey, Alex," I say, my voice a mix of anticipation and anxiety.

"Hey, Cole is with you, right?" Alex asks.

"Yeah, he's right here," I reply.

"Okay, let me add Jamie. One sec." There's a pause, and then, "Okay, Jamie, you there?"

"Yeah, I'm here," Jamie responds.

"Alright, I've got Autumn and Cole on the line," Alex says, setting the stage.

"Hi, Autumn," Jamie begins, his tone slightly amused. "It's kind of odd that this is the first time we've spoken through all of this, and I don't think I've seen you in person in, what, twenty years? But I've got news for you."

"Hey, Jamie," I reply, my nerves easing slightly at his laugh. "Thank you for everything. Alex has mentioned you over the years, but yeah, I'm pretty sure the last time I saw you was at their wedding."

Jamie chuckles again, and I feel a glimmer of hope. Laughter usually signals good news, right?

"So, I've got a bit of a mixed bag—some not-so-great news about what we've uncovered, but also some very good news, and more good news after that. You ready?"

"For good news? Always. For the rest, well... we'll see," I say, trying to keep my tone light.

"At the prosecutor's request, I was allowed to submit a written statement on your behalf during the bond hearing. I detailed the incident in Chicago, the flowers sent to your house, and the cease and desist violation in Nashville. Now, this next part is a bit of mixed news," Jamie continues. "Cole, I think it's important for you to hear this. The prosecutors provided evidence that Dr. Gabari had a conversation with Drs. Stein and Hochner about two minutes before they approached Julio. This information is not only in their statements but also captured on video."

At this, Cole drops his head into his hands, elbows resting on the kitchen island, and takes a deep breath.

Alex cuts in, trying to reassure him. "Cole, we talked about this. It should give you some peace of mind, but it also shows even more intent on Gabari's part."

"Yeah," Cole murmurs, his voice heavy with emotion.

I reach out, rubbing Cole's back as he keeps his face buried in his hands.

Jamie continues, his tone serious. "You both need to understand that even if there had been private security, Gabari might have found a way to distract them. His determination, coupled with the deserted surroundings that created a false sense of security, even someone like Danny or myself could have been susceptible to diversion if someone asked for help. You both need to recognize how cunning he was that night."

We sit in silence, absorbing the weight of his words.

"Now, here's the not-so-great news from the investigation," Jamie says, his tone softening. "This is excellent for building a case against him, but it won't be easy for either of you to hear." Cole lifts his head, meeting my eyes before we both look at the phone, bracing ourselves. "The video, which you have the option to view but may not want to, clearly shows Gabari was surprised to meet Autumn in the bathroom doorway. He was intent on actually making it all the way inside. If Autumn hadn't walked out when she did, things could have been much worse." I swallow hard, my stomach churning. "I know it's unsettling, but from a prosecution standpoint, it's a crucial detail. It factored heavily into the bond decision and will carry weight at trial."

I manage to respond, "I don't think I want to see the video, but knowing that... it's helpful, in a way."

Jamie doesn't miss a beat, moving on to what I hope is the good news. "Now, onto the best news after that scary part—the judge denied bail."

I glance at Cole, and he looks back at me, relief flooding his features before he drops his face into his hands again, this time with a different emotion.

"The defense presented their expected arguments," Jamie explains. "They claimed his violations of the cease and desist order were part of routine business, highlighted his clean record, and emphasized his prestigious career. But the prosecutor countered by pointing out that this case isn't just a 'he said, she said' situation. There's substantial video and physical evidence, and four reputable witnesses, all with professional backgrounds, supporting the case. They also argued that Dr. Gabari's blatant disregard for the cease and desist order made it unlikely that a protective order would provide sufficient protection. We're still pursuing it, of course, but it might be just a piece of paper to him."

"I agree," I say, my voice barely above a whisper as I swallow the lump in my throat.

"The prosecutor also emphasized Gabari's nearly limitless resources and property holdings in Europe, suggesting he has the means to flee the country. They brought up the evidence of intent with the drugs and the fact that he pulled Cole away. Finally, they reiterated the point I just shared—that the indisputable video evidence indicates intent beyond the immediate incident, even without other witnesses or the drugs. Taken together, these factors led the judge to deny bail," Jamie concludes.

We're silent again, the gravity of the situation settling in.

"There's more good news," Jamie continues. "They're expediting the protective prder. While it might not have much impact with him in jail, there's still the possibility of contact—from letters, emails, phone calls, or even gifts sent from jail or prison. I'll be in court tomorrow morning to secure it, and there shouldn't be any reason for them to deny it."

"Okay," I say, realizing I hadn't even considered the possibility of him contacting me from jail. The thought sends a chill down my spine.

"The preliminary hearing is scheduled for October 14," Jamie begins, "where the judge will decide if the State has enough evidence to proceed with charges. Given the overwhelming evidence, that shouldn't be an issue. His arraignment will be set during that time, and they won't consider a plea bargain until then. So, he'll remain in jail for at least another three or four weeks. Honestly, Autumn, the evidence is substantial. I've got connections in the prosecutor's office, and I doubt they'll entertain anything less than a stalking charge. But there's a strong possibility he'll face multiple felony charges."

"Autumn," Alex chimes in, "even if he takes a plea deal, he's going to prison. His resources and fancy lawyers won't change that. The evidence is just too strong, and his actions are too egregious."

Jamie adds, "Alex is right. We can't predict exactly what will happen—judges can be unpredictable—but I don't see a scenario where he doesn't go to prison. I'm also filing a complaint with the Illinois Department of Public Health today. Cole, you might want to see if your company is willing to file one too. Mine will be on behalf of Autumn, but your company could file one as well. He will lose his medical license over this, and I will fight until that happens."

"Autumn, do you have any questions?" Alex asks.

"That was a lot of information, but I think I understand it all," I say, my mind spinning. "If this goes to trial, I assume they'll want me to testify."

"Honestly, Autumn," Jamie replies, "you could, but you wouldn't have to. The video evidence, combined with testimony from Drs. Stein and Hochner, who aren't emotionally involved, and Julio's testimony will be more than enough. But you should make a statement—both of you should—at sentencing. If his lawyers are worth anything, they'll probably agree to a plea deal, reducing the charge from aggravated stalking to stalking, with a sentence of two to three years in prison. But the judge has the final say. If he's found guilty, whether by trial or plea deal, he likely won't get more than five years, but the judge could sentence him to up to ten years."

"Also," Alex adds, "they're looking at adding more charges before the preliminary hearing. He could be charged with violating the cease and desist order, unlawful restraint, assault, battery—there's a long list. These additional charges could increase his prison sentence."

"I don't know what I'd be doing right now without you both," I say, my voice cracking as the emotions start to overwhelm me. "Jamie, I can't thank you enough for all of this, and Alex, thank you for calling in your resources and friends."

"Autumn," Alex says softly, "I'm just glad you're okay. I don't want to watch the video either, but I trust Jamie when he says it's bad, and that the intent was there for something far worse."

Tears sting my eyes, and I blink rapidly to hold them back.

"Yeah," Jamie adds, his voice serious. "I don't want to make this harder on you, but I'm so glad you walked out of that bathroom when you did and that you didn't back up further into the bathroom when he approached you. He might have gotten you out of view of the cameras. You stayed where you were in public view, and that's what kept things from escalating even further."

"I do have a question," Cole says quietly, his voice almost tentative.

"What's that?" Jamie asks.

"In your experience, what are the chances that he could get out of prison in a couple of years and start all this again?" Cole's worry is evident.

Jamie sighs, a long, heavy sound. "Honestly, he might. But the protective order will still be in place, and we can file for a new one if necessary. We'll need to be hypervigilant for a while. Most of the time, in cases like this, the offenders don't reoffend—they learn their lesson. But this guy is persistent, and when he's released, we'll be prepared for the worst. But, Cole, that's years down the line, and we'll cross that bridge when we get to it."

"It's a good question, Cole," Alex says, backing him up. "I asked Jamie and Claire the same thing."

Jamie continues, "I'm actually hoping he violates the protective order while he's still locked up. If he sends her letters or emails, just twice, that's another felony. And if it's the same victim, which in this case it would be, they could add years to his sentence. So, in a way, if he's not going to stop, it's better if he messes up sooner rather than later, when he can't physically harm Autumn."

The line goes quiet for a moment, the weight of everything settling in. Cole drops his face into his hands again, clearly overwhelmed. I'm processing what Jamie just said, and I imagine Alex is too.

The silence stretches, growing uncomfortable, so I speak up. "I know I already said it, but thank you both. I really appreciate everything you're doing."

"I'm glad I could help," Jamie says, his voice warm. "Most of my clients aren't people I know personally, so this one means a lot to me too. I'll keep fighting for you until it's no longer necessary."

"Thanks, Jamie," Alex says. "And, Autumn, I'm glad I had these resources for you. Cole, you doing okay, buddy?"

"Yeah," Cole sighs, still processing. "Just trying to wrap my head around everything."

"You've got my number, use it if you need to," Alex says. "I'm also going to send you both Jamie's contact information."

"That sounds good, thanks," I reply. "And Alex?"

"Yeah?"

"Can you give the kids an update? Leave out the scarier details?"

"Of course," he says. "I'll call them."

"Thanks," I say, feeling a bit of relief.

"Alright, take care, you two," Jamie says. "We'll be in touch in a couple of weeks, probably around the preliminary hearing."

We all say our goodbyes, and I hang up the phone. Cole's face is still buried in his hands, leaning on the kitchen island. I gently run my fingers along his forearm, and he opens his arms, pulling me into him. He just holds me, his face in my neck and buried in my hair.

"You okay?" I ask softly.

"I should be asking you that," Cole replies with a gentle laugh, leaning back to meet my gaze. "But yeah, I'm okay. I don't think I realized how worried I was until I finally had a reason to feel relieved."

"It was a lot to take in," I admit. "It makes me sick knowing that the video was even worse than I imagined. And the fact that he wanted me actually *in* the bathroom—it's terrifying, Cole. Even when you came back, you wouldn't have known what was happening for a while. That thought is terrifying."

"I know," he says quietly, pressing a kiss to the top of my head. "It's terrifying to me too."

I hesitate before voicing the thought that's been nagging at me. "You know what else I keep thinking about?"

"What's that?"

"If there weren't an us, there still would have been a Tony. How different would all of this have been?" I ask, feeling the weight of the hypothetical. He kisses the top of my head again, and I continue, "I still think you, Pete, Mark, and Julio would have intervened, but maybe not as much. And that night in Chicago, would you still have driven me home?"

Cole sighs, his eyes softening. "It's hard to imagine a reality without us, but I want to say it wouldn't be much different. Just without the... well, without the sex. That night in Chicago, though—if you hadn't already caught my attention, you definitely would have that night." He laughs lightly. "We probably would have gotten you a room at the hotel, and maybe I would have taken you home, but it's hard to picture."

"I think you're my knight in shining armor," I say, leaning in to kiss him.

He smiles, but there's a hint of regret in his eyes. "I would have been a better one if I hadn't left that hallway."

"Cole, you heard what Jamie said. You can't keep blaming yourself."

"I'm trying," he says with a small smile.

"You were my knight in shining armor that day too, in so many ways. The rest isn't your fault," I reassure him, kissing him again.

"Autumn, I'm just so glad you're okay," he breathes, his voice barely above a whisper. "The thought that something worse could have happened to you—"

"But it didn't," I interrupt gently. "And that's because of you."

Our eyes lock, and I see a familiar hunger wash over Cole's face. He pulls me closer, his lips finding mine as he starts backing me toward the bedroom. He kicks the door closed behind us, a small gesture that makes me wonder if Matthew is home, but I quickly forget as Cole's intensity takes over.

"Autumn," he murmurs against my lips, "I love you, but right now, I *need* you." His words send a shiver down my spine, turning into a deep heat in my core.

"I need you too," I whisper, my hand slipping to the nape of his neck as I pull him back into a kiss.

His kisses are deep and filled with a longing that ignites something primal in me. By the time his hands start to wander, I'm already aching for him. His touch sends electric shockwaves through my body as he trails his fingers over my arms, down my ribs, and across my back. He's not teasing me—this is him cherishing me, worshiping every inch of my skin.

I feel loved as he slowly undresses me, his fingers tracing every part of me as he goes. Once my clothes are gone, his mouth moves to the sensitive spot on my neck, then down to my collarbone, each kiss stoking the fire inside me. My body responds with an increasing heat, the ache for him growing with every touch. And we're still standing.

With a gentle push, he lays me down on the bed, his movements growing more urgent. Instead of meeting my mouth, his lips trail down my inner thigh, starting near my knee and working their way up to my center, his fingers brushing the other thigh in rhythm. When he finally reaches the place where I need him most, he hovers just above it, leaving me throbbing with want. My hands find his hair, pulling him closer as he kisses up to my navel, then back to my breasts.

Fingers explore me, finding me wet and ready. He teases me with delicate touches while his mouth works my nipples, driving me wild. When he finally moves back to my mouth, his fingers plunge inside me, and I gasp, my body arching toward him. My hands clutch him—one holding the back of his neck, the other gripping his arm, feeling the flex of his muscles as he moves.

He pushes deeper, his fingers curling at just the right angle, sending me spiraling toward the edge. His mouth never leaves mine, and I trail my fingers down his back, over his chest, and back up again, savoring every inch of him. As I reach the peak of pleasure, my head tilts back, eyes closed, and I feel his mouth move to my neck. My nails dig into his arms, and I bite my lip to keep from crying out. He groans, a sound thick with desire.

His fingers leave me only to be replaced by him, driving inside me with slow, powerful thrusts. Every movement is perfect, both inside and out, and his eyes meet mine with a look that makes my heart swell.

"I love you," he whispers before his lips capture mine again, his hand threading through my hair, holding me close.

As he reaches his release, his head drops to my shoulder, and I pull him to me, holding him as his weight presses into me. It makes me feel safe, protected, loved.

I run my fingers through his hair, down his neck, and whisper, "I love you too."

CHAPTER FORTY-ONE
THE COVENANT & THE BOOKSTORE

We lie there in each other's arms, basking in the quiet intimacy, until the soft vibration of Cole's phone on the floor pulls us back to reality. He groans slightly, remembering that he's supposed to be working.

"Sometimes you're distracting," he says with a playful smile, kissing me before he gets up to find his phone.

"I think this whole situation has been distracting," I reply, returning his smile.

Checking his phone, he sees a missed call from Andy. Sighing, he assumes it's related to the situation with me, so he calls him back, putting the call on speaker.

"Hey, Andy, sorry I just missed you," Cole says when Andy picks up.

"No worries," Andy replies. "I was calling about the Dr. Gabari and Autumn situation." I roll my eyes at being reduced to a 'situation,' but Andy continues, "Have you spoken with her today?"

Cole smiles at me. "Yeah, I have."

"Good. Do you both know about the hearing this morning?"

"Yes, her brother and her attorney updated her," Cole confirms.

"Okay, I'm really glad he isn't getting out this afternoon," Andy says, and I can hear the relief in his voice.

"Definitely a collective sigh of relief there," Cole agrees.

"So, here's the thing," Andy continues, his tone turning more serious. "This upsets me, Cole, especially with the timing, so I'm sure it'll upset Autumn too. I wanted to talk to you first, and then we can decide how to approach her—whether you want to do it, or if Lauryn, Pete, or I should."

Cole glances at me, and I see the anxiety returning. "This doesn't sound good, Andy."

He takes the phone off speaker, but I shake my head at him, silently insisting he put it back on. He does so, albeit reluctantly.

Andy sighs before continuing. "I get it from a legal perspective, but it's still insensitive. The contract attorneys we use for HR legal issues want Autumn to sign a covenant not to sue the company over this."

Cole looks at me, and I shake my head, feeling more confused than anything.

"Wait," Cole begins, "they're worried she's going to sue Quisenbelt over this?"

"Yeah," Andy sighs again. "I don't know how worried they are, but they want her to sign the covenant not to sue. There's more in the agreement—a lump sum settlement is involved, though the exact number is still being finalized. We'd go over everything with you or whoever talks to her before bringing it up."

I have to stifle a laugh. Cole responds, "Okay, Andy, honestly, I don't mind talking to her about it, but I think it needs to wait a couple of days. And just so everyone is aware, her brother and sister-in-law are both corporate attorneys. I'm sure she won't sign anything blindly. But I don't think she's going to sue Quisenbelt over this. She'll probably sign it, unless her brother or attorney advises her otherwise."

I nod, agreeing with his assessment.

"I think that's part of what's worrying them," Andy explains. "I haven't been involved in all the conversations, but it's not common for a victim to have their own attorney at a bond hearing—those are typically handled by the state. That raised some red flags for them."

"That's understandable," Cole acknowledges. "But just to clarify, she didn't hire an attorney for this. Jamie went to law school with her brother, was a groomsman in his wedding, and has connections in the prosecutor's office. It's more about personal relationships and, I guess, privilege than her actively seeking legal representation."

"That's helpful information, Cole. I didn't know about the personal connection. We knew she had hired him for legal representation and security after the incident with the flowers, but I didn't know the background." Andy pauses. "I'll make sure everyone is aware of that and see if it changes anything. I'll also get a firm number on the settlement. It's insurance-based, so it's not negotiable, but I'll find out and call you back, possibly tomorrow."

"That sounds good, Andy. I get their perspective, but I agree it's pretty lousy timing."

"I hear you," Andy says. "I'll keep you updated."

After the call ends, Cole shakes his head in disbelief. I'm still wrapped in a sheet, and he's only in his boxer briefs—it's an odd setting for such a serious conversation. He looks at me and says, "Well, that was not what I was expecting. I'm not sure what I was expecting, but definitely not that."

I laugh softly. "Me either. I'm going to call Alex."

Alex picks up after one ring. "Hey, baby sister."

"Hey, do you have a minute? I need to run something by you."

I put him on speakerphone and quickly explain the conversation with Cole and Andy. As always, Alex proves incredibly helpful in breaking it all down.

"Autumn, believe it or not, this might actually work in your favor. I deal with these situations regularly because, unfortunately, injuries in the logging industry are not uncommon," he says with a humorless laugh. "This could be a silver lining for you. It's part of the liability insurance settlement process. Serious injuries and crimes against employees probably aren't routine in your field, which might explain why your CCO had trouble explaining it. Essentially, they're offering you a settlement from their insurance, and it might be a substantial amount for a felony. You'll know soon, but the catch is they'll want you to agree not to sue them for more. They're fronting you the money they'd eventually pay after a lawsuit. Make sense?"

"I think so," I respond, processing the information.

"If you decline to sign, they'll keep the money. They might let the insurance company handle it if you decide to sue, but they'll use that same amount to settle based on a judge's decision. Honestly, Autumn, Quisenbelt might not have much liability here. They covered their bases with the cease and desist, had executive management support you, removed you from Dr. Gabari's account, and made reasonable efforts to ensure you were never left alone with him. A lawsuit probably wouldn't get you more than what they're offering."

"Okay," I say, starting to understand.

"It might feel callous, especially to you, Cole, and even your CCO, but the fact that they're already discussing settlement numbers on a Monday after an incident on Friday says a lot about their HR and people management approach. In my line of work, this process usually takes weeks, if not longer. It shows they acknowledge the severity of the situation and want to make amends the best way any corporation can—with money."

I glance at Cole, both of us feeling more at ease. "That was incredibly helpful, Alex."

"Now you're talking my language, not Jamie's," he laughs. "But before you sign anything, send it over to me. Claire and I can review it, though I suspect it's just standard procedure."

After I hang up with Alex, Cole and I talk it over and agree that Alex is probably right. This kind of thing doesn't typically happen in our industry.

Cole has to get on a couple of sales calls with clients, so I take a shower and let him work. I call Tara and give her the full details, leaving out most of the parts involving Cole. She's shocked and a little scared, but I remind her that this kind of thing doesn't happen often. We talk for a while, and I feel a little better after talking to her.

Andy calls back around five, and this time, he's more thorough, explaining everything in greater detail. It's clear he's gathered more information since the last conversation. He breaks it down in a way that echoes what Alex had said earlier, and then he drops the number—forty-five thousand dollars. The settlement offer is much larger than I expected, and I can tell from Cole's expression that he's just as surprised.

"Andy, that all makes a lot more sense now," Cole says, nodding. "Go ahead and send it over to me, and I'll talk to her about it. I'm sure she'll want someone else to review it too."

Andy agrees and emails the documents almost immediately. Cole forwards them to my personal email, and without even reading them, I send them to Alex for review.

"I think you should take me to a bookstore now," I say with a playful smile as Cole shuts his laptop.

"Well, aren't you demanding?" he teases, his eyes sparkling with amusement.

I shrug, feigning innocence. "Sometimes."

"Want to get dinner too?" he asks, closing the distance between us and planting a soft kiss on my lips.

"That sounds perfect. It's been a day," I sigh, leaning into him. "What about Matthew?"

"Let me check in with him," Cole says, pulling out his phone.

It turns out Matthew won't be home until late, so Cole decides to take me out to a nicer restaurant, suggesting that we should celebrate the bail decision, among other things. The evening unfolds into something truly special.

We wander through the bookstore together, and I talk to Cole about my eclectic taste in books, which, much like my taste in music, spans a wide range of genres. While I enjoy many types of literature, I tend to gravitate toward romance and crime dramas with romantic elements. I even give him a little crash course in dark romance, watching with amusement as he flips through a few pages of the more intense scenes, his eyebrows knitting together in surprise.

"Geez, Autumn," he mutters, shaking his head, and I can't help but laugh.

We chat about his reading preferences too, and I'm pleasantly surprised to learn that he reads more than I expected—though not as much as I do. His focus has been mostly on autobiographies, non-fiction history, and books about leadership and business. I end up buying a few books while he refrains this time.

As we drive from the bookstore to the restaurant, Cole turns to me with a question that seems to have been weighing on his mind. "When are you going home?"

I take a moment to consider. "I'm not sure, honestly. When you brought me here, I knew I might be staying for a while, and that's kind of where I'm at mentally. I'll definitely stay through this week—you have to work, and I won't make you drive me home until the weekend. Maybe not even then. But I do need to be back before Megan's birthday."

"That's coming up, right? When is it?"

"The sixteenth," I reply. "Apparently, Steve wants to throw some kind of joint party," I add, rolling my eyes. "So, I'll have to reach out to him about that."

Cole chuckles. "I see the eye roll, but honestly, even that is something my kids have never had."

I shrug. "Have any of them talked to her?"

"As far as I know, no, they haven't," he says, mirroring my shrug. "I've taken the lead from you on that—I don't ask. I let them say what they want, but I don't push for details."

"Life is easier that way," I laugh.

He takes me to a nice steakhouse, and as we enjoy our meal, we share little touches and talk, the stress of recent days momentarily lifting. For a while, life feels blissfully normal.

I smile at him across the table. "Cole?"

"Autumn?" he replies, mirroring my tone with a playful grin.

"Thank you."

"For what?" His smile widens.

"For just existing."

He laughs. "Yeah?"

"Yeah, seriously, you're so fucking good for me."

He raises an eyebrow, a smirk playing on his lips. "Fucking good, or good fucking?"

I throw my napkin at him, wrinkling my nose in mock annoyance. "Okay, maybe both."

"I'd say it's both for me too," he says, his expression softening. "In all seriousness, Autumn, I can't imagine a life without you now."

"I hope neither of us ever has to," I reply, my heart swelling. "Also, in all seriousness—has Pete said anything yet?"

"No, he said he'd set up a meeting with me later in the week, once some of the emotion from Friday had died down. So, I'm just waiting."

"Are you going to bring it up if he doesn't?" I ask, watching him closely.

"Maybe, we'll see," he says with a thoughtful nod.

"It makes me anxious for you," I admit, frowning. "I'm not really worried about me, but I'm nervous for you."

"Same," he laughs. "But in reverse. I'm worried about you, not so much about me. I think you'll be fine, but I can't help but worry."

"In all honesty, Cole, I do like my job, but I have a safety net. So don't stress too much," I say, reaching over to touch his hand.

"Well, apparently you're about to have a bigger safety net," he jokes.

"That's so weird to me, but I'm not going to argue." I shrug. "I didn't ask for it, but I'm not turning it down."

"I don't think many people would," he says with a grin. "I've been thinking about getting you home—"

"I think about getting you home all the time," I tease, smiling at him. He rolls his eyes but laughs.

"Seriously, woman," he says, still smiling. "You know what I mean—taking you back to Wisconsin."

"Oh, that's boring. My plan was way more exciting," I joke, making him laugh.

"I think you should stay for two weeks," he suggests. "It'll give us time to hang out with the boys, and we can get you back before Megan's birthday. Then maybe I'll stay with you until I have to go to St. Louis with Mark and Tara. That would be about two weeks too."

I laugh. "Why does it feel like we're splitting custody of ourselves between our kids and our houses?"

"Because we are," he says, laughing too. "It's either that or spending time apart right now. And as crazy as it sounds, Autumn, for this relationship that's all of, what, six weeks old? We're eventually going to have to decide what we're going to do about that."

"You mean about the fact that we don't want to be without each other and we have two houses hundreds of miles from each other? That part?"

"Yeah, that part," he agrees, smiling.

"Cardboard box, Cole," I say, grinning at him.

"God, I love you," he says, his voice warm.

"I love you too."

We finish dinner and head back to Cole's house. He mentions wanting to shower since he hasn't had a chance since we left my place. While he's in the shower, Alex calls me.

"Hey, Alex," I answer.

"Hey there. Claire and I both read through the document, and we think you should go ahead and sign it. That's a generous amount of money, and there's nothing in the fine print that seems out of the ordinary."

"Okay, I trust you both, so I'll go with that," I say, relieved.

"Is Cole around?" Alex asks.

"He's in the shower," I reply.

"Are you still happy? Even with all this drama and stress?"

"I am, Alex. Really. It's still so intense, but I'm happy," I confess, and I mean it.

"Megan and Sami said you were still very happy, which, given everything, is impressive," he says with a soft laugh. "And, Autumn?"

"Yeah?"

"Megan mentioned the night Cole drove you home after Gabari said those awful things. She said you'd clearly had too much to drink, but she hasn't told anyone besides me about it. She said Cole was an absolute gentleman that night, and that it set the bar for her. She didn't give me details, but she said he genuinely just wanted to take care of you. And, Autumn, that's all I've ever wanted for you."

My eyes burn with unshed tears. "Alex," I say softly, my voice thick with emotion, "that was such a horrible night, but also incredible. She's right—he just wanted to take care of me, to make sure I was okay." I sniffle, trying to keep my composure.

"So intense," Alex laughs lightly. "I'm happy for you. I've talked to him enough to know he's a genuinely good guy. Not that you need my approval, but you have it."

"Alex, that means a lot. You're right—I don't need it, but it does mean a lot because I know you probably care about me more than anyone else."

"Autumn, you have Mom and Dad and the kids," he says with a laugh.

"Alex, you know you've been my rock for over a decade now," I say, my voice full of gratitude.

"I think I'm ready to hand over those rock duties," he jokes.

Just then, Cole comes out of the bathroom, a towel wrapped around his waist, and I find it hard to focus on the conversation.

"I'm glad you like and trust him that much," I say, letting my eyes linger on Cole as he moves around the room, intentionally exaggerating my gaze so he notices.

"I do, Autumn. He's good for you."

"I agree completely," I say, watching Cole, who narrows his eyes and tilts his head at me. As he walks closer, I grab his towel and pull it off, making him turn and give me a playful, challenging look.

"Okay, I know it's late there, so I'll let you go. Keep me posted, okay?" Alex says.

Cole is already pushing me back onto the bed, sliding his hands under my shirt. "Okay, Alex. Thank you. Love you, talk soon."

"Love you too. Bye," Alex says.

I hang up, drop my phone on the bed, and fully enjoy the consequences of my actions.

CHAPTER FORTY-TWO

THE MEETING & THE ISLAND

Tuesday morning starts with the sound of Cole getting ready for his endless stream of meetings. The clicking of his keyboard, the quiet hum of his voice—it's a rhythm I've come to know well. I stir, tempted to join him, but he leans down and kisses my cheek, his lips warm against my skin.

"Sleep a little longer," he whispers, his tone tender yet firm. I don't argue; instead, I sink back into the pillows, savoring the extra minutes of rest.

A few hours later, I stumble out of the bedroom. Cole is sitting at the dining room table. He's wearing a button-down shirt and talking to someone; he barely smiles at me, so I assume it's a client. I grab a bottle of water from the fridge and lean against the island, just watching him work.

"Autumn, you're so distracting," he teases, his eyes twinkling with mischief.

I raise an eyebrow. "What do you mean?"

He laughs, a sound that sends warmth through me. "Look at you," he says, stepping closer. "Standing there in your tank top and underwear, fingers on your mouth, making me want to kiss you."

"Is that so?" I challenge, a smile playing on my lips. "Just me standing here is that tempting?"

"You have no idea the things you do to me," he murmurs, closing the distance between us. His hands find my waist, pulling me into him, and I melt into his embrace.

"Good morning," I whisper before our lips meet in a soft, lingering kiss.

"Good morning," he echoes, his voice a low rumble as he hugs me closer, our bodies fitting together perfectly.

I pull back slightly, my fingers smoothing his collar. "You know," I begin, my voice thoughtful, "I like watching you work. You're so confident, so charming. Maybe I had more feelings for you before July than I realized."

He grins, the kind of smile that reaches his eyes. "Well, as much as I'd love to keep you watching, I have another sales call in five minutes. You might need to be a little less distracting."

I sigh, exaggerated for effect. "That's too bad. But later, you're all mine."

His laugh is light, full of affection. "Always. I'm yours."

"Except when you have a sales call," I tease, pressing one last kiss to his lips before straightening his collar once more. "Go on, get back to it."

As he returns to his work, I slip away to put on something a bit more "presentable"—leggings and a t-shirt will do. I grab my phone and a new book, curling up on the couch. I can still hear Cole's voice, and it's enough, for now. My mind drifts to the tasks of the day, particularly the need to finally deal with Steve about Megan's birthday.

Me

Hey, sorry I didn't reach out earlier, what did you want to do about Megan's birthday

Steve

Autumn, how are you? You doing well?

Me

I'm good, Steve, hopefully you are well, Megan's birthday?

Steve

I'm well too, and yes, I'd like to throw her a big party

Me

Yeah, she mentioned something to me, only concern I had was we didn't do anything like that for Kevin

Steve

I talked to him about it, he's good - I wanted to do it at the country club, are you good with that?

Me

That's fine, what do you need from me?

Steve

Just your presence and your guest list

Me

Nothing else?

Steve

Nope - we'll hire a caterer and a bartender, planning on an open bar - it is her 21st birthday

> **Me**
>
> Okay, if you're sure, want me to email you a guest list, or can you give me the information and I'll invite and get you a count?

> **Steve**
>
> Option two is fine, I'll email you the information - I'll need a headcount by the fourteenth

> **Me**
>
> Okay, I'll look for the email

> **Steve**
>
> Thank you Autumn, take care

So then I reach out to Megan.

> **Me**
>
> Hey there, just talked to your dad about your birthday, he wants a guest list any requests from my side of the world?

> **Megan**
>
> Family should be obvious, but Cara, her people and Cole's boys, I'll take care of my friends

> **Me**
>
> Okay, that's easy

> **Megan**
>
> You doing okay?

I set my phone aside, the notifications fading into the background as I reach for the soft blanket draped over the back of the couch. The fabric is warm, comforting, and I settle into it with a contented sigh. One of my new books is waiting, the crisp pages inviting me into a world far removed from the one I'm in. I open it, letting the words pull me in, but the quiet rhythm of the house keeps me grounded.

After a while, Cole joins me, his laptop balanced on one knee, much like how we used to sit together in my family room. It's a familiar scene, one that brings a sense of calm. He stretches out, propping his feet up on the coffee table, and I instinctively curl up, resting my fuzzy-socked feet against his thighs. There's a simple intimacy in the way our bodies fit together, even as we focus on different things.

Every so often, he reaches over, his hand warm as it glides over my feet or gently squeezes my leg. It's a wordless connection, his touch grounding me as he continues typing out emails and sales reports. I glance over at him, watching the way his brow furrows in concentration, but I don't interrupt. I know how much he has on his plate, so I let him work, content with the quiet moments we share.

The next few days unfold in a comforting rhythm, a blend of familiarity and newness that I hadn't expected to embrace so fully. I curl up on the couch with my book, letting the hours slip by as Cole immerses himself in his work. This week, he's particularly busy, his schedule packed with meetings and deadlines, yet there's a quiet intimacy in the way we share the space. Every evening, without fail, he works out before dinner. I often find myself watching him, appreciating the strength and focus in his movements.

Matthew joins us for dinner most nights, bringing with him an infectious energy. It's in these moments that I realize how comfortable I've become in Cole's home. It starts to feel like I truly belong here, and I can sense that Cole is getting more at ease with my presence as well.

By Friday morning, the week has settled into a familiar pattern. After his morning meeting, Cole receives an untitled invite for a call with Pete. The tension in the room shifts slightly as Cole inhales deeply, a clear sign that this is the conversation he's been dreading but knows needs to happen.

"Do you want to eavesdrop, or would you rather not?" he asks, his voice casual but laced with underlying nerves.

I respond without hesitation. "Oh, I want to," I admit with a grin, "but if you don't want me to, I can go somewhere else."

"It's fine," he reassures me, "you can listen, but maybe I'll sit at the dining room table, and you can stay out here. I'll be on camera, and I don't even want to be tempted by your facial expressions." He chuckles.

I smile, amused by the thought. "Oh, now I'm tempting just with facial expressions?"

"Yeah, especially when the conversation is about you, with my boss and the second-in-command of the whole company," he says, his tone more serious now. "And hopefully, by the end of it, I'll still have a job."

I frown, sensing the weight of the situation, but I lean in to kiss him on the cheek. "Okay, I'll sit out here and be quiet," I promise, offering a soft smile. "Good luck, but whatever happens, we'll figure it out."

Nodding, he replies, "I know we will."

I hear the familiar beep as Cole joins the meeting, followed by Pete's voice a few seconds later.

"Hey, Cole, how are you doing?" Pete asks, his tone friendly yet businesslike.

"I'm hanging in there, what about you?" Cole replies, the polite exchange masking the tension underneath.

"Not too bad. I heard some of those sales leads from the weekend are panning out," Pete continues, easing into the conversation.

"Yeah, it's been a busy week, lots of sales calls," Cole confirms.

"Good, I'm glad," Pete says, then clears his throat, shifting the conversation. "So, here's the thing, Cole. I've been thinking a lot about you and Autumn. I haven't talked to anyone about it, except Laura. I've discussed it with her quite a bit, actually. Why don't you tell me what your plan is—or was? I've known you for a long time, and you've always had a plan."

Cole exhales slowly, the weight of the question evident. "Honestly, Pete, I didn't have one at the beginning—one of the few times in my life that I didn't have a plan. But later, my plan, as flawed as it might be, was to finish out this conference schedule, or at least get close to the end of it, and then talk to you, maybe Lauryn, and try to figure out a solution." Cole pauses, collecting his thoughts. "I know one of us will have to move, and I've been watching the open positions for something that might be a good fit for either of us."

That is news to me, and I find myself listening even more intently.

Pete sighs, a deep, thoughtful sound. "So, Cole, here's the thing. I'm in a tough spot with this, and I know you understand that. But I've known you for two decades, and you've always been nothing but professional in the workplace. More than that, Laura and I consider you family, like a nephew or even a surrogate son," he says with a small laugh. "Even with the drama in Chicago, we've never seen you as happy as you were with Autumn. You've always been charming with clients, but when you're with her, you're genuinely happy. We both see it."

I hear Cole clear his throat, a mix of relief and apprehension. He doesn't interrupt, allowing Pete to continue.

"So," Pete says, "I'm going to go out on a limb for you here. I'm not going to say anything to Lauryn, Andy, or anyone else—for now. But I need you both to be careful until we find a place for one of you to move to."

"Pete, you don't have to—" Cole starts, but Pete cuts him off.

"Cole, I do. This is a balance for me between work ethic and seeing you as a person outside of work—a person I've watched struggle on a personal level for a long time. Professionally, you're outstanding, but you're also a workaholic. You've taken more time off in the last three months than you did in the last three years." He laughs lightly. "I checked. There's a solution here, I think, if you two can stay under the radar for basically as long as you were already planning."

"Yeah?" Cole asks, hope creeping into his voice.

"Yeah. Michael Parker is retiring at the end of February. That could be a position for you. We could plan ahead with succession, and it wouldn't be a big deal. If that doesn't interest you, the account executive team is expanding in Q1, and Autumn could move there. You both can still work here; she just can't report to you. But I think you know that."

"I do know that," Cole says, exhaling heavily. "But Pete, Michael's job isn't a lateral move; it's an upward move."

"It is," Pete agrees, "and one you deserve. But I just need you to stay off the radar with Autumn until then. After what happened this past weekend, people will expect you two to be more bonded—especially Julio, who was there. And you're only scheduled together at one more conference between now and February, so you don't have many opportunities to mess this up."

"Pete, I honestly don't know what to say. Thank you," Cole says, gratitude and relief evident in his voice.

"Well, thank Laura, and make sure she's invited to the wedding, or she may hunt you down," Pete jokes.

I can't help but smile at that comment.

Cole laughs too, though there's a hint of nervousness in it. "That might be putting the cart before the horse, but yeah."

"I think it's a possibility," Pete says with a knowing tone. "So, first question—do you want Michael's job? Because we can start that process now, even though we can't move you until February."

"Pete, I'd be stupid to turn it down, even outside of this situation," Cole laughs, the tension easing slightly.

"Okay. I'll talk to Lauryn and Richard, and we can start that process. Rich already asked if you were interested as soon as Michael put in his retirement notice, so this shouldn't be hard."

"Well, this is not how I thought this conversation would go," Cole admits, a bit of wonder in his voice.

"I'm sure it's not. Next question—how's Autumn doing?" Pete asks.

"She's doing okay, actually. The bond hearing result was a relief for both of us. But she's holding up okay," Cole replies, his tone softening as he talks about me.

"We were all relieved he didn't get bail, that's for sure. Is she there with you in Fort Wayne?"

"How much plausible deniability do you want?" Cole jokes, though there's an edge of seriousness.

"I'll take that as a yes, but don't tell me," Pete laughs. "Just take care of her, and take care of yourself. Keep off the radar."

"I will, and we'll do our best. Pete, I can't thank you enough," Cole says, and I can hear the sincerity in his voice as I quietly move closer, still out of sight.

"Cole, just make it worth the risk, okay?" Pete's voice is gentle but firm.

I step around the corner, my eyes meeting Cole's. "That's the plan," Cole says, locking his gaze with mine as they exchange goodbyes and he closes his laptop.

He leans back in his chair, exhaling deeply as the tension begins to slip away. I walk over, and without a second thought, he grabs my hand, pulling me into his lap. His arms wrap around me, and he kisses me, the warmth of his lips lingering as he murmurs, "Well, that was a pleasant surprise."

I can't help but smile at him, feeling the ease in his voice. "I just have one question that I probably should already know the answer to." I laugh softly, teasing. "Who is Michael Parker?"

Cole chuckles, his eyes crinkling at the corners. "He's our Chief Experience Officer, the executive over the account executive team and a few other projects. You do know who Rich is, right?"

I nod, smiling back. "Yeah, he's our CEO. That one, I do know. So, you might be looking at a major promotion?"

"That's a possibility, apparently."

A mischievous grin spreads across my face as I lean in closer. "Well, maybe you should stay off the radar with me—behind the bedroom door." I punctuate the suggestion with a kiss, slow and tempting.

He groans softly, the conflict clear in his eyes. "Tempting, and I wish I could, but I have another meeting in five minutes," he says, kissing me again, a little more urgently this time.

I wrinkle my nose in playful disappointment. "So disappointing."

Laughing, the sound warm and rich, he replies, "Trust me, I'm disappointed too."

Standing, I smooth down my clothes and meet his gaze. "You relieved?"

He sighs, nodding. "Yeah, although it still leaves us in a spot where we could get caught, and getting caught could still have consequences."

I grin, a playful glint in my eyes. "Yeah, but there's something a little exciting about the risk, isn't there?"

He shakes his head, laughing. "Seriously, Autumn, what am I going to do with you?"

"For now, nothing," I tease, glancing at the clock. "Because you have a meeting in like thirty seconds."

He opens his laptop, a smile tugging at his lips. "You're right. Now go away, you're distracting me."

I feign hurt, putting on my best pout. "Ouch." With an exaggerated sigh, I leave him to his work, unable to keep the smile off my face.

You have no idea - especially when it comes to you

Cole

Okay maybe bedroom, then dinner and a movie

Me

Yay!

Cole

How was that one word the funniest and sexiest thing you said in this conversation?

Me

Because you like that I get excited for you?

Cole

How excited?

Me

You really want me to answer that while you're on camera?

Cole

Try me

Me

Brave, Mr. Waters, that is brave

Cole

...

Me

Excited enough that I should probably go change my thong, maybe even my leggings

Cole

You telling me you're already warmed up?

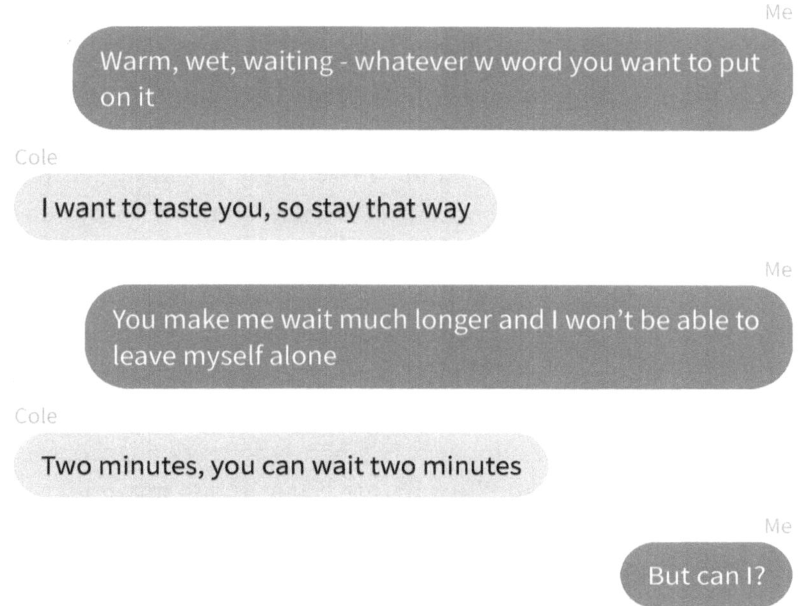

I don't give him a chance to respond. Leaving the comfort of the couch, I saunter over to the kitchen, positioning myself where he can see me from the dining room. I lean against the island, my eyes locked on him. His gaze flicks up from his laptop, and I catch the faintest hint of a smile tugging at his lips. I lift my shirt deliberately, letting my hand slip inside my leggings in a slow, provocative motion. His eyes darken, and I notice the subtle shake of his head—almost imperceptible, but telling.

The voices from his meeting begin to wrap up, and as the final goodbyes echo through the room, Cole slams his laptop shut and strides toward me. I expect a kiss, but instead, he surprises me. He grabs my hand from inside my leggings, bringing my fingers to his mouth. His eyes never leave mine as he wraps his lips around them, his tongue teasing my fingertips.

"Autumn," he murmurs, dropping my hand, his voice thick with desire, "you're going to be the death of me."

Before I can respond, he fists his hand in my hair, pulling me into a fierce, hungry kiss. A groan escapes him as my hand slides down his pants, finding him hard, harder than usual. His grip tightens in my hair, the other hand slipping under my shirt, his touch grazing my back with electrifying warmth. The absence of a bra allows him to brush his thumb along the side of my breast, sending a fresh wave of heat coursing through me.

In one fluid motion, Cole's hands move to my hips, and with a surprising grace, he lifts me onto the kitchen island. Now eye-to-eye, I loop my arms around his neck, pulling him into another kiss, this one slower, deeper. He tugs at the waistband of my leggings, and I shift my weight, helping him slide them off. My shirt follows, and in moments, I'm fully exposed on the cool surface of his kitchen island.

Sapphire blue eyes devour me, tracing over my body like I'm a masterpiece meant to be admired. His hands follow his gaze, gliding over my arms, ribs, legs, and hips before lingering on my inner thighs. He strips off his shirt, and with a gentle push, he guides me to lie back on the island. My hips meet the edge as he leans over, his breath hot against my skin before his mouth finds me, fulfilling every delicious threat he's ever made.

My body responds to him instinctively, every touch, every stroke of his tongue igniting something deep within me. He worships me with his mouth, finding every sensitive spot with practiced ease. His facial hair brushes against my skin, adding an extra layer of sensation as he works his tongue in circles over that sensitive bundle of nerves. I can't help but grind toward him, my body craving more, encouraging him. The muscles deep inside me tighten, and when I try to close my thighs around him, he holds them open, keeping control.

Before he even touches me with his hands, he draws a powerful orgasm out of me, using only his mouth. He doesn't stop, letting me ride out the wave, his tongue coaxing every last bit of pleasure from me. When my body finally stops convulsing, he plunges three fingers inside me, finding that sensitive spot within. His mouth returns to that swollen nerve, and I'm lost to him, to the way his fingers hook inside, massaging me just right, while his tongue continues its exquisite torment.

Everything about him feels like it's meant for me, perfectly in tune with what I need, what I crave. As I feel the sharp edge of another intense orgasm approaching, I grab the edges of the island, needing something to hold on to as my body releases. Cole moans, the vibrations sending me over the edge as the island beneath me and my thighs become even slicker with the evidence of my satisfaction.

His hand slides up my body, and he grabs my wrist, pulling me up to him. The sight of him, his mouth and beard glistening with my pleasure, only heightens my desire. He pulls me into a fierce kiss, his arms wrapping around my hips, bringing me to the edge of the island again. One hand frees the waistband of his sweatpants and boxers, letting them fall to the floor.

My arms remain wrapped around his neck as our mouths find each other again. I feel him, hard and ready, pressing against my thighs. As he finds my center and pushes into me, I moan, but my lips don't leave his. He holds my hips close, keeping me steady on the island as I cling to his back, biting and kissing his neck. His pace quickens, each thrust driving us both closer to the edge of release.

As he nears his climax, he lightly pushes me back down onto the island, lifting my knees over his arms. The intensity builds until he stills, his body convulsing with the force of his release. When he finally relaxes, he gently pulls me back up, wrapping me in his arms for a long kiss that leaves me breathless.

CHAPTER FORTY-THREE

THE BIRTHDAY PARTY

The next week flies by in a blur of meetings and catching up on work after my week off. Cole sets me up in William's old bedroom so we can work from different parts of the house, ensuring privacy for our numerous calls. Initially, the team is a bit awkward with my return, but by Wednesday, Tara and Mark have warmed up, and even Julio and Tom begin acting more normally.

By Friday afternoon, we're packing up Cole's car to head back to Milwaukee for Megan's birthday. The following Friday, William will drive up with Tyler and Matthew for the party, and we'll have all our kids together for a couple of days.

When we get home, Megan leaps into my arms. The chaos of our departure two weeks ago and her concern for me have left her missing me intensely.

"Kevin and Sami will be here tomorrow," Megan says, showering us both with hugs and even kissing Cole on the cheek. "They're staying until Sunday dinner, then they'll be back next week for the party."

"I'm glad I'll get to see you all this weekend," I say, feeling the warmth of her affection.

We settle in, organizing and unpacking, both so exhausted by Friday night that we simply curl up together and fall asleep.

Saturday begins busily, as I'm woken up by Kevin calling at nine in the morning. It's unusual for him to call instead of text, and my heart races momentarily.

"Hey Kev, what's up?" I ask, my voice still heavy with sleep.

"Hey Mom, sorry, did I wake you up?" He laughs softly.

"Yeah, but it's okay," I say, reaching over to run my fingers through Cole's hair as he stirs awake.

"Okay, sorry. Um, I have news."

"What kind of news? Good news?"

"I think it's good news, just news."

"What's up?"

"You know how I've been dating someone?"

"Yeah, your big secret," I laugh.

"Well, I'm going to bring her with me this weekend, unless you don't want me to."

"Kevin!" I nearly shriek. "Why wouldn't I want you to?"

He laughs. "Just making sure. Are you going to make us sleep in separate bedrooms?"

"Kevin, you're almost twenty-three years old, no."

He laughs again, and I hear a female laugh in the background, which makes me smile. Cole is fully awake now, his fingers lightly tracing up and down my thigh, sending shivers of pleasure through me.

"Are you going to tell me her name?"

"I would have thought Megan would've spilled by now," he laughs. "But I guess not. Her name is Kalisha, she's twenty-two, and she's a nurse at St. Mary's. And we've been dating longer than you and Cole."

We both laugh. "Kevin, I'm so happy for you. I can't wait to meet her."

"You know what I'm going to ask next," he says hesitantly.

"You might have to help me out here, Kev."

"Really?"

"I just woke up, Kevin," I laugh.

"What did we do the first night Sami and I met Cole?"

It hits me. "Are you going to make me do a lasagna night?" I laugh.

"Yeah, Mom, I am. I can pick up dessert. Are you gonna make bread?"

"Let me see what time Samantha will be here and I'll let you know. It's a good thing your sisters and I love you."

Cole rolls toward me, his hand wandering up my inner thigh, dangerously close to the apex. I almost slap his hand away, but his devilish smile and the look in his eyes stop me.

How can he do that with just his eyes?

"I'm glad you all love me. I'll see you around two. Let me know about the bread," Kevin says, pulling my attention back to him.

"I will, love you, Kev. See you soon."

"Love you too, bye, Mom."

I hang up, put my phone on the nightstand, and turn to Cole, my mouth finding his in a passionate kiss.

He smiles against my lips, his voice a low whisper, "Sorry, the morning wood made me."

I laugh softly, my breath mingling with his. "I'm not complaining."

Eventually, we make our way down to the kitchen. I call Sami to check when she'll be arriving and let Megan know that Kevin is bringing Kalisha. Her eyes light up with excitement at the news. Sami will be here around noon, so I decide there's plenty of time to make bread. I quickly text Kevin to confirm.

"Hey, Megs?" I ask.

"Yeah?"

"Wanna take a look around Kevin's room and make sure there's nothing too embarrassing lying around?" I chuckle.

"Uh, eww, but okay," she laughs back, rolling her eyes as she heads upstairs.

When Sami arrives, we share big hugs, and then she and Megan head off to the store. With everything prepped, all that's left is to wait for Kevin and Kalisha to arrive.

As soon as Kevin walks through the door, Megan is all over them, hugging both him and Kalisha with enthusiasm. Sami introduces herself, and then Kevin introduces Kalisha to me and Cole. I ask if I can hug her, and she smiles warmly before wrapping her arms around me.

Kalisha is strikingly tall, just an inch or two shorter than Kevin and Cole. She has a graceful figure—thin but with curves in all the right places, reminiscent of Tara's build, though much taller. Her skin is a beautiful sepia tone, flawless from what I can see. Her hair is styled in long, thin braids with hints of blue at the ends, a detail she later shares matches the color of her hospital scrubs.

Lasagna night is a success, filled with lively conversation. Kevin explains that he wanted Kalisha to meet us this weekend because she'll be at Megan's party next week, and he wanted Sami and me to get to know her beforehand. We learn that Kalisha works three twelve-hour night shifts, so they get creative with their time together—occasionally sneaking in breakfast dates and adjusting to her unpredictable schedule. Seeing Kevin dote on her fills my heart with happiness, especially after all my worries about him becoming like his father.

When I find a quiet moment while Sami and Megan have Kalisha distracted, I pull Kevin aside. "Kevin, I just wanted to tell you that you're doing great," I say softly.

He looks at me, his eyes softening. "Mom, I appreciate that."

"I just want you to know you're doing what you need to do. Megan and Cole both mentioned you had concerns about that," I add with a laugh. "It's funny though—when you told Cole, you were already dating her, but, Kevin, you're an amazing guy. You're doing just fine."

He pulls me into a hug, holding me tightly. Megan notices us and starts walking over, a curious look on her face. "What are you two whispering about over here?" she asks with a grin.

"Just telling Kevin what an awesome boyfriend he is," I reply, smiling.

Megan beams at her brother. "I agree. But awesome boyfriend, come back over here and stop ignoring your girlfriend."

Kevin laughs, and we all head back into the kitchen. Cole gives me a questioning look, and I shrug, offering him an 'I'll tell you later' glance. He pulls me close, pressing a tender kiss to my temple.

Later, as we all head to bed, I can't help but feel a small pang of awkwardness sending Kevin off to his room with Kalisha. But the feeling passes quickly, replaced by a deep sense of contentment as the house settles into a peaceful silence.

The next day, after a cozy dinner at my parents' house, we exchange warm hugs with Kevin, Kalisha, and Sami, saying our goodbyes with the comfort of knowing we'll all be together again next weekend for Megan's party. The evening flows easily, and it isn't until we're back home, settling in for the night around nine, that I'm reminded of what tomorrow holds. The realization only hits when I see a text from Alex flash on my phone.

Alex

Hey Autumn, sorry it's late for you, I forgot to text earlier and time zones lol

Me

It's okay, just getting in bed now, what's up?

Alex

Tomorrow is the preliminary hearing, if you want to, you can watch it, they live stream all the courtrooms

Me

I'm not sure I want to, but I'll talk to Cole about it, I assume you and Jamie will

Alex

Jamie will for sure, I'm going to try, but we'll see how the timing works out, Jamie said they're adding charges, but I'm not sure what those are

Me

Okay, maybe Cole will watch, I don't think I want to

Okay - I'll call you if anything major happens

alright, thank you

I glance at Cole, the realization hitting me. "I totally forgot the preliminary hearing is tomorrow."

"I didn't," he replies, matter-of-factly. "That Alex?"

"Yeah," I nod, glancing at my phone. "He said we could live stream it, but I'm not sure I want to."

Cole's expression shifts slightly, his eyes narrowing in thought. "It might just make me angry, so I'm not sure I want to either."

"Alex mentioned they added charges, but he doesn't know what they are yet." I shrug, the weight of it all settling in.

"They'll let us know after the fact," Cole says, rubbing my back. "Maybe I'll want to watch the arraignment, but not this one." His hand continues to soothe me, and gradually, we drift off to sleep.

The next morning, we slip into our usual work routine. By mid-morning, I'm deep in emails when my phone rings—it's Alex. With Cole in a meeting, I close my office door for some privacy and answer the call.

"Hey, Alex. What's up?"

"Hi there, I wanted to update you on the official charges," he says, his tone a mix of seriousness and something else I can't quite place.

"Okay, what did they end up charging him with?" I ask, bracing myself.

"He's been charged with aggravated stalking, which we knew—a class three felony—and unlawful restraint, a class four felony. But Autumn, they also added aggravated battery and aggravated sexual assault, both class X felonies. Those are huge. Each charge could carry a sentence of up to thirty years."

"Seriously?" My voice wavers between shock and a strange sense of relief.

"Yes. The fact that it happened in a public place where you had an assumption of safety and that he drugged you escalated the charges. It could be reduced to battery in a plea deal, so I don't want us to get our hopes up too much. But even the minimum sentence for aggravated battery is six years. If the judge orders the sentences to run consecutively, he could be in prison for at least eight years, maybe longer. Parole is possible, but those last two charges are serious, and even Jamie didn't expect them."

"So you're saying this wasn't just some favor he called in?" I chuckle softly, the tension easing just a bit.

"No, this was all on the prosecutor's office and maybe the detectives. His arraignment is set for October 30th. He could plead down then, but hopefully, we'll have more information before that."

"Thanks for the update, Alex. I really appreciate it."

We chat briefly about family and the kids before I head out to find Cole in the dining room. He's still on a call, so I just give him a smile and retreat to the kitchen. A few minutes later, he joins me, his expression curious.

"Hey, I only have a couple of minutes," he says, pulling me close and kissing the top of my head.

"It's okay," I say, leaning into him. "I just wanted to update you—Alex called."

I fill him in on the details, and Cole's surprise mirrors my own. We both feel a sense of relief, though the looming concern of what happens when he eventually gets out still hangs over us. But for now, knowing he might be locked away for a long time brings some comfort.

The week feels like it drags on. Megan's birthday is on Tuesday, and since it's her twenty-first, she goes out with friends and stays the night at Stacey's house. She does text me to let me know she got there safely, which eases my mind. The rest of the week is fairly uneventful.

Saturday arrives, and it's finally party day for Megan. Sami, Kevin, and Kalisha arrive around noon, filling the house with warmth and excitement. Not long after, William, Tyler, and Matthew show up, and the house is soon overflowing with chaos—a beautiful kind that fills my heart.

As we're getting ready, Cole asks, "How often do you and Steve do these kinds of things together for the kids?"

"Not too often, usually just for big events," I say, pausing to fine-tune my mascara. "We did a combined one for Samantha's high school and Kevin's college graduation here at the house, and I think the last time before that was probably Megan's high school graduation."

Cole shakes his head, the idea clearly foreign to him. "That's still weird to me, Autumn. I can't imagine crossing Michelle's threshold or her crossing mine."

I shrug, understanding his perspective. "There was a time when it would've been like that for me too, but we've figured out how to make it work. We're not friends by any means—we mostly fake it for the kids. Trust me, having him here wasn't comfortable for me either, but they wanted a pool party, so we made it happen."

"So that was the only time he's been here?"

"Yep, that's the one and only time he's ever been inside my house," I say with a shrug. "He's been in the driveway and up to the front door countless times though."

"Up until the boys could drive, Michelle and I always met at a neutral location to exchange them," Cole says, matching my shrug with his own.

"We used to meet at my parents' house for a while, but eventually, we stopped that," I reply, and Cole comments again on how different our lives have been.

Once we're ready, we pile into too many different cars and head over to the Country Club. Steve's a member there, and though my dad was at one point too, I haven't been there in ages. Steve is surprisingly welcoming when we arrive, especially when meeting Kalisha for the first time. He's pleasant, which I appreciate.

With both families and Megan's friends present, the crowd is large enough that we're not stuck talking to anyone we'd rather avoid. Megan has a great time, drinking just enough to enjoy herself without going overboard. She introduces us to some of her college friends I haven't met before, but Cole seems surprised by how many people I know.

I catch his look and smile. "Acquaintances," I laugh. "Remember that conversation?"

He nods, laughing along. "It's Megan," I explain, smiling fondly. "I wouldn't know Sami's or Kevin's friends nearly as well. They didn't bring them home or talk about them with me the way she does."

"That makes sense," he says, chuckling.

At one point, while I'm chatting with Stacey's mom, I glance over and see Cole and Steve deep in conversation. Curiosity piqued, I make a mental note to ask about it later.

When I finally do, I ask, "What was that about?"

"With Steve?" he asks, a smile playing on his lips.

"Yeah."

"I think you and Cara would call that gaslighting," he laughs. "He was telling me how genuinely happy he is that you have someone in your life now and how lucky I am." He clears his throat, adding, "He even said letting you get away was a mistake."

I raise my eyebrows, surprised. Cole just shrugs. "He asked a little about my background with Michelle, but that was about it."

"Weird," I say, wrinkling my nose.

"Well, I am lucky," he says, his smile softening as he looks at me.

The evening is filled with more than a few public displays of affection, and I might be a little more free with them than usual. We spend much of our time catching up with Cara and Blake, getting to know each other better.

Eventually, it's time to head home. Megan asks if some of her friends can come back to the house and hang out around the firepit. I have no objections, so we head back. "Some" of her friends turns into about twenty, plus Cole's kids, Sami, Kevin, and Kalisha—soon, we have around thirty people on the patio. But I don't mind at all.

I order pizza for everyone and tell them they're free to help themselves to beverages. Then I leave them to it, trusting them to be the adults they are. Plus, I have cameras now, so I can check on them without hovering. Cole and I head to bed, content to let the kids enjoy the night.

"I still can't believe how nice it is when all six of our kids are together," Cole says as I snuggle up to him in bed. "It makes me wish we'd gotten together earlier, so they could've had even more time together."

I laugh softly. "They might have driven each other crazy as teenagers, but I do love watching them all now."

"Megan and Matthew definitely have a bond that will last," he muses.

"I agree," I agree, feeling a warm sense of contentment.

"Tonight wasn't bad," Cole continues. "I don't know what I expected—maybe I was imagining how awkward it would be if Michelle and I tried to do something like that. But it wasn't nearly as uncomfortable as I thought it might be."

"He was on his best behavior," I say with a shrug. "He's gotten better now that the kids are adults and he's not entitled to their time. He has to earn it. The most important thing is that Megan had fun."

"She definitely did," Cole chuckles. "And she's still having fun out there."

We turn on a movie, letting the sound drown out the noise from the backyard as the kids continue their night. Eventually, we drift off to sleep, the warmth of the evening still lingering between us.

CHAPTER FORTY-FOUR

THE ARRAIGNMENT & THE ST. LOUIS SEPARATION

The next week and a half with Cole is wonderful. We settle into a comfortable rhythm, and Megan gets plenty of quality time with us. I notice something during those days—Megan and Matthew share a unique connection with us, simply because they live with us. We just know them better than the other kids.

Cole and I watch the arraignment together, and it's more shocking than either of us expected. I can see the surprise on Jamie's face in the courtroom, and Alex calls me right after to fill in the details. Anthony Gabari fired his attorneys, decided to represent himself, and entered a plea of not guilty to all charges. A trial date is set for December 10. Jamie tells us later that the prosecutor offered Gabari a plea deal, and even his attorneys wanted him to take it, but he's insisting that he's not guilty and claiming everything he did was consensual.

"He's delusional," Cole says, shaking his head.

"That's the general consensus," Alex replies. "This might get interesting, but since he didn't take the plea deal, I'm pretty sure the prosecution is going to throw everything at him. It's going to be a jury trial."

The situation feels surreal, but I take some comfort in knowing the legal process is moving forward, even if it's heading into uncharted territory.

The next day, Cole heads home to pack for his trip to St. Louis with Tara and Mark. It's his first conference without me since that fateful night in Dallas, and saying goodbye feels almost as bittersweet as it did the first time he left my house. He lingers by his car in the garage, clearly not wanting to leave.

"Seriously, Autumn," he pauses, his voice thick with emotion, "I don't know how I'll fully function without you."

I smile, leaning in to kiss him. "You'll manage, just like you did six months ago."

He chuckles. "I don't even remember what that was like."

"Me either," I admit, kissing him again. "I'll see you soon, at your place."

The plan is for me to drive down to his house on Sunday afternoon. He lands around nine that night in Indianapolis, and I'll spend a couple of weeks with him before heading back home just in time for Thanksgiving.

"Besides," I add with a playful smile, "it might be fun to see how distracting I can be from a distance."

He squints at me, a mischievous glint in his eye. "You're going to make this even harder, aren't you?"

"This, or you?" I tease.

He rolls his eyes, but the next moment, his arms are around my waist, pulling me flush against him. The kiss that follows is deep, filled with longing and love. As he pulls back, he whispers, "I'm going to miss you, Autumn. I love you." His voice is soft, yet it sends heat straight to my core.

"I'll miss you too," I whisper back, kissing him again. "And I love you. I'll see you on Sunday."

Throughout the day, he keeps me posted on his flight, letting me know when he lands and gets to the hotel. He's having dinner with Mark and Tara, and I can't help but feel a twinge of jealousy—I'd love to see them both, but I'd also love to be there with him. He promises to say hi for me.

Later that evening, he calls me from his hotel room.

"Hey, you," I answer, smiling at the sound of his voice.

"Hey, beautiful," he replies, that familiar warmth in his tone making me feel instantly at ease.

"I miss you. How was dinner?"

"I miss you too. It's weird being in a hotel room without you," he laughs. "Dinner was good. Mark was full of innuendos about us, so that was interesting."

"Oh yeah?" I ask, amused.

"Yeah. Tara tried to calm him down, but even she said, 'I can't believe neither of you has done anything about that yet.' I didn't even know what to say, so I finally changed the subject to Tara's wedding."

I laugh, imagining the scene. "I'm sure Mark was worse with just you than when I was there."

"For sure," Cole says, his voice a mix of humor and exasperation. "How was your day?"

"It was okay. Just the usual—emails, meetings, nothing too exciting," I laugh. "Cara came over and had dinner with Megan and me."

"Nice. Some girl time?"

"Yeah, it was nice."

"See? You do okay without me," he teases.

"Maybe," I reply playfully. "I survive."

"I love it when you laugh," he says, his voice dropping a notch. "It turns me on more than anything."

"Yeah? Well, maybe you shouldn't make me laugh when you're so far away."

"Maybe you shouldn't be so far away," he counters, and I laugh again.

"Maybe you shouldn't be so funny."

"Oh, woman, what am I going to do with you?" he asks, laughing.

"That's a loaded question," I say, my voice taking on a flirtatious tone.

"Oh, I know," he replies, his voice dripping with intention. "It was intentional."

"What do you want to do with me?" I ask, letting my voice soften, teasing.

He groans softly. "Everything. I want my hands on you, everywhere. I want to taste you, feel you. I know how you taste, and I want more."

"Cole, I think you're turning me on," I say, my voice coming out in a breathy whisper.

"That's the plan," he says, his voice low and challenging. "I want to keep you wet until I get home and can do something about it."

"That might require a lot of dirty talk," I laugh, feeling the heat between us rising.

"Oh, I can do that," he says, his tone darkening. "And I can get dirtier if you're not careful."

"Maybe I'd like that," I tease.

He laughs, a little darker this time. "Knowing you, you probably would. You're surprisingly dirty for such a sweet little thing," he says, and I laugh, a bit softer this time.

"What did I tell you about that laugh?" he asks, his voice full of desire. "I can think of things to do with that mouth that would make it impossible for you to laugh."

"Me too," I reply, my voice barely a whisper, "and I'd probably like it."

"I would love you on your knees, Autumn, but I want to take care of you first. I want to fuck you with my fingers and mouth until you come so hard you shake," he says, his voice so deep and sultry that it sends shivers through me.

"I think I'd like that too," I murmur seductively, "and then I can taste you."

"I'd want to fuck you first, so you can taste yourself on me," he replies, his breath coming quicker.

"That's hot. I like it," I say, feeling the electricity between us. He inhales sharply, and I recognize what's happening on his end. "Cole, are you—?"

"Picturing you, yeah. Keep talking."

"That's so hot," I say, my own breath catching. "I want to ride you until I'm done, and then I want you to flip me over and fuck me so hard I have to brace myself against the headboard."

"Fuck, Autumn," he groans, the sound of it sending another wave of heat through me.

"But then I don't want you to finish in me," I continue, my voice soft and teasing. "I want you to finish on me. I want it to be messy and dirty."

He groans again, and I can hear the desire in his breath. I keep going, "Then we can shower, and you can wash yourself off of me. And when I get you all hot and bothered again, you can have me on my knees. I want to worship you until you're done, and then I want to taste you."

There's only the sound of his breathing on the other end, and I know exactly what that means, so I keep going. "I want you to tie me to the bed so you can pleasure me while I can't move, and then I want to do the same to you. I want you to leave my body wrecked, weak, and shaking."

He groans one last time, and I know he's reached his limit. I hear him shift, and then he speaks, his voice soft and full of emotion. "Fuck, seriously, where the hell have you been all my life?" Despite the dirtiness and profanity, there's so much love in his words that it makes my heart swell.

"I don't know if you could've handled me when you were younger," I joke.

"You're probably right," he laughs.

"Feel better?" I ask, a smile in my voice.

"Better and worse. You might want to hide from me on Sunday because I might treat you like prey."

"I'm pretty sure that's exactly what I want, so there will be no hiding," I say, grinning.

"I really hate being in this hotel room without you," he says, the longing clear in his voice.

"Well, Mr. Fancy Pants, future executive, you might have to get used to it," I tease. "And I'll be going off to conferences without you too."

"We'll see," he laughs. "We both can work remotely, so we'll see."

"Cole Waters, are you planning to follow me around the country while I work?"

"If I can, yeah, I think I will," he says, laughing. "And I'll take you with me to the executive and board functions anytime I can get away with it."

I laugh, feeling warmth spread through me. "I think you might be a little obsessed with me."

"More than a little, Autumn."

"Well, it's a good thing I like you, or that might be creepy," I tease, both of us laughing together. "It's okay. I'm obsessed with you too. I do miss you."

"I know. I miss you too. But I should sleep now," he says, laughing softly. "Though I think I need a shower first."

"Okay, you go do that," I say flirtatiously. "Picture me while you're in there."

"I think I picture you everywhere, woman. I love you."

"Love you too. Goodnight."

"Goodnight, beautiful."

When Cole gets out of the shower, he'll find a message waiting for him—an explicit picture of me with my favorite rabbit. I roll over, sated and happy, and drift off to sleep with a smile on my face.

I wake up to a message from Cole.

I was fast asleep when he replied, so I don't see his response until the next morning. As I open my eyes, I realize it's already well into the day, and I know damn well he's standing in our booth at the conference.

Cole

Aren't you? The booth is slow this morning, we're toward the back

Me

Meh, my boss is out of town so I slept in

Cole

Careful about that special treatment there, Autumn

Me

Oh, I slept in when he was at conferences before I was sleeping with him, so there's no special treatment there

Cole

I don't doubt that

Me

but I would like different kind of special treatment from him

Cole

Yeah?

Me

Yeah, the kind that makes my panties wet

Cole

You do know I'm in public right now?

Me

You do know you challenged me to make your life harder, right? Or was it to make you harder? I don't remember

Cole

lol - you're going to make me put my phone on do not disturb

Me

Oh, I know better than that, it's still a weekday and you're still working, you can't do that - you're stuck with me texting you

Cole

Sigh, well be good

Me

If I'm not good will you punish me?

Cole

I literally lol'd, but how about if I reward you if you're good, and nothing if you're not?

Me

Oooh, what kind of reward?

Cole

The kind that leaves you shaking and weak, falling asleep in my arms

Me

I think you're talking my language now

Cole

Good, now be good

Me

I'll try - love you and miss you

Cole

Love you and miss you too

I decide to leave him alone for the rest of the day, figuring he knows I miss him and that I've tortured him enough. Tara texts me, saying she wishes I were there to do her hair for the cocktail hour tonight. I laugh, telling her to keep me posted on how it goes and to skip the heels.

Later, just before heading down to the cocktail hour with Tara and Mark, Cole texts me, a brief check-in that makes me smile, knowing he's thinking of me even in the middle of all the conference chaos.

Cole

> Hey, I just want you to know I'm thinking about you, headed to the cocktail hour, I'll call you when I get back to the room

Me

> Okay - love you

Cole

> Love you too

He calls me that night, and it's clear from the first slurred words that he's drunk. The combination of worry and amusement I feel is almost overwhelming as he blurts out, "I love you so much, please don't leave me."

"Cole?" I ask, trying to gauge how far gone he is.

"Autumn?" His voice is thick, unsteady.

"How much did you drink tonight?" I ask, my pitch rising with concern.

"Enough... enough to maybe forget you weren't here... or there... whatever."

"Cole..." I draw out his name, a mix of affection and worry in my tone.

"Mark kept buying drinks for me, and he also kept asking about you, about us," he sighs heavily, the words tumbling out.

"What did you tell him?"

"Maybe too much, but I don't think so. I think I just told him you're the best thing that's ever happened to me."

"Cole..." I say his name again, this time with a blend of worry and endearment.

"I didn't tell him we did anything, just that you're amazing and you still torture me," he laughs, the sound almost boyish.

"I don't think I've ever seen—or heard—you this drunk," I laugh softly.

"Usually, I leave the drunken debauchery up to you," he jokes, and I can't help but laugh with him.

"I can't believe you can even say 'debauchery' right now."

"Me either," he laughs again, the sound more relaxed.

"Was Tara with you?" I ask, curious about the night.

"Yeah," he replies.

"Did you tell her all that too?" I probe gently.

"Probably," he admits.

"Cole, no more alcohol this weekend," I say, my voice playful but firm.

"Yes, ma'am," he pauses, his voice softening. "I wish you were here."

"I wish that too, but since I'm not, drink some water, maybe take a shower, and get to sleep, okay?"

"Autumn?"

"Cole?"

"I love you so much," he says, the longing in his voice unmistakable.

"I know you do, I know. Now go drink some water, okay?" My tone turns a bit maternal, guiding him gently.

"Okay... I'll talk to you tomorrow."

"Yes, call me in the morning."

He hangs up, and I immediately text Tara, needing to check in on him and make sure he's okay.

Me

Hey Tara, how was the cocktail hour?

Tara

> Interesting

> **Me**
> Is there a story? Lol

> **Tara**
> There is, but I don't know if you want to hear it

> **Me**
> Tara?

My phone rings, and Tara's name flashes across the screen. I pick up quickly, sensing it's more than a casual chat.

"Hey," I answer.

"Hi, Autumn, sorry, I just couldn't text this all," she says, and I realize how much I've missed the sweet lilt of her Oklahoma accent.

"No, I get it. What's up?"

"Cole was a mess tonight, like... I don't even know how to explain it," she begins, and my heart starts to race.

"Tara, he called me. I know he's drunk—that's part of why I texted you."

"Let me tell you the whole thing," she breathes out, and I brace myself. "This afternoon, this very flirtatious hospital rep came by the booth."

Wait—what?

I didn't see this coming, and suddenly, I'm on edge. Memories of Steve's betrayal surface, twisting in my gut, but I force myself to focus on her words.

"Cole mentioned he'd met her at a conference last year. She made a big deal about seeing him again. Then Mark started asking questions about you."

She pauses, and I can feel the tension in her voice. "Autumn, I don't know the full story between you two, and it's not my business, but Mark was teasing Cole—maybe a little too much. Mark said he's done that when the three of you were together, so I doubt it's surprising."

She hesitates again before continuing. "At the cocktail hour, that same woman approached us and was clearly trying to pull Cole away. He was adamant about staying with Mark and me, but when she walked off, Mark made a comment about how Cole should go take out his sexual frustration over you with her."

My jaw drops. "He basically told him to have a one-night stand to get you out of his system. Cole got... well, not angry, but as close to angry as I've seen him. He doesn't really get angry," she adds with an uncomfortable laugh. "Then he downed three Long Islands in a row, fast, and didn't leave my side for the rest of the night."

"Tara..." It's all I can manage to say, but she must hear the storm of emotions in my voice.

"I know," she sighs. "And Mark said you know Cole is attracted to you, so I hope I didn't say anything I shouldn't have."

"No, it's fine," I assure her. "That much I know. It's... complicated," I add with a laugh.

"Obviously," Tara echoes. "But something about Mark encouraging him to go off with that woman just set him off. I feel like these cocktail nights are full of drama, and maybe we just shouldn't go anymore," she jokes, trying to lighten the mood.

I laugh too, feeling the tension ease just a bit. "It does seem that way."

"So, Cole called you?" she asks, probing gently.

"He did," I confirm, offering no further details.

"Like a drunk confession call?"

"Kind of," I admit. "I mean, I've known how he feels, and honestly, Tara, it's reciprocated. But he's still my boss, and he's trying to figure that out. I don't think he'd want to go off with some other woman."

"I know it's reciprocated. I've seen the way you look at him," she laughs. "And I won't ask if anything happened because I want to maintain plausible deniability. But something about what Mark said tonight really got to him."

I'm at a loss for words, so I just listen.

"Autumn, he did say that knowing you is the best thing that ever happened to him. And he was drunk, so you know it was honest," she says with a soft laugh.

"He can be a bit of a romantic when he wants to be," I reply, chuckling.

"I'll keep an eye on him tomorrow and let you know if there's anything you need to be aware of."

"Thanks, Tara. I appreciate you, and I'm sure he does too."

After we hang up, I text Cole before drifting off to sleep, my mind still spinning but a little more at ease.

Me

> Hey, I love you, I talked to Tara, she filled me in, call me in the morning?

Surprisingly he answers.

Cole

> I love you, I'll call you in the morning, but I'll be dreaming of you

Me

> You have me blushing here, I'll dream of you too

> I love you more

Cole

> I don't know if that's possible, but I'll let you try

Me

> Call me in the morning, when you're hopefully sober

Cole

> I will, goodnight beautiful

Me

> Goodnight

I leave my phone ringer on so I can hear if he calls in the morning, and just before seven, he does.

CHAPTER FORTY-FIVE
THE WORKOUT BENCH

"Hey, you. Feeling better?" I ask, trying to keep my voice light.

"I've got a killer headache, but I'll survive," he replies with a groan. "You talked to Tara?"

"I did. I asked her a general question, and she ended up calling me. I don't know if she told me everything, but it was enough. She had me worried for a minute in the middle of her story—I thought she was going to say you went off with some woman."

"You should know better than that," he says softly, his tone reassuring. "But I can see how, mid-story, it might've sounded that way."

"I think I do know better," I admit, though there's a hint of doubt in my voice. "But you know how jaded I am."

"I know," he says gently. "I don't think I told Tara anything I shouldn't have."

"You didn't, or at least not that she mentioned. She knows we're attracted to each other. She said she wouldn't ask if anything had happened so she could maintain her plausible deniability. But she did say Mark pushed you too far last night."

"Yeah, well, no... I mean." He hesitates, searching for the right words. "He wasn't coming from a bad place. Honestly, if we hadn't acted on this, he kind of made sense, at least in a locker-room banter sort of way. Maybe he was testing me to see what I'd do. But yeah, it felt like too much."

"It just needs to be March already," I say, half-joking, half-wishing.

Cole laughs softly. "That would make everything easier."

"Cole?" I ask, my voice tinged with a vulnerability I can't quite hide.

"Autumn?"

"If there wasn't an us... what would've happened last night?" The question hangs in the air, heavy with the emotion I'm trying to suppress.

"Autumn," he sighs, the sound full of empathy. "Nothing. Nothing would've happened—just like nothing happened a year ago with the same woman or with any other woman who's approached me at these conferences over the last ten years."

I feel the tension in my shoulders ease a bit, and I exhale deeply. "Okay, I was just wondering."

"I'm yours, Autumn. You have no competition," Cole says firmly. "Please don't think like that."

Suddenly, the emotions I've been holding back come rushing to the surface, and my eyes start to burn with unshed tears. I sniffle, trying to keep my voice steady. "Okay, it's just that when Tara was telling me last night, all those old emotions from being cheated on came flooding back, and—"

"Autumn, sweetheart, don't," he interrupts gently. "I understand, I really do, but I need you to trust me."

"I do," I say, sniffling again.

"I wish I could hug you right now," he says, and the tenderness in his voice is so different from the playful banter we've shared over the last few days. I can tell it's intentional, a deliberate shift to reassure me.

"I love you," I murmur, my voice thick with emotion.

"I love you too," he replies softly. "I have to go meet Tara and Mark now, but I'll talk to you later today. And I'll see you tomorrow."

"Okay, but no more alcohol," I say with a weak laugh.

He chuckles. "Not like that again, I promise. I'll talk to you soon."

We say our goodbyes, and while I feel a bit better, the fight-or-flight response is still buzzing through my body, leaving me with restless energy. Needing to do something to shake it off, I start cleaning, doing laundry, and packing for my trip to Fort Wayne the next day.

As I'm scrubbing the bathroom, my watch vibrates, pulling me out of my thoughts.

Tara

Hey, I have a funny-ish story for you, you have a minute?

Me

Sure

"Hey, Tara," I answer, sensing something urgent in her tone.

"Hey, I only have a minute—I told them I was going to the bathroom," she says with a laugh, the sound light but hurried.

"Okay, what's up?" I ask, bracing myself.

Tara lowers her voice. "So, that woman came by the booth again this morning, and Cole shut her down hard. He asked her straight up if she had any interest in the products, and if not, she should move along. Then she pulled me aside and asked if she'd done something to offend him. I told her he's in a relationship and wouldn't entertain anything outside of business. She goes back to him and says something like, 'You could have just told me you had a girlfriend or whatever.' Cole looked at me like, 'What the hell?' but then turned back to her. She asked if it was serious, and he didn't even hesitate—just deadpanned, 'The most serious thing I've ever done.'"

I feel a mix of pride and relief, but Tara's voice grows even quieter as she continues.

"Then she says, 'You're not distractible then?' and I swear she batted her fucking eyelashes at him. Cole looked pissed. He said, 'I couldn't be distracted if Venus herself walked in here.' And then he added, 'Nobody should have to tell someone more than once that they're not interested. If you want to hear about the products, you can work with Tara,' and he legit turned his back and walked away."

I take a moment to process. "First of all, what a persistent bitch," I say, unable to hide my frustration. "But the rest of that was... kind of sweet. Was Mark there?"

"Yeah, and I think he was a little stunned," Tara laughs. "I've never seen Cole close to angry until yesterday and today."

"Well, you know his ex-wife cheated on him, and honestly, this woman is like the female version of how Dr. Gabari started with me. I'm sure he has zero patience for that right now."

"I didn't even think about that, but you're right. He wouldn't have any patience for that now," she agrees, her voice dropping lower. "I need to go, Autumn, but I'll keep you posted."

"Okay, Tara. Thanks. Talk soon," I say, hanging up, still turning over everything she just told me.

As I sit there, I can't shake this nagging feeling of insecurity. I know, deep down, that Cole loves me more than anything and would never entertain another woman. But why do I still feel this way? Is it the shadow of my history with Steve? Or maybe it's my own insecurities flaring up. Even hearing how Cole handled the situation, I can't help but feel unsettled about him getting relentless attention from someone else. I pick up my phone, needing to connect with him, needing to remind myself of what we have.

Me

> Hey you, I just want you to know I'm thinking about you - I miss you and I love you

Surprisingly, he answers me right away.

Cole

> Were your ears burning? I miss you and love you too

Me

> Were you talking about me? Lol

Cole

> Yep, in all the best ways

Me

> No kissing and telling lol

Cole

> Never, just how much I adore you, not how much I show it lol

Me

> Awww, I know you're probably busy, but I wanted you to know I was missing you

Cole

> You can text me anytime, as long as it's not too distracting lol

Me

> I'll be good I promise, just need the connection right now

> I'm glad I'll see you tomorrow though, I'm still feeling a little insecure over here after all the shenanigans

Cole

> I'm not going anywhere or with anyone, you're my whole world, but I do know what you're saying and I will happily make you feel more secure tomorrow

I channel all my nervous energy into cleaning, scrubbing away the unease that still lingers. When Cara texts, asking if she can come over for dinner, I'm more than happy to have her company. She's still there when Cole calls that night.

"Hey," I answer, trying to keep my tone light.

"Hey, beautiful. How was your day?"

"Uh, productive. Had a lot of energy to burn. Cara's here now, just so you know."

"Okay, tell her 'hi' for me," he laughs. "Why so much energy?"

"Fight or flight response kicking in over some bimbo hospital rep trying to get you to her hotel room last night," I half-joke, though the seriousness seeps through.

"Autumn, she's nothing, no one. She's gone. I told her off completely today," he says, his voice firm.

"I know, Tara told me."

"Tara told you?" He sounds a bit surprised.

"Yeah, she called me."

"Why? Wait—does she know?" There's a note of concern in his voice.

"Like I said earlier, she assumes. She doesn't care, she doesn't know for sure, but she assumes." I pause, choosing my words carefully. "Cole, she's an ally in this."

"Okay, I guess that is what it is," he concedes. "But she told you what happened today?"

"She did, and I trust you. I just don't know why I'm still feeling so insecure, why I'm stuck in fight or flight mode." I sigh, feeling the weight of my emotions.

"Maybe it's just that we're apart," he says softly. "I love you, Autumn. And seriously, I went twelve years—you're my only temptress."

"I guess I just have to get used to women hitting on you. You are pretty sexy," I laugh, trying to lighten the mood.

Cara overhears and shouts, "Yeah, you're hot! I mean, if I'd seen you in a bar before you were Autumn's, I would've hit on you."

Cole laughs as I launch a throw pillow at her.

"And how Cara used to be is exactly why I would've turned her down," he says quietly, almost conspiratorially. "Don't tell her I said that."

I laugh. "I won't, but yeah, I know what you're saying."

"Seriously, Autumn, I get what you're feeling, but I would never—"

"Not for Venus herself?" I interrupt.

He chuckles. "I don't know if I want to thank or kill Tara for that, but yeah, not even for Venus herself. I am yours, unconditionally, indefinitely, undeniably, and unmovably yours."

"Cole," I say softly, touched by his words. "I love you."

"I love you too, Autumn."

"I'll see you tomorrow," I say, smiling now.

"I can't wait to get my hands and lips on you," he laughs, his tone playful.

I laugh too. "I'm not responding to that right now."

"You don't want Cara to hear you talk dirty to me?" he teases.

"Not tonight," I reply, grinning.

We wrap up the conversation, and Cara and I return to our usual banter over dinner. That night, I sleep well, feeling more at ease, and the next morning, I get up, ready and excited to head to Cole's house.

I start my day with a long, hot shower, shaving, exfoliating, and doing everything that makes me feel sexy. I spritz on enough perfume to last the drive and keep my makeup light and natural. I slip into a new black lace thong and bra set that Cole hasn't seen yet, then pull on his favorite jeans and the green shirt with the angel sleeves he loves. I grab a black cardigan because November's chill is in the air. Megan helps me load my bags into the Audi, gives me a tight hug, and sends me off to Fort Wayne.

Cole calls as soon as he lands in Indianapolis to check where I am. I'm about an hour from his house, and he's still more than two hours out, so I'll definitely get there first. That's fine—it gives me time to settle in. When I arrive, I let myself in, unpack, and set up my work things in William's bedroom. Matthew is out of town, so the house is quiet, giving me time to make myself at home.

Cole keeps me on the phone from the moment he exits the highway until the garage door opens. I hang up just in time to meet him as he steps out of the car. The garage door is still closing behind his SUV when I launch myself into his arms, not even giving him a chance to shut the car door.

Our mouths collide, and I can't remember ever needing to kiss someone so desperately. I lose myself in him. One hand is on my bare back, the other on my ass, while my arms wrap around his neck, and I grab a fistful of his hair.

He leans back against the car, and I can feel the hard evidence of his arousal pressing against my stomach. His hand moves up to my hair, pulling me even closer, though I didn't think it was possible.

With his free hand, he unties the back of my shirt, letting one shoulder fall, then the other. Our mouths separate briefly as he glances down, admiring my breasts. He cups one, tracing the lace along the top of my bra before his hand returns to my neck, pulling my mouth back to his.

I tug at his shirt, and he lifts his arms, breaking our kiss just long enough to pull it over his head. When he pulls me back to him, his eyes meet mine, filled with hunger and emotion. He kisses me softly before trailing his mouth along my jaw to my neck, nibbling on my earlobe as he pushes me away just enough to unbutton my jeans. My hands explore his chest and arms as his fingers skillfully slide my jeans down to the garage floor.

He runs his hands over my ass, leaving the thong in place. I work on his belt and pants, and as they fall around his ankles, he kicks them off along with his shoes. He gasps as I push down his boxers, sinking to my knees in front of him. I stroke him, then run my tongue up and down his shaft before pulling him into my mouth, drawing the first words from Cole since we hung up the phone.

"Fuck, Autumn," he groans, his left hand wrapping in my hair as he braces himself on the open car door with the other. I look up at him, meeting his eyes, and he lets out a deep growl.

I feel his thighs tense, and he gently pulls me up by my hair, saying, "I need more of you before I'm done."

He guides my mouth back to his, then backs me up toward his weight equipment. With a deft hand, he unhooks my bra as we move, pulling it off and wrapping it around his right hand. He gently pushes me onto an inclined weight bench, brushing my cheekbone before trailing his fingers down my arm to my hand, his eyes locked on mine the entire time.

Once he reaches my hand, he grabs both wrists, pulling them above my head and tying them to the bench press bar with my bra. With the weights on the bar, there's no way I'm moving. I moan as his hands travel back down my body.

My legs straddle the bench, leaving them weak, and my hands are securely tied above my head. He takes a moment to admire me, deciding where to start. His thumbs hook into the sides of my thong, dragging it down and lifting one leg at a time to remove it. He glances at the panties in his hand, then back at me.

"Did you buy new underwear for me?" His tone is teasing, a little wicked.

"Mmmhmm," is all I can manage.

I'm so turned on that I can feel the slickness on my thighs.
Cole sniffs the balled-up panties before tossing them aside, sending another wave of heat through me. He runs his hands up my inner thighs, following with his mouth. The electricity coursing from his mouth to my center is intense, but he doesn't waste time teasing me. The roughness of his facial hair on my inner thighs heightens every sensation as his mouth finds its target, devouring me with a hunger that's all-consuming.

The bar above me clangs loudly as I try to pull my hands down to tangle them in his hair. He works me with his mouth until I'm teetering on the edge, and as the orgasm rips through me, he enters me with his fingers, giving my muscles something to clench around. My moans are loud, and the bar clangs again as my body tries to close in on itself. The fact that I can't bring my hands down makes the release even more intense, and another climax builds as his mouth and fingers work together. I feel the gush of fluids beneath me.

Cole groans, a primal sound, as he laps at me like I'm the last source of water on earth. He runs his hands and mouth back up my body, untying my hands, which immediately wrap around him. He kisses me deeply, the taste of myself on his lips electrifying me more.

He moves quickly and gently, trading places with me. He sits on the bench, bringing me down on top of him. The incline brings us closer, almost face-to-face. I stroke him against me, sliding him between my folds, his eyes dark with desire as he watches me. His hands wander my body, sending sparks through my nerves. I wrap my fingers around him, guiding him into me, and as I drop down onto him, he fills me perfectly. I gasp loudly with pleasure, biting my lip to stay quiet. His hands find my breasts, massaging them, rolling and pinching my nipples as I move up and down on him, our hips moving in sync.

As I approach another climax, I lean in to kiss him, then whisper against his lips, "Come with me."

He kisses me deeply before I sit back up, and as we both chase our release, I finish just before him, collapsing into his embrace. My cheek rests on his collarbone, my face buried in his neck. He gently runs his fingers through my hair, then down my back.

He kisses the top of my head and murmurs, "I missed you."

I rake my fingers through his chest hair and whisper back, "I missed you too."

His hands continue to gently caress my naked, wrecked body as he whispers, "The reason Venus herself can't compete with you is that I'm pretty sure you are my Venus."

He lifts my chin, bringing my lips to his, and I melt into him.

Later that week, as I watch Cole work out on that same bench, it turns me on more than usual, the memory of that night still fresh in my mind.

CHAPTER FORTY-SIX
THE RABBIT & THE TURKEY

Over the next two weeks at Cole's house, we're practically inseparable. The only time we're in separate rooms is when we both need to be on camera for work at the same time. We both sense that something has shifted between us—intensified in a way we hadn't anticipated. It's not just physical; there's a deepening emotional intensity that neither of us can ignore. We spend a lot of time in the bedroom, maybe more than we should, but we're ravenous for each other. We don't fully understand why things have ramped up, but neither of us is fighting it.

When I'm not working or playing Venus, I'm planning out Thanksgiving with everyone. We all decide to have our Thanksgiving celebration on Friday instead of Thursday. This way, Cole's boys can visit their grandparents and see their mom for the first time in months, and Kevin and Kalisha can spend the holiday with her family. The day doesn't matter to me as long as we're all together.

Cole and I pack up and head back to Milwaukee the Saturday before Thanksgiving, taking both of our cars. It really feels like we're splitting custody—between our houses and our children, though it's just Matthew and Megan at this point, and they're only home part-time. Megan is job hunting in hopes of getting an apartment with Stacey soon, and Matthew spends many nights crashing with friends near campus.

Once we arrive at my house, we take a few hours to get settled in. It's like a mini-move every time we switch houses—organizing clothes, toiletries, and everything else. The recent snowfall has blanketed the area, giving the cold air both a magical and bitter quality. My house, older than Cole's, has windows that let in more of that cold air, but I tell him it's just a good excuse for cuddling.

On Sunday, we have dinner at my parents' house, and it's a warm, pleasant evening. All three of my kids make it, and Kalisha joins us too. Sami is home for Thanksgiving break, and Kalisha has the day off. It's a genuinely enjoyable dinner. As our family gatherings have become less frequent, my parents, especially my mom, seem to appreciate them more. My mom makes a roast with all the trimmings, and by the time the six of us leave, there are no leftovers.

Cole and I only work on Monday and Tuesday, eagerly anticipating the long five-day weekend. On Tuesday afternoon, we have a team meeting that's more like a Thanksgiving party. It gets a little awkward when people start asking about Thanksgiving plans, and Cole and I both keep our answers simple, just saying we're spending it with our kids. We didn't anticipate that question, and it catches us off guard. After the call, Tara asks me to stay on.

"Hey, Autumn, I've been meaning to ask you something," she starts. "I know we've only met in person once, but we talk all the time, and I consider you one of my closest friends. So, I wanted to ask if you would be one of my bridesmaids."

"Tara, yes!" I reply excitedly. "I'm honored, absolutely. I'd love to."

"Great!" She beams. "I'll send you some info on dresses. You can pick your own, but it needs to be black and follow a few guidelines."

I already know her wedding colors—black, white, and red—for her Valentine's Day wedding. "No worries at all. Seriously, I'm honored."

"I'm so happy to have you. The wedding is on a Friday, but can you be here by Wednesday for the rehearsals and everything on Thursday?" she asks.

"I'm sure I can. I'll clear it with Cole, but I don't think it'll be an issue. Maybe I just won't go home since we'll be in San Francisco the weekend before."

"That makes sense too. We'll figure it out," she says, smiling. "Okay, text me your personal email address, and I'll send you all the details."

"Sounds good," I reply.

We wrap up our call, and I let Cole know what Tara wanted to ask me. He's a little surprised but agrees that I should fly from San Francisco to Seattle, taking off whatever days I need. He mentions that he has a board meeting at corporate headquarters in Columbus as part of his transition on that Wednesday, so he won't be in Seattle until Wednesday evening. I suggest maybe spending a couple of days with Alex in Portland between San Francisco and Seattle, and Cole agrees it sounds like a good idea and makes geographic sense.

I get an email from Tara with all the details—hotel information, dress guidelines, and the schedule for Thursday and Friday. She's not a bridezilla at all, just organized, which I appreciate. The dress needs to be black, not too full, below the knee, and if it's strapless or backless, it needs to have a cover-up for the ceremony like a short jacket or a shawl. She wants a picture of the dress but isn't overly concerned.

Thursday morning, there's a bridesmaids' brunch, followed by the rehearsal and rehearsal dinner that night. I can bring a plus-one to the rehearsal dinner. I look at Cole and say, "It won't be March yet."

"No, it won't," he sighs.

"So, we're going to be at a wedding, on Valentine's Day, together, but not together?" I wrinkle my nose. "That's going to be... not fun."

Cole laughs. "At least she made it so I won't be tempted to touch you during the ceremony. I'll just have to admire you from afar."

"True," I laugh. "I guess it's not that different from a conference. We'll survive."

I continue reading Tara's email. We'll have our hair and makeup done at the venue at noon, followed by pictures. The wedding is at six, with dinner and a reception scheduled to go until midnight, though she doesn't expect us to stay that late unless we want to. I give Cole the hotel information so he can book a room at the same place.

I text Tara to let her know I'll find a dress in the next couple of weeks so she can approve it. She's not worried about my choice but just wants to keep everything consistent.

On Wednesday, Cole spends a lot of time on the phone with his boys. Tyler and William had both called their mom ahead of Thanksgiving, and neither conversation went well. Still, they want to see their grandparents and cousins, so, as Tyler put it, they're going to "suck it up and go." Matthew, on the other hand, plans to attend without even speaking to his mom, which makes Cole a little nervous.

As we sit together on the couch in the family room, I notice the tension in his expression after he hangs up with Matthew. "Cole, we can't control any of it," I say gently. "We can just be there for them afterward, especially Matthew. He's been talking to Megan a lot. I think he's predicting a blowup, but I hope he doesn't cause one intentionally."

Cole sighs. "I don't think he will, but he's done with her nonsense, so he won't just sit back and take it."

"I get that," I say, offering a reassuring smile. "I know you want to protect them from all of it, but you can't." I reach over, tracing my fingers along his cheek. He grabs my hand, kissing my palm.

"I know," he murmurs. "But it's still hard."

"I know it is," I say softly. "They're your babies. You never want anything bad to happen to them."

Thursday is all about Thanksgiving prep. Sami, Megan, and I, with some help from Cole, dive into making cranberries, stuffing, peeling and soaking potatoes, and preparing several other side dishes. We bake pies and chat as we work, enjoying our time together. For the most part, Cole leaves us to it, sensing the epic girl time and the genuine joy we're finding in each other's company.

Cole doesn't hear from his boys all day, which he takes as a sign that things either went okay or were handled as best as possible.

Later, when we're alone in the bedroom, he confides that he's never experienced Thanksgiving prep like this before. His parents never did anything like it, and his foster mom used to get charitable Thanksgiving dinners delivered.

When he was married to Michelle, they'd go to her parents' house, where everything was already prepared. For the last decade, he either didn't do anything or went to various friends' or siblings' houses, but he was never part of the process. He admits that he feels a little overwhelmed by the whole thing.

"What did I say before?" I tease, pausing for effect. "Welcome to my world."

"I love your world, and I love you," he whispers, his thumb tracing softly across my cheekbone.

"I'm just glad the girls were here to help. It's a lot of work on my own, especially since we're making over double what we used to." I laugh, feeling the weight of the day's work but also the warmth of his affection.

"My boys are going to appreciate it too," he says, his lips brushing lightly over mine. "Thank you."

"You're welcome." I smile back. "But maybe taste it first before you get too excited."

"I've had your cooking before, Autumn," he chuckles. "I'm not worried. But right now, what I really want is to taste you," he whispers, his voice dropping to that familiar, tantalizing tone. A shiver runs down my spine, sending a spark from my neck to my core.

He lifts my mouth to his, and I lose myself in the kiss, letting everything else fade away.

I reach to tug at his shirt, but he grabs my wrists, whispering against my lips, "No, we're going to focus on you first." A mix of excitement and nervous anticipation surges through me, but the ache and wetness I instantly feel tell me my body is anything but scared.

He pulls my shirt off with a swift motion, quickly following with my leggings and underwear, leaving me standing naked before him. He draws me close, kissing me deeply as his fingers explore every inch of my skin with soft, gentle touches.

Guiding me backward toward the bed, his hand finds its way to my inner thighs, and when he feels the wetness there, he groans while I gasp. He pushes me back onto the bed, and I feel the familiar brush of his facial hair against my inner thighs before his mouth reaches its destination, pulling a moan from me. His fingers quickly join in, entering me and curling up just right, and I can feel that knot tightening, ready to unravel at any moment. It doesn't take long before my body convulses under his skillful touch, rewarding him with the rush of fluid he craves.

"Fuck, Autumn," he breathes against me, the warmth of his breath sending shockwaves through my body as I arch toward him.

Taking the cue, he spreads my lips and blows gently, causing my hips to rise off the bed, making him chuckle. His tongue wets me again before he blows, repeating the cycle until I'm begging for more.

"Please, Cole," I whisper, desperate, and he takes me fully into his mouth, his fingers plunging into me again. I'm quickly pushed to the edge, my hips grinding against him, against his mouth and hand. When I finally release, he groans, lapping up every bit of my arousal.

Then I hear my nightstand drawer open.

"Cole?" I ask breathlessly.

"Shhh," he murmurs. "I thought it was time we broke into your arsenal."

Holy fuck, this man is going to kill me by orgasm.

I laugh softly, but the sound catches in my throat when I hear the hum of the vibrator. He presses the rabbit into me, the vibrating ears hitting my already sensitive nerves. I gasp as he holds it there, moving up my body, still fully clothed. He kisses me before whispering in my ear, "Show me how you use it."

His words, combined with the sensations at my core, rock me to my very soul. I manage to whisper back, "You want me to show you or teach you?"

He laughs a little wickedly. "Both. It's so fucking hot, Autumn."

I reach down, my hand covering his as I turn on the rotation and adjust the vibration. My hips begin to move on their own, seeking more, as I position it perfectly. I place his hand back on it, whispering, "Just hold it still. It does all the work for you."

He follows my lead, letting me control the rhythm as I grind against the rabbit. My body is so sensitive that a chain of orgasms quickly follows, each one more intense than the last, until I'm left completely spent. Cole watches, captivated, as I convulse beneath him, his mouth finding mine in between, his lips and tongue exploring my breasts.

I'm at my breaking point, feeling dizzy from the intensity. I reach up, grabbing him by the neck and pulling him close. Before kissing him, I whisper, "If you want to fuck me, you should probably do it before I pass out."

He pulls the rabbit out, and I feel a wave of relief. "Autumn Flynn, did you just ask me to fuck you?"

"Yeah," I breathe. "I believe I did."

He stands, leaving me feeling vulnerable and empty for a moment as he strips off his clothes. Then he climbs back over me, trailing kisses up my body. His mouth meets mine just as he buries himself inside me with one quick thrust, and I feel whole again.

Wrapping my legs around him, I pull his mouth to mine. As he nears his climax, he sits up, and I brace us on the bed as he thrusts hard, his pace quickening. When he finally releases, he leans down, brushing the hair out of my face and kissing me deeply.

"I hope that was good for you," he says with a laugh.

"I think you tried to kill me by orgasm," I whisper, rolling into him. He laughs again and kisses my forehead.

I look up at him with a smile. "Still doesn't beat Nashville, though."

He laughs, pulling me closer, and we just lie there, content in each other's arms.

Eventually, I have to get up, so I slip out of bed and head to the bathroom. When I return, Cole has put on his underwear and sweatpants, and I find my way to the closet, pulling on a tank top, underwear, and shorts. I climb back into bed with him, and he encourages me to lie on his chest, gently rubbing my back.

"I think you might have just checked another thing off my list of teenage boy sex dreams," he laughs.

"Oh yeah?" I ask, laughing along with him.

"Yeah," he says, kissing my hair. "But seriously, I love everything about you. Your heart, your mind, your body, and the way it responds to me. All of you."

"I love you too, even if you do try to kill me with sex," I laugh.

"I seem to remember you telling me I was speaking your language when I said I wanted to leave you shaking and weak, falling asleep in my arms," he says, laughing as he kisses my head again.

"I'm pretty happy with shaking and weak, then falling asleep in your arms." I pause, smiling. "Even if it might kill me, at least I'll die happy."

Eventually, we drift off to sleep, his arms securely around me, and I don't think we move all night.

By noon, the house is buzzing with activity. Cole's boys arrive around eleven, with Kevin and Kalisha close behind. The boys quickly debrief about their Thanksgiving, and it sounds like Michelle was her usual difficult self, but the rest of the family kept her in check. They were super supportive of the boys, which pleasantly surprises Cole and makes him happy.

The turkey has been in the oven for a while, and Kalisha joins us in the kitchen to work on the rest of the Thanksgiving meal. There's some playful joking about gender roles, but I know Kevin is comfortable in the kitchen, and Cole's boys aren't clueless either. They're in and out of the kitchen, helping where they can. My parents, Cara, her kids, and Blake arrive about an hour before the food is ready.

When we finally sit down for Thanksgiving dinner, my dining room is at full capacity. I've never had this many people here, and I find myself both grateful for having a dining room this big and wondering how we'll manage in the future when there are more partners and grandkids.

By the time dinner is over, my heart is full. My parents handle the large group well, not seeming overwhelmed, but they do leave early, even before we break out the pie. Kevin starts talking about Christmas, which gets me thinking.

"So, while everyone's here," I suggest, "how about you all pull the Christmas stuff out of the basement? I bet the foyer tree will go up really fast with all you tall guys, instead of Kevin having to run up and down the stairs twenty times."

Kevin loves the idea, and although the other guys are a bit hesitant, they agree to do it all on Saturday. I love the idea of having them all here, helping decorate the house for Christmas.

The next morning, they seem motivated. Kevin takes the lead, having done this for me for years, especially since Alex moved to Portland. Sometimes, Kevin's friends would help, but this year, the Waters men quickly understand what I mean. We have a thirty-foot artificial tree that goes up in the foyer next to the grand staircase. It's prelit and comes in multiple pieces. Kevin uses the staircase instead of a ladder, but it's still a lot of up and down. With all five guys helping, and some assistance from Kalisha, they get it up and lit in about twenty minutes. Sami and Megan run the garland around it with a little help, and just like that, the tree is done. Cole asks if that's where we put presents.

"No," I reply with a smile. "We have a smaller tree in the family room for all our sentimental ornaments. That's where we open presents."

Kevin runs the realistic, prelit, evergreen garland up both sides of the staircase, and suddenly, it really feels like Christmas in the foyer. Cole and the boys are a bit awestruck.

Kalisha looks around and says to Kevin, "Yeah, we're definitely taking pictures in this foyer—it's gorgeous."

"Anytime," Kevin says, hugging her close and kissing her temple.

They bring up the rest of our Christmas decoration boxes but leave the actual decorating to Megan and me. The hard part is getting everything upstairs from the basement, so we're grateful for the help.

By Saturday afternoon, all our extra kids head back to their own lives. Tyler, William, and Kevin all have work on Monday, Matthew and Megan have classes, and Kalisha works Sunday night. They need to return to their routines.

Matthew asks Cole when he'll be back, and Cole says he's not sure. We hadn't discussed it yet. Matthew jokes about continuing to make grocery orders, and all is well. After everyone leaves, I ask Cole the same question.

"I don't know, Autumn," he says, pausing. "The trial starts in a week and a half, and then our company Christmas party is a week and a half after that."

We received the invitations just before Thanksgiving. It's a black-tie event at a hotel near our corporate headquarters in Columbus, and it's the first time I'll be going since I wasn't invited in my previous role. Employees can bring a guest, so the rest of our team will be there with their significant others.

I look at Cole, uncertain. "I'm not sure it's a great idea for both of us to go."

Stepping closer, he drags his thumb along my cheekbone before tilting my chin up to meet his gaze. "Autumn, I think we'll be okay. We can call it practice for Tara's wedding."

Laughing, I remember he managed to keep his hands off me that night Megan thought it would be impossible. "I guess you mostly managed to behave in the blue dress."

"I'm pretty sure for a black-tie event, you'll look even hotter," he teases with a grin.

"And I'm pretty sure you will too." I smile, kissing him. "Okay, we'll deal with the trial first and see where we are. But your house is much closer to Columbus."

"That's true, but we'd stay in Columbus for the party," Cole says. "We'll figure it out when the time comes."

CHAPTER FORTY-SEVEN

THE CONTINUATION & THE WALL

Over the next week, I find myself on the phone with the prosecutor's office, Jamie, and Alex several times. Dr. Gabari has hired new attorneys, which doesn't surprise anyone. No one thinks I need to be in the courtroom until sentencing, but there's still a difficult conversation with the prosecutor and Jamie, both on the call.

"Autumn, if you're going to watch the trial, you need to see the video beforehand," Jamie says. "They'll show it at trial, and it's better if you don't see it for the first time in the courtroom."

The prosecutor adds, "It's not just the video of the actual event, but footage from around the conference too—exhibit rooms and other areas that show his intent, his waiting for an opportunity."

I take a deep breath. "Okay, so how does that work? Can you send it to me?"

Jamie responds he can send it over to me and he doesn't think I would want to do it anyway, but he advises we shouldn't share it with anyone else or let it go public.

"There's no way I'd want it public," I assure him.

"Just needed to say it," Jamie replies.

"Are you sending it to Alex too?" I ask.

"Yes, he'll need to see it before the trial as well," Jamie confirms.

The prosecutor goes over more details, preparing me for what's ahead.

When the video arrives, Cole and I decide to watch it together. The anxiety building inside me is intense, but Cole, calm as ever, puts his arm around me before we press play.

The footage plays in chronological order, starting with clips of Dr. Gabari watching our booth, clearly waiting for the right moment to make his move. Then, it shifts to the footage of me walking into the bathroom, with Cole waiting in the hallway. We see Dr. Gabari talking to Drs. Stein and Hochner, then circling around to approach the bathrooms from a different direction after Cole leaves.

I lean into Cole, and he kisses my temple, his right arm wrapped around me while his left hand holds mine.

I don't want to see this.

The video continues. Drs. Stein and Hochner approach Julio, who then calls down the hall to Cole. There's no sound, but I see Cole hesitate before squeezing his hand. As soon as Cole turns the corner, Dr. Gabari appears. According to the timestamp, Cole is gone for only eighty-five seconds, which feels unbelievable to me. But we watch it all—no sound, but I know exactly what we both said.

As I watch, anger bubbles up. I'm annoyed with myself for not fighting back harder, for not running, for not screaming. But it happened so fast, and I have to remind myself that he drugged me.

Three different camera angles capture the entire interaction between us. It's clear his initial plan was to follow me into the bathroom. He hesitates when I walk out, but then he sees me. Everything happens as I remember and as Cole described. The body language shift is evident as soon as Cole and Julio turn the corner. Dr. Gabari quickly releases me, raising his hands as if to claim innocence when he hears their voices.

Julio reaches him a second before Cole, and they both pin him against the wall. Julio then defers to Cole, likely because Cole is physically bigger, and Julio moves to check on me. Dr. Hochner tries to console me, placing his hand on my shoulder, but I sharply flinch and back into the wall, sliding down it.

There's a brief exchange between Cole and Dr. Hochner before Julio and Dr. Hochner secure Dr. Gabari. Cole crouches beside me, trying to talk to me, and it's a full twenty seconds on the timestamp before he touches me.

I watch my reaction—how I pull away from him—and I squeeze his hand, feeling the tension in my chest. He kisses my temple again.

On the video, my body collapses into his arms as he leans against the wall, holding me. Dr. Stein eventually leaves to find hotel security, and when he returns with them, the footage ends.

"That wasn't as hard as I thought it would be," I say, looking at Cole. "The hardest part was watching how I reacted to you."

Pulling me close, he kisses my temple. "You didn't know it was me, and once you did, your reaction was completely different. But I'm glad that was the hardest part for you. Watching the parts where I wasn't there was rough, but I already knew, so it was easier than I expected."

He squeezes my hand, offering reassurance.

"Eighty-five seconds," I say, shaking my head. "You can't beat yourself up over that."

Cole smiles, but it's tinged with guilt. "Oh, I can—and I have been."

He pulls me in, kissing my temple again.

"I love you," I whisper.

"I know, I love you too," he replies, closing the laptop.

The next morning, jury selection is supposed to begin, and just seeing Dr. Gabari on screen stirs up an anxiety that I can't shake. Fortunately—or unfortunately—I get a reprieve. Dr. Gabari's attorneys file for a continuance, claiming they need more time to build a defense. The court grants it, pushing the trial to the end of March.

As soon as we hear the news, Alex calls.

"Hey, Alex," I say, putting him on speakerphone so Cole can hear too.

"Hey there," he replies. "So, it's going to drag out, but at least he'll stay locked up until then."

"Yeah," I say with a small laugh, "good for my immediate anxiety, not so great for the long-term."

"I get it," he says, then pauses. "Cole?"

"Yeah?" Cole responds.

"You should take her out and do something fun tonight," Alex suggests, and I can hear the smile in his voice.

"Already thinking about that," Cole replies with a grin.

"Good," Alex laughs. "We'll see what happens with all this down the line. Love you, Autumn."

"Love you too, Alex. Thanks for everything."

"That's what brothers are for," he says, and we hang up.

Cole looks at me, his eyes full of mischief. "Alex stole my thunder, but how about we do something fun tonight?"

"Sure, what are you thinking?" I ask, leaning in to kiss him.

"I don't know... smash room? Ax throwing?" he suggests with a laugh, which makes me laugh too.

"Do you have some testosterone to burn off?" I tease, still laughing. He grins. "Maybe I do."

"We can do that if you want," I say, still smiling, "but I can think of a few other ways to put that energy to good use."

It takes him a second to catch my meaning, and when he does, his eyes narrow playfully. "You want me to take out all this built-up energy on you?"

"I wouldn't mind," I reply, laughing softly.

We're still sitting at my desk in separate chairs, but he reaches out, gripping the nape of my neck and pulling me toward him for a deep, lingering kiss. When he finally pulls back, he says casually, "Unfortunately, I promised your brother we'd go do something fun."

"Cole, is playing with me not fun?" I challenge, my voice teasing.

"Autumn, that's not playing fair," he says, smiling.

"I never said I play fair." I laugh. "How about we have fun my way first, then we do something your way?"

He studies my face, clearly torn between the two options. His hand lifts to my face, his thumb brushing over my bottom lip.

"Autumn, that laugh of yours is going to be the death of me," he murmurs, leaning in for another kiss. Despite our earlier talk, the kiss is soft and gentle, sending waves of electricity from my lips to my core.

I pull back slightly, my voice a whisper. "Does this mean we get to have fun my way first?"

He chuckles softly. "Do you really think I can say no to you?"

"Well, you never know," I say, laughing again, just as his lips meet mine.

I reach down between his legs, feeling how ready he is, and he gasps.

"I think you want to have fun my way too," I whisper against his lips, pulling my hand back and wrinkling my nose playfully.

"You can keep your hand there," he says, his voice low as he grazes his lips along my jaw.

"Oh yeah?" I slide my hand back down, and he groans in response.

"Come here," he says, guiding me to stand. I know there's no way I can straddle him in the office chair, but as I move around, he pushes my hips against the desk in front of us. He pulls down my leggings, then quickly removes them, his hands moving up my legs without hesitation. His fingers find my entrance, and I gasp, looking down at him just as he leans in, his mouth joining his fingers.

My hands tangle in his hair as he consumes me. The tension from the trial that didn't happen, the buildup of stress and anticipation, all make my body tight and resistant to release, but Cole is patient, his fingers and mouth working in perfect harmony.

I feel my core start to relax, and then it tightens as the orgasm builds. The stress melts away first, and then I fall over the edge, my body convulsing around his fingers as he moans in response. His other hand moves up my body, pulling me down to kiss him. I taste myself on his tongue, the sensation sending another shiver through me as he stands, lifting me into his arms.

He glances at the cluttered desk behind me and laughs. "I'd use the desk, but there's a lot there."

I laugh too. "Good thing there's a couch in here," I say before kissing him again.

He guides me to the couch, where I help him out of his shirt, and then push his sweatpants and boxers down. He kicks them off as he sits down, pulling me on top of him. Usually, when we end up like this, it's my idea, but I'm definitely not complaining.

My mouth meets his as I grind against him for a moment before letting his hand between us to position him. I slowly sink down onto him, and we both moan at the sensation, feeling complete and connected. I move slowly, savoring the moment, trying to make it last.

"Fuck, Autumn," he rasps, pulling my mouth to his, kissing me hungrily, as if he's trying to consume me entirely.

I get lost in the kiss, forgetting to move my hips until he grabs them, thrusting up into me, reminding me. I grind against him, still lost in the kiss, and then he tips us onto the couch. I wrap my legs around him as he drives into me, slowly at first, but soon picking up the pace. Eventually, he sits back, gripping my thighs, pumping faster, fucking me until I'm dizzy with pleasure. As he nears his climax, I pull him back down to my mouth, wanting to kiss him as he finishes inside me.

He laughs softly. "Autumn, I think you just wanted to kiss me."

"I wanted all of you," I smile, "but the kissing was pretty nice." I pull his lips to mine again.

Once we're dressed and recovered, Cole asks me again what I want to do tonight.

"Surprise me," I say, smiling. "Just tell me what I need to wear."

"Let me think about it," he says, smiling as he kisses my forehead before heading off to clean up.

As I'm sitting on the couch in my office, texting away, Cole walks back in. "Hey, beautiful," he says with that warm smile that still makes my heart flutter. "Just wear some jeans tonight, we'll leave around six."

I look up at him, curious. "You're not going to tell me where we're going?"

"It's not a big surprise, but no," he replies, grinning and throwing in a wink. That wink. It still melts me every time.

"We're going to eat, right? Because I'm starving," I say, feigning a little whine.

"Yes, Autumn, I won't let you starve," he laughs. "But it's twenty-six degrees outside, so keep that in mind. We won't be outside much, but still."

"I've lived here my whole life," I mock, raising an eyebrow.

"I know, but I'm still a little protective of you," he says with a smile. "I know you're a big girl."

"I appreciate you," I reply, wrinkling my nose playfully at him.

He grins back. "I'm going to call Pete and fill him in on the latest if he doesn't already know."

"Okay," I say, holding up my phone. "I'm catching up with the kids and Cara."

"Figured it was either that or Alex," he chuckles.

I shrug. "My circle is small, but I like it that way."

"I know," he says with a nod. "Alright, I'll make my call. Be ready by six."

I set my phone down and head off to get ready for our night out. I pull on Cole's favorite jeans and slip into a new bra, then make my way to the bathroom to freshen up my makeup. Cole walks in as I'm finishing up and smiles at me in the mirror.

"I hope you're planning on wearing more than just that," he says, wrapping his arms around me from behind.

"Oh, definitely. I thought twenty-six degrees was perfect for just a bra," I joke, rolling my eyes as I apply my mascara. "I'll put on my sweater after my makeup's done."

"I kind of like you like this," he says, his eyes meeting mine in the mirror with a playful glint.

"Well, I can stay like this and we can skip going out," I tease.

"No, I'll just strip you down later tonight," he replies, his voice dripping with sinful promise.

"Is that a promise or a threat?" I challenge, raising an eyebrow.

"Maybe both," he says, moving to lean on the counter in front of me.

"I'm pretty sure I'll enjoy it either way," I laugh, finishing up my makeup and slipping into a royal blue sweater that brings out my eyes.

"You ready?" he asks.

"Ready," I say, grabbing my jacket. "We taking your car?"

"Yep." As I walk out of the bedroom, he gives me a playful smack on the ass, making me laugh.

We get into Cole's car, and it doesn't take long for me to realize we're headed out of Wisconsin and towards Chicago.

"Where are we going?" I ask, leaning in closer to him, my hand finding its way to his thigh.

"It's a surprise," he says, glancing at me with a grin.

"Are you kidnapping me? Taking me across state lines?" I joke.

"I don't think I need to kidnap you to get you to go anywhere," he laughs.

About two hours later, we pull up to a cozy Italian restaurant near downtown Chicago. The meal is delicious, and the conversation even better. After dinner, Cole surprises me with tickets to an improv show at a nearby comedy club. We laugh so hard that by the time we're back in the car, we're both happy and relaxed, feeling like this night out was exactly what we needed.

As we drive home, Cole places his hand on my thigh, and I wrap my arm around his, resting my head on his shoulder. In this moment, everything feels perfect, like the world has finally aligned.

"Thank you," I murmur in the quiet of the car.

"You're welcome, Autumn," he says, his thumb gently stroking my thigh. "I love you."

"I love you too."

As we turn off the main street and near the house, I let my hand slide down his thigh, inching up to where his legs meet. He inhales deeply, the sound of it sending a thrill through me.

"Autumn," he warns, his voice tinged with playful caution.

"What?" I laugh, feigning innocence. "We're almost home."

He chuckles. "Yes, but I'm still in control of a two-ton piece of metal."

"I don't know, there might be some fiberglass in there too," I tease, leaning closer to press my lips to his neck, then his earlobe.

He laughs again, this time accepting his fate.

I move my hand gently, feeling his body's immediate response to my touch. His hand, in turn, moves up my inner thigh, his pinky grazing the spot where all the seams of my jeans meet, just below my center. I moan softly, continuing to kiss along his neck, jaw, and ear.

Somehow, he manages to park the car in the garage. We barely make it into the house, just far enough to disarm the alarm. As soon as I'm done, Cole turns me and presses me back against the wall next to the alarm panel. It's not painful, but it's aggressive, raw, and incredibly hot. I love it when he lets go like this.

His fist wraps around my hair as he kisses me, the kind of deep, passionate kiss that makes everything else disappear. My hands find his hair, and his free hand starts working on the button and zipper of my jeans. The moment he gets them open, his fingers slip inside, his palm rubbing against all the right places. I can feel how wet I am, and it only turns me on more, making me moan into his mouth.

When he pulls back, the hunger and lust in his eyes are almost overwhelming. I don't think I've ever seen him look at me like this before. His left hand lets go of my hair and moves to my jaw, tilting my head to expose my neck. His mouth follows, his tongue and lips finding the most sensitive spots, making me moan again.

"Autumn," he growls against my neck, right above my pulse point, the vibration of his voice sending shockwaves through me. "I need you to come for me."

His words ignite something deep inside me, and quickly, my body is convulsing around his fingers. My head falls back, and my nails dig into his back as the orgasm takes over. He growls against my neck, his mouth trailing up to find mine again.

When his hand finally leaves my jeans, I almost whimper in disappointment. But then his wet fingers find my lips, and I can taste myself before he kisses me again, a primal growl escaping him.

He doesn't waste any time, stripping off my shirt and bra, his hands rough and needy. I tug at his shirt, and he quickly pulls it over his head, our eyes locking as he grips my hair again, his mouth crashing down on mine. There's something violent in the way he kisses me, as if he can't get enough.

Strong hands move to my jeans and thong, pulling them down in one swift motion. I kick them off, along with my shoes and socks, as he does the same with his pants and boxers. He pulls me close, our bodies flush against each other, my softness melding with the hard lines of his chest. One of my hands wraps around his neck, the other rests on his side. He takes my wrist, guiding it to his neck before pushing me back against the wall.

Our mouths part just long enough for him to grip my thighs, lifting me effortlessly and wrapping my legs around him. I'm momentarily stunned as he presses me against the wall and thrusts into me. I push my weight against the wall and use my arms for balance, letting him take control. The strength in him, the way he uses it to love me, makes me feel safer than I ever have with anyone.

He buries his face in my cleavage, and I feel a deep, vibrating groan as he reaches his climax, driving me to my own. We stay there for a few seconds, catching our breath, before he gently lowers me to the ground, one leg at a time. His mouth is hungrier than ever as he kisses me again, still with that fierce intensity.

It takes a few minutes for the waves of calm and quiet to settle over us.

"You okay?" he whispers against my lips, his voice softer now as he moves to kiss my neck.

I laugh softly. "I'm great. Are you okay?"

"I'm great too," he says, his fingers gently tracing the marks he left on my thighs. "But I'm pretty sure you're going to have bruises from tonight."

He pulls back to look at me, his fingers grazing my cheek with a tenderness that contrasts with the passion we just shared.

I smile up at him. "If I do, that's fine," I say with a shrug. "Honestly, I thought that kind of thing only happened in movies. I'm kind of impressed."

He smiles, pressing a quick kiss to my forehead. "Another first?"

"Uh, yeah," I laugh.

"Well, in all fairness," he gestures around us, "this is as far as we made it into the house, and there aren't a lot of options."

Laughing, I kiss him again, deciding not to ask if it was a first for him too. I don't want to know if it wasn't.

The next morning, I wake up feeling a little sore, the bruises from his hands and fingers marking my thighs and breasts. But instead of feeling regret, I'm strangely turned on by the sight of them.

CHAPTER FORTY-EIGHT

THE COLUMBUS TRIP

On Wednesday, we drive back to Cole's place ahead of the Christmas party on Saturday. We leave his car at my house and take the Audi because he wants to bring it to Columbus. It's a surreal feeling—like I've left home, but also like I'm somehow returning home at the same time. Matthew is thrilled to see us, and we enjoy a cozy dinner together. We make plans to have dinner with all his boys on Sunday when we're back from Columbus.

Thursday and Friday are typical workdays, but by Friday evening, we're on the road to Columbus. Pete mentioned we only needed one hotel room, reassuring Cole that nobody would notice. It feels like a small victory, a step forward for us.

Friday night, we have dinner with Pete and Laura. It's a relief to be out with people who know about us, where we can be a little more ourselves. Even though public displays of affection are off the table—under it, though, seems to be fine, as Cole's hand is a constant presence on my thigh and our fingers frequently intertwine.

The evening is pleasant. I learn more about Laura—she teaches creative writing at a local community college and also at a rec center, where she runs classes for kids and seniors. Pete and Cole delve into work talk, most of which flies over my head, but I understand bits and pieces. I know I'll learn more as time goes on.

Back in our hotel room, Cole is relaxed, a soft smile playing on his lips. "Autumn, it feels so good to be somewhat normal with you around them. Do you know how many times I've had dinner with them, just me?"

I laugh. "I'm guessing a lot or none, based on that question."

"A lot," he chuckles, meeting my gaze. "It was really nice to have you there."

"Well, I'm glad you like having me around," I tease, reaching up to fix his collar before wrapping my arms around his neck.

His arms encircle me, pulling me close for a kiss. "I think I more than *like* having you around. Want? Need?" He pauses, searching for the right word. "Love? Yeah, I *love* having you around."

My heart swells as I smile at him. "I love you."

"I love you too," he murmurs, pressing a kiss to my forehead. "But I really do love having you here."

"Oh yeah? Why's that?" I ask, playful curiosity in my voice.

"There are way too many reasons to list. I'd be at it all night," he laughs, his eyes sparkling with mischief. "And I can think of better things to do all night."

"As long as those things involve me," I say with a grin, my voice dropping to a whisper, "and all my favorite parts of you, I think that's acceptable."

He raises an eyebrow, his expression both amused and intrigued. "All your favorite parts, huh? What exactly are those?"

"I think you know," I laugh softly.

"My personality? My brain? My heart?" he continues playfully.

"Oh, I love those too. I love all of you," I reply, kissing him quickly. "But I was thinking more about your mouth," I kiss him again, "your hands, and of course..." I trail off, my hand slipping between us to feel his readiness, leaving the rest unsaid with a suggestive shrug.

Cole doesn't need any more encouragement. He pulls me to the bed, and what follows is slow, tender, and deeply intimate. The emotions radiating from him are overwhelming. It's one of those moments where I can feel how much he loves me, how much he desires me, how much he needs me. When he spoons me afterward, holding me close, I sense his vulnerability. Publicly and professionally he's so strong and confident, and I know that seeing this side of him is a testament to how much he trusts me. I lace my fingers with his around my waist, and together, we drift off to sleep.

The next morning, we sleep in and order breakfast to the room. The team wants to get together for lunch, which is both exciting and nerve-wracking. We have to be careful with our movements, it feels unnatural, but Cole arranges a light lunch before the party tonight.

It's nice to see everyone. I'm especially excited to see Tara and meet Max, but it's also a pleasure to meet Mark's wife, Leona, Julio's wife, Cassie, and Tom's wife, Mary. Nobody asks Cole or me about our plus ones, so I assume those conversations were already had before lunch.

I sit between Tara and Cole, with Mark on Cole's other side. This setup relaxes both of us a little. Cole even places his arm on the back of my chair a few times as he leans over to talk to Tara and Max. His hand finds my thigh on occasion, but only for brief moments. His occasional winks in reaction to conversations warm me inside.

Mark and Cole have several quiet conversations, and while I'm not sure they're about me, I have a feeling they are.

At one point, Mark pats Cole on the back and says, "I'm happy for you, man."

Right after that, Cole's hand squeezes my thigh for just a second before he catches my eye and then pulls his hand back to the table.

We eventually part ways with the team, everyone heading to their rooms to prepare for the black-tie affair tonight—a holiday dinner and ball for the upper echelons of our company, with the Board of Directors, our executive and senior leadership teams, and a few select invitees in attendance.

I'm taken aback when I find out that Cole actually *owns* a tuxedo. He got it for this party and the New Year's Eve events our CEO often invites him to. Apparently, it was cheaper to buy one than to rent one as frequently as he needs it. Cara, Megan, Sami, and I had gone dress shopping together, and we found the perfect one.

The dress is a soft, matte satin in a striking scarlet red—a color I usually avoid, given my skin tone and hair, but this one works. It screams 'Christmas' with its bold, festive hue. The dress is strapless, with intricate boning in the front, so no bra is necessary. Soft, off-the-shoulder sleeves add a delicate touch, more for aesthetics than support. The skirt flares just enough to twirl, but it's tight enough to highlight my hips and ass. The neckline has a subtle sweetheart shape, drawing attention to my cleavage without being too revealing.

Starting by straightening my hair, I then curl it—a funny ritual we women sometimes do. The large, soft curls cascade down to the bottom of my shoulder blades, even when pulled up into a loose, flipped ponytail at the back of my head. I leave a few sweeping strands to frame my face.

I go heavy on the makeup, painting on smoky eyes and a bright red lipstick to match my dress. I slip into the dress, managing to zip it up, but I'll need Cole's help with the hook and eye at the top. Tonight calls for heels, and I have the perfect pair—red, strappy three-inch heels that match my dress. We'll be sitting most of the night, which makes wearing them more bearable.

For jewelry, I choose dangle, tear-drop diamond earrings that Alex gave me for my thirtieth birthday. I skip the necklace, thinking it'll draw Cole's eyes straight from my lips to my breasts. Part of me feels a sense of pride in being so temptingly dressed. I finish with a delicate diamond tennis bracelet and leave my watch behind. My kids have Cole's number, so there's no need for me to carry a phone tonight.

I step out of the bathroom just as Cole is fixing one of his cufflinks. He freezes, his jaw dropping slightly.

"Hey," I say, smiling.

"Geezus, Autumn," he rasps, his eyes raking over me, "I never thought you could outdo that night in the blue dress, but damn. What am I going to do with you?"

"Well, right now, I just need you to clip the back of my dress," I reply with a grin.

"Okay," he breathes, his voice thick with emotion. "Turn around."

His hands on my bare back send electric tingles across my skin, straight to my core.

After he secures the dress, he leans in close, his breath warm against my neck. "At least now I know how to get it off you later. And by the way, you smell amazing."

A shiver rushes down my spine, and I ache for him in that moment.

Smiling, I turn to meet his gaze. "Thanks, it's my fancy perfume. But first, we have to get through dinner and the ball."

"Yes," he says, kissing my forehead. "But tonight, you're all mine."

I smile back, my voice dropping to a breathy whisper as I lean closer to his ear. "Tonight, and every night."

"God, I love you, Autumn."

"I know," I tease with a playful shrug, earning a laugh from Cole.

"I'd kiss you, but I don't want to mess up all that hard work you put into your makeup," he says with a chuckle.

"Probably a good call," I agree, "but here." I unbutton his shirt slightly, pulling down his undershirt to kiss his chest, leaving a bold lipstick mark behind. "There, now you have my kiss to carry with you all night."

His hand cups my face, his thumb brushing tenderly along my jawline. "I think you meant that to be playful, but that was actually kind of amazing, Autumn. You always manage to surprise me."

Kissing my cheek, then my forehead, and finally my other cheek, he then lightly brushes his lips against mine. We both want more, but he respects the makeup.

Once he's finished getting dressed, I straighten his tie. I can't help but admire how he's cleaned up his beard and mustache earlier; even with the roughness of his short facial hair, he looks sharp. I reach up, my palm resting against his beard as I brush my thumb along his cheekbone.

"You look pretty good yourself," I purr, and he really does—he's fucking sexy tonight.

"Next time we're invited to this party, we can walk in as the sexy, power couple we are." He grins.

"Well, aren't you confident," I tease back.

"Oh, I'm very confident that we'll be a power couple," he says with a playful smile.

"We'll see," I laugh softly.

"You ready?" he asks.

"As ready as I'll ever be." I pause, then remember something. "Hey, I'm not carrying a purse, and my dress doesn't have pockets. Think you've got room in your pocket for my lipstick?" I ask with a smile.

"I think I can manage that, Autumn," he replies, tucking the lipstick away. "Anything else?"

"Nope, that's it," I say, feeling ready to take on the night.

We meet Pete and Laura as planned so we can enter together without making it obvious that we're doing so. Laura is stunning in a black strapless, A-line gown, almost sparkling with the diamonds she's adorned in. It's more than I would choose to wear at once, but she pulls it off beautifully.

Pete leans in to greet me with a gentle kiss on the cheek, and Cole does the same with Laura. Laura squeezes my hand, her eyes shining as she tells me how beautiful I look.

She then turns to Cole with a playful smile. "Good luck tonight."

Cole laughs, a touch of nerves in his voice. "Thanks, I think I'll need it."

As we walk into the dinner, I notice the seating assignments—Cole and I are placed with his team, while Pete and Laura are at a table with other executives.

Cole leans in close, his voice low and teasing. "See? Power couple. Tell me we won't look better than everyone else at that table."

I nudge him lightly on the arm, laughing softly. "Mostly because we're younger. Someday, people will talk about us like that."

He whispers back, his tone confident, "I'm pretty sure we'll always be the couple people talk about. We're perfect together."

"How can I argue with that?" I smile at him, feeling a warmth spread through me. "You were made for me."

As creatures of habit, our team sits at the dinner table in the same arrangement as we did at lunch—Tara to my left, Mark to Cole's right. Dinner is delicious, and though there's an open bar, I take it easy on the wine, limiting myself to one glass with dinner and another with dessert. As the dessert is served, a DJ starts playing music, and the dance floor lights up. The playlist is filled with songs we all know, catering to the crowd mostly in their forties and fifties.

Cole leans close, his breath warm against my ear. "I'll dance with you before the night is over," he whispers.

"Oh yeah?" I smile, intrigued.

"Yeah, but I'll make it count," he says, casually brushing his thumb along the bare skin of my shoulder as he pulls his arm off the back of my chair. The touch sends shivers down my spine, though I doubt he notices.

Pete approaches our table, introducing Laura to those who haven't met her. I sense a subtle tension between Tom and Pete. I've never seen them interact in person before, but there's a chilliness between them that makes me wonder if there's more history there than I know.

As people begin to get up and dance, the tables start to empty. Standing tables surround the dance floor, where people gather to socialize. Cole seizes the opportunity to introduce me to more executives, bringing Mark and Leona along, perhaps to avoid raising any red flags. He introduces us to our CEO, Rich, who is completely down-to-earth. His wife compliments my dress and hair, and I return the favor. After the introductions, we circle back to Pete, where Cole confides in me, right in front of Pete, that Mark is being groomed to take his position when he moves up at the end of February.

"Oh, so that's why you wanted to introduce him to everyone," I say with a knowing smile.

Cole returns my smile. "Yeah, and it was also an excuse to introduce you too."

I grin in response to his smile. "Is there bad blood between Tom and Pete?" I ask quietly, while Pete is engaged in another conversation.

"Sort of," Cole replies, hesitating. "Tom had a certain trajectory before the merger, and both Pete and I got in the way of that." He pauses, taking a sip of his wine. "Tom's going to be pissed when

Mark gets promoted over him, but not everything is about seniority or tenure," he adds with a shrug.

I nod thoughtfully. "Mark does seem like a better salesperson, but I don't see all the numbers you and Pete do."

"No, you're right," Cole agrees, glancing at his glass. "Mark's numbers are better, but more importantly, he can connect with a wider range of people. He makes everyone feel comfortable, while Tom can come across as a bit too cocky, which puts some people off. It's one thing to be a great salesperson, but it's another to lead a sales team."

"I get that," I say, smiling at him. "People bring their own drama."

Cole nods, just as Pete turns back to us. "Who's causing drama?" Pete asks, clearly catching the tail end of our conversation.

"Nobody," I say with a laugh. "We were just talking about the difference between leading people and being a worker bee. I'm pretty sure there's less drama when you're not in charge."

Pete chuckles. "That's true, and when you're middle management like Cole, you get drama from both above and below."

Cole raises his glass in agreement.

"Well, he handles it well," I say, my tone sincere.

"And that's why he's moving up," Pete says, giving Cole a friendly pat on the back.

A slow song starts playing, and Laura pulls Pete onto the dance floor. Tara and Max are out there too, moving gracefully to the music.

Cole looks at me, a wistful smile on his face. "Next year," he says softly.

"Yeah, I know. I'm kind of used to this down-low thing now," I reply with a laugh. "Hey, Cole?"

"Yes, Autumn?"

"Did you tell Mark? At dinner?"

He looks at me with mock innocence. "Tell Mark what?" His lips curl into a slight smile.

"About us, but you knew that," I say, giving him a playful look.

"I plead the fifth," he says, then grows more serious. "No, I didn't tell him directly. He asked, and I told him I wasn't going to answer. Whatever he inferred from that is on him."

"Not answering is still an answer, Cole," I laugh.

"Isn't that the same thing that happened with you and Tara?" he asks, raising an eyebrow.

I shrug, scrunching my nose a little. "Maybe."

"As you said about her, Mark is an ally, and we may need those someday," he says with a smile.

"So, are you telling me that Mark is going to be my boss at some point?"

"That's the plan," he says, his tone light. "And the best part about that is, it means I won't be anymore."

"I don't know, I kind of like sleeping with the boss," I tease with a shrug.

"Oh, so should I be worried about Mark now?" he asks, feigning a hurt tone.

"Nah, he and Leona are too cute to mess with."

"That's the only reason I shouldn't worry?" he asks, mock seriousness in his voice.

"Well, I kind of have this serious thing going on, so there's that," I say, grinning at him.

"Kind of have?" he laughs.

"Well, you know, in the finally met the love of my life kind of way," I say, my smile widening.

He chuckles softly. "Yeah, I guess that does sound like a kind of serious thing."

Just then, Tara and Max come over to chat with us. Cole excuses himself, promising to be right back. I watch him go, then turn my attention to Tara and Max. We talk about their wedding plans, and soon Pete and Laura join us. They ask a few questions about the wedding, and Tara shares that I'll be one of her bridesmaids. Pete comments on how nice it is when work friendships blossom into something more.

Cole returns, exchanging pleasantries with everyone, but there's something in his demeanor—a glint in his eye, a softness in his smile—that catches me off guard. It's rare that he surprises me, especially in public, but tonight he does.

Without a word, he wraps his hand around my forearm, his touch gentle but insistent, and begins to guide me toward the dance floor.

"Come on, I made a request," he murmurs, his voice low and enticing, his eyes holding a promise that sends a thrill through me.

CHAPTER FORTY-NINE

THE DANCE & THE COUNT

I glance back at Laura, who gives me a knowing smile as Cole gently pulls me toward the dance floor. The opening notes of "Wonderful Tonight" by Eric Clapton begin to play, and I feel a rush of warmth as he wraps his right arm around my waist, drawing me close. With his left hand, he brings my right hand to rest over his heart, and we start swaying together, perfectly in sync with the music. We're keeping a respectable distance, enough to pass any parochial school ruler test, which is probably wise, all things considered.

"You requested this?" I ask, a smile tugging at my lips.

"I seem to remember it being on your shortlist," he replies, his eyes twinkling.

"You remember correctly." Our conversation falls away, and we simply dance. It's the first time we've ever danced together, and the moment feels almost surreal.

After a few moments of comfortable silence, Cole breaks it. "Plus, you do look wonderful tonight."

I laugh softly, taking him in. "Well, this sight of you in a tuxedo might just haunt my dreams when you're not around."

He chuckles. "Yeah? Too bad there aren't many excuses to wear one."

"No, definitely not everyday wear," I agree with a laugh.

He pulls me a little closer, and I'm pretty sure we'd fail the ruler test now.

"You have no idea how much I want to kiss you right now," he whispers in my ear, his breath warm against my skin. The sensation sends a wave of heat through me, pooling low in my belly.

I glance over and catch Laura and Pete watching us.

As Cole leans back, I smile up at him. "Oh, I think I have some idea," I tease. "We'll be alone soon."

"Not soon enough," he murmurs, his smile full of longing.

"Hey now," I laugh, "I seem to remember I was the one who wasn't so sure about this idea and you thought it would be fine."

"It is fine," he laughs softly, "but you are incredibly tempting."

"Tempting, huh?" I smile, enjoying this playful banter.

"Again, you have no idea," he laughs, the sound low and warm.

"If you pulled me all the way into you right now, I think I'd have a pretty good idea," I say, raising my eyebrows suggestively.

"Autumn Flynn," he laughs, shaking his head. "You know Pete's watching, just waiting for me to mess this up, and you're making it harder."

"Cole, did you hear what you just said?" I can't help but smile, trying to stifle my laughter.

He rolls his eyes. "Woman, you have a one-track mind."

"Yeah, that track is you. Do you want me to have more tracks?" I ask, testing him.

"God, no," he says firmly, his voice low. "You're mine. You're only mine."

"Aren't you the confident one?" I tease, enjoying this back-and-forth.

"When it comes to how much I love you, yeah, I'm pretty certain," he says, his smile tender.

"What about how much I love you?" I ask, locking eyes with him. "You certain about that too?"

"More certain than I've ever been about anything," he says, his voice filled with quiet conviction.

His thumb moves slightly on my back, giving me a subtle taste of the familiar, intimate touch we usually share in private. I mirror the gesture, running my fingers under his lapel, both of us savoring this stolen moment.

"Cole?" My voice comes out raspy, thick with anticipation.

"Autumn?" He turns his gaze to me, curiosity flickering in his eyes.

"You should tell me what you're going to do to me later," I whisper, a teasing smile playing on my lips.

He breathes my name, almost as if he's savoring it, shaking his head as if trying to resist something. But then a devilish smile tugs at the corners of his mouth. "To you or with you?" he asks, his eyebrow arching suggestively.

"Either. Both." I shrug, playing along.

He leans in, his breath warm against my ear. "You sure you want to do this?"

"Yeah, pretty sure," I reply, my voice steady, filled with confidence.

His eyes travel slowly down my body and back up again. "Well, first, we'd have to get you out of that dress," he says with a laugh.

"Pretty sure that will take less time than getting through your layers—jackets, shirts, ties, and cummerbunds," I laugh back, feeling the playful energy between us.

"You might be right," he concedes, his smile turning wicked. "But I don't necessarily need my clothes off for most of what I want to do to you." His voice deepens as he speaks, sending a wave of heat through me.

"Oh yeah?" My cheeks flush as his words sink in.

"I want to trail my hands over every inch of your body, then follow with my mouth," he whispers, his breath hot on my neck. He pulls back slightly, looking me in the eyes, a teasing glint there. "But I'm not going to touch you where you want me to—not until you're hot and wet and begging for it."

"Cole," I challenge him, a mix of excitement and frustration in my voice.

"If you're going to torture me on the dance floor, I can torture you in the bedroom." He winks, the promise in his voice unmistakable. "You begged for it in Nashville, and I'll make you do it again."

Electricity pulses through me, my palms tingling as a new intensity of need settles low in my belly.

He leans in closer, his voice a low, seductive whisper in my ear. "After you beg for it, I'll give you my mouth and my fingers until you shake. You'll taste yourself on my fingers and my tongue. And when you're on the very edge, I'll fuck you, and I'll fuck you everywhere."

I clear my throat, trying to regain some composure. "Cole?"

"Autumn?" he responds, his thumb tracing a soft circle on my back.

"If I were wearing underwear, they'd be soaked right now," I admit, my voice barely above a whisper, "but instead, my thighs are slick."

His eyes widen, darkening with desire as his fingers press more firmly into my back.

Shaking his head slightly, his voice is a low growl. "Autumn, you're a bad girl. A true temptress."

I lean in close, my lips brushing his ear as I whisper, "Only for you."

The song draws to a close, the last notes fading away as we step off the dance floor. We walk back to Pete and Laura, who greet us with knowing smiles. Pete leans in to say something to Cole, while Laura comments on how much fun we seemed to be having and how much we smiled at one another. I glance at Cole, a secretive smile tugging at my lips.

Cole leans in, his voice low. "You want to find everyone and say goodnight?"

I laugh softly. "Sure, and good thing you waited until this late to request that song."

"Yeah." He grins. "I actually put some thought into that one."

Our goodbyes feel drawn out, lingering with each member of our team. It's been a pleasure to spend this time with them, getting to know their significant others, but the night is winding down, and we're both trying to avoid the obviousness of leaving together. We get separated by conversations a couple of times, but finally, we find ourselves alone in the glass elevator, heading up to our room.

"If this elevator wasn't glass..." Cole's voice trails off as his gaze travels slowly over me, untying his tie with a deliberate slowness.

I smile, feeling a spark of excitement. "Just a short walk down a hallway."

"How are those wet thighs?" he asks, his voice deep, but he can't help the laugh that escapes him.

"Still pretty wet." I laugh back, feeling the thrill of our shared secret.

"You're laughing now, but I meant it—I plan on torturing you," he says with a wicked grin.

"Oh, I hope so," I reply, my laughter mingling with anticipation.

He shakes his head, a look of playful exasperation on his face. "Seriously, woman, you're going to be the death of me."

"I'd like to think I breathe life into you," I counter, meeting his gaze.

He pauses, studying me with an intensity that makes my heart skip a beat. "That's probably a much more accurate statement," he murmurs just as the elevator doors slide open.

Holding the door for me, as I step out, he leans in close, whispering in my ear, "Game on." His words send shockwaves through me, electrifying every nerve.

I turn, catching his hand in mine, and walk backward down the hallway, leading him to our room. When we reach the door, I press my back against it, waiting as he pulls up the key on his phone.

"I remember the last time you had me backed against a hotel room door," I say, my voice breathy, filled with the memory of that night.

His eyes lock with mine, and his voice drops to a whisper, full of emotion. "Probably the best night of my life," he says, unlocking the door with a soft click.

Much like that night five months ago, he turns me around, pressing me against the wall behind the door, but this time, there's no hesitation. His lips find mine instantly, and my hands tangle in his hair, pulling him closer. His hands brace against the wall, not on me, but the intensity of his kiss is enough to make me forget anything else. His lips, his tongue—they're intoxicating, driving every thought from my mind until all I feel is him.

I push his tuxedo jacket off his shoulders, and he quickly shrugs it off, tossing it aside before returning his hands to the wall. His kisses trail along my jaw to my ear, then to that sensitive spot on my neck. Heat blooms in my core, radiating outward, and I feel the tension building between my legs, the need for him growing stronger with every touch.

Pausing, he leans back to meet my eyes, his voice soft but filled with hunger. "When I take this dress off, how much more will I need to remove?"

I smile, breathless. "Nothing, just the dress... and the shoes," I manage to say before his mouth claims mine again, more ravenous than before.

Slowly, he drops to his knees in front of me, his hands finally making contact with my waist before sliding down my legs. My fingers weave through his hair, holding on as he unstraps one heel, then the other, carefully removing them.

His right hand lingers on my inner ankle, and as he stands, he runs his hand up my leg, his touch sending shockwaves through me. When his fingers graze my inner thigh, he finds the evidence of my arousal and groans.

"Fuck, Autumn," he whispers, his voice thick with desire.

Hovering his fingers just millimeters from where I crave him most, he pulls away, leaving me aching. He braces himself against the wall again for a moment before his left hand wraps around my waist to pull me close.

With his right hand, he unhooks the top of my dress, and then slowly, agonizingly, slides the zipper down my back. When it reaches the bottom, he releases his hold on me. I let my arms fall, and the dress slips down, dropping in a soft red pool at my feet.

His deep sapphire eyes devour me, traveling from my feet upward, lingering on every inch of my exposed skin. When our eyes meet again, he moves with purpose. His hand tangles in my hair, pulling me to him, our bodies pressing flush against each other as his mouth crashes into mine. Kissing him is like taking a potent aphrodisiac, and I feel my strength melting away, my body surrendering to his.

Fingers trail down my spine, sending electric jolts through me, leaving a path of goosebumps in their wake. I moan against his lips, and I feel the corners of his mouth lift in a satisfied smile.

Bringing my hands between us, I fumble with the buttons on his shirt. He breaks the kiss, glancing down to watch my progress. His hands meet mine, and for a moment, I think he might stop me, but instead, he trails his fingers up to my shoulders and then back down, his touch gentle, reverent. My skin responds instantly, the tiny hairs on my arms standing up, goosebumps spreading across my body, all of it heightening the aching peaks of my breasts and the throbbing need between my legs.

I unhook his cummerbund and untuck his shirt, his fingers still tracing patterns on my skin. I can feel his eyes on me, burning with intensity, as I focus on undressing him. When his shirt is fully unbuttoned, I ease it off his shoulders, and he lets it fall away, leaving him in just his undershirt.

"You were definitely wearing more clothes than me," I say, a playful smile tugging at my lips as I glance at his undershirt.

"Not by choice," he replies, his voice deep, seductive, and filled with that alluring edge I've only heard a few times.

I start working on his belt, and he pulls his undershirt over his head, revealing the chiseled lines of his torso. I kiss him again, pressing my lips to the lipstick mark I left earlier, as his pants and belt fall to the floor, joining the pile of my dress. He still has on his boxers, socks, and shoes, but I start at the waistband of his boxers, ready to remedy that.

Grinning, he brushes his thumb along my cheekbone. "Sorry, I didn't get the memo that this was a commando event," he teases.

I laugh. "It was supposed to be a surprise, so there was no memo."

Quickly, he strips off his remaining clothes, and in a matter of seconds, we're both completely naked. I take a moment to admire him—the strong muscles of his arms, the solid thickness of his thighs, the chest hair I love to run my fingers through, and of course, the undeniable evidence of his desire for me, hard and ready.

He draws me away from gazing at his groin, his fingers gently finding the bottom of my jaw, guiding my eyes back to his. His thumb traces along my jawline and then lightly brushes my bottom lip before he leans in to kiss me, soft but full of promise. His other hand glides down my arm, from my shoulder to the small of my back, pulling me flush against him. The warmth of his body against mine is electrifying. He then turns us around, backing me toward the bed, and just as the backs of my legs hit the mattress, he breaks the kiss, gently pushing me down onto the bed. Leaning over me, he reaches behind my waist, helping me move up toward the pillows.

Settling between my legs, he kneels, and I can tell he has no intention of rushing this. My body, however, is acutely aware of his presence, the anticipation heightening my ache for him. His fingers start at my ankles, trailing slowly up the insides of my legs. Each touch is a tease, stopping just short of my core before sliding back down to my knees. He repeats this torturous path, building my need with every stroke. Then, as his fingers trace up once more, he brushes oh-so-lightly against the outside of my folds, just enough to make me gasp, but not enough to satisfy any need. My hips lift off the mattress, seeking more, but he places his hands on the outsides of my hips, firmly guiding them back down as he continues his exploration up my body.

Leaning over me, he reaches up to my collarbones, and I can feel him hovering tantalizingly close to where I want him most. My hips rise instinctively, desperate for contact, but his hand quickly presses down on my pelvis, keeping me in place.

"Stay," he whispers, a teasing smile on his lips.

That strong, commanding hand begins to move again, tracing featherlight paths across my abdomen and up to my breasts. He teases around the hard peaks, his fingers trailing down my ribs, across my stomach, but never where I want them most. Leaning over me, he meets my eyes, a spark of mischief in his gaze, before lowering his mouth to the side of my breast. He kisses in slow, deliberate circles around each nipple, never quite touching them, the anticipation driving me wild. My breasts ache for release, and my back arches off the bed as he gets closer.

I feel him smile against my skin, his breath warm. "Say please," he murmurs, his voice dripping with playful dominance.

My hands tangle in his hair, gripping tightly. "Please, Cole," I whisper, surprised by the breathiness and need in my own voice.

His mouth engulfs one of my swollen peaks, his hand finding the other, and I moan, unable to control the way my back arches in response. The sensations are intense, his mouth and tongue working in perfect tandem with his fingers. The relief is almost overwhelming as the tension in my core tightens. My hips rise again, instinctively seeking more, but he shifts slightly, keeping himself just out of reach while his mouth and hands switch sides.

The knot in my core tightens, and I feel it start to unravel, the release washing over me in waves. My legs instinctively try to close, but he holds me still, letting the convulsions ripple through my body. The orgasm is powerful, leaving me breathless, and I feel the wetness spreading beneath me on the bed.

"One," he whispers, his voice thick with satisfaction. He leaves one hand on my breast, his touch electrifying me, as his mouth begins to travel down my body, lingering teasingly at my navel before continuing lower.

As his mouth reaches my pubic bone, he moves down to my inner thigh, almost grazing my knee. His lips find one thigh while his hand, having trailed down from my breast, caresses the other. His tongue slowly travels up one leg as his fingers glide up the other, teasingly close to where I ache for him the most. Just inches from my core, he switches sides, his mouth descending the opposite thigh as his fingers follow the same path. The wetness from me, combined with the heat of his mouth, intensifies every sensation. He repeats this torturous dance twice more, each time building the anticipation until it's almost unbearable. But I know when he finally indulges me, the pleasure will be even more profound.

As he crosses over me one last time, he blows gently across my aching center, and I gasp, my hips rising off the bed. He continues his path down my leg, then, on his way back up, he blows again, the cool air making me shudder, before he inhales deeply, drawing a sharp breath from me.

"You smell so good, Autumn, so sweet," he murmurs, his voice vibrating against my sensitive skin, causing me to moan and lift my pelvis, desperate for more.

His breath teases me again, and then I feel his fingers barely graze the outer lips between my thighs, still teasing. His tongue trails up the outside of both lips, and I moan, my hips moving instinctively, trying to press closer to him.

"You ready to beg yet, Autumn?" he asks, his deep voice vibrating through my core. I don't answer, too lost in the sensation, and he traces the crease where my ass meets my thighs, his fingers agonizingly close to my entrance before sliding back up along the outside of my lips.

I can't take it any longer. "Please, Cole," I breathe, my voice thick with need.

Laughing softly, and a little wickedly, he savors my surrender.

His hand trails up my inner thigh from knee to center, pausing for a tantalizing moment before plunging three fingers inside me. I gasp, the feeling so intense; my body craves him so desperately that even his fingers feel like a lifeline.

Shifting, the full weight of his body moving up my side, he half-crushes me as our lips meet. My hands find his hair and his upper arm, and his fingers move expertly inside me. Almost immediately, I feel another orgasm building, and when he curls his fingers just right, it sends me over the edge. My body throbs and convulses around his hand, my nails dragging across his arm as I unravel.

Breaking the kiss, he whispers against my lips, "Two."

His kisses trail down my jaw, across my collarbones, then down to both breasts, lingering just enough to drive me wild before continuing toward my center. His fingers move slowly in and out of me while his mouth teases, tortures. He looks up at me one last time before his tongue finally dips between my folds.

I inhale sharply, moaning as he licks me from his fingers upward. He pulls one lip of my folds into his mouth, sucking and nibbling playfully. The pleasure is so intense it borders on pain. His tongue quickly moves across my most sensitive spot, repeating the same attention on the other side. My hips push against his fingers and mouth, desperate for more.

Holding me open with one hand, he finally gives me what I've been craving. His tongue circles the bundle of nerves between my folds, his fingers spreading me to grant him full access. He withdraws two fingers, leaving me wanting more, but the one finger he keeps inside moves with gentle precision. His tongue works me like he's been studying for this moment his entire life, every stroke driving me closer to the brink.

Just when I think I can't take any more, he pulls away, leaving me on the edge. But then he blows across me, and I gasp, my thighs trying to close around him, but his elbows push them apart. His tongue returns, the intensity heightened by each teasing blow, until I'm ready to come for him again. This time, when I grind against him, he takes the hint. His tongue circles me with the perfect pressure, his finger still working inside me. He pulls the bud between my folds into his mouth, sucking, nibbling, licking—never letting up. The sensation is overwhelming, both too much and not enough at once.

As the orgasm builds, I reach down, tangling my fingers in his hair, my pelvis grinding into him. When I finally come, the release is powerful, my body convulsing around his finger as he pushes more inside, giving me exactly what I need. His tongue moves down, plunging into me as his fingers withdraw. He moans against me, the vibration sending aftershocks through my already spent body.

"Three," he whispers before licking up my slit again. I shudder as he moves up my body, kissing me deeply. The taste of me on his tongue, on his lips, reignites the desire within me, even though I should be completely spent. "You're not shaking yet," he murmurs against my lips, a smile playing at the corners of his mouth. "I'm not done."

His mouth finds my breasts again, while his hand works between my thighs once more. This time, he starts with three fingers, hooking them just right to make me fall apart. His thumb circles my sensitive spot, and then I feel him add a fourth finger, stretching me in ways I've never experienced before. His mouth releases my nipple, and our eyes meet—his gaze mischievous, almost wicked. I don't know whether to be scared or excited, but the way my core clenches tells me I'm excited.

Slowly, his thumb moves down to join his fingers inside me, gently pressing in. He looks into my eyes again, perhaps seeking permission or maybe checking if I want him to stop. But as I feel myself stretch around him, the only words that escape my lips are, "Fuck, Cole," in a breathy moan and I push toward him. He takes that as permission, pushing his whole hand deeper inside me.

He groans, and as he starts to move, a sharp, strong orgasm begins to build. I've never felt anyone this deep inside me, and the sensation is entirely new, overwhelming. My head falls back, my toes curl, and I grip the sheets, trying to hold on, trying to make it last. But his hand feels so good, I can't fight it off for long. When I finally come undone, the orgasm wrecks me completely. As he slowly and gently pulls his hand out, I feel a rush of fluid follow.

"Fuck, Autumn," he breathes, his voice low and drawn out.

He trails his wet hand up my body, his fingers brushing across my lips. I let his fingers slip into my mouth, tasting myself on him, and he lets out a hushed growl.

"Four," he whispers against my lips before kissing me again.

Now, my legs are shaking, and I feel lightheaded, euphoric, and utterly spent.

"Cole?" I whisper, my voice trembling with need.

"Autumn?" he replies, a devilish smile playing on his lips.

"Can I beg you to fuck me now?" I breathe, the words spilling out of me.

"You want me now, do you?" he teases, his smile widening.

"Always," I whisper, the truth of it echoing in my chest.

He kisses me, and I can still taste myself on his lips and tongue—it's intoxicating. He sits up on his knees, pulling me closer, and I can feel him, hard and ready, hovering just outside my entrance. I push toward him, and he chuckles softly, but then he thrusts into me, burying himself deep. My body feels like it might explode, every nerve in my core tingling, heightened by the orgasms he's already wrung from me.

As he pushes deeper, I feel whole, that same connection that I've never felt with anyone else, just him, only him. I moan as my head falls back, and his thumb begins to circle that sensitive spot between my lips while he thrusts, and the knot inside me tightens again. I didn't know I had anything left to give, but my body does—it always does for him.

Under the movement of his thumb and the feel of him driving into me, my body releases. He pulls his hand away, bracing himself as he leans down to kiss me, his mouth claiming mine while my core convulses around him, still hard, still moving inside me. Our mouths part, and he looks into my eyes.

"Five," he murmurs before sitting back on his knees.

Everything is messy now—the sounds of wet skin on skin are erotic, filling the room with the rawness of our connection. We're both drenched in the aftermath of my chain of orgasms, the rush of fluids from the most intense one, and my overwhelming arousal. I can feel the wetness beneath me, around me, on him—it's everywhere.

He pulls out, and I feel a pang of emptiness, but then he moves back toward my now not-so-forbidden entrance, gently pushing in. His eyes meet mine, and I push toward him, inviting him deeper, drawing a low growl from his throat. He quickly thrusts his full length into me, and his fingers find my more familiar entrance. My head falls back again as his fingers slide between my folds, dipping into the wetness at my core.

He pulls my left leg up onto his shoulder, bracing us both, and his other hand moves in sync with his hips, thrusting into me. He's true to his word—he fucks me everywhere, and he fucks me hard.

The sensation is euphoric. As his fingers hook up and find that sweet spot inside me, I lose control of my body. My eyes roll back, my head falls back, and I release him, my hands gripping the pillows and sheets around me.

Then his voice, deep and commanding, pushes me over the edge. "Let me know when you're going to come, baby, because I'll fall with you."

It only takes a few more thrusts, his fingers curling just right. "Now, Cole. Come with me."

And he does. I feel him throbbing inside me, the flexing of his muscles as my core tightens around him. He groans, a deep, primal sound that sends one last wave of pleasure through me.

"Six," he whispers, collapsing beside me on the bed, both of us shaky, satisfied, and utterly spent.

We lie there in silence for a long time, our fingers laced together, basking in the afterglow.

Cole finally breaks the silence, still a little breathless. "Did that at least compete with Nashville?"

I smile at him, warmth flooding my chest. "I'm pretty sure it at least tied."

He leans over, kissing me gently. "I love you, Autumn."

"I love you too. Maybe tomorrow you can just make love to me and let my body recover from this," I say, gesturing to my thoroughly satisfied but slightly sore body.

Cole laughs, his eyes twinkling. "I think soft and gentle can be arranged," he says, kissing me again.

"That's good because I'm pretty sure I'm going to have more bruises on my thighs." I smile at him. "Also, I'm pretty sure that's the first time you called me baby."

"I'm pretty sure it's the first time I've called *anyone* baby," he laughs. "But I kind of liked it."

"I kind of liked it too," I admit with a shrug.

We get up, clean ourselves up, and go through our nightly routines—washing faces, brushing teeth, doing all the things that need to happen before bed. We both put on minimal clothes before crawling back under the covers.

I fall asleep with my head on his chest, his arm wrapped around me. I feel safe, completely satisfied, and utterly loved, even if I am a little sore.

CHAPTER FIFTY

THE YACHT & THE HOTEL

We sleep in the next morning, and I wake to the soft caress of Cole's fingertips tracing lazy patterns on my back. I moan softly as my eyes flutter open, the sensation warming me from the inside out. His lips press a tender kiss to my forehead.

"Good morning," I murmur, still half-dreaming.

"Hey, beautiful," he replies, his fingers never pausing in their gentle exploration of my skin.

"If you keep that up, you might just turn me on," I tease, a smile tugging at my lips.

"Maybe that's my goal," he says, a playful edge in his voice that tells me he's entirely serious.

He shifts beneath me, rolling over so he can kiss me, his fingers continuing their sensual assault. When he makes love to me, it's soft, tender, and gentle—everything the night before wasn't. Yet both experiences leave me feeling deeply loved.

After a long, warm shower together, we meet our team, along with Pete and Laura, for lunch. Somehow, we manage to keep our hands off each other. Afterward, it's time to head back to Cole's.

"Hey," I start, breaking the comfortable silence as we drive. "I just want you to know this weekend was one of our best. I love you."

He steals a quick glance at me, his eyes softening. "It was for me too. I love you too, and thank you. Thank you for being in my life, for letting me love you, for loving me back, for letting me be your anchor, and for anchoring me," he says, lifting my hand to his mouth and kissing my fingers.

"Cole," I say softly, touched by his words, "that was so sweet. You're welcome, but I'm grateful for you too—for all of those things."

Squeezing my hand, his voice turns more serious. "I know you are. But, Autumn, it still feels so surreal that someone like you would love me. Sometimes, I feel like I don't deserve you. Like I'm just waiting for the other shoe to drop."

"Cole," I say, my voice gentle but firm, "I don't know where you got the idea that you don't deserve love, but you do. You're an amazing man, an amazing father—really, an amazing human being," I say, squeezing his hand. "I love that you can be so vulnerable with me, but you also radiate confidence. Sometimes, I think you just doubt yourself."

He laughs softly. "I think it's more than just sometimes, Autumn. I doubt myself and second-guess myself a lot."

"Well, when it comes to me, please don't," I say, squeezing his hand again. "It feels surreal to me too, but I'm not going anywhere. You *are* my anchor, and I'm pretty sure if I lost you, I'd just float around, lost at sea."

He kisses my fingers again, then wrinkles his nose with a smile. "That was a little cheesy."

I laugh, leaning closer. "I know, but that doesn't make it any less true."

We spend the next few days at Cole's before heading to my place for Christmas. To our amazement, we manage to have all six kids together under one roof for four days. Kalisha even joins us the day after Christmas. The family time is nothing short of magical. Matthew, Megan, and Sami stay with us for their entire winter break, and Cole and I are completely overwhelmed by how well our children continue to bond. It's the first Christmas in years that feels like everything I've ever wanted—a true sense of warmth, love, and togetherness.

The season is laced with romance, too. The soft glow of the Christmas tree and decorations casts a candlelit aura over our lives. Mistletoe kisses, fireside snuggles, and the chilly bedroom that urges us to keep each other warm—every moment heightens our connection. I find myself falling more in love with Cole every day.

But reality looms. Cole has to leave the weekend after New Year's to return home before attending his first board meeting in his new interim role in Columbus. He'll stay there for a couple of weeks, learning the ropes of his new position, having dinners with other executives and board members. The thought of being apart for two weeks feels unbearable, especially after the closeness we've shared.

Determined to make New Year's Eve unforgettable, Cole insists on something special. I keep telling him I'd be perfectly happy spending the evening on the couch in our pajamas, but he's set on creating magic. When he finalizes our plans, he's like a kid who's just been told he can get a puppy, his excitement contagious.

"Hey, beautiful," he says, walking into the kitchen where I'm making tea, his smile so genuine and wide that I can't help but grin back.

"Hey, you," I reply, a flirtatious note in my voice. "What's got you so excited?"

"I figured out our New Year's plans," he says, wrapping his arms around me, pulling me close.

"Oh yeah?" I ask, raising an eyebrow.

"Yeah." He beams. "We'll have to drive to Chicago, but I booked us a dinner and fireworks cruise on a yacht in Lake Michigan."

"A yacht?" I ask, surprised.

"Yeah," he says, his eyes lighting up. "Dinner, drinks, dancing, fireworks, and then a hotel room on the Magnificent Mile so we don't have to drive back. I booked the hotel through the third so we can spend some more time away from reality," he says, leaning in to kiss me.

"I'm assuming this is a fancy affair?" I laugh.

"Cocktail attire, yeah," he nods. "But I like you all dressed up."

"I think you like undressing me," I tease, smiling.

He shrugs, eyes playfully drifting toward the ceiling as if in deep thought. "Yeah, I kind of like that part too. I won't deny it."

I wrinkle my nose, smiling back at him. "I kind of like you undressing me too."

A few days later, we prepare to head to Chicago. I choose the blue dress Cole never got to fully appreciate. Megan styles my hair in the same waterfall braids as before, and we drive to the hotel, where we get dressed. Cole looks incredibly sexy in his suit, but the look on his face when he sees me is even sexier. The desire in his eyes alone is enough to turn me on.

"You still look a little untouchable," he says, his hands resting on my waist, his gaze raking over me.

"I think the word you used before was 'disheveled,'" I laugh. "You didn't want to dishevel me."

"Yes, that night I didn't want to dishevel you," he smiles, "but tonight I kind of do. But I won't—at least not yet," he adds with a wink that melts me from the inside out. "You're gorgeous, Autumn. Stunning. I'm a very lucky man, and not just because you're beautiful."

"I think I'm pretty lucky too," I say, straightening his tie and giving him a gentle kiss.

The cruise is nothing short of amazing. One of the best meals I've ever had, paired with unique and delicious cocktails. We dance together without a care, free from the need to be discreet. As the countdown approaches, Cole finds us the perfect spot on deck to watch the fireworks. For the first time in years, I share a New Year's kiss, and it feels like the most meaningful one of my life. The coming year promises so many wonderful things for us.

As the fireworks explode in the sky, Cole runs his thumb over my cheekbone and kisses me again before turning me around so my back is flush against his chest. We watch the fireworks together, his arms wrapped tightly around my waist.

"Megan was right—fireworks are pretty romantic," he whispers in my ear.

I lean back into him, his breath warm on my ear and neck. Heat courses through my veins, pooling in my core. The way this man can ignite a fire within me with just a breath still catches me off guard. His arms pull me in tighter, and though the lake air is cold, I feel nothing but warmth in his embrace.

We return to the hotel around two in the morning. The first thing I do is kick off my heels, relishing the relief, while Cole patiently watches as I let my hair down. He's busy shedding layers of his own—his tie, his jacket—by the time I step out of the bathroom. When I turn the corner, I see him standing there, looking much like he did that unforgettable night a few months ago. His tie hangs loosely around his neck, his shirt is half unbuttoned and untucked, and, God, if he doesn't look even sexier like this. Just the sight of him stirs the ache between my legs.

He catches the hunger in my eyes and narrows his gaze, tilting his head slightly. "What?" he asks, his voice husky, sending a shiver down my spine.

"I'm just lucky, and I love you," I say as I step toward him.

Moving toward me at lightning speed, his hand finds the small of my back, pulling me against him while his other hand tangles in my hair, guiding my mouth to his. The kiss is deep, passionate, and I can feel the intensity of our connection through every brush of our lips, every flick of our tongues.

My hands hang at my sides, overwhelmed by the sensations coursing through me. But as I begin to regain some control, one hand slides up his arm while the other glides up his chest until they both find their place around his neck. My fingers tangle in his hair, and we're lost in each other, the vibrant energy between us like a livewire, powerful and intoxicating.

Our mouths part for just a breath, and Cole gazes into my eyes. He cups my face with one hand, then pulls me back into another searing kiss. I don't know how long we stay like this, lips and tongues locked together, but it feels like forever and yet not nearly long enough.

When he finally pulls back, his thumb trails down my throat, his eyes following the path of his hand as his fingers gently trace across my collarbone. He tucks a loose strand of hair behind my shoulder, his sapphire blue eyes studying my skin, my body, as if trying to memorize every detail.

His other hand reaches down, gently tugging the zipper on the side of my dress. He slips his hand inside, helping to release the corset, and the dress falls to the ground in a soft, satin heap. Instantly, he closes the distance between us again, pulling me flush against him, his mouth capturing mine. His fingers graze my back and arms, their touch so light it feels like feathers dancing over my skin.

I manage to get my hands between us, working on the buttons of his shirt. He pulls back, watching my hands, then gently tucks another stray piece of hair behind my ear. Once the buttons are undone, he shrugs off his shirt, and I help him pull his undershirt over his head.

His hand finds the nape of my neck, kissing me again, while his other hand wraps around my waist before trailing down to caress the soft curves of my ass. I work on the waistband of his pants, pushing them down as he groans softly against my mouth.

In one fluid motion, he turns me toward the bed and lays me down. His mouth finds my navel, and he begins his slow, deliberate journey up my body. When his warm mouth and tongue reach the hard peaks of my breasts, I gasp, arching into him. His lips meet mine again as two of his fingers dip inside me, reigniting that livewire sensation. His fingers find the perfect spot, and his wrist presses against the most sensitive part of me.

I grind against him, and he moans into my mouth, feeling my body respond, but he doesn't break the kiss. The band of tension in my core tightens, my climax building as I move against him, chasing that release. He hooks his fingers just right, and the band snaps. My core contracts around his fingers, and my head falls back as his mouth moves to the sensitive skin of my neck.

He kisses me again as he withdraws his fingers, leaving me momentarily empty. Then, with a swift motion, he rolls us over, and I find myself straddling him. I angle myself above him, slowly lowering onto his length. He inhales sharply, his eyes closing, head tilting back in pleasure.

Quickly, he refocuses on me, watching as I ride him. The first words he utters come out as a guttural groan, "Fuck, Autumn."

His hands grip my thighs, and he bites his lower lip, encouraging me to continue the rhythmic movements. I feel his thighs begin to tense, and he sits up, wrapping an arm around my waist. His mouth finds the pink bud of my breast, and I continue grinding into him, feeling his muscles tighten beneath me.

I rise, pulling off him, leaving him on the edge. But I have no intention of stopping. I trail kisses down his chest, following the line of fine hair that leads to my goal. When I take him into my mouth, I moan at the taste of myself on him. My tongue swirls around his head as my hand and lips stroke him in unison. He leans back, his hand in my hair, groaning again—a sound so masculine and primal that I can't resist. I suck and lick harder and faster, and he rewards me with another groan as he stills and throbs. I taste him on my tongue before swallowing, letting him become a part of me.

Pulling me back up to him, his mouth crashes into mine. My hair falls around us like a curtain, and his fingers continue their exploration of my back and arms, while his mouth devours mine, never getting enough.

After a few more minutes of kissing, he gently turns me onto my side next to him. His fingers weave through my tangled hair, the gentle movement stirring nerves and leaving me tingling. He kisses my forehead, and my fingers trace patterns across his chest as we lay in contented silence.

Cole's raspy voice breaks through the quiet. "Autumn?"

"Cole?" I respond, my voice equally raspy.

"I just want you to know that I'm pretty sure I can't live without you anymore," he says, kissing my head. "You're my oxygen, my life force. I don't just love you, I need you. You really do breathe life into me, and I wish I'd met you earlier so we could have had more years together."

I prop myself up on my elbow, meeting his gaze. "In the words of Shakespeare, 'What's past is prologue,'" I say with a smile. "Cole, you are my everything now, and even though I wish we had more years together too, I'm glad we have so many chapters of our story left to write. If it weren't for the prologue, we wouldn't be who and where we are now. We have chapters, sequels, spin-offs—all still ahead of us. We might be older than the characters in most great love stories, but that doesn't mean we can't have one. I think we already do. You're my prince charming, my fairytale ending, the hero who comes back and rides off into the sunset with the girl—you're all of it."

He studies my face for a moment, then pulls me into a gentle, tender kiss. Our tongues explore each other's mouths softly, savoring the connection.

As our lips part, his hand traces my cheekbone. "I love you, Autumn."

"I love you too," I reply, snuggling down and using his chest as my pillow.

The next few days in the hotel, we barely leave the bed. Cole had plans for fancy dinners, but knowing we're about to spend two weeks apart, we're completely wrapped up in each other. We talk, touch, kiss, make love, and just lose ourselves in each other's presence. The TV stays off, our phones are ignored, and all our meals are delivered to the room.

On Sunday morning, we drive back to my house, and Cole packs up to head back to his. While I'm sad to see him leave, I'm also excited and proud of him—and of us—that he's starting this new chapter in his career. The secretive nature of our relationship makes it too risky for me to go with him to Columbus, so it makes sense for me to stay at my house.

Once his things are loaded in the car, he pulls me into a tight hug. I inhale his scent, my fingers tracing the edges of his muscles, committing them to memory. His hand wraps around my hair, and he kisses me deeply. For better or worse, we've gotten better at goodbyes. They're inevitable, and we've learned not to fight them so hard.

I watch him back out of the driveway, my arms wrapped around myself, feeling the sting of his absence. But when I step back inside, I find Megan in the kitchen, and I'm grateful that I'm not alone.

CHAPTER FIFTY-ONE

THE DENVER CONFERENCE

For the next two weeks, I immerse myself in work, and Cole is doing the same in Columbus. The days blur together, moving both fast and slow. Finally, it's Wednesday—the day before our conference in Denver.

That evening, Cole calls me. "Hey there, beautiful. I'm pretty excited that I get to see you tomorrow."

"Yeah? How excited?" I tease, unable to hide my own excitement.

He chuckles, his voice taking on a playful, challenging tone. "Excited enough that I hope you can handle it."

"Oh, I can handle anything you throw my way," I reply, just as flippantly.

We laugh together, the sound filling the distance between us, and finalize our plans to meet at the airport. We're landing in two different concourses at almost the same time, so we decide to meet in the terminal just outside the secure area before baggage claim.

The next day, Megan drives me to the airport. After making my way through security, I send Cole a quick text, anticipation bubbling up as I wait for our reunion.

I make it to the terminal before Cole and patiently wait for him, but our plans hit a snag when Tom appears first, catching me off guard. We hadn't known he was flying in at the same time. He spots me immediately.

"Autumn," Tom says as he approaches, offering a soft hug. "Waiting for someone?"

"Uh, yeah," I reply, hesitating for a moment. "Cole, actually. We were going to share a ride to the hotel. I don't think he realized you were flying in at the same time."

"I wasn't going to, but I found an earlier flight on a different airline," he explains with a smile. "I guess we can all ride together."

"Yeah," I respond, forcing a smile while rolling my eyes internally. "I'm sure we can."

Just then, I see Cole approaching. I smile, but I catch the brief drop in his expression when he spots Tom. The moment passes quickly, and he slips on his professional mask, returning Tom's smile.

Cole pats Tom on the shoulder, offering a handshake. "Hey, good to see you, man. How are you?"

"Doing good," Tom replies.

"I thought you were flying in later today?" Cole asks, his tone casual.

"I changed my flight," Tom answers with a nod, and Cole turns to me.

He pulls me into a half hug—one that leaves us both wanting more. "Hey, Autumn," he says, his voice strained with the effort to keep it even.

The familiar scent of him washes over me, and my body hums with the desire to be closer.

"Hey," I respond, trying to keep things light. "Yeah, Tom was saying we could all share a ride to the hotel since we're here together."

Cole's expression remains neutral, but I know he's feeling the same frustration as I am. "Sure thing," he says smoothly. "Definitely the fiscally responsible decision."

He glances at me. "Did you check a bag?"

"I did," I confirm. "Did either of you?"

They both shake their heads, so we head to baggage claim for mine. Cole plays the gentlemanly boss, lifting my bag off the belt before we head to find our ride share. The drive is filled with small talk, a thin veil over the tension simmering beneath the surface.

By the time we arrive at the hotel and check in, I'm more than ready to get my hands on Cole. Because Tom is checking in with us, Cole doesn't get the chance to request adjoining rooms, but he does ask for rooms close to each other on the same floor for all three of us. As we walk to the elevator, he discreetly slips me one of his room keys. I stifle a laugh, torn between finding the situation exciting and mildly annoying.

When we reach our floor, my room is closest to the elevator. Cole winks at me before continuing down the hall with Tom. I smile, entering my room, the anticipation buzzing in my veins. About five minutes later, my watch vibrates with a message.

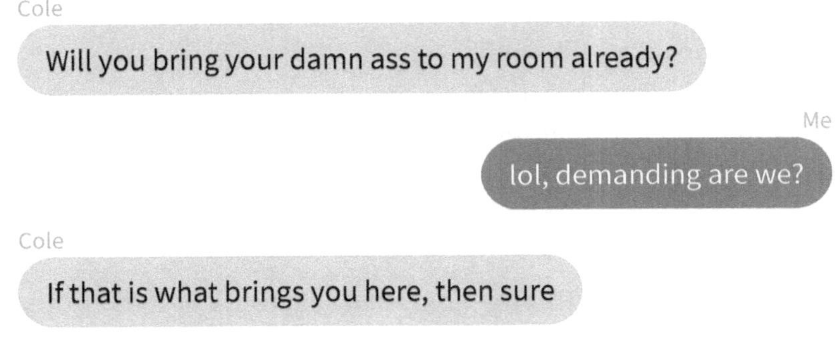

I text him as I'm walking out of my room.

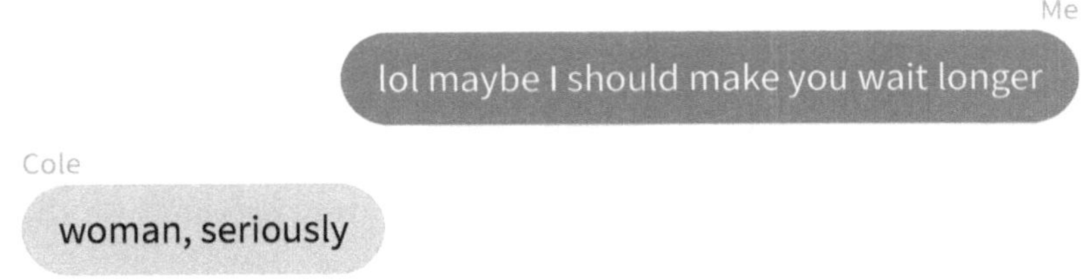

I scan the key and receive the last message just as I open the door. Cole closes the distance between us in an instant, the door barely clicking shut before his mouth is on mine, his hands exploring my body. He tastes like vanilla and coffee, and the combination of his taste, scent, and touch overwhelms my senses, sending waves of desire and lust coursing through me.

Breaking the kiss just long enough to smile at him, I say, "I missed you too."

His only response is to capture my mouth again, backing me into the wall as his body molds against mine. I feel the hardness of his desire pressing into my abdomen, igniting an even deeper need within me. One of his hands braces against the wall above me while the other wraps around my waist, pulling me closer. My hands find their way to his hair and neck, and I lose myself in the intoxicating rhythm of our kiss.

Nothing turns me on as much as kissing Cole. The rush of lust travels from my mouth through my veins, awakening every nerve in my body, pooling into a growing wetness between my legs. His mouth moves from my lips to my jaw, then to my neck, kissing right over my pulse point. The light scratch of his facial hair against my skin heightens the sensations already flooding through me.

He continues down to my ear, then behind it, his hand moving from the wall to tangle in my hair, giving him better access. I tilt my head, inviting more, as his mouth trails to my collarbone and then across to the other side of my neck. When he reaches that sweet spot just under my ear, I can't help but whimper quietly, and I feel him smile against my skin.

Fingers grip my waist tighter, pulling me even closer as he leans back against the wall, taking me with him. He holds me there, his eyes locking onto mine as the back of his fingers graze my cheek, making my eyes flutter shut.

"Fuck, Autumn, how does this get even more intense as time goes on?" he whispers, his voice full of wonder.

"I don't know," I breathe, meeting his gaze. "But I'd rather trust it than fight it."

He pulls me into another kiss, this time slower, more tender. His hands glide up and down my ribs, leaving a trail of goosebumps in their wake. The lust between us hasn't diminished, but every move he makes now is deliberate, gentle. His mouth and tongue explore mine with a newfound softness, and his fingers trace tender caresses along my skin. Eventually, his hands find their way under my shirt, his fingers savoring the bare skin of my back and sides.

Slowly, I slide my hands down from his neck and begin unbuttoning his shirt. He takes the cue, gently pulling my shirt over my head. As soon as my bra is exposed, he runs a single finger along the lace top, his eyes following the path of his hand, causing my breath to hitch.

I push his shirt off his shoulders, and he lets it drop to the floor. I quickly remove his undershirt, my hands running up his hard chest, fingers threading through his chest hair. As I follow my hands with my eyes, he cups my jaw, tilting my face up to meet his gaze.

He kisses me softly on the forehead. "Sometimes you don't feel real," he murmurs before pressing a tender kiss to my lips.

Hands loop around my back, unhooking my bra and letting it fall to the floor. As I bring my hands back up, I pause at his waistband, unhooking his belt and undoing his pants. They fall to the ground, and he kicks them off, his feet already bare.

Cole's hands trail down my ribs to my waistband, unbuttoning my jeans and peeling them off along with my thong. I kick off my shoes, stepping out of my pants. He pulls me close for a moment, our bodies pressed together, before guiding me backward toward the bed.

When the bed brushes the back of my legs, Cole turns us around and sits on the edge, his hands firmly on my hips, silently telling me to stay. My hands wrap around his neck, and his right hand travels down the outside of my leg to my knee, then slowly up the inside of my thighs, brushing against both as he goes. When he reaches my core and feels the heat and wetness, he groans quietly.

He looks up at me, meeting my eyes and holding them, before plunging two fingers inside me. His other hand wraps around my ass, and as he curls his fingers in that maddening, come-hither motion, my head falls back in surrender. He leans his head against my abdomen, his hand on my ass pulling me closer while his head presses into my belly, creating a delicious tension between wanting to move closer and needing to stay still.

My body responds instantly to his touch. As the wetness builds, I grip his neck and hair tighter. He adds another finger, his thumb finding that sensitive bundle of nerves on the outside, his movements patient and consistent. The tension coils tighter and tighter within me until I can't hold back any longer. My body convulses around his fingers, and I feel the flood of wetness between my thighs as I tug at his hair, my body seeking release.

As the waves of my orgasm subside, Cole pulls his fingers out, leaving me empty and hungry for more. His hands return to my hips as he scoots back on the bed, guiding me down on top of him. My hair falls around our faces like a curtain as he pulls my mouth back to his, his other hand moving between us to position himself beneath me.

We move together, my body sinking down onto him as he pushes up into me. His mouth breaks from mine for a moment, and he inhales sharply before letting out a moan, resuming our kiss. We find our rhythm, savoring the feeling of him filling me completely.

As he nears his climax, he flips us over, his thrusts becoming faster, deeper, more urgent. I feel him tense, his body tightening as he throbs inside me, groaning as his release overtakes him. He captures my mouth with his once more, our kiss sealing the moment.

When he finally collapses beside me, his hand lazily tracing patterns across my body, he whispers with a hint of humor, "Yeah, I missed you."

We don't have much time to linger in the afterglow. Tom texts Cole about dinner plans, reminding us that we need to meet him soon. I quickly get dressed, stealing a quick kiss from Cole before slipping back to my room to freshen up for dinner.

A little while later, I meet both Tom and Cole by the elevators, and we head out together. We're seated at a four-top in the restaurant, with me positioned between Cole and Tom. The atmosphere feels strained, awkward. Tom was with us at the Christmas party in Columbus, but aside from that, we haven't seen him since Dallas. He's the only one on the team who doesn't seem to know there's something more between Cole and me.

Julio hasn't said anything to us directly, but he was in Chicago with us and likely has figured out something. Mark has been informed that he'll be trained to take Cole's place, but I'm not sure if Tom knows that. The entire situation feels tense. Tom is a nice guy, but he's not Mark or Julio, and sitting there between them, I can't shake the feeling of discomfort.

After dinner, we head back to our rooms. Almost as soon as the door closes behind me, Cole texts, letting me know he'll be over in about ten minutes. I brush my hair, kick off my shoes, and wait. When he knocks lightly, I let him in.

"Hey," he greets me with a gentle kiss on my temple. "I'm not sure how we're going to handle this weekend with Tom here," he says, brushing a stray hair from my face. "It's just... tricky."

"Yeah, me either," I admit. "You can sleep here, but we can't both walk out in the morning."

"I know," he sighs, looking a little defeated. "Maybe I'll just get up early and go on a coffee run."

"Just a few more weeks," I say softly, offering him a reassuring smile.

"I know," he murmurs, kissing me softly.

That night, he sleeps in my bed, and we cuddle, which is all I really want. In the morning, he gets up early and goes for coffee. When I step out of my room, I find him waiting outside, just like those first mornings in Dallas.

I laugh a little, taking the chai latte he hands me. "This feels like a bit of time travel."

"I know," he says with a smile. "But at least now my stomach isn't in knots with anxiety trying to figure you out."

"Aww, did I make you anxious?" I tease, leaning into him.

"Um, yeah," he admits with a grin. "As I recall, I went through an entire mini-bar in two nights."

"You made me anxious too." I smile, wrinkling my nose playfully.

We head down to breakfast, where we meet Tom a few minutes later. Over coffee, Cole outlines the plan for the conference. With a few major clients in attendance, he emphasizes the importance of showing up at the cocktail hour on Friday night. The temperature outside barely reaches twenty degrees, so we're all grateful that everything takes place within this sprawling hotel, conveniently close to the airport. The Denver skyline looms in the distance.

The first day goes smoothly. Cole and I keep our interactions professional—minimal touching and flirting, but not entirely hands-off. We make the rounds, greeting some of our major clients who are pleased to see us there in person. To our surprise, Drs. Stein and Hochner stop by, delighted to see me thriving. I hug them, expressing my gratitude for all they've done to help me get to this point.

Around four o'clock, I head up to my room to get ready for the evening, leaving Cole and Tom to tie up loose ends. I slip into my green dress—the same one I wore in Dallas—with its delicate, multi-strap shoulders and deep V-back. It's my favorite dress, both stylish and comfortable, complete with the all-important pockets. I pin my hair half-up and darken my makeup, adding the final touches just as Cole sends a message in the group chat with Tom.

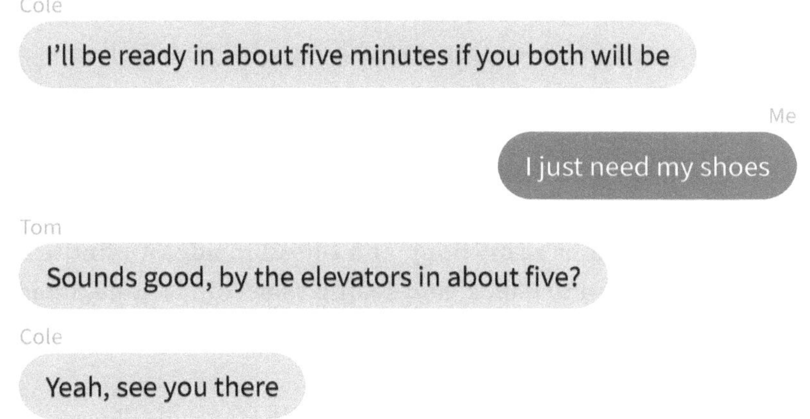

I step out of my room just as Cole exits his. He pauses for a moment, his eyes sweeping over me from head to toe.

"I remember that dress," he says with a smile that sends a flutter through me.

"I'm sure you do," I reply with a soft laugh.

"Pockets?" he asks, raising an eyebrow.

"Pockets, comfort, and no need for heels," I say with a grin.

As he closes the distance between us, he leans in, his voice low and teasing. "Don't worry, it'll look good on the floor too."

A flush of heat rises to my cheeks, and I give him a playful swat on the chest.

We wait by the elevators for Tom, who soon joins us, and then we head down together. Tom compliments my dress as well, and I realize he's only ever seen me in this one and the red one from the Christmas party.

The cocktail hour turns out to be a great move. We get to mingle with current and potential clients, and I watch as Cole turns on his charm and charisma. It warms my heart to know that this confident, charismatic man is mine. I get to see him at his most vulnerable, and even in his weaker moments, I still find him captivating.

I follow his lead, though I'm cautious after the Dr. Gabari incident. I know I'm an attractive woman, and being around the same age as most of the people we're talking to, I use that to my advantage. I ask about their families and, when appropriate, share stories about my own children. This is the first event of its kind that actually feels like what it's supposed to be—a true social hour with peers, clients, and potential clients.

One group in particular, a physician group from Denver, spends a lot of time talking with Tom. On the elevator ride back to our rooms, Tom is buzzing with energy, excited about the potential sale.

We all say goodnight at my door, and I head inside. A minute later, I crack the door open to check, and seeing that Tom is gone, I head to Cole's room and scan the key. He's tugging at his tie with one hand, and with the other, he pulls me into a hug.

"You were on fire tonight," he says, smiling down at me.

"Are you saying that as my boss or my man?" I tease.

He looks up, feigning deep thought. "Pretty sure it's both," he replies with a grin.

I laugh. "It was nice to see your charismatic sales side too."

He kisses me gently, his voice turning more seductive. "You know, I've had dreams about taking this dress off you ever since I first saw you in it."

I feel the warmth in my cheeks as I laugh softly. "Is that so?"

"Yeah," he murmurs, trailing his hand down my arm. "That night, when you called my name to tell me it had pockets, I was really hoping you'd say something else. But you were so adorable the way you said 'pockets,' I couldn't even be upset."

"I'm pretty sure I wanted to say something else that night too," I admit, smiling. "That night changed everything."

He kisses me deeply, and I feel heat and energy coursing through me. He pulls back, his eyes taking in the sight of me one more time before he slowly and gently pushes the shoulder straps of my dress aside. They slip down to my elbows. I take his hand and guide it to the side zipper, and he unzips it slowly. The dress falls to the floor, but there's a thud when it lands. Cole looks at me, puzzled.

"Pockets." I shrug with a grin. "My phone."

He chuckles softly and then tugs the strings on my backless bra, letting it fall to the floor as well. He pulls me close for another kiss, but just as our lips meet, there's a knock at the door. We both freeze, listening as the knock comes again.

"Cole? Hey, it's Tom. I just wanted to talk to you real quick."

Cole sighs, shaking his head slightly. "Fuck," he whispers under his breath. "Let me talk to him, see if I can get him to leave."

I nod, and Cole calls out, "Hold on, Tom. Just a second."

Quickly, I kick my dress and bra out of sight, hiding them behind Cole's suitcase, and tiptoe toward the bathroom. On my way, I grab one of his button-down shirts from the closet and slip into the bathroom, closing the door gently behind me. I hear Cole clear his throat, trying to sound normal.

"Hey, Tom," he says, his voice steady. "What's up?"

"I just heard from the chief medical officer of that practice—they want to have dinner with us Sunday night," Tom says, sounding excited. I hear the door close behind him.

Fuck. He's in the room.

"Really?" Cole responds, maintaining his calm. "That's great. You should set that up."

"Definitely, but I wasn't sure what your and Autumn's plans were for flying home," Tom continues.

"I fly home Monday midday, and I think Autumn flies home Monday morning," Cole says.

I pull Cole's shirt over my shoulders, buttoning it up quickly. Even though no one can see me, I feel exposed and vulnerable.

"Let me call her real quick, and let's get on the same page," Tom says.

"Really, Tom, we can talk to her about it tomor—" Cole starts, but he's cut off by the sound of my phone vibrating against the wall where I left it on the floor.

Fuck, fuck.

"Do you need to get it?" Tom asks.

"No, it can wait," Cole says, trying to keep the situation under control. "Look, let's just talk to Autumn in the morning. I'm sure she can do whatever you plan with them."

"I just want to make sure. I'll try once more," Tom insists.

I roll my eyes so hard I'm sure the entire world could feel it, and then my phone starts vibrating again.

And then, everything unravels.

"Isn't that your phone?" I hear Tom ask.

The vibrations stop, and I can practically feel the pieces clicking together in Tom's mind. I know Cole's phone is on the dresser by the TV, and if my phone is the one vibrating...

"Cole," Tom says, his voice laced with shock. "Isn't that Autumn's dress? What the fuck is going on?"

Fuck, fuck, fuck.

"Look, Tom," Cole begins, his tone steady but pleading. "I can explain. This has been going on for a while. I'm transitioning to a new position soon. Just, please, don't overreact."

"Overreact?" Tom's voice rises in anger. "This is totally unethical. Is she here now? She has to be—where are you hiding her?"

"Tom," Cole's voice shifts to something more authoritative, "I'm sorry if this is disconcerting for you."

"Disconcerting? Seriously?" Tom snaps. "It's unprofessional, unethical, and immoral."

Fuck, I can't let Cole handle this alone. I'm a consenting adult, and I need to face this with him.

"Tom, let's calm down and talk about this," Cole says, trying to defuse the situation.

"Cole, you've got to be fucking kidding me," Tom growls.

I take a deep breath and step out of the bathroom, wearing just Cole's shirt, which luckily falls to mid-thigh, and my thong. Tom's back is to me.

"Tom," I say calmly. Cole shakes his head slightly at me, his eyes closing as Tom turns to face me. I lean against the bathroom door. "No one is kidding you. I'm sorry to put you in this position, but as Cole said, he's transitioning to a new role soon. We're both consenting adults."

Tom glares at me, his expression a mix of disbelief and contempt. He turns back to Cole, shaking his head. "Unbelievable," he mutters before storming out, the door slamming shut behind him.

CHAPTER FIFTY-TWO

THE FALLOUT

"Fuck, fuck, fuck," Cole mutters, his voice low but tense as he runs his hands through his hair, pacing the room. I walk toward him and wrap my arms around his waist, trying to ground him.

"Cole, just call Pete. Take a deep breath and call him," I say softly, my voice steady even as my heart races.

He slowly wraps his arms around me, pulling me close. "You should've stayed in the bathroom," he murmurs, his voice heavy with regret.

"Cole, he saw my dress on your floor—the same dress he saw me wearing ten minutes ago. It was over the moment he walked in, whether he saw me or not," I reply, trying to reassure him. He kisses my forehead before grabbing his phone.

"I know, but you didn't need to subject yourself to it," he confesses, and I realize that his statement was more about protecting me than changing the outcome.

It's nearly midnight in Columbus, and Cole knows Pete is probably asleep. The call goes to voicemail, so he tries Laura instead. She answers and hands the phone to Pete.

"Pete, you're going to want to kill me," Cole begins, pausing to gather his thoughts. "No, no, maybe not kill me, but probably close. Tom just... completely caught us—me and Autumn."

There's a long pause as Cole listens to Pete's response, his face tense. Then he explains everything that happened, every detail. I feel exposed, vulnerable, but I understand why he needs to be thorough.

"Okay, I get it," Cole says, nodding. "Call me back in the morning. But we still have two more days of the conference." He glances at me, his eyes heavy with concern. "I'll tell her," he says after another pause. "Yeah, I don't know what else to say. I'm so sorry, Pete."

He hangs up, tossing his phone onto the bed, then runs a hand over his face, his frustration palpable. I move to stand in front of him, gently running my fingers through his hair as he wraps his arms around my thighs.

"Talk to me," I say gently, wanting to ease his burden.

"Pete's going to message Lauryn and Andy tonight to try to get ahead of whatever Tom might say or do, but it's late, so there's only so much he can do right now," Cole sighs. "Pete wants you to work the booth alone for the next two days. He thinks it's the best way to keep the conference running smoothly and keep Tom away from both of us, without it looking like Pete is giving either of us—or Tom—special treatment."

Cole takes a deep breath. "He's going to text Tom and tell him that he's investigating the situation. You'll handle the rest of the conference, and we'll reconvene on Monday."

"What do I need to do?" I ask, my voice calm.

"Nothing," Cole replies, looking up at me. "Like I said from the start, there's no policy against you having a relationship with someone you work with. The issue is with me and my subordinates."

"And what do you need to do?" I press gently.

"I'll probably have to catch a flight home Sunday, maybe even Saturday, and be in Columbus on Monday. Pete will let me know in the morning. He's got a lot of damage control to do, not just with HR but also with Rich. He needs to get ahead of whatever Tom might do."

I sit down next to him on the bed, curling one leg under me. "I'm sorry," I say softly, my heart aching for him.

"I knew I was playing with fire," he says, his voice filled with a mix of regret and resignation. "We were so close to the finish line—I thought we'd make it."

Looking over at me, a small smile tugs at the corners of his mouth. "You do look pretty hot in my shirt."

I glance down at myself and smile. "I'm kind of surprised this is the first time I've ended up like this," I say, then look back at him, concern creasing my brow. "Are you okay?"

"Not really," he admits, his voice heavy with the weight of the situation. "But hopefully, Pete will have some news tomorrow that takes some of the pressure off." He reaches over, gently running his fingers over the sleeve of his shirt that I'm wearing.

"Should I go back to my room?" I ask, knowing the answer but needing to hear it from him.

"At this point, it doesn't really matter," Cole sighs, his voice softening. "I'd prefer you stay."

"Me too," I say, wrinkling my nose in agreement. "Especially if you have to be in Columbus for the week."

Cole pulls me closer, his fingers tracing the curve of my cheekbone before he leans in and kisses me, a kiss that promises comfort in the storm we're facing together.

Cole and I spend the night wrapped up in each other, finding comfort in the closeness we both desperately need. It's not the night we'd planned, but it's what we need right now. By the time we wake up the next morning, Pete has answers—it's Saturday, but since our entire corporate office is on Eastern Time, the day has already begun for them. Cole receives a text from Pete asking him to call, and when Cole asks if he can put Pete on speakerphone, Pete agrees, making me a part of the conversation.

"Okay," Pete begins with a sigh, "I went out on a limb here. I told them you had informed me about your relationship, which is true. I also said that because we were planning for your succession to the CXO position, we saw this as a natural end to any HR concerns, and *I* made the decision not to escalate it further, which is also true." He pauses, his tone serious. "So, Cole, I just need you to know that while I didn't lie, I kind of threw myself under the bus with this."

"I understand," Cole replies, regret lacing his voice. "Pete—"

"Cole, it's fine. We both made adult decisions," Pete cuts him off. "I talked to Rich this morning, and I'm okay with how things are playing out. I think you'll be okay too. But, Autumn, let me tell you what I need from you first."

"Okay," I say, my voice smaller than I intend. Cole reaches over, taking my hand and gently rubbing his thumb over the back of it.

"Autumn, I need you to run the booth today and tomorrow like nothing is going on," Pete instructs. "If anyone asks, say there was a work emergency that pulled Cole and Tom away. Did you meet anyone from that local practice Tom mentioned?"

"Yeah, I met a couple of them, but I didn't do much talking," I admit.

"Alright, if they come by the booth, let them know that I'll personally set up a dinner with them in Denver later this week or next. I've already reached out to Tom's contact, but I haven't heard back yet."

"Okay," I respond, trying to stay composed.

"Autumn, really, what Cole and I need from you is to keep doing your job as usual," Pete says, his tone reassuring.

"I get it. I can do that," I manage to say, adding a small smile at the end.

"Good, I'm sure you can," Pete says, pausing briefly before continuing. "Cole, here's the deal—and Autumn, this doesn't really impact you, but you can hear it because Cole will probably tell you anyway." Cole gives me a small shrug. "Cole, I need you to get home—either tomorrow or even today. I don't know if they'll want you in Columbus on Monday, but it's best to be prepared. Full transparency, probably too much transparency, but Tom was very vocal in his report of the situation. He emailed everyone on the executive team, and I'm really glad I copied Rich on my message last night."

"Everyone?" Cole asks, his voice tightening.

"All nine of them, plus he copied all of HR and everyone under Andy."

"Fuck, Pete, I'm so sorry," Cole says, frustration evident in his voice.

"Well, he also accused me of giving you special treatment, so I guess he wanted everyone to see that," Pete says with a hint of exasperation. "And, sorry, Autumn, for the language, but when I called him this morning—Lauryn was on the line too—he told me, 'You better not let that little bitch have my commission.'" Cole shakes his head, rolling his eyes. "So, clearly, he's not in a productive headspace."

"Wow," Cole mutters, disbelief in his voice. "I can see him being pissed at me, but Autumn didn't do anything."

"He seems to think you've been helping her bump her sales and giving her leads you're not sharing with the rest of the team."

"Pete, that's bullshit," Cole snaps, running his fingers through his hair.

"I know it is," Pete replies calmly, "but now we have to navigate the HR and legal protocols. Honestly, I really *do* think this will turn out okay. HR and Rich weren't upset with me for keeping this under wraps—they understood my reasoning. Legal might review it today, but we probably won't have more information until Monday. That's all I can tell you for now."

"Okay," Cole says, looking at me with a mixture of concern and resignation. "I'll check flights and keep you posted."

"I will too. And, Autumn?" Pete adds.

"Yeah?"

"Call me tonight with any updates from the conference and the usual numbers that Cole would have reported. It's just you now, so you'll need to handle that."

"Okay, I can do that," I reply, trying to keep my voice steady.

We say our goodbyes, and Cole turns to me, a mix of worry and weariness in his eyes.

"I really think it's going to be alright," I say, trying to project optimism. "It's just going to be bumpy for a few days, maybe weeks."

"You're so optimistic," he says with a faint smile that doesn't quite reach his eyes. "I wish I could have that kind of outlook."

I pull him into a long hug, followed by an even longer kiss. He decides to stay at the hotel for the night to be with me but checks out of his room so it won't be a company expense.

As he holds me close, I can feel the weight of the uncertainty pressing on us both, but in this moment, all I want is to hold on to him, to remind him that we're in this together.

Running the booth by myself feels a bit strange, but it goes smoothly. When Tom's sales lead practice comes by, they've already spoken with Pete, but I still spend time chatting with them, making sure to charm them as best I can.

Midday, I get a text from Cole letting me know his flight is scheduled for four o'clock on Sunday, which means I won't see him again after I leave the room tomorrow morning. It's a bittersweet realization.

That night, we order room service and spend our time together, just loving and reassuring each other. There's a quiet intensity in the way we connect, knowing that the next few days will be uncertain. When I leave the room on Sunday morning, Cole kisses me deeply, a kiss filled with both hope and worry. I can feel the weight of what's ahead as I walk out, leaving him to pack while I head to work the last day of the conference alone.

After the booth is cleaned up, packed, and ready to ship, I head back to my room and call Pete. Cole is probably still in the air. I give Pete my report for the day, and he offers more encouraging words, reassuring me that everything will turn out okay.

Later, Cole calls me when he's in his car in Indianapolis.

"Hey, you," I answer.

"Hey," he says, his voice tired but steady. "Just wanted you to know I made it back okay. Still have to drive home, though, and there's no plan for tomorrow yet, so I'll probably sleep like shit."

"Me too," I admit softly. "I'm sorry."

"None of this is your fault, Autumn. It's okay. *We'll* be fine, no matter what happens."

"I know we will. I love you."

"Love you too. I'll call you when I get home."

And he does. We talk through different scenarios, including the possibility of him losing his job. By the end of the conversation, I feel like we've prepared for almost every situation—except the one we end up facing.

The next morning, I notice our usual call is missing from the calendar, replaced by one at the same time without Cole or Tom, but with Pete and Lauryn instead. Anxiety creeps in as I prepare to join, but I push it aside, trying to act as normal as possible. I'm grateful to still be included, though I know this won't be easy. When I log on, Mark and Pete are already there. Pete greets me with his usual demeanor.

"Hi, Autumn," Pete says, his tone familiar.

"Good morning, guys," I reply, forcing a smile. Mark gives me a supportive nod.

Even though I'm dreading being on camera, knowing that Mark, Tara, and Pete are on my side brings a small measure of comfort. In the next few seconds, Tara, Julio, and Lauryn join the call. After some brief pleasantries, Lauryn starts the meeting.

"Alright, let's get started," Lauryn says, her tone professional. "I know meetings like this can make people nervous, but I'm here to support Pete and answer any questions he can't."

Julio raises an eyebrow, sensing the tension. "Well, this doesn't sound good," he comments, and I swallow hard.

"This isn't an easy discussion," Pete says, his voice steady but serious. "I just need you all to trust me right now." He pauses, and the silence hangs heavy. "First, I have an announcement. Both Cole and Tom are on administrative leave for now, and it could be for several weeks. In the meantime, the four of you will report directly to me. Lauryn will update the system this morning."

Pausing again, he takes a sip of his coffee. "I know this is sudden, but I'm in touch with Cole about some pending matters, so I may need to reach out with some sales leads that I'll hand off to you."

Pete's expression grows more somber as he continues. "I also need you all to refrain from contacting either Cole or Tom. I know your team is close, and that might be difficult, but it's crucial that you remain radio silent with them until we get this sorted out."

This better not fucking apply to me.

Lauryn steps in, her voice firm but gentle. "There's an HR investigation in progress. I don't want any of you to make assumptions or assign blame, but it's vital that you don't reach out to either of them. If they contact you, please don't respond. We're trying to contain this situation and prevent it from escalating."

Mark, Julio, and Tara look shocked, while I drop my face into my hands, trying to process why I'm not on administrative leave too.

"Our calendars are up to date," Pete adds, "so if you need to talk privately with Lauryn or me, schedule some time. Just keep in mind we can't discuss the details of what's happening."

"Any questions?" Lauryn asks.

We all shake our heads, too stunned to speak.

"Alright then," Pete says, "that's all for now. Please keep this to yourselves—clients and other departments don't need to be involved. As far as anyone else is concerned, Cole and Tom are simply on leave. Autumn, can you stay on with Lauryn and me for a few minutes?"

"Yeah," I reply quietly, nodding.

"Okay, the rest of you are free to go. We'll be in touch," Pete says.

The others drop off the call, leaving just the three of us. Lauryn speaks first.

"Autumn, I know this is difficult for you," she begins gently. "I have a couple of questions I need to ask, even though Pete has already provided some answers."

"Okay," I say, my voice barely audible.

"Was your relationship with Cole consensual?" she asks.

I nod firmly. "Yes, completely consensual."

"And there were no promises made in exchange for favors, promotions, or raises?" Lauryn continues while Pete drops his head slightly.

"No, Lauryn, nothing like that," I respond, a bit stunned by the question.

"I'm sorry, Autumn, but I have to ask," Lauryn says, pausing. "I also need to inform you that the no-contact rule applies to you as well."

Fuck.

"Cole has been told the same thing. Violating this could impact the outcome of the investigation and, more importantly, his job. Do you understand?"

A tear slips down my cheek, and I wipe it away quickly. "Yes, I understand."

"Autumn, I'm truly sorry, but we have to follow the rules," Lauryn says, her tone softening.

"I get it," I say, holding back more tears.

"That's all I needed from you," Lauryn says.

"Can I ask a question?" I say, trying to steady my voice.

"Of course," Lauryn replies.

"This might sound ungrateful, but why am I not on administrative leave?"

"Because, in this situation, you're considered a victim," Lauryn explains gently. "Even though I know you don't feel like one, you didn't do anything wrong. Cole, however, did, according to company policy."

"Can you tell me why Tom is on administrative leave?" I ask, a note of confusion in my voice.

"I can't give specifics," Lauryn says carefully, "but it's related to this situation."

"Okay," I nod.

"Please reach out to me if you need anything," Lauryn offers.

"I will. Is that all?" I ask.

"Actually, Autumn, could you stay on with me for a minute after Lauryn drops off?" Pete asks, and I see a brief flash of confusion on Lauryn's face before she masks it.

Though I'm on the verge of breaking down, I agree. "Sure, that's fine. Thanks, Lauryn."

"Goodbye, Autumn," she says, then exits the call, leaving just Pete and me.

"Autumn, I just wanted to talk to you for a minute. I wish we could do this in person." He runs his hand down his face, and holds his chin. "I am putting myself at risk here, I need you to know that."

I nod, unable to stop more tears from falling.

"Tom is on administrative leave because he made threats—it's either Cole or him. He essentially gave us an ultimatum—fire Cole, or he'll quit and likely sue us. So, we put him on leave while we investigate," Pete explains.

"Okay," I whisper, trying to absorb the information.

"Autumn, I need you to trust me. You know I care about Cole like family, right?" he asks, his voice sincere.

"I do," I reply, my voice shaky.

"I'm going to find a way to make this right, but I need you and Cole to follow HR's rules. It's crucial that Cole, especially, shows he can comply with what's being asked of him," Pete says, his tone urgent.

"Okay," I say, my voice cracking. "Pete?"

"Yeah, Autumn?"

Another tear slips out. "How is this going to impact his move to the new position?"

"I honestly don't know," Pete admits. "But Rich is on your side. He's even talking about changing the policy—he thinks it's outdated and archaic. He believes consenting adults shouldn't have to worry about their jobs. I think it'll be okay, but I don't know for sure, and I can't say when I'll have a clear answer."

"How long do you think this will take?" I ask, needing some sense of a timeline.

"I'm hoping just a week or two, but a lot depends on Tom," Pete says, and I look at him, confused. "I think they're going to try to settle with him."

"Like, pay him off?" I ask, letting out a small laugh despite the tension.

"Not exactly how the lawyers would phrase it," Pete says, managing a slight smile, though it doesn't reach his eyes. "But that's the general idea."

I feel a bit of relief wash over me. It means they're trying to protect Cole, and I'll confirm that with Alex later.

"You have my number, right?" Pete asks.

"I do," I reply.

"And Laura's?"

"Yeah, I have hers too," I say.

"Good. Please reach out if you need anything. I know it might be easier to talk to Laura, but trust me to make this right," Pete says, his tone reassuring.

"I'll try to be patient," I promise.

"Take care, Autumn. If you need a day or two off, just take it. You don't need to use your PTO—just take care of yourself and text me if you'll miss any meetings."

"Thank you, Pete. I really appreciate that," I say sincerely.

We say our goodbyes, and I exit the meeting. As soon as I close my laptop, I drop my face into my hands and let the tears flow. After a few moments, I pull myself together and text Cara.

Me

Hey, you busy?

Cara

Unfortunately, yes, with a client for another hour or so

Me

Can we do a girls' night either tonight or tomorrow?

I look at my phone. I know what they said, but seriously, I have to just reach out. I open my thread with Cole.

I don't expect him to text me back—he's a rule follower through and through. I don't want to tempt him into doing something that could make things worse, but I just needed to tell him I love him.

After sending the message, I text Pete to let him know I'm going to take some time today. He responds quickly, saying it's fine, and I head upstairs to my bedroom. Curling up in bed, I let the exhaustion wash over me and fall asleep almost instantly.

I sleep through most of the day and all night, waking up with a heavy realization: I'm seriously depressed. I hope it's just temporary, something I can shake off, but, because of my history, I know I'll need to keep an eye on it.

The next morning, I drag myself out of bed and dive into a couple of meetings with clients. They go relatively well, and I start to realize that maybe what I need right now is to try to maintain some sense of normalcy. It's not easy, but it's a start.

I notice a few missed texts and a missed call from Tara that I've been avoiding. Part of me has been too overwhelmed to deal with it, but I know I can't keep putting her off. With a deep breath, I decide it's time to reach out.

Me

Hey, sorry I didn't get back to you earlier, you have a minute now?

Tara

I do, I have about an hour

When Tara answers my call, her voice is filled with concern. "Hey, Autumn."

"Hey, Tara. I'm sorry I didn't get back to you yesterday. I just needed to breathe for a bit," I say, trying to keep my voice steady.

"I get it, but that's why I was trying to reach out," she says, her words coming out in a rush. "I just wanted to make sure you're okay. I mean, I know I don't know all the details about you and Cole, but, c'mon, I know there's something there. I don't know if this had anything to do with you, but I was worried about you."

"Tara, I'm holding up for now, but this is tough. I'm not sure if I'll be okay for long," I admit, feeling a bit more vulnerable than I intended.

"You two can't talk to each other, can you?" she asks gently.

"No, that's what they told us. And Cole hasn't reached out, so it's clear we really can't even console each other," I sigh, the weight of it settling in again.

"Do you know what this has to do with Tom?" Tara asks, her curiosity piqued.

"I know, but I can't share that right now. I'm sorry," I say, hating that I have to keep things from her.

"Well, someday you'll be able to tell me," she says, her voice soft and understanding. "Are you still planning to come to San Francisco?"

"Pete hasn't told me otherwise," I say, "and of course, I'll be at the wedding."

"That's not optional, Autumn," she laughs, the sound a bit of lightness in a heavy day.

We wrap up our conversation and get back to our workdays. Tara checks in on me frequently, and I'm grateful for her support. I end up handing over some of my sales calls to her because there's just work I can't focus on right now.

Later, Cara arrives with ice cream and pizza, her usual way of cheering me up.

"Hey, my favorite bitch," she greets me as she walks in.

I hug her tightly, then fill her in on everything that's been going on.

"Wait, so you're not allowed to talk to each other? That's so fucked up," she says, her disbelief mirroring my own.

"Yep, I agree. I'm just hoping it all blows over in a few days." I shrug, trying to stay optimistic.

"Well, I'm here for you, however long it takes," Cara says with a reassuring smile.

"I know, and I love you for it." I smile back, feeling a little lighter.

"Did you tell Alex?" she asks.

"Actually, no, I probably should. I meant to ask him about it."

"Uh, yeah, you should. Also, that's weird, Autumn," Cara says, giving me a questioning look.

"What do you mean?" I ask, puzzled.

"You tell Alex everything almost as soon as it happens. Why not this?"

"I don't know. Yesterday I slept all day, and today I was busy with work. But you're right, it is kind of weird I haven't told him," I laugh, realizing she's got a point.

We spend the evening eating pizza, indulging in ice cream, and laughing. Cara's presence is good for my soul. She leaves around nine, needing to get some rest before work the next day. After she's gone, I decide it's time to call Alex.

"Hey, baby sister," he answers, his tone instantly comforting.

"Hey," I reply, my voice softer than usual.

"What's wrong?" he asks, picking up on my mood immediately.

"That obvious?" I ask, trying to laugh it off.

"I've known you since you were born, so yeah, it's that obvious."

I take a deep breath and tell him everything—about Denver, the conversations with Pete and Lauryn, the team meeting, and the separate talks that followed.

"Autumn, I know it's not what you want to hear, but you need to listen to them," Alex says, his voice firm but kind. "And if it helps, if I were in Cole's shoes and it was me and Claire, I'd do the same. So if you're thinking about being mad at him, please don't. Honestly, Autumn, I like the guy, and I think he'll do whatever it takes to make this right for both of you, even if it feels awful right now."

"I know," I say, my voice tinged with resignation. "He trusts Pete so much, and he's the kind of guy who follows the rules. I just miss him."

"I get it, I really do. Hopefully, this is resolved soon. It sounds like this is more about Tom than Cole."

"That's how it sounded to me too," I sigh, the uncertainty still gnawing at me.

"There's not much you can do other than what you're already doing. But keep me posted, okay? If there's anything I can do..."

"Thanks, Alex. I'll keep you updated."

We exchange goodbyes, and just after we hang up, I get a text from him.

Alex

Chin up baby sister - it'll be okay

I open my thread with Cole, he did read my last message. He left me on read, but he did read it. I take a chance; it has been about thirty-six hours since the last message I sent.

I go to bed that night, but I can't sleep. The next few nights, I don't sleep well. I reach out to Pete and he says he has no update on the timeline.

On Friday, I finally call my doctor and schedule an appointment. When I see her, she listens carefully, her concern evident in the way she studies me. After nearly twenty-five years as my physician, she knows me well—she's the same doctor who helped me through my separation from Steve. Back then, she prescribed me an antidepressant and something to help me sleep, which I ended up taking for about two years.

Now, she prescribes the same medications, but with the reassurance that this time it will likely be much shorter. She knows me well enough to recognize that I'm in a rough spot, and she doesn't want me to struggle unnecessarily. Her support feels like a lifeline, reminding me that it's okay to ask for help, even when I think I should be stronger.

CHAPTER FIFTY-THREE
THE LUNCH & THE SAN FRANCISCO CONFERENCE

The meds help. The tears come less often, and I finally manage to get some sleep. I spend the next week burying myself in work, reading, and cleaning the house—anything to keep my mind occupied. Then, on Friday, I get an unexpected phone call from Pete's wife, Laura.

"This is Autumn," I answer, a little surprised.

"Hi, Autumn, it's Laura, Pete's wife," she says, her tone carrying a hint of uncertainty, like she's not sure how I'll react.

"Hi, Laura. How are you?" I ask, trying to sound more composed than I feel.

"I'm good, but more importantly, how are you? This whole thing must be so hard," she replies, her concern clear.

"I'm hanging in there," I admit, taking a deep breath. "But it hasn't been easy."

"I can only imagine," she says softly. "Listen, I'm going to be driving through your area tomorrow on my way to St. Paul. I was wondering if you'd like to have lunch? Maybe I can give you a little insider information—and an ear if you need one."

"Laura, that sounds great. Just let me know the time and place," I say, feeling a slight sense of relief at the thought of talking to someone who understands.

"Okay, great. I'll text you the details either tonight or in the morning," she says.

"Alright, I'll see you tomorrow," I reply, hanging up and feeling oddly reassured.

The next day, I meet her at a charming little café near Madison. I figure I can visit Kevin afterward. As soon as I see her and she pulls me into a hug, I feel tears sting my eyes, but I manage to keep them at bay. After we order, she dives right into the reason she's here.

"Autumn, are you really okay?" she asks, her eyes searching mine.

"No." I laugh to keep from crying and shrug. "I miss him."

"I'm sure you do," she says sympathetically. "I haven't spoken to him, but Pete has, and I don't think he's doing very well either. But I know he trusts Pete."

"Do you know anything? About the timeline or what's happening?" I ask, needing any piece of information.

"Yeah, that's part of why I wanted to see you," she says, taking a sip of water. "The lawyers are deep in negotiations with Tom and his legal team. Tom's only a couple of years away from retirement, but he's claiming that you received special treatment. Pete says if anything, it was the opposite—probably trying to overcompensate for the relationship. But these things take time. Contracts go back and forth with no set deadlines. It's just a waiting game right now."

"What are the chances Cole could lose his job or the promotion?" I ask, the question heavy with worry.

"Slim to none, according to Pete. But until it's all settled, there's always a chance," she says, sighing before taking a bite of her food.

"I know he could find another job, but he's worked so hard here for so many years," I say, my voice wavering. "I don't know how he'd handle it if he lost that."

"Autumn," she says, her tone thoughtful, "I think it would be harder for him to lose you." She smiles softly. "At the Christmas party, the way you two were together—God, it looked like you were always meant to be. I know you did a good job of not being inappropriate, but I'm pretty sure you'd be an even more impressive couple if you weren't holding back. You two are the stuff fairytales are made of."

I feel my eyes start to burn again. "It certainly felt like a fairytale, at least until two weeks ago."

"I don't think what happened in Denver changes that," she says gently. "You're a reader, right? Cole mentioned that to Pete. I teach creative writing, and I think this is just the 'ordeal/darkest night' part of your hero's journey."

I laugh softly. "I would've thought the ordeal was Dr. Gabari and all that insanity—or maybe Cole's crazy ex-wife—but I can see that."

"I think those were your 'tests, allies, and enemies.' This is the last challenge you have to face before you can finally be happy," she says with a smile. "In a month, Cole won't be your boss. This will blow over. Dr. Gabari is behind bars, and you two can finally be the power couple you're meant to be."

"I hope your optimistic outlook comes true," I say, smiling through the anxiety. "I'm so tired of feeling like I'm living in a soap opera."

Laura laughs. "Soap operas are just endless cycles of the second act of the hero's journey. You need to get to the third act," she says with a wink, making me laugh.

"Tell me about Cole before I knew him," I say, curious to hear more about the man I love.

"He's always been a gentleman, a sweetheart," she begins, her voice warm with fondness. "I met him a little over twenty years ago, back when Michelle was pregnant with Matthew. We were at a company picnic, and Cole was a good father, a good husband—honestly, too good for Michelle. Nothing he did was ever enough for her, even in front of others. I can only imagine how much worse it was behind closed doors."

She pauses to take a few bites of her meal, then continues. "The divorce was rough on him, whether it was the betrayal or just the process itself. He was too nice to her, even then. He let her keep everything and lived with furniture he found on the side of the road.

When he finally bought his house a few years later, Pete was so happy for him."

"It's a really nice house, and he's so humble about it," I say, smiling at the memory of Cole showing me around.

"Right? I helped him pick out his kitchen appliances during the build," she says with a grin. "But after the divorce, he was just a shell of who he used to be. It always made me sad because Michelle wasn't worth that. He should've been celebrating being free of her. He was still a great dad, but he threw himself into work, nonstop, for years. I'd ask him about dating, and he'd just say he wasn't interested, that women weren't worth it."

She shrugs, then adds, "At company events, he'd smile and seem happy, but compared to how he is with you, it was all a mask. There was no light in his eyes when he smiled or laughed. That first time we met you in Chicago, he had changed—everything about him had changed."

Laura pauses, thinking about how to put it into words. "Before, he was polite and businesslike, charming and charismatic in that perfect sales mode. But with you... it's like he's whole again. There's light in his eyes. Even when he was angry at Gabari, he was so focused on you. And at the Christmas party—I don't know how either of you kept your composure, but you did. Pete was just waiting for one of you to slip, but you didn't. I'm sure once you got out of the public eye, though, he probably had you out of that dress so fast," she says, laughing.

I blush and laugh with her. "Laura! But yeah, it was a good night," I admit, smiling even more. "That's not an area where we're lacking."

"Well, enjoy it," she says with a smile. "Because, you know, as you get older, it's just not the same. It slows down."

"You and Pete still have a lot of chemistry—I can see it," I say.

"We never had anything on you two. You two have that fairytale kind of chemistry, the kind most of us never find," she says.

"It feels that way. We were just drawn to each other. There was no fighting it, for either of us," I say, laughing at the memory of how inevitable it all felt.

We finish our lunch, chatting about our kids and getting to know each other better. When we walk out to our cars, Laura gives me a warm hug and tells me to call her anytime. As I drive away, I feel infinitely better about everything. This lunch was one of the best things I've done for myself in a long time.

After lunch, I head to Kevin's apartment. I've only been there a few times since he usually comes home, but today it feels right to visit him. Kalisha is working, so it's just the two of us, and we have a nice dinner together. It's a good distraction, and it's rare to have this time alone with him. That night, I sleep better than I have in weeks.

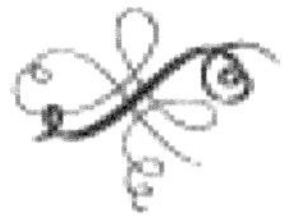

Being alone in the house on Sunday feels like a weight pressing down on me. I try to keep busy, tackling housework and losing myself in a book, but it doesn't take long before I start spiraling again. I tell myself that a shower will help, that the warm water will wash away the heaviness clinging to me, but it doesn't. Instead, I find myself sitting on the shower floor, tears mixing with the water streaming down my face. Even with the meds, I can't stop the flood of emotions.

The water turns cold before I finally force myself to stand up. I wrap myself in a towel and head to the bed, not even bothering to get dressed. I just lie there, letting the exhaustion pull me under until I drift off to sleep.

When I wake up in the middle of the night, the house is dark and silent, the kind of silence that makes everything feel even more empty. I know I shouldn't, but the need for some kind of connection, some reminder that I'm not completely alone, is too strong. I reach for my phone, open my text messages, and scroll down until I find Cole's name.

The screen glows softly in the darkness as I hover over his name, my thumb hesitating for a moment. I know I shouldn't contact him, but the longing to hear from him, to feel connected to him in some way, is overpowering. Finally, I give in and type out a simple message.

Me

> I miss you so much, I love you

He reads my message right away, and my heart skips a beat. It's one in the morning here, two for him. My heart aches, picturing him struggling not to respond. I can almost see him, the way his hands hover over the phone, the familiar furrow in his brow as he fights the urge to reach out.

Despite the silence, I feel an intense connection to him, even though the message goes unanswered.

The next day, I ask Kevin to reach out to him and Megan to reach out to Matthew, hoping for some word. Megan tells me later that Matthew confirmed Cole is alive and that he sees him daily, but that's all he can say. It's not much, but it's something, a small piece of comfort. Kevin doesn't get a response.

Wednesday arrives, and I pack my bags, getting ready for the whirlwind trip to San Francisco for a conference, followed by time with Alex in Portland, and finally, Tara's wedding. I'll be gone for almost two weeks, and the thought of holding myself together for that long feels overwhelming, but I have no choice.

Early Thursday morning, I drive to Chicago for my flight—there are no nonstops out of Milwaukee. I park my car and check in my three suitcases, prepared for the long trip ahead. I sleep through the entire five-hour flight, exhaustion catching up with me. When I land, I'm relieved to see a text from Tara. She's waiting for me at baggage claim, ready to share a ride to the hotel. The hug she gives me is warm and reassuring, and I cling to that comfort.

At the hotel, we meet Mark for dinner. He doesn't bring up Cole, and I'm grateful. We talk about the conference, work, and Tara's wedding instead. I appreciate that they both steer clear of topics that could unravel me emotionally. I know they're aware of what's going on—Tara more than Mark—but they respect my need for normalcy.

The conference is intense, busier than any I've attended before. Friday night, we're all exhausted, and we agree to skip the Meet and Greet. Saturday is just as hectic; I'm grateful for it. After a quick dinner at the hotel, Mark heads up to his room early, leaving Tara and me some time alone.

"You hanging in there, Autumn?" Tara asks, her eyes full of concern.

"By a thread," I admit with a tired smile.

"You haven't heard from him at all?" Her surprise is genuine.

"No, nothing. The only update I have is through Matthew, who told Megan that Cole's alive. I've texted him three times since that meeting with Pete and Lauryn, and he hasn't responded once. It fucking sucks, Tara. I won't lie."

"I can only imagine," she says softly. "I'm going to reach out to him. He's still RSVP'd for the wedding, and I want to confirm if he's coming, but I'm not allowed to reach out to him either. I'm sure you'd like to know too."

"I'd love to know," I say, the thought of seeing him again giving me a flicker of hope. "It would give me something to look forward to."

"You're still bringing your brother?" she asks.

"That's the plan, unless one of us gets some good news from Cole." I smile faintly.

"You're going to Alex's first, right?"

"Yeah, I'll fly to SeaTac tomorrow, and he'll pick me up and drive me to Portland. Then, we'll head up to Issaquah on Wednesday afternoon," I explain. "I feel bad for taking him away from Claire on Valentine's Day, but he says it's just one in their relationship."

Tara smiles. "It'll be hard, but hopefully, your brother will help."

"He's my rock. I'll be okay," I say, trying to convince myself as much as her.

The next day is just as busy, and I have to leave Mark and Tara to break down the booth so I can catch my flight. I feel guilty, but they reassure me it's fine. It's a rush to the airport, but I make it to the gate on time. The flight from San Francisco to Seattle is a short two hours, and I spend it aimlessly scrolling through my phone, trying to keep my mind occupied. When we land, I'm greeted by a light snowfall and a peaceful blanket of white on the ground—a stark contrast to the whirlwind inside me.

CHAPTER FIFTY-FOUR
THE BEST BROTHER & THE WEDDING

As I step off the plane at SeaTac, I feel like I'm moving in a fog. I've been here and in Portland several times since Alex moved, but today, I'm so emotionally drained that it feels like I'm floating outside of my own body.

The moment I leave the secure area and spot Alex waiting for me, I break. I hadn't expected him to come inside the airport, and the sight of him shatters me into a million pieces.

He stands there, his dark, dirty blond hair trimmed neatly as always, those warm brown eyes filled with concern. At six feet tall and built like the mountain biker he is, he's dressed in a long-sleeve button-down with casually rolled-up sleeves and slacks. It's clear he came in his church clothes. His jawline and upper lip are covered in facial hair, something new and different, but he's still the same brother I know and love.

Tears flood my eyes and spill over as I rush to him. I hug him tightly, and he just holds me, letting me finally release all the emotions I've been bottling up *for weeks*. I've been trying so hard to stay strong for my kids, to remain professional at work, to keep my composure, but now, in my brother's arms, I finally let go.

"Hey, baby sister," Alex says softly, his voice full of warmth. "Autumn, you're going to make all these people think this is either some grand reunion or that someone died," he adds with a laugh.

I manage a small laugh through my tears, pulling back to look at him. "Sorry, I've been holding it together, but you're, well, you."

He just smiles and brings me into another hug, holding me even tighter. A few minutes later, he kisses my forehead, and I wipe my eyes as we head to baggage claim. Alex spots my bags and pulls them off the belt with ease, then walks me out to his car. Because of the snow, he's driving his Infiniti SUV instead of his little Audi. He hugs me again and kisses my forehead before opening the car door for me.

As soon as we're on the freeway headed south to Portland, he glances over at me and says, "I know what you need."

I give him a puzzled look as he fiddles with the touch screen and turns up the volume. The first song that blares through the speakers is "Last Resort" by Papa Roach, and Alex immediately starts headbanging and dramatically drumming on the steering wheel. Despite myself, I laugh through the tears and start singing along.

Next up is "Paddy's Lament" by Flogging Molly, and every once in a while, Alex exaggerates singing the lyrics and playfully punches me on the shoulder. By the end of that song, I'm genuinely laughing, and my tears have dried.

For the next two hours, as we make our way to his house, the car is filled with the sounds of our favorite alternative, punk, and Irish tunes from our teens and twenties. Alex skips any ballads, keeping the energy high, and I find myself feeling lighter, more like myself.

By the time we pull into his garage, I feel almost normal again. Alex has always been so good for me, and I appreciate him more than ever. He lifts my bags out of the car and carries them to the guest house. If anyone thinks my house is big, they should see his—it's at least twice the size.

Claire meets me in the kitchen and pulls me into a tight hug. She lets me know that Kiersten will be joining us for dinner tonight and that she's planned a girls' day for Tuesday—nails, hair, massages, the works. I'm so grateful for both of them.

I apologize profusely to Claire for taking Alex away on Valentine's Day, but she waves it off. "It's just another day, Autumn. We'll be fine. I'm not lacking in any spoiling from your brother," she says with a laugh. It's true—they just returned from a week in Paris.

"Hey, Autumn?" Claire asks.

"Yeah?"

"Alex told me not to ask about Cole, but I want you to know that if you *want* to talk about it, I'm here. I didn't want you to think that I was avoiding the subject."

I'm sure my face falls a little. "I appreciate it, Claire. I might take you up on that, but not right now."

"No pressure, but I'm here," she says, reaching over to squeeze my hand.

"Thank you, Claire," I say, forcing a smile.

Dinner is pleasant, and I focus mostly on Kiersten, who's thriving in the biomedical and genetic research field. I only fully grasp about three-quarters of what she tells me, but I can tell she's passionate about it.

The next day, Claire, Kiersten, and I enjoy our spa day. While the mani/pedi is nice in preparation for the wedding, the massage is what I truly need. I've been carrying so much stress and emotion that I have to fight not to cry on the massage table. I mostly succeed, though the therapist assures me that crying during a massage is common.

Kiersten heads back to school on Tuesday night, needing to be in the lab the next morning. That evening, Claire and Alex take me to a fantastic seafood place. I'm not usually a big seafood person, but the fresh catch from the Pacific Northwest is a treat.

On Wednesday, Alex works a half day, and then we head up to Issaquah. The car ride is fun, bringing back memories of when we were teenagers or when he'd come home from college, and we'd drive around trying to find something to do. When we pull up to the hotel to check in, the person at the front desk assumes we're getting a room together.

Alex grins. "No, she's just my little, bratty sister."

I narrow my eyes at him, and he wraps an arm around me, giving me a light noogie, just like when we were kids. I laugh, genuinely, for the first time in weeks.

He tells the front desk that adjoining rooms might be good and insists on picking up the tab for both. I argue, but I don't win. They manage to get us adjoining rooms, which could be helpful if I need assistance with my dress or anything else.

As we head back out to the car to park and bring in our luggage, Alex wraps an arm around me, kisses my temple, saying, "It's nice to hear you really laugh again."

"It's nice to really laugh again," I admit, smiling up at him.

He hugs me even closer before we drag our luggage inside. He takes most of it, leaving me with just my laptop bag and the garment bag holding my bridesmaid dress.

It's almost six by the time we settle into the hotel, so Alex suggests we try the hotel restaurant for dinner. We'd seen it on the way in, and it looked nice, so I agree. We both freshen up and head downstairs.

Over dinner, Alex finally gets serious. I can tell he feels this conversation needs to happen before the wedding festivities begin.

"Autumn, really, are you doing okay?" he asks, pausing. "Is being at a wedding and doing this all on Valentine's Day going to be too hard?"

"I'm not going to lie, it's going to be hard," I admit, taking a deep breath. "Not only have I not heard from him in four weeks, but he was supposed to be here. My whole team is going to be here. It's just a giant fucking reminder."

I take a big sip of my wine.

"I know we talked about this, but I'm pretty sure, given everything I know, I would have done the same thing if I were in his shoes," Alex says, pausing to think. He reaches over and puts his hand on mine. "I don't know him as well as you do, but Autumn, I'm pretty certain he's just following the rules. And I know the rules suck royally right now." He shrugs, taking a sip of his own wine. "But that night in Chicago when he called me, I knew he loved you. I've never even seen the two of you together, but I knew. And I still believe in that. You haven't heard otherwise, and there hasn't been any resolution from anyone else at work. I think he's just following the rules."

"I know," I say, fighting the sting in my eyes. "I'm just having a hard time believing he could stay away." I swirl my wine, trying to hold back tears. "And the hardest part is that he told Matthew not to tell Megan anything. Those two are so bonded—they actually remind me of you and me." I laugh softly. "The fact that whatever he said to Matthew is stopping that communication too... I don't know." I look up, still fighting back tears. "I know we have to keep up appearances here, but are they going to pull his cell phone records?"

"Actually, if Tom takes this to court, they could," Alex says, putting his hand back on mine to get me to look at him. "I don't think they would or that it would make a difference, but they could."

"Seriously?"

"Seriously," he says, taking another sip of wine. "Cole's boss told you he had a plan and that you just needed to be patient, right?"

"Yeah," I say, poking at my food with my fork. "And I believe him. Did I tell you his wife took me out to lunch?"

"No, you didn't. Cole's boss's wife took you out to lunch?"

"Yeah, they consider him like a son or nephew or something. Pete, Cole's boss, is about twenty years older than Cole, but Cole has worked for him for almost two decades. Anyway, she took me out to lunch to check in on me in a way Pete can't and to reassure me that Pete is pretty certain they can fix this."

"Autumn, that's actually pretty nice, and it was a risk they both took," Alex says. "I really do think it'll all be okay. I just hope they can speed up the timeline," he adds with a smile.

"Yeah, me too." I pause. "Another hard thing about this weekend is that Cole is still RSVP'd as coming. He hasn't told Tara otherwise, but he's not supposed to talk to her either, so I don't know." I laugh a little. "Part of me—the part that's read too many romance novels and watches too many movies—" I stop and roll my eyes. "Never mind."

"Autumn, it's me. Just tell me."

I take another sip of wine. "There's part of me that thinks—more like wishes—he would just show up here in some grand romantic gesture. I mean, Pete said that everything would be resolved by the end of this week, so whether he still has a job or not..." I trail off and shrug.

"That might be a little wishful thinking," Alex laughs softly, "but it's also possible. I mean, if I were in his shoes, I might do that—show up and try to sweep you off your feet." He laughs again. "Not that it would take much sweeping."

"Yeah, I'm already pretty swept," I laugh.

We finish up dinner and head to bed relatively early. Back in my room, I open my text thread with Cole and see all the messages I've sent him that he hasn't responded to. It's been two weeks since I last reached out. I think about sending another, letting him know I wish he were here, but instead, I just shut off my screen. I take a shower, cry out as many tears as I can, and then take my sleeping pill and go to bed.

Thursday morning, I get up and prepare for the bridesmaids' brunch. Alex plans to work from the hotel room while I take his SUV for the morning, and then he'll join me later for the rehearsal and dinner.

The brunch is lovely, with five of us in total. Tara's sister, Julie, is her Matron of Honor, and the other bridesmaids are two cousins, a friend from Oklahoma, and me. We spend the morning getting to know each other, and I manage to sidestep questions about my significant other by mentioning that my plus-one is my brother. One of Tara's cousins asks if he's single, and that quickly changes the subject.

Tara gifts each of us a delicate silver necklace with an open-heart pendant holding a small pearl—something we'll all wear at the wedding. It's a thoughtful gift and fits my style perfectly. As we're getting ready to leave, Tara pulls me aside to check in. I tell her I'm doing better, thanks to spending time with Alex. She seems genuinely relieved.

"Have you heard from him?" I ask, trying to sound casual.

"No, he's still RSVP'd as attending. We have a place card for him," she says with a shrug, offering me a sympathetic half-hug. "I'm sorry, Autumn."

"It's okay, I'll be fine. Alex is great, and I couldn't ask for a better support system here."

She smiles and hugs me again before heading back to the hotel with Julie.

The rehearsal goes smoothly, much like the other wedding rehearsals I've been in. Alex sits in the back with some of the other significant others and plus-ones, watching quietly but always checking in with me. The rehearsal lasts about an hour, followed by a pleasant dinner where I meet more of Tara's family. There are a few heartfelt toasts, and though Alex doesn't engage much, he's a constant, reassuring presence.

As we drive back to the hotel, Alex asks if I think I'll be able to get through the wedding without crying.

"I *think* so," I say, considering it. "I can compartmentalize it. Tara and Max are great together. She's so happy, and I think she'll stay that way. I can focus on that."

"Okay, well, you know I'm here for you if you need me," he says with a smile.

"You've been my rock for a long time, Alex. There are so many times in my life when I don't know what I would do without you," I admit. "That's why I lost it at the airport—because, for the first time in *weeks*, I felt safe because you were there."

"Autumn, I'll be there for you and your kids until the day I die, but I'm ready to hand over those rock duties, and I think Cole will take them when he can," he says, glancing at me. "He's not Steve." I laugh softly at that. "Steve was more like Dad—couldn't handle shit himself and would pay someone else to do everything. Cole's a man's man, and as sexist as it sounds, I think that's what you need to feel safe. I think that's why you've always leaned on me so much, even when you were still married to Steve. Dad and Steve couldn't give you that. Kevin can, but you shouldn't lean on him unless you have to. Even with everything that's happened these last few weeks, I have a lot of respect for Cole, and I understand the decisions he's made. I just need this all to get cleared up so you can be happy."

"Me too," I laugh, though it's tinged with a bit of sadness. "And I agree with you, but first, he has to talk to me." The words sting, and my eyes start to burn. "Okay, now I'm going to cry, so let's change the subject."

Alex looks at me, then turns on the music. Blink-182's "Dammit" comes on, and we both start laughing and singing along. I'm still laughing when we get back to the hotel, grateful for my brother and the temporary relief from everything else.

The wedding day is a whirlwind. Alex plans to be there about forty-five minutes before the ceremony. He'll be sitting with Julie's husband and a few other guys he has bonded with. By noon, a team arrives to do our hair and makeup. The stylist compliments my hair, especially the color, and manages to create a beautiful updo that frames my face perfectly. We all have red and white baby's breath woven into our hair, and it looks stunning. The makeup is light, designed to bring out the teal in my eyes. They use a dark blue eyeliner that subtly enhances the blue without being too bold—it reads as gray or black from a distance. Once we're all dolled up, we help Tara into her dress.

My black bridesmaid dress has a sweetheart neckline with spaghetti straps and an asymmetrical mid-length skirt that flares slightly when I spin but isn't too full. I have a shawl for the ceremony since the dress, though not strapless, shows a lot of skin. All our dresses are similar in cut, with slight variations in the sleeves and straps, creating a cohesive look.

Helping Tara into her dress is a poignant moment for me—it makes me think of Megan and Sami someday getting married. The first look before the ceremony for pictures is sweet, something I didn't do with Steve, and it touches me in a way I didn't expect. We spend about an hour and a half taking pictures, then whisk Tara away to hide before the ceremony begins. Julie and Tara retreat to the bridal dressing room while the rest of us help seat guests, including our plus-ones, before we too slip away.

Max's cousin, acting as a wedding planner, gets us ready with our bouquets—beautiful arrangements of white and red roses tied with black ribbon. Tara's bouquet is a striking bunch of red roses with trailing black ribbons, contrasting beautifully with her white dress.

We hug Tara one last time before her dad arrives to walk her down the aisle. The procession music is an electronic remix of "Pachelbel's Canon," which I love. Max's youngest brother and I walk down the aisle together, second to last in the procession. When we reach the front, I glance at Alex, who winks at me, making me smile.

But then, as "Here Comes the Bride" begins and Tara steps into the aisle, my heart nearly stops. Beyond Tara, I see Mark and his wife, but it's the person next to them who captures my attention—Cole. Our eyes lock briefly before he looks away, and my heart races.

I try to focus on the ceremony, but my mind is in overdrive. I want to run to Cole, to jump into his arms, to kiss him. I want to tell Alex, to know if Tara noticed him. My thoughts are a jumbled mess.

I catch the vows and feel my eyes sting with emotion, but I manage to keep it together as Julie and some of the guests in the front rows tear up. The vows are sweet and romantic, and when Tara and Max finally kiss, the music swells, and we all walk back down the aisle. I glance at Cole again, managing a small smile, but he looks down and away from me, his expression unreadable, and my heart sinks. He's never looked at me like that before.

Something is wrong, and I can't shake the feeling.

The ushers start excusing the rows from the front, so Alex reaches me before Cole is even standing. I pull him aside and whisper in his ear. He smiles and jokes about my getting a romantic movie ending, but I tell him something is off.

"Alex, he wouldn't even look at me, and when he did, he didn't smile. I'm going to need to talk to him, but I don't know what's going on. Something isn't right."

"Autumn, don't overreact or overthink," he says, kissing my forehead gently.

As I turn, I see Mark and Cole leaving the ceremony area. Our eyes meet again, but Cole sets his jaw and keeps walking. I hand Alex my bouquet and shawl, asking him to place them at the head table where I'm seated. He nods, his expression concerned.

I greet Mark and his wife with hugs, trying to keep my composure, but then I look at Cole. "Hey," I say softly.

He shakes his head, not saying a word.

"Cole," I try again, fighting the urge to cry, "what's wrong?"

My heart is pounding. Everything in me wants to wrap my arms around his neck, to hold him close, but he's so distant.

"Autumn, don't," he says sternly, his voice cutting through me.

We're almost at the receiving line where Tara and Max are standing, so I step back, biting my lip to keep from crying. Cole hugs Tara and shakes Max's hand, putting on a smile that doesn't reach his eyes. Tara catches my gaze, and I shrug, unsure of what to do. She mouths, "I'm sorry," and I feel a wave of confusion wash over me.

After Cole makes it through the receiving line, I grab his wrist, sending a flurry of butterflies to my stomach. I pull him aside, determined to get some answers. "Cole, talk to me."

He looks around, avoiding my eyes. "Not here."

I have no idea what's happening. A flicker of hope rises in me—maybe he's just trying to keep his distance in public—but why would he act like this?

"Okay, give me a minute. I think I know where we can talk."

He doesn't respond, just nods and pulls his hand away from me.

What the hell is going on?

I'm barely holding back tears as I find Julie and whisper my request to use the bridal dressing room to talk to Cole. She agrees, and I signal to him, barely getting him to acknowledge me, before leading him down a back hallway. Julie walks with us, but as soon as we're out of public view, I reach for him. He flinches, the look he gives me filled with something close to hatred. The first tear I can't hold back slips down my cheek.

CHAPTER FIFTY-FIVE

THE CONFUSION & THE CONFRONTATION

We step into Tara's bridal dressing room, and Julie gives me a small, encouraging smile before she quietly shuts the door behind us. Cole walks over to the windows, his back to me. The room is heavy with unspoken tension, and I don't have the faintest idea why. I watch him, waiting for a clue, anything that might help me understand what's going on in his head.

Finally, he turns to face me, though his eyes never quite meet mine. "I thought this was special, Autumn, you and me," he says, running a hand through his hair. He crosses his arms over his chest, starting to pace, and I recognize the telltale signs of him trying to rein in some powerful emotion.

"Cole, it was special. It *is* special," I correct him, my voice soft but firm. "I don't understand why you're so upset. You're the one who hasn't responded to me."

"Dammit, Autumn," he snaps, the frustration in his voice cracking the air between us. "I couldn't respond without risking both of us. I told you I'd fall on that sword, and I meant it." He pauses, his voice lowering as if the weight of his words is too much. "I came here to tell you that Pete and I fixed everything. I wanted to surprise you, to tell you in person." He looks at me briefly before glancing away, and I can't fathom why any of this would make him angry.

Then his voice drops even lower, almost a mumble. "But I never thought you'd move on, Autumn. I never thought I'd come out here to surprise you and find—fuck." He stops, turning away to look out the window, his shoulders tense with restrained anger.

My heart sinks as I realize what he's saying. "Cole, I don't understand," I say, my voice faltering.

He turns back to me, his expression a mix of confusion and pain. "Autumn, don't look at me like that. I was going to surprise you a couple of days ago, but I saw you checking into the hotel, at the restaurant, and then here." He gestures sharply toward the door, his frustration boiling over.

Suddenly, it clicks—the hotel, the restaurant, the way Alex and I were together. Of course, Cole saw us and jumped to the worst possible conclusion. I take a slow, deliberate breath and step toward him, hands raised in a calming gesture, trying to reach him through the storm of emotions I see brewing in his eyes.

"Cole, that's Alex," I say, my voice gentle, almost pleading.

His frustration peaks as he raises his voice again. "I really don't give a fuck what his name is."

I flinch, the harshness of his tone cutting through me. Just then, the door opens, and Alex steps into the room.

"Julie told me you were in here," Alex says, his tone concerned as he closes the door behind him. "Are you alright, Autumn?"

Cole turns on him instantly, his anger flaring. "We really don't need you in this," he snaps. "She'll be back with you shortly, and then I'll be gone."

Alex looks at me, confused, and I give him a look that says more than words can. With a deep breath, Alex pieces it together and realizes what Cole must be thinking.

"Wait," Alex says, his voice laced with a mix of disbelief and amusement as he looks between us. "You think she and I...?" He gestures between the two of us, and a short laugh escapes him.

Cole glares, still not understanding.

I take another step toward Cole, my voice even softer now. "Cole, this is Alex."

He looks confused, but there's a flicker of recognition.

Alex steps forward, his tone soothing. "Cole, buddy, you know me. We've talked." He extends his hand for a handshake, trying to break through the tension. "Alexander Liam..." He pauses, then emphasizes the last word, "...Flynn."

The room seems to freeze as Cole's eyes dart between us. His brow furrows as he slowly processes what Alex just said. "This is your brother?" he asks, his voice barely above a whisper.

Tears spill from my eyes as I nod, unable to speak. Cole turns away, looking up at the ceiling, and covers his face with his hands. I glance at Alex, signaling with a tilt of my head that he should leave.

Alex lowers his hand, squeezes my shoulder reassuringly, and heads for the door. Before leaving, he pauses and turns back, directing his words at Cole.

"What I've been doing is trying to console my sister as her heart was breaking. I really hope you're here to fix it," Alex says, his voice firm and unyielding. "If you're here to hurt her or make this any worse, you and I *will* have a problem." With that, he walks out, leaving Cole and me alone.

Cole turns away from me again, one hand still covering his face, the other resting on the back of his neck. I stand there, waiting, giving him the space he needs to process everything. I can see him taking deep breaths, trying to calm down, and all I can do is hope that we can find our way back to each other through this mess.

Why is he not just laughing about how ridiculous his assumption was? Or apologizing? Why does he still seem so pissed off?

The longer Cole remains silent, the more the hurt and anger churn inside me, like a river swelling dangerously against its banks, threatening to overflow. His silence is unbearable, each passing second a painful twist in my heart until finally, I can't hold back anymore.

"Why didn't you write back or call me?" My voice trembles, the words rushing out, propelled by the pent-up emotion. "Why didn't you at least tell Tara whether or not you'd be here?" The tears start streaming down my cheeks, hot and unstoppable. "You haven't talked to me for four weeks, Cole. Four fucking weeks. Whatever you felt when you saw me with Alex—" My voice cracks, and I'm on the verge of breaking down completely, my chest heaving with the effort to keep the sobs at bay.

I pause, the room thick with tension, tears flowing freely now. I don't even bother wiping them away. Finally, Cole turns to face me, looking as if he's about to say something, maybe even yell at me, but the moment he sees my tear-streaked face, his expression softens, the anger dissolving into something that looks like pain.

Slowly, he starts to close the distance between us, his eyes reflecting a deep sadness. He reaches out, his thumb gently brushing away a tear, but it's futile—the tears keep coming, a relentless stream of everything I've held back. His touch sends a jolt of electricity through me, an undeniable connection despite everything.

Then, to my surprise, he falls to his knees in front of me, his hands grasping my hips as he presses his face into my stomach. I stand there, arms wrapped around myself in a protective cocoon, unmoving, unsure of what to do or say.

"Autumn," he whispers, his voice trembling with regret. "I am so sorry. I fucked this up so much."

I remain silent, my body still, guarding my heart. He takes a few deep, shaky breaths before looking up at me, and then he stands, backing away slightly as if to give me space.

"I didn't write or call you, or Tara, or anyone back because they told me that if I did, it would impact both of us—and others too," he explains, his voice thick with guilt. "They said it would be best for everyone if I just stayed silent. They told me they told you that too."

"They did," I whisper, my voice barely audible, but then it rises as the hurt spills over. "And I knew we had to keep some distance, but I didn't think you'd go completely silent on me. Fuck, Cole, I had Kevin and Megan reach out to you. Matthew wouldn't even tell Megan anything. You could've answered someone."

"I'm sorry," he says quietly, his eyes filled with regret as he stands. "Lauryn told me that if I talked to anyone—anyone—until this was all sorted out, we'd both likely lose our jobs. She made it clear that even people like Tara could be affected."

I just stare at him, my tears slowing, but the pain is still raw, still stinging.

"And then on Monday, Pete called me," Cole continues, gesturing with his hands as he speaks, his words tumbling out in a rush. "They figured it out. They found a solution for us." His voice softens, and I see the flicker of the man I know underneath the anger. "I had this grand plan to surprise you, to tell you everything and sweep you off your feet. It's Valentine's Day, for fuck's sake. I thought—" He stops himself, realizing he's raising his voice again. He takes a breath, runs his fingers through his hair, and turns away, staring out the window.

"I completely fucked this up. I was waiting for you at the hotel, and then I saw you with Alex, and I jumped to conclusions," he says, turning back to me. "Obviously. And when I saw you together at the hotel restaurant, it cemented those conclusions. I wasn't even looking for you that night; I was just headed out to the car to find food, and there you were, with Alex. He grabbed your hand, and then later, he kissed you, and, Autumn, what the fuck was I supposed to think?"

His voice rises again, the frustration evident, and each word cuts deep, like a knife twisting in my heart.

Is he seriously blaming me for this? Because my brother hugged me and comforted me?

I don't respond right away, not because I'm at a loss for words, but because I'm so consumed by anger and hurt that I know anything I say now might be too harsh, too raw.

"Autumn," he says softly, almost pleading, his voice filled with regret.

I take a deep breath, steeling myself. "Cole," I reply, my voice stern, and I see him flinch at the sharpness in my tone. I pause, letting the silence hang between us before I continue, my words spilling out quickly, "Maybe you should have started by trusting me—trusting that you know me, that I love you, and that there's no way I'd move on from us that fast. Maybe you should have remembered that I have a brother who lives three hours from here, a brother you've talked to and even seen pictures of. Yes, he has a little facial hair now, but it's still him."

I choke up, tears streaming down my face again. "Maybe, when you knew on Monday, you should have told someone, like Tara or Megan, that you were coming. They could have told you that I was bringing Alex."

I'm crying too hard to continue. My emotions are overwhelming, the weight of the past weeks crashing down on me.

Cole steps forward, moving slowly, cautiously, as if he's approaching something fragile. When I don't pull away, he wraps me in his arms, holding me close. I keep my arms folded around myself, but I can't help sobbing into his chest. Despite everything, it still feels like home. He's still my anchor, still my sanctuary. He places one hand around my waist and the other on my upper back, gently rubbing the skin above my dress.

"I'm sorry," he whispers, his voice filled with remorse as he kisses the top of my head. He repeats it over and over, "I'm sorry, I'm sorry, I'm sorry," until my sobs start to subside. Then he simply holds me, letting the silence stretch between us, grounding me in his presence. When my breathing finally steadies, he whispers, "I love you, Autumn."

I pull back, wiping my face, but I don't respond. It's not that I don't love him—I do, more than anything—but I need time. I can't bring myself to say it back, not right now. I move to the nearest chair and sit down, trying to collect myself.

A soft knock at the door breaks the silence, and Julie steps in, her eyes gentle and understanding. "Tara wanted me to check on you, Autumn," she says softly, clearly sensing that things are far from okay.

"Hey, Julie," I say, my voice a little hoarse. "Can you find my brother and send him in here?"

I notice Cole's posture stiffen, a flicker of something—worry, maybe—crossing his face. I know he's thinking the worst, that I want Alex to intervene in some negative way.

"Sure," Julie replies with a small smile. "I'll send him in with a box of tissues."

I manage a faint laugh. "Thanks, Julie."

As the door closes behind her, I turn to Cole. "Will you please stop assuming the worst? I just need him to grab some things for me."

Cole turns back toward the window, crossing his arms over his chest, and we lapse into silence again until Alex comes in.

"Hey, Autumn," Alex says as he steps into the room, concern etched across his face. "Julie sent me in here. She's looking for tissues." He glances at me—at what must be my tear-streaked, mascara-smeared face—then at Cole, who's still standing with his back to us. "Are you okay?" His voice is gentle, filled with brotherly worry.

I manage a shaky laugh, sniffing back more tears. "Yeah, despite how I look." I try to smile, though it probably doesn't reach my eyes. "But could you do me a favor?"

"Of course," Alex replies, his gaze shifting back to Cole briefly before returning to me. "What do you need?"

I chuckle a little, wiping at my face. "Could you grab my makeup bag from my room and bring it here?" I hand him my key.

"Yeah, I can do that. Anything else?" he asks, his tone warm and reassuring.

"Maybe those tissues and my hairbrush," I say, giving him a half-hearted smile, acknowledging I'm a pain in the ass.

Alex walks over, giving me a small hug and a kiss on the top of my head. He shoots another glance at Cole, who still hasn't turned around, then heads out to get my things.

As the door clicks shut, I can't hold back the frustration anymore. "You don't have to be rude to him," I snap at Cole, my voice laced with irritation.

He finally turns to face me, stepping closer with a look of raw emotion. "I'm not trying to be rude," he says softly, his voice thick with regret. "Fuck, Autumn, I don't even know where we stand right now. I don't know how to handle any of this. Nothing in my life has prepared me for this."

I let out a bitter laugh that turns into a sob. "You think I'm prepared for this?" My voice rises with every word, the hurt and anger boiling over. "I'm crying in a bridal dressing room on Valentine's Day with the man I'm in love with, who hasn't talked to me for four fucking weeks and apparently thought I was cheating on him—with my brother."

His expression shifts as if the full weight of my words hits him. He takes a tentative step closer. "Man you're in love with?" he asks softly, surprise flickering in his eyes. It's the first time since this whole ordeal began that I see something other than anger or pain in his face.

"Yeah," I say, the bitterness returning to my voice as I look down at my hands. "Did you think that changed?"

"Yeah," he admits quietly, looking almost defeated. "I thought it might have. You were so mad, and when I said it—you didn't say it back."

"Cole, I wouldn't be this upset if I didn't care," I snap, my voice cracking. "All this pain, all these tears—it's because I care. This is more hurt than anger."

The room falls into silence, the air between us thick and charged with emotion. I can feel his anger melting away, replaced by a palpable sense of regret.

Cole exhales loudly, then takes another deep breath before speaking again. "Autumn," he begins cautiously, taking another step toward me, his arms still crossed. "I know I made mistakes, and I know you probably don't want to hear that I thought they were for the right reasons, but in my mind, they were. I was trying to protect you, to keep my promise from that first night we were together, and then I wanted to surprise you. Looking back, maybe I should have done things differently, but I didn't—I can't change it. All I can do now is tell you that I'm sorry and that I love you."

He moves even closer, his voice thick with emotion. "Please tell me how to fix this, or at least understand that I'm trying to. I love you more than anyone or anything. These last four weeks have been torture for me too, and I'm so, so fucking sorry."

I'm about to respond when the door opens, and Alex steps in, his arms full of my things. He sets them down on a nearby table, standing just a couple of feet in front of me, while Cole stands right beside me.

Cole clears his throat, his voice still raw with emotion. "I'm sorry about earlier and everything that's happened. It's just... a lot." He extends his hand to Alex. "I'm Cole, in case that wasn't clear," he adds with a small, uncomfortable laugh.

Alex shakes his hand, his tone calm but firm. "Alex, obviously." He pauses, looking at me with concern before turning back to Cole. "Autumn's my baby sister. I'll always do whatever I can to keep her happy and safe." He gives me a small smile, brushing a strand of loose hair from my face.

"That's a well-known and undisputed fact," Cole says as Alex heads for the door.

Surprisingly, Alex turns back to Cole with a smile before leaving. "Your family is pretty amazing, Autumn," Cole says softly. "You really drew a good hand with them."

"I did," I agree, grabbing a tissue and noisily blowing my nose. I laugh, the sound shaky. "I'm sure that was sexy."

"I'm not worried about sexy right now, Autumn," Cole says, his voice soft but insistent. "I'm worried about *us*, about the pain I've caused you, and about how to fix this."

I meet his gaze, my voice steady but laced with sadness. "This is going to take time, Cole. I was so happy when I saw you, my heart nearly stopped. I was excited—I thought you were here to surprise me." I look down at the tissues in my hand. "But then you were so cold, and I didn't understand."

I look back up at him, my eyes filled with pain. "When you got angry, all the hurt from the last few weeks came rushing to the surface. It hurt so fucking much, Cole, to be ignored like that, for that long."

Cole drops to his knees in front of me, holding my wrists gently, his eyes filled with regret. "Autumn, I'm so sorry. I love you," he whispers, pulling my forehead to his. "And I should have figured out that was Alex. My trust issues clouded every bit of judgment I should have had. I jumped to conclusions, and I hurt you even more. I'm sorry."

I stay silent, my heart aching.

He squeezes my wrists, his voice pleading. "I'm also sorry I didn't respond to anyone. There were nights I almost drove up to see you, a few times I even got on the freeway. But I didn't want to make the situation worse. I told Pete I'd resign, and he promised to find a solution, but I had to stay off the radar. I didn't want what happened in Denver to end your career. I'm so, so sorry."

I take a deep breath, not moving, just letting his words sink in. Cole waits, giving me time, not pushing, not speaking.

"Cole?" I finally whisper, my voice weak.

"Autumn?" he replies, his voice still heavy with sadness.

"Don't ever do that to me again. Don't disappear, no matter the circumstances." My voice cracks, and I stop, unable to continue as a small sob escapes.

He reaches up, wiping the tears from my cheek, and I fully meet his eyes for the first time since Alex had walked in. "Never," he promises, "never again."

He looks down at my mouth, grazing my bottom lip with his thumb before leaning in to kiss me—lightly at first. As he starts to break the kiss, I reach around his neck, pulling him into a deeper, emotional kiss.

"Never," I whisper against his lips as I lean back and look at him, his eyes now just as red-rimmed as mine.

"I love you," he whispers, his thumb tracing my cheekbone.

"I love you too," I whisper back, and with my words, a few tears spill from his eyes.

CHAPTER FIFTY-SIX

THE RECEPTION

Now that the tension has eased, I want to savor this moment with Cole, but I know I need to get back to Tara. I've probably been away too long.

"Cole?" I say softly.

"Autumn?" His voice is calm, almost soothing.

"I have to get cleaned up and head back out there." I give him a small, apologetic smile.

"I know," he replies, understanding in his eyes.

I walk over to the large mirror where Tara had carefully placed her veil earlier. My face is a bit of a mess, but somehow, my eye makeup and hair have held up surprisingly well. The rest of my face, I can fix. Cole leans against the table beside the mirror, watching me with a mix of affection and concern.

I blow my nose a few more times, silently thanking myself for being prepared for tears. The makeup artist had used waterproof mascara and eyeliner, so despite everything, my eyes still look decent. I grab my eye drops from my bag and carefully apply them, watching as the redness in my eyes starts to fade. I find my powder foundation and gently reapply it to my cheeks, nose, and upper lip.

"Autumn, you're beautiful," Cole murmurs, his voice warm and sincere. "You don't look bad at all, especially after everything."

I glance at him, a soft smile tugging at the corners of my lips, then return my focus to the mirror. I add a touch of blush and lip stain before stepping back to straighten my dress. I take a moment to check the back of my dress in the full-length mirror, making sure everything is in place. As I turn, Cole wraps his arms around me.

"Autumn, I missed you so much," he whispers against my ear. "Let's go enjoy this night together. We'll have time to talk about everything later."

I look up at him, our eyes locking for a brief moment before I let my fingers trail down his arm. I wrap my fingers around his, then look back into his eyes. Without a word, I start walking backward, leading him toward the door.

As we step into the hallway, we find Alex leaning against the wall, scrolling through his phone. He looks up as we approach, his expression softening when he sees me. There's a silent exchange between us, a question in his eyes, asking if I'm okay. I nod and smile, reassuring him.

Alex glances at Cole and tilts his chin up slightly, a hint of humor in his voice. "Some day, this will be funny, but I know that day isn't today."

Cole chuckles softly, the tension from earlier finally dissipating. I shake my head, smiling at the two of them.

"What did I miss?" I ask, gesturing toward the reception hall.

"Not much," Alex replies. "Just them walking into the room. I think they took some pictures with extended family. Everyone's eating now, so I don't think anything else will start until after dinner."

"Thank goodness," I breathe out in relief, grateful and very relieved I haven't let Tara down too much.

Alex looks back at Cole, a playful glint in his eyes as he tries to lighten the mood. "Tara wasn't sure if you'd be here, but she sat us next to each other, at a table with all your other people. And, Autumn, you're at the head table."

"Yeah, I knew that," I say with a smile.

Alex turns to Cole, trying to dissolve any lingering awkwardness with a joke. "Don't worry, she doesn't have to stay there the whole time," he laughs.

I lead the way into the reception hall, Cole following close behind, with Alex bringing up the rear. Tara and Max are seated, already enjoying their meal. My place has been set, and I'm relieved to find it's right at the end of the table, making it easy for me to slip in without causing too much of a stir. The other tables seat six, so it's perfectly arranged with Alex, Cole, Mark, Julio, and their wives.

Tara leans forward, her eyebrows raised in a silent question. I give her a reassuring smile and nod, and she smiles back, relief washing over her features. The last thing I want is for her to worry about me tonight, so I'm glad we're in a better place.

Dinner is filled with moments for Tara and Max to share sweet kisses, followed by heartfelt toasts. Julie's speech is laced with humor, while Max's brother delivers a serious, emotional toast that brings tears to many eyes around the room. Both fathers follow with their own words, each one heartfelt and perfectly fitting the occasion.

When it's time for the first dance and special dances, we all leave the head table. There are extra chairs near the dance floor, and I spot the table where my people are sitting, conveniently close to the action. Alex, ever the telepathic brother, sees me heading that way and pulls over an extra chair, placing it between him and Cole.

As soon as I sit down, Cole wraps his arm around me, pulling me close and kissing my temple. I look up at him, curious.

"They all know, everyone knows," he says with a smile. "Pete had a conversation with Mark and Julio on Tuesday. The only reason you and Tara weren't on that call was because you were both out for the wedding."

I have so many questions, and I know he can see them on my face. He squeezes my shoulder gently. "Later, Autumn. I have so much to tell you, but for now, just know there's no more hiding."

The DJ announces the first dance, and as the music starts, I recognize "Take Forever" by Cooper Alan. I know Tara loves country music, though it's not exactly Max's favorite, so this song feels like a beautiful compromise. It's a perfect reflection of their relationship. After the father-daughter dance, Alex quietly asks Cole to step away with him, leaving me to slide over and sit next to Mark.

Mark leans in, his voice low. "I'm really happy for you and Cole, Autumn. I'm glad everything at work and whatever was going on here got straightened out." He then grins, a teasing light in his eyes. "Next work wedding I go to will probably be yours."

I smile at him, too overwhelmed for words, but grateful for his kindness.

As the special dances come to an end, Alex and Cole return. They're standing by the wall, and Alex gestures for me to join them. I get up and walk over, feeling Cole's fingers gently graze my arm as I reach them.

"Hey, baby sister," Alex starts, his tone affectionate. "I'm going to head out. If I leave in the next hour, I can make it home while it's still Valentine's Day to surprise Claire."

I smile at him, feeling a warmth spread through me. "So you think I'm in good hands then?"

He laughs. "Yeah, I think you're in good hands. But I did tell Cole you should come down for dinner tomorrow night. I know you're not flying back until Monday afternoon, and neither is Cole, so come down, or Claire and I can meet you somewhere in between."

"Okay, I'll text or call in the morning," I say, then pause, my voice softening. "And Alex?"

"Yeah?"

"Thank you, for everything," I say, hugging him tightly. "You know you're the best brother ever."

He chuckles. "Well, you're a pretty good sister too. Makes it worth it."

"One more favor?" I ask, my tone slipping into a slight whine.

Alex laughs again. "What's that?"

"Can you update the kids? At least Kevin?"

Alex glances at Cole, then back to me. "Yeah, I'll see if Kev can talk while I'm driving, if he's not out with Kalisha. I'll call Megan and Samantha too." He pauses, giving Cole a knowing look. "I'll make sure they know everything's okay."

He kisses my forehead and shakes Cole's hand. As he hands me my room key, which he still had from earlier, he gives me a wink. "You might need this."

I laugh. "Drive safe."

"I will—probably fast, but safe." He winks again.

Before he leaves, Alex stops by to say goodbye to Tara and Max, then he's gone.

I turn to Cole, curiosity burning in my eyes. "What was that look my brother gave you?"

He shrugs, trying to play it off. "I don't know."

I squint at him, not entirely convinced, but let it slide. "You survived my brother and even gained his approval, after everything. I'm impressed."

Cole smiles, a hint of relief in his expression. "I don't think I ever lost his approval. At least not the way he tells it."

"That's true. You never lost it," I concede, looking up at him. "And you never lost mine either."

We're tucked away in a far corner of the room, but Cole still surprises me by wrapping his hand around my neck and leaning in for a kiss. It's tender and gentle, but I can feel the desperation behind it. When he pulls back, he rests his forehead against mine.

"I missed you, Autumn, so much."

"I know," I whisper, my voice thick with emotion. "I missed you too."

As the cake-cutting begins, Cole and I turn our attention back to the room. Tara and Max are adorable, carefully feeding each other without a hint of the usual cake-smashing antics. Everything about them is picture-perfect.

With the formalities out of the way, the party shifts into full swing. I can't help but smile when Julio and his wife hit the dance floor for the line dances. It reminds me of that first conference with Cole, and when I glance up at him, I can tell he's remembering it too.

The music follows a pattern—three fast songs, two slow ones—and when the opening notes of "The Dance" begin to play, Cole doesn't hesitate. He takes my hand and pulls me into his arms on the dance floor. My hand rests on his heart, his covers mine, and his other arm wraps around my waist, holding me close. I nestle my head against his chest, letting him guide us in time with the music.

When the song ends, Cole places a gentle kiss on my forehead, ready to return to our table, but I stop him as I recognize the first few notes of the next song.

"I listened to this a lot over the past few weeks," I admit, my voice soft. "Maybe with some tears." I shrug, trying to downplay the emotion that bubbles up.

He looks at me quizzically but doesn't say anything, just wraps me back into his arms. As Jason Mraz's "I Won't Give Up On Us" fills the room, I see a flicker of recognition in his eyes as the lyrics resonate with him. A couple of tears slip from my eyes, and he tenderly wipes them away with the back of his fingers. He kisses my forehead, then lifts my chin to plant a soft kiss on my lips. As the song fades and a faster beat takes over, he leads me off the dance floor, holding me close.

"I love you, and I'm sorry I ever doubted you," he whispers into my hair, his voice thick with emotion. "I know you're mine."

I laugh softly, trying to keep the tears at bay. "Unconditionally and indefinitely."

"Yes," he echoes, his voice full of conviction. "Unconditionally and indefinitely."

Julio interrupts us with a grin. "You two might want to tone it down a bit. You're showing up the bride and groom with all this love and sweetness."

We laugh, and Cole responds, "I don't think we have much control over that, especially since we haven't seen each other or even spoken in weeks."

He glances at me, then back at Julio. "But we can try."

The evening passes in a blur of socializing and laughter. When it's time for the final events, Max expertly snaps Tara's garter into the crowd of eager men. Cole opts out, joking that he has no interest in touching something that had been around Tara's thigh, making us all laugh. But when it's Tara's turn to toss the bouquet, I don't even have to reach for it—it practically lands in my arms. Tara gives me a knowing smile before crossing the dance floor to hug me and whisper in my ear.

"I'm pretty sure that was the most accurate bouquet toss ever."

I laugh. "We'll see, Tara. We have a lot of talking to do, but you might be right."

As I walk back to Cole, he glances at the bouquet in my hands and smiles, pressing a kiss to my forehead.

We send Tara and Max off under a sky of bubbles, their faces glowing with happiness. As the night winds down and we say our goodbyes, Mark asks if we'll be in the meeting on Monday, even though we're technically off. Cole doesn't hesitate before saying yes.

"It's really good to see you two together," Mark says, hugging me before shaking Cole's hand.

After the farewells, Cole turns to me, his eyes warm. "Your place or mine?"

"Oh, we're not going to our own rooms?" I deadpan, watching as his serious expression falters for a moment before he catches on.

"Autumn," he says, his voice carrying a hint of challenge.

I smile, relenting. "Either is fine. I just need to grab my things from the dressing room. Walk with me?"

He nods, and we head toward the dressing room together. "I think we should go to my room," he suggests. "We can grab whatever you need from yours."

"Okay," I agree, my heart fluttering. "Honestly, I don't care where we go, as long as I don't have to let you out of my sight."

"I feel that in my core right now," he laughs.

After gathering my things from the dressing room, I grab a few essentials from my room—some clothes, my phone charger—and hand them to Cole, who's already carrying a bag with my other items.

When we reach Cole's room, he scans his key and opens the door, letting me step in first. The sight that greets me takes my breath away. My jaw drops as I take in the hundreds of red and white roses scattered throughout the room, the bed covered in red rose petals, and the soft glow of electric candles lighting up the space.

"Cole—" I manage to say, my voice barely a whisper, as I turn to look at him.

He's standing behind me, a soft smile on his lips. He gently takes my hand and turns me toward him, his eyes filled with warmth and love.

"Autumn Flynn, will you be my Valentine?"

CHAPTER FIFTY-SEVEN
THE VALENTINE & THE GIFT

I nearly leap into his arms, and he catches me effortlessly, his lips finding mine in a tender kiss before he pulls back to look into my eyes.

"Is that an answer?" he asks softly, a touch of humor in his voice.

"Yes," I breathe, my lips brushing against his, "Yes, of course, I'll be your Valentine."

His arm tightens around my waist as he draws me closer, his lips capturing mine in a kiss that starts slow and deepens, his hand cradling the back of my neck as our tongues explore one another. A rush of electricity shoots down my spine, and I feel the heat spreading through my veins. He's still so intoxicating.

"How? You were so mad," I murmur when our mouths part, turning to take in the room.

The suite is massive, much larger than my room, and filled with an overwhelming number of roses. It looks like he bought out an entire flower shop.

"This isn't even your real gift," he laughs. "As for how... well, I think I had more hope than I think you realize. And Alex."

I turn to him, eyebrows raised. "Alex?"

"Yeah, I had everything, but it wasn't set up. Alex did that for me before he left. He even sent me pictures to make sure it was just right before driving back to Claire."

"Cole, this is insane," I say, my jaw practically on the floor. I wouldn't notice if bugs flew in. "You had all of this planned?"

He nods, a playful smile tugging at his lips. "Like I said, I wanted to surprise you. Grand romantic gesture and all that." He leans against the wall, loosening the knot of his tie.

"Well, mission accomplished," I say, grabbing his hand and pulling him the rest of the way into the room.

"Not exactly the way I envisioned it," he says, kissing my forehead before fully removing his tie. "It wasn't my intention to make you cry sad tears. Happy tears? Sure, but not sad ones." He pulls me into a hug, his arms warm and solid around me.

I rest my head on his chest, listening to the steady rhythm of his heartbeat. It's a sound I've missed so much. I breathe him in—earthy, spicy, and velvety, all the things that make him feel like home. He feels like forever, and that thought sends tears rolling down my cheeks again. I sniffle, trying to hold them back, but it's no use.

"Hey," Cole says softly, unwrapping his arms from around me and tilting my chin up so our eyes meet. "What's this?" he asks, gently wiping away the tears with the back of his fingers.

His touch, his concern, only makes the tears flow faster. I shake my head, and he pulls me back into his embrace, my head resting once again on his chest.

"Autumn, sweetheart," he sighs, his voice thick with emotion. "I'm so sorry. I love you."

"No." I step back, shaking my head and laughing through the tears. "I mean, not 'no'... I just—" I pause, trying to collect myself, glancing up at the ceiling as I fan my face with my hand. He waits patiently, his eyes never leaving mine. "I love you too," I finally manage to say, my voice trembling. "These are happy tears. I just..." I take a shaky breath, but it's no use; the words spill out between sobs. "I just missed you so much."

As soon as the words are out, he pulls me into him again, holding me tightly. He kisses my hair and lets me sob against his chest, the tears coming harder now than they did in the dressing room, harder than when Alex picked me up from the airport. It takes what feels like forever to calm down, but Cole doesn't rush me. He doesn't ask questions or say anything; he just holds me, letting me release everything I've been holding in.

When I finally regain control, I take deep, cleansing breaths and feel my breathing slowly return to normal. I step back from him, wiping my eyes, and laugh a little.

"I'm not sure where that came from," I sniffle, a faint smile on my lips. "But that wasn't sadness. That was just a whole hell of a lot of emotion."

Cole watches me closely, his eyes filled with a mixture of concern and confusion, as if he's trying to understand the storm of emotions swirling inside me. "Mostly relief," I say, my voice barely above a whisper, "I think. I love you," I meet his gaze, "I missed you so much, so, so much, and this," I gesture to the room around us, "is amazing. You are amazing, even with everything that happened earlier today. Cole, I—"

Before I can finish, he crashes into me. One hand grips the back of my neck, and the other wraps tightly around my waist as his mouth claims mine with a kiss so deep and hungry that stars burst behind my eyelids. My body melts into his, the softness of me yielding to the hardness of him. I'm lost in the sensation, our tongues and lips exploring each other with a fervor that makes the rest of the world disappear. It's just him—his touch, his taste, his warmth.

Heat floods my veins, and my skin tingles with electric sparks that all converge at the center of my desire. A moan escapes my lips as I grab a fistful of his hair at the nape of his neck, trying to pull him even closer, needing more of him.

His hand moves from my waist to the bare skin of my back, his fingers grazing my spine in featherlight touches that send shivers through me. He finds the zipper of my dress and slowly, teasingly, pulls it down. His fingers trail over my exposed skin, igniting every nerve as he pushes one strap of my dress off my shoulder.

His hands cup the back of my neck, his thumbs tracing along my jawline and pulse points, before one hand slides across my collarbone to nudge the other strap down. I loosen my grip on him just long enough for the dress to slip off and pool at my feet.

I lift each foot to remove the straps of my heels, kicking them off and feeling the significant drop in height. Cole laughs softly against my lips, the sound vibrating through me. His hand finds my back, unhooking my strapless bra. Our bodies are so close that the bra doesn't even have a chance to fall away. His fingers dance across my skin.

My hands find their way between us, unbuttoning his shirt as he hooks his thumbs under the waistband of my thong, slowly pushing it down over my hips. His fingers skim my skin, avoiding my most sensitive spot, drawing a whimper from deep in my throat. He pulls the fabric lower until it, too, falls to the floor, leaving me completely bare.

Our mouths part, and I start to push his shirt off his shoulders. Cole's hands come between us to unfasten his cufflinks, giving me the opportunity to unbuckle his belt and pants. His shirt lands on the floor with my dress, and he pulls his undershirt over his head. I repay him for his earlier teasing, letting the back of my hands brush lightly over his length as I push his boxer briefs down. He kicks off his shoes and socks, and then we stand there for a moment, completely exposed to each other.

Then, in an instant, he's on me again, crashing into me with that same ravenous kiss. My hands find the pins in my hair, pulling them out one by one, letting my hair tumble down my back and shoulders. I know the baby's breath will be tangled in there, but I don't care.

Once my hair is free, I wrap my arms around him again, and he tangles his fingers in the loose strands. His mouth leaves mine, trailing hot kisses along my jaw and down the side of my neck. He guides the tilt of my head, his hand firm yet gentle in my hair, as his lips travel across my throat and up the other side before meeting my mouth again in a soft, tender kiss.

His eyes lock onto mine, intense and searching, as he begins to back me toward the bed. The comforter brushes against the backs of my calves just before he lays me down gently, hovering over me with one arm supporting his weight.

His sapphire blue eyes, now dark with desire, study my face for a few seconds before he moves down my body. His warm mouth closes over one of my breasts, his tongue skillfully teasing the sensitive peak. My back arches off the bed, and his hand finds my other breast, pinching and rolling the nipple between his fingers.

His other hand slides down between my thighs, finding the wet heat there. He growls softly, a sound of pure need, as he dips three fingers inside me, sending a shockwave through my body.

My nails dig into his back, trailing up to his shoulders as his fingers begin a rhythm that leaves me breathless. My pelvis tilts toward him, desperate for more, and his mouth returns to mine, our lips crashing together in a kiss filled with the urgency of our need.

I feel the tightness building in my core, the pleasure winding tighter and tighter until I'm on the brink of release. Cole's fingers don't falter, maintaining the perfect rhythm as his mouth moves to my neck, sending jolts of electricity straight to my core.

And then I'm falling, my body contracting around his fingers as I cry out, the orgasm washing over me in waves. He holds me close as I ride it out, his lips brushing against mine before he rolls us over, pulling me on top of him.

My hair falls like a veil around us as I kiss him again, sitting up on my knees and moving my hips, rubbing his length against me. He moans, his eyes dark and filled with desire as his hands roam up and down my sides.

I lean down, kissing him once more before shifting my hips, positioning him at my entrance. Cole stills beneath me as I slowly lower myself onto him, taking him in inch by inch. A deep groan escapes his lips as I start to move, rocking my hips in a slow, steady rhythm.

I feel whole again, complete, as he fills me. I pick up the pace, and he shifts beneath me, matching my movements as we both chase the edge of our pleasure. Then, he flips us over, driving into me deeper and harder, sending me spiraling into another orgasm.

I wrap my legs around him, bracing my hands against the headboard as he thrusts into me, his rhythm strong and sure. As he nears his release, he leans down, his mouth finding mine once more before moving to my neck, his breath hot against my skin.

"I missed you too," he whispers, his voice rough with emotion.

When he's spent, he rolls off me, pulling me with him to rest my head on his chest. His fingers trace scattered patterns on my back, making me shiver as I laugh softly, picking rose petals off our skin.

"God, I missed the sound of that laugh," he says, holding me closer.

I laugh more as I untangle a petal from my hair. He kisses the top of my head, his fingers gently combing through my hair, working out the tangles with such care that it makes my heart swell. We lie there in comfortable silence for a long time before Cole finally speaks again.

"Autumn?"

"Cole?"

He pauses, swallowing hard, as if gathering the strength to speak. "I think," he begins, "I think that everything you felt back then, just before... you said relief?"

"Yeah, that's what most of it was," I reply softly, sensing the struggle in his voice.

"I think that's what I was feeling downstairs when you all finally got through to me about Alex," he murmurs, pressing a gentle kiss to the top of my head. "That's why I didn't talk for so long, and I know that made things worse," he adds, another kiss brushing through my hair. "I was relieved, and then all the excitement to see you rushed back, but so did a flood of regret. My mind was overwhelmed, processing too much all at once. I'm sorry," he says, hugging me closer, his lips brushing my hair once more.

He swallows again, struggling with the memories. "I think my headspace at the time, with all the adrenaline, wanted to be angry because I'd been hurt and angry for days. The pendulum swung, and my stress response was so confused that I just froze," he admits. "The last thing I wanted was to hurt you more, but I got defensive. Part of me was convinced you were gone, so yeah, when you didn't say you loved me when I said it, and then when you asked Tara's sister to get Alex, I made assumptions."

I trace my fingers over his chest and abdomen as he continues, his words tumbling out like confessions. "I was scared, Autumn," he exhales, voice cracking, "terrified of losing you, terrified of making everything worse."

"Shhh," I whisper, propping myself up on my arm so I can meet his bloodshot eyes. "I'm here. I'm not going anywhere. The only thing that really upset me was that you thought I was even capable of—"

"I know, Autumn," he interrupts, his voice filled with remorse. "The second I realized it wasn't true, I knew how deeply that would cut you, and I'm sorry."

He takes a deep breath, exhaling slowly. I rest my head back on his chest, feeling the rise and fall of his breathing. "My whole life, people I loved betrayed me. I know you're not them, I *know* that," he says, taking another deep breath. "I've played through the last few days in my mind, and I'm not sure where I could have changed my response." He chuckles softly. "I joked with Alex that if you all had pulled up in his Audi instead of the SUV, that might have done it," he sighs. "I have a list of things I should have done differently, and I know I can't take that back, but much like those eighty-five seconds in the fall, I'll think about them for a long time."

"Perseverate," I say gently.

"Um, what?" Cole laughs softly, confused.

"That's the term for it. When you think about something over and over, especially when you can't change it."

I feel him shake his head with another soft laugh before I speak again. "Cole, I do understand. We both had a picture of what this would or could look like. You, I think, had a much more detailed picture of that," I laugh lightly, "but still, all of this just makes me love you more."

"Autumn," he groans, my name almost a question, filled with longing.

"Trust me," I whisper. "We're okay. I know I came at you with all those questions about not responding, not talking to me, and yeah, that hurt. But I knew it wasn't your choice. And Alex was your ever-present advocate, constantly telling me he would be doing exactly what you were. He even got a little heated about it with Kevin."

Cole hugs me closer, kisses my hair again. My fingers continue tracing random lines across his chest as I go on. "I know you were trying to do the right thing. You don't need to convince me of that. It sucked, a lot, but I know that's what you were doing. I don't want you to feel guilty, despite what I said earlier. I'm sorry I questioned you." I take a deep breath. "I guess I was just trying to say that if you had talked to someone, anyone, they could have told you I was here with Alex." I shrug lightly.

Cole swallows, his voice barely above a whisper. "There was a night you texted me, about two weeks in," he says, drawing his hand down his face and exhaling. "I think it was the night after Laura took you to lunch, but it was super late, more like early morning."

"I remember," I say quietly.

"Autumn, after I read that text," he pauses, "I was halfway to Chicago before I turned around. And honestly, I don't even know how I found the strength to turn back or why I did," he confesses, lifting my hand to his lips and kissing my palm before lacing our fingers together and resting them back on his chest. "I should have followed my instincts that night."

We fall into a comfortable silence, the only sound between us the steady rhythm of our breathing. After a few minutes, I speak softly. "Cole, I remember that too, because I remember seeing that you read it nearly the second I sent it, and my heart dropped. I felt bad that I might have made things worse for you, but I also felt this crazy connection because I knew we were both staring at our phones at the same time, and... I don't know," I sigh. "That was a rough night, like really rough."

"It was for me too," he admits, lacing his fingers in and out of mine. "That's why I was staring at my phone at two in the morning."

"I had cried myself to sleep that afternoon, and that's when I woke up," I say with a shrug. "I didn't even realize what time it was until after I sent it."

"Autumn..." he sighs my name, the weight of regret heavy in his tone.

"Don't, Cole," I sigh, "I didn't say that to make you feel bad, just to let you know where I was."

"I wasn't going to tell you about that night because I didn't want you to feel bad about texting me, but I just want you to know that none of this was easy for me," he says, his voice thick with emotion.

"I didn't think it was," I whisper, and then we lay there in the quiet and the candlelight, letting the silence speak for us both.

As the night winds down, we decide it's time to clean up and think about sleep. Cole suggests we shower together, and I can't bear to be apart from him, not even for a moment, so I follow him into the bathroom. The water cascades over us as he tenderly pulls the petals and fragments of flowers from my hair. His touch is soft, his kisses plentiful, and for the first time in what feels like forever, everything feels right again.

Cole finishes first and steps out, slipping into his boxers and sweatpants with ease. I stay behind, taking my time finger combing conditioner through my hair, then towel drying it until it's just damp. Once I'm dry enough, I throw on a tank top and shorts and make my way back to the bed, still in awe of the room. The sheer amount of roses—everywhere, their fragrance filling the air—leaves me stunned.

"Cole, seriously, this is incredible. So many roses... This must have cost a small fortune," I say, sitting on the edge of the bed, my fingers absently running through my wet hair, trying to towel it dry.

"Maybe," he murmurs from behind me, the mattress dipping as he moves closer, "but you're worth every penny. And like I said, this wasn't even your real present—this was just setting the scene," he adds with a soft, slightly mischievous laugh.

One hand trails down my back, while the other appears in front of me, holding a small gift bag.

"Happy Valentine's Day, Autumn. I love you," he whispers, moving to sit beside me, one leg tucked under him, the other draped over the edge of the bed.

I look at him, curiosity in my eyes.

"Go on, open it," he encourages, his fingers playing with a tendril of my hair before sliding gently down my back.

I set the towel I had been using on my hair aside and begin to pull the tissue paper out of the bag. My hands find a square box, slightly larger than my palm, and I know immediately it's a jewelry box. I glance at Cole again, and he just gives me a soft smile.

When I open the box, my breath catches. Inside, perfectly displayed, is a sapphire and diamond necklace. My eyes widen as they meet Cole's, his smile deepening as he watches my reaction. My jaw drops, and I quickly close it, turning my gaze back to the necklace. Twelve teardrop-shaped sapphires are set on what I'm certain is a white gold chain, each sapphire separated by a delicate diamond.

"Cole," I breathe, my voice so soft I barely recognize it.

Before I can say anything more, I turn to him, still holding the box, and wrap my arms around his neck, kissing him deeply.

He smiles against my lips. "I take it you like it?"

I pull back slightly, glancing down at the necklace in my hand. "I love it. It's stunning, and exactly something I would choose for myself," I laugh softly, "but also probably a small fortune."

"A few multiples of the roses," he admits with a laugh, "but that doesn't matter, Autumn. I saw this necklace, and I could picture it on you. Originally, I wanted you to have it before the wedding, so you could wear it if you wanted."

"Well, if it makes you feel any better," I say, smiling up at him, "Tara gave us necklaces to wear, so I wouldn't have been able to wear it anyway." I reach up, gently cupping his face, my thumb tracing his cheek before I kiss him softly. "I love you. Thank you."

His eyes search mine, and he leans in to kiss me again. "You're welcome. I love you."

Eventually, we manage to blow out most of the candles and snuggle into bed together. I fall asleep curled up against him, the little spoon in his arms, and it's, by far, the best sleep I've had in weeks.

CHAPTER FIFTY-EIGHT

THE BEST FRIEND & THE KIDS

We sleep late the next morning, wrapped in the warmth of each other, not stirring until around noon. I wake to the soft brush of lips trailing down my neck and shoulder, the whisper of gentle fingers tracing the curve of my ribs.

I turn to Cole, my voice still hushed and groggy from sleep. "Good morning. I'm glad to see you're real and that yesterday wasn't just a dream."

Smiling, he offers a tender expression that melts any lingering doubt. "Good morning," he murmurs before capturing my mouth in a long, deep kiss.

His lips and tongue begin their journey down my body, and I savor every moment of his presence, the weight of him, the warmth. We keep our hands on each other, neither willing to let go, as if the act of separation might cause us to disappear. He makes love to me with a tenderness that is exactly what I need, grounding me in the reality of us. When we finally come up for air, it's already past one in the afternoon.

"Alex wanted to have dinner with us," Cole says, his voice tinged with amusement. "We should probably figure that out," he adds with a light laugh.

"I don't even know where my phone is," I admit, smiling as I realize how disconnected from the world I've been. "And I'm starving."

He kisses me softly, the kind of kiss that lingers long after it ends. "You find your phone, I'll hunt down the room service menu."

I locate my phone, nearly dead, and plug it in to charge. Cole hands me the menu, and I quickly decide what I want before he places the order.

"Food will be here in about forty minutes," he informs me.

"Perfect," I reply, leaning back into the pillows. "What do you want to do about Alex? Before I call him."

Cole gives me a curious look.

"I mean, do you want to drive all the way to Portland, or should we meet somewhere in between?" I clarify.

"I'm okay with the drive," he says with a shrug. "It might give us a chance to talk without too many distractions." He laughs and kisses my cheek, his tone turning more serious. "I really do have a lot to tell you."

I nod, and then call Alex to arrange dinner. He suggests a nice steakhouse near their house, and with that settled, Cole and I enjoy our meal before heading back to my room so I can pick out something to wear. Luckily, I've packed plenty of nice clothes. I pull out the green dress I wore on our last night in Denver and hold it up, glancing at Cole with a question in my eyes.

"One of my favorites," he says without hesitation.

"Yeah, but I feel like it's bad luck or something," I say, hesitating.

"It wasn't bad luck the first time I saw you in it." He smiles. "Wear it. If you think it's bad luck, let's change that."

"Okay," I agree, smiling back at him.

I gather a few more things, and we head back to his room. As we get ready, I can't help but laugh at the sheer volume of roses that still fill the space.

"What are you going to do with all these when we leave?" I ask, amused by the extravagance.

"I figured I'd tell the front desk that anyone who wants them can take them. They're quality flowers, meant to last about a week, so someone else can enjoy them too."

Nodding, I smile and hand him the box with the necklace. "Help me put it on?"

He takes the box from me, smiling with a warmth that lights up his entire face, his eyes sparkling. "I'm not sure if sapphires go with your dress," he says, a hint of doubt in his voice.

"They'll be fine," I assure him, smiling as I lift my hair to give him access to clasp the necklace. "It's emerald green—it's a jewel tone."

He carefully fastens the necklace, then steps back to admire the result. His eyes flicker down to the necklace and then back to my face, his fingers grazing my cheek with a tender touch. "It does look beautiful on you."

I grin, teasing him lightly. "I just hope you have it insured."

He rolls his eyes, smirking. "I do, actually. Traveling with it made that a must."

I slip on the sapphire tennis bracelet Alex gave me, and it complements the necklace perfectly, toning down its boldness against the green dress. Cole, looking irresistibly sexy in his shirt and tie, checks his watch, signaling it's time to go. We're both ready, excitement and a sense of new beginnings in the air as we head out for our drive.

"So, I feel like you've probably already told me everything, but is there anything I need to know before we do this?" Cole asks, chuckling softly.

"Claire is the absolute sweetest person in the world," I begin, a warm smile tugging at my lips. "Tara reminds me of her—despite their wealth, she's just so down-to-earth. She's perfect for Alex."

I glance down at my hands, gathering my thoughts. "They're not pretentious. Sure, they like nice things, but they're genuinely humble. If they invite us back to their house, just know that their place makes mine look like a dollhouse." I laugh, trying to downplay the opulence.

"Seriously?" Cole raises an eyebrow in surprise.

I sigh, nodding. "Yeah, they've lived there for a long time, so it feels comfortable to me now, like a real home—my brother's home. But they have a guest house, they're on the waterfront... no pool, but there's a putting green, a basketball court, and honestly, I don't even know what all they have. If we go back after dinner, it'll probably be for drinks, and we'll likely stay in their kitchen since it's too cold to be outside by the water."

Cole glances at me, curiosity in his eyes. "I'm going to ask something that might sound off, but it's just out of curiosity," he says carefully. "I know they both do well, but where does that kind of money come from?"

"Mostly hard work," I reply with a shrug. "Claire had a windfall from a great-aunt or something that helped them pay off their law school loans and put money away for Kiersten's education. But the rest? That's all them."

Cole's hand rests on my thigh, and I give it a reassuring squeeze. "But here's a little secret—well, not really a secret, but something that's not usually discussed openly. Claire makes about three times as much as Alex. He holds the benefits because she works on contract, no employer benefits, but she's constantly flying all over the world for corporate mergers. So... everything Alex has done for me, it's only possible because of her."

Cole looks at me, clearly impressed. "Wow, I just always assumed it was more him."

"Most people do," I laugh, "because the world is still pretty sexist. But they also don't go out of their way to correct it. I think they honestly don't care. We just don't talk about it."

"She must love you too," Cole says softly.

I nod, my smile softening. "She's an only child, and Kiersten is an only child. I'm really the only family they have besides Kiersten. Claire and I were closer when they lived nearby, but she's like an older, wiser sister to me."

"Is Kiersten intentionally an only child?" Cole asks, his tone gentle.

"That's a good question," I say, clearing my throat. "Kiersten is adopted, so yes and no. Claire lost several pregnancies, and it was hard because I had Kevin during the tail end of that struggle, just before they decided to adopt." I swallow, squeezing Cole's hand a little tighter. "Claire has also told me that while she knows there's nothing lacking between Alex and Kiersten, she thinks Alex's close relationship with Kevin has something to do with the fact that Kevin is both a boy and genetically related to him."

"Do you think that's true?" Cole asks.

"I think the boy part is accurate. I also think Alex recognized very quickly that Kevin would need a father figure besides Steve," I say with a shrug. "Claire might be right, but there are so many factors at play that it's hard to say for sure."

"I get that," Cole nods, understanding.

Just then, my watch vibrates, and I see it's Cara calling. I show the screen to Cole before answering. "Hey, Cara."

"Autumn, bitch, what the fuck?" Cara's voice is both exasperated and playful.

"What the fuck what?" I laugh, already knowing where this is headed.

"You're kidding, right? Alex sent the kids pictures. Megan sent them to me. Were you not going to call and tell me that you had a Valentine's Day fantasy? That Cole went all grand romantic gesture on your ass?"

I laugh lightly. "I would have told you, eventually. I'm still living it."

Cole looks at me, eyebrows raised in question. I just shake my head at him, smiling.

"Eventually?" Cara echoes, clearly not satisfied.

"Yeah, like when things calmed down a bit." I pause. "Look, Cara, I'm sorry. I haven't even seen the pictures you're talking about, but I was there in person, so you know," I laugh again.

She sighs. "Also, Tara tagged you in wedding photos, and there are a couple of you and Cole that are pretty good."

"On Facebook?" I ask, laughing at her insistence.

"Yeah, and Instagram," she says, like it's the most obvious thing in the world. "Have you not checked anything?"

"Honestly, no, Cara. I'm pretty sure I didn't even look at my phone for a full twenty-four hours, and when I did, it wasn't for long."

"Well, you should look. And you should talk to your children," she scolds, her tone softening with concern.

"Cara," I say firmly, "can you not?"

Cole gives me an amused look as I roll my eyes. He squeezes my thigh in solidarity, a small laugh escaping his lips.

"Autumn," Cara's voice is more empathetic now, "everyone was worried about you—so worried. And then everything is just fine, and they're still worried. I was worried."

"Do you think you could say 'worried' one more time?" I tease.

Cara sighs, exasperated but not really mad.

"Okay," I sigh back, "I get it. We're on our way to Portland right now, but I'll reach out. Just know that everything is good."

Cole squeezes my thigh again, his touch comforting.

"Okay, love you, bitch."

"Love you too, Cara," I say, hanging up the phone.

"What was that all about?" Cole asks, a grin playing on his lips.

I chuckle. "Hurt feelings, mostly. She's the friend I called about two seconds after you walked out of my hotel room that first night, so she feels a bit left out. And apparently, the kids are worried too. But Alex sent them pictures, and there are already photos from the wedding on social media."

Since Cole and I started our relationship, I've been less active on social media. Our relationship had to be private, secret, and with the kids mostly out of the house, there wasn't much to post besides the occasional funny meme. Over time, I found myself looking at it less and less.

I text Alex, asking what pictures he sent, and his response is to send them to me.

"Okay, so Alex just sent me the pictures he shared with the kids. They're probably the same ones he sent you of the room," I laugh, showing Cole the photos.

"That makes sense," Cole says as I start opening up my social media apps.

I begin scrolling, narrating for Cole since he's driving. "Looks like the pictures were posted by Julie. These are from the cameras on the tables, not the professional photographer." I pause, then laugh. "Cole, there are a lot of us in these."

"Seriously?" he asks, amused.

"Yeah, I think a lot were taken by Julio and Mark, but yeah, maybe what Julio said was right. I guess I should text the kids."

I open the group chat with my kids, hoping they're not as upset as Cara. They all prefer texting over talking, so this will be the easiest way to catch up with them all at once.

Me

Hey kids, sorry I've been way non-communicative

I know Alex updated you, but I'm good, we're good, Cole and I are on our way to Portland, but I will call each of you tomorrow, I promise

Kevin

Are you sure you're okay? Because you were not okay when you left here?

Me

Yes, I'm sure, I'm pretty sure outside of time there was only one thing that was going to make me be okay and I have that now

Megan

Well, that's cheesy

Sami

lol

Megan

Kev, by the pictures from the wedding alone I think she's fine

Kevin

Does he still have a job?

Megan

Do you think he could have bought like four thousand dollars in roses if he didn't?

Me

Kids

Sami

Facepalm - seriously? Roses are that expensive?

Me

Yes, he still has a job, but we haven't really talked about that yet, so I have no other details

Megan

Yeah - for that quality especially, it's over one hundred per dozen, more on Valentine's Day

Kevin

How was that not the first thing you talked about?

Sami

Kevin - if you hadn't seen Kalisha in four weeks would money be the first thing you would talk about? Or do?

Megan

Seriously … plus money and jobs don't matter if she's happy, and she is

Me

Okay - don't argue with each other, Kevin I love you, I'll call you tomorrow, maybe later tonight, just know I'm okay

Megan

Oh so you love Kevin, but not us?

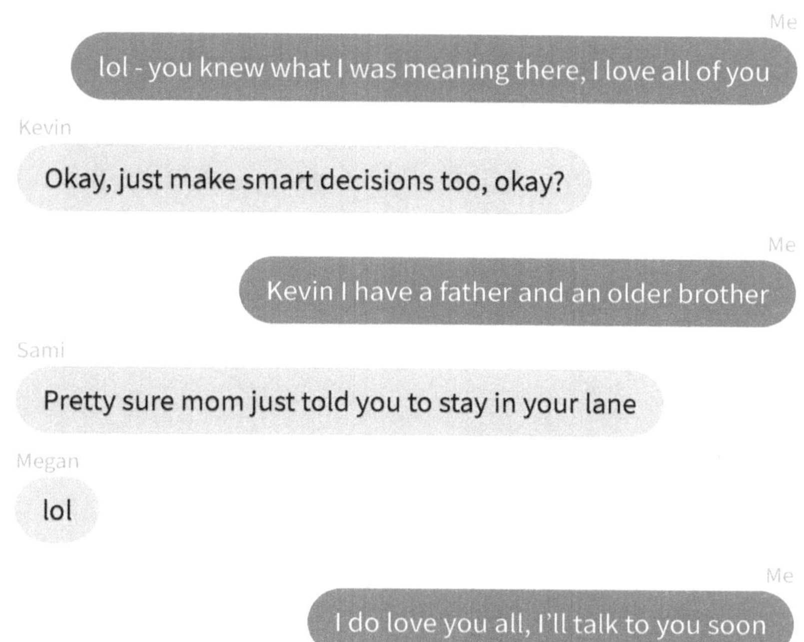

I lean back, staring up at the car's ceiling with a deep sigh.

"Everything okay?" Cole's voice is gentle, his concern evident.

"Yeah," I exhale, though the weight of the situation lingers. "The girls are fine, but Kevin... Kevin's a different story." I squeeze his hand, needing that connection. "You might have to help me with this one."

"Really?" he asks, his tone a mix of curiosity and concern.

"Yeah, unfortunately," I admit, pausing to gather my thoughts. "I think he just needs to vent, but I'm not sure. Alex has been trying to keep him calm these past few weeks, but he's still clearly pissed."

"Do you know why he's so much more upset?" Cole asks, his thumb tracing comforting circles on my thigh.

"I don't know for sure, but I have a few ideas," I say, swallowing the lump in my throat. "He's definitely the most worried about our jobs and what happened there, which, honestly, I don't even know the full extent of yet," I add with a small, humorless laugh. "But Kevin was the most aware of where I was when Steve and I split up, and these last few weeks probably triggered those memories for him. He has always been so protective of me. I think kind of like what you said about having the anger built up, he has built up this anger towards you, and it's going to take some time for him to let go of that."

Cole squeezes my hand in response, his voice tender. "I love you, Autumn. I'm sorry."

"I know," I say, feeling the sincerity in his touch. "I'll talk to him, but before I do, I need to have some answers." I laugh softly, knowing how true that is.

"About work?" Cole asks, his concern shifting.

"Yeah," I nod. "I need to have those answers first."

CHAPTER FIFTY-NINE

THE CAR RIDE TO PORTLAND

"That's actually what I wanted to talk to you about on this drive," Cole says, his tone shifting as he changes lanes on the freeway. "So, it's an appropriate segue," he adds with a brief pause. "Honestly, I thought that would be the first thing Alex would bring up, but he didn't even mention it."

"He probably assumed it was resolved and didn't care much about the details," I say, smiling at him. "What did he want to talk about, then?"

"Mostly, he just wanted to reassure me that we're good, that despite everything that happened after the ceremony and over the past few weeks, he still respects me, understands the decisions I made, and thinks I'm good for you." Cole steals a quick glance at me, a smile tugging at his lips. "It was more about our relationship and not so much about you. Then we talked about him leaving, and I went out on a limb and asked if he could help set up the room. He was honestly delighted to help. He told me you'd mentioned hoping I'd do exactly what I was planning, so he was overjoyed to make that happen for you."

I laugh, shaking my head. "He probably was, even though having my brother spread rose petals on a bed for me is something I never imagined in my wildest dreams."

Cole laughs with me before his expression turns more serious. "Anyway, the big news is that Rich and Vanessa, Lauryn's boss, rewrote the policy. So, there's no longer a rule against us having a relationship. There's still some language about avoiding special favors and the potential appearance of impropriety, but it's no longer against company policy, which is why it doesn't matter that it's not March yet."

"I assume that means you're still changing positions in March?" I ask.

"Yes," he nods. "I've been learning the ropes, but it's not terribly different from what I've been doing—just managing existing clients instead of mostly new ones." He pauses again. "The contracts and official job offer have all been signed. It's a done deal, just waiting for the next two weeks to pass."

"At least this didn't impact that," I say, feeling a surge of relief.

"No, it didn't. In fact, Rich said the way I handled everything solidified their decision."

"I guess that's a silver lining."

"Yeah, and Autumn?" he says, his tone shifting slightly.

"Cole?" I respond, mimicking his seriousness with a playful lilt.

"There's a signing bonus, and I'll now be eligible for executive bonuses, on top of a pretty substantial pay increase. So whatever worries Kevin has about that, I'm sure we'll be okay."

"A signing bonus? Even though you're internal?" I ask, raising an eyebrow.

"Yeah, but there's a reason for it, and it's something I need to talk to you about." He glances at me again before changing lanes.

"That doesn't sound good," I say, bracing myself.

"It's not bad, but it's not necessarily good either," he admits, swallowing before continuing. "They're going to need me in Columbus a lot more frequently, probably a couple of weeks out of each month, or at least several days within those weeks."

"Do you have to move?" I ask, my mind already spinning with what that could mean for us and our kids.

"Not necessarily, but they're strongly suggesting I get an apartment or condo there," he says, pausing as if weighing his words. "I've been thinking... and this feels like an entirely inappropriate conversation to have after the last few weeks." He laughs a bit awkwardly, his thumb tracing soothing patterns on my thigh. "This is going to sound really forward."

"I'm pretty sure you've been forward with me before," I laugh. "Remember, I gave you a key to my house on our first date."

"True," he chuckles. "But I think we should live at your house, and I can get a condo in Columbus for when I need to be there."

"Cole, that's like a seven-hour drive," I point out, my practical side kicking in.

"Well, I'm glad that's the part you're objecting to," he laughs, clearly relieved.

It takes me a second to process what he's saying. "Oh, you thought I'd object to you moving in with me?"

"Well, yeah, potentially," he admits with a smile, though there's relief in his tone.

"We've pretty much been living together unofficially, except when work kept us apart, and honestly, I still don't want you out of my sight if I can help it," I laugh.

"I didn't know if this would have changed that," he admits. I squeeze his hand and in reassurance. "There are at least five direct flights from Chicago to Columbus every day—short and cheap flights. So, yeah, the drive is long, but there are options," he says. "When you don't have conferences, you could come with me to Columbus if you want. There will be times when I'd want you there for social business events, dinners, gatherings. It wouldn't just be that I *want* you by my side; it would be beneficial for you to be there."

"A condo and executive parties do sound better than the cardboard box I once said I'd need to be happy with you," I tease, smiling at the prospect.

Cole laughs, his eyes sparkling with affection. "Yes, it would be. And you can help me find one—make it yours too. It'd be the first place that feels like ours, not just yours or mine, from the very beginning."

"You're right. That would be nice." I smile at the thought, then ask, "What would you do with your house?"

"I was thinking I'd rent it to Matthew, maybe him and some friends. He wouldn't be able to cover the full mortgage, but it would give him some stability and give me a reason to keep the house—besides just wanting to."

"And you can afford both? You're sure?"

"Yeah, honestly, Autumn, when I sat down with Rich and Vanessa—and by the way, there still wasn't a resolution to our situation when they handed me those contracts—Rich was confident there would be, but when I saw the numbers, I'm pretty sure my jaw hit the table," he says with a laugh.

"That much, huh?"

"I knew it would be a pay raise, and I knew my bonus structure would change, but it was *a lot* more than I expected. Rich said he wanted to reward my loyalty and hard work, that it was time I got paid what I'm worth." Cole pauses to change lanes, then continues. "The signing bonus alone is probably enough to put down at least fifty percent on a one-bedroom condo in downtown Columbus, which is exactly what it's intended for—either that or a full relocation."

"Well, that explains why you thought Valentine's Day was worth spending an absurd amount of money," I tease, laughing.

He glances at me, his expression softening. "Not Valentine's Day—you. *You* were worth an absurd amount of money."

His words leave me momentarily speechless. "Cole, about that cardboard box..."

He smiles, understanding. "I know, Autumn. And yeah, this one was special, probably not an annual thing. But part of why you're worth it is that I could have given you a candy necklace, and you would've reacted almost the same way."

I smile, my heart swelling with affection. "So, what happened with Tom?"

Cole sighs, the lightness in his voice dimming. "This is the not-so-fun part. He didn't follow the rules. First, he filed complaints, not just about you supposedly getting special treatment from me, but also about me getting special treatment from Pete. When HR told him not to talk to anyone, he still sent group messages to Mark, Julio, and Tara, and emailed them at their personal addresses."

"Seriously?"

"Yeah, he was trying to out us—out me, I don't know—but they all knew, or thought they knew. Mark and Tara pretty much knew from us, and Julio had made his own assumptions but wasn't surprised. They all immediately forwarded everything to Lauryn," he sighs deeply, "But HR's reaction to that is part of why I was so rigid about following the rules. I knew you wouldn't tell them if we talked, but Tom's actions pretty much shut down all his arguments."

I squeeze his hand, feeling the tension in his voice. "Pete told me the most important part of the non-communication rule was proving *you* could follow the rules," I say, shrugging. "That's part of why I thought I could get away with texting you, even though you wouldn't write me back," I add, catching his glance as his thumb and fingers trace soothing patterns on my thigh.

"Yeah, that's pretty much what they told me too, and they emphasized it even more after Tom did what he did. Anyway, Tom was less than two years away from retirement age, whether he planned to retire or not. He hired lawyers, trying to argue that I should never have been in the position I was in—that Pete was biased. But legally, our relationship became a moot point quickly because I'd reported it to Pete months ago. Plus, Tom's commissions and bonuses were more than yours, so he had nothing to stand on. He tried to argue that it was because you'd been in your role for less time, but it didn't hold."

I laugh, shaking my head. "I don't know if I should be mad or happy that he was getting bigger bonuses than me."

Cole smiles, a hint of relief in his eyes. "I get that. In the end, after a lot of legal back and forth, Tom left with a pretty substantial severance package. He signed a non-disclosure agreement, so he can't talk about the company, including Pete, you, or me. But before he signed, he burned all his bridges—said some pretty nasty things to the team. Basically, he told them they weren't worth anything."

"I'm surprised Tara didn't tell me," I say, shaking my head slightly.

"I'm not," Cole replies. "They were explicitly told not to mention it to you. That was one of the reasons Pete wanted Laura to have lunch with you that day."

"To see what I knew? Or to see if I'd talk?"

"Yeah, partly. But the main reason was to check on you—for my sake. So someone could see how you were really doing." He sighs. "I was *so* worried about you. Laura said you weren't yourself, that there was no light in your eyes, but she said you were holding up."

"She was lovely that day, honestly. I asked her about you, and she did tell me you weren't doing well either."

"I wasn't," he admits with a dry laugh. "But I felt a little better after she told me you were hanging in there."

"Well, I was also medicated," I say with a shrug.

Cole's eyes widen slightly. "Medicated?"

I clear my throat. "Yeah," I sigh. "The Friday after Denver, I just wasn't okay. I wasn't sleeping, wasn't eating, was crying almost constantly, and barely working. I'm grateful Pete let me slack off for weeks, and Tara took half my sales calls, telling clients I was sick. But that Friday, I saw the doctor. She put me on an antidepressant and gave me prescription sleep meds." I laugh, though there's no humor in it. "She wanted to give me Ativan, but after Dr. Gabari... I just couldn't."

"Autumn," he says, my name heavy with apology.

I squeeze his hand, offering a small smile. "I'm not saying this to make you feel guilty. Those medications exist for a reason."

Without a word, Cole changes lanes and pulls off to the shoulder of the highway.

"Cole? What are you doing?"

"I just need to give you my full attention for a minute." He unbuckles his seatbelt, turns toward me, and reaches out, his fingers tracing the curve of my cheekbone, then brushing my lower lip. He leans across the console, kissing me deeply. I unbuckle my belt to turn fully toward him, the kiss becoming more intense, more emotional.

"I'm so sorry, Autumn," he whispers against my lips.

"We're okay," I murmur, swallowing the lump in my throat. "I did what I needed to do, and I'm better for it. It would've been so much worse if I hadn't."

He studies my face for a moment, then kisses me again, this time softer. "No wonder Kevin's so pissed," he says, leaning back in his seat and staring at the car's ceiling.

"It's still not your fault," I say, gently placing my hand on his.

"It is, but I appreciate you saying that," he replies, his smile tinged with sadness.

"So, by the time I saw Laura, I'd been on medication for about a week. I was probably the best I'd been in two weeks," I explain. "That was my point, I guess."

"You didn't tell her?"

"No, I didn't. I put on my brave face," I say, laughing softly. "Honestly, did Alex tell you about the airport?"

"No," he says, his eyes searching mine.

"I had been holding it together for three weeks, trying to be strong for the kids, to keep them from worrying more than they already were. I was trying to stay professional at work, even during the conference in San Francisco. Just trying to maintain some sense of normalcy when everything was far from normal." I pause, swallowing hard. "Alex was my first safe place. When he met me at the airport, I hugged him, and I completely lost it. I, shattered, I cried and cried—not as much as I did last night, but close. It was the first time in almost four weeks that I didn't feel like I had to pretend everything was okay. I knew Alex was strong enough to handle it and supportive enough of you not to hold it against you."

Cole reaches over, his fingers gently twisting a strand of my hair. "I'm so sorry," he says again, his voice full of regret.

I shake my head. "It's just information now, Cole. There's nothing to apologize for. Spending time with Alex was therapeutic. He cheered me up and continued to be supportive of us—of you." I pause, hesitating before asking, "Where were you when we pulled up to the hotel?"

Cole takes a deep breath and exhales slowly. "I was in my car, in the parking lot."

"When we finished checking in and went out to get our luggage, that was the first time I genuinely laughed since Denver," I admit, the memory bringing a small smile to my face. "I'm pretty sure you couldn't hear us because Alex even said something like, 'It's good to hear you laugh again, baby sister.' Laughing was not something I did much of for a while there. And ironically, the banter that led to that moment started because the front desk person thought we were a couple."

Cole chuckles softly. "Apparently, that was a thing that morning."

"Yeah, well, I think Alex was overly affectionate because he knew the wedding would be hard for me." I shrug.

Cole takes another deep breath, leaning over to kiss me softly. "I guess we should start driving again."

As we merge back onto the freeway, I steer the conversation back to work. "So, does that mean Mark is my boss now?"

"Not yet," Cole replies, shaking his head slightly. "Not until I officially transition in March. But yes, he will be."

He pauses, glancing over at me. "There's something else I wanted to tell you. That transition is going to be a slow process. You might know a bit more than the others, but there's a lot I do that the team doesn't see, and I need to train Mark on all of it. Plus, the sales team is down two people until he can hire and train replacements, so..." He throws me a quick, mischievous smile. "For the foreseeable future, I'll still be on the conference schedule and helping with sales leads. Everyone higher up is fine with us being at the same conferences during that time. So, essentially, I'll be with you everywhere—unless there's a conflict with something else important, but with conferences mostly happening on weekends, that won't be an issue often."

"Seriously?" I ask, a bit surprised.

"Yep," he confirms, his tone light. "And even after the team is back to full strength, there'll still be training. Honestly, Rich mentioned that Michael should have been better partnered with the sales team. He's hoping that's something we can improve with this transition—that Mark and I will have a stronger working relationship than Michael and I did. Which also means I'll have excuses to travel with you beyond the foreseeable future."

"Well, that all sounds fantastic," I laugh, feeling a wave of relief and excitement.

"You might get sick of me," Cole jokes, his eyes sparkling.

"Not anytime soon," I reply, smiling back at him.

CHAPTER SIXTY

THE DINNER & BACK TO REALITY

An hour later, we pull up to the restaurant and meet Alex and Claire in the foyer. Introductions are made, with hugs and handshakes exchanged. Once we're seated, wine and water in front of us, Alex wastes no time bringing up work.

Cole gives a concise version of what he told me earlier in the car. Alex listens carefully, then turns to me. "Do you feel comfortable with all of that?"

I nod, smiling. "Yeah, I think it's honestly the best possible outcome."

Alex glances at Claire before continuing, as if sharing an unspoken understanding. "I just want to share something from our own experience, so you have all the information," he begins. "You know we tried that—where I worked halftime in Portland and we tried to stay in Milwaukee. Now, Portland is *a lot* farther from Milwaukee than Columbus is, but after about eighteen months, we realized it was just too much. I'm not saying it's impossible for you, but we've been down that road, and we know how challenging it can be."

I clear my throat, knowing my response might surprise Cole. "I thought about your situation almost immediately," I admit, glancing at Cole. "I think we'll see how it goes, but there are a few things we—more like I—have to consider. Mostly Mom and Dad. I feel like we can't both be that far away, but if I'm already far away more than half the time..." I shrug. "I also know the kids see our house as a forever home, a place they want to be able to come back to. But at some point, it might not make sense anymore, and moving to Columbus could be something we'll need to consider."

Cole gently runs his fingers through my hair. "Autumn definitely has more roots than I do, so a lot of that will depend on her comfort level, especially with her parents."

"I had the comfort of knowing you were still blocks away from Mom and Dad when I moved away," Alex adds with a smile, "which made that decision easier."

The conversation shifts to work, with Claire explaining more about her job to Cole, and Cole sharing insights into some of the up-and-coming medical devices in research and development—things even I'm not fully aware of.

"Kiersten would love to hear all this," Alex says, his eyes lighting up.

"She would," Claire agrees with a smile.

"We're planning on coming out in July with Kiersten," Alex continues. "Figured we'd spend the Fourth with the family. She'd love hearing about all of that."

"We'd love to have you," I say, smiling warmly.

"Does that boat you went out on for New Year's Eve do the same thing for the Fourth of July?" Alex asks, turning to Cole.

"Oh, she told you about that?" Cole grins, glancing at me before nodding. "Yeah, they do the Fourth too."

"Maybe we can find a way to take the whole family," Alex suggests.

"It was pretty magical—the girls would love it," I say, already picturing the celebration.

"I also want to see Kevin in Madison, see his apartment and office, and everything while we're there," Alex adds.

"I'm sure that can be arranged," I reply with a laugh. "And Kalisha is such an amazing woman—I'm hoping he hangs on to her."

"Yes, I'd love to meet her too," Alex says, his smile widening.

We continue talking about Alex's plans for his visit to Milwaukee. They'll be there for two weeks, plenty of time to visit everyone and do everything he wants. As dinner winds down, Alex mentions that they'd invite us back to the house, but they both have early mornings. We exchange hugs, and Claire tells me she's genuinely happy for me.

On the drive back, I decide to reach out to Kevin. It's late in Wisconsin, but I text him anyway, asking if he has a minute to talk. A minute later, my phone rings.

"Hey, Kev," I answer.

"Hey," he replies, his voice still tinged with agitation.

"Kev, I love you," I say, sighing softly.

"I know, Mom. I love you too," he sighs back. "Did you find out about work? Both yours and his?"

"I did," I reassure him, then go over everything I'm comfortable sharing, including the plans to split time in Columbus. When I finish, he changes the subject.

"Mom?"

"Yeah, Kevin?"

"Are you happy? Like, honestly happy?"

I glance at Cole, his face illuminated by the passing streetlights. "I am, Kevin. Very much so."

"I just don't know how you can forgive that," he says, the frustration evident in his voice.

I take a deep breath. "Kevin, I'm not going to try to explain what Alex has already tried to. Sometimes adults have to do hard things," I say as Cole reaches over, his thumb tracing soothing circles on my thigh. "Especially when they create the situation. It's the 'you made your bed, now lie in it' scenario. Cole and I knew we were playing with fire, and while things are fine now, we did get burned."

Kevin is quiet, his breathing the only sound on the line. I wait, giving him the time he needs.

"Mom," he finally speaks, his voice softer. "I was just so worried... so worried it would be like when Dad left, only worse because I believe you love Cole more than you ever could have loved Dad."

I laugh, almost a snort. "Kevin, that's true. I'm okay, we're okay. It was a temporary thing, and we're okay now."

"You promise?"

"I promise," I say, smiling. "How about we figure out a weekend that works and get everyone together for dinner or something?"

"I'd like that," he laughs, a bit of the tension easing from his voice. "Maybe a lasagna night?"

"Maybe." I smile. "Kevin, we okay?"

"Yeah, we're okay. I was just so worried and scared."

"I know you can't help it, but remember, I have a father—and a brother who thinks he's my father half the time—so you don't need to take that on."

"I know, but it doesn't change how I feel."

"I get it. I love you."

"Love you too."

After I hang up, I drop my phone into the console and glance at Cole.

"Better?" he asks, his eyes meeting mine.

"Yeah, better," I say, feeling a sense of peace. "He's good."

Monday morning, we join the team call, with everyone present except Tara. Pete kicks off the meeting by formally announcing Cole's transition and Mark's new role. He reiterates what Cole and I already knew—Cole's transition will be gradual, as he hands off tasks to Mark and continues to support the sales team, which will be short-staffed for a while.

Mark and Cole are tasked with revising the conference schedule based on the events the company has already committed to, with a deadline to finalize it by the end of the week. Beyond that, it's business as usual.

As the meeting wraps up, I turn to Cole with a smile. "That was easy."

He grins back. "Tom was the only one who could've made it difficult."

Two weeks later, we host a lasagna night at my house with Cara, Blake, all our kids, and Kalisha. Cole's boys are becoming pros at these gatherings, and their smiles when they see me are even bigger than I expected. Those four weeks apart clearly affected them more than Cole let on.

Over dinner, the conversation naturally turns to Cole's upcoming move into my house. Megan and Sami are thrilled, knowing it means I'll be home more, even with the time spent in Columbus.

The boys, however, are quick to tell Cole he needs to hire movers for his workout equipment, which sparks a lot of laughter.

"I love you, Dad, but I am not packing and carrying all that," Tyler says, shaking his head.

"Where are you going to put it all?" Megan asks, looking between Cole and me.

I glance at Cole, a smile playing on my lips. "I was thinking the basement."

"Me too," Cole agrees. "We'll need the garage space, so it makes the most sense."

The conversation shifts to Matthew staying at Cole's house. He jokes about keeping his bedroom because it would feel weird to sleep in Cole's room after we'd been there together.

Cole leans in, whispering with a mischievous grin, "Probably shouldn't tell him about the kitchen island."

I nearly spit out my wine, laughing as Cole chuckles beside me.

By the end of the night, I'm overwhelmed with gratitude for all of them, my heart full and content.

Another two weeks pass, and Dr. Gabari files for another continuation, requesting an additional ninety days for the defense. The court grants the request, but due to the availability of the courtroom, judge, and prosecutor, the trial date is pushed to August.

The day after the continuation is granted, Cole finishes moving the last of his things into my house.

"So, I guess that means we're officially cohabitating," I say, smiling up at him.

"I guess so," he laughs, pulling me into his arms. "There's nobody else I'd rather live with. Also," he pauses, his tone turning playful, "I think we should just disable the camera by the pool for now."

"Oh yeah?" I ask, feeling the warmth of his embrace as he kisses me.

"Yeah," he says with a mischievous grin, "there are still things I want to do with you out there—fantasies, you could say."

"I can't wait," I reply, kissing him deeply.

That night, in the quiet hours after midnight, Cole leaves me speechless again. His fingers trace slow, deliberate lines down my back, and his voice, though confident, is soft.

"Autumn, I've been thinking about something for a while."

"Yeah?" I respond, curious.

"A few months ago, before all this drama, there was a moment in this room," he says, glancing around my bedroom.

I laugh softly. "Cole, we've had a lot of moments in my bedroom—and yours."

He draws me closer, pressing a sweet kiss to my forehead. "That's true," he says with a hint of humor, "but I'm talking about the time you asked me to change your last name."

I hold my breath, unsure of where he's going with this.

"Don't freak out on me," he laughs, sensing my tension. "I'm not asking that question right now."

I exhale, my fingers tracing gentle patterns on his chest as his lips find the top of my head.

"But that night, you planted a seed," he continues, his voice tender. "And it's been growing ever since. I know we're only six months into this, but I want you in my arms as you drift off to sleep for the rest of our lives. I want the world to know that you're mine, and I'm yours."

Pausing, he swallows as if gathering the courage to continue. "But the part I really want you to know is that I swore I would never go there again. I told my brothers, my boys, my friends—everyone—that I'd never get married again. And almost the second I kissed you for the first time, I started rethinking all of that."

He swallows again, his voice filled with emotion. "Autumn, you broke me in all the right ways. You shattered the walls I'd built to keep people out. You woke up parts of me I didn't even know existed. You've changed me in all the best ways, and I'm so, so grateful for you."

It takes me a moment to find my voice, but when I do, the words come from deep within. "Cole, I don't think you broke or shattered me, but you did awaken me. There are parts of me I thought I'd never feel or see again, and others I never knew existed that I now experience almost every day. I love you, unconditionally and indefinitely."

"Unconditionally and indefinitely," he echoes, pulling me into a slow, gentle kiss that seems to seal a promise between us.

EPILOGUE

The July heat is oppressive as Cole and I pack up the car, ready to head to the airport. We've spent the last week at our beautiful new condo in Columbus, but today, my brother and his family are flying into Chicago, so we're heading back to Milwaukee, with a stop in Chicago to meet them.

The plan is simple—we'll meet Alex and his family at the airport, though they'll rent a car and drive up to our house. We land about thirty minutes before they do, so it makes sense to see them at the airport first. Our car situation has worked out well since we started splitting our time between Columbus and Milwaukee—Cole keeps his SUV in Columbus, while my SUV and the Audi stay in Milwaukee. Long-term parking fills in the gaps.

With the Fourth of July falling on a Friday this year, it's shaping up to be a full family weekend. Cole's kids are driving up on the third to join us, making it an even larger gathering.

Kevin and Kalisha are still dating, as adorable as ever. Megan has been seeing someone new for a few months now, a guy named Austin. And William is in what Megan and Matthew jokingly refer to as a "situationship" with a sweet but incredibly spunky girl named Chloe.

Cole and I don't pry, but we like Chloe and think she's good for him—definitely not the kind of girl either of us would have ever pictured with him, but so good for him.

Alex is bringing his wife Claire and their daughter Kiersten, so we'll have fourteen people in total, plus Cara and Blake, for the weekend celebrations. Alex and Cole have pooled their resources to charter a yacht for our family to watch the Chicago fireworks on Lake Michigan. They've been handling all the planning, and since I'm not footing the bill, I've stayed out of it unless they ask for my input. Claire and I have talked about it, and she feels the same way—they're handling caterers and bartenders, and it all seems more complicated than it needs to be.

We meet Alex, Claire, and Kiersten at baggage claim, grateful we flew into Midway instead of O'Hare. Hugs are exchanged all around, and Claire introduces Cole to Kiersten, who's eager to hear about Quisenbelt's research and development. About two hours later, we're all back at my house, though Alex, Claire, and Kiersten will be checking into a hotel. Our house will be full of six kids and three of their partners, and that would be a bit much for my brother and his family to handle for three or four days.

Sami is home from college for the summer, so the girl cousin group is excited to spend some quality time together. The seven of us enjoy a nice dinner out on the first night. Alex and Claire have plans to visit other friends and some of Claire's extended family, so we won't see them every day while they're here, but the time we do spend together is precious.

On Thursday, I receive a call from an unfamiliar number. When I answer, I'm surprised to hear a very frantic Chloe on the other end.

"Autumn, you have to help me," she pleads, her Bostonian accent thick with anxiety.

"What's wrong, Chloe?"

"William said this event is formal and I need cocktail attire. Autumn, where I'm from, we don't use those words! I just smiled and nodded at him, but I have no idea what I'm supposed to wear on Saturday."

"Chloe," I say, trying to soothe her panic, "did you ever go to homecoming or prom?"

"No, I didn't, but is that the kind of dress I need?"

"Yes, more like homecoming than prom, but that's the idea."

"Autumn, I don't have anything like that. I've *never* worn anything like that. Maybe I just shouldn't go," she says, her words tumbling out so quickly it takes me a moment to catch up.

"Hold on, Chloe," I say gently, "I'm going to put you on speaker so I can text Sami. Do you think William can take you into Gary on the way here?"

"Yeah, probably," she responds, her voice a little steadier now.

Me

Hey Sami, any chance you can meet Chloe on your way through Gary to help her find a dress for the Fourth of July?

Sami

Sure, send me her number

"Okay, Sami will meet you there. If you don't find anything, we can look in Chicago or Milwaukee. We'll get you sorted," I reassure her.

"Autumn, I can't afford that," Chloe says, her voice tinged with sadness.

"I've got it covered. You'll need shoes too," I say firmly.

"Are you sure?" she asks, sounding a bit hesitant.

"Yes, I'm sure. I'll send Sami your number so you two can connect."

We wrap up the call just as Cole walks into the room.

"What was that about?" he asks, curious.

"Girl problems," I laugh. "Chloe has nothing to wear—not in the usual way women say it, but I think she's never really worn a dress."

Cole sighs, amused. "So you're sending Sami to help her out?"

"Yeah, hopefully William doesn't mind meeting her at the mall," I reply with a grin.

"He shouldn't," Cole chuckles, then leans in to kiss me. "What about you? What are you wearing?"

"I don't know. I have so many dresses, it doesn't seem worth it to buy a new one," I say, wrinkling my nose.

"I think you should wear the blue one," he suggests with a smile.

I laugh, shrugging. "Okay, I can do that."

"Also, just so you know, Pete and Laura are coming, and I invited Mark, Tara, and Julio," he says. "Julio can't make it—kid stuff—but Mark and Tara might."

"The more, the merrier." I smile.

"Well, good, because I also invited my brother Carson and his wife," he adds.

That surprises me. "Oh, really? A fancy boat party for their first time meeting me?"

He smirks, pulling me in for a long kiss. "Yep, that's the plan."

I call Sami, giving her instructions and a spending limit for Chloe, but I also remind her to make Chloe feel like family. Sami is perfect for the task.

By Thursday afternoon, Matthew and Tyler arrive at the house, with everyone else trickling in on Friday afternoon. Austin won't join us until Saturday, but by Friday night, we have ten adults under one roof. With all the chaos, we decide to order pizza instead of attempting to cook.

Later, Chloe and Sami pull me aside to show off the dress they found. Chloe looks absolutely adorable—there's no other word for it. She's older than William, almost twenty-eight, but she's barely five feet tall and full of spunk. Her raven hair complements her tawny skin and chocolate-brown eyes perfectly. The dress they chose is a simple, elegant little black dress. Sami said they wanted something Chloe would feel comfortable wearing again. She also found a pair of shoes, a clutch, and a shawl to complete the look. I know she'll look fantastic.

Saturday afternoon, Austin arrives at the house, carrying a garment bag. He's a great match for Megan, though he's a few years older. His hazel eyes and blonde hair, with a subtle hint of red—not quite as strawberry as Megan's and mine—add to his easygoing charm. He stands about six feet tall with an athletic build, and there's a gentleness in the way he interacts with her that's rare for their age. There's something about him that we can't quite put our finger on—an air of mystery. It's clear he has money, but he's humble, and we know there's more to the story that Megan hasn't shared.

Our caravan, filled with all the kids, Alex and his family, and Cara and Blake, heads to Chicago. It's a long procession of cars, but we're grateful Jamie's office is near Navy Pier, offering us free parking for the afternoon and evening. Alex rented a seven-passenger SUV, so he shuttles everyone from Jamie's office to the yacht.

Alex, Claire, Cole, and I are the last to board, allowing all the kids to get on first. I shouldn't have expected anything less with Alex and Cole planning it, but the yacht is impressive. There's a catered buffet, a fully stocked bar with bartenders and servers, and a DJ playing soft music, which I suspect will pick up once we're out on the water.

I smile at Cole, leaning into him. "You guys did good."

"We tried," he says, wrapping his arms around me.

Earlier, Megan had styled my hair in waterfall braids, just like that night in Chicago when Cole first saw me in this dress. He had told me I looked untouchable, but I assured him he was allowed to dishevel me. Now, as he runs his fingers over the necklace he gave me, he repeats how beautiful it looks, especially with this dress.

Cole introduces me to his oldest brother, Carson, and his wife, Maria. The resemblance between Carson and Cole is unmistakable;

they're clearly brothers. Maria is quiet but sweet, and Cole mentions they've been married for over twenty years.

Mark and Leona, along with Tara and Max, join us as well. We were expecting Pete and Laura, who also make it on board, but it's nice to see everyone together outside of work. We've met at conferences and other work events, but this feels different—more relaxed, more personal.

As the evening unfolds, we eat, drink, and enjoy the music. The kids make song requests and dance, and it's heartwarming to see Kevin, Megan, and William more at ease with their significant others. Even though it's a formal event, the atmosphere is casual and intimate, surrounded by family.

About twenty minutes before the fireworks are set to begin, Megan pulls me aside and asks if we can talk. I kiss Cole on the cheek and excuse myself, following her to the far end of the boat where we're alone. It's the perfect spot to watch the fireworks, with a stunning view of the Chicago skyline.

"What's up, Megs?" I ask, curious.

She starts to tell me everything about her relationship with Austin. Some details surprise me, others don't, but she answers all the questions I've had, and I'm grateful for her honesty. We're laughing together when I suddenly notice the music. We hadn't been able to hear it out here before, but now it's clear, and I look at Megan with a raised eyebrow.

She grins and says, "Turn around, Mom."

I do, and my breath catches. Somehow, while I was engrossed in Megan's story, an entire scene has transformed behind me. Hundreds of roses—just like Valentine's Day—adorn the deck. Party lights suddenly flicker on, illuminating the space. I see all our family and friends gathered on both the upper and lower decks, and standing just a few feet in front of me is Cole. He must have been right behind me a second ago. My jaw drops.

Cole steps forward, takes my hand, and smiles. "Autumn, you know I love you more than life itself. There was a moment in an elevator in Columbus when I told you that you were the death of me, and you said you'd like to think you breathe life into me. Truer words have never been spoken. And, Autumn," he pauses, taking a breath, "I want you to breathe that life into me for the rest of the time I have on this earth and, God willing, beyond."

He drops to one knee, pulling out a box and opening it to reveal a ring. "Autumn, will you marry me?"

Tears spill down my cheeks as I nod. "Yes, yes—a thousand times yes."

Cole stands and slips the most beautiful sapphire and diamond ring onto my finger before kissing me. Cheers and whistles erupt from everyone around us, and as if perfectly timed, fireworks begin to explode over Lake Michigan. He gently unwraps his arms from around me and wipes the tears from my cheeks.

"Happy tears?" he asks.

"Extremely happy tears," I laugh.

"Did you just quote *Pride and Prejudice* when you said yes?" he asks, amused.

I think about it and laugh. "I did, but it wasn't intentional."

He kisses me again, and we turn to watch the fireworks together. For the rest of my life, I'll be grateful to this group of friends and family who helped Cole pull off this magical moment. He pulls me to him, my back flush with his chest and Austin joins Megan as we watch the explosions in the sky.

After the fireworks, there are endless congratulations and admiration for the ring. It has twin teardrop-shaped sapphires surrounded by diamonds—stunning and unique. Cole tells me he had it custom-made with Alex's blessing on the design and the proposal itself. He also shares that he asked for my dad's blessing, though my parents didn't want to come out on the boat.

When the boat docks and it's time to head home, I realize Cole's surprises aren't over. A limousine waits for us at the dock. Cole tosses our car keys to Alex, and we exchange hugs and handshakes with everyone who came out, not just for the Fourth but for us.

"Cole? Where are we going?" I ask, curious about the next surprise.

"Just to a hotel, nothing too extravagant," he says with a smile. "But with so many people at the house right now, I thought we might want some time just for us."

As soon as we're in the limousine and it starts moving, I pull him close and kiss him deeply. "I love you so much," I whisper when our lips part.

"I know you do, and I love you too," he says, gently running his thumb over my cheekbone.

"I have a question," I say, raising an eyebrow. "How long have you been planning this?"

"Planning to propose to you? Probably since the night you asked me to change your last name," he laughs. "Planning this proposal? Since Tara's wedding."

My eyes widen in surprise. He laughs, clearly amused by my reaction.

"Autumn, part of me wanted to propose that night, as part of the grand romantic scheme, but I didn't think the timing was right—not after everything that happened. I thought we should be together a little longer. But honestly, since you let me into that hotel room in Dallas, I've known I never want to be parted from you, ever."

I pull him back to me, and we kiss again, losing ourselves in the moment like teenagers after prom until the limousine finally comes to a stop.

Cole already has the keys to the room, and I don't want to know how that happened since I'm pretty sure he's been with me all day—though it occurs to me that Alex hadn't. He scans the lock and opens the door, and I'm instantly transported back to Valentine's Day. The room is filled with white roses and blue baby's breath. I take it all in and then turn to look at Cole.

"I think you can dishevel me now," I say, smiling. He laughs, a low, almost sinful sound, as he loosens his tie.

"You know, this is starting to become an expectation. I might have to up my game," I tease.

"Oh, I've already thought about that." He grins.

"How long do we have this room?" I ask, curiosity piqued.

"Two nights, but if you want to stay longer, I got us both out of work all of next week," he says, smiling.

"We left all those kids alone in our house," I point out, and he just shrugs before gently bringing my mouth to his, his hand resting on the back of my neck.

"They're not kids," he whispers against my lips.

He slowly pulls down the zipper of my dress, letting the fabric fall away from my body. As the corset slips to the floor, he looks up at me. "Do you need to deal with your hair before I dishevel you further?" he asks, smiling.

"Maybe, but it won't take long since, you know, I'm sober," I say, reaching up to remove the two hidden hair ties and gently pulling out the plaits with my fingers. "See?"

He laughs, then wraps his hand in my hair and kisses me again. His lips travel across my jaw and down my neck, sending sparks across my skin. He kneels in front of me, his hands gliding down my body as he slips off my thong and carefully removes it from my ankles.

As he stands, his hand trails along the inside of my leg, warmth coursing through me. When he reaches my center, he gently slides two fingers inside, making me inhale sharply. I realize he's still fully dressed while I'm left wearing only my heels, and I laugh softly.

Cole looks at me, curious, and I shake my head, starting to unbutton his shirt. He continues to work his fingers inside me, curling them to hit that sweet spot he knows so well, the heel of his hand applying perfect pressure.

As his movements quicken, I lean into him for balance, trying to steady myself in my heels while delaying the inevitable orgasm building inside me. I finish unbuttoning his shirt and move to his belt, trying to stay focused. Once his pants drop, he kicks them off along with his shoes. I lean into him, savoring the feeling of his expert touch. My hands grip his hair as I drop my head to his shoulder, my body convulsing around his fingers.

He brings his fingers to my mouth, and I clean them with my tongue, drawing a low growl from him. I push his shirt off his shoulders, and he quickly sheds it along with his undershirt before pushing me onto the bed. He removes my heels and his socks before climbing on top of me.

"I love you, Autumn, but right now, I need you," he says, tracing my features with his fingers.

"I love you too. And if you need me, then take me," I whisper, and he kisses me deeply as he thrusts inside me, drawing a sound between a gasp and a whimper from my lips.

His mouth moves to my neck, kissing and nibbling as my fingernails find his back and the muscles of his upper arms. He savagely fucks me, hard and intense, leaving me feeling wanted and needed. I feel him release inside me, and he kisses me again.

As he leans back, meeting my eyes, he laughs softly. "I promise I'll make up for that one, but there was a lot of adrenaline going into tonight."

"Well, you've got forever." I smile. "Adrenaline, huh?"

"Yeah," he breathes, laying down beside me and pulling me onto his chest. He lightly rubs my back and plays with my hair.

"You worried I'd say no?" I laugh.

"No," he chuckles. "*That* I wasn't worried about. If I had been, I wouldn't have done it in front of thirty people. But I was worried something would go wrong. Megan played her part perfectly."

"So, my fiancé," I say with a smile, feeling his lips press against my hair again, "since you have all these big master plans, how long are you planning on being engaged?"

Laughing, he runs a hand down my back. "Actually, I'm not sure. But there's something I want to do first."

I prop myself up on my elbow, resting my chin on my hand so I can look at him. "What's that?"

"I want to try to find all my siblings—at least establish some communication with them," he says, swallowing as he rakes a hand through my hair. "Alex said Jamie could help. But if they don't want it, that's fine. I'm not going to push anyone, but I want to at least try."

"You want a family reunion at our wedding?" I ask with a smile.

"Something like that," he says. "But either way, we'll be able to set a date soon."

"Okay, well, that sounds like a project and a mission," I say, smiling. "I'll help you any way I can."

I kiss him softly, and we lay there in the quiet until I drift off to sleep in his arms.

Afterword

Dear Reader,

Thank you for diving into *Breathing Autumn*! I'm so grateful to have shared Autumn and Cole's story with you. This book marks the beginning of an exciting saga, one that explores not only their future together but also the love stories waiting to unfold for their children.

While this book wraps up with a happy ending, there's so much more to uncover—new challenges, new connections, and new adventures that will bring their families closer together. I can't wait to take you on this journey as their worlds expand and their kids discover happiness of their own.

Your support means everything to me, and I'd love to hear your thoughts! If you enjoyed this book, please consider leaving a review or reaching out—I love connecting with my readers.

Stay Naughty ♥ Mae

The Prophecy of Vyrdanor:
The Echoes of Shattered Realms & *The Echoes of the Prophecy*
Epic Romantic Fantasy | Coming of Age | Political Intrigue | Unique
Magic System | Unique Pantheon

The Roll For Love Trilogy:
Initiative | Roll For Love Book One, Advantage | Book Two, End Game |
Book Three
Why Choose Web | Romantic Comedy | Contemporary Romance |
Polyamory Love Story | Dungeons & Dragons As A Mirror to Their
Story

The Vallyn Duet
Vallyn in Chains & *Vallyn Unchained*
A Dark Romantic Suspense | Stalker to Romance to Rescue to
Vengeance | This Duet Has Serious Content Warnings for Trauma,
Violence, and Sexual Assault, Please Read the Author's Note Before
Diving In

The Unbinding Trilogy
Unbinding Desire, Unbinding Fate, & Unbinding Forever
The Unbinding Omnibus With Bonus Content
Why Choose | Lovingly called a healthy & non-toxic why choose | A polyamory love story

The Fated Love Saga:
Breathing Autumn | Fated Love Saga Book One & Embracing Autumn | Fated Love Saga Book Two
A refreshing, classic romance, about finding love a little bit older |Our main characters are in their forties |Boss/Employee romance |Most of the drama comes from outside the couple

Fighting For Evangeline
A story of survival and empowerment after domestic violence | This book does contain serious trigger warnings for violence and sexual assault | Please read the author's note before diving in

A Veil of Execration
Dark Romance | Taboo Romance | Age Gap | Stalker | Romantic Suspense

For updates on future releases, sign up for
Maelana's Newsletter
or visit her website at:
www.maelananightingale.com